I0762131

For Tony and Tyler,
my pillars of strength.

Frost Giant Territory
hinterland Ice-Drifts
Scarbroath Ridge
Icewall Cliffs
Twisted Bone Forest
Sunder Run
River Torle
Mount helgunth
Well of Eyes
Mount Alderath
Brynmoor highlands
Duenthorn
BELDERETH
Springs of Almsdeep
Dragon's Bite
Loch Windmere
NORTh ENDLUND
Kildaer Peak
Ridge
Raven's Run
Forest
Feldoril Forest
River Torle
Shoreless Bay
Mystwitch Woods
Moors
Glyndaer
Swamplands
Glorm Mountains
SOUTh ENDLUND
Shadowless
River Torle
Feldoril
Shytuckle
SERPEN EMPIRE
Mount Fargrum
Wanderer's End Bay
Innith Tine
Graven's Tideway
Dreaded Oak Wilds
Bloodthirsty Oak
Stormfront Channel
ASGAR
OCEANU
CIAThR

TRITON'S DEPTHLESS EXPANSE
OLDWILDE
&
SHALAMORAIZE
Elzanar Kingdom
MIRAJARAN
Natreehla Oasis
DESERT
Feadhl-Ree Gateway
N
W
E
S
Teeth of Killkush
BIRAKTAR
DUNEBALA
Desert of the Living Sands

BOOK 3 OF
HER DARK DESTINY

T. RAE MITCHELL

PRAISE FOR HER DARK DESTINY SERIES

"FAN'S OF GAIL CARSON LEVINE AND CASSANDRA CLARE WILL WANT TO ADD T. RAE MITCHELL TO THEIR READING LIST."

~ Readers' Favorite Editorial Review ★★★★★

"THIS FANTASY HITS ALL THE RIGHT SPOTS."

~ Artistic Bent ★★★★★

"EVERYTHING I'VE BEEN MISSING IN THE YOUNG ADULT SCENE."

~ The Passionate Bookworm ★★★★★

"BRILLIANT, WITTY AND FUNNY, A JOY TO READ"

~ Book Traveller ★★★★★

"A HIGHLY ADDICTING SERIES... BE PREPARED TO LET THE REST OF THE WORLD GO BY"

~ Amazon Reviewer ★★★★★

"DELIGHTFULLY ENTERTAINING AS WELL AS INVENTIVE"

~ Award winning author, Kay Gregory ★★★★★

"NOT YOUR TYPICAL YOUNG ADULT NOVEL."

~Top Knot Librarian ★★★★★

"LOVED IT! ACTION UP THE WAZOO! THIS WILL BE ONE I WILL READ AGAIN AND AGAIN"

~Netgalley Reviewer ★★★★★

Original Mix Media Inc.
1685 H Street #1046
Blaine, WA 98230
www.originalmixmedia.com

Ordering Information:
Quantity sales. Special discounts are available on quantity purchases by corporations, associations, and others. For details, contact the publisher at the address above.
Orders by U.S. trade bookstores and wholesalers. Please contact Big Distribution:
Tel: (604) 725-4284 or visit www.originalmixmedia.com.

Printed in the United States of America

Library of Congress Cataloging-in-Publication data
Mitchell, T. Rae.
Fate's War / T. Rae Mitchell.
p. cm.—(bk. 1)

Summary: As Keep Guardian, seventeen year old Fate Floyd must confront the dark forces stealing the immense power stored within the Keep. But a deadly game of deceit is playing out behind the scenes, unleashing what may be an even greater threat. As war bears down upon Fate and her companions, her only hope is to plot a perilous course that will propel her directly into a firestorm of battles she can't possibly win.

ISBN 978-1-7771472-1-1 (hardcover)
ISBN 978-1-9990241-4-7 (paperback)
ISBN 978-0-9917987-9-7 (ebook)

[1. Supernatural–Fiction. 2. Myths–Fiction. 3. Legends–Fiction.
4. Secret Portal–Fiction. 5. Fairies–Fiction. 6. Druids–Fiction.
7. Magic–Fiction. 8. Sorcery–Fiction. 9. Romance–Fiction] 1. Title.

10 9 8 7 6 5 4 3 2 1

I
DOOMSDAY

FATE PULLED BACK THE arrow, straining the bow, directing the sum of all her failures through the muscles of her arms and down the steel shaft. She held the full draw until her bow arm trembled. Inhaling deeply, she relaxed her shoulder and released the arrow.

The shot cut the air, slicing through the holographic Chimera's leathery wing.

"Damn," she muttered. Another soft shot. Thirty arrows in, and she still hadn't hit the creature's vulnerable underbelly. She couldn't seem to relax her fingers on the release and kept dropping her shoulder too much.

She could easily make herself feel better about her rusty archery skills by choosing an easier target, but this was one mark she needed to conquer. When she'd faced the real Chimera a few weeks earlier, she'd had to be rescued by her best friend who'd had far less experience with monsters than Fate.

Fate's heart grew heavy, as it always did, at the thought of Jessie and what she must be suffering as a prisoner of the power-hungry sorceress, Kaliena. Was she being tortured? Or was she still the unfeeling automaton Kaliena had turned her into? The last time she'd seen Jessie, there'd been nothing left of her childhood friend. Kaliena had taken control of the Dragon Eye Jessie had been wearing. She shuddered at the memory of Jessie's vacant stare as her friend had idly watched Kaliena unleash a fiery storm onto Fate that had nearly killed her.

Was Jessie even alive? She hated to think it, but it probably didn't matter if she was. Either way, her best friend was gone.

The tightness in her chest increased. "When reality sucks, the tough get fighting," she muttered under her breath. Fate nocked another arrow and let it fly. The dying roar of the holographic Chimera as it thrashed at the arrow stuck in its belly gave her little satisfaction.

Working herself into the ground to sharpen her combat skills would only get her so far. At this point, all she had to show for it was increased fatigue and aching muscles. Dropping the bow at her side, Fate sighed tiredly as she tilted her head to stare at the electric daylight shining from the training arena's arched ceiling. She was up against too much. Kaliena's reach was growing. She'd taken over three-quarters of the Keep already. It wouldn't be long before she controlled every inch of the arcane storehouse of magical objects.

The dread Fate woke with intensified each morning, wondering whether that would be the day Kaliena finally mounted her attack upon them. She knew deep down inside she would lose if it happened now. The only way she could protect her loved ones was if she possessed powers equal to Kaliena's.

The shadow of her failures inevitably darkened Fate's thoughts to desperate levels. They haunted her daily. If she hadn't lost the extraordinary powers she'd gained from a war goddess during her time in the *Book of Fables*–as well as the courage those powers had given her–she would've saved herself from that Chimera. Had she been as swift as before, she could've rescued Lincoln from being devoured by a dragon. If she'd been stronger, she could've prevented Jessie from falling under Kaliena's control.

Everything would be different...better, if Fate hadn't been reduced to her normal human frailty. She clenched the bow with all her strength. She didn't know how she would do it, or when, but she was determined to get a major upgrade in the very near future.

"Nice shot, love."

Startled by Finn's voice, Fate glanced over her shoulder. He crossed the expanse of the training court in long easy strides. His cotton shirt breezed loosely against his tapered waist as her gaze trailed over him. His hair had grown while they'd been apart. The burnished gold of his wavy hair now grazed his broad shoulders. Her heart raced as the sight of him chased back the darkness like nothing else could. Dropping the bow, she shrugged off the quiver with a clatter of arrows falling over the stone floor and went to him.

Finn smiled, his eyes glittering like emeralds as he took her in his arms. She sank against him, breathing in the woodsy scent of sandalwood soap lingering on his skin and tightened her hold on him. She didn't think she'd ever get used to the thrill his presence incited after suffering his absence for so long. Their relationship had been riddled with hardships from the moment they'd first met, and even though Finn assured her they would always be together, she couldn't shake the feeling he would be taken from her again.

He nuzzled his face against her neck. Waves of excitement rippled along the length of her spine. "You missed breakfast with everyone." His voice grew husky with desire. "I missed you. How long have you been down here?" The heat of his breath on her skin made her knees go weak. Dizzy with longing, she swayed backwards. He held her closer to keep her from falling. "If you're feeling light-headed, you should eat," he warned.

Fate leaned her head back and looked at him with a drowsy smile. "I'm only hungry for one thing."

Finn tried to hide his amusement behind a scolding look. The effort was entirely ineffective. "Stop trying to coax the devil out of me." His eyes gleamed an even brighter green as his gaze traveled over her face. The Elder race runes inked on his skin had blessed him with power over the elements, as well as superhuman strength and speed, which he used only when needed. But there was another side effect that was always evident. The runes had turned his irises into mood rings. The more excited he was, the more luminous his eyes became. Something she loved seeing. "You're making it impossible for me to keep my promise to your father."

The mention of her father was every bit as unwelcome as a pail of cold water splashed in her face. "You never should've made that promise in the first place. It's not up to either of you to protect my virtue. The decision as to when I give my virginity away is up to me." She broke free of Finn's embrace and bent to pick up the mess of arrows she'd left on the floor. "I can't believe you two. You're both being completely... antediluvian."

"Which means?"

"Outrageously old-fashioned."

Finn shifted his weight from one foot to the other as he tried to form a defense.

"Oh, don't bother. I can't bear to hear the whole spiel on earning his respect all over again." Having gathered up the bow and arrows, Fate stormed across the court to put them away.

Finn jogged to catch up with her. "Don't be mad, fireball."

Fate stopped and glared at him. He shut his eyes and raked his hand through his thick locks. She crumbled inside knowing her anger hurt him. Finn was simply caught in the middle and doing what he thought was best for everyone concerned. She really needed to stop taking her anger out on him. It wasn't his fault her father had so thoroughly convinced him she was still a fragile little girl in need of protection.

Frustration boiled in her chest. It was time she and her father had a talk. Ever since Eustace had extracted his ridiculous promise of honor and respect from Finn, she had directed no more than a few curt words at her father over the last few weeks. Dropping her scowl, she stood on tiptoe and gave Finn a light peck on the cheek. "Sorry for being such a bear."

Before she could take another step, he pulled her close. His heart thudded hard beneath the palm of her hand. "Whoa, lass. You can't leave me with a granny kiss."

Fate laughed, a harsh sound betraying her irritation. "Hey, I'm not the one who made this bed. You did, so you're just going to have to lie in it." She headed for the exit before glancing back to flash him a bitter smile. "Alone."

Fate entered the library, her gaze sweeping over the six story high ceiling and full surround of terraces filled with collections of scrolls, tablets, grimoires and vast accumulation of texts. She spotted Sithias on the top level. The unusually large ivory-colored snake slithered by the shelves, his head bobbing up and down as he read the spines of each book. She sensed his excitement with whatever he was reading by the way his golden-brown wings fluttered and twitched. A ghost of a smile formed on her lips. Was Sithias narrowing in on the solution she'd asked him to find for her?

Resisting the urge to call out to him, she dropped her gaze to the main floor, which was as large as an Olympic-sized skating rink, interrupted only by islands of huge tables and chairs. Her smile faded when she saw Eustace sitting at one of the tables near the far end of the library. He hadn't noticed her presence. He was engrossed in reading and the stacks of leatherbound books on the table blocked his line of vision.

Finn stole silently in beside her. The walk between the training court and library had been tense and quiet between them. "How about we head to the galley so you can get something to eat before we spend the rest of our day in here researching how we're going to defeat Kaliena. If you take care of the basics, you can handle any–"

Fate silenced him with a look. "Who's being the granny now?"

At the sound of voices, Eustace rose from his seat. He was a tall man, and always meticulously groomed, but from this distance he looked smaller somehow and unkempt in the way his silver-dusted hair hung over his glasses. Fate caught the hopefulness in his eyes as he stared at her.

Two parts of her battled with one another. The little girl who wanted to run into her father's arms and have everything be what it used to be–unconditional love and acceptance–but the woman she was becoming could not forgive the boundary he'd crossed.

She tore her gaze away, but not before she saw the light go out of Eustace's eyes. Her throat constricted and she lost the courage to speak her mind to him altogether. The subject matter was simply too uncomfortable. She'd thought she was ready to confront him, but in truth, she wasn't.

She looked at Finn. "Can you see if Eustace needs any help with his research? I'm going to see what Sithias has found."

"Fate, you can't keep freezing him out. He's your father."

She shook her head at Finn's pleading gaze. "Stop pushing me. I need more time."

The corners of Finn's mouth turned downward before he nodded and walked away. Fate willed herself to keep from stopping him. Any amount of sadness she caused him cut like a knife, but on the same note, she needed him to understand the effect his promise to Eustace was having on them.

Forcing down the pain of hurting the two people she loved most in the world, Fate scaled the terraces to the top level. She used to complain about the library's lack of stairs or ladders. The architects of the Keep had provided two librarian automatons–robots designed to climb the walls and retrieve all requests. But Fate had developed excellent wall climbing skills ever since she'd been forced to spend an exorbitant amount of time in the library. Most of all, she enjoyed increasing her speed to beat her last climb.

She jumped over the balcony rail, startling Sithias when her boots hit the floor behind him. "Sweet! Thirty seconds faster than last time."

"How wonderful for you, though not for my rampaging heart." Sithias waved his tail in front of his face while trying to steady his breathing. "You really must stop sneaking up on me, misss."

Fate shook her head and smiled. While Sithias had somehow managed to lose most of the hiss in his speech since they'd last been together, he hadn't stopped exaggerating his so-called fragility. He liked to think of himself as a lover, not a fighter, but he was much tougher than he let on. "You can take it." She glanced at the two stacks of books sitting next to him. "Anything in there for me?"

Sithias grinned wide, baring his fangs as his amber eyes twinkled with inspiration. "Ah yesss, I believe there is." He pointed at the first stack with his tail. "After much laborious cross-checking, between what's stored here in the Keep, against all historical texts documenting war goddesses, I've narrowed your options down to two deities."

Fate leaned against the railing. "I'm listening."

Sithias lifted a book from one stack and opened it to an etching of a dark-haired woman whose hooded cloak swirled into a murder of crows. "This is the Morrígan, once revered as the goddess of battle and later known as the phantom queen. She is listed among the Tuatha Dé Danann as the granddaughter of King Nuada. You'll be interested to know, the Morrígan was instrumental in defeating the Fomorians."

Fate stiffened at the thought of the Fomorians. She'd experienced the repulsive, reality warping creatures first hand. The memory, though blurred and distorted, was unpleasant to say the least. "The phantom queen's got my vote so far. What are her powers? Did she blast the Fomorians away with some sort of reality rejection mojo?"

"Well, I don't think so. I do know she's associated with fate in the way she foretold doom and death in battle by taking the shape of a crow and flying over the battlefield…" Sithias turned the page and skimmed the text.

Fate fidgetted while she waited. "If there's one thing I can relate to, it's the fate thing. Having the name's been more of a curse than anything else. Did I ever tell you about the time a meteor landed on the car my dad gave me for my birthday? I never even got to drive it." She waited for his reaction but he was too intent on reading.

"Ah, I found it." Sithias looked up from the book. "It appears the Morrígan used her feminine wilesss to great advantage to win the war against the Fomorians."

Fate wrinkled her nose. "Really? That's it? She batted her eyelashes at the right person? Not impressed."

"Well, she did a little more than that, misss."

When she realized what he was alluding to, heat rushed to her face. "Oh, she…"

"Kept a tryst with the powerful druid, Dagda."

Fate's thoughts rushed to Finn. Her longing to share more than a kiss with him flowed through her veins like quicksilver. She gulped dryly. "What's the other option?"

"You don't like the Morrigan?"

"Not if I have to tryst with some stranger to get the results I want."

"Don't underestimate the power of female sexuality, misss. Many a war has been lost and won because of a woman who was able to harness that wild force of nature."

"Nope. Next."

Closing the book, Sithias set it down and took a tome from the other stack. "All right then, you might like this goddess better, though I haven't completed my research." He showed her an illustration of a fierce looking woman holding a spear and shield. She wore a breastplate over a long dress. Thick golden locks flowed to her waist from beneath a winged helmet.

Fate liked the balance of strength and feminity in the portrait. "Tell me more."

"This is, Freya, the Norse goddess of war and death, and leader of the Valkyries."

Fate leaned forward with interest. "I've heard of the Valkyries–expert battle maidens with kickass supernatural abilities."

Sithias nodded. "Yes, and like the Morrígan, they too determine the fates of fallen soldiers in war, as well as escort their spirits to the afterlife. While Freya possesses these same abilities, as well as the usual superhuman strength, speed and invulnerability, she is sssupremely powerful in warfare and makes the Valkryies seem like playful puppies on the battlefield."

"Now that's what I'm looking for. How do I get me some of that?"

"One of the vaults is holding Freya's armament, one of which is the legendary Brisingamen–a magical necklace made of gold filigree, ambers and rubies."

"Hmm, sounds like it'll match my eyes."

"Uh, before you get excited about the necklace, you should know it was crafted by four dwarves." Sithias squirmed with discomfort.

"So? What's wrong with that?"

"Freya trysted with them in exchange for the necklace. She was famous for trysting rather freely."

"Ew! Is that all those goddesses did back then?" Fate chewed on her bottom lip. The Morrigan was sounding better by the minute. At least she was sacrificing herself for the benefit of others, while Freya sounded like a party girl. Albeit, a powerful one. "What does the necklace do?" she asked with reluctance.

Sithias glanced down at the book. "It says here the Brisingamen gave her the power to create treasures. When her tears fell on the earth, they turned to gold, and when she wept at sea, they turned to amber." He lifted his gaze. "Apparently she cried a lot, especially when she was searching for her missing husband."

Fate understood that kind of sadness. The memories of her desperation to get back to Finn and free him from the *Book of Fables* were still fresh. She let out a heavy sigh. "I don't know. The necklace sounds lame. What else is in the vault?"

Sithias closed the book he was holding and referenced a new volume, which looked like a log of records. "Well, there's her sword and shield, but you'd need superhuman strength to wield them since all goddesses were giantesses..." He scanned further down the list. "Ah, there are three other items. A crown, a gauntlet and a girdle."

"A girdle? Sounds uncomfortable. Who wears a girdle anymore? What does the gauntlet do?"

"It grants the wearer the strength to wield weapons of colossal size."

"I suppose that solves the problem of being able to use her sword and shield, but I don't exactly see myself hauling around a shield the size of a dining room table and a sword that's taller than me. What about the crown?"

"Hmmm," Sithias mused as he read the description. "The crown appears to amplify the magical powers of the wearer."

"Which is useless to me, since I'm magicless." Fate huffed. "I guess we're back to the girdle."

Sithias nodded as he searched for the item's attributes. "Oh my, I think you're going to like this. The girdle imbues the wearer with Amazonian powers."

"Ooh, me likey. Wonder Woman's an Amazon and she *never* has to give herself away to get business done."

Sithias shook his head at the page. "Thisss doesn't make any sense. Why would a Norse goddess have a girdle of Hellenic origin?"

Fate shrugged. "The lady got around. She probably laid it down to get her hands on that one too."

"Possibly." A shadow of concern crossed Sithias's face.

Fate frowned. "What?"

"You're being rather blasé about assuming the powers a goddess once wielded. Are you certain you want to risk being changed into something else entirely? Remember Bremusa's plight from the *Book of Fables'* story of *The Lightning Sword*? The gods and goddesses of old were famous for leaving behind fragments of their power in which to slip back to this world for a chance to unleash their might."

How could Fate forget? She'd lived through that fable. But what Sithias was overlooking was how Fate had been embued with a war goddess's powers, which was exactly why she'd survived that particular story.

Sithias set the book down. "Pleassse, give it more thought before you go through with this."

The metallic clicking of a librarian robot sounded from below. Fate leaned over the railing to see Gerdie riding piggyback on one of the robots as it traversed the wall of shelves with its six arms, moving as easily as a spider. Catching sight of Fate, Gerdie waved before directing the robot to climb over to her.

The wispy, twelve-foot librarian made of blinking gold lights, brass coils and porcelain face, stepped over the railing and placed the little girl gently on the floor. Gerdie's frizzy, fawn-colored hair fluttered around her impish features with the delicacy of a dried dandelion. Her brown eyes moved from Fate to Sithias, and to the stacks of books sitting next to them. "Whatcha doin'?"

Fate shrugged. "The usual. Searching for something to help us kick

Kaliena's royal blue butt."

Despite her six-year-old appearance, Gerdie had spent untold centuries evading the clutches of a child-eating monster and now was forty-five pounds of pure stubbornness. The wise old soul stared, unconvinced. "Mmhmm. If that were true, you'd be down there with Eustace. He's collected all the books we need."

Sithias squirmed under Gerdie's stare. "We're exploring other avenues of thought."

Gerdie bent to read the spine of one of the books. "What does *Lebor Gabála Érenn* have to do with the Sanskrit Vedic texts we've been siftin' through everyday for the last month? Celtic myths won't give us the answers we need." She glanced at the book Fate was holding. "The same goes for Norse legends."

Sithias huffed. "Why did I ever teach you to read?"

"Too late to take it back now."

He tsk, tsked. "I've created a monsssster."

Gerdie crossed her small arms and looked at Fate. "Spit it out. What're you up to?"

Fate gulped. Just as she hadn't told Finn of her intentions to power up, she couldn't tell Gerdie either. Especially Gerdie. Her great-aunt had witnessed how power had corrupted her older sister, Brune, when she'd become obsessed with the Orb of Aeternitis. Gerdie's grandmother had died because of Brune's use of the magical object, and Brune's obsession was the reason Gerdie had been suspended in time and trapped inside the *Book of Fables*.

But what choice did Fate have? Gerdie wouldn't let this go. She could only hope she didn't tell the others. Fate looked at Gerdie. "Well, we were–"

"What're those books you're lookin' at?" Gerdie stooped and read the spines. "Celtic and Norse myths? What's that got to do with the Sanskrit Vedic texts we've been siftin' through everyday for the last month?"

Fate and Sithias exchanged a baffled look. Then she remembered Gerdie had been researching forgetting spells. "Gerdie, did you happen to try one of those forgetting spells you've been digging into?"

Gerdie's expression went blank. "I think so…"

An alarm blared throughout the expanse of the library, making all three of them jump.

Sithias looked at them round-eyed with fear. "Oh dear. Do you think this is the day?"

Fate's heart hammered as she threw her leg over the railing. "I don't know."

Gerdie climbed onto the back of the robot. "Fate... "

The tone in her voice held Fate in place. "Yeah, Gerdie?"

Gerdie stared then shook her head. "I…I forgot what I was gonna say."

Fate nodded. "It's okay. You'll remember if it's important." But she hoped the forgetting spell wouldn't fade too terribly soon. She couldn't let anything get in the way of taking action on what she'd learned from Sithias. Not with the alarms ringing out what may be the doomsday she'd been dreading all along.

2
LAPIS PHILOSPHORUM

THE CURVED SANCTUARY WALLS were awash in flashing crimson lights when Fate, Sithias, Gerdie, Finn and Eustace raced through the door. Farouk sat in his cage, his monkey-sized body kicked back in a relaxed pose and fox-like face strangely serene under the noisy barrage of warning bells.

Brune was there too, leaning against the wall with arms folded. She was dressed for a mission, decked out in full body armor and blonde hair pulled back in a tight bun. Fate's stomach tightened at the sight of her. Only a few short weeks ago, an infection had mutated Brune into a Gorgon. But then Farouk had miraculously cured her, and this was after informing everyone that finding a cure in time was highly unlikely.

Suspicious indeed.

The snakes covering Brune's head were thankfully gone, along with the scales and fangs, all replaced by flawless features, bedroom eyes and full lips. Not that her good looks bothered Fate. Though she could've done without the double take Finn had given Brune upon her remarkable transformation.

What troubled her most was the secrecy going on between Brune and Farouk. She'd interrupted too many hushed conversations, and had even caught Brune coming in from two scouting missions after Farouk had explicitly warned against any such outings.

They were working on something together. Fate knew it in her bones, and she hated being left out, especially since she was Keep Guardian. It was her duty to know everything. Just because Brune had held the position before, didn't mean Farouk should be deferring concerns and strategies to her during this time of looming war. They'd both assured her this was not the case, but she wasn't buying it.

Fate slowed her pace when she saw how relaxed each of them looked. Was this some sort of cruel joke? She didn't know what to think anymore when it came to those two.

Farouk's vast history with the Keep may have made him the guiding force behind every group decision, but Fate had never been entirely at ease with the sly creature. Anyone who mixed perfectly good words into his own convoluted versions was suspect in her mind. It was amazing she was able to understand his odd speech patterns in the first place. And for all she knew, there might be all sorts of double meanings behind everything he said.

As for Brune, Fate would never fully trust her cantankerous great-aunt the way she had come to trust Gerdie. Not after Brune had chucked Fate into the *Book of Fables* without a single care for whether she survived or not. She'd said it was to save the Keep, but she'd really done it to save herself from rotting away.

Plus Brune was once again pushing to be Fate's proxy. Fate's desire to be free of her oath as Keep Guardian was stronger than ever, but not if that freedom meant dying. She didn't trust that Brune would be content with being a stand-in. She could easily hold the position permanently if Fate met with an untimely end–a temptation for murder Fate wasn't about to hand over.

Darcy and Mason burst through the door in a panic. Both looked mussed, as if they'd just climbed out of bed, which they probably had. Ever since Mason had found the courage to stand up to his hen-pecking girlfriend, they'd been getting along like never before. Fate could hardly stand being around them. They were always kissing and inevitably disappearing to their room, a romantic indulgence she wished she could share with Finn.

Renewed frustration set in. It wasn't fair. Darcy was the same age as her and no one was concerned about protecting *her* virtue, least of all Mason.

Darcy did her best to smooth the black fringe of her bangs back into place. She tried for her standard Cleopatra expression of cool detachment, but failed since her pale complexion was made clownish by the smear of her dark red lipstick and heavy eyeliner. Mason's geometric haircut, which he used to gel into stiff Anime spikes, fell in dark, irregular points over his fine Asian features. His shirt was on inside out and his shoes didn't match. Obviously they'd both dressed in a hurry.

Everyone gathered around the large table, which through some means of anti-gravity, hovered a foot off the floor in the center of the room. Gerdie stood on her footstool with her ears covered. "Can somebody turn that off?" she yelled.

Farouk straightened and pressed a button on the keyboard of his control panel. The alarm and flashing red light ceased, dropping them into instantaneous silence.

Fate frowned at him. "Is there a real emergency here, or were you just torturing us for a laugh?"

Farouk stood and leaned with the point of his nose close the bars of his cage.

“That was a drill, of which you messbacled.” His slanted gaze slid to Brune. “Please explainate their shortgoings.”

Brune pushed away from the wall and strolled down the length of the table before stopping in front of Fate. “For starters, you failed to show up in full armor and gear. You do realize you’re nothing without them.” She glanced at Finn, particularly at the runes inked on his temple. “Unlike your boyfriend here, whose weapons and protections are already built-in.”

Fate ground her teeth together.

Brune moved on, focusing her forbidding gaze on Gerdie, Eustace and Sithias. “And you three…what do you have to show for three weeks of research on Kaliena’s weaknesses?” She gave them no time to answer. “Zero, zip, zilch, that’s what. In the meantime, Kaliena has seized another three hundred and fifty-five sectors.”

She gestured to Farouk, who held his bronze pointer stick poised over the detailed map of the Keep’s two hemispheres spread over the table’s surface. He tapped each circle, triggering the 3D projections of both halves of the Keep, where they rotated above the map. One half was dark and only a small portion of the other half was lit.

“As you can well see, Kaliena now ownjugates over eighty-five percent of the Keep,” Farouk informed them. “I previsionate she’ll have full governation of the Keep within the next five days or less.”

Fate’s pulse quickened. “Why the sudden acceleration? Just a few days ago, you told us we had at least a month.”

Farouk’s devil-pointed ears sagged a little. “That was when I still had connectifications with over half the Keep. After losing these latest sectors, I can no longer be exacturate with my diagnostifications.”

“If that’s the case, how do you know we only have five days left?” Finn asked.

“Because of this.” Farouk triggered the schematic of the Keep and the massive rings sweeping around it. One of the rings was no longer rotating.

The full ramification of what this meant slammed in and Fate’s nerves skittered. The Keep was located in the darkest edge of space, a place called the Chaos Region. The rings protected them from the harmful emanations of a roiling ocean of wild, multidimensional magic and psychic energy storms. Before the Golandon had put the rings in place, droves of their population had succumbed to the destructive energies and had gone on killing rampages. Thousands of the insane had been imprisoned underground. Eons had passed since then, but Fate wondered if their bones were still piled somewhere deep inside the Keep.

The warm touch of Finn's hand on the small of Fate's back woke her to the present moment as Farouk explained the importance of the protective rings to all the others. "Are you all right?" he whispered in her ear.

She nodded. Smiling, he dropped his hand and returned his attention to the meeting. Her skin grew cold where his palm had been. She shivered with the need to rest against him and forget the trouble pressing in on them from all sides.

She was tired, and not just physically. Her exhaustion ran as deep as the soul. She'd been dealing with one crisis after another from the moment she was first trapped inside the *Book of Fables*. The six months she'd spent within the book's hidden realm of Oldwilde had been harrowing. Had it not been for Finn, Sithias and Gerdie, she never would've survived.

Yet even after escaping the cursed book, surviving was all she'd been doing since then. Most of all, leaving Finn behind in Oldwilde had broken something deep down inside. Her determination to get back to him had been the driving force behind everything she had done since entering the Keep. That's what had kept her alive when forced to face the monsters it contained. Now that Finn was back with her, the tenacity she'd come to rely on for fuel was no longer required, leaving her emptied of all energy reserves.

She needed to find a way to recharge. And fast.

"The Chaos Region is the source of many omnivasive entities, some of which are known in your myths and legends as gods and demons," Farouk continued. "Most of you are already acquaintiformed with the *Mortcarion Apocrypha*, but we should revisit for Sithias and Finn's sake."

Fate noticed the telepathicgram projector in his hand before he plugged it into his control panel. She wanted desperately to excuse herself. She'd experienced the horrific recording two times already, but she held still and braced herself as a sheet of misty particles formed over the center of the meeting table.

The image of the three-eyed seer, Vasha, flickered into view. Her dry voice scraped the air, grabbing hold of everyone's minds as she guided them through the story of the Keep's origins and its builders, the Golandon, an exotic blue-skinned race born with six arms. Fate tensed when Vasha's narration came to the birth of the chaos god. The intensity of the images gripped hold as she was forced to witness, once again, the entity's churning mass of darkness destroy the Keep's protective force field and merge with the High Priestess. She clenched her fists as the dark power transformed the woman into the fierce, black-eyed Kaliena they had all come to fear and hate.

Farouk stopped the recording. "I guesstimate Kaliena's plan is to bring the force field down by blockending all six rings."

Fate pressed her fists into the surface of the table until her knuckles ached. "That's crazy. She knows what the energies will do. She watched her people go nuts and kill each other. I know she doesn't care about us, but why would she risk her own sanity?"

"I suspiciate she plans to wake another chaos entity and governate it to merge with her, as she did before."

Fate's blood froze. They were all dead meat if Kaliena managed to pull that off.

Eustace cleared his throat. "I have a differing thought on that."

All eyes fixed on him and Fate grew hopeful. Her father had always been her pillar of strength, forever providing the firm ground on which she had stood for most of her life. Being at odds with him had only shaken her foundation even more.

"I don't believe Kaliena's physically strong enough to be the vessel for such an immense energy as a chaos entity," Eustace offered. "For some time now, I suspect she's been working on achieving the legendary alchemical substance known as the *Lapis Philosphorum*."

"Do you mean the Philosopher's Stone?" Fate asked.

Her father's expression softened into surprise when she spoke directly to him. A sad pang spread through her chest as he nodded.

"Whoa," Mason exclaimed as he rubbed his eyes and looked suddenly awake, "that makes total sense! *He Who Must Not Be Named* used the same thing to restore his body and power."

Eustace frowned. Fate could see her father's patience had run thin with her fellow fantasy geeks. Mason and Darcy were the last relics of her old life as a writer. They were fans of an accidentally successful book she'd authored. Unfortunately for them, they'd made the innocent mistake of following Fate into danger. Worse yet, there used to be three of them. A golden Chinese dragon had eaten Lincoln. Poor, overly enthusiastic, yet brave, Lincoln.

It was time Mason and Darcy returned home, where they'd be safe again. Hopefully, Gerdie would find the right forgetting spell soon, so they could be sent back without worrying they would remember the Keep and expose its entrance to the entire world.

"I hardly think we can compare the stuff of fiction to the very real and miraculous achievement of transmuting base metals into an elixir of life," Eustace insisted.

"Uh huh." It was clear Mason didn't see the distinction.

"Even if we could compare this to pure fiction, which would be preposterous," Eustace muttered the last part with a roll of his eyes, "the necessary amounts of elixir required to restore any sorceress in a degraded state such as Kaliena–or wizard, as you've mentioned–would be gargantuan. As far as I know, that wasn't the case."

"But he did it all the same," Mason insisted.

Eustace's shoulders sagged with exasperation. "Yes, well, you have a point."

Before Mason could press the subject any further, Darcy rubbed against his arm like a purring cat and shushed him. A far cry from what she would've done only a few weeks before, which would've been to berate her boyfriend in front of everyone.

Farouk's spine straightened as he narrowed his eyes on Eustace. "Why didn't you notellify me of this opinionation earlier?"

"Well, it's not my opinion. It's more of a theory, and has remained so, up until I finished my research of the *Great Work* this morning. There's still one stumbling block though. Crystal is the base compound for the formula, and Kaliena would need a lot of it. I've searched the records for any vaults storing that much crystal and there are none."

Farouk sank into his chair, his snout pinched as he stroked his tail anxiously. "That may not be absopletely true…" he trailed off, deep in thought.

Brune edged closer to his cage. "You're thinking of the core, aren't you?"

Farouk shook off the blank stare he'd fallen into. "Yes, and it would explainate why one of the rings has stopped moving."

An instant knowing came over Fate, something she'd grown accustomed to since her initiation as Keep Guardian. She could've done without the excruciating download of all the Keep's history into her brain, but she certainly enjoyed being able to ask any question concerning the Keep and know the answer in a blink. Though this particular knowing wasn't from the download. This was a memory from when she'd been wearing the helmet of Hermes Farouk had given her to wear during her initiation. After the download, the helmet had freed her consciousness to go anywhere her thoughts would take her.

Her overzealous curiosity about who had built the Keep had taken her into the bowels of the arcane structure. That's when she'd first seen Kaliena, asleep in her shrine. Or so she'd thought. A Golandon cyborg scientist had revived her at that same moment with some sort of liquid he'd concocted in his mad scientist laboratory. Kaliena had woken and had sensed Fate's presence. She was none too happy about it.

Fate had had to make a hasty retreat.

Looking back, Fate wondered if what she'd witnessed was the making of the elixir of life. Before discovering the scientist's laboratory, she'd seen the maintenance robots delivering glowing sapphires, which the scientist had used to make the liquid. The Keep's core was a mystery, even to Farouk, though he'd often theorized it was most likely comprised of solid crystal.

Fate pushed away from the table. "Dad's right. Kaliena has the elixir of life and she's been mining the crystal from the core to do it."

Brune looked at her like she was deranged. "How would *you* know? It's not like you've ever been down there. None of us have. The core's impossible to get to."

Farouk stood and gripped the bars of his cage. "Fate knows. She was there." Brune opened her mouth to argue, but he raised a hand to stop her. "We must work speedidly. Any further flawmage to the core's crystal will bring all the rings to a grinding halt."

Sithias, who still looked horrified after listening to Vasha's story, whiffled his wings nervously. A brown feather fluttered to the floor. "What happens if all the rings ssstop rotating?" Farouk leveled his gaze on the 3D projection of the Keep. "We descend into madness, which usually begins with severical paranoia, followed by prolongated fits of terror and the need to protect oneself from what is perceived as danger."

Sithias shivered. "You mean we'll end up killing each other the way the Golandon did?"

"Disfortunately, you are exacturate."

3
Where You Go, I Go

FATE TUGGED AT THE breastplate of her armor to keep it from digging into her armpit. She'd chosen one that was too small, but there wasn't time to run back to the armory to change. Brune, on the other hand, was already dressed and armed to the teeth with every weapon she could carry.

And so was Finn.

An involuntary sigh escaped past Fate's lips as she looked him over. Finn wore the armor like he'd been born to it. The shaped leather fit the sculpted contours of his muscles like a glove. The tarnished bronze and gold tones of the cybernetically enhanced gear covering the arm and leg bracers, shoulder pads and breastplate seemed molded to his form. The sleek helmet fit like a crown.

He caught her staring and smiled. Heat flooded into her face and she didn't know what to do with the sudden rush of emotion surging through her. She dropped her gaze and reached for her aeronaut pack.

"The aeronaut packs are not obligessary for this mission." Farouk ambled his cage into the middle of the sanctuary as the three of them gathered in front of him. He pushed his hand through the bars, displaying a small gadget in the palm of his hand. "You'll be teleporting to the core with this."

"Did I hear you say teleport?" Fate asked. "As in vanish from one spot and show up in another?"

Farouk's devil-shaped ears slanted with annoyance. "What otherelse could I potentiably mean?"

"The king of word salads has to ask?"

Finn stepped forward to look at the device. "How does it work?"

"The instrument connectifies to the brain. The only way to make it work properly is to envisionate where you wish to teleport."

"What happens if you don't have a clear idea of where you're going?" Finn asked.

Farouk touched his snout to his shoulder and gave him a sidelong glance. "You could restructalize inside solid matter, such as a mountain, or you could transhift into another dimension, either of which would be...displeasurable."

"More than just a little." Finn's stance grew rigid. "I don't like it. Sounds too risky."

"I've already tested it." Brune shot him a challenging stare.

Fate narrowed her gaze on Brune. "Is that what you were doing when I caught you coming into the sanctuary, even though we've been in lock down?"

Brune and Farouk exchanged another one of their secretive looks. "Someone dispensable had to test the teleporter. It's not like we could risk our precious Keep Guardian." Resentment dripped from Brune's tone.

Fate ignored the jab. Brune was obviously trying to distract her from the real issue. She wanted to push the subject, but this wasn't the time to get into what Brune has been really doing outside the sanctuary walls. She'd only continue to evade or lie. "How will we all visualize the core if none of us have actually seen it?"

"You may not have seen the core, but I suspiciate you were close to it during your initiation," Farouk explained. "Otherelse, you wouldn't have seen the crystals being disported to the laboratory by the robots. That's why you'll be the one to triptivate the positionality to Brune and Finn's teleporters."

Fate's stomach swirled with nervous energy. "I don't suppose there's any way to know if Kaliena will be down there waiting to jump out at us from behind a couch when we arrive? I really hate surprises." She muttered the last part.

Farouk shook his head. "I'm unable to diagnosticate anything other than the few sectors left under our control."

Mason rushed into the room. He was dressed in full gear. "Sorry I'm late. I had to wait until Darcy fell back to sleep."

Brune sauntered over to him. "And where do you think you're going?"

"With you guys."

Brune's eyes glazed over with disinterest. "Negatory. Without the Dragon Eye, your super soldier days are over."

Mason raised his chin, his gaze defiant. "I'm trained. I can do this without the Dragon Eye."

"You only think you can."

Mason gripped the hilt of his sword. The blade stuck in the scabbard. He yanked twice before it came free. Holding it out in front of him with the blade wobbling, he glared at Brune. "Come on! Spar with me. I'll show you what I've got!"

Unable to watch any further, Fate half turned, but even as she did, her gaze was dragged back to Mason. She knew how he was feeling. The Dragon Eye headgear had given him instantaneous superhuman speed, strength and expert combat skills. To be deprived of that kind of power after growing used to it, was not only frightening in the ensuing powerlessness, but also humiliating.

"That's not fair!" Mason complained. "Just let me wear the Dragon Eye. You guys need all the help you can get out there."

"No way," Brune told him. "The Dragon Eye controls the brain. That's like putting a sign on your back that says, 'Hey Kaliena, make me your stooge.'"

"Jessie's gear got infected," Mason argued. "I'll make sure that doesn't happen to mine."

Brune's impassive expression remained unchanged. "How?"

Mason opened his mouth, but a high-pitched screech interrupted whatever he was about to say.

"*What are you doing in here?*"

They all turned to see Darcy standing in the doorway. She was wearing black pajama bottoms printed with pink skulls and a t-shirt that read, 'Oh my Goth!' Her fists were clenched and she was shaking with rage.

"You promised me you wouldn't go out there again!" Her blue, charcoal rimmed eyes turned into angry slits. "So that's why you feather tickled my arms this morning. To get me back to sleep so you could sneak out!"

The sword slipped from Mason's hand and clanged on the floor. "I just wanted to help, Dimples."

Darcy shrieked, turned on her heel and shoved the big steel door open. Mason ran after her, letting the door slam behind him. As bad as Fate felt for him, she was relieved Darcy's anger was aimed elsewhere. She'd withstood the brunt of far too many accusations that she was trying to get Mason killed everytime he joined their previous missions.

Fate looked at Finn. "Does Darcy have dimples?"

He shrugged. "She doesn't smile enough to be able to tell."

Brune turned back to them. "Something needs to happen to those two. They're useless and getting on my nerves."

"Gerdie's been researching forgetting spells so we can send them home without any memory of the Keep or what happened here," Fate assured her. Brune was forever threatening to end them by some sort of unpleasant means. "So far Gerdie hasn't found anything strong enough to make the forgetting permanent. We need to give her more time."

"Time is something we don't have," Brune grumbled.

"Exacturacy." Farouk stared intently at Brune. Secrets floated on the air between them, though something had changed. Fate sensed resistance between them she hadn't picked up on before. Farouk tore his heated gaze from Brune and held the teleporter out to Fate.

She took the device, turning it at different angles to figure out how to wear it. "I give up. Where does it go?"

"You hook it over your ear," Farouk instructed.

Fate eyed the brass tube encircling the intricate circuitry overlaid with cogs and wheels, before finally seeing the ear shape. She hooked it over the top of her ear and turned the little screw to tighten the fit. "That's not so bad. Now wh–"

Cold metal snaked through her ear canal, followed by an explosion of pain spreading through the right side of her skull. Sparks of light flashed before her eyes as the room tilted.

Finn was by her side in an instant, holding her upright. She blinked as he came into view. Concern hardened the planes of his handsome face as he spoke to her, but she couldn't hear his words. She closed her eyes. A buzzing cut through the silence before the muffled sound of Finn's voice grew louder and clearer.

"Fate, can you hear me?" Finn's tone was tight with panic. He shot Farouk a black look. "What did you do to her?"

Fate found her footing and stood straight. "I'm fine. It was just a dizzy spell, a mere side affect of the *stabbing pain* in my brain." She scowled at Farouk and Brune. "Thanks for the warning."

Brune shrugged. "Is it better to dread what's coming, or just deal with it when it happens?"

"None of it's better, especially since I'll be dreading the brain jab everytime I have to put this thing back on."

A cold smile crept onto Brune's face. "Oh, didn't we tell you? Once this is on, it only comes off through major brain surgery."

Fate stopped breathing.

Finn stormed toward Brune. "You evil witch," he seethed.

Farouk raised his cage and clambered between them. "I constructified the teleporter, not Brune."

The muscles in Finn's jaw flexed as he clenched his teeth. Darkness stole the brilliant green of his eyes. "Why the hell would you make it permanent?"

"The unimerging of organic tissue and micro circuits must be uncontinuous for the atoms to discatter and restructalize in proper order. Any delay in connectification would result in perpetual discatterment."

Finn's pained gaze moved to Fate.

Brune moved into his line of sight and tapped the side of her helmet. "It's your turn. Unless of course, you've decided to opt out."

Panic raced through Fate and she found her voice. "No, Finn, don't do it."

Finn swallowed. "Where you go, I go." He took the teleporter receiver Farouk offered. The moment he adjusted the tightness of the instrument onto his ear, he winced, gripping the edge of the table for support. The muscles in his back bunched as he breathed deeply, silently enduring the pain Fate knew too well and wished she could save him from.

At last he straightened, his expression dark and somber. "I'm ready. Let's do this."

Farouk looked at Fate. "You know where to take them. Now, close your eyes and envisionate the laboratory."

Nodding, Fate squeezed her eyes shut, tuning everything out and she traveled back in her mind, picturing the red glow of the furnaces burning deep within the depths of the Keep. She visualized the tunnels filled with steaming pipes and complicated machinery. Once she saw it clearly in her mind's eye, she honed in on her memory of the laboratory with its complex system of glass beakers connected by reams of copper tubing.

All of a sudden, her skull filled with a horrible buzzing. Clamping her hands over her ears, she looked at Finn who was doing the same. He locked eyes with her, each of them unable to form a single word, as the buzzing became a paralyzing full body vibration. The sensation of pins and needles covered her skin, making her want to scream.

Then Finn disintegrated into billions of tiny particles and smoke. Within the same instance of seeing him destroyed before her very eyes, Fate burst into a cloud of atoms.

4
SHE'S RAISING AN ARMY

THE AWFUL FEELING OF insubstantial nothingness lasted for a split second before Fate's awareness caught up with her scattered particles, speeding through space like tiny grains of sand. Materialization happened every bit as swiftly, bringing with it an alarming sense of veins and nerves spidering through organs, anchoring to bone, muscle and skin.

Fate grabbed at her body to check for missing parts. Sighing with relief, she blinked at the hellish fires of the giant furnaces fueling the engines deep inside the Keep. The roaring sound of flames filled the narrow tunnel she stood in. Finn and Brune appeared instantaneously from within bursts of sparking smoke. Fate rushed to him as he adjusted to his surroundings.

She smiled. "Glad to see you made it in one yummy piece."

He kissed her. "Likewise, love. I would've been upset if you were missing those delicious lips."

"Oh please, spare me," Brune grumbled.

Fate stepped beside Finn with a sigh. She glanced each way down the length of the tunnel, filled with pipes dripping with condensation and oily panels of machinery. "Hmm, I'm not sure which way to go."

"Of course you're not. Why should any of this be easy?"

Finn looked at Brune. "There's no need for that. We'll get along a lot better if you can–"

"What? Turn my frown upside down?"

"Aye, that'd be a good start."

"Right." Brune turned her back to him. "I'll go this way. You two go the other. Radio me if you find the lab."

"Gladly." Fate started down the tunnel with Finn.

"I've mostly been in the library since I got here. Is she always this unpleasant?" he asked.

"Actually, this is a good day for Brune."

Brune's voice crackled in the headphones built into their helmets. "I can hear you. Turn off your coms so I don't have to listen to you two prattling on."

Fate flicked the switch, as did Finn. "Yeah, Brune's a real sweetheart."

"How do you stand being around her knowing she's the one who threw you into the *Book of Fables*?"

"It was nearly impossible at first. But she opened up one time and told me her side of the story." Finn stared at her in disbelief. "Believe me, the last thing I wanted to do was give Brune–of all people–the benefit of the doubt. But in the end, I could see she was telling the truth. As for her tossing me into harm's way, every decision she made was based on what was best for the Keep. It's what we guardians are hardwired to do."

Fate glanced down at her palm, where the guardian seal glowed beneath the surface of her skin–a round symbol spinning within moving interlocking rings. It was her very own tiny version of the Keep, a built-in reminder of the blood oath she'd taken.

They slowed down to squeeze between two pipes impeding their path. "She wants the Keep Guardian position back, doesn't she?" Finn asked.

"Almost as much as I want to be free of it."

"Why don't you let her have it then?"

Fate stopped and spoke in a hushed tone. "I was totally ready to have her be my proxy, but my spidey senses have been going off lately. Brune and Farouk are keeping a secret. Until I know what they're up to, I can't hand over my position."

"What do you think they're hiding?"

Fate stared into the darkness. "I don't know, but something tells me it's bad."

"We need to find out. With Kaliena taking over and building weapons, we can't have dissension going on between us. We need more eyes on Brune and Farouk. When we get back, we'll bring Sithias and Gerdie in on this." Finn nudged her chin, raising her gaze to meet his. "And your father."

The tight knots in Fate's stomach loosened and she nodded. "Sounds like a plan." She rose on tiptoe to kiss him, when she noticed a blue spark out of the corner of her eye. "Hey, I see something." She darted in the direction of the glinting lights, leaving Finn kissing air.

They caught up to a long line of spider bots carrying luminescent sapphires. Stepping over them, they pushed forward to the front. After several minutes, a round hatch stopped them from going any further. The spiders continued to scrabble forward through a small hole next to the entrance.

Fate surveyed her surroundings. "This looks familiar. I'm pretty sure the laboratory is behind this door." She pressed the radio on. "We found the lab, Brune."

"I'll be right there."

Finn ran his hands over the hatch and doorframe. "I'm not seeing any way to open it. The door probably unlocks from the inside."

Fate noticed a small panel off to one side of the tunnel. It looked like the ones she'd seen on many of the vaults. Lifting her hand, she waved her palm over the surface. A series of beeps and lights flickered. The sound of compressed air releasing and grinding iron filled the narrow tunnel as the hatch's iris rotated open.

Drawing their laser guns, Fate and Finn stepped cautiously through the opening. A humid smell of ozone clung to their skin. A complex system of glass beakers boiling with a luminous aquamarine liquid took up the vast portion of the laboratory. Spider bots delivering the sapphires crawled over hundreds of buckets filled with gemstones.

A sudden movement from the other side of the room had them aiming their laser guns in the direction of the noise. Unintelligible jabbering resounded through the room as a robot staggered back and fell onto the buckets of gemstones. A sparkling carpet of blue stones spilled across the floor.

"That's the scientist robot." Fate inched forward to get a better look.

Much like the librarian robots, this one was spindly with six arms, but its head was humanoid, fleshy and blue tinged. Its flat, wrinkled features narrowed into a pointed chin. Glowing, bulgy eyes stared back at them as it scrambled to stand.

"I'd say it's more of a cyborg since its not all machine," Finn offered.

Brune rushed in. "So this is what's been making Kaliena's trouble juice." She stormed over to the robot. "Take us to the core."

The scientist shrank from her, talking a mile a minute in a language none of them understood.

Brune took a small instrument from her utility belt and clicked it on. The robot's voice amplified with a fuzzy, crackling sound. A few seconds later, the words began to make sense. She looked at Fate. "Did you forget about your transmodulator? You have one too."

Fate glanced down at her belt. Leave it to Brune to make her feel like an idiot.

"Who are you?" The scientist asked. "You don't have the proper authorization to be here. You've disrupted my work. Timing is crucial. The distillation process must remain uninterrupted. You have to–"

"Stop talking and listen." Brune pressed her laser gun against his forehead. "And don't pretend you can't understand me. The transmodulator works both ways."

The robot nodded.

She dropped her aim. "Did you know your work is destroying the core?"

The robot blinked, its gleaming eyes roving the room as it considered her question. "No, this is illogical. Neither my values or my program, would ever allow for the destruction of any part of the Obiectis."

Fate remembered Vasha's recording. This was the Golandon's best scientist–chosen to be cybernetically enhanced for life extension–stored in stasis if the time ever came when something broke that could not be fixed by the maintenance robots. Kaliena was that broken thing. Vasha had predicted he would find a way to wake her. If only he knew that what he'd woken was bent on reclaiming her godhood at any cost.

Fate turned on her transmodulator. "We know your job is to fix what can't be repaired by the maintenance robots, but you have to believe us, the core is damaged. One of the rings has stopped rotating."

The scientist juddered over to a blank wall. Waving several hands, he triggered a 3D rendering of the Keep with its turning hoops, except for the ring that had gone still. He gave a little yelp and then brought up a schematic of the interior workings of the Keep. The scientist flipped through layers and layers of intricate images, until at last, he stopped to stare at a round vault holding what looked like a ball of energy. Twisting his hand and fingers as if turning a dial, he subdued the light enough to display the details of a deep blue crystal.

"Is that the crystal core?" Fate asked.

The scientist didn't answer. He was intent on magnifying the image. Sliding his hand, he turned the crystal rendering, surveying the smooth surface, his head hunched forward in concentration. He stopped and went rigid when he came to a gaping hole, crawling with millions of spider robots. He turned stiffly to them with a stunned expression. "I was assured the crystals were being delivered from a surplus source."

Fate stepped forward. "Who told you that?"

"The High Priestess, Kaliena. Her health was deteriorating. She required tremendous amounts of elixir to regenerate."

"Is she back to normal health now?"

Squeaks came from the scientist's neck as he nodded. Fate couldn't help feeling sorry for him. Isolation had made him vulnerable to manipulation, and he appeared to be in need of a little repairing of his own.

"If Kaliena's healthy, why are you still making the elixir?" she asked.

"Kaliena requires elixir for the others."

Fate's stomach tightened. Wodrid was one of them. Unbeknownst to her, the sorcerer had stalked her for years, waiting patiently for her to be summoned to the Keep so he could sneak in as one of her fans. After he'd revealed his true identity, they'd all discovered he was Kaliena's lover. In their last confrontation with Wodrid, Jessie had killed him, but Kaliena had used the Orb of Aeternitis he'd stolen from them to reanimate him. He was undead now, just as Brune had been, and would remain so, unless Kaliena could fully restore him. But she would need the Rod to do that.

Fate reached for the chain holding the tiny gold Rod beneath her armor. Eustace had tried to convince her to lock the Rod in a safe place, but she'd refused. She was beginning to think maybe she should have. Kaliena already possessed the Orb. If she got her hands on the Rod, it would be game over, not just for them but for the universe at large.

Whosoever unites the Orb and Rod of Aeternitis lives as a god.

From all accounts, it appeared Kaliena was forming a contingency plan to this ultimate goal. With enough elixir, she could restore Wodrid back to the living. But who were the others?

Finn moved in toward the scientist, his eyes darkening with concern. "Can you calculate how many others there are, based on how much elixir Kaliena has asked you to make?"

The scientist counted silently, all the fingers of his six hands moving rapidly while gazing at the ceiling. After a few seconds of this, he looked at Finn. "At least two hundred thousand."

Fate stared back with mouth agape.

Brune was the first to break the silence. "Your numbers are off. There aren't that many people–or creatures for that matter–here in the Keep."

The scientist tilted his head with a soft clank and thought for a moment. "True, there are not that many living organisms readily available."

Finn visibly tensed. "Do your subjects need to be alive for the elixir to work?"

"No, they do not. Large quantities of elixir will regenerate dead matter as well."

Fate gulped. "Please tell me there isn't hundreds of thousands of dead matter lying around inside the Keep."

"Not in the hundreds of thousands," the scientist assured her. "During the Dark Tide period, we imprisoned approximately fifty thousand of the insane in the lower cells. The corpses are relatively intact."

"Relatively?" Fate squirmed with discomfort. "As in partially rotted?"

"While reanimation is instantaneous. Decayed flesh regenerates over time, as long as the elixir is administered consistently."

Fate made a face. "Oh great, he's talking zombies."

Brune shot Fate a dismissive scowl before aiming her annoyance at the scientist. "Fifty thousand isn't even close to what you calculated. Where would all the other bodies come from?"

The scientist teetered from one foot to the other as he turned to her. "The ship graveyard, which has littered the Chaos Region since the galactic Thousand Year War, of course. From there I can use freshly thawed corpses from the deep freeze of space."

It was Brune's turn to teeter. She grabbed a nearby table for support. "There's no more guessing what Kaliena's been planning. She's raising an army."

5
PRIME DIRECTIVE

"YOU'RE COMING WITH US," Brune ordered the scientist. "Kaliena can't build her army without you to make the elixir."

Raising all six arms in surrender, the scientist shook his head violently. The squeaking metal made Fate want to find some oil to grease his neck. "I cannot leave. I must reprogram the droids to repair the core."

Brune glanced down at the floor before returning a hardened gaze. "I'll give you as long as it takes me to flash back to the sanctuary and have Farouk assemble another teleporter to get you out of here." Holstering her gun, she looked at Fate and Finn. "You two stay and make sure he gets the job done."

She vanished within a puff of glinting smoke before either of them had a chance to reply. The scientist lurched across the laboratory to a long panel of gleaming buttons, which he began pressing. Four hands typed furiously, while he massaged his temples with the other two.

Fate inched toward him. She didn't want to interrupt, especially if he had a headache, but there was a question she had to ask. "Did you give the elixir to Wodrid?"

The scientist continued his frenzied typing, but this did not keep him from turning his head to look at her. "Describe this Wodrid, please."

"Well, he's not bad looking. He's actually quite beautiful, with an elfin face and delicate pointed ears poking through long silvery hair and eyes the color of ice."

"Careful," Finn warned with a playful smile, "you sound like you're crushing on him."

Fate's face warmed with embarrassment. "Ew, never!" Shaking off the repulsive thought, she turned back to the scientist. "He's also undead and being kept alive by the Orb of Aeternitis."

Recognition registered on the scientist's pale blue face. "Yes, I administered the elixir to one such subject."

Fate waited for more information, but none was forthcoming. "Did it work? Is he back to being the narcissistic, power hungry sorcerer we've all come to know and hate?"

"The one you described is currently regenerating. He requires more elixir to restore his depleted multi-dimensional reserves."

"Do you mean his ability to use magic?"

"Correct."

Fate sighed with relief. "That's good news. Wodrid's as ordinary as the rest of us." She glanced at the rune marks on Finn's temple. "I take that back. He's as powerless as me."

Finn stepped close and took her hand in his. "Hardly. You're one of the strongest amongst us. You face danger without any advantages other than your well-honed skills and courage."

Frustration gripped hold. She was tired of mustering the nerve to face each day. She wanted to know without a doubt she was every bit as powerful as her enemy. She wanted absolute confidence and fearlessness. She hated the word courage. All it meant was not running from what she was afraid of, even though that's exactly what she wanted to do. "That's easy enough for you to say. Try being normal again." Her sharp tone took her by surprise and she felt terrible for directing her resentment toward Finn.

"Hey, I know what that's like. I lost my ability to fly same as you."

"Don't remind me," she grumbled. While they'd been inside the *Book of Fables*, she'd come to rely on flying almost as much as walking.

"At least we've got these handy dandy jets built into our armor now," he reminded her.

"It's not the same. I still haven't mastered balancing the speed between the rocket fuel shooting from my boots with what's bursting from the backpack. The other day I turned myself upside down into a nosedive. I was in serious jeopardy of becoming one with the floor."

Finn winced. "You didn't need to tell me that."

"Not exactly my proudest moment."

A flurry of activity distracted them from continuing the conversation. Thousands of the spider-shaped droids skittered into the laboratory and swarmed over the bins of crystals. Swiftly and efficiently, they gathered as many crystals as each could carry, exiting the laboratory, while more streamed in to replace those leaving.

"Looks like the reprogramming is in place." Finn returned a concerned gaze. "What's really bothering you?"

"Nothing." How could she tell him she was planning to level up her abilities with something that was once used by a goddess? He'd never allow her to put herself at risk, even if the benefits outweighed a few minor side effects. Besides, this was her decision and no one else's.

"I don't buy that," he pressed. "Tell me–"

The hatch ground open. Grateful for the interruption, Fate glanced over her shoulder expecting to see Brune.

It wasn't her.

A dark soldier stormed through the opening. Fate drew her laser gun and shot. The air wavered in front of the soldier, a force field that deflected the beam. In the span of time it took Finn to pull her down behind the table with him, she recognized Jessie.

Her best friend's body was completely covered by an exoskeleton haloed by a misty aquamarine light. Bronze-toned armor fit the contours of her legs and arms like a second skin. Ribbed metal wrapped her torso and steel spikes grew from the spine of her armor. A helmet of fine metallic webbing fit snugly to her head, concealing the whole of her face, except for one beautiful hazel eye. The yellow Dragon Eye covering Jessie's other eye moved in tandem with her gaze, making it all the more disturbing.

Fate's chest tightened with a confusing mixture of relief and fear. Jessie was still alive! But what had she become? Kaliena's infection inside the Dragon Eye had obviously spread and multiplied into more machinery, completely transforming her friend into a mechanized weapon.

"It's Jessie," Fate whispered to Finn.

"Aye, I was afraid of that."

"Stay down, I'm going to see if I can talk to her." Before Finn could stop her, Fate stood. "Jessie, it's me, Fate."

Without looking at her, Jessie lifted an arm, pointing it in her direction as the armor plating reshaped into a long-barreled laser gun. Before the blast of energy struck, Fate focused her panic into being on the other side of the laboratory. Her teleporter activated, and in the flash second of scattering through space, she was standing by the hatch, staring at the black scorch on the opposite wall.

The scientist yowled and reeled, his six arms flailing. He was definitely having a bad day.

Jessie marched over to him. "Reprogram the droids to continue mining." Her voice sounded modulated and monotone through the mouthpiece.

Dropping all arms to his side, the scientist shook his head with a loud, pathetic squeak. "I cannot. Repairing the core is my prime directive."

"Kaliena's order is your *only* directive."

Finn edged out from behind the table and made his way over to Fate. "Where's Brune? We need to get the scientist out of here," he whispered. "Now!"

The scientist trembled and his knees clanked together as he turned back to the control panel and began typing.

Loyalty to the Keep surged through Fate. As much as she wanted to avoid fighting Jessie, the oath she'd taken as Keep Guardian would not allow her to stand by and do nothing. She drew her sword and struck Jessie's head from behind with the flat part of the blade. The sound of metal clashing on metal made Fate sick to her stomach. She didn't want to hurt Jessie, just knock her out.

Jessie staggered to one side, but swiftly regained balance. She turned, rushing at her with incredible speed. Fate braced for the impact, but Finn rammed into Jessie, taking her to the floor. They rolled, each struggling and grappling to gain the upper hand.

Fate watched helplessly, fearing for them both. Then she realized Finn was the one in greatest danger. Jessie's armor shifted. The gun slotted back into the arm bracer. With a series of clicks and sliding steel, daggers formed from the hard surface of her gloves and Jessie punctured Finn's armor, stabbing him in both shoulders.

Growling in pain, he vanished in a streak of sparking smoke, appearing next to Fate within the next second. "She's too strong and fast. And deadly." He winced, touching his injured shoulders.

Jessie was on hands and knees, her head turning this way and that when he disappeared from beneath her. She jumped to her feet, her claws shifting into swords, and charged toward them.

"Back to the sanctuary!" Fate yelled.

In the instant her transporter initiated, her last glimpse was of Finn nodding and Jessie's swords coming down over his head.

6
WE'RE TALKING ZOMBIE APOCALYPSE

FATE MATERIALIZED INSIDE THE library. "Finn!" Her scream echoed throughout the expanse. Her knees buckled and she hit the floor, sobbing into her gloves.

Arms folded around her and she heard her father's comforting voice.

She lifted her head to look at Eustace. Tears blurred his face. She blinked them away, swallowing the painful lump in her throat. When she tried to speak, the air stayed trapped in her lungs.

"Breathe," Eustace told her. "Just breathe."

Fate took two shaky breaths.

"That's good." Eustace removed her helmet. Her hair spilled down over her shoulders. He was quick to smooth back the stray hairs clinging to her forehead.

"Wh-what am I doing here? I was aiming for the sanctuary." Fate glanced from side to side, startled when Sithias landed next to her.

"Misss?" Sithias weaved his head low, his amber eyes round with concern. "Did something happen?"

The tap of Gerdie's shoes rapped loudly on the polished marble as she ran over as fast as her little legs could carry her. She slid to a stop. "What happened?"

Fate's eyes watered up again, making the three of them swim behind her tears. "I left him. I just left him there."

"Finn?" Eustace asked.

Squeezing her eyes shut, Fate nodded.

Eustace stiffened and he fell quiet for a few seconds. "Was it Kaliena?"

Fate shook her head. "It was Jessie."

Her father's complexion paled.

"She was completely covered in this weird, crazy armor." Her words came in gulps. "It looked like the metal had grown around her. Like it was part of her. I only recognized her by the one eye that wasn't covered."

"I take it she's still under Kaliena's control then."

"Oh yeah, Jessie's part of the Borg." She choked back more tears. "We've lost her, Dad. Jessie's gone."

Eustace stood and helped Fate to her feet. "Let's go to the sanctuary. Farouk and Brune need to be briefed."

Fate couldn't move. "I can't." She teetered, and Eustace steadied her. "It's all too much," she cried. "This isn't how it was supposed to be. I can't go on anymore. Not without Finn. I don't have it in me to keep fighting."

Eustace cupped his hands on each side of her face. "You're stronger than you think."

Fate clung to his every word.

"You've proven that, time and again. Since we've been here, I've been amazed by your bravery and determination. I know I've gotten in the way of that by being overly protective, but that's what fathers do and I'll never apologize for that." He let out a heavy sigh. "But I can see my job is done. You don't need me, or anyone else, for that matter. Not even Finn. You have the strength to carry on and do what needs to be done, regardless of what comes."

The strength in Fate's legs returned despite the incredible ache in her chest. She stepped into a hug and held her father tight.

Now she knew why she'd teleported to the library. She may have intended to go to the sanctuary, but her heart had taken her to where she knew her father would be. She could always count on Eustace–her strong pillar of strength–to ground and renew her.

Eustace winced and groaned. "Doodles, you're squeezing a little too tight."

Fate released him from her cybernetic grip. "Sorry, I always forget how much stronger the armor makes me. You okay?"

Eustace forced a smile, but it was pained. "Just a bruised rib or two." He turned and walked stiffly toward the exit.

Fate, Sithias and Gerdie followed. The walk to the sanctuary was a silent one, each of them deep in thought beneath the pall of unspoken grief over losing Finn.

When they pushed through the heavy door, Fate went dizzy with shock.

Finn was standing at the big table with Farouk and Brune. He'd removed his armor and the shoulders of his t-shirt were bloodstained. The second he saw her, he rushed over and scooped her up in his arms.

"I went mad with worry when you didn't show up here in the sanctuary." He buried his face against her neck. "Where were you?"

"I teleported to the library by mistake."

He set her down and Fate stared at him, intent on burning every detail of his face into her mind. He was here. He was really here. She wasn't imagining him. Then she touched his shoulders, happy to see that Farouk's rescue potion had already healed his stab wounds. Relief and joy flooded through her like a drug.

"Now that we have that messbacle rectisolved, we have much work to do," Farouk interjected, his voice blaring through the transmodulator attached to his cage.

Fate glared at him. "Ow, turn that down before you make us all deaf."

Farouk reached for the dial on the device with a self-satisfied smile. "I had to get your noticement somehow."

Finn held Fate's hand and led her to the table. "I filled them in on everything."

Eustace rubbed his side with a pained expression. "What exactly is everything? We know about Jessie, but it sounds like there's more."

Sithias flitted in next to Eustace, while Gerdie took her usual place on the footstool. "Yesss, please enlighten us. My scales are quivering, which is *never* a good sign. We're in even greater danger, aren't we?"

"Aye, Kaliena's been mining the core for her elixir." Finn looked at Eustace. "You were right on all counts. She has the Golandon scientist making huge amounts so she can revive the fleets of armies in the ship graveyard outside the Keep."

"And I think she's already tested the elixir on the bodies in the lower cells," Fate added.

"The scientist didn't actually say that," Finn pointed out.

Fate shook her head. "He said the corpses *are* relatively intact. He didn't say the corpses *should* be relatively intact."

"Aye, you have a point there."

"Let's just hope they haven't used the elixir on all fifty thousand of them."

"Fifty thousand!" Eustace's eyebrows shot up in alarm.

"That's not including the two hundred thousand or more corpses in the ship graveyard they plan to reanimate," Fate said. "We're talking zombie apocalypse here."

"Stop calling them zombies," Brune scolded. "Having been one of the undead and decaying at an alarming rate, it's offensive. Nobody asks to be traumatized to that degree. I certainly didn't."

Fate stared at her in surprise. "Sorry, I had no idea your feelings were so delicate."

But she wasn't sorry. Brune's reliance on the Orb of Aeternitis to keep her at the age of nineteen for seventy-five long years was bound to backfire on her, given that she'd used it without the Rod. Though she couldn't condemn Brune completely for using the Orb to solve every problem that came along. After all, if she hadn't used the Orb to summon Fate to be the next guardian with the *Eyes of Eros* spell, Finn never would've come into existence.

She gave Finn a sidelong glance and smiled. Would she ever get used to the fact she'd spent years imagining the perfect boy, writing about him in minute detail, creating an entire world and story around him that was only real to her? Yet here he was, in the flesh, thanks to a spell that had inadvertently combined her deepest desire with the creative forces of the Orb.

Finn caught her smile and his eyes lit a bright green. She leaned against him, but her armor got in the way. With an impatient huff, she unbuckled the arm bracers and gloves, slid them off, and discreetly rubbed her forearm against his, reveling in the warmth of his skin.

"Kaliena's building an army we'll never beat!" Sithias's wings twitched nervously. A large feather fluttered to the floor.

"Who's Kaliena?" Gerdie asked, wide-eyed and without a clue.

Sithias eased his head next to hers. "I'll tell you all about her when we get back to the library."

Gerdie smiled and nodded. "Okay. I like her name. It's pretty."

Farouk pressed his snout through the bars. "We'll all expirate against these kind of numbers, unless..." When his gaze slid to Brune and they locked eyes, Fate caught a disturbing red glint in his pupils.

Brune was quick to counter. "We have a billion different options. For starters, we could alter all the maintenance robots and drones into killing machines. There's at least a hundred thousand of them running on autopilot. And there's a ton of decommissioned robots in salvage we could repair."

Farouk appeared unimpressed. "Unachieveless. It would take years to retroquip each robot with weapons and artillery."

Brune refused to accept his argument and her voice rose to a shout. "Don't tell me that! I know you could program a smaller number of robots to retrofit the others. I'm sure they could get it done within days."

"Unlikely and highly riskilous." Farouk eased back in his chair with an air of confidence that was unsettling. "Have you forgotten Kaliena can taintfluence machinery and take control? If we do that, we might as well constructify an army for her."

Fate sensed a shift between Brune and Farouk. They might still be sharing a secret, but they were definitely having a battle of wills.

"Then we raid the vaults for magical objects powerful enough to destroy

Kaliena," Brune pressed.

Fate jumped on the idea. "I agree. There's got to be something out there in the Keep that'll crush Kaliena and her zombie army."

Taking offense at the 'z' word, Brune frowned at Fate, but at least she didn't disagree like she usually did.

Eustace cleared his throat as he removed his glasses and cleaned them with his handkerchief. "I've been researching everything available in the library, attempting to narrow in on Kaliena's greatest weakness, while also cross checking the vault records." He set them back on the bridge of his nose. "So far I haven't found anything that will effectively stop her, especially now that she possesses the Orb."

"The only reason Kaliena has the Orb is because someone refused to lock it up." Brune shot Gerdie an accusatory glance.

Gerdie's expression remained innocent. She'd obviously forgotten she'd stubbornly held onto the Orb, which had given Wodrid the opportunity to kidnap her and steal it for Kaliena.

"Which reminds me." Brune's gaze shifted to Fate. "It's time the Rod comes off your neck and goes in lock up."

Fate frowned and grabbed at the chain. "That depends on where you plan on putting it and who holds onto the key."

Farouk stood and held out his furry hand. "I'll governate the details of that."

"No way," Fate argued. "Not until I see where, and the security you have in place."

"The Rod's locationality is best kept secretential. If you're seizurated by Kaliena, you can't tell her what you don't know."

Fate ran her finger over the warm metal of the Rod. There was a time when she'd been under Brune's spell, an overpowering directive, which had forced her to get the Rod at any cost. The spell had also placed a mania upon her to keep the Rod for herself. Fortunately, the spell's effects had faded, but Fate had grown accustomed to being its owner.

And there was an even more important reason she wanted to hold onto the Rod. Gerdie had once told her that when Brune was in the height of her obsession with the Orb, she'd experimented with bringing dead animals back to life. Only they were never right afterwards. They were moving carcasses. Brune had even played with the weather until she wreaked havoc, and she'd made plants grow from seed to full size in an instant. The fruit had been ripe and beautiful, but rotten on the inside.

Fate glanced at Finn. He was a creation of the Orb without the benefit of having the Rod to do it properly. She tried not to think of it too much, but there was always a worry at the back of her mind, like a sliver she couldn't remove, that something might go wrong with Finn at any given point. She prayed the day never came, but if it did, she would move heaven and earth to get the Orb back from Kaliena and use the Rod to unlock its full power to restore him.

Fate stared down Farouk. "I'm Keep Guardian and I'll decide who holds onto the Rod. Until you can show me a place I agree is safe enough, it stays with me."

Farouk's mouth stretched back in a silent snarl.

"Look who thinks she's the big boss," Brune said.

Finn reached for Fate's hand and gave it an encouraging squeeze. She fixed her gaze on Brune. "I *am* the boss, so get used to it."

Brune's smug expression vanished, a sight that filled Fate with a surprising amount of satisfaction. She had allowed Brune to bully her and make her feel inadequate for the job of Keep Guardian for far too long. It was time she took hold of the reins completely.

Part of that involved taking care of that upgrade she'd been planning.

"Our first order of business is to get the scientist out of Kaliena's clutches, though she'll have moved him by now," Fate continued. "We have to find him and stop all further production of the elixir. Secondly, we need to locate where Kaliena's storing the elixir they've already made. If she's planning on raising over two hundred thousand soldiers, her supply will be astronomically huge, and most likely, difficult to hide. I say we find it and destroy it."

Everyone around the table nodded, their eyes trained on Fate, alert and at attention. Even Brune. Eustace looked proud and pleased. Gerdie appeared lost.

"That means teleporters for everyone," Fate told Farouk. "Including Darcy and Mason. With diagnostics cut off from the majority of the Keep, we need all hands on deck for this. It'll be strictly recon missions. In and out. Nothing more. Once we've located the scientist and elixir stores, Finn, Brune and I will take care of retrieval and blowing the supply to kingdom come."

She paused to look at each one of them. "Got it?"

Everyone was agreeable, except for Gerdie. "What's all this about a scientist and elixir?"

Fate called her father over. "Dad, could you take Gerdie to medical and see if there's anything that can be done to flush the forgetting spell out of her system?"

"Agreed, I'll see what can be done. We need her sharp." Eustace took Gerdie's hand and led her from the sanctuary.

"Finn, can you please roust Darcy and Mason from the love nest and bring them up to date? We need to get on this, stat."

"Aye, will do." He leaned close and whispered in her ear. "I'm proud of you, love. Leadership looks good on you."

Fate's face flushed with warmth as she watched him leave.

She glanced back at Farouk and Brune to ensure they were engaged with gathering supplies to build additional teleporters. Instead, she found them in another hushed conversation. Curiosity burned hot, but it wasn't like she could casually walk over and listen in.

She crooked her finger at Sithias, who slithered over. "I'll be needing the exact location and description of Freya's vault," she whispered. "I'm going to get what I need while we're out doing reconnaissance."

Sithias hesitated. "Misss, are you sure you really want to do this?"

"Stop asking me that. I'm not strong enough for what we're up against. I have to be every bit as powerful as Kaliena to win this."

Sithias shook his head sadly.

"What?"

His amber eyes welled with tears. "I fear you'll be changed into something I won't know, and I would miss you terribly."

7
I'M STILL ME

TENDRILS OF COLD MIST flowed from the steeples of Freya's ice vault. A biting chill pooled around Fate's boots, seeping into her feet. Shivering, Fate removed her glove and waved her palm over the panel to activate the opening with her guardian seal. The thick doors of ice swung inward. With a quick glance over her shoulder to ensure none of the others were close by, Fate ducked inside.

Frost clung like thick layers of sugar to pillars stretching up to a high, arched ceiling of translucent ice. A deadly threat of icicles dripped overhead, any of which could break and spear a person clean through. Ice sculptures in the form of snarling wolves, dragons, trolls, elves and dwarves flanked her on each side. Her breath crystallized in the air in white puffs, the snow crunching beneath her steps as she moved toward the altar.

A thick blanket of gold coins lay over the raised slab of ice, where the amber gemstones of the Brisingamen necklace sparkled under the light. While it was beautiful, Fate resisted the temptation to try it on. She skimmed over the gauntlet and crown, fixing her gaze on the girdle she'd come for, which was more of a corset than the granny girdle she'd dreaded. And it was a breathtaking one at that. Gleaming with an inner light, the darkly bronzed metal was tooled to perfection with intricate designs laced across the front and sides in shapes of interlocking serpents and raptors.

Fate ran her hand over the glimmering surface. It was warm to the touch, firm and strong, yet pliable. She lifted it, surprised by how light it was in her hands. It didn't weigh any more than a cotton shirt.

She unbuckled her shoulder pads, arm bracers and breastplate, letting them fall in the snow. The frosty air rushed in, biting her skin. Her hands shook from the cold as she loosened the strings on the back of the corset. Lifting it over her head, she wriggled it over her clothes, grateful for the heat coming off the metal. Fate closed her eyes, waiting for the sensation of power she was expecting to be imbued with.

Nothing happened.

The weight of disappointment set in as she glanced down at the corset through angry tears. Was she doomed to be ordinary forever?

Swearing under her breath, she pulled at the corset to slip it off over her hips. Her thumb hooked in her trousers and the corset touched her skin. Electricity raced across the exposed area. Fate pressed the metal against her skin again. The zap made her jump.

Feeling encouraged, she pushed the corset down over her trousers so she could remove her leather jacket and shirt. Taking a deep breath, she hiked the corset back over her hips.

As soon as it rested around her bare waist, the laces tightened of their own accord. Fate gasped as the material hugged her ribs, molding to her form like a second skin. Heat sparked at her belly button, spreading across her ribcage, shooting up her spine. Her back arched, throwing her arms out to the sides as a living fire flowed up her spine, hot and mercurial, flooding her brain with molten energy.

Her vision darkened, and for one terrifying moment, she feared she'd gone blind. Stars shattered the blackness. Light throbbed behind her eyes. Her surroundings took on a luster and clarity she hadn't known since the time she'd been knighted into Murauda's army. Though this was different. Her sight ran deeper than that. She could see the life force energy pulsing beneath the skin of her hand.

She looked down at the corset, astonished by how the pliant metal had contoured itself to her torso. Its bronzed surface was translucent, shining its inner light over her skin with the luminescent pattern of snakes and eagles etched on the curves of her waist and solar plexus.

The power hummed deep inside, as if every cell in her body was singing. Yet it was a quiet, strengthening force that was rebuilding her, making her... unbreakable. The fatigue in her muscles was gone. Erased entirely. All the tiny human aches and creaking bones no longer existed. She felt light as air.

Fate smiled. She didn't know exactly what kind of superhuman abilities she could expect to be endowed with, but she welcomed the opportunity to test herself.

A voice called out to her from outside the vault. It was Sithias, and he sounded worried. Grabbing her clothing, Fate dressed hurriedly, surprised by how well the corset fit beneath her undergarments. Sithias continued to call out as she strapped on her cybernetic armor and buckled it down. Not that she needed it anymore, but she couldn't let onto Finn, or anyone else that she'd upgraded. At least not until she'd figured out what powers she possessed.

Fate opened the ice doors and shut the vault behind her. Flapping his wings, Sithias lifted off the snow surrounding the vault and landed on a nearby moving walkway. Fate leapt over the low-lying wall and joined him. "What's all the hollering about?"

Sithias blinked sleepily. "For starters, the chill coming off that vault very nearly put me into a long winter sssleep."

"Sorry, I forgot about how your snakiness doesn't do cold weather."

"And that's exactly my problem, I was trying to–" Sithias stopped and stared at her, round-eyed with wonder. "Oh my, something's different about you, misss. I take it you got what you came for."

"How can you tell?"

"You're positively glowing."

Fate frowned with worry. "Glow in the dark glowing? Or glowing like a pregnant woman?"

Sithias grew pensive as he moved around her, his head weaving this way and that as he studied her. "A little of both, I'd say."

"Terrific, I suppose it'll be impossible to keep it a secret then."

"By the way, where is the girdle? Or did you decide on one of the other items?"

"Let's stop calling it a girdle. That's so old-timey. It's a corset, and actually quite comfortable."

"You're wearing it?"

Fate nodded with a proud smile. "Yup. When I put it on it sort of molded itself to my body, and you almost can't see it against my skin. Not that I'm going to strip and show you."

Sithias looked horrified. "I don't like the sound of that!"

"Jeez, am I that repulsive?"

"I meant what you said about the girdle–excuse me, corset. Do you even know if you can remove it?"

"I barely just got it on and I haven't had the chance to test it out to see what it does. But yes, I'm sure it comes off. Why wouldn't it?"

Sithias's anxious expression didn't fade. "I don't know, misss. This could very well be a situation where the corset wears you, instead of the other way around."

The power flowing from her core surged into her chest, reminding her of her ultimate goal. She was doing this for the good of the Keep and everyone concerned. "What was it you were going on about? You mentioned a problem?"

"Oh right. As you well know, I'm not just a snake. I'm a multi-faceted artist with a need to express myself in various creative forms and personas.

So while I was researching war goddesses and their possessions for you, I happened upon information of a siren's vault that stores a mere few thousand glamours within its walls. I wasn't going to bother you about it, but I couldn't get inside. Apparently, I need a Keep Guardian for that."

"Oh, you just happened upon a vault with a bunch of glamours, huh?" Fate smiled, relieved to have distracted Sithias from focusing on her.

If Sithias could blush, his ivory scales would be a deep shade of red. Instead, he smiled sheepishly. "Truth be told, I actively hunted for anything that would allow me to shapeshift again. I've become accustomed to doing so, and it's been horribly trying without it."

Fate gave him a wave of her hand. "Say no more. I feel your pain. There's nothing worse than having kickass powers and suddenly being without them."

Sithias sighed with relief. "I knew you'd understand, misss."

She winked. "The way you understand me."

He nodded. "Of course, so long as you're sssafe."

"Worry wart. Where's this siren's vault, anyway? Do you have a visual on it? You might as well go ahead and transmit the locale–"

Before Fate could finish her sentence, Sithias triggered the teleporter and she disintegrated into a flurry of atoms, though the experience was different this time. Instead of losing herself, the power brewing at her core united her awareness with her scattered particles and her consciousness expanded beyond the Keep, to glittering constellations, rocketing comets and spinning galaxies. She was a whirling dazzle, speeding between the world and the shadows of its energetic constructs.

Before she could comprehend what was happening, her body coalesced from the ether and she was pure substance again, standing in front of a vault made entirely of coral. Crimson and salmon-colored branches of hard coral curved high into a natural dome. The rounded entrance was tiled with pearlescent, blue-toned abalone shell.

Sithias appeared in a swirl of twinkling smoke. "Oh my, teleportation is terribly unsettling," he muttered to himself as he wavered in place, staring into space before he noticed Fate. "Oh, how did you get here before me? That's not supposed to happen."

She patted her stomach, where warmth simmered beneath the corset. "I guess the upgrade's working." Without elaborating any further, she stepped over to the entrance to open the door with her guardian seal.

The pearly door rolled aside, revealing a dark cavern with a still pool. The briny scent of the ocean washed over them in humid waves. Droplets of water fell from the wet ceiling, sounding a musical note as each drop splashed into the pool. Sea-green hues of light gleamed from somewhere deep inside the well. Strewn in a generous pile upon a large boulder cresting the water's surface were countless necklaces made of pink pearls and polished coral. They were exactly like the glamour the siren from the *Book of Fables* had given Fate.

Sithias flapped his wings, rustling a breeze against Fate's face as he lifted off and flew over to the rock. Scooping a glamour with the tip of his tail, he looked over at her with a triumphant smile. "Prepare for the new me to emerge."

His voice echoed off the grotto's walls and Fate noted a disharmonious ring to the musical water drops.

With an excited giggle, Sithias started back toward her. He didn't get far. A long sinewy arm and clawed hand burst from the water, gripped his tail and yanked him out of the air. Sithias yelped, disappearing in the sudden froth of roiling water.

Fate dove in after him. The siren was dragging Sithias down into the depths where the light grew stronger. The siren was a hideous bulgy-eyed creature with a fishy grin, gills and body covered in slime and barnacles. Sithias struggled to free himself from her claws, but she was too strong and quick. The spiked dorsal fin rising from her spine twitched as she gnashed at Sithias. He managed to evade the deadly bite of her shark's teeth, but he wouldn't last much longer. If she didn't eat him first, he would most certainly drown.

Fate swept both arms in one broad stroke, a move that catapulted her through the water like a missile. She caught up to them within seconds, shoving her hands into the siren's bony chest. Cracked ribs scraped Fate's knuckles. She grabbed the siren's beating heart, squeezed and pulled it from the hole.

Blood gushed from the ragged cavity, staining the pristine water a dark red. The siren went still, her seaweed hair floating around her vacant stare and slack, lipless mouth. Fate released the heart and let it float from her grasp. She pushed off the body and dove for Sithias. He was limp, his huge wings splayed wide as he drifted in the currents.

Grabbing hold of his tubular body, Fate swept her arm in one downward stroke. The motion shot them straight to the surface. Within seconds, they burst through the water and Fate dragged Sithias to the pool's edge. She jumped out and heaved him onto the stone.

"Sithias, wake up." When he didn't respond, she wedged her fingers beneath him and shook hard. His head thumped over the hard surface.

"Wake up!" she screamed.

Sithias coughed and sputtered, his amber eyes blinking as he looked around, lost and disoriented. "How did I survive?"

Fate couldn't stop the tears filling her eyes. "I saved you, silly."

"Then why are you crying?"

She shook her head and smiled. "Because you scared me."

"I scared you? Did you see that siren?" He coughed out more water. "*She's* what was scary. It's no wonder they stockpile those glamours."

Fate wiped her eyes and drew a shaky breath. "I thought you were dead."

Sithias rose into a coil and flapped the water from his wings. "Me, dead? Pleassse! It would take a lot more than a deadly siren to do me in. Have you forgotten I survived Elsina?"

"You have a point." Fate could only imagine the dangers of being romantically involved with a territorial, narcissistic and possessive sorceress.

"That's right." Sithias searched the wet stone. "Oh no, I dropped the necklace."

Fate pulled the glamour from her pocket and held it up. "I wouldn't let you go through all that without making sure we got what we came for."

Sithias smiled as she slipped the necklace over his head. His smile faded when he saw the siren floating face up in the bloody water, clearly displaying the hole in her chest with ribs splintered outward. His expression grew troubled. "Did you do that, misss?"

She hadn't had a moment to reflect on how easily she'd torn into the siren and she was surprised by a complete lack of empathy. If anything she felt a sense of rightness because Sithias was alive, and that's all that mattered.

"She would've killed you, Sithias. I had to do something."

"But you ripped her open with your bare hands?"

"I'm wearing cybernetically enhanced armor. You know how much stronger that makes me."

Sithias stared at her through veiled lids. "Not that strong. This is the girdle, isn't it?"

"Corset. And yes, I suppose I'm a bit stronger, and maybe a little faster. But that's a good thing. That's exactly what I wanted. And it's what we need to win the war Kaliena's about to crash down on us."

"Maybe so, misss, but there was a time–only hours ago, in fact–when such an action would have made you sick to your stomach. From what I'm seeing, you're what I'd have to describe as nonplussed."

Fate set her hands on her hips. "You're entitled to your opinion. In fact, I'll be the first to agree I'd normally be turning myself inside out with disgust over what I just did. But maybe it's time I toughened up and stopped falling apart when faced with the ugly acts of war we're constantly plagued with."

Sithias released her from his vigilant stare. "It's sad to say, but you may be right."

Fate reached out and smoothed the scales around his face. "Don't worry, I promise, I'm still me. I'm just new and improved. Like you'll be now that you have a glamour to play with again."

The snake glanced down at the necklace and smiled, though there was worry in his eyes when he returned his gaze to her. "Yesss, unfortunately life has a way of pushing us into recreating ourselves, whether we desire it or not."

8
TABULA SMARAGDINA

FINN'S HEAD SPUN FROM the dizzying sensation of his atoms and molecules reassembling. He widened his stance to stay balanced, at the same time fighting a deep-seated fear, which had become impossible to ignore. He couldn't move past the feeling he was being uncreated each time he teleported.

Clenching his fists, he pushed the worrisome thought aside, convincing himself the teleportation device was safe. These were old fears, surfacing because of how he'd come into being. He thought he'd come to terms with being born of magic, but the disturbing experience of teleportation was a continual reminder he'd been created from nothing but a random combination of Fate's imagination and the unpredictable power of the Orb of Aeternitis.

He shook his head. "Stop dwelling, boyo. This is no time for reflection."

He'd materialized into pitch black, a cold place thick with the rank odor of dead flesh, mold and rot. The back of his neck prickled as his throat closed around the cloying stench. He knew that smell from his time in the *Book of Fables* when he'd been in Asgar, the enchanted kingdom of illusions, whose people had unknowingly fed off their dead.

Finn reached for the cadastral gramographer Farouk had given him and pressed the button. Lasers of light displayed a map of the lower prisons. He blinked into the dark, trying to determine if the antechamber he'd entered branched off into the cellblocks he was seeing on the map.

Releasing a tense sigh, he searched his utility belt for a sun disc and clicked it on. It zipped into the darkness in front of him, shining a brilliant beam over greasy walls. Shadows along the floor moved in response to the sun disc's sudden radiance, slow and sluggish. As Finn's eyes adjusted to the light, he stiffened with terror.

Skeletal forms stirred, their bony arms spidering over the walls as they pulled themselves off the floor. Pale, blue-tinged flesh clung like damp, wrinkled gauze to their bones. Skulls with patches of stringy hair turned toward the light. The hollows of their eyes gleamed with an unholy blue-green light.

A chill slithered down Finn's spine. He was completely surrounded by the undead Golandon prisoners Kaliena's scientist had raised. He'd expected them to be locked in their cells, where they'd been left to die thousands of years before. Farouk had made a calculated guess the scientist might be in the antechamber, where he could administer the elixir. Based on how little the walking corpses had been regenerated, it appeared as though the scientist's work had begun and then ended abruptly. But why?

Every muscle tensed with revulsion as Finn drew his laser gun. There were too many of them to shoot at once. But they seemed not to have noticed him. They were moving with mindless purpose. Until they sniffed the air and every vacant gaze shifted to him. Grotesque faces twisted, cankered mouths stretching back from rotted teeth as their howls and snarls echoed throughout the antechamber.

Chaos erupted. The undead descended on him at once. Clawing, biting, tearing from every angle. Finn went down, the air slamming from his lungs with the shock of it all. Kicking and straining to break free, he flailed like a drowning man struggling to rise to the surface. For every corpse he threw off, another rushed in to fill the gap.

Remembering the laser gun, he squeezed the trigger, slicing into three inmates scratching at his armor. Sweeping his free arm in an arc, he blasted through a wide swath of shambling corpses, hewing them clean in half. Pieces fell to the floor with sickening wet thuds.

When another mob surged past the carnage, Finn knew he was wasting his time. Picturing the sanctuary, he braced for the sensation of his body unraveling and his atoms dispersing. The horrors crowding in on him vanished in the same instance, shifting to the welcome interior of the sanctuary.

Farouk was there with Eustace. They both looked up from the massive tome they were focused on. Finn yanked off his gloves and slapped them on the table. "Well, your theory was wrong, Farouk. The scientist was nowhere near the lower prisons."

Eustace looked him over with a grimace. "I can see you found *something* down there, as evidenced by the refuse splattered over your armor."

Finn nodded tiredly. "Aye, from the numbers, it looked to be about every prisoner ever locked down there by the Golandon. They were rabid. I wouldn't call them much of an army, so much as an undead wild horde. I'm guessing that's why Kaliena had the scientist abandon the treatment early on."

Farouk scratched under his chin. "Hmm, the lower prisons were filled with those who'd gone insane before the rings were constructified to filter the harmful energies coming from the Chaos Region. It would most likely proquire more elixir than Kaliena is willing to sacrilinquish to fully restructify their minds."

"Which means she'll focus on resurrecting bodies from the fleets in the ship graveyard," Eustace agreed. "Those are all military vessels, aren't they?"

"Yes," Farouk replied. "And too many to count after a thousand-year war."

Eustace's frown was solemn. "Kaliena will have her pick of soldiers and commanders. Clearly, the prisoners were simply a test to see how much elixir is needed to make the corpses functional."

"Aye, I fear that's the main goal." Finn's stomach tightened. He needed to know Fate was safe. He was tempted to radio her, but they'd all agreed to radio silence unless it was an emergency. "Have you heard from Fate and the others? Has anyone else returned yet?"

The words were barely out of Finn's mouth when Mason appeared in a burst of gleaming smoke. His eyes were wide with excitement as he hopped up and down. "I found the elixir! Vats of it, filling the courtyard!" He pointed at Farouk. "The Franken hamster was right about the Caledonian castle vault being the most likely storage place."

Farouk stared at him through half-veiled lids. "Of course I was exacturact, though I was hoping not to be."

"And I can see why." Mason's exuberance faded. "The walls are heavily guarded, lined with ugly gobliny dudes carrying pikes. Kind of looked like a gang or something. All their caps were red."

"Redcaps," Finn muttered.

"What was that?" Mason asked.

"Redcaps. I know them well. I had a run-in with one a few years back." Finn ground his teeth together. The redcap memory wasn't actually his. It was part of the story Fate had made up for him. He frowned. Why were these old resentments resurfacing? He thought he'd overcome the anger he'd first felt when he'd learned of his origins.

It was the teleporting. Being dismantled in the flash of a second was a frightening reminder of how he could be unmade as easily as he'd been created.

"Dude," Mason said, snapping Finn back to the moment. "You were saying?"

"They're murderous fairy folk who kill regularly to keep their caps dyed wet with the blood of their victims. It's said if their caps dry out, they die.

They'll even go after each other if they run out of plain folk to kill. Kaliena must be paying them in blood, though I'm not sure whose. It's the only way they'd agree to let her store her supply there and keep it under guard."

Mason wrinkled his face. "How are we supposed to go up against a vicious bunch like that? With cordless blow dryers?"

Finn raised his brows in surprise. "Hmm, that's not a bad idea."

Mason stared back like he was crazy, when two flares of glimmering smoke appeared behind him, causing him to jump. Finn's disappointment increased when he saw it was Darcy and Brune.

Darcy stared daggers into Brune. "You didn't need to yank me out of there. I could've handled it."

Brune stared back, her mouth pressed in an angry line. "Those weren't the orders. Recon only. Remember?"

"If you would've just let me get closer, we'd have the scientist right now!"

"No, you'd be dead right now."

Eustace stepped in between them. "You located the scientist?"

"In Sector 683." Darcy held her chin high. "I'm the one who found him."

"And nearly blew it," Brune added. "She was about to teleport into a hornet's nest of maintenance drones retro-fitted–Kaliena style–into war machines. If I hadn't stopped her when I did, Kaliena would know we're narrowing in on her master plan."

Eustace held his hands up in an attempt to calm them both. "Thankfully, that didn't happen. I suggest we focus on which vault she's taken the scientist to."

Brune unbuckled her holster and dropped it on the table. "She has him in Alexander the Great's tomb of Hermes."

Farouk ambled his cage around the table. "Ah, Hermes Trismegistus, the Egyptian adept king who docuscripted the *Tabula Smaragdina.*"

"The famous Emerald Tablet?" Eustace asked.

"Exacturately," Farouk replied grimly.

"All the alchemists I researched based their knowledge and processes on the Emerald Tablet," Eustace continued. "The tablet is at the root source of all alchemy. The philosopher's stone could never be made without its foundational knowledge."

"Kaliena moved the scientist to the tomb for a reason." Farouk crossed his arms, pulling at his fur nervously. "This is a disfortunate devolvement." His slanted gaze slid to Brune.

Finn caught a flash of red in the creature's eyes and noticed Brune's quick turn of the head to avoid his stare. Fate had said they were keeping a secret. She wasn't wrong.

"What more could they possibly do with the tablet in hand?" Eustace asked.

"The Emerald Tablet holds the secretentials of *prima materia*, the first matter, and *anima mundi*, which is the oversoul of the universe," Farouk explained. "The true natures of *prima materia* and *anima mundi* are mislost from most alchemical texts, and for good reasdom."

Mason snorted. "Doesn't sound all that threatening to me."

Darcy elbowed him. "Shh, this is big."

Farouk grabbed the bars of his cage, fixing his gaze on Mason. "With the exacturact knowledge in the hands of a scientist who comprestands alchemy, Kaliena won't need an army, she could create a titan. And as many as she likes."

Mason's smirk vanished. "Like in the movies?"

"Worse. Now be quiet," Darcy snapped.

Eustace gripped the edge of the table. "What exactly are you saying, Farouk?"

"With the Emerald Tablet, Kaliena has the power to create gods and later use them to become one."

The room fell quiet. They were running out of time. And where was Fate? She should've been back by now.

As if in answer, Fate and Sithias appeared in flashes of glinting smoke. Finn let out a relieved sigh, but his breath was squeezed off with renewed tension. Fate seemed changed, radiant beyond her normal beauty. Her skin gleamed with an otherworldly luster, and her eyes shone with an inner flame. He'd seen this type of radiance before, when she'd been taken over by the war goddess, Murauda, and imbued with the power of wind and lightning.

He wasn't the only one to notice. Farouk pushed his snout through the bars of his cage to squint at Fate suspiciously. Brune stared with a mystified frown as well.

"Okay, what did we just bounce into?" Fate asked. "Did someone drop a grumpy bomb in here?" She looked at Darcy. "It was you, wasn't it?"

"No." Darcy scowled at her. "We're having a tense conversation, which you should've been part of. Why are you two so late, anyway?" She grew quiet, which was out of character for Darcy, once she got going. She narrowed her dark rimmed eyes at Fate. "Something's different about you."

Sithias weaved away from Darcy's stare as Fate dropped her gaze. "Not sure what you mean."

"Are you using a new face cream? You look... less plain than usual. And more awake."

"Thanks, I think. And yes, I am." Fate kept her head down while fumbling with the buckles of her armor. "It's something I had the replicator whip up for me. I'll make sure you get some. It'll bring some much needed color to your face." She glanced up for a quick second and smiled when Darcy had nothing else to say.

Fate went back to stripping off her armor. "So, is anybody going to fill us in on what we missed. Sithias and I are all here to be tense with you. You know, solidarity and all that." She punched her fist in the air.

Finn moved in next to her. "The meeting's over, and I'm sure you're as tired as the rest of us." He glanced at the others. "I'll bring these two up to date while we head back to our rooms. Come on, Sithias."

Before Fate could say a word, Finn took her by the arm and whisked her toward the door with Sithias trailing reluctantly behind.

"What's with the bum's rush?" Fate asked as he marched her down the hall at a brisk pace.

Sithias caught up to them. "He knows, misss."

Fate threw the snake a warning glare. "I don't know what you're talking about, Sithias. There's nothing to know."

Finn stopped and grabbed her by the shoulders to make her face him. "What did you do, Fate?"

His anger increased as he watched her fight to keep her secret hidden. Fortunately, she was a terrible liar. "What are you talking about?" she asked.

"You did something to yourself. I can see the light under your skin and behind your eyes." He closed his eyes, allowing his awareness to fully open to her as he probed with his senses. Power sizzled off her in waves, an energy that at first curled away from his touch, then lashed at him with the force of a tiger's rage.

Finn lurched backward, staring at Fate in shock. Her jaw was set with defiance, her brown eyes filled with a fiery resistance that might as well have been a punch to the gut.

Her expression softened lightning-quick, completely unaware of what had lashed out at him. "What just happened? What's wrong? Are you all right?"

He stared at her in disbelief. "You didn't feel that?"

Wordless, Fate looked from him to Sithias. "Did you see anything?"

Sithias blinked at her round-eyed in an attempt to stay impartial.

"Tell me," she pressed.

"Well... I'm not sure what that was exactly, misss. If I had to put it to words, I'd have to say a flare of sorts came off you and pushed Finn away."

Fate placed her hand over her diaphragm. "That doesn't sound good."

Finn took a step closer. "It's not. Whatever you did, Fate, you need to undo it now."

"You're right." She fell into a run down the hallway. Finn and Sithias rushed to keep up with her but she was faster than normal. She skidded to a stop in front of her bedchamber. "Stay here, I'll get this off and be right out."

When the door slammed shut, Finn rested his back against the wall, inhaling slowly to calm his nerves. "Sithias, I want details. What is it she has to take off?"

"A girdle–I mean corset–once owned by the Norse goddess, Freya." Sithias grimaced with worry. "Fate said it fit like a second skin."

"What kind of powers is it supposed to pass on?"

"Amazonian powers. I found it rather odd that an item of such origin would end up in the vault of a Norse goddess."

Concern churned in Finn's chest. "Weren't Amazons male-hating warriors?"

Sithias gulped. "I don't know. My research didn't cover Amazons. Though looking back, I should've included them before I gave Fate the description of Freya's vault."

Finn pushed away from the wall and paced. What was taking Fate so long? Surely she should be done by now. He stopped in front of the door. "I'm going in."

"Sssir, a lady is changing inside."

"It's been too long."

Sithias slithered away and stopped several doors down. "Enter at your own risk."

Finn reached for the handle, but the door opened. Fate stood in a robe, out of breath with panic. Her face was flushed, her skin luminous and glistening with sweat. She'd never looked more beautiful. He swallowed hard, resisting the urge to gather her up in his arms and cover her in kisses.

"Finn." Her voice came in a breathless gasp. "There's no way to get it off."

"Do you need help unloosening it?" His pulse quickened at the thought of helping her undress. He shook his head. What was he thinking? This was no time to lose focus.

Fate shrank from him, pulling the robe tight around her waist.

Finn's heart sank. Why was she suddenly afraid? "I can get someone else to help. Gerdie, or Darcy... "

"No, don't tell anyone else about this!"

Sithias inched up behind Finn and peeked over his shoulder. "Misss, what's wrong?"

Tears welled in Fate's eyes and her chin trembled. "You were right, Sithias. I'm not wearing the corset. It's wearing me. I can't even see it anymore. It melded into my skin. It's part of me now."

9
CRASH

FATE LEANED OVER THE railing of the tower balcony adjacent to the Caledonian castle to study the layout of the courtyard. Surrounded by a moat of oily black water, the castle itself was unusual, in its triangular shape. Lichen stained its rough walls and age had darkened the pink sandstone to a blood red. Within the heart of the castle's inner courtyard, and glowing a bright aquamarine, stood vats of the elixir. Short, stocky creatures with large hooked noses and snarling mouths paced the ramparts. Their huge pikes knifed the air with each step. The red caps clung to their malformed heads, glistening with fresh blood in the pale light.

The urge to launch into the air and land in the middle of the Redcaps to strike them down surged through Fate's nervous system. She clamped down on the driving force burning in her core, but with great difficulty. The plan was to wait until everyone else was in position and make their surprise attack from all sides in ten minutes time.

Fate breathed deeply, but each inhale came in excited bursts. She wasn't sure she could hold out another minute, let alone ten. Closing her eyes, she thought back to the fight she'd had with Finn the night before.

He'd been furious with her decision to make herself a stronger, more capable warrior. His anger was so great he'd said hurtful things. Like how she'd summoned the Green Man when they'd been trapped in the *Book of Fables*, the very action that had caused him to be interred within the oak to pay for her rash mistake. He'd accused her of being reckless. He'd said she was utterly without care for the consequences of her actions to herself and everyone else.

When Finn saw how deeply his words had cut, he'd tried to take them back. His voice had dropped to a soft whisper as he'd said how sorry he was for losing his temper. He'd moved in behind her, wrapping his arms around her as he pressed his mouth to her ear. Shivers of heat ran down her neck even now as she remembered his hot breath feathering against her skin. She'd wanted to give in and tell him she understood his anger.

But a wall of resistance had risen from a cold, dark place inside she hadn't known existed before that moment. The emotion had been so sudden and strong she'd broken free of his embrace and pushed him across the room. She should've been upset to see him hit the wall, but she'd been filled with blinding defiance.

They hadn't spoken since then. During the strategy meeting that morning, she'd avoided his gaze and had been out the door before he could say a word. She wanted more than anything to soften to Finn, but something was stopping her, filling her head with too many reasons not to forgive so easily. She was tired of the men in her life constantly trying to control her, sick of being told what she could and couldn't do. Most of all, she was fed up with being second-guessed and told her choices were always wrong.

The timer on her watch beeped. Fate's eyes flashed open as the bloodlust she'd been holding back fully erupted and coursed through her veins. Without thinking, she leapt from the balcony. She hadn't tested herself in this area yet, but she knew the laws of gravity no longer applied to her. How she knew was a mystery. Only that as the air rushed past her, she knew in her bones she could direct the speed of her fall toward the parapet she was aiming at.

She landed firmly on both feet behind a Redcap. The creature glanced over its craggy shoulder, growling, bearing a row of yellowed fangs. Fate whipped her sword, severing the Redcap's head from his neck in one smooth motion. Two more charged with pikes aiming to run Fate through.

Fate ran straight at them, and at the same time hurled her sword into the air. Her hands reached for the daggers strapped to her thighs, as if of their own accord, and flung them. One Redcap caught a blade between the eyes, the other a blade to the throat. More Redcaps rushed in to replace the three she'd taken down. Without looking up, Fate caught the sword on its descent, cutting through four Redcaps in a powerful sweep. They fell in a heap, trying desperately to keep their innards from spilling out.

Leaping over the fallen Redcaps, Fate drove her sword into the heart of the last one standing, immediately snapping around with the blade when she sensed another sneaking up from behind. His head fell to the floor and rolled off the rampart.

Fate glanced from side to side. The area was clear. Across the way, Brune darted and weaved amidst a pack of Redcaps in a storm of steel and iron. Finn was on the third wall, moving with unnatural speed and grace, eluding the onslaught of spears. Like a phantom, he vanished from one place in a seeming blur and reappeared in another, the slash of his wind blade felling Redcaps like trees.

Having cleared his section, he sprinted along the parapet, scaled to the next level and joined in the fray to help Brune finish off the last of the Redcap guard. An anguished groan pulled Fate's attention back to the carnage near her feet. Bending to pick up a pike lying near her feet, she drove it into a surviving Redcap. Letting go of the pole, she ran and jumped from the edge. Keeping her gaze trained on the ground, she landed in the inner courtyard next to the vats of elixir.

Without wasting a moment, she planted explosives around the outer edges. Finn and Brune caught up with her when she was near the end of her personal supply. She straightened and looked only at Brune. "I've got the outside covered. You two place your charges in the center."

Giving her a nod, Brune navigated her way between the vats.

Finn started to follow, then stopped. "Fate, how long are you going to freeze me out?"

She finally met his gaze. Pain shone clearly in his eyes when all he met was ice. "This isn't the time or place for us to talk."

"When we get back then," he said.

She didn't answer, but instead glanced at the tower balcony and jumped to it while Brune had her back turned. She wasn't ready to expose her newfound powers beyond anyone but Finn and Sithias. Grabbing hold of the railing with one hand, she leaned out into space to look out over the courtyard. Finn stood amidst the glowing vats, his face upturned to stare at her in disbelief. He lingered for only a moment, then turned to join Brune in setting the charges. When they were finished, they jetted up to the balcony.

Fate continued to hold herself poised on the outside railing. She liked this vantage point. The Keep's constantly moving landscape of architectural marvels stretched out for miles in every direction. She had no trouble seeing the details of each vault cresting as far as the horizon or hearing the sounds of the enormous gears grinding beneath the surface, the fiery roar of the furnaces, and the crackling of the titanic revolving rings grazing the firmament overhead. All her senses had intensified and expanded beyond their normal reach.

She turned her awareness inward, to the power collecting beneath her ribcage, where it spilled into her solar plexus and sat like a bottomless well. Streams of energy coursed along her spinal chord, illuminating her brain with brand new neural activity. She felt herself rebuilding on a molecular level. Extraordinary strength and skill were already evident, but she wondered what else she was capable of.

Brune held the detonator up for grabs. "Who wants to do the honors?"

Fate continued to hang out over space. "Be my guest." She was mildly surprised by her detachment toward everything. Normally, she'd be fighting to assert her authority as Keep Guardian. In truth, she could hand her position over to Brune without a single qualm. She wasn't even bothered by Brune and Farouk's hush hush conversations anymore. They could have their secrets. She was above their petty concerns, evolving into something greater.

Finn stepped in next to her. "Come onto the balcony, Fate. The shockwaves from the explosion could knock you off balance."

Fate gave him a sidelong glance. "Don't tell me what to do."

"Ooh, do I detect trouble in paradise?" Brune asked.

Finn shot her a frown. "Nothing of the sort."

Brune shook her head at him. "Men... you really don't like your women strong and independent, do you?" Though when her gaze returned to Fate, she looked her up and down suspiciously. "Only thing is, you're way more puffed up with yourself than usual. I can't put my finger on it, but there's something off about you."

Finn stiffened. "How about you stay out of this, Brune?"

Fate swung her leg over the railing and landed on the balcony. "Yeah, just push the button, Brune. Let's blow this thing and get back to the sanctuary before Kaliena notices what we're up to. Remember, this is her sector. She might've detected us already."

Brune's smug expression vanished. "Here goes nothing." She pushed the button on the detonator.

Fire spewed from below and a deafening boom echoed throughout the expanse. The tower rumbled and shook. Blue-green flames rose high from within the castle walls, licking the air, filling the air with indigo smoke. Strangely, the scent of fresh rain on a cool breeze wafted past them as the elixir sprayed skyward.

Within seconds of the explosion, the whirring of hundreds of drones sounded in the distance like a fleet of helicopters. Dark shapes with blinking lights littered the skyline as they flew toward the castle.

"Kaliena's war drones are on the way. Time to go." Brune vanished in a streak of smoke and sparks.

"You too," Fate said to Finn.

"You first," he insisted.

"Go. I'm right behind you."

Lines of doubt furrowed Finn's brow. "You better be." With that, he activated his teleporter and left her standing there.

Fate turned to face the swiftly advancing machines–perfect for testing her new powers. She singled out a maintenance robot outfitted with metal wings, staring at it while the power collected in her solar plexus. When the energy swelled to bursting, she directed the power to swat the machine out of the air. The robot dipped but quickly corrected its course.

She was encouraged, but hardly satisfied. Inhaling through clenched teeth, she imagined a fist slamming down on the robot. Its wings wobbled and it nearly spun out of control. Frustrated, Fate gripped the railing and squeezed. The power wasn't obeying her literal intentions, though she could tell her imagination was somehow rearranging the immense force building inside her core.

Maybe she was trying too hard.

Fixing her gaze on the robot again, she spoke one word, "*Crash*."

The machine slammed into the castle walls, shattering into glinting shards of metal. The pieces fell and clattered over the stone. She smiled. "That's more like it."

Most of the large drones were dousing the flames with ash collected from the furnaces. But a small fleet of drones equipped with lasers turned toward the tower she was on. A torrent of red-hot beams cut through the railing and sliced into the balcony.

Fate jumped and pressed her back to the wall, her heart hammering with excitement. "*Shield*," she said, fully expecting the power to throw a protective force field around her.

A laser knifed through her armor. The hot slice of the beam drilled pain all the way to her hand and up her shoulder. She screamed, more with fury at her own stupidity than from the actual pain.

The experiment was over. It was time to leave.

But then the drones stopped shooting and hovered in place. The machines parted, allowing a dark figure to rush into view. It was Jessie. Fate couldn't tell how she was flying. There was nothing to indicate she was wearing an aeronaut pack, and there wasn't any jet fuel coming from her boots. Either way, Kaliena had indeed upgraded Jessie's gear to a new level.

"Surrender or die." Jessie's modulated voice was amplified to an ear-piercing pitch that reverberated against the wall Fate was cornered against.

The power unfurled from within Fate's core, rising in defiant waves. She stepped to the edge of the balcony. "I could say the same to you," she shouted back.

Yet her heart fought back. This was Jessie, the girl who'd befriended Fate in kindergarten by giving her the silver and gold crayons from her box so she could finish coloring her unicorn. As Jessie had put it, "There's no magic without silver and gold." They'd been inseparable ever since. They had everything in common, even in what they didn't like. Neither of them liked gym class or sports. As they'd grown up together, they'd become masters at ditching physical exertion in general. Many wonderful days were spent together in detention, daydreaming fantastical stories and drawing pictures for them.

How had they come to be in this awful place?

Jessie held her arms out in front of her as the armor covering her forearms reshaped into long barreled guns. "Surrender or die."

Love for her best friend surged through Fate. She had to save Jessie from this horrible life. The Jessie she had always known was in there somewhere. She simply had to find her.

Fate leapt from the balcony, hurtled through the air and grappled onto Jessie. They tumbled downward, smacking into the hard surface of one of the winding walkways. Jessie was on her back and Fate was on top. Taking advantage of her position, Fate gripped the gun barrels, tearing them from Jessie's armor.

Jessie brought her boot up against Fate's back, a jarring blow that sent her flying against the low-lying wall of the walkway. Fate rolled onto her knees and jumped to her feet. Jessie was already upright and storming toward her. Dodging a punch, Fate ducked low and swung her fist into an uppercut strike. The sharp ridges of Jessie's armor bit into her knuckles.

They circled each other.

"Jessie, you don't want to do this. You're not just my best friend, you're my *sister*. We grew up together."

Fate looked into Jessie's eye, the one human part of her not covered by armor. Yet there wasn't an inkling of recognition or emotion. Fate's gaze moved to the Dragon Eye. The only way to get Jessie back was to rip the thing off her face. The Dragon Eye was how Kaliena was controlling her.

Fate charged Jessie, pushing her back with one arm as she grabbed hold of the Dragon Eye and pulled. Jessie screamed as blood spilled from the loosened device. This was a human cry, not the robotic tone she'd been using.

Fate let go of the Dragon Eye, horrified to find that the device was now embedded into Jessie's eye. If she continued to pull, she might blind and possibly even kill her.

Fate jumped to the rooftop of a pearlescent mausoleum passing by. Clinging to its spire, she glanced back at her lost friend with tears in her eyes.

Jessie didn't pursue her. She stood very still, then lifted off and flew back in the direction she'd come. The drones rushed toward her with lasers blasting. Picturing the sanctuary, Fate triggered the teleporter, escaping the onslaught of cutting beams by a few spare seconds.

10
Heaven Will Have to Wait

QUIET ANGER VIBRATED THROUGH every inch of Finn's body. He'd had to wait a torturous eternity for Fate to return from the surface of the Keep. When she'd finally arrived and he'd found out she'd fought with Jessie, he'd lost his temper all over again, a reaction that had driven the wedge between them even deeper. She'd turned even colder–if that was possible–and had stormed out of the sanctuary.

He pushed through the huge doors of the library and marched across the marble floor to where Sithias huddled behind a stack of books immersed in reading. He'd shifted from snake form into the pale, freakishly tall young playwright Finn had grown accustomed to when they'd been trapped inside the *Book of Fables*.

Finn stopped in front of the table. "Is this why you did it?"

Startled, Sithias reared back in his chair with a gasp, his long arms flailing as it tipped over. He fell onto his back then jumped to his feet, towering over Finn like a skinny tree.

"All so you could get the siren's glamour?" Finn demanded to know.

Sithias grabbed at his chest in an attempt to catch his breath. Flushes of pink stained his pasty complexion. "Wha-whatever do you mean, sir?"

"Don't play daft with me, Sithias. You know what I'm talking about... helping Fate to find the object of a war goddess to make herself stronger."

Sithias stood, though his bony knees quivered. "I tried to warn her against it. Honestly, I did."

Finn poked his forefinger into Sithias's chest. "You never should've done the research in the first place."

Sithias raised his hands like someone being held at gunpoint. "I know, I know." Dropping his arms, he hung his head behind the long wisps of his flaxen hair.

Finn stopped poking him and sighed. "I'm done, Sithias. Sit down and relax."

Sithias set his chair upright and eased himself down, though apprehension lingered in his amber eyes.

Finn grabbed a chair and sat down next to him. "Now then, what are you going to do to make amends for helping create this tangled mess?"

"Oh, I'm already on the job, sir." Sithias reached excitedly for a leather-bound book and opened it to the bookmark. "I've been studying up on the Amazonian warriors. According to the *Book of Herodotus*, the Amazons were not men haters, as you first assumed. Quite to the contrary, they were open to having men in their lives, as long as the men wished to adopt their nomadic horse-riding lifestyle of hunting, raiding and fighting, all while making their home beneath the open sky."

Sithias stroked his goatee into a curled point as he leaned in and whispered, "Actually, the Amazons were well known for being passionate lovers."

Finn leaned back and crossed his arms. "If that's the case, why is Fate freezing me out?"

"Well, the Amazons were also fiercely independent. They didn't like being told what to do. By anyone."

"Aye, I've been getting that message loud and clear."

Looking uncomfortable, Sithias cleared his throat. "There's more, if you'd like to hear it, though you won't like it."

"What choice to do I have? Keep going." Finn slumped in his chair as Sithias skimmed the page.

"The real trouble began when the Amazons earned the attention of the gods, notably Ares, the god of war. He sired a whole new generation of Amazons who grew to be militaristic savages. They lived only for the blood drawn in battle. He gave his first daughter, Hippolyta, a magical girdle that made her queen of the Amazons. She ruled with an iron fist, that is until Hercules killed her for the girdle." Sithias raised his gaze from the book. "I fear this is the very same girdle Fate is wearing."

Terror iced through Finn's veins. He sat stiffly in his chair. "Tell me you're not thinking Fate has to die to remove the blasted thing."

Sithias stared back with renewed fear and gulped. "I would, but I can't think of any other alternative."

Finn pushed his chair back and stood. "No! There has to be another way."

"Agreed. I'll keep looking into it, sir." Sithias reached for the pile of books next to him. "The answer is here somewhere. I'm certain of it."

Sounds from the entrance had Finn turning to see if it was Fate. Instead, Gerdie and Eustace entered the library. "Keep working on it, Sithias. I'll head these two off. It's best they don't know what Fate's done unless it becomes impossible to hide."

Wiping the frown from his face, Finn headed over to them. "Fancy seeing you here, Gerdie. How's the memory? Is it back?"

Gerdie stared up at Finn wide-eyed. "Who are you?"

Eustace bent slightly to speak to her. "You remember Finn, don't you?"

She tilted her head to one side as she studied Finn. "Nope."

Finn leaned close to Eustace. "Is it just me, or has she gotten worse?"

"Yes, unfortunately, her memory appears to be disinte-grating day by day."

"Who's he?" Gerdie pointed at Sithias. "He's funny looking. His skin's real white. Why does he look like a stick of chalk?" Giggling, she ran across the room and stopped at Sithias's table.

"Uh, Finn, can I speak to you for a moment?" Eustace asked. "Aye, what can I do for you?"

"It's about Fate."

Finn braced for the impending question of her sudden change. How was he supposed to tell him Fate possessed the powers of an Amazonian queen who'd been the daughter of the god of war?

Eustace shifted his weight from one foot to another, obviously feeling as awkward as Finn. "I've been thinking about that promise I extracted from you. It was wrong of me to meddle in your relationship with Fate. She's more woman now than she is a child. It would seem the innocence I've tried to preserve in her has already been taken by the terrible experiences she's had to face of late. Given that, I think it's time I stepped aside and allowed her to make her own choices, concerning... well, you know the matters of consenting adults."

Finn opened his mouth to speak, but Eustace cut him off. "I hope you'll recognize she's been through a lot since you two met, and it would ease my mind greatly to know you have her very best interests at heart."

Finn nodded. "Aye, sir, I understand your concerns. I only want what's best for Fate."

"Good. I trust you'll pass this onto her? It's been very difficult being on the outside of my daughter's affections these last few weeks."

"I will. And believe me when I say, I know exactly what you mean by that." Finn started to leave, when Eustace stopped him.

"Have you noticed anything different about her lately?" Eustace asked. "She seems changed somehow. There's a restless energy simmering beneath the surface–a look in her eyes I've never seen before. The intensity is... unsettling."

Finn swallowed. Was it possible Eustace couldn't detect the full radiance lighting Fate from within? Darcy had noticed a difference in Fate's skin as well, but she'd been willing to accept Fate's excuse of a new face cream. Was it because they were ordinary humans and had never been touched by magic? "I'd say it's too much stress that's causing the restlessness," he offered at last.

Eustace looked doubtful at first, but accepted the explanation with a nod of his head. "You'll let me know if it's something else though?"

"Of course." Finn turned away and headed for the door before Eustace could catch the lie in his eyes. He respected the man and didn't enjoy deceiving him. But what else could he do? The last thing he wanted was to get in the way of Eustace making peace with his daughter. Fate hadn't voiced her feelings, but he knew she was miserable about the rift between her and her father.

Finn started down the hall toward the residence quarters then stopped and took the hallway to the training court. He couldn't stand the thought of going back to his room, knowing he'd end up pacing a deep groove in the floor. His time was best spent training for imminent war. As well as burn off some extra steam.

Fate was already there when he arrived. He slowed down and kept his steps light as he eased toward the courtyard–sunken in the center of the vast chamber. Inching close to the edge, Finn watched Fate's movements in amazement.

Dressed in nothing more than a loose shirt and leggings, she was stunning to behold. It was like she was dancing. She spun and slashed her sword in sweeping motions, piercing the holographic targets darting around her with perfect accuracy. She moved so fast her face was a blur, her hair streaming in the air like fiery ribbons of silk.

Finn's heart thudded at the sight of her and his throat dried. His beautiful warrior lass. No one else stripped him of all his defenses the way Fate did, leaving him utterly open and vulnerable.

She stopped abruptly and turned. Lifting her chin, she met his gaze. He noticed the struggle to hide her feelings behind her long, thick lashes. Standing still, she breathed hard as he fell into the depths of her cinnamon brown eyes. Love swelled in his heart. In that moment, he lived for a smile on her lips. Something to tell him she had softened toward him.

Filled with hope, he jumped down into the court and walked over to her.

She sheathed her sword. "I'm finished. The court's all yours."

He caught her by the wrist before she could escape. "Stay and train with me."

A mixture of wonder and confusion played across her face as she pulled away. Bending to retrieve a towel, she wiped the sweat from her brow. Tiny beads glistened over her top lip. He longed to kiss them off. The shining luster of her skin made her all the more irresistible.

When he raised his gaze from her mouth, he was met with a cold, obstinate stare. "It's best you train on your own. As you keep reminding me, I'm not myself and I wouldn't want you thinking I've done something horribly out of character again." She jerked her wrist from his grasp and turned to leave.

"Fate, don't go. We need to work this out."

She turned back with fists shaking at her sides. "And how do you propose we do that? By me going back to what I was? Weak and useless? Is that how you like me?" She didn't give him a chance to answer. "You really can't stand me being stronger and more powerful than you, can you?"

Finn shook his head. "You know it's not about that. Can't you see I'm afraid for you? You're changing into something else, and I'm afraid whatever that is will consume you entirely."

Fate bit down on her lip. "No, I think you're mourning the loss of the girl you want me to keep being. I'm not the selfish one here. You are, by not letting me become who I want to be. Let me set you straight on this. I don't exist for your entertainment."

Her words shot straight to the heart and tore a hole in him. "Oh, I see. It's all right for me to exist purely for your happiness, but I don't deserve the same from you."

She fell silent and stared at the floor.

Feeling terrible for throwing an angry barb back at her, he closed the space between them. "Hey," he whispered softly, "don't you know your strength and power had always astonished me? And I'm not talking about what's coming from this magical girdle–"

"Corset."

"Aye, that thing around your waist." He tapped her collarbone lightly with one finger. "What I'm talking about is the strength and power you were born with. That deep well of courage and determination is what's gotten you this far. It's what I fell in love with. I could care less if you can leap mountains, throw boulders and crush them into rubble. I love you just as you are, Fate Floyd. And I always will."

She lifted her gaze as tears stood on her lashes. "I'm sorry. I've been awful to you." Leaning against his chest, she sobbed.

Finn folded his arms around her and held tight. All the tension he'd been carrying melted away as he buried his face in the soft fold of her neck. "As long as we're together, we can face anything."

Fate nodded wordlessly and stood on tiptoe to kiss him. The honeyed taste of her mouth sent delicious shivers along his spine and he returned the kiss hungrily. Waves of desire flushed through his center, shooting to his brain, hot and dizzying. Until now, he hadn't realized just how much he'd been craving her touch. How much he'd missed the heat of her breath against his skin.

Framing her face in his hands, he kissed the corner of her mouth before brushing his lips over her jaw and down the curve of her neck. Gasping softly, Fate dug her fingers into his back, pressing her body against him with astounding strength. The force behind her grip took him by surprise, but he had to admit he liked it. He no longer needed to keep his own strength in check for fear of hurting her. Nor did he have to worry about breaking his promise to her father. He was finally free to act on the love overflowing for his sweet bonnie lass.

Breathing in the perfume of her skin, he drank of the salty ambrosia glistening at the base of her throat. Fate moaned and pulled him to the floor. Feeling lightheaded, as if he was floating, he sank down beside her. The air grew hot and thick between them, pulsing with energy. She clutched at the front of his shirt and arched against him.

Every nerve ending in his body lit up, magnifying her touch. Sliding his hand over the slope of her hip and past the hollow of her waist, he reached for the top button of her blouse. Her breathing grew shallow as he undid each button. A blush spread from her neck until her face burned feverishly. She lay bare, offering herself to him, heart, body and soul. Awestruck by her beauty, he traced his gaze over the graceful lines of her face and secret curves of her body, doing his best to commit her to memory before the moment passed.

Finn descended to her mouth, kissing gently at first. When her kisses matched the ravenous desire building inside him, he surrendered to the crashing tides of unbridled passion and devoured her. The voluminous chamber faded and vanished until all that was left was the space between them and the wild beating of their hearts.

The ear-piercing scream of a siren drilled into Finn and the paradise they'd created together shattered into a million tiny pieces. Fate jolted to a sitting position, clutching her shirt tight across her chest. She glanced around wild-eyed, panting from a mixture of passion and panic. "Farouk sounded the alarm again."

Finn clamped down on the frustration burning in his chest. "Do you think it's for real this time?" He reached out, but he'd already lost her. Fate rose to her feet and buttoned her shirt. Determination and purpose hardened her expression. Gone was the look of love and longing he'd enjoyed only seconds before.

"It's real. Something's wrong. I can feel it."

"That's fine, but can't it wait just a few more seconds?" he pressed. "We made a piece of heaven together. I know you were there with me."

She stared at the exit, her stance tense, like a horse ready to bolt as soon as the reins loosened. "I was, but heaven will have to wait." Without looking at him, she sprinted across the courtyard and headed up the ramp.

As Finn watched her leave, a deep sadness sank in. Fate was lost to him. He'd been fooling himself. She would never be his. Not as long as she was bound by her oath as Keep Guardian and under the influence of a powerful object of magic only a goddess could, or should wield.

II
A WEE BIT BAD

FATE RACED DOWN THE hall toward the sanctuary at a speed that was startling. She'd be pleased with this if she weren't in such turmoil. She felt awful for deserting Finn the way she had, but she'd needed to leave. The temptation to stay with him and ignore the insistent, duty bound urgings of her oath ripped her in two. Even now, the sweet tender memory of what they'd shared flowed through her system like quicksilver; touching off pleasure centers she'd almost forgotten. She'd wanted more than anything to let go and tumble into paradise with him, never to return to the nightmare she was now running toward.

Frustration poured into her chest, bitter and foul. She was powerless to resist the call of the Keep. The shrieking alarm scratched at the inside of her skull like a wild animal thrashing in its cage. Defying her oath caused actual physical pain that only worsened the longer she held out.

She burst through the door to find most everyone gathered in the sanctuary. Darcy clung to Mason's arm anxiously. Gerdie wandered the outer edges of the room, glancing around as if this was the first time she'd ever seen it, which was worrisome. Brune and Eustace hunched over the table, staring at the 3D projection of the Keep. Farouk held his usual position at the head of the table. When he saw her, he switched off the alarm.

The projection showed two more rings had stopped rotating around the Keep. A total of three stood at a complete standstill. Stifling a streak of panic, Fate joined them at the table. "I take it destroying Kaliena's store of elixir hasn't done a thing to stop her from moving forward with her plans."

Sithias rushed into the sanctuary, arriving out of breath and wobbly on his new human legs. A smile tugged at the corners of Fate's mouth. She was happy to see he'd taken on the form of the gangly, awkward Sithias she'd grown so fond of during their time together in the *Book of Fables*. He lurched between the door and the table, the snowy wisps of his hair moving like wind-ruffled feathers as he grabbed the edge to steady himself.

"Glad to see the old Sithias is back," she whispered.

He stood a little taller by stretching his neck like a crane and smiled. "I thought you might appreciate thisss particular persona." He winked with a twinkle in his amber eyes. "I've always been rather partial to this one myself. Elsina's Mr. Romance was boringly perfect, and while I've experimented with many other interesting characters, this one feels the most natural."

Finn entered the room. Fate's heart hammered out of control and her face flooded with heat. He only glanced at her for the briefest second, but in that instance, the sorrow in his eyes infused her with grief. She wanted to grab him by the hand and drag him out of there so she could chase the sadness away, but duty rooted her feet to the spot.

The Keep was in danger. They were all in danger. That was all that mattered in the moment.

Farouk banged the end of his pointer on the table. "This is a predica-mergency of the highest order. I have retroquipped the sensors on the operactional rings to visually capture images outside the Keep. As you will see, there is much to be concerned about."

He pointed at the last three turning rings, which generated images of space debris and derelict ships floating well outside the perimeter of the Keep's rings. Fate leaned forward with a building dread. Some of the ships were lit up and appeared to be forming concentric lines around the Keep.

Her voice cracked, betraying her fear, when she spoke. "It looks like Kaliena has already reanimated enough soldiers to repair and man those ships. I don't understand. We blew up all the elixir she had."

A sarcastic snort came from the other end of the table. "Obviously, she had more than one reserve." Brune rolled her eyes, a gesture that had a way of making Fate feel like a knucklehead. But not this time.

Raising her chin, Fate stared back at Brune. "If it's so obvious, why didn't you locate all those other reserves the last time you were out on one of your mysterious scouting expeditions for Farouk?"

Brune chose to remain silent, but the sidelong look she gave Farouk spoke volumes.

Farouk banged the end of his pointer on the table. "This is not the time for suspiciations!" A snarl twisted his snout as he pushed his face through the bars of his cage. "We must prepurate for an attack. We are about to be occuvaded by armies unlike anything you have ever faced."

"Do you mean right now, this minute?" Fate asked.

"No, as long as one of the rings is operactive, the ships are unable to breakture the forcefield and protective atmosphere." Farouk's pointed ears sagged. "Kaliena is no doubt working on shutting the other rings down as we speak. Her fleet will occuvade the moment the rings stop moving."

"What do we need to do to prepare?" Eustace asked.

Her father's face was drawn and lined with worry. He hadn't looked like his usual buttoned-up, neat self for weeks. Not since they'd been at odds. Fate's heart ached knowing she should have prevented him from coming to the Keep with her. Even if that meant he'd be angry with her for the rest of his life. She'd grown up without her mother and she'd lost Gran. The thought of losing Eustace and being orphaned, slayed her.

"I say we send everyone who isn't a Keep Guardian back to Earth, where they'll be safe," Fate announced. "And we need to do it now, in case the portal is damaged in the attack."

An immediate debate broke out, with everyone talking at once. Eustace argued that Earth would not be safe if Kaliena succeeded. Finn flat out refused to leave. Mason wanted to stay and fight. Sithias reminded her of his promise to stick together, though his knees were shaking when he said it. Gerdie wondered why everyone was upset, while Brune remained silent, knowing her place was with the Keep. Darcy ran to the portal entrance, yelling for someone to activate it so she could go home.

A loud and distant rumble sounded. A jarring thrum reverberated through the floor and walls. All light vanished, plummeting them in darkness. The arguing stopped and all noise ceased, save for frightened cries from Gerdie and Darcy. Remembering that Gerdie had been standing next to her before the lights died, Fate reached out and grabbed her hand. "It's okay, Gerdie. I'm right here."

Gerdie sniffed. "I'm scared of the dark."

Someone brushed against Fate's arm. "Take this Gerdie," she heard Brune say. "Push the button."

The bright light of a sun disc flew from Gerdie's grasp and hovered in the air. She gasped and clapped at the day glow spotlight shining down on her.

"That was nice of you," Fate told Brune.

"She's my little sister."

Fate nodded. "Now what?" she asked Farouk, who was busy typing on his keyboard with an unusual frenzy.

"I'm attempting to destructalize Kaliena's governations over the sanctuary. If the interpediment is successful, we'll have continulonged life support and possibly take back control of at least one ring to generate a forcefield. A weak one, but it will at least hinder all remaining ships from infilcrossing."

Fate ran over to the armory section. "Time to suit up!" Her hands shook with nervous energy as she slipped her legs into one of the leather suits. She glanced at Eustace, who had taken it upon himself to comfort Gerdie and keep Darcy from freaking any more than she already was while she, Finn and Mason donned their gear. As always, Brune was already in uniform and dressed to kill. "Farouk, is there somewhere safe Eustace can take the girls?"

"Let Farouk concentrate," Brune told her as she marched over to her father. "Go to the very end of the residence quarters. There's a shelter there, which locks from the inside."

"Like a panic room?" Fate asked.

Brune nodded. "I never understood why it was there until I heard Vasha's recording. The Golandons must have installed the shelter in case the large population of insane ever busted loose and breached the sanctuary walls."

Fate checked the fuel gauge of her laser gun. Satisfied it was full, she holstered the gun and turned to her father. "I'll see you after this is over, okay?" She did her best to project a positive face, but she couldn't hold it when she saw the fear in Eustace's eyes.

He stepped forward and gave her a hug. "Please be safe, Doodles, and come back from this." He kissed the top of her head, stepping back with tears glistening in his eyes.

She'd placed her life on the line as Keep Guardian more than once, but this was the first time an internal quaking gripped hold. A sense of terrifying change and doomed endings rattled around her. She held still as the sanctuary walls closed in around her like a giant coffin. The last time she'd had that feeling was when she'd been summoned by a spell and trapped inside the *Book of Fables*.

Everything was about to go very bad indeed.

She pushed the premonition away and nodded at her father. "I will," she assured him, but her words came out more willful than confident.

Gerdie tugged on her arm. "You look like a soldier. Are you going to war?" Her face crumpled into worry. "I hope not. My daddy lost his arm in World War I."

Fate bent low. "I didn't know that, Gerdie. I'm sorry that happened."

"Be real careful... what's your name again?"

"Fate." She straightened. Maybe it was a blessing Gerdie couldn't remember anything. At least then she'll be saved the pain of loss that was sure to come. Her gaze returned to Eustace.

"LYF," he said, struggling to smile, but the corners of his mouth turned down.

Fate gulped down the painful lump in her throat. "LYF."

Eustace tore his gaze away and steered Gerdie toward the door.

Darcy lingered behind. "I'm not going to say goodbye to Mason because this isn't goodbye." She hugged her arms and glanced over at him, where Brune was implanting him with a teleporter device. "Please, Fate... keep an eye out for him. All right?"

"Of course," Fate promised.

Sithias tripped over something on the floor, most likely his own feet, and stopped in front of her. "Should I suit up and go with you?" His eyes were round with dread.

"No, I need you to stay and keep my dad and the girls safe."

Sithias nodded enthusiastically. "I can do that." He started to leave, then turned back. "Do be careful, misss."

"I will." Fate tried to sound convincing despite the foreboding feeling taking root in her gut.

Sithias caught up with Darcy and followed Eustace and Gerdie through the door, taking the light of the sun disc with them.

Fate reached for one of the sun discs slotted in her belt just as Finn closed in behind her with a whisper. "It's all good, love. We'll get through this fine."

She wanted nothing more than to sink against him and stay hidden in the darkness where she could pretend everything really was fine. "I wish I could believe that, but there's something different this time–"

A deafening blast of rending steel stole her words. Blinding light blazed through a jagged hole where the hatch used to be. Superheated waves of energy and howling air hit Fate with the force of a hurricane, ripping her from Finn's arms. She slammed against the back wall, instinctively deflecting debris careening through space with her forearms. In a moment of shock, she realized her armor was shredded, but her skin and bones remained unharmed.

She searched for Finn, seeing with unmeasured relief that he'd created a protective shield of wind to avoid being impaled by the metal shards flying through the air. Brune had taken shelter behind Farouk's cage, which repelled the deadly shrapnel with an electric forcefield. Mason was nowhere in sight. Had the impact from the explosion thrown him outside? Her heart clenched with sorrow to think he was probably dead.

No, she couldn't lose another soldier. Fate jumped to her feet and rushed to the sanctuary wall's mangled hole. She leaned over the edge in search of Mason, but her blood ran cold as she surveyed the Keep. Legions of strange, antiquated ships swarmed the air, blotting out the sprawling landscape of vaults far below. Many of them appeared to be dirigible airships. Vessels which obviously had the ability to traverse both space and the atmosphere within the Keep, while other ships were much smaller and sleeker in design, propelled by such things as fans, wings and fins.

A massive ship rose into view, designed much like an ocean liner with a small city of elaborate buildings and towers built upon its platform. An intricate network of machinery and spinning fans beneath the hull of the airship kept it hovering in place, while tall spires exceeding the height of its towers whirled with rotating blades.

As the ship sailed closer, Fate noticed a line of cannons aimed at the sanctuary. Standing on the bow just above the masthead of a growling bronze wolf, was Kaliena. Adorned in a flourished helmet and long black dress with ornate armor covering her torso and multitude of arms, her blue skin glowed with vibrant health. The last time Fate had seen Kaliena, she'd been sickly, using a mechanical, centipede-like contraption to give her the mobility she'd required while on life support.

Wodrid stood tall and strong next to Kaliena. He'd lost the zombie gray pallor from their last encounter. His crimson robe and long white hair blew in the breeze churned by the other airships. The red jewel crowning his staff burned with an ethereal fire, an unsettling sign that his magic was back in full force.

Fate wasn't surprised that Kaliena had used the elixir to restore herself and her lover, but the two had been hard enough to fight when they were in a weakened state. She couldn't imagine going up against them when they were both juiced up with the curative powers of the Philosopher's Stone.

Jessie flanked the other side of Kaliena. Nothing had changed about her. She was still the souped up cyborg soldier Kaliena had turned her into.

An army filled the deck behind the three of them. While many of the warriors appeared human at first glance, a better look proved they were nowhere near human. Heads were oversized and distorted. Some had horns. Bodies were disturbingly disproportionate, and ranged in size from giants to dwarves.

Finn stepped in beside Fate. "This is bad. Very, very bad."

"Uh huh," she muttered as she stared at the ships, "and I think we lost Mason."

"I know."

Kaliena's ship advanced, stopping within fifty feet of them. Her voice boomed throughout the expanse, every bit as loud as the explosion that had punched a hole through the iron wall. "Surrender the Rod of Aeternitis and I will allow you to live."

Fate reached for the Rod hanging from the chain around her neck and backed into the shadows of the sanctuary.

"Wow. She actually thinks we'll hand over the Rod and give her the key to becoming a god."

"Aye, but I can see why she believes she has the upper hand," Finn replied as he stared back at Kaliena with a grim expression. "By what I'm seeing, I have to agree with her."

Farouk crabbed his cage over the debris and stopped behind them. His ears stood straight and quivered when he saw Kaliena's ship and her massive fleet. "We're out of time! Give me the Rod, Fate. I'm the only one who can keep it safe now."

Fate clutched the tiny gold bar. "The Rod's safest with me."

Farouk's ears flattened against his head and his slanted eyes narrowed into slits. "You are the most instubbordinate guardian I've ever had the botherance of working with." He turned to Brune. "Unlock my cage. Now!"

A look of guilt and fear filled Brune's eyes as she edged along the wall. A sickening sense of betrayal spread through Fate's stomach.

"We made a bargain when I curified you of the Gorgon's monstramorphosis," Farouk reminded Brune. "It's time to pay."

The hairs on the back of Fate's neck stood on end as Brune withdrew a key and stepped toward the cage. Fate blocked her way. "What's going on, Brune? Why is–"

Finn grabbed her arm. "There's no time for this. Look, Kaliena's ordered her goons to move in."

Fate neared the ragged edge of the sanctuary. Several smaller ships moved past Kaliena's flagship and advanced toward them. They slowed and hovered within a few hundred yards of the hole. Lines shot from their bows with grappling hooks that clanged against the walls. Most fell away, but several lodged on the twisted metal of the blasted opening.

Finn dragged Fate away from the hole. "Get back, we're about to have company!"

The words were no sooner out of his mouth, when a tangle of electricity lashed through the hole, knocking him across the room. A helmeted head lifted up over the edge. The mouth below the visor gaped with fangs dripping ichor. The stench of rotten meat wafted from its decayed torso, which was covered in a breastplate of bones.

Farouk's furry little arms worked the levers to hurry his cage off to one side as a dozen more undead soldiers followed the first in, each of them in varying stages of decomposition.

Fate drew her laser gun and shot. The beam sliced into the necrotic flesh, but did nothing to stop them from advancing. Using weapons that shot wild bolts of electricity, they struck with frightening speed. Giving up on the gun, she dodged their deadly strikes with superior speed and drew her sword.

One of them swiped Farouk's cage. He went hurtling to the back of the sanctuary, crashing into the wall with a loud clamor. Brune charged with her sword, hacking through his arm before more soldiers swarmed, backing her into a corner with crackling beams poised to strike.

Finn's voice filled the room with the deafening roar of giants of old. Red-gold micro-sparks poured from his mouth as he used the Elder race runes to call upon the element of Air. A wild and terrible wind rushed in, sweeping the soldiers across the room, where they smashed into a wall.

Fate rushed in, slicing her way through torsos, severing heads wherever she could. These things couldn't be killed, but dismemberment seemed to debilitate them. Finn transformed his flute into a wind sword with a few quick notes and leaped in next to Fate. They set their backs to each other, sweeping their blades with a unified frenzy that fired adrenaline up Fate's spine.

It was over within seconds.

She wiped her forehead dry and smiled at him. "That wasn't so bad."

Finn started to smile back when a headless body clawed his ankle and held on. Swinging his air blade down like he was swatting a fly, he shook his leg to kick the appendage off. "Aye, not bad at all."

The humor in his expression vanished as the sound of Kaliena's voice echoed outside the walls of the sanctuary. "Kill them and bring me the Rod!"

His gaze darkened and moved past her shoulder. "I take it back, love. Looks like things are about to get a wee bit harder."

Fate turned around and gulped.

She had no idea what they were, but from where she stood, it looked like an army of demons pouring in through the hole, with no end in sight.

12
CURIOUS CREATURES IN CAGES

HORNED CREATURES OF MELTED scales over meat and bones surged into the sanctuary. Acrid smoke drifted off their dark slender bodies, filling the room with the smell of hot metal. With bony spikes bristling from their backs, their chests glowed red-hot like the embers of a fiery forge. Inhuman eyes blazed white with fury.

Fate knew these creatures were otherworldly, but if she had to put a name to them, she'd call them the devil's minions. What else could they be?

"Holy hell," Finn murmured, echoing her thoughts exactly.

One of the demons stepped forward, its wrathful stare aimed at Fate. It pointed a shiny black claw at her. "Give me the Rod," it hissed.

Finn angled in front of Fate. "Get behind me so I can blast these–"

Before he could speak another word, let alone summon the elements, the demon lanced him in the chest with a fiery whip. The blow threw him back, knocking Fate off to one side.

Fear catapulted Fate into action. She jumped even as she was running, high into the air with her sword targeting the demon's chest. Calling on all her strength, she brought the blade down, piercing its decayed scales. But when the steel slipped into the creature's burning core her sword melted into silvery molten drops.

The demon lashed its fiery whip, striking her on the back before she landed. Heat seared her spine. She faltered and stumbled as the burst of pain transformed into rage. Fate spun around. She closed the space between them in a heartbeat and punched her fist through its craggy breastbone. Fire engulfed her hand, shooting agony up her arm, but she held it there, her fingers digging for its heart. When she reached the pulsing organ, she squeezed the life force from it. Jerking her arm back, she tore the heart from its root. The demon collapsed as she held the oozing black pulp up for the other demons to see.

She glanced at her charred, bloody hand and forearm. The skin was fast turning pink, healing within seconds, the pain abating just as swiftly. The other demons fanned out, tilting their horned heads as they narrowed in on her.

Fate stood her ground, counting their numbers in her head as they spun whips of fire from the tips of their claws. Thirty-three. The air was growing hot and acrid, making it difficult to breathe. There were too many of them to take on all at once. Any attempt at holding them back would be like trying to hold back a meteor shower.

She'd have to pick them off one by one. After all, she was the only one who could survive hand-to-hand combat with these things.

The split second decision triggered something in her head, throwing sparks up in front of her eyes. In a flurry of motion, she leaped forward, moving faster than any human ever could. Jabbing her fists into the first two demons she met, she ripped their hearts from the smoking holes in their chests.

A thrill flooded her bloodstream, when she discovered how easy it was. Everything seemed to slow as her awareness sharpened into the ability to see the tiny particles of ash scattering from the demons like snowfall. Next to her movements, theirs were sluggish. She darted and weaved through the gaps between them, using the spikes on their backs like the branches of trees to climb them. Grabbing at the nearest horns, she twisted downward, dragging one to the ground by its head, downing the demon like a bull at a rodeo before wrenching its black beating heart from the brittle husk of its ribcage.

Fate did this over and over, first confusing them by feinting in one direction, while targeting the other. They chased with their whips, sometimes lashing each other. Smoke rolled off their burning bones. Fiery embers rained from their dark sulphurous clouds, burning her eyes, singing her skin. Yet she reveled in the power coursing through her limbs, elated by the fearlessness she embodied. Invincibility was her shield. It didn't matter how much damage she received in the battle. She would recover.

She owned the power of a god, and it was her job to eviscerate those who attempted to extinguish her light.

Fate moved like a machine through the hot acrid stench and narrowed her vision on the remaining demons. Her fury rose. Blood rushed in her ears, pounding like a war drum. Instead of charging at her with their whips, the last three demons shrank toward the hole in the wall. She wasn't about to let them escape. Blindly, she tore into them. But it wasn't enough to simply take their hearts. This time she pulled them apart, ripping limbs from torsos, heads from spindly necks.

Finn's voice cut through the tumultuous ruin in her head, distant at first, before growing louder and more urgent. She finally stopped stabbing a demon with its own bony spike and let the appendage drop at her feet.

Mangled bodies littered the center of the sanctuary. The floor was slick with char and ichor. She looked at her hands, thick with putrefaction and began to shake. The smell of blood and rot and sulphur turned her stomach.

Finn eased up next to her. "It's over, love. You did it. They're gone, at least for now."

She raised her gaze to his. When she recognized fear in his eyes–fear when he looked at *her*–she ran to a far corner and vomited. Convulsions of shame shuddered through her torso. Finn was afraid of her.

Farouk's voice cut through the silence. "I knew you monstramorphosized yourself! What did you do, Fate? What did you do to be this omnipowerful?"

Fate lifted her head and swallowed back the bile in her throat. Farouk hung by his tail from the bars of his tipped over cage. His slanted eyes were nothing more than slits as he glared at her. Brune stood next to his cage with a tense frown as she glanced back at the hole.

Fate grabbed a polishing cloth from the armory table, wiped her mouth and cleaned her hands of the fetid demon blood. "Does it matter? We'd all be dead right now if I hadn't taken measures to be on par with what Kaliena just threw at us."

Brune's shoulders shook as she clenched her fists. "Haven't you learned there's always a price to pay for using magic? Especially when it's for your own benefit!"

"I did this to protect us all!" Fate shouted, but even as she flung the words at them, she knew it was a half-truth. How could she tell them she'd become exhausted with being afraid all the time?

"No, no, no!" Farouk shook his head so hard, his whole body swayed from where he swung. He shot Brune an anxious look. "Set me upright!"

Brune lifted his cage back onto its mechanical crab legs and Farouk dropped into his seat. "What happens if this power you've pilferized takes over and turns on *us*? The Keep would be without a guardian, that's what! I demand you make Brune your proxy. *Now!*"

Fate's first impulse was to resist with an unequivocal no, but this was no time for arguing, and he was right. She glanced nervously at the hole. "Fine, let's do it."

"I'll get the contract." Brune ran to one of the far cabinets, upended but still miraculously intact. She returned with the page shaking in her hand and handed it to Fate.

"Stamp it with your seal," Brune said without taking her eyes off the hole. "And hurry."

Fate hastily passed the guardian seal embedded in her palm over the page. The seal flashed its image onto to the paper, faint but visible. "Is that it?" She'd expected to feel lighter, like a weight was gone, but she didn't feel any different.

Folding the contract, Brune nodded and stuffed it up the sleeve of her armor.

Farouk pushed his snout through the bars to look at Fate. His eyes sparked red as he held out a grasping hand. "Give the Rod. Only I can prevent it from falling into Kaliena's hands."

"Right, because your cage just tipped over and you needed help to roll it upright." Fate shook her head.

"You have no idea what I'm miscapable of." Farouk's gaze slid to Brune. "It's time. Unlock my cage."

Fate moved in front of the cage. "Hold on, Brune. How about we have a meeting between the two guardians and discuss this?"

Brune shook her head. "Out of my way." The panic in her eyes scared Fate.

"Don't be rash, Brune," Finn joined in. "There's a reason curious creatures in cages aren't allowed to roam free."

Fate nodded anxiously. "Couldn't have said it better myself. You two really need to let us in on this secret you've been keeping."

Brune squeezed the key until her hand shook. "If you haven't noticed, there's an entire legion out there ready to come down on us all at once. Kaliena's been toying with us so far. Once she loses patience, it's over. Farouk's our best hope now."

Fate looked from Brune to Farouk. "What exactly is being let out when the cage is unlocked? At least tell me that much."

Brune started to speak, but Farouk held up his hand. "Leave this to me to explainate." He paused, staring into space, seemingly transported to another time and place. Straightening his back, he pulled himself away from whatever visions had called him away.

"I am not what I seem," he began. "This cage was constructified with specilicious spells to hold me in stasis. It has kept me from appearializing in my true form for thousands of years. In here, I am forced to make the Keep my only priority."

"Are you saying you're like those cute little mogwai that turn into ugly gremlins if water spills on them?" Fate hid the beginnings of a nervous smile behind her hand.

Farouk's ears angled back. "I am far more magniposing than those lesser demons. You would do well to show some respect."

All humor vanished. "Are you saying you're a demon?"

Farouk seemed unsure for the briefest moment, but then he shook his head. "In all my investispections, I've found nothing in the records to define what I am or where I come from."

"That's worse than knowing what you are." Finn's frown turned incredulous as he looked at Brune. "Why would you ever consider letting him out? We're in enough trouble without worrying about what he'd do to us once he's out."

Brune stared back, but not with her usual defiance. Instead, fear was driving her. "Better to deal with the devil you know than the one you don't."

"That's just it," Finn argued, "we don't know the devil you'll be letting out. We only know what's in the cage. And to be honest, I've never been all that impressed."

Farouk stiffened and he started to speak, but an explosion from a fireball launched through the hole cut him off. Flames and sparks shot from the projectile as it rolled forward, dying down to a black ball smoldering with a noxious green gas.

The air filled with a corrosive haze. Finn and Brune succumbed to the fumes, each collapsing on the floor, gasping to breathe.

Fate's lungs burned like she'd inhaled acid, but unlike them, she withstood the incredible pain and damage. Brune crawled toward her, holding the key up, her face contorted in agony. Ignoring the key, Fate grabbed them both by the arms and dragged them to the door. Pushing it open, she rolled them out into the hall.

"I'm going back for Farouk. I'll be right back." She turned to leave, when Brune gripped her ankle.

"Take the key. *Please*," she rasped.

Fate swiped it from her grasp. "Fine, I'll take the damned thing, but I'm not using it."

Shutting the door, she rushed over to Farouk's cage. He appeared to be fine. "Why aren't you affected by the gas?" She coughed, waving a hand through the toxic green mist. "This stuff hurts like hell."

He sat in his seat with his arms crossed. "My cage has a defensative shield."

"Lucky you."

"Not so much." His eyes rounded and his ears stood straight as he pointed at something behind her. "It won't stop them."

Fate turned as a horde of wraithlike creatures swarmed through the hole. The stink of dry blood and rotting corpse flooded in. Hoarfrost spread from their feet. Their decayed muscles, white as bone, gleamed from beneath gray, desiccated skin. Skulls hung open at the neck where jaws had been torn away. Torsos gaped wounds of shredded ribs with blackened cinders for organs. Spiked gauntlets were all they wore for armor, and every one of them carried barbed spears and sabers.

Spine-tingling shrieks issued from their maws as they thundered over the bodies littering the floor. Terror stretched Fate's nerves to the breaking point, knowing this would never end. Kaliena would send wave after wave of her undead armies until they drowned under the deluge. Was Brune right about Farouk? Was he really the lesser of two evils?

She tried to swallow the fear down, but her throat was full of needles and her strength was waning. The caustic gas stripped away her lungs faster than they could regenerate. It was becoming harder to breathe by the second.

With her hand shaking, Fate slotted the key into the lock on Farouk's cage.

He jumped off his seat and gripped the bars of his cage. "Hurry!"

Fate gave him a warning frown. "Don't make me regret this," she wheezed.

Farouk's eyes gleamed with the same red spark she'd glimpsed in the past and had always been uncomfortable with. Doubt blazed in her heart, but she turned the key anyway, and the door of his cage sprang open.

13
KEYS TO THE KINGDOM

FAROUK'S EYES FLARED LIKE hot coals in the darkness, his body growing, elongating into a monstrous thing of bristling fur, horns and fangs that filled his cage until the bars bent and broke. Straining his sinewy muscles, he shrugged the cage off his back like the cracked shell of an egg and stretched to a full height of twelve feet or more. Silver foxfire ran along the tips of his claws as he loomed over Fate. His massive lupine head tilted curiously, fixing a harrowing, incandescent gaze on her. Malice dripped from the growl rumbling deep inside his throat as his long, barb-tipped tail twitched behind him.

Terror streaked along Fate's spine as she shrank from him. The very air vibrated around him, as if his presence disturbed his surroundings on an atomic level. She felt dizzy and sick to her stomach. Sharp spasms drilled into the forefront of her brain, making it hard to focus on him. Her eyes kept sliding away from him, as if forced away.

A guttural voice invaded her mind, imperious and jeering. "*Fate, you really are the worst guardian I've ever had the displeasure of knowing.*" Horrified by the intrusion, she fought to hold his gaze. He bent toward her, his snout curling back in a venomous snarl. Tendrils of smoke smelling of sulfur drifted past his fangs. "*Torturing you will bring me tremendous–*"

His head jerked upright as several spikes drove into his side and back. Hoarfrost spread over his fur, freezing his gushing blood into long red knives. Letting out an unearthly roar, dark smoke rolled from his gaping mouth, the black ring of his muzzle quivering with absolute rage.

Farouk dislodged the spikes as if the ensorcelled weapons were mere splinters. Fate ducked to avoid being hit by a bloodied spike and backed against the wall as Farouk dove into the onslaught pouring into the sanctuary.

His movements were faster than she could track. He was a force beyond comprehension, descending on the enemy like a demon hurricane of gnashing teeth and slashing claws. Fate inched along the outer edges of the room toward the exit as body parts slammed into the walls. The carnage she'd wreaked was nothing in comparison to Farouk's devastation.

Trembling all over, she reached for the door handle, praying he was too distracted to sense her leaving. She was well inside the doorframe when he twisted round with a hissing growl. His muscles bunching as he angled toward her, every movement as measured as a hunting lion coiled and ready to lunge on its prey.

Fear locked Fate in place. She should know what to do, but his lasered attention muddied her thinking, paralyzing her well-honed instincts and making her forget all avenues of escape. The pain in her head increased to a pounding thrum. Nausea snaked through her center until she doubled over in weakness.

Content to have her back in his thrall, Farouk slunk forward. Fate squeezed her eyes shut, knowing she was about to die in the next few seconds.

An enraged howl pierced her ears. Fate opened her eyes to Farouk writhing to pull free of a half dozen pikes stuck in his backside. He suddenly launched backward through the hole, pulled by ropes attached to the pikes in his back. His claws burst with quicksilver lightning as he dug into the iron floor, gouging ribbons of curling metal as he fought to gain purchase.

Farouk's power over her ebbed, vanishing altogether the moment he went flying through the hole. A roar filled with rage and fury echoed out over the Keep.

Relief flooded through Fate's limbs as her strength returned. She never thought in a million years she'd be grateful for yet another of Kaliena's attacks. If this were a perfect world, Farouk and Kaliena would kill each other off. But she knew that was too much to hope for.

At least Farouk would be distracted for a time. She could count on that much. Kaliena would no doubt lose a good number of her undead army, but Fate wasn't naïve enough to think either of them would be eliminated this early on in the fight.

Closing the door, she turned to find that Finn and Brune were still unconscious. Worry raced along her frayed nerves as she checked Finn's pulse. Letting out a sigh, she checked Brune's. They were both alive, but she needed to get them medical attention immediately. Visualizing the infirmary, she transmitted the coordinates to their teleporters. The activation was immediate as the dizzying effect of teleportation took hold of her senses.

The stark white interior of the room was a welcome sight after the bloodbath she'd left behind in the sanctuary. Fate sat down to catch her breath and regain her equilibrium while the med bots administered to Finn and Brune. She rubbed her palms over the tops of her legs back and forth absentmindedly, staring at the shiny black floor.

Disbelief pooled alongside increasing terror. She didn't know if she was more afraid of Farouk or Kaliena. They appeared equally threatening, though Farouk was beginning to win out. She'd witnessed a lot of violence recently, but never the kind of raw savagery Farouk had displayed in his true form. The menace coming off him made her shiver even now. There was no question he'd become as much an enemy as Kaliena was to them, and all in one fell swoop. Worse yet, he knew all of their personal strengths and weaknesses. Not to mention, none of them could ever hope to surpass his knowledge of the Keep and its inner workings.

Brune had been wrong to think he would help them after he was set free. *Fatally wrong*. Everything inside Fate screamed a warning each time she remembered the smoldering embers of his malevolent stare. Farouk was bent on nothing less than wanton destruction.

A soft moan from Finn brought Fate back into the room. Rising on shaky legs, she hurried over to his bed. "How're you feeling?" she asked.

"Like I swallowed a bucket of rusty nails." He cleared his throat with a pained grimace. "Other than that, I'm dandy." He started to smile, but his expression turned to one of concern as he touched the wet blood on her face. "I think the more important question is, how're you feeling?"

"Not good," Fate replied as she grabbed for a cloth and wiped her face clean. She turned back to him and gulped. "I panicked... I opened Pandora's box."

Finn raised himself on one elbow. He looked queasy. "You let Farouk out?"

Haunted again by Farouk's vicious transformation, Fate stared into space and nodded. She blinked the image away. "He changed into something really, *really* scary. I'd even go so far as to say he's worse than Kaliena and everything she's been throwing our way."

"That's because he's a demon," Brune croaked from the bed next to Finn. She sat up with some effort and rubbed her eyes.

Fate walked around the bottom of Finn's bed. "Didn't I ask if he was a demon earlier?"

"Obviously I didn't want Farouk to know what he is." Brune coughed and patted her chest. "His records were sealed and hidden by the first guardian. It took me forever to locate them, and even longer to break the seal so I could actually read them."

"So that's what all those trips out into the Keep were all about," Fate stated.

Farouk healed me of the Gorgon's infection in exchange for me finding the key to his cage. You would've done the same thing if you knew you were sentenced to being a scaly freak for the rest of your miserable life."

Fate could hardly argue with that.

"For the record, I had no intention of keeping my end of the bargain. Not after what I discovered," Brune continued. "But later, when I realized we didn't stand a chance against Kaliena, I knew Farouk was our only chance to survive."

Finn rose and hung his legs over the edge of the bed. "We need to know what we're dealing with. What did the records say about him?"

"He was only a few months old when the first guardian found him. Apparently, he'd crawled through one of the gateways during the twilight openings and became lost inside the Keep. She did her best not to grow attached to him while she spent months searching the library for what kind of creature he was. When she couldn't find any information on him, she deemed him harmless and kept him as a pet. She taught him to speak, and when he started showing an aptitude towards integrating multidimensional magic with technology, she schooled him on everything pertaining to the Keep. He eventually became her assistant."

Fate paced between the beds. "What you're saying is, she basically gave the keys to the kingdom to a mystery furball."

"Yup, and she came to regret it. Years later, when Farouk grew to be his full height of three feet–"

"Scratch that," Fate corrected her, "he's at least twelve feet tall now."

"Oh." Brune's eyes grew round with dread. "Anyway, when Farouk hit puberty... at least that's what the guardian described it as, he became rebellious and sullen. One day he wanted his cupcakes from Earth and thought he should be able to leave and get them himself. When the guardian refused to let him go, he threw a teenaged fit, which turned him into what you saw."

Fate stopped her. "Hold on. Are you saying he pulled an incredible hulk over cupcakes?"

"Most definitely. Farouk's hopelessly addicted to cupcakes. Cloud Nines are his favorite. Back home there's a little bakery near the bookstore that bakes them. I've been making cupcake runs twice a week for decades."

Fate knew the bakery well. "Why not just use the food simulator?"

"Farouk can taste the difference."

Fate thought back to the spongy mystery curd the simulator had given her when she'd ordered popcorn. "Yeah, it's not always exact. So how come I didn't know about this baked goods fixation of his?"

"Maybe because we've been in triage mode since you got here."

Fate filed this bit of knowledge away in the useless information pile. "What happened to the guardian after his tantrum?"

"He attacked her, and came quite close to killing her. She made it to the infirmary, but later realized it was only because he let her. During her recovery, he tormented her with cruel mind games that made her question her sanity. When she was strong enough, she barricaded herself in the library with wards, determined to find out what he was and how to stop him."

Chills raced over Fate's skin when she remembered Farouk's threat to torture her. "I take it that's when she found out her adorable pet was a demon."

"A Persian Shedreakai demon, to be exact. They've been called by other names, such as the Hinn... very rare, and extremely deadly. As we've learned, the young are harmless, but when they mature, watch out."

"Is that why his speech is so convoluted?" Finn asked.

"You nailed it," Brune confirmed. "His first inclination is to deceive and manipulate, even when the spells built into his cage are forcing him to tell the truth. That's why the transmodulator on his cage mixes his words."

Finn pushed off the bed, his jaw clenched with tension. "We have to cage him back up. If it was done before, we can do it again."

Brune stood and headed for the door. "Follow me, I have all the notes the first guardian left on how to build the cage and trap him, but it won't be easy with Kaliena attacking us from every side."

Fate fell in step with Finn right behind. "Kaliena's the least of our worries at the moment. Farouk's the main threat. He did something to weaken me."

"Shedreakai demons are particularly disruptive to time and space. Unless they're cloaking their power by holding it in, the dark magic they emanate warps reality, making those around them feel sick and disoriented."

"That's not supposed to happen to me though," Fate argued. "I should be immune to... pretty much everything."

"Why?" Brune eyed her suspiciously. "Is that because of the upgrade you swiped from the Keep? What is it exactly?"

"Hippolyta's magical girdle," Finn answered for Fate when she hesitated.

"You mean the girdle Ares made for his daughter?" Brune's laugh was sharp when Finn nodded. The sarcasm in her smile turned to anger as she gave Fate a sidelong glance. "There's your answer. Demons have always been the counterbalance to the gods, and since your powers are derived from Ares, you're even more vulnerable than us."

Fate wanted to disagree, but how could she? Farouk's malignant energy had brought her to her knees. "He's going to come after us as soon he's done making minced meat of Kaliena's army."

"You don't have to tell me." Brune increased her pace down the hall.

"What can we expect from him once his attention's back on us?" Finn asked.

Brune stopped abruptly. Her face was pale and drawn with stress. "Your worst nightmare." Her voice was a whisper filled with dread. "Shedreakai demons are masters of illusion and deception. They're wielders of the blackest magic, and delight in destructive mischief. But only when it's on the grandest scale. They'll actually build you up with false hopes and then destroy everything you put in place. All for the fun of watching those hopes die. If that doesn't satisfy them, or if they become bored with the game, they'll revert to their base instinct... "

"Which is?" Finn pressed when Brune trailed off with a terrified stare.

She looked at him. "The Persians used to call Shedreakai demons man eaters."

"You're saying Farouk will eat us after he's had his game of cat and mouse?"

Brune nodded.

"Okay then." Fate forced an upbeat tone of voice, which came out as a high squeak. She was shaken by Brune's open display of fear. Her disagreeable great aunt was usually quite calm and cool in the face of danger. "We're just going to have to make sure that doesn't happen. Right?"

"Aye," Finn agreed.

Brune remained silent and continued walking the hall, though with less determination. It was as if she'd talked herself out of any hope of stopping Farouk.

"Where are these notes you mentioned?" Fate asked.

"In my quarters," Brune muttered.

"All right then, we swing by your place, get the notes and head to the shelter. We'll regroup there and get everyone working on this. Except maybe Gerdie. She's been pretty out of it."

"I don't think Darcy will be much help either," Finn added. "Not after we tell her we lost Mason."

Fate gulped. "Oh yeah." Her heart grew heavy again. How many more would they lose before this was all over?

Brune stopped in front of the door to her residence. "Wait here. I'll be right out."

Finn stepped close to Fate and nudged her chin to get her to look at him. "I can see the worry in your eyes. Stay strong. We can't let fear get the best of us."

She nodded and inched closer to kiss him.

"Got it," Brune announced before they could touch lips. She looked away with a disgusted frown. "Does anything ever stop you two from going at it?"

Finn kept his gaze trained on Fate and smiled. "Only enormous spans of space."

Fate smiled back as they fell in step behind Brune, who marched as if she couldn't get away from them fast enough. They passed through several sets of doors after leaving the residence quarters and entered a rounded tunnel Fate had never seen before. Not that she was surprised. With her attention on training and researching, there was much she had left unexplored. When they finally reached the tunnel's end, they stopped in front of a hatch with no visible handle or control panel to open it.

"How do we get in?" Fate asked.

"Normally, we wouldn't be able to get in after the hatch has been locked from the inside." Brune tapped the teleportation device implanted in her ear. "Fortunately, we have these."

Before Fate could say another word, the tunnel swirled and disappeared, replaced by a dimly lit vault. They were in a large, mostly empty chamber. One end was filled with winding pipes and tubes glowing a soft yellow from a wall of utilitarian equipment. A floating table and cluster of airborne chairs sat off to one side. A metal screen blocked the rest of her view.

"Warn people before you activate their teleporters," Finn growled under his breath. The color had left his face as he held the wall.

"Yeah, a heads up would be nice." Fate agreed out of concern for Finn.

"Babies," Brune muttered as she walked over to a chair and sat down.

Eustace and Sithias rushed over to them. Sithias was all arms, his hands waving frantically. "Misss! Sssir, you're alive!"

Eustace remained quiet, but the look of relief on her father's face was evident.

"We feared you'd been killed in the explosion." Sithias looked her over as if he expected to see missing limbs. "You appear quite fine. You all do."

"The explosion was the least of our worries." Fate made her way over to a chair and slumped into the seat. "Kaliena sent in one army of freaks after the other. It was pretty touch and go there for a good while."

Eustace finally found his voice. "Were you able to lessen their numbers? How many are left?"

Finn patted his shoulder on his way over to a chair. "There's too many to count. We hardly made a dent."

The bad news cast a heavy pall over the room and no one spoke for several minutes. Gerdie appeared from behind the metal screen and tiptoed her way into the middle of the gathering. "Why's everybody so upset? Did someone die?"

Fate stiffened in her chair. She'd been dreading this moment. "Where's Darcy?"

"Right here." Darcy walked out from behind the screen. Her charcoal rimmed eyes widened with questions. "What is it? What's wrong?"

Fate stood, searching for the right words to tell her Mason had perished in the explosion. She stared at the floor, unable to hold Darcy's gaze. "I have to tell you something, but I don't know how–"

"How to what?"

Fate looked up in shock when she heard Mason's voice. "Mason?"

"Yeah, it's me." He swept his hands in front of his body and smiled. Other than his black hair being mussed, no doubt by Darcy, he seemed to be perfectly fine. "Did you think I bit the dust?"

Fate looked at Finn and then Brune. Both of them appeared equally shocked. She turned back to him. "How'd you make it out?"

"Teleported my ass out of there at the first sign of danger." He gave them a sheepish look. "Not on purpose, of course. It was sort of a knee-jerk reaction. Sorry about that. I know I should've stuck around."

Fate held her breath. She should be overjoyed to see Mason alive and well, but instead she felt caught off guard and on edge about it.

Darcy stepped in next to Mason and put her arms around him. "I for one am glad you bolted. Who knows what could've happened to you," she cooed.

Mason squeezed her back then looked at Fate with an apologetic smile.

Doing her best to shake off her uneasiness, Fate smiled at Mason nervously. The leftover adrenaline pumping through her system was obviously clouding her thoughts and emotions. That was all it was.

14
SPLITTING UP NEVER WORKS IN THE MOVIES

FINN PRESSED HIS FISTS against the surface of the table, staring Fate down from where she stood on the other end. Everyone else watched the heated debate in silence. "We have too many enemies. No matter how many of Kaliena's abominations we eliminate, she'll always have more to throw at us. And all this while Farouk's out there plotting god knows what. I'm telling you, this onslaught will never end as long as we're holding the Rod of Aeternitis in our possession."

Fate's face flushed with heat. "I said no! I'm not letting you dangle the Rod under Kaliena's nose so you can lure her and that fleet of monsters away from here. It's suicide!"

"I can round up more than enough help in Oldwilde to fight her off. Maybe even defeat her."

"You don't know that yet. What if Rudwor refuses?" She was grasping at straws and she knew it. Finn was like a son to Rudwor and he would do anything for him.

Finn straightened, relaxing his shoulders. "He'd never turn his back on me."

Fate's chin trembled, knowing he spoke the truth. But she wasn't about to admit it because of what it meant for them. She pressed her lips into a stubborn line to stop the tears rising in her eyes.

"His kingdom has the strongest army in all of Oldwilde," Finn relented. "You know this better than anyone. You were a Beldereth warrior."

Fate continued to fume in silence. Why was he so eager to leave her? Their recent reunion was still fresh and new after being apart for far so long. She wasn't about to lose him again.

"Rudwor has powerful allies. He can amass the numbers we need to weaken Kaliena's position." Finn waited for her to agree, but obstinance won out.

Eustace cleared his throat. "Fate, we've been at this for hours. I know you don't want to hear this from me, but Finn's plan is the most sensible so far."

Fate tore her gaze from Finn and glared at her father through angry tears. "Splitting up never works in the movies, so what makes you think it'll work in real life? We have to stick together."

"Normally I'd agree with you, but we have two opposing forces bearing down on us. One of them needs to be eliminated so each team can focus on the best defense."

"Finn has my vote." Brune waved a pair of pliers in the air from the other side of the vault, where she was working on building a new cage for Farouk. Gerdie sat on the floor at her feet, humming a childish tune while twisting thin copper wire into the shape of a pig.

"And ours," Darcy chimed in with a smug smile.

Mason shook his head. "No offense, Dimples, but I'm not sure I'm totally down with this one."

Darcy frowned at him. "What? Have you lost it? You were almost killed by those zombie freaks Kaliena sicced on us. We need them all gone, and *now*. Let Finn deal with them anywhere else but here."

Sithias raised his hand, though with obvious apprehension. "I agree with the young lady, and I volunteer to go with you, sssir. I'm well accustomed with the politics of Oldwilde, and feel confident I can be of help."

Fear hammered through Fate's chest. She wasn't willing to lose anyone else. Her heart simply couldn't take it. "No, Sithias, you're not going, and neither is Finn! There has to be another way!"

Sithias inched closer to her. "Misss, I don't want to do this anymore than you want us to, but you know we have to act on Finn's plan."

Fate's breathing came in fits and starts as she shook her head. "No, no, no, no, no–"

Finn rushed to her side, folding his arms around her firmly. "We'll get through this, love. I promise."

She struggled to catch her breath. "Stop making promises you can't keep."

"All right then, I promise I'll do everything in my power to get back to you as soon as this is over." He stepped back, cupped his hand under her chin and gently wiped away a tear that escaped.

Frustration burned through her immediate fear, leaving anger in its place. "That's not good enough." She frowned at Sithias. "I forbid you to go unless you can both guarantee you'll survive."

Sithias smiled sadly. "I only wish we could, but you know that's impossible, misss."

"Fine! Go!"

"What's the next step, Finn?" Eustace asked.

Finn looked torn, but he released Fate and resumed his place at the table.

"First, we locate a portal into Oldwilde, one that'll allow Kaliena's fleet through as well."

"Good luck with that." Everyone turned to look at Brune. Sparks flew from the soldering iron in her hand. She didn't bother to look up.

"Care to share why?" Finn asked.

Brune straightened and pushed her goggles onto her forehead. "The portals can only take six bodies at a time."

"Well, that's a problem."

A relieved, almost hysterical sound escaped from Fate's throat. "I guess that means we'll have to nix the plan after all."

"Not necessarily." Brune set the soldering iron down on the workbench. When Gerdie moved to grab it, she moved it out of reach. "All we need is something to amplify the portal and widen the opening. Of course, that's Farouk's area of expertise, so I suppose we're back to being out of luck."

"Would the Golandon scientist be able to create this amplification?" Eustace asked.

Brune considered the question, but Fate already knew the answer. "The scientist could do it in his sleep. If he sleeps."

"That's all well and good, but we don't know where Kaliena's keeping him," Fate added.

"Yes we do."

Fate's frown deepened into a scowl. "And why don't I know this?"

Brune frowned back. "Because you were busy getting your upgrade at the time."

"What upgrade?" Darcy asked.

Brune ignored the question. "The scientist is in Sector 683."

"That's right," Darcy jumped in, now distracted by the matter at hand. "I'm the one who found him. And we'd have him right now if Brune hadn't stopped me from bringing him back."

Brune rolled her eyes. "We've been over this. Kaliena's war drones would've mowed you down before you even got close."

"Oh, so he's heavily guarded," Fate muttered with feigned disappointment.

"Yup." Brune turned back to the table and grabbed the soldering iron to resume her work.

"Sounds like we'll have to go in and get him." Finn began sliding on his armor. "Give me the coordinates, and I'll take care of it."

"Not alone, you're not. I'm going with you," Fate insisted. Finn looked ready to argue, but she stopped him by pointing at her face. "See this? You should know by now this is my don't-argue-with-me face. Do not mess with it. Unless you want to see me get real ugly."

He held his hands up in surrender. "Aye, you can go with me."

Finn did his best to ignore the distressing sensation of his atoms spreading thin across space and time, but it was impossible. The instantaneous materialization of his body hammering back into form was every bit as violent. Grabbing his knees, he bent and hung his head, waiting for the residual vertigo to subside.

Fate appeared next to him in a dark drift of glittering mist. The dark bronze color of her leather armor stood out in stark contrast to her softly illuminated skin. As much as he disliked what she'd done to herself, he couldn't help admiring how she embodied the war goddess as if she'd been born and bred that way.

She scanned her surroundings before dropping her gaze to meet his. Concern clouded her expression. It was the first time since their last argument that he'd seen anything other than anger and frustration.

"What's wrong?" she asked. "Are you sick?"

He straightened before he was ready to do so, a dizzying move that had him grabbing the wall. "A wee bout of dizziness is all. I see you're not bothered by teleportation anymore," he said, not letting on how deeply disturbed he was by what felt like the shredding of his very soul.

"I'm sure you'll find your sea legs soon enough." She looked a little sheepish, like someone caught cheating at cards, before edging close to the window of the small tower room.

Finn joined her. According to Brune, they were above the scientist's newly located laboratory, which was situated upon a structure with a spindly base that widened into stacks of connecting towers. The balconies lining each turret were in full view since they were at the very top. Multitudes of what had once been working drones cluttered the air, hovering around the towers. They'd been reconfigured into war machines, each outfitted with heavy artillery.

"I can teleport into the laboratory if you need more time to recover," she offered.

"Or we could do it the old-fashioned way and climb through this trap door."

"That works too." She leaned down to grab the latch.

Finn stopped her by holding onto her arm. He angled her so she could no longer avoid his gaze. "I know you're upset with my leaving, but we should be making the best of what time we have left."

"You mean the five minutes before you say goodbye to me again? Oh wait, you never said goodbye the last time, because I was unconscious and couldn't stop you."

"That's unfair. I gave myself up to the Green Man to save you."

She pushed away from him. "You can't hold that against me. If we're comparing, *that's* unfair. I never would've let you sacrifice yourself for my mistake. Just like I don't want you making yourself bait for Kaliena. It's too dangerous! Why do you keep doing this?"

"Because it's what needs to be done, and you know it." He stepped closer, needing to make things right between them. "Neither of us knows how much time we've got left together, so let's make it count."

Her eyes widened and her breathing increased. "Spend the night with me."

His pulse raced at the thought. "Aye... " His voice was a hoarse whisper.

Fate's cheeks blushed a beautiful rose-red and her brown eyes sparkled with excitement. She never ceased to surprise him. He leaned in to kiss her, but she bent to lift the trapdoor at the same moment to survey the room below. If he didn't know better, he'd swear she'd just ducked him.

He shook his head. Her mercurial moods were certainly a challenge to adjust to. With the Keep forever calling her to duty, mixed in with the unpredictable influence of the war god energy in the girdle, her soft, cuddly edges had certainly sharpened.

She was a far cry from the timid, uncertain girl she was when they'd first met. God help him, none of it made any difference. He loved her all the same.

She stood, while keeping a downward gaze. "I don't see any drones. I'm going in." With that, she dropped through the trapdoor, landing as light as a cat.

Finn jumped down next to her, landing on a platform at the very top of the laboratory. A spiraling staircase led the way down to two other levels. He moved to the edge to have a look. All sorts of inventions in varying degrees of development filled a collection of large tables spread about the bottom floor. The scientist was nowhere in sight.

Fate started down the stairs and Finn was about to follow when a rapid thud sounded behind them. He turned to see a round little bot with large feet and curved, long paddles attached to its small head, which looked like ears.

"Does that look like a rabbit to you?" Fate asked.

The bot's ears angled, as if perked to attention before hopping closer, the two lenses for eyes turning as it focused on them.

"Aye, I suppose at the very least, it's an attempt at a rabbit."

Fate smiled at it. "Cute little guy."

"It's a machine."

"Cute, all the same." Her smile didn't last as she descended the stairs gripping the hilt of her sheathed sword while glancing warily from side to side.

Finn fell in step behind her.

Something darted past their heads, making them both duck. Before Finn could react, Fate had her sword out, muscles tensed and poised to fight. Finn caught sight of the culprit high above them. A mechanical swallow, which circled the ceiling, then dove to the lower floor, where it perched itself on the head of a bronze horse.

"You can stand down." He pointed at the horse. It was the most intricate piece of work so far. A graceful form consisting of an elaborate network of cogs and wheels, fine chains and clockwork mechanisms. The maker had even added wings, which made Finn wonder if the horse could actually fly.

The horse shook its head, sending the swallow flying back to the ceiling, where a robotic owl sat perched in the overhead beams. Fate sheathed her sword and walked over to the horse. "It's beautiful." She ran her hand along the horse's muzzle. "I wonder who made it?"

A voice jabbered from what seemed like no particular direction, startling them. They both turned as the Golandon scientist juddered from the shadowy recesses of a work area. He was blue-skinned with six arms like Kaliena, though the resemblance stopped there. His facial features were flat and his skull was large and bulbous. The rest of him from the neck down was machine and blinking circuitry, much like the librarian and medical robots.

A mechanized tiger slinked alongside him, growling lowly. Fate reached for her sword again, but relaxed her grip when the scientist gestured for the tiger to lie down.

She clicked on her transmodulator. "What did you say?"

"I answered your inquiry." He waved three spindly arms at the horse. "These automatons are the last remnants of the great inventor, Daedalus." The rabbit hopped from the stairs and stopped next to him. "Excluding this one. This was my failed attempt at mimicking the master. Apparently, having access to the same tools and plans here in his workshop, does not endow one with the same skill and artistry."

Fate stooped to pat the rabbit on one of its perked ears. "If it makes you feel any better, I think the rabbit's adorable."

"Correction, that is a doggit, though the mistake is understandable since the canine aspects are not visible. Those characteristics are innate to its programming."

"Do you think you could make me a pet?" she asked. "I really miss my cat, Oz."

"If you provide me with the parameters of its personality and physical characters, I should be able to build an approximation."

Fate gave him the thumbs up. "Done."

Finn cleared his throat. "Maybe we could talk about that another time? Right now we need to speed things along." He turned to the scientist. "We're going to need you to come back with us."

The scientist cocked his head to one side, aiming the bright gleam of his glowing eyes at him. "Why would I leave? The High Priestess has ordered me to stay hidden here. From you people, in particular."

Finn restrained his building impatience. "Are you aware that Kaliena invaded the sanctuary by sending in her resurrected army?"

The scientist fiddled with the narrow point of his chin, staring into space as he considered this. After a few seconds his beaming gaze focused on Finn again. "The sanctuary is crucial to maintaining order within the Obiectis. Did it sustain damage?"

"Aye, there's a hole the size of this room in the sanctuary wall. And we've lost the... " Finn searched for the right word to describe Farouk, "caretaker in the battle. We've been left without anyone to handle the necessary repairs."

"This does not compute." The scientist's blue-tinged face wrinkled into a frown. "Why would the High Priestess cause damage to something integral to operations?"

"Because the woman's demented," Fate interjected.

The scientist wobbled like she'd bumped into him, and he appeared all the more confused. Finn could tell they were losing him. He would be useless to them if he didn't come willingly. Logic was the only way to win him over. "I understand your prime directive is to fix that which cannot be repaired by the usual means. And you were successful in saving Kaliena from certain death, but since her restoration I'm sure you've noticed her choices have been damaging. Such as the mining of the core. Did you know five rings have stopped turning, and only one is left moving?"

The scientist yelped and staggered in place. Fate moved in to steady him while the rabbit bot hopped close to one leg to prop him up on the other side. "How can this be? She assured me the core is being repaired now that she has enough elixir."

"I take it your equipment is back in your lab? Fate asked.

"Correct. Kaliena moved me here after you two breached my laboratory. I'm currently unable to access any activity within the Obiectis." He hugged his six arms close to his body with a fretful expression playing over his features.

Finn spotted the perfect opening. "Would you like to have access to that equipment?"

The scientist nodded. "Yes. Diagnostics must be run, followed by a plan for immediate repairs."

"Come with us and we can supply you with everything you need," Finn offered.

The scientist looked over his shoulder fearfully, as if he expected Kaliena to step into the room and take them by storm. For a prolonged moment it seemed as if he might refuse, but then he straightened his bony shoulders. "Yes, take me with you."

Finn gave Fate a conspiratorial smile. But she brushed past him with a stony expression, intent on implanting the scientist with the teleportation device they'd brought with them.

A sharp ache snaked through his chest. Had she changed her mind about spending their last night together? He didn't think his heart could take the disappointment if she'd changed her mind. He had suffered an eternity of hell to find her, surviving on the vision of holding her in his arms. But since his return, all they'd had were a few stolen moments together and too many arguments. He fully accepted the blame for allowing honor to come between them, but surely she'd forgiven him for that.

Finn considered reaching out with his senses to read her shifting emotional state but fear stopped him. All he wanted from her was love. He couldn't bear the wall of resistance he was able to see with his own two eyes.

15
THIS DOES NOT COMPUTE

BACK IN THE SANCTUARY, Fate could hardly contain herself. Her excitement over spending the night with Finn was all she could think of. From the moment they'd agreed to be together, she'd barely been able to look at him without becoming wildly distracted. A delicious haze of desire took hold everytime she did, making her feel like she was floating outside of herself. She enjoyed the heady sensation and wished she could lose herself in it entirely, but there was work to be done.

To counter the distraction, she'd taken to avoiding his gaze and keeping her distance. The mere brush of his arm against hers, even the heat of his body standing next to her, sent her senses reeling.

"Do you have everything you need?" Fate asked the scientist. She stepped closer to attach the transmodulator onto his metal chest and stubbed her foot into the doggit. The bot's bunny ears angled downward as it hopped to one side.

The scientist took over with fastening the device and then bent over a workbench, his many arms moving all at once as he repaired the control board they'd salvaged from Farouk's demolished cage. A laser beam shot from his glowing eyes, zapping the circuitry with precision. He then clicked the last pieces together and tapped a few keys to test the board.

"Uncertain at present," he finally answered. "I will know in eight, seven, six, five, four, three, two, one… " The lights on the control panel lit and he turned to her with a satisfied expression. "Yes, after a few more modifications I will be able to access all operations within and without the Obiectus."

He bent, hitting the keys with a blur of fingers. "I am now overriding Kaliena's directives blocking the ground sensors, while running diagnostics on the core. I will instigate solutions once the report is complete." He looked up from the keyboard. "I have also ordered the maintenance drones to begin immediate repairs in the sanctuary. It is imperative we seal the wall and build barriers enhanced with defensive wards, per my design."

Fate stared in awe. "Wow, how did we ever get by without you?"

Brune joined them. Her face was grimy with sweat. She looked grumpy. "That's terrific, wonder boy. How about you finish building Farouk's cage for me too? Given how fast you fixed that board, I'm sure it'll only take you another minute or two."

The scientist's glowing eyes moved to the cage and he started over to Brune's messy work area, when Fate stopped him. "Whoa. We need to check into the status of the Keep and determine Kaliena's latest position. Brune, you can keep working on the cage for now. If you're not finished by the time we've taken care of more urgent priorities, I'll send him over. And don't call him wonder boy."

Fate ignored Brune's displeasure and returned her attention to the scientist. "By the way, what's your name?"

The scientist gave her a blank expression and blinked. "I... cannot seem to retrieve a name from my memory banks. I would have had one... "

"I suppose we'll have to find a name for you then."

Sithias, who had been watching from the galley, swooped in. "Oh, let me do the honors! As you know I'm well accustomed to coupling the perfect names with the famous characters from my plays. Of course, you're welcome to join in. I'm sure you wouldn't mind stretching your writerly muscles again."

"That's all right, those particular muscles are atrophied, in exchange for building real ones, as a matter of survival." Quite happy to give him something to do, Fate stepped out of the way.

Poor Sithias had been bored with being cooped up in the vault. He'd been entertaining himself and others by performing his plays. Pulling this off by using his glamour to shift into all the various characters. His stamina had finally given out though, and he'd returned to reading. That is, until restlessness gave way.

Circling the scientist, Sithias tapped his chin while looking him up and down. "Hmmm, you're an odd specimen. Part machine, part man... or something close to that. All of which leaves one wondering what you are... " He trailed off, perplexed for the moment.

The scientist stared back with a quizzical gaze. "I am composed of fifteen percent organic matter and eighty-five percent cybernetics. My brain was enlarged with Nimawel DNA and transferred into one of their skulls in order to download the extensive Golandon engineering logs. My brain stem was preserved with–"

"Ah hah!" Sithias jerked his arm above his head, pointing a finger at the ceiling. A move that startled the scientist so much he teetered in place, his mechanical knees squeaking as he did so. "There's no disputing your intellect and scientific genius. That is what we'll focus on!"

Sithias turned to pacing. "I will name you after someone from the vast annals of history. Someone who is highly respected in your field, and preferably well known."

"How about Spock?" Fate added.

"Who?"

"Never mind, I suppose it only works if you're a Trecky," she mumbled.

Sithias continued to pace the floor, now and again stopping to peruse the befuddled scientist. Fate took the opportunity to check on the others. Her father was at the table reading a story to Gerdie. She smiled at the sight, remembering back to all the bedtime reads she and Eustace used to have.

As she watched them her amusement shifted to concern. Why wasn't Gerdie's memory returning? She'd been so proud to have finally learned to read and write, and here she was being read to. By all appearances, the hundreds of years of experience Gerdie had endured within the *Book of Fables* were erased from her memory, and everything else that had happened since then.

Fate rounded the metal screen dividing the room. Cubby-holes filled with bedding lined the wall in ten rows of five. Darcy and Mason were cuddled up in one of them. Seeing them lying with their limbs laced together as they whispered and laughed turned her thoughts to Finn. Her heart pounded with anticipation as she glanced around for him. He wasn't lying in one of the cubbyholes, so she checked the lavatory. When she found the room empty, she walked over to the passionate couple.

"Have either of you seen Finn?"

Darcy rolled over to look at Fate. "Really? This place is cramped enough without you invading other people's personal bubbles."

"Maybe you should respect the fact that I can see straight through your bubbles and am terrified I'm going to witness something that'll scar my psyche forever."

Mason rose on one elbow. "Sorry, we'll do our best not to get too carried away." He squirmed under Fate's harsh stare. "Uh, I was kinda distracted at the time, but I think Finn might've teleported out of here."

Fate did her best to remain calm. "When?"

He shrugged. "Maybe a half hour ago?"

She could hardly believe her ears.

"He seemed upset about something too," Mason added.

Fate turned on her heel and stormed out of the barracks. Eustace glanced up from his book, noticing she was upset. Rising from his seat, he handed the book to Gerdie and walked over to her. "What's wrong?"

"Finn's gone. He left without telling me where he was going and why."

"He's probably out scouting."

"Without a word to anyone? This is no time for rogue behavior. It's too dangerous for that."

Eustace patted her shoulder. "Finn can take care of himself. I'm sure he'll be fine."

"You don't know that." The dread she'd been holding at bay burst free. "None of us know if anything will ever be fine again!"

For the first time in her life, Eustace appeared to be at a loss for words. And uncomfortable.

"What?" she pressed, when he remained quiet.

"I'm getting the impression this runs deeper for you."

"No." She bit her lip and frowned. "Well, maybe."

"Is there trouble between you two? Mind you, I don't want to intrude. I meant it when I said I've stepped aside when it comes to your relationship." He pulled at the collar of his dress shirt like it was strangling him. "I know this is something you'd normally share with Jessie, but since she's... well, you know."

"I do. I can still feel the boot in my back from our last meeting."

"Just know I'm here for you."

He was right. Jessie was the only one she would ever talk to about her mixed up emotions over Finn. She missed her best friend terribly, but the loss was especially magnified. Fate had made one of the most important decisions of her life, and as excited as she was, it made her feel unreasonably vulnerable.

She let out a heavy sigh. "Thanks, Dad, but I think it's best I save you from being Jessie's stand-in."

Relief washed over Eustace's pained expression. "I understand."

"I have it!" Sithias exclaimed. He turned to his audience with a dramatic wave of his arm toward the scientist. "It is my pleasure to introduce you to the highly regarded engineer, physicist, mathematician and inventor, Archimedes." He nodded at them, his amber eyes lit with excitement as he waited for the applause.

Fate looked at Eustace. "I don't know. Does he really look like an Archimedes?"

Her father glanced at the scientist and grimaced. "Well, there's no arguing he's... unique."

"What?" Sithias squawked. "The name suits him to perfection. In fact, I'd go so far as to say he surpasses–"

He stopped when the scientist tottered back toward his workstation.

Sithias lurched after him, grabbing one of his many arms and dragging him back. "And where do you think you're off to, Archimedes?"

"I have diagnostics to run. And what relevance does Archimedes have to my work? Other than the fact that many of my calculations are based upon his mathematical theorems."

"Archimedes isss your new name," Sithias hissed insistently.

Fate pulled Sithias aside. "I love the name, but how about we call him Archie for short? That way he won't get himself mixed up with his mathematical forefather."

Sithias lifted his arms and stomped his foot, which always made him look like a stork trying to take flight. "How do you get Archie out of the name when the 'h' is silent?"

"Creative license?"

"I like it," Eustace added.

"It has my vote, if it'll put an end to this asinine conversation," Brune called from the other side of the room.

Gerdie skipped over to them. "He looks like an Archie to me." She stooped to pat the doggit on its head.

Sithias moped. "I don't even know what an Archie looks like."

Gerdie pointed at the scientist. "Like him."

"Minus the red hair and freckles." Fate smiled at the confusion on Sithias's face and was glad for the momentary diversion.

Sithias glanced back at the scientist, his expression serious. "Oh fine, you will be known as Archie from this time forward."

"Affirmative. I will now answer to Archie. May I return to my work?"

"By all means, yesss." Sithias waved him off with a superior air. A short-lived attitude that was destroyed the moment he squealed with a start because Finn appeared beside him in a sudden burst of glimmering smoke. Breathing hard, he patted his chest. "There should be some sort of early warning signal on those teleporters to let others know someone is jumping out of nowhere!"

Finn winked at him. "Ah, but that would ruin our advantage and the element of surprise they provide."

"For the enemy, which I'm not!" Sithias huffed and marched off toward the barracks.

"What's wrong with him?"

"Boredom's making him cranky." Fate frowned in spite of her relief at seeing Finn. "You left without telling anyone."

"We'll leave you two to talk." Eustace took Gerdie by the hand and led her back over to the book he'd been reading her.

The playful glint in Finn's eyes vanished. "I told Mason to let you know I'd be back shortly. Didn't he tell you?"

"Really? You're actually going to try lying your way out of this?"

Finn looked hurt. "I'd never lie to you. Especially about something so small."

"Mason wasn't sure when you left. He said you looked upset."

Finn's brows furrowed in confusion. "That's not how it happened. I swear."

"Then answer me this. Why did you leave without telling me?"

Finn took her hands in his, smoothing his thumbs over hers. Her skin tingled, as tiny bolts of electricity raced up her arms. "I was getting my room ready for tonight. I figured we could sneak out for a few hours. I wanted everything to be perfect. It was supposed to be a surprise."

Fate's defenses crumbled. "That's what you were doing?"

"What did you think I was up to?"

She shook her head. "I don't know... I guess I thought you changed your mind."

He smiled. "Funny, that's what I was worried about. You've been avoiding me like... like I was one of your dreaded worms."

She laughed at the absurd idea. How could he possibly mix himself up with her worst phobia? "No, I've just been trying to focus and stay in control." A wave of heat rushed to her face. "Everytime I look at you and think about tonight... I get sort of dizzy in the head and all hot and restless. I couldn't focus."

He inhaled deeply, as if he'd been holding his breath, and stepped close. "I feel the same."

The air grew hot between them. They each took a step closer, when Archie rambled across the room toward them, talking too fast to understand.

"Whoa, slow down. Where's the fire?" Fate asked, doing her best to slow her own breathing down.

He stopped in front of them, off balance and swaying as he spoke. "No fire. I have visuals from the clean up crew in the sanctuary. This does not compute with the head count I took here in the shelter."

"I don't understand."

Archie pointed at the 3D image of the sanctuary being projected above his workstation. "They cleared the necrotic bodies from the battle. All but one, because it was a fresh kill and an Earthling, like you."

Fate stared at the projection as she moved closer. She was amazed by how fast the demolished room had been brought back into order. Even the hole in the wall was close to being fully patched. She focused in on the body, which had been laid carefully on the table. She gulped. "Can you zoom in on it?"

Archie trundled back to the control panel, pressed a few buttons and magnified the body lying on the table.

Mason's face came into view.

Fate teetered with shock. "Oh my god!"

Finn placed his hands on her shoulder to steady her, his grip tightening before he let go. "If that's Mason's body in the sanctuary, who's locked up here in the vault with us?"

16
WHAT'S ALL THE WHISPERING ABOUT?

FINN WATCHED FATE QUIETLY gather her father, Brune and Sithias together to tell them what Archie had discovered. As devastating as the news surrounding Mason was, Finn couldn't ignore his crushing disappointment about letting go of his plans for one precious evening with Fate. He'd been overjoyed while lighting his room with candles and adding a profusion of fresh-cut flowers from the garden to infuse the air with their intoxicating perfume.

Reluctantly, he joined the tense huddle.

"How can this be? Mason's right over there," Eustace whispered while pointing toward the barracks. "This can't be. Don't you think Darcy would've realized it's not him by now?"

Fate waved her hand dismissively. "Not if *it's* being the perfect Mason."

"*It*?" Eustace stiffened. "We've got to get Darcy out of there. She's in terrible danger."

"As long as we stay holed up in here with that thing, we're all in danger." Brune thumped the pliers she was holding against the palm of her hand as she glanced over at the barracks.

"Do you think this is Kaliena's doing?" Finn asked.

Brune shook her head. "No, Kaliena is always direct in her attacks. This stinks of trickery."

Fate rubbed her arms, suddenly chilled. "You're thinking this is Farouk in the other room?" Her whisper turned into a squeak on the last word.

"What? Are you saying Farouk can shape shift?" Sithias shivered, making his tall, skinny form quiver from head to foot like a beanstalk in the wind. "Ew, what a horribly spooky thought."

"How is that any different than you using your glamour to shape shift?" Fate asked.

Sithias appeared momentarily offended. "What I do is for art's sake. I do not use it to go around terrifying others with cruel deception."

"Point taken."

Gerdie poked her head in between their legs. "What're you all whisperin' about?"

"We're planning a surprise," Brune was quick to say. "You can help by making more of your animals from the wire I gave you. Why don't you make a doggit?"

Gerdie's face brightened. "I bet no one's ever seen a wire doggit before!"

"Better get to it then." Brune watched her little sister skip over to the supplies before turning back to them. It was impressive to see how protective she'd become of Gerdie.

"What makes you think it's Farouk?" Finn asked. "This could be Wodrid. Don't forget how he fooled you all into thinking he was Steve."

Eustace nodded. "Finn's right. Not to mention, Wodrid knew Mason and his relationships with us well enough to mimic him perfectly."

"The logic's sound," Fate agreed, "but I'm going to have to go with Brune on this one. I have the same sick feeling in the pit of my stomach from when I released Farouk from his cage. The only question is, how did he get inside the vault before we did? Especially when he was busy fighting Kaliena's entire fleet when we first left the sanctuary?"

Archie made excited noises from his workstation, which meant he had news. They all rushed over to see what he'd discovered.

"Visuals outside the sanctuary have been restored," Archie announced as they gathered around the rotating 3D image of the Keep.

The destruction was shocking. The legions of airships that had previously blotted out the Keep's surface were burning. More than half of them had crashed. Fires raged from the grounded vessels. Columns of black smoke filled the atmosphere with a thickening haze. The dirigibles still hovering in the sky flickered with flames and drifted aimlessly. The only vessel left intact was the lead ship carrying Kaliena, Wodrid and Jessie.

"Give me a close up on this one," Fate instructed.

Archie magnified the colossal vessel. The intricate buildings sitting atop the massive hull came into view. On closer inspection, they revealed smashed windows, pulverized walls and collapsed towers. It looked like it had been struck by a hurricane.

The bow of the ship, where they'd seen Kaliena, was littered with broken bodies.

"See if you can find Kaliena and Wodrid." Fate's voice grew low and tense.

Finn could tell she was thinking of Jessie, but she was probably too afraid to add her name to the list. It would kill her to see her childhood friend lying amongst the dead. As Archie enlarged the area and narrowed in on the mangled corpses, thankfully, Jessie's face did not appear.

"No matches for Kaliena or Wodrid," Archie confirmed.

Fate breathed an audible sigh of relief.

Eustace leaned in to study the projection. "I'm still trying to wrap my head around this. Are you saying Farouk caused *all* that destruction?"

"I wouldn't believe it either, if I hadn't seen it with my own eyes. Not that I stuck around to watch it get to what we're seeing here." Fate turned to Brune. "Do you really think it's possible Farouk could've done all that and beat us back here? I mean, it was probably no more than an hour between the time it took for me to get you and Finn to the infirmary before we entered the vault."

Brune spoke in hushed tones, forcing them all to crowd close together to hear better. "If there's one thing the first guardian stressed when it came to Farouk, when he was in full demon form, was to never underestimate what he was capable of. When he's unchained, Farouk becomes multidimensional. That means he might be able to control the speed of time. He might even be able to live outside of time. If that's the case, he can manipulate reality as we know it. Who's to say this isn't all an illusion? We might only believe Kaliena's army was decimated, when in truth, it's still–"

"What's all the whispering about?"

Startled by Mason's voice, they all broke from the circle and turned to see him standing behind them with Darcy.

"Don't you know it's rude to keep secrets?" Darcy planted her fists on her hips. "Especially when we're crammed in here like prisoners on a sinking ship. And here I thought things couldn't get any suckier."

The room fell quiet for several awkward minutes. Mason pointed at the projection of the Keep's surface and the derelict ships. "Are those Kaliena's ships? What happened to them? They look totally FUBAR."

Finn gripped his flute, ready to transform it into a wind sword if need be, and stepped forward. "Aye, you can blame Farouk for that damage."

Mason nodded. "Impressive. Glad he's on our side."

Fate stepped in next to Finn. Her hand was poised over the hilt of her sword as well. "Is that what it looks like to you, *Mason*?"

Mason tilted his head to one side and frowned. "Why'd you say it like that?"

"Not sure what you mean."

"You said my name like you were mad, or trying to make some sort of point."

"Yup, I heard it too," Darcy joined in. "What's your problem, Fate?"

Fate answered her, but continued to stare at Mason. "You should probably ask your boyfriend about that."

Concern replaced Darcy's smug expression. "What are you talking about?" She grabbed Mason's arm and looked at him with growing alarm. "Mason, what's going on here?"

Mason muttered something with a shrug, but Finn didn't hear what he said. Something about the movement bothered him. The shadow Mason cast on the wall hadn't moved in tandem with him. Instead, the dark silhouette stood straight-shouldered, while growing and looming higher than it should.

Finn blew two sharp notes into his flute, igniting a deadly blade of air. He whipped the wind sword back and forth. "Darcy, move aside. That's not Mason."

Fate drew her sword and circled to the right while Brune did the same, flanking Finn on the opposite side. Sithias and Eustace edged to the far wall, taking Gerdie with them. Archie stayed at his workstation, his head cocked to one side as if observing an interesting experiment.

Darcy placed herself between them and Mason. "Back off! Have you all lost your minds?"

Crimson sparks danced in Mason's brown eyes as he laughed. His mouth stretched wide, well beyond what was natural. Black smoke sifted past a row of exposed fangs. When his laughter deepened to a malignant growl, Darcy stiffened and her face went blank. Slowly, she turned to look over her shoulder.

Fire flared from Mason's body, burning away his clothes like it was tissue paper, charring his skin black, scorching his hair from his scalp. Muscles bulged beneath his cindered skin, bones cracked as his form stretched, bristling with coarse fur. His features distorted into something unrecognizable, until a feral, wolfish face stared back. Darcy's mouth opened in a silent scream as she stumbled away from the daggered tail snaking toward her.

Finn grabbed Darcy by the arm and flung her behind him.

"*Careful, that's my girlfriend you're pushing around.*" Finn reeled from the invasion of Farouk's voice in his head.

Darcy found her voice. "I'm not your girlfriend, you creep! What did you do to Mason? Where is he?"

Her response surprised Finn. Farouk was invading all their minds at the same time. Fear streaked along his spine. He could read their thoughts too.

Farouk feigned injury with his red burning gaze aimed at Darcy. "*That hurts my feelings. Are you forgetting the tender moments we shared together?*"

Darcy grabbed her stomach and winced. "I think I'm going to be sick."

"Leave!" Fate yelled. "Before we slice you into pieces."

Farouk's fiery gaze slid to Fate and his tail flicked the same way a cat's tail twitches with irritation. "*Haven't we already been through this? You know you don't have the power to make anything happen to me.*"

"Maybe so. But we can make it too miserable for you to overstay your welcome."

She advanced, slicing her sword in threatening arcs. After two steps, she stopped and doubled over in pain.

Farouk's hunched shoulders shook with silent laughter. "*You really should've focused on governing a strong will over your newly acquired divinity, rather than honing mundane military skills.*"

Fate straightened and staggered forward, barely able to lift her sword.

Wagging his head in pity, Farouk pointed at her. Silvery bolts crackled from the ends of his claws. "*I didn't think anyone could be more stubborn than Brune, but you win, Fate. A character flaw that will be the end of you one of these days.*"

Keeping his eyes on the beast, Finn sidled over to Fate. "Get behind me and sit this one out."

Fate's expression twisted with frustration, but she didn't argue and backed away.

Finn rushed at Farouk, yelling the Elder race runes to ignite the internal fire he needed to increase his own strength. Heat erupted at his core, flooded through his chest. Power flowed through his limbs as he lunged at the demon. Finn sailed through the air, swinging the blade of his wind sword down over Farouk's head and waited for the moment of impact, but it never came. He never even registered Farouk's movements. They were faster than his senses could detect. Finn smacked against the floor and turned to see Farouk off to one side of the vault, next to where Brune was building his cage.

"*What's this?*" Farouk picked up the platform to the cage. "*I've been hearing whispers of a new cage for me. Could this be it?*" He turned the large piece over to examine the intricate circuitry worked into the underside.

Brune inched forward with a look of panic.

"*Is this your work, Brune? Hmmm, I see you've added extra security. The entire floor is an electrocution plate, most likely remote controlled. Now why would you do that?*"

Brune's arms shook as she held her sword ready to defend herself. "All we want is to have you back. Everything can go back the way it used to be. No harm, no foul."

"No harm?" Darcy shouted. "That thing pretended to be Mason!" She glared back through a heavy smear of black mascara tears. "We still don't know where Mason is. We have to find him!"

Finn hesitated to be the one to tell her the truth and started to speak when Farouk ripped the platform of his new cage in two like it was cardboard and flung the pieces against the wall. "*Poor, poor, Darcy. Didn't they tell you?*"

Darcy sniffed and wiped her wrist across her wet cheek. A streak of mascara stained her shirtsleeve. "Tell me what?"

Farouk picked up a curved bar from a stack obviously meant for his cage, all of which Brune had recently engraved with binding symbols. Gripping the metal, he ran his claws along its length. Steam billowed from his grip, melting the bar into a bronze puddle at his feet. He gave Darcy a sidelong glance. "*Mason's dead. He died in the explosion.*"

Darcy wavered in place. Strangled noises rose from her throat as her eyes rolled back in her head. Fate ran over to catch her before she hit the floor. "If you're not here to kill us, what do you want from us?" Fate yelled.

Farouk continued to melt the bars of his cage, one by one. "*Like any living thing, to be free and do what I want.*" When he was finished destroying the bars, he dropped on all fours, slinking past Brune and Finn like the predator he was. He stopped in the middle of the vault. "*You have no idea what it's like to be caged for thousands of years, while having your true nature suppressed the entire time. Helplessness and rage does not begin to describe what I felt.*"

Fate set Darcy's limp form gently on the floor and stood. "Oh boo hoo. You had free reign of the Keep. How can you call yourself a prisoner when you were able to come and go as you pleased?"

Farouk swung his large head to look at her with a hair-raising growl. His muzzle wrinkled into a vicious snarl wreathed in dark swirling smoke. "*Didn't I warn you from the beginning not to get on my bad side?*"

The slightest tremor of fear showed in Fate's eyes, but she stood her ground. "What are you going to do? Kill me?"

Finn's heart hammered in his chest. What was she trying to do?

Farouk's ears flattened to his head. His growl intensified, filling the vault with a violent rumble that shook the floor. His eyes burned red through the sulphurous haze exuding from his snout. Just when it looked as if he would lunge at her, he turned and fixed his sights on Finn.

Farouk appeared in front of Finn so fast he hadn't even seen the demon move. Claws raked across Finn's breastbone. Fiery bolts drilled through his body, collapsing his strength. He fell, quaking and unable to move. Shadows swarmed in, dimming his vision. He heard Fate crying out from a far away place, until at last her voice faded and all he knew was the snarling of the beast and the smell of its fetid breath choking in his throat.

17
ON THE OFFENSIVE

FATE FLEW AT FAROUK the moment he overtook Finn. The aim of her sword was true, targeted straight at his spine. But when her blade came down the monster dematerialized, leaving wisps of black smoke stinking of rotten eggs and burnt rubber in his place.

She dropped to her knees, placing her hand on Finn's bloody chest. His green eyes were open, staring blankly at the ceiling. Fear drained her of all courage as she leaned over him. "Finn, can you hear me?"

He looked at her and reached for her hand. Grimacing in pain, his grip tightened around her fingers.

"Archie!" she called out. "Get the remedy kit!"

Eustace and Sithias crowded around. Sithias wobbled like he was ready to faint when he saw the blood. "Oh dear. Will he make it?"

Eustace gave him a stern look. "Of course he will."

Brune seemed doubtful. "I don't know... he's losing a lot of blood." Gerdie ran over, but Brune steered her away before she could fully see Finn's injuries. "Go to your bed." When Gerdie resisted, she pointed at the barracks. "Take the doggit with you and play fetch. It likes that."

Archie tottered back with a wooden box. He set it on the floor, opened the tiered drawers and reached for a bottle of liquid sparkling with golden light. Fate cut away the tatters of Finn's shirt, gasping at the long rake of gaping wounds. More scars to add to the ones he'd received from a wolverine during their time in the *Book of Fables*. Tears filled her eyes.

Archie poured the gleaming liquid over the deep gashes. Finn winced, arching his back as the wounds fizzed and smoked. The potion worked fast, turning the inflamed red marks to a healthy pink. The tears closed, leaving four welts across the wolverine scars, though these new ones were much less noticeable, and would no doubt fade completely with time, thanks to the miraculous remedy. Her gaze shifted to another scar over his heart. The Elder race rune Tove had burned into his skin.

"How do you feel?" she asked.

Finn rose stiffly to a sitting position. "Like a trashed scratching post."

Eustace circled behind Archie and extended a hand. Finn took the help he offered and stood. "How do you feel otherwise?" he asked Finn. "Any adverse effects we should know about?"

Finn found his footing with surprising ease. "Nothing I'm aware of."

Fate breathed easy and smiled weakly.

"I wouldn't be so sure." Brune scrutinized Finn like he was on the witness stand. "The first guardian wrote that his bite caused hallucinations."

Finn frowned at her. "I feel fine. Besides, this was a scratch, not a bite."

"I'd call it more of a gouge," Fate corrected him.

"The first guardian's notes would sound like the ranting of a paranoid schizophrenic to anyone who hadn't experienced Farouk in full demon form," Brune continued. "But she was as sane as any of us. Her warnings are explicit. Every move Farouk makes is measured and calculated. There's a purpose behind everything he does."

"What was calculated about that attack?" Fate asked. "If anything, it seemed impulsive. Like he was trying to hurt me by hurting Finn. And all because I've gotten on his bad side."

"Maybe," Brune conceded. "Either way, it's still early in the game. Farouk's just getting started, so watch for any side effects." She paused to study Finn again, before looking away. "And the rest of you get ready, Farouk has more in store for us."

Sithias worried his hands together. "Like what?"

Brune gulped. "I could read you the litany of cruel tricks he played on the first guardian, but it wouldn't help morale."

"It couldn't be worse than what I'm imagining already." Sithias fanned his face. "Are you aware I'm blessed with a wildly creative imagination? Though cursed in this case."

Eustace patted him on the back. "I agree with Brune. We shouldn't be focusing on the worst possibilities. We need to be proactive here."

"Until the worst does happen! And then what?" Sithias clapped his hand over his mouth. "I'll be quiet now," he muttered against his palm.

"What's happening? Why am I on the floor?"

They all turned to see Darcy struggling to a sitting position. Darcy rubbed the top of her head and blinked.

"You fainted," Fate reminded her as she bent to help her stand.

Darcy stared blankly. Until the moment it all came back to her and her face crumpled with grief. "Is it true? Is Mason really gone?"

"I'm so sorry, Darcy." Fate didn't know what else to say. She'd lived in fear of what Darcy was going through and knew she'd be just as inconsolable if she lost Finn.

"You're sorry?" Darcy yelled. "That's rich coming from you! It's your fault Mason came here in the first place. He's dead because of *you*!"

Darcy had been blaming Fate since the beginning, so this was no surprise. But the undiluted hatred she radiated was.

Eustace stepped in. "Come with me, Darcy. Let's get you cleaned up and settled more comfortably." He glanced back. "I think it's best we take a moment to give this the attention it deserves and reconvene in a few hours. Sithias, will you see to making suitable arrangements for our fallen soldier so we can pay proper homage to the dearly departed?"

"That, I can do," Sithias agreed, seemingly eager for something to put his mind to other than worrying as he trotted over to Archie's workstation.

Brune shook her head and started cleaning up the debris of her destroyed project.

Fate looked at Finn. "Thanks for having my back on that one."

"What did you expect me do? Tell her to lay off? She's hurting, Fate."

"I know she is, and I feel terrible for her. I just don't see why everything always ends up being my fault. It's not like I ever said, 'Hey, come to the Keep with me and get yourself killed. It'll be fun!'" She huffed with frustration. "They were being snoopy and got sucked through the portal. It's that simple."

"You do realize they should've been sent back the minute they arrived."

"To make it clear, it wasn't up to me. Brune and Farouk wouldn't let anyone leave."

"But weren't you the Keep Guardian?"

"Technically, yes, but I was a complete bumpkin when I first arrived. I didn't know my armored knee pads from my cybernetic shoulder pads."

Finn smiled. "Sorry, love, didn't mean to make it seem like I was calling you out. I guess I never fully understood how Darcy and Mason came to be here." He took her in his arms and held her close.

His touch cooled her temper and she relaxed enough to sink against the warmth of his body.

"Do you still want to spend the night with me?" he whispered in her ear, sending tingles down her neck and spine with the heat of his breath.

She pulled away as much as he would allow. "Don't you think it's too soon after everything that's happened?"

"No. If anything, we need this to strengthen us. It'll help us face what's to come."

Fate nodded eagerly. "When?"

He winked. "How about now, while the others are making arrangements for Mason?"

The inkling of excitement that had begun to spark flat lined. "I don't know. I feel weird sneaking off to be together in the middle of a terrible tragedy."

"If not now, then when?" Finn asked. "It's not like we have the best track record when it comes to finding time to be alone together."

"Yeah, I know," Fate agreed, but she was still unsure.

The muscles in Finn's jaw clenched, showing his impatience. "Did Mason and Darcy stop loving each other while we were separated and you were miserable about it?"

"Well, no. If anything, Darcy was quite fine with rubbing it in my face."

Finn nodded. "I'm not saying that's what we're doing here. We're keeping this private. We'll be back before anyone notices we're gone."

Fate couldn't resist any longer. She'd been waiting for this moment for what felt like an eternity. "Yes," she whispered.

Finn smiled and glanced around. "Let's slip out now while no one's looking."

"Emergency!" Archie announced. "Kaliena's army has increased. They are on the offensive."

Fate sighed and looked at the ceiling. "Why am I not surprised? Hold that thought," she told Finn as they both rushed to the workstation, where Archie and Sithias were staring at the 3D projections. Brune rushed over to join them.

"Look what they're doing!" Sithias exclaimed.

A whole new armada floated in regimented rows within the Keep's atmosphere. A ship with a battering ram in the shape of a dragon's head hovered outside the sanctuary. Blue vapors breathed from the iron dragon's mouth as the ram beat at the walls rhythmically. The booming sounds reverberated through the layers of walls standing between them and the exterior, stopping when the horns pierced the patchwork wall of the sanctuary and held. Corrosive fumes billowed from its maw, until pieces of the wall broke away on the horns, allowing the ram to return to its steady hammering.

Sithias turned to Archie. "Will the barricade hold long enough for your drones to retrieve Mason's body?"

Brune stared at him like he was nuts. "The real question is, will the wards hold at all? If they get through, they'll take over the entire station."

Archie's hands moved in a flurry of motions over the motherboard he'd modified from Farouk's original control panel. "Kaliena is wise. She's equipped the battering ram with her own ensorcelled manna."

"Her what?" Fate asked.

"The fuel she generates to connect with the Obiectus, and in turn control or destroy any of its working parts."

"You mean the blue glowing liquid I saw pouring out of her hands when she was enshrined?"

"Correct."

"Are you saying her manna will eat a hole through the barrier?"

"No."

"But... you said Kaliena is wise. Doesn't that mean she's going to win this one?"

Archie's neck creaked as he gave her a sidelong look with his beaming eyes. "Kaliena may be wise, but her intellect is no match for mine. This chosen method of invasion will prove ineffective. My barrier is designed to rebuild itself."

Fate smiled. "Nice thinking, Arch."

Finn pointed at the other projection. "What's this? Is that the glass dome of the garden I'm seeing? What are those things crawling all over it?"

"Orgknights from the Drozeer dimension." Archie enlarged the image to show black, crablike creatures with tiny heads peering from beneath the humps of spiked shells. They were striking the glass panes of the dome with their heavy front pincers. "Kaliena summoned them. They're extremely adept at rupturing shields made with multidimensional magic. Their job is to weaken the integrity of the wards fired into the glass so it can be eventually shattered."

Fate chewed on her bottom lip. "Can they do it?"

"Given time, yes." Archie's tone was matter-of-fact.

"Isn't there some sort of snazzy defense for the dome too?"

"I did not design the dome."

"Oh." Fate clenched her hands into fists, both alarmed by this frightening new development and frustrated her efforts to be alone with Finn were once again thwarted. "Well," she sighed, "time to gear up, people."

Archie turned away from the controls. "You are no match for Orgknights."

Fate slumped. "Hey, you're not supposed to defeat us before the fight. It's terrible for morale."

Brune crossed her arms. "I second that."

Archie's blue brow furrowed with confusion. "I'm merely providing necessary information."

"Crushing despair is more like it." Brune shook her head.

"Let's not throw in the towel so soon. Have you forgotten I have super powers?" Fate avoided Finn's gaze as shame pushed to the forefront. She wasn't proud of the bloodlust she'd allowed herself to be overtaken with during the last battle.

If she could erase from his mind the sight of how she'd zealously torn into the enemy, she would. Unfortunately, she could not. Unless she tried a forgetting spell on him, but Gerdie was living proof that would be a horrible mistake. Either way, she was hooped. He'd most likely witness the same ugliness again, regardless of how much she tried to restrain herself in the next battle.

"I should be able to handle this crab infestation on my own," she offered. The beginnings of her inner war drum were already pounding through her bloodstream at the thought of being free to unleash her powers without Finn there to judge her actions. "Right, Arch?"

"I know nothing of any extraordinary powers you may possess. Therefore, I would not recommend taking on more than one Orgknight alone. As of the last count, there are eighteen."

"Is it the hard shells that make them so formidable?" Finn asked.

"The shells are not indestructible, simply difficult to damage because Orgknights live between dimensions. A state that makes them intangible on this plane of existence. Simultaneously, they can pierce through the veil with their pincers to wreak enormous damage on our physical plane." Archie trundled over to his cluttered workbench and reached for a rifle with a fluted barrel plugged into several brass canisters. "Your odds of defeating them increase exponentially with one of these."

Brune took the rifle before Fate had the chance. She studied the intricacies of the tubes and canisters built into the barrel. "Looks like the casing is an atomizer condenser." Looking impressed, she nodded at Archie. "Smart. Parabolic stabilization of the particles forms the center of mass we need for engagement."

Fate stared at them. "You're going to have to dumb that down for the rest of us."

Brune shrugged. "It's simple. Point, shoot, and they become solid on this side of the veil."

"Which makes them available to fight, and hopefully kill," Finn finished for her.

"Exactly." Brune reached for her armor.

"Finn and I can handle this."

Brune stopped to frown at Fate. "We're outnumbered at three, yet you want to go in with only two?"

"Finn and I are best equipped for this one. We've got the speed and strength to make up for our lack of numbers." Fate didn't want to elaborate that she had other supernatural skills she was only just becoming accustomed to and was anxious to test without Brune around. "Besides, you need to be working on Farouk's cage. The sooner we lock him down the better."

Brune shifted her weight back and forth from one foot to the other, demonstrating her pent-up energy like she was the one who was caged. "Building another cage isn't going to work. He'll destroy that one too. We need to think outside the box on this one."

"Nice pun, but I suppose you're right," Fate agreed. "You and Archie put your heads together on this one and see what you come up with."

"Put our heads together?" Archie blinked at her. "What logic is there in doing that?"

Fate smiled at him. "Oh Archie, for all your knowledge, you have much to learn." Archie's confusion remained, and no amount of explaining would clear that up, so she began suiting up, while Finn did the same.

As she buckled down the shoulder pads, she realized none of her armor was necessary. She'd already proven she was invulnerable. Was she wearing it out of habit, or for the benefit of everyone else? If she had to answer that question, she would have to admit to the latter. After Finn's fearful reaction to her recent battle fervor, she wasn't ready to let on just how powerful she had become. She couldn't bear to see the same fear in his eyes. The same went for her father and everyone else.

Fate reached for the atom condenser rifle and turned to Finn. "Ready?"

He returned her gaze with a grim stare. "Aye, ready as I'll ever be."

18
HEART TO HEART

FINN WEAVED THROUGH THE garden's thick jungle and dove under the cover of a giant mushroom to stay hidden from the Orgknights. Fate was already there, waiting for him to catch up. He'd suspected her strength and speed had surpassed his, but this confirmed it. He felt the sting of inferiority for a split second and understood a little better why she'd risked everything to be as strong as he was. Though there was no telling the full extent of her new powers. She'd barely scratched the surface, and that bothered him more than anything. There was no way to know if she could control them.

"Have a look," she said. "You can see the damage clearly from here. It's extensive."

He inched out to the edge of the cap, glancing up at the garden's domed ceiling. A long fissure ran along one side of the dome, while more fractures spidered from the main vein. The Orgknights were clustered around the widest part of the rupture, hammering at the glass with their pincers. With every strike, glimmering waves of multidimensional magic rippled in all directions.

He drew in a sharp breath. "The dome's going to cave any minute. We need to get up there."

She held the rifle out to him. "You make them solid while I crack some crab shells." She smiled. "I love seafood, how about you?"

"Aye, I like a good crab cake now and then." He pushed the rifle back into her hands. "But how about you shoot, while I do the cracking?"

She frowned and her bottom lip pushed out in the most irresistible way. "Why?"

Desire clouded his mind as he reached out and traced his thumb over her pouting mouth. "Can't let you have all the fun."

"Is it because of how the last battle went?"

Finn withdrew his hand and looked away. He dreaded seeing her lose control again. What if the bloodlust became permanent? There was no way to know how another intense battle would affect her. He wasn't about to find out. Which was why he was determined to do whatever was necessary to give Sithias more time to figure out how to separate Fate from Hippolyta's magical girdle safely.

He returned his gaze. "I just don't want to see you lose yourself like before."

"Was it really that bad?" She cringed. "Don't answer that." She cocked the rifle. "Fine, I'll shoot, you do the cracking."

Relieved, he nodded. "Good. We go in on the count of three."

"Kiss for good luck?"

Finn's pulse raced as he stared at her moist lips, but he stopped himself at the last second. It was best he keep his head about him. "Better yet, let's make it a victory kiss. *After* this is done."

She thought about it. "Hmm, incentive. Works for me."

Finn held three fingers up and silently counted by curling one finger down at a time. The moment he flexed his fingers into a tight fist, Fate disappeared in a whirl of dark stardust. Gulping back his fear of teleporting, he visualized the exterior of the dome, tensing against the sensation of every atom exploding.

Bones, blood and muscle pounded back into form within an instant. Ignoring the dizzying sick feeling sweeping through his body, he focused on finding his footing to keep from falling over. Lifting his head, he fixed his sights on the curve of the dome, where the Orgknights worked to weaken the glass. Their bulky forms wavered in and out of visibility.

Fate raced over the rounded surface, slid to a halt and pulled the trigger. A blast of shimmering silver surged from the rifle's barrel as strong and forceful as water from a fireman's hose.

The spray penetrated the dimensional veil, covering the Orgknights with a thick mercurial fluid. They stopped hammering. Tiny heads with numerous red eyes and fanged mouths shrank into their shells, each swiveling to peer at her.

Finn blew the two rune notes into his flute to create a scimitar-shaped wind blade. Letting out a loud roar to distract them from Fate, he charged forward. The Orgknights crabbed toward him with pincers knifing the air.

Finn leapt high, landing on the humped shell of the closest Orgknight, bringing the windsword down to slice into the head recoiling beneath his feet. The creature staggered to one side. Finn jumped off before it toppled over, ducked the deadly sweep of another Orgknight's snapping pincers and spun round to open its soft underbelly. A thrill shot through him, awakening a darkness he thought he'd left behind.

He stormed into the fray with a clarity he hadn't realized he'd been missing until that moment. His windsword seemed to come alive in his hand, swinging where it needed to go, slicing with perfect precision and astonishing speed. Severed appendages lay in craggy piles at his feet as he tore through their numbers like a wild force of nature. He felt indestructible, as if nothing could touch–

A pincer bit into his back, knocking the air from his lungs, a painful blow that had pierced his armor and cut him to his knees. He heard Fate's cry. In a blur of motion, she was next to him, her sword slashing in streaks of flashing silver, downing five Orgknights with what looked like hardly any effort. The Orgknights along the outer ring, angled backward, their pincers held in defensive positions, but they did not advance. If anything they seemed to be fading from sight. Finn blinked to clear his eyes, then realized they were slowly retreating into their own dimension.

Fate's movements stilled as she watched the creatures vanish completely. Seconds later, she turned around, her face clenched with fear. "I'm getting us out of here."

Finn's surroundings collapsed without warning. When he rematerialized beneath the giant mushroom, a nauseating dizziness took hold. Grabbing the stem for support, he focused his breathing. In the same instant, Fate appeared next to him in a burst of glittering smoke. He quickly straightened to hide his discomfort, but the jabbing pain in his back prevented him.

She hurried to check his injury, her expression relaxing upon inspection. "I'm happy to say, it looks like you're going to live. It's just a flesh wound, but we should get you to the infirmary to get it cleaned. You never know, an infection from an Orgknight might cause you to grow a crabshell on your back." She smiled jokingly.

Wishing to stay a little longer, Finn dropped his gaze to the profusion of flowers and greenery. He'd grown weary of being bound by iron walls, still air and the ever-present drone of simulated lights. He missed the Earth's blue sky and the winds that brought whispers from distant lands. At least here in the garden, the air moved and was filled with sounds of birdsong and buzzing insects. "I'm in no real hurry to leave if it's just a scrape."

Fate leaned outside the shelter of the mushroom's cap and peeked at the ceiling. "Well, I suppose we could stay a few more minutes. I don't think Kaliena's noticed the Orgknights are gone yet. Not that it matters. We saved the dome, and thanks to Archie, I see the maintenance bots are already making repairs from the inside." She scanned the perimeter of the garden. "Wait, what about Farouk? Our fight outside the dome had to have drawn his attention."

"No need to worry about that. I placed repelling wards around the garden earlier." He didn't bother to mention the garden had been part of the romantic evening he'd planned for them. Kaliena's latest attack had put an end to that.

"When we get back, you should put them around the shelter too."

"Aye, I've been intending to, but I haven't been able to find enough pulverized chicken bones to match the size of the shelter. You wouldn't happen to know of a supply, would you?"

Thinking of the food replicator, Fate chewed on her lip. "Do they have to be real chicken bones?"

"Aye, and the chickens need to be alive and blessed by a Grand Druid before slaughter. Though I could probably get away with doing that part myself."

"That could be a problem. Unless old MacDonald's farm happens to be in one of the vaults stored here in the Keep."

"I thought as much." Biting down on the pain snaking through his ribs, Finn tucked his flute into the holster of his belt. He tried mustering a smile. "Thanks for coming to my rescue up there."

"I'd do anything for you." Fate stared back with an incredulous expression. Her face was still flushed from the battle. "And you've always done the same for me. More times than I care to admit."

"You'll always have my protection, love." He grimaced with pain. "So long as there's breath in my body."

She closed the space between them. "Don't worry, I'll make sure you keep breathing." Mischief played across her features as she clasped her lower lip between her teeth and smiled. She had no idea what that look did to him.

His palms began to sweat. Feverish heat rose beneath his skin as he traced his gaze over the curves of her face. Hopelessly drawn in by the gold flecks shining in her cinnamon-brown eyes, he loosened her braid and tangled his fingers gently into the satiny curls of her hair.

Her eyes glistened with unbridled desire. She was awash in it. The intoxicating scent of passion on her skin came to him on the air. His blood pumped hard, enlivening every inch of him, banishing the pain. She caught the look in his eyes and blushed an even deeper color of rose, an alluring sight that shook him to the core.

"I want you, Finn." Her voice was little more than a trembling whisper.

Despite trying to keep the full magnitude of her emotions hidden, she was failing miserably. Her longing stare clawed at him. He'd never seen her more open and vulnerable than in that moment. All he wanted was to take her into the cover of his arms and hold her closer than he ever had in the past. Heart to heart, skin to skin.

He needed to touch her so badly his body ached with the absence of her.

They each took a step closer. Their breastplates clanked against one another, a reminder of the wall of armor between them. Fate rushed to unbuckle her shoulder pads from the breastplate. She let the pieces fall to the ground, then fought with the straps of her arm and leg bracers in her hurry to remove them. Finn did the same to catch up with her.

Shrugging her undercoat off, Fate stood before him in a tank top and leather breeches. Finn's throat went dry and he gulped loudly as she sidled closer. She rose on her toes as if to whisper something in his ear. Instead, she took the lobe of his ear into her mouth. The wet stroke of her tongue lanced jolts of electricity down his spine, overriding the pain in his back enough to ignore it. She let go, her mouth skimming over his cheek and then his lips with a touch as light and silken as the brush of flower petals.

She stepped back, gazing up at him, her pupils every bit as wide and untamed as a cat's. Her lips parted, a wordless invitation he could no longer resist. Finn descended on her mouth and their tongues met in an achingly sweet caress.

His head spun with the heavenly taste of her. He drew her closer, feeling the rise and fall of her breasts against his own chest. Running his hands over the smooth skin of her arms, he whispered her name and told her he loved her, again and again. Her breath fanned against his neck as she breathed the tiniest of sighs–angelic music that sang to the deepest part of his soul.

Finn lifted her off her feet and lowered her gently down onto a bed of flowering woodland moss. The perfume of her skin mingled with the scent of fragrant blooms and dewy earth beneath them. He rested on one elbow, trailing his other hand down one side of her face. She was luminous, unearthly in the way her auburn locks splayed like wildfire over the green moss. Fate had always taken his breath away, but this was different. Her heart was fully open. Her spirit was shining through, brighter than any sun in the universe, a blinding sight that left him utterly breathless.

Time stopped.

Fate was all that existed. This was how it felt to stand at the very center of creation itself. They had defied heaven and earth to be together. And here they were, two souls sharing this sacred space in one precious fragment of time.

Heart to heart at last.

Allowing his body to flood with raw desire, Finn surrendered everything he had to Fate.

19
TIED TOGETHER, ALWAYS

FATE'S HEART SOARED AS she rested her head on Finn's shoulder, soaking in his warmth. Every inch of her body hummed with blissful joy. So much so, she could barely contain it. Filled with exuberance, she tangled her legs together with his and tickled the bottom of his foot with her toes. When his knee jerked reflexively and his eyes popped open in surprise, she giggled.

He chuckled sleepily. "Saucy minx." The green of his eyes lit to brighter hues as he engaged in a tickling foot war.

After a few more minutes of mischief, they fell silent again. Finn stifled a wince as he positioned his injured back against the broad stem of the giant mushroom as comfortably as possible. Fate leaned against him with her head tilted upward, gazing at the blanket of stars glittering beyond the umbrella sheltering them from view. Being with Finn in this way, feeling the dense, hard muscle of his chest against her bare back, and the weight of his arm wrapped loosely around her waist, was as natural as if they'd been lovers from the very start.

A rare peace came over her. All her troubles and concerns seemed a million miles away. She was home.

If only she could stay in this safe place forever. An impossible wish, but she wished it all the same. She turned her head to give him a playful sideways glance. "Play me some music."

He raised his eyebrows. "You've never asked me that before."

An old sadness rose unbidden. Fate dropped her gaze and drew a spiral pattern over the back of his hand as the painful memory returned full force. "When you were trapped inside the oak, all I had the strength to do was lie at the bottom of the tree trunk. Sounds nutty, but I wanted to be near you. I was pretty weak from blood loss at the time and mostly slept. Sometimes you would come into my dreams and play your flute until the pain I was in went away."

Finn caressed her arm and kissed the top of her head. "Sorry, love, I don't recall any of that. I was part of the Earthmind, which is so much larger than either of us. Are you sure it wasn't just a dream?"

She wriggled around within the crook of his arm to face him. "No, you were there with me. I know it, because I wasn't always asleep. When I was awake you sometimes spoke to me through the wind and the birds. Like when I came to say goodbye, I heard your voice in my heart. I remember the words clearly. You said, 'We are–'"

"Tied together, always," he finished for her.

It was her turn to look surprised. "You remember."

"Not from the time you're telling me, but it's something I always told myself when we were apart. It's what kept me going."

She kissed him. "Promise me we'll never be apart again."

Finn's gaze moved past her, his eyes filling with a sudden sadness. "You know I can't. We don't know what's ahead, or what will be asked of us."

His words left her cold and feeling suddenly exposed. She reached for her clothes and began dressing.

Finn slid into his trousers. "I didn't mean to upset you."

"I'm fine." Her voice sounded tight, even to her ears. She shoved her arms into her undercoat and zipped it all the way to the throat. Tears stung at the backs of her eyes and she was about to leave when the lilting notes of Finn's flute filled the air.

The soothing melody held her there, hushing her inner turmoil. The birds fell quiet too, as if to make room for his song. A tear slipped down her cheek as she turned back. Finn's eyes were closed, his long fingers gently tapping the wooden flute, creating the music in his heart.

Love swelled from the notes, carrying a message only the soul could hear and understand–a song of eternal love, trust and endless devotion. The music floated around her, shivering over her skin, soft as feathers. The notes vibrated through her body, soaking into the rush of blood in her veins, filling her with an unwavering sense of being held and protected.

A profusion of butterflies lifted off the foliage all at once and fluttered over her. All the colors of the rainbow shimmered and flashed upon their delicate wings. They hung in the air in a spectacular cloud of moving color, and Fate gasped with delight as she realized they had formed the shape of an undulating heart.

The music trailed off into one long, sweet and fading note. The butterflies dispersed and Finn moved the flute from his lips and smiled. She ran to him, kissing him over and over until they fell into a passionate tangle of limbs upon the moss. "Thank you," she whispered between kisses.

"Do you understand now that nothing can ever truly separate us?" His voice grew husky with the depth of his emotions.

"I do." Her words came in breathless fits between each kiss. "I'm sorry

I doubted–"

Brune's voice cut in, a sharp interruption that was almost physically painful. "What's with you two? You do realize there's a war going on outside these walls, right?"

Fate pushed off of Finn and jumped to her feet, her heart pounding with a chaotic mixture of desire and shock at being discovered. She hugged her arms, grateful for the fact she was fully dressed. Irritation set in. "Ever heard of knocking?"

Brune crossed her arms. "Knock on what? This mushroom you chose to... " She raised an eyebrow at the strewn armor and Finn's bare chest. "Liaise under?"

Fate didn't bother to answer and began strapping on her armor.

Finn stood and pulled his shirt over his head. Tucking the loose ends in, he buckled his belt and glanced up. "What's the big rush, Brune? Archie said the sanctuary is holding, and we took care of the Orgknights in short order."

"It's been four hours since then. Others were growing concerned, meaning Eustace." Brune smirked at Fate. "He was getting ready to come out here. I told him I'd go instead. Even though I now feel the need to wash my eyeballs. Do you two ever come up for air?"

Finn ignored the remark. "It's been that long?"

"Yup."

Fate gulped, thankful her father hadn't been the one to find them in such a compromising position. Eustace may have said he was stepping aside to allow her to make her own choices, but she was certain he wasn't emotionally prepared to see outright evidence of what those choices were. She would've thanked Brune for saving both father and daughter from a world of humiliation, had it not been for the smug expression on her face.

"Diagnostics for the core are in, and it's not looking good," Brune continued.

Fate cinched down the buckles of her boots and grabbed her helmet. "Has the last ring stopped turning?"

"It's best if Archie explains." Brune looked them both over. "Have you got everything? Nothing on backwards? No mix up of clothes? Hair's straightened?"

Finn strapped the last of his gear on. "We're good. You two go ahead. I'll catch up."

Fate's gut tightened. "We should go together."

"I'll be along." He smiled, but the clench of his jaw betrayed his tension.

"Go ahead, Brune," Fate told her. "We'll be right behind you."

Brune narrowed her eyes. "You better be." She vanished in a drift of shimmering smoke.

Fate stared at Finn. "What's wrong?"

"I'm done using the teleporter."

"Why? Given the dire situations we've been in so far, it's exactly what we need right now."

Finn shook his head. "It's not right for me."

"Tell me why."

Pain splashed across his face. "It's difficult to explain, except to say it feels like I'm unraveling thread by thread each time I teleport."

"But you're not," Fate argued. "You're as solid and whole as I am."

He frowned. "I'm not made of the same stuff as you." His jaw tightened again as the shade of green in his eyes dimmed to the color of seaweed. "I was brought into being by the Orb. We both know its creations have always gone sideways at some point. I can't help feeling like using the teleporter is increasing the odds of whatever will go wrong."

"Don't talk like it's inevitable. You're perfect and there's nothing wrong with you." She could see her words did nothing to assure him. Fate unclasped the Rod of Aeternitis and dangled it from the chain. "I should've given you this the moment we were back together."

"What good will it do me without the Orb?"

"Maybe nothing. Maybe everything." Fate clasped the chain around his neck. She stepped back. "Feel anything different?"

"I wish I could say I did. Either way, I'm not teleporting anymore. I've decided to have Archie remove it."

Fate's heart jumped with fear. "No, Farouk was very clear on the subject. The teleportation device is permanent. I remember quite clearly him saying something about perpetual discatterment."

"That was before we had Archie on our side."

"I suppose, but..."

Finn headed for the exit.

"Where are you going?"

"Back to the shelter, the old fashioned way. Some people like to call it walking."

Fate caught up to him. "What if we run into Farouk?"

"Then we fight, like we always have."

"Are you forgetting the swipe he took at you and the way he weakened me just by being in the room?"

"No, but that should tell you how badly I don't want to teleport."

Fate had run out of arguments. They left the safety of the tranquil garden and walked the long dark halls past the residence quarters and the training chamber, each on guard for any sign of Farouk. When they passed the infirmary, she remembered Finn's injury. "Let's make a quick stop to have your latest scratch attended to."

Finn waved her off and kept going. He'd increased his speed and she could see by the muscles working in his jaw, he was growing tense. "I'm sure Archie can take care of it."

Fate decided not to press him. When they reached the outside hatch, she radioed Brune through the comm of her helmet to open the latch from the inside.

Brune's voice crackled in the headset. "I'm not opening it. Teleport inside."

"We can't."

No reply.

"We have a malfunction."

A few seconds ticked by. "There better be, otherwise you're jeopardizing the safety of everyone else."

The sound of grinding metal echoed through the corridor as the large hatch juddered open. Glancing over his shoulder, Finn gestured for Fate to enter before following her inside.

Brune palmed the panel, closing the hatch behind them. "Which one of you has the malfunction?"

"I do." Finn marched over to Archie's station to address his needs.

Fate stepped around Brune to follow, but Eustace rushed over. "Are you all right?" he asked, his brow twisted with concern.

She was more than all right. Her face warmed with remembered passion, followed immediately by burning spots of embarrassment dotting her cheeks and forehead. "I'm fine," she insisted.

Eustace caught the range of emotions across her face. When he realized what he was seeing, he forced a blank face. They stared at each other for what seemed like an uncomfortably long time before he cleared his throat and removed his glasses to clean them. "Very good, I'm relieved all is well."

"Me too," she managed to squeak.

Eustace replaced his glasses and looked everywhere in the room but at her. He finally anchored his frenzied gaze on Archie. "Sorry to say, you've returned to some rather bad news."

Eager to move on as well, Fate nodded. "That's what I hear. I suppose it's time to get the low down on everything."She moved stiffly toward Archie's station, careful to avoid meeting Finn's gaze since it was impossible to mask the emotional high he ignited in her.

The 3D projection of the core hovered over Archie's control panel. He turned around to face them all. It didn't seem possible, but his beaming eyes actually appeared dimmer than usual. "I've determined the core is beyond repair," he announced. "The damage from the mining is far too extensive. With only one ring in operation, very little of the Chaos Region's harmful emanations are being filtered out. I would like to examine each of you to determine current cognitive functions."

Avoiding her father and Finn, Fate glanced at Sithias and Brune. Darcy and Gerdie hadn't joined them. "Everyone seems fine to me," she said. "Except maybe Gerdie, but her memory loss has nothing to do with what you're talking about." Her stomach tightened at the thought of everyone she cared about going insane the way most of the Golandon population had before they built and installed the six protective rings.

"We're in the early stages of exposure," Archie explained. "It's only a matter of time before we begin seeing signs of degradation. Irritability will be the first, followed quickly by irrational thinking and uncontrollable rage or terror. Or in some cases complete apathy and depression, which were known to lead to mass suicides."

Sithias gasped and fanned his face. "I think I've succumbed! Ever since we locked ourselves in this horrible vault, I've been quite sad."

Fate patted his skinny arm. "We're all less than thrilled about being cooped up in here. If anything, I'd say boredom is what's getting to you." She glanced over at the barracks. "Darcy's the one we really need to watch. If anyone has reason to be depressed, it's her."

"Yes, losing Mason has thrown her into a very dark place," Eustace agreed.

"Plus we've all witnessed her tantrums," Fate added. "This could push her into going postal any minute now."

"I'm more concerned about Archie losing his marbles," Finn said. "The last thing we need is a genius mad scientist sabotaging the technology we rely on for our very survival."

The point was well taken, and everyone fell silent, Archie included. His metal neck creaked as he tilted his bulbous head with a pensive expression creasing his blue skin. "I'm unfamiliar with any marbles I may possess, though my programming would never allow me to initiate any action that would result in sabotage of Obiectus technology. As well, I was genetically engineered to withstand the emanations from the Chaos Region and will remain immune regardless of how saturated the Obiectus becomes."

The room filled with a discernable sense of relief.

"Now that we've got that question out of the way, what's next?" Brune asked.

Archie turned back to the projection, his many hands flying over the keyboard, which swiftly produced an intricate star map. "The safest option is to remove the Obiectus from the Chaos Region."

"You can do that?" Fate asked.

"I can navigate the Obiectus through a wormhole. I estimate it would take fifty of your Earth years to reach the nearest one."

Fate made a face. "Fifty years? Is that with or without warp speed?"

Archie considered her question. "Define warp speed."

"Never mind," Fate muttered impatiently. "Listen Arch, that's not going to work. We won't last fifty years. If Kaliena doesn't wipe us out in the next few weeks, Farouk will."

Sithias whimpered.

"Fate's right," Brune agreed as she glared at Archie. "It's time we get down to the real reason we brought you here. We want you to amplify one of the Keep portals and widen the opening enough to allow the entire structure to pass through. Do you think you can handle that?"

Archie teetered and blinked rapidly. Had Brune overloaded him with too much information? Fate moved in closer in case she needed to catch him. Just when it seemed steam might spew from his ears, he stopped swaying and stared straight ahead. "Initial computations give your theory a ninety-five percent success rate. I'll need to know the accessibility of the portal and its final destination before I can confirm the theory is sound and one hundred percent actionable."

"The portal you're looking for leads to Oldwilde," Finn told him. "It's a hidden realm on Earth."

The tension seemed to lift somewhat amongst the others, but not for Fate. Her recently acquired pink bubble of happiness popped in that instant, replaced by a brick of ice settling in the pit of her stomach. As soon as Archie located the portal to Oldwilde, Finn would be gone.

20
AS GOOD AS COMING HOME

FINN SHRUGGED OFF HIS aeronaut pack, glancing skyward as he did so at the fleets of ships blotting out the stars beyond the Keep's artificial firmament. He ducked in beneath the shadows of a nearby vault made of intricately carved ivory before turning off the visibility disruptor Archie had provided. Sithias landed nearby with a loud thud, followed by the clank of his aeronaut pack and vibrating wings clattering against the walkway.

"Ow, ow, my foot! I think I may've broken it," Sithias complained.

Finn edged forward with his hand outstretched, feeling the air for Sithias. When he found his arm, he dragged him into the shadows. "Stop your grousing, Sithias, and be quiet!"

He heard a click and Sithias blinked into view. He was on the floor, whimpering and rubbing his ankle. "It may just be a light twissst," he whispered. "We can only hope."

Fate appeared next to him in a flurry of smoky stardust. She kneeled next to Sithias when she saw he was injured. "What happened?"

"He crash-landed." Finn couldn't hide his irritation. He was upset with having to leave Fate so soon. He thought they'd have at least another day together before Archie located an accessible portal to Oldwilde, but the scientist had found it within a matter of minutes.

Sithias's white brows angled into sad lines and his amber eyes rounded. "Well excuse me for wanting to challenge myself with something new."

"I don't know why you didn't just go with your own wings. It's what you're used to." Finn attempted a less irritable tone. "The aeronaut packs are tricky at best."

Fate helped Sithias to a standing position. He leaned against her, draping himself over her shoulder like a wilted beanstalk before testing his weight on the afflicted foot. "Ow, ow, ow... oh, hold on. I think maybe... yes, I can stand." He grinned with relief. "It's working. I'm fine."

Finn pressed his mouth into a smile. "Well, there's one less worry."

Fate smiled affectionately at Sithias, but it vanished when she looked at Finn. His spirits sank. She wasn't dealing well with his all too abrupt departure, which was further inflamed by the location this particular portal opened onto. They'd all agreed his mission was imperative to their ultimate survival, but leaving Fate behind to face constant danger without him, ripped him to shreds. And it didn't help she was protecting herself by withdrawing. She was already slipping away from him. He couldn't leave without making things better between them.

He'd prepared something special to give her when they'd been alone in the garden, but Brune had come along before he'd had the chance to present the gift. Apparently, the ideal place and time would continue to elude him, so this would have to be it.

"Sithias, can you excuse us for a minute?" he asked.

Sithias glanced at Fate and made a small 'o' with his mouth. "Certainly, sir, I'll sneak over there by that marbled unicorn. You know me, I've always been an admirer of beautiful art."

"Thanks." Finn watched him tip toe beneath the out-cropping of the vault keeping them hidden from view. If there was one thing he could count on when it came to Sithias, it was his love of romance.

Fate's stare was aloof when he turned to her. "I suppose this is where you tell me everything's going to be fine, even though this could be the last time we ever see each other."

Finn unbuttoned one of the pouches in his utility belt to retrieve its contents. He stared at the braided cords of the two bracelets he'd made.

"What are those?" Fate's voice softened.

He glanced at her. "Do you remember that time in Asgar when we joined the ribbon dance beneath the Maytree?"

"How could I forget? You tricked me into it."

He smiled. "Remember what you asked me after the dance was over?"

Her brows knitted together. "Not really."

"You asked if the dance meant that we'd tied the knot. I explained the meaning behind the ribbon dance, that we were bound by an unspoken promise to wed, but that it wasn't official unless the ceremony was consummated before next Beltane."

Her face flushed a lovely shade of red. He took her hand and slipped one of the bracelets onto her wrist. "As far as I'm concerned, it's official."

Her long lashes veiled her emotions as she ran a trembling finger over the blend of silk and wool. When she looked at him, her eyes glistened with tears.

"I know it's not a real wedding," he rushed to say. "If we had the time we'd do it right. Your father would be there to give you away. You'd be wearing the dress of your dreams and I'd play my flute to have songbirds carry your train, and butterflies to decorate your bouquet of flowers. And–"

She put a finger to his lips to stop him. "I love the idea of having a real life Disney wedding. Really I do, but this is every bit as perfect." She took his bracelet and slipped it onto his wrist, her hand lingering warm against his skin.

His pulse calmed.

Fate pulled at the silk ribbon on his bracelet. "Is this the one you gave me? I thought I'd lost it. I hadn't wanted to tell you until I could be sure it was long gone."

"Aye, I stole it to braid together with strips of the kilt from the uniform Rudwor awarded me when he made me First Knight. I would've used my own clan tartan, but that's back in Scotland." He swallowed down the dark thoughts that followed. *Not that there's anything real for me in Scotland. Not my grandda, my heritage, or my home.*

Fate fingered the silver charms hanging from the ends. "Tell me about these."

"This one's the Tree of Life. It represents the inter-connection of all that is. When you look at it, you can know that we're always together, never truly apart." He lifted the other charm. "This is the Celtic Love Knot. It stands for eternal love and fidelity. I had them specially made. You can thank Archie for that."

"Apparently I have much to thank Archie for." She attempted a smile but the corners of her mouth turned down. "Like taking you straight to Tove."

Running his hand through his hair, Finn clenched his jaw. What was it going to take to convince her that his heart belonged to her and her alone? He gripped her by the arms, a forceful move that startled her. "Fate, you have nothing to worry about. Any feelings I had for Tove are gone. Erased by you. You're the only one for me. Why can't you see that? What more do I need to do?"

She crumpled into tears. "Don't go. That's what you can do. Just stay with me until Archie's done building the amplifier. We'll go through the portal together and rally the armies after we get to Oldwilde."

Finn shook his head. "You know that's not going to work. The armies have to be in place. If they're not, Kaliena's legions will destroy Oldwilde, and us with it."

Sorrow seeped into every part of his being as he held her close and she shook with sobs. Her pain opened the old wounds of their last separation. All the loneliness he'd suffered during that horrible time rushed back in.

What was he thinking? Facing the actual reality of leaving was agonizing and more than he could bear.

"Please don't cry," he whispered in her ear. "I can't stand to see you in pain. I'll stay. We'll make another plan."

She pulled back to look at him, blinking furiously to see through all the tears. "Really?"

"Aye, I can't leave you. Not again. Not ever."

"You would do that? You'd stay just for me?"

"Of course. Don't you get it? I'd do *anything* for you."

Hope washed away the pain in her eyes. But then a shadow crossed her face, heavy and oppressed, when at last, defeat set like stone in her gaze. "No, that would be incredibly selfish of me. You have to go. I've always known you would leave and that I would stay behind."

They had fought so hard to be together and had since shared countless small delights since their reunion. But there had to be more than this tiny taste of heaven. Were they not destined to share the great joy of resting in each other's arms for the remainder of their lives?

"You're not being selfish," Finn assured her. "It's time we made us the priority."

Fate stared at him with more love than she ever had, if that were even possible. "I wish we could, but we both know the powers-that-be won't let us." The tears returned, but this time her eyes were free of turmoil. "Thank you for being willing to stay for me. It means *everything*."

Finn's voice caught in his throat. He wanted to argue, but she spoke the truth.

She stroked the fabric of the bracelet with a brave, sad smile. "I love this. It couldn't be more perfect. We are tied together, always."

"*Always*," he whispered, unable to find his voice for the tightness in his throat.

"We'll never say goodbye... " She trailed off as she rose on her toes to kiss him. The softness of her lips and the sweet taste of her drew him into a swirling vortex of desire. He knew in that moment he'd suffer a lifetime of hell for whatever bits of time he could steal with her.

Finn moved to pull her close, when his arms suddenly swiped through nothing more than air. He opened his eyes to the lingering drift of stardust Fate had left behind. If Archie hadn't removed the teleportation device as requested, he would've used it in a heartbeat to chase after her. Glancing skyward at the fleets of airships he'd be forced to navigate through again, he swallowed down the desperate urge to take to the air. Fate had teleported away without warning to save them both the misery of saying goodbye.

If he didn't leave now he never would. In his heart he knew it was for the best of all concerned.

Sithias snuck back over to him. "Where did Fate go? Don't tell me she left without saying goodbye."

Finn stared into space. "She didn't want this to be goodbye," he managed to say after several long seconds. He felt gutted, utterly hollowed out.

Sithias looked him over. "Wise choice. We mustn't jinx our luck. It's always best to trust we'll meet again." His expression softened with compassion. "It must be hard leaving her after being apart so very long and everything you went through to finally reunite."

"A hell of a lot harder than I thought it would be," Finn agreed. The timing had been all too quick. There was so much left unfinished.

Sithias said something else that didn't quite register. Finn shook his head, focusing in on Sithias's mouth, as if reading lips was the only way he would understand him.

"What did you say?"

Sithias replied, his white goatee bobbing on his chin as he chattered on. But it was all mere noise against the strained buzzing in Finn's head. "Say again?"

"I spotted the vault in question while you were both not saying goodbye." At this point Sithias was miming every word, his long skinny arms waggling as he did so. He hopped to one side before rounding a corner, which teased Finn into following. His gesticulating movements came to a halt as he held one hand up to present his findings. "If this isn't the vault holding the tree troll cave, I'll eat my socks."

"Right," Finn answered, but his thoughts were chasing Fate and not on his surroundings. He was worried about the volatile power she'd risked everything for. It was getting stronger. What if she lost control? He wouldn't be there to rein her in. He interrupted Sithias's ramblings. "Where did you leave that research you were doing on the Amazonian girdle?"

"Oh, I uh..." Sithias gave him a sheepish look. "I know you told me not to tell Eustace about what Fate did, but when I found out I'd be joining you, I thought it best to inform him of the situation. I left all my research and books with him."

Finn breathed easier. "Good thinking, Sithias. If there's anyone who can figure out a way to remove the girdle without killing Fate, it's her own father. No offense."

Sithias let out a loud sigh of relief. "None taken, sir. I'm glad you agree with my decision."

"I don't know why we didn't bring Eustace in on the dilemma from the very beginning."

"You were trying to protect both father and daughter."

"Aye, I suppose." Feeling more assured with Fate's situation, Finn surveyed the vault Sithias had pointed out. At first glance it appeared more like a gigantic knot of burlwood than any sort of built structure. On closer inspection, he noticed a craggy head carved over the mouth of the entrance. The face emulated the same kind, wise visage of his good friend, Grysla, the last known tree troll in all of Oldwilde. Moss and vines clung to the dark entrance, covering most of the Elder race runes etched along the edges of the opening.

The familiarity of the runes and the thought of seeing his old friend soothed his heartache somewhat. "Good work, Sithias."

Finn activated his visibility disruptor and leapt onto the moving walkway. Sithias did the same and clamored in behind him, grunting with some misstep Finn couldn't see. They waited until they were in line with the tree troll vault before jumping off.

Finn welcomed the soft give of earth beneath his feet and the grounding scent of wood and moss moving through the air. His head cleared and his sense of purpose crystallized as he picked his way between large rocks stained gray with lichen.

Sithias stubbed his toe and squeaked with pain. Finn stopped to check on him, when Sithias bumped into him, rocking him off balance.

"Sorry, sir. As nice as this invisibility is against the enemy, it makes it impossible to know where you are, so you'll have to forgive me."

"It's fine, Sithias."

Anxious to move on, Finn hurried over to the entrance. The opening was much larger than it had looked from farther away. Big enough to allow a giant to pass through, with nothing barring the way, and therefore, no need to have Fate open the vault.

From where Finn stood, the opening appeared to be a long tunnel leading deep inside the massive knot of wood. A damp smell tinged the air. He stepped inside the shadow of the entrance before deactivating the visibility disruptor.

Sithias shuffled in next to him with sounds of fumbling and grumbling before he flashed into view. He smiled with relief and wiped his brow. "Whew! We made it." He glanced over his shoulder nervously and scanned the sky. "And it would seem all's clear."

"Aye. Let's make sure we're well inside before we use any lights."

With a nod, Sithias followed Finn through the tunnel. The darkness was absolute and they had to feel along curved walls to find their way. From what Finn could tell they seemed to be moving in a spiraling fashion. After walking a fair distance, a warm glowing light finally crested the end of the rounded tunnel, which spilled out into a large cavern.

The ceiling was high and etched deep with Elder race runes glimmering with golden light. At the center of the cavern rose a perfectly domed mound with a spiraled path cut into it.

"Where's the portal?" Sithas asked worriedly. "I don't see anything that looks like a gateway. Did we risk our lives to come here for nothing?"

Finn walked around the bottom of the mound until he found the beginning of the path. He stepped onto the well-worn groove and followed its spiraled pattern as it rose toward the top of the mound. "Keep in step, Sithias. I wouldn't want to leave you behind."

Sithias scrabbled after him. "How can you tell this is the portal?"

"Let's just say I know tree trolls and how they use their troll mounds." The spiraled path brought back memories of a clear and beautiful wintry night he'd shared with Grysla and her human daughter, Tove. Finn slowed to a reverent pace. This was a sacred place and it deserved a show of respect.

When he arrived at the top of the mound, he knelt and spoke the rune for Fire. Sparks flew from his palm and landed at the center of the spiraled path, where a ball of golden flames floated over the ground.

Sithias gasped in wonder as the runes on the ceiling flashed bright in response. "What happens next?" he asked.

Before Finn could answer, gold dust drifted from the runes, showering down light as snowfall. Unsure what to do next, he thought it might be best to call on the other elements to balance the energy of Fire, but he couldn't seem to remember the commands. A drowsy stupor had taken over.

He glanced at Sithias, who was blinking sleepily and swaying like a drunk. Finn reached out to keep him from falling over and missed. Sithias flopped to the ground like a rag doll. Despite his gangly legs being bent behind him and arms flopped at odd angles, he appeared to be comfortable enough since he was snoring up a storm.

Struggling to stay alert, Finn took a step to leave the immediate area. Instead, his knees bent and he landed face down next to Sithias. He opened his mouth to extinguish the Fire he'd summoned, but all that came was a satisfying yawn. He blinked once, then twice, before his eyes sealed shut for good.

"*Pleassse*, w-wake up!"

Wanting to remain in asleep, Finn resisted the insistent urgings. Fingers dug under his arms in an attempt to lift him. When that failed to work, he was jiggled from side to side until irritation disturbed him enough to wake him. "Stop, would you!"

Sithias bent over him, his eyes squinted and teeth chattering. "How c-can you sleep in this ungodly t-temperature?"

Finn breathed in crisp, frosty air and knew instantly he was in the Twisted Bone Forest. Rising to a sitting position, he surveyed the snow-covered hills dotted with the crooked trees the region was named after. They were strange trees, leafless with huge deadly thorns growing from their bent, white branches.

Finn smiled and gazed at the starlit sky. Next to Scotland, this was as good as coming home. This land was where he'd learned to master the Elder race runes. Grysla had given him her ancestral gift, and Tove had taught him how to control the earth magic contained within the powerful runes she'd so carefully inked into his skin. They were his family. More so than his grandda, who didn't actually exist, except in his mind and heart.

Finn touched his left temple, where three runes marked the family knot, the only evidence of his true family.

"This f-fire's doing nothing to warm me," Sithias com-plained as he squatted next to the golden ball of fire floating at the center of the troll mound's spiraled path. He held his hands close to the flames before returning them to his mouth to warm them with his breath.

Finn shifted his attention to the fire, noting for the first time that the troll mound they'd been transported to was completely bare. The magic within the portal had cleared the snow from the rounded hill to reveal the sacred spiral. "It's not that kind of fire."

Anxious to see Grysla and Tove, he stood, turning in circles to spot the correct direction of their cave. "Let's go Sithias, the cave's that way. And it'll be plenty warm."

"How far is it?"

"A few miles."

"A few m-miles? I'll freeze before then!"

Finn bit down on his impatience. "Not if you change into a caribou again."

Sithias's mouth dropped open, his jaw trembling and goatee flapping. "What? Is this so you can get out of walking? N-no, I swore I'd never be a b-beast of burden after that last time in Duenthorn!"

"I have no plans of ever riding you again," Finn assured him. "The only reason I suffered that humiliation was because Gerdie needed to be kept warm."

"The humiliation was all mine, believe me." Sithias quaked and rubbed his arms. "I suppose I c-could be a polar bear. There's an animal that's equipped with plenty of fur." He smiled with growing excitement. "And you know me. Being an adventurous sort, I always like to try n-new things."

Finn resisted the urge to roll his eyes. "Aye, you're a real daredevil."

"Excussse me while I concentrate." Sithias closed his eyes. After a minute of nothing happening, he opened them. "I'm still f-freezing. Are there any visible changes?"

"None that I can see."

Sithias frowned. "I'm out of practice using the siren's g-glamour. It's quite different from the shape shifting powers I grew accustomed to." He shuddered. "S-slow to respond and in need of my full attention, versus instantaneous transformation on command."

Finn's patience had run out. "I'm going to start walking and leave you to catch up."

"No, wait! Aren't you worried about leaving me too far b-behind?"

"Not a bit. At the rate bears run, you'll no doubt beat me there."

"But you have super human speed."

Finn spoke the unmaking rune to extinguish the ball of gold flames and took the downward spiraling path. "I'll take it slow," he called over his shoulder. "And don't cut through the path when you leave. Walk all the way back down the mound. It's considered bad form if you don't."

"Oh, well I w-wouldn't want to offend a mound of dirt."

Finn stopped at the end of the path and glanced back. "It's more about tangling with the energies. You wouldn't want to have your luck turn, would you?"

Sithias shook even more. "N-no, I would not."

"You'll be fine."

Finn stepped into the deep drifts. The icy press of snow seeped through the thick fabric of his army pants, but it wasn't intolerable. The Elder race runes had given him the resilience he needed to withstand severe arctic weather, though it would be nice to have an extra layer of furs like the ones Tove had made him.

His thoughts turned to her. Memories of their time together flooded in and he was back chasing her over the snowy drifts with barely a footprint left behind, sharing in her reverence for the circle of life during their deer hunts, soaking up an even greater connection with all living things through her eyes. Most of all, she held a special place in his heart for saving his life by showing him how to keep from being consumed by the darkness possessing him at the time.

Remembering all that Tove had taught him, Finn pushed his senses out into every particle of the air until he felt the breathing wind and the messages it carried from all corners of the world. A surge of joy raced through him. He'd missed this deep connection with the elements, but he hadn't been willing to admit just how much until now. Excitement spurred him on, increasing his speed until he was skimming over the snow like a ghost, dodging the barbs of the crooked trees as they blurred by. He needed to see Tove and Grysla. He wanted to go home.

Finn slowed when the light of the cave appeared in the distance. His heart leapt and he moved to cross the last stretch of space when something knifed into his right side with the force of a raging bull. Staggering and unable to catch his breath, he looked down to find he'd been shot with an arrow.

21
A TOTALLY RANDOM UNBIRTHDAY

FATE RETURNED TO THE shelter and headed straight for the barracks. Gerdie stopped chasing the doggit to give her a cheerful wave. Brune was working on something with Archie and didn't bother to look her way. Eustace glanced up from a book and looked ready to speak, but remained quiet when Fate avoided his stare and kept walking.

Darcy was laying in one of the cubbyholes, buried under a pile of blankets, the very activity Fate had in mind. Her heart hurt too much to deal with anyone or anything else at the moment. Stripping off her armor, she kicked off her boots and crawled into the cubbyhole tucked in the furthest corner of the room. Comforting darkness swarmed in as she pulled the blankets over her head and curled into a ball.

Despite having relinquished her role as Keep Guardian, an entrenched sense of duty nagged at the back of her mind, telling her to jump to attention and get the latest status report from Archie. Restless, she fluffed her pillow and turned over. "It's Brunes problem now," she grumbled under her breath.

After a few minutes, she relaxed somewhat. If only she could lessen the agonizing ache of Finn's departure as easily, but that pain would plague her until their reunion.

If they ever reunited.

Angry tears stung her eyes. It was wrong to be defeatist before they'd even begun. But she couldn't stop thinking of all the countless ways in which everything could go terribly wrong.

Starting with Tove.

Fate would never forget the possessiveness in Tove's eyes when she'd seen her with Finn. Nor could she put from her mind the way Tove's eyes had turned dark and threatening when she'd discovered Fate was competition for Finn's heart. Yet he seemed to think she would welcome him back and join his cause. That's only because he never witnessed the resentment Tove radiated when Finn had made the decision to leave her for Fate.

A woman scorned was a dangerous one, and Finn was forgetting that about Tove. What if she turned on him? Tove was far more practiced in her use of the Elder race runes, and every bit as fast and strong as Finn. She could end him if she wanted to.

Every muscle in Fate's body tensed into tight bands. She rolled over and flung the covers off her head. Eustace stood nearby with a cake in his hands. It was lit with candles. Her first impulse was to dive back under the blankets, but she couldn't bring herself to do it.

"Did I miss the invitation for someone's birthday?" she asked.

Smiling, he sat down on the edge of her mattress. "It's pretty hard to miss your own birthday. They have a stubborn way of following us around."

Fate sat up and rested her back on the wall. "It can't be my birthday. Where are the Halloween decorations, the bowls of yucky candied corn and all the costumes?"

"Well, from what I've been able to calculate, it's not October 31st back home yet. There's still a few more months to go. But as you've said more than once, after being trapped inside the *Book of Fables* for over half a year, you're technically eighteen." He placed the plate on her lap. "I thought we might at least celebrate this important milestone."

Fate dipped her finger in the chocolate frosting and tasted it. "Mmm, nice job with the food replicator."

"This is my tenth attempt."

"Yeah, chocolate's a challenge. Although, Jessie knew how to get a mean batch of brownies out of it." She smiled with a heavy sigh.

Eustace nodded sadly. "You've been through a lot, Doodles."

Tears instantly sprang to her eyes. Struggling to contain her emotions, she stared hard at the candles.

"I know you're fearing the worst when it comes to Finn, Sithias and Jessie. I'm confident we'll get them back," he assured her. "Everything will work out as long as we hold good thoughts for everyone."

Fate tore her gaze from the mesmerizing flames of the candles. She wanted desperately to believe he was right, but her stalwart father was out of his depth. He couldn't make any promises in this case, nor would she hold him to it.

"You better blow those out before the wax melts over the icing," he urged. "Remember to make a wish first." He peered at her over the top of his glasses. "Make this one count."

Fate closed her eyes and pictured a time in the future when everyone she loved was gathered in celebration. Their eyes sparkled with joy and they were laughing at all the troubles they'd left behind. Eustace was carving a turkey, while delicious food was being passed around a big table. Sithias was in his glee, entertaining anyone who would listen with his stories. Jessie glowed in a lovely dress that made her look like a princess. Gerdie was back to being her wise old self. And Fate could almost feel the touch of Finn's arm brushing against hers. She could see his face and the love lighting his leaf green eyes.

"This is my wish," she whispered.

Breaking from the vision, she opened her eyes and blew on the eighteen candles. The flames blinked out. Except one. Panicked that her wish was ruined, she drew breath and blew it out as quickly as possible. A shadow of despair set in as wisps of smoke drifted over the cake.

Eustace patted her leg. "Not to worry, Doodles. Isn't there a five second rule on blowing every candle out?"

She sank back against her pillow in defeat. "I think that only pertains to dropped food."

"I'm sure this wish will come true." He gave her ankle a squeeze and rose. "I'll get a knife and some plates. A generous dose of chocolate is just what you need."

Fate tried to smile but failed.

Gerdie hopped over with the doggit in tow. "Whatcha doin'?" She didn't wait for an answer. "Are you havin' a birthday party?"

"Not exactly."

Gerdie stared at the cake and licked her lips.

Eustace arrived with a stack of plates and utensils. "Would you like a piece, Gerdie?"

"Yes please!"

Fate cracked the tiniest smile. As much as she missed Gerdie's down-to-earth words of wisdom and guidance, she found having a child around refreshing. It was so easy for kids to be happy, even in dire circumstances, as long as they felt cared for. In many ways she was glad Gerdie had been given the opportunity to recapture some of her lost innocence. She'd been robbed of her childhood from the first day she'd stepped inside the *Book of Fables*.

Eustace served up the cake and delivered it to everyone, whether they wanted a piece or not. Darcy emerged from her hideaway in a disgruntled mess when he woke her to have some cake. Holding her plate, she aimed a mascara smeared gaze at Fate. "What's wrong with you?"

"We're celebrating her birthday," Eustace interjected.

"Looks more like a funeral to me." Darcy took a big bite. "Is this the official day?"

"Not exactly." Eustace winked at Fate. "It's one of those time traveling conundrums, where it's already happened in one place and not in another."

"Oh, in other words it's a totally random unbirthday." Darcy smirked with frosting splotched in the corners of her mouth. A far cry from her usually perfectly lined lips. She really had lost all care. "I suppose that's fine as long as it isn't one of those stupid birthday months where we have to break out the party hats on a weekly basis until the actual day."

"No, this is it," Eustace confirmed.

"What about presents?" Gerdie asked. "I don't see any."

Eustace reached in his pocket. "Well, I actually have a little something here. Close your eyes and give me your hand," he told Fate. He placed what felt like cold metal into her palm. "Okay, have a look."

Fate gasped in surprise at the miniature clockwork cat curled in her hand. Raising its head, the cat rose to a sitting position and looked at her with sparkling eyes of emerald. With a soft meow, it purred, sending rhythmic vibrations pulsing through her hand.

"I tried to get Archie to add orange striped fur to make it look more like Oz," Eustace explained, "but he said the hair would get caught in the cogs and wheels."

"Thanks, Dad, I love it." Homesick for her old cat, Oz, and the comfort of home, she gave Eustace a big hug. "I'll call him Poz."

"As in cat paws?"

"Short for pocket Oz."

Eustace smiled. "Perfect."

Gerdie wedged in between them. "Can I play with Poz?"

"Sure." Fate handed her tiny cat over with surprising reluctance. "He sleeps with me though."

With a nod, Gerdie cupped the cat in her small hands and skipped away.

"Do you think we'll ever get Gerdie back to normal?" Fate asked Eustace.

"Probably not," Darcy said before he could answer. "She was working on permanent forgetting spells to use on me and Mason, right? Oh, you didn't think I knew? Well, I did, and I think you've all gotten what you deserve. No one has a right to erase someone's memory."

Fate swung her legs over the edge of the cubbyhole. "For your information, we weren't going to use it on you without asking first. And we didn't tell you because we were waiting for Gerdie to find the right spell first."

Darcy crawled back into her messy cubbyhole and buried herself under the blankets. "Whatever."

Riled, Fate stood and paced. "I know she's going through stuff, but she makes it next to impossible to feel sorry for her."

"Pain often makes us act in ways we shouldn't." Eustace dropped his gaze to Fate's wrist. "What's that you're wearing?"

Fate stopped to see what he was staring at and gulped when she realized it was the bracelet Finn had given her. "Uh... Finn made it for me... a parting gift to help say goodbye."

"Looks like more than a mere bon voyage present to me." He was quiet a minute. "Does it mean what I think it means?"

She raised her brows. "I'm not sure what you're thinking. Mind reading isn't one of my super powers."

"He's Celtic, and I know how old-fashioned he is. Did he give you that in lieu of a handfasting ceremony?"

Fate's throat went dry. Why was she afraid to confirm his suspicions? "Um... more like an engagement ring?"

"No, I don't think so."

Fate swallowed. "You're right. It's the whole deal."

Eustace appeared as though he had more to say. Instead, he pulled out his handkerchief, cleaned his glasses and wiped his eyes before she could see what was going on behind them. When he replaced his glasses, he gave her a blank nod. "Thank you for being honest."

"Are you upset?"

He didn't answer immediately, but when he did, his voice was tight with restrained emotion. "No father lives for the day he must release his precious daughter into the care of someone else. But I've grown to respect Finn, and if you've chosen to commit yourself in that regard, I'm grateful it's him."

She should be relieved by his acceptance of the situation, but she couldn't help feeling as though everything had changed between them. "I'm sorry. I should've told you right away..."

Eustace busied himself with clearing the plates. "It's all right. I haven't exactly made it easy for you to approach the subject of your relationship with Finn." Holding the stack of dirty plates, he stood straight with the same blank expression. "I'll leave the cake with you in case you feel the need for another chocolate fix."

Fate felt a wholly new pang of sadness as she watched him walk in the direction of the galley. She'd ruined his attempt to lift her spirits, and instead, had dragged him down into the nosedive she was in. She winced. Causing Eustace pain was inexcusable. She had to find a way to make things better. Starting now.

"Time to get over yourself," she muttered as she pulled on her boots and cinched them tight. She straightened her shoulders, resolved to fake a better attitude until she believed that all would be well–in every way–very soon. Until then, she'd hold it together. No matter how bad it got or how much she felt like running away from it all. She wasn't going to lose it the way Darcy had.

Fate grabbed a slab of cake and took a big bite. "Mmm!" She choked it down, despite a complete lack of appetite. "That's *the* most yummy, delicious cake I've ever tasted."

Eustace glanced over his shoulder with a confused smile.

"Thanks again, Dad. It took awhile to kick in, but it's exactly what I needed."

His troubled brow smoothed and the tension between them lightened.

Fate left the barracks and started to head over to Brune and Archie to check in on their progress when she noticed Gerdie huddled in the far corner over by the locked entrance. The doggit was sitting next to her, its long ears twisting and turning as if to listen. Something in the way Gerdie held her little shoulders, while glancing nervously from side to side, made Fate uncomfortable. This was odd behavior, even for Gerdie.

Fate stole across the common area. As she closed in, she heard Gerdie speaking softly.

"That's funny! Do it again." She giggled, but then covered her mouth. "If you don't want them to hear me, you shouldn't make me laugh so hard. I can't help it."

Fate inched closer, squinting to see what Gerdie was talking to, but there was nothing but shadow in the corner.

Queasy unease settled in Fate's stomach. "Gerdie, who are you talking to?"

Gerdie jumped and turned around with a guilty expression. "Nobody."

"It didn't sound like nobody."

Gerdie stuffed her hands into the pockets of her dress and frowned.

Fate kneeled next to her. "You can tell me. I'm an expert at keeping secrets."

Gerdie's mouth remained a stubborn straight line, but she finally gave in and glanced at Fate. "I'm not supposed to tell."

"It must be hard keeping it to yourself though."

"Really hard."

"You can trust me. Your secret's safe with me."

"I have a new friend."

The queasiness in Fate's stomach twisted into a knot. "Does this friend have a name?"

Gerdie smiled. "Boo. I call him that because he's always startlin' me."

"Do you know what Boo is?"

Gerdie shrugged. "I'm not sure. He can make himself into all kinds of funny lookin' things. Except for when he loses his temper and gets all fangy and dark. Truth be known, I think he might be a Bandersnatch."

Fear trickled down Fate's spine. This was sounding more like Farouk all the time. But Gerdie had completely reverted back to her childhood. Maybe this was straight out of one her favorite stories. "Do you mean like the one from *Alice in Wonderland*?"

"You know any other stories with a Bandersnatch?"

Feeling slightly better, Fate surveyed the corner behind Gerdie. There was nothing there, but she was afraid to let it go. "Do you remember the monster that pretended to be Mason? The one that attacked Finn?"

Gerdie thought for a minute and then her face brightened. "No, I didn't know Finn was here. Where is he? How'd he get out of the oak?"

Fate studied Gerdie with growing sadness. If she'd already forgotten about Finn's release and all the time he'd spent in the Keep with them, then maybe this really was just a little girl's attempt at escaping the sheer boredom of being locked away.

"Well, I guess Boo must've left, because I don't see anything here that looks like a Bandersnatch."

Gerdie glanced back. "Nope. He's still here."

Goose bumps raced over Fate's arms. "Come on, Gerdie, I don't see anything."

"That's because he doesn't want you to see him."

"Well I'd sure like to see Boo. Go ahead. Tell him."

Gerdie shook her head and pointed. "I don't have to. He's standin' right here. He can hear you."

Fate stood and patted Gerdie's fine fluffy hair. "All right, I give up. I'll let you two get back to playing."

She turned to leave, when a glint in the dark corner stopped her. Fear iced along Fate's nerves as she looked over her shoulder. Two burning coals for eyes stared back from the darkness, floating in space over a fanged grin.

22
KEEP YOUR WAR

THE CROOKED TREES TILTED and the world spun. Finn collapsed in the snow, his breathing painful and ragged. The arrow had hit a lung. He tried to rise and couldn't. His strength had abandoned him. The right side of his chest burned with each inhale. He couldn't get enough air. Wheezing, he lifted his head to see where the shot had come from. Rolling onto his back, he stared at the stars, his mind racing in directions he didn't want to go.

His gaze returned to the shaft of the arrow. The hawk feathers on the fletching were shield cuts and tipped with red. These were Tove's arrows. He'd know them anywhere. But why? Why would she shoot him? They were bound by the family knot rune. An attack like this flew in the face of everything the Elder race runes represented.

The crunch of footsteps on snow jarred him back to the present. He turned his head, squinting as a hazy figure crested the hill, arms held in the position of someone aiming a crossbow. Something about that seemed wrong. Tove had only ever used a bow and arrow.

"Tove," he rasped. "Please stop. Just talk to me."

A man's gruff voice echoed over the forest. "Talk? No, you die making my sister hurt!"

Finn recognized the thick Norse accent immediately. It was Tove's brother, Leif, and his English was still as bad as ever. He squinted at the fast approaching figure, big and bear-like because of all layers of furs he was wearing. "Leif?"

"Ah, you remember." Leif stopped in front of Finn and spat a gob of tobacco, which melted a revolting brown hole into the snow. His weather-beaten face hardened with hatred as he loomed over Finn with crossbow targeting his heart.

"I thought we were friends," Finn wheezed.

"No. Not after you leave Tove with broken heart!"

Finn raised his hand in a plea for forgiveness. "I never wanted to hurt Tove. I thought she," he gasped for air, "understood."

"She never smiles. Not since you go."

Finn didn't know what to say, and it seemed Leif wasn't interested in talking it out. His blue eyes turned stone cold as he stared at Finn, his finger caressing the trigger of the crossbow. There was nothing Finn could do but accept the consequences of his actions.

A vicious growl cut through the silence, followed by a blur of white that knocked Leif off his feet and tore his crossbow from his hands. Leif screamed beneath the weight of the polar bear and the claws digging into his chest. Struggling to breathe, Finn tried to tell Sithias not to kill Leif, but he couldn't get enough air in his lungs to form the words. He reached out, wanting to intervene. Instead he tumbled toward death along with Leif.

Finn's right side pulsed with heat, a pleasant sensation that lured him back into sleep. "Did you see that? His eyes twitched," he heard Sithias say. "I think he's coming around."

"He should let death take him," Leif's voice bellowed. "He won't like how I kill him later."

"Threats like that will get you bitten again, and I can't promise to miss an artery this time," Sithias warned.

"I don't fear a yappy stick!"

"The bear can make another appearance." Sithias threatened, his tone pitching high with false bravado. "Go ahead! Dare me!"

Unable to drift back into the nothingness he'd found so very comforting, Finn forced his eyes open. The light of a fire flickered over rough cave walls covered with Elder race runes. This was Grysla's cave. Blinking drowsily, he turned to see Sithias sitting next to him. He'd resumed his gangly human form and was wearing a hooded fur coat and leggings, which were five times too big for him. He was basically swimming in the winter wear bearing Tove's artful stitching in the handiwork.

Finn cleared his throat. "Would you mind keeping it down? I'm trying to sleep here."

Sithias's eyes lit up. "Sir! Oh thank goodness. They told me you'd survive that barbarian's pathetic shot, but you've been out for some time and I was beginning to have my doubts."

"I meant to wound him. For slow torture," Leif argued.

Finn lifted his head to get a good look at Leif, but cool hands brushed over his forehead and gently pressed him to lie back. He glanced up; surprised to see Tove crouched over him.

Her long ebony hair fell in a straight, silken curtain around her fine, elfin features. Firelight danced over the rune marks inked on her olive skin. The moment they locked eyes, her irises shifted from an earthy sage to a fiery jade. His breath caught in his throat for a fraction of a second. Her otherworldly beauty transcended the faded archives of his memory.

"You must rest and allow the healing runes to do their work." She kept her voice low and devoid of emotion. But she couldn't fool him. The shining green of her eyes betrayed her excitement.

"It's good to see you. Really good," he whispered. "Where's Grysla?"

Tove lifted her gaze to the ceiling. Finn tilted his head back at the same moment the tree troll leaned forward from behind him. Her crown of twisted roots preceded the rough bark of her craggy face. When their eyes met, she smiled with deep affection, her enormous arms sweeping as she scribed runes into the air and welcomed him home.

He smiled. "Thank you, it's good to be back." He glanced at Leif, who was nursing his wound with a mug of ale. "Well, mostly."

Grysla signed while using troll speak in her deep, soothing voice, saying she sensed Finn's visit was one of urgency.

"I never could fool you, Grysla." Finn fell back into troll speak naturally, even though he hadn't spoken the ancient language since his departure. "Unfortunately, you're right. I've come with bad tidings."

"What I say?" Leif hollered. "He's a dunga!"

Tove shot him a barbed look and let out a low growl. Leif went back to his drink. It was comforting to see she wasn't happy with the whole shooting incident.

"Is there any possibility of switching back to English?" Sithias asked. "I'd appreciate being part of the conversation, especially if this ruffian is the only one I'm able to understand. Though I'd be happy enough if you could at least gag him."

"Sorry, Sithias," Finn said. "I forgot you don't know troll speak. I was just telling them of the bad news we bring."

"Oh yesss," Sithias chimed in. "The whole of Oldwilde is in terrible trouble. An undead army is on its way to annihilate everything in its path."

Finn stared at him in horror. "I was planning on working my way up to that part."

Sithias covered his mouth. "Oh dear, I suppose that's a lot to take in all at once."

Tove crossed her legs and leaned forward. "How can this be? There have been no disturbances in the air or in the earth."

"That's because this impending danger is on the other end of the universe," Finn explained. "But I can promise you, they're coming to Oldwilde very soon."

"What is this army?"

Overwhelmed by the full breadth of the answer he needed to provide them, Finn shook his head. He couldn't gather his energy and thoughts together, and instead, stared at the firelight playing over the ceiling of the cave. His mind strayed back to the ancient Keep. He was so far away from Fate and that terrified him. Was she still safe? So much could've happened between the time of his departure and now. She was literally surrounded by danger. What if Kaliena had broken through all of Archie's defenses?

And then there was Farouk, the most unpredictable threat of them all.

He clenched his eyes shut and rubbed them. This was no time for indulging in the nightmares festering at the back of his mind. He was on a mission and needed to move forward in the knowing that if he did his part, Fate would do hers. Though it didn't help he was suffering a temporary weakness of mind and body, thanks to Leif's vendetta.

Finn returned his attention back to Tove's question, grateful to find Sithias had jumped in to fill them in about what the Keep was, and Kaliena's rise to power and the legions of undead armies she'd gathered in force.

"Why would this Kaliena want to come here to Oldwilde when it sounds like what she wants is to take back the Keep?" Tove asked.

Finn reached for the chain around his neck and pulled out the Rod of Aeternitis. "Because she wants this. She wants it over all the magic the Keep contains. If she gets one of her six hands on it, she'll be able to combine the Rod with the Orb of Aeternitis, which will grant her the godlike powers she's been so hungry to regain. At that point, the entire universe will be at stake."

Tove stared at the tiny piece of metal. "She knows you have this?"

"Not yet." Finn swallowed back the painful lump in his throat. "She still thinks Fate has it."

Tove frowned at the mention of Fate's name. "Then why not let Fate deal with this Kaliena? Why bring this war to Oldwilde?"

Anger burned hot in Finn's chest. "Because Fate doesn't stand a chance against an army of that size."

Tove's expression remained cold and detached. "Will it be the end of all existence if Kaliena defeats Fate?"

The air went out of Finn as surely as if Tove had pierced him with another arrow. He couldn't speak. If Fate was gone, it meant the end of his existence.

Tove took his silence for an answer. "Then you should let Fate's war against Kaliena wage itself on the other side of the universe where it belongs."

Sithias gasped. "For your information, it's been prophesied by the Djinn that there will be a great battle between Kaliena and Finn in the Marajaran Desert. There's no avoiding the unavoidable." His face pinched up in distaste. "We should leave, sir. It's plain to see we won't be getting any help here."

Finn lifted himself on one elbow and flinched at the effort. "Is it true?" he asked Tove. "You'd actually refuse to help?"

Tove's stare was as inscrutable as stone.

"My sister has point." Leif piped up from the back of the cave. "Keep your war and–"

Grysla startled them all with a gruff sound. For the first time ever, Finn saw fury in the tree troll's wizened face and her soft green eyes grew black and stormy. Her massive arms swept the air in a gesture of displeasure as she reverted back to troll speak. "Finn is family," she said, her furious gaze fixed on her daughter.

Tove's rigid posture wavered as she looked away in shame.

The darkness in Grysla's eyes eased to a grassy green as she returned her gaze to Finn and spoke in English. "Your fight is our fight, Shining One."

Finn laid his head back down on the bed furs. All the tension he'd been feeling drained away as he smiled and signed his gratitude to her.

Grysla bent over him and spoke the rune for deep sleep. Sparks of white light poured from her mouth and fluttered down over him like snowflakes. The affect was powerful. His eyes closed, and as he drifted off into a peaceful slumber, he was vaguely aware of a voice... Sithias he thought...

"Who'sss the Shining One?"

23
INSIDIOUS

"GERDIE, COME OVER HERE please." Fate held her arms out to coax her out of the corner.

Gerdie didn't budge. "No, I wanna stay and play with Boo."

"Gerdie," she spoke more firmly, "get over here right now."

Gerdie's face crumpled and tears stood on the brink of falling. "You're bein' mean. And you're scarin' Boo!"

The gleaming eyes rose within the shadowy corner. The mouth opened impossibly wide, looming over Gerdie's head, ready to bite down.

Fate leaped forward, grabbed Gerdie's arm and yanked her away as gaping jaw and fangs snapped shut. Adrenaline fired through her veins as she pushed Gerdie behind her, while reaching for her sword. She grasped air. Her scabbard and sword were lying on the floor in the barracks.

Gerdie cried out and ran across the common area, calling out to Brune.

The shadows in the corner coagulated, becoming dense around the disembodied eyes and mouth. Farouk's hulking shape emerged, bringing with it, the disturbance of every particle of air, distorting the walls into twisting lines. The more Fate tried to focus on him, the more her vision blurred, forcing her gaze away.

Fighting the dizziness his emanations caused, she willed herself to stare straight at him.

Silver fire crackled from his claws and the stink of sulfur stained the air. His burning gaze fixed on her as his black lips curled back in a vicious snarl. Black smoke sifted between his fangs as he laughed, an eldritch sound that shivered along her spine. His barb-tipped tail jerked impatiently as he slunk forward.

Farouk's voice snaked into her mind. "*I'm sorry, did I catch you off guard?*" His sinewy shoulders shook with quiet amusement. "*A good Keep Guardian would know better than to be caught unprepared. Especially when she knows her enemy can come and go as they please.*"

"Out of the way, Fate!" Brune shouted.

Fate staggered to one side, barely stepping aside before Brune marched forward, her laser gun on full charge.

The red ray sliced into Farouk. He shrank from the initial blow with a growling howl, dematerializing before Brune's laser finished him. He reappeared behind her, swiping his charged claws in a burst of silver lightning across her back. She arched backward, and fell face down.

Farouk turned back to Fate. *"Now there's a good guardian. Brune always was my best.*" His fiery gaze shifted to her dead body. "*It's a shame she had to be retired... again.*"

The stench of sulfur drifted toward Fate, burning her eyes, filling her with a wave of nausea. She edged closer to the wall for support, her heart thundering in her chest. She hated how Farouk reduced her to a ball of quivering nerves. Fear wasn't supposed to touch her anymore. Her newfound power should be making her invincible, but was instead her Achilles heel, where Farouk was involved.

Farouk moved in, his mouth opening in a malicious smile, fangs dripping. *"Time to retire you–"*

A large grapple hooked Farouk by the neck and dug in. Bolts of electricity raced over his bristling fur. Growling, he whipped around and yanked on the cable, jerking Archie off his spindly legs. Released from Farouk's malignant thrall, Fate raced forward to help, but Archie had to keep pulling the trigger of the grappling gun to keep the electricity flowing and was being dragged across the floor.

Fate stopped, afraid to risk Farouk turning his full attention back onto her when she had no means of defense.

Eustace rushed in next to her and thrust her sword in her hand.

"Thanks, Dad."

He gave her a nod of encouragement that was suddenly cut short. His body went rigid as a look of surprise filled his eyes. "Oh dear," he whispered, so softly she barely heard him. The smallest point of color appeared at the corner of his mouth, forming a red trickle down his chin.

Eustace fell forward and Fate caught him in her arms. His head tipped forward and that's when she saw the bloody tip of Farouk's tail withdrawing from his back.

Her strength drained and her father's limp body slipped from her weakening grasp. Fate fell to the floor with him. "Dad?" She shook him. "Wake up. Please wake up," she pleaded.

Eustace stared past her with eyes that looked into a faraway place she was not part of.

A clamorous sound like the wheels of a train screeching over the rails filled her head.

"NOOOO!"

The scream ripped her chest open, scorched the sides of her throat. *Not Eustace. No. Not him, not my father... never.* The idea that he was gone was too massive and agonizing to grasp.

An icy chill gripped hold and she shook like she'd never know warmth ever again. The noise in her head grew louder, threatening to unbalance her mind unalterably.

Another scream joined the clamor in her mind. It was Gerdie. She was clawing the sides of her face, sobbing at the sight of Eustace and Brune's slain forms.

Darcy stumbled into the common area, her mouth open in shock, but when she looked at Fate, she glared. "Why are you just sitting there? Do something!" she yelled. "Archie's in trouble!"

Fate glanced over as Farouk grabbed hold of Archie's mechanical leg, tore it free and flung the limb against the wall. Reaching for her sword, Fate rose, stepped over her father's body and strode slowly toward Farouk. His focus was centered on dismantling Archie. The stream of electricity bombarding Farouk was obviously hampering his ability to dematerialize. She could tell by his stiff, sluggish movements.

Staring at the protruding bones of Farouk's spine, Fate brought her sword down. The same place he'd struck Eustace in the back. A shrieking growl bit through the uproar in her head. Blood sprayed against her face. She licked her lips, tasting the sulphurous tang of her enemy.

The noise in her mind grew quieter.

Swinging her blade in a crisscross, she flayed Farouk's hide open. Another unearthly screech rumbled through the room. Farouk raked at the floor, silver sparks flying from his claws as he attempted to escape the next blow, and then the next.

Fate lost herself in a black frenzy of hacking, slashing, slicing and stabbing. After awhile she realized she was killing a pool of bloody pulp spreading itself over the floor at her feet.

She dropped the sword. The clang of metal echoed against the walls, reminding her of the emptiness in the room, an awful, horrid emptiness that spread to her chest. Fate inhaled a racking sob and the tears finally came, a flood that would never stop.

"Fate, wake up. You're having a nightmare."

Gasping for her next breath, Fate opened her eyes. She was lying in the cubbyhole of the barracks and Eustace was leaning over her.

What kind of cruel joke was this? "No, this isn't real. You're gone. You're gone!" she cried.

Eustace gripped her by the shoulders. "I'm right here. It's a bad dream, that's all."

"No, it happened. He killed you." She couldn't breathe for the knifing pain in her chest. "Farouk killed you."

"I'm alive and well, Doodles. Please, stop and look at me for a minute."

Tears swam before her eyes, distorting Eustace's face like a circus house mirror. She blinked, rubbing her eyes to see clearly.

He smiled down at her. "See? I'm fine. It was all just a terrible dream."

Fate wanted to believe him more than anything in the world, but she was afraid to hope it was true. What if this was the dream and she woke up to the horrible reality that Farouk had taken her father from her? She couldn't survive the same heartbreak all over again.

She reached out and touched Eustace's arm.

Solid. Real.

Relief flooded through her limbs. She sat up and hugged him tight, never wanting to let go. "You're alive!" She started crying again, this time from tears of happiness. Eustace squeezed her in his arms and suddenly she was in the safest place in the entire universe.

After awhile, he gently let go and handed her his handkerchief. She took it and wiped her face, all the while staring at him in wonder. "Was I really asleep this whole time?"

"Oh yes. You've been out for a good five hours since you got back from seeing Finn and Sithias off. I suppose saying goodbye took it out of you, and the upset of it no doubt triggered the nightmare."

She shook her head. "It was so incredibly vivid... I've never had a dream that felt *that* real before."

Eustace patted her leg. "All you've been doing is surviving these past six months, and without a single moment to process everything you've been through. That's bound to come out through a bad nightmare here and there."

"I suppose... " Fate stared at the blanket and pulled at a thread. She stopped when it unraveled all too easily.

"Are you hungry?" Eustace asked. "We've all eaten, but I set a plate aside for you."

She nodded. "I'm starving."

"Good, and then Archie can show you the progress he's made with the portal amplifier."

Fate tossed the blankets aside and swung her legs over the edge. "Finally, some good news for once."

She slipped off the mattress; glad to see she was still wearing the same clothes. The very confirmation she needed to know the nightmare was just that. A nightmare. She pulled a boot on one foot, stopping when she noticed the ribbon bracelet. Hastily, she tucked the bracelet beneath the sleeve of her top to avoid reliving a conversation about why she was wearing it and pulled on the other boot. She started to step over her discarded armor, but decided to put it back on. She may have had a nightmare, but what Farouk had said in the dream still rang in her head.

"A good Keep Guardian would know better than to be caught unprepared."

Fate tightened the last buckle of her armor and followed her father into the galley. Her tortured heart reached out to him, wanting desperately to return to their old lives. Quiet dinners on the sofa while watching their favorite shows and debating whether science fiction was better than fantasy. She missed those days, when life was simple.

And safe.

Darcy was sitting at the table pushing a mangled square of lasagna around with her fork. She raised her head to look at Fate and scowled through oily, black strands of hair. "She finally wakes. Did you have yourself a good cry?" Her tone was taunting.

Eustace retrieved Fate's plate from the warmer and set it on the table as she took a seat at the farthest end of the bench. "She's bouncing back," he said, saving Fate from having to respond.

Darcy continued to point her misery in Fate's direction. "As she should. *Her* boyfriend's not dead. He's just gone for awhile."

Fate ground her teeth together. Why wasn't Darcy still hiding under the blankets where she didn't have to listen to her? She pushed the plate away and stood. "I think I'll see what Archie's been up to," she told Eustace.

He nodded. "Sure, I'll keep Darcy company while she finishes dinner."

Fate marched out of the galley, utterly irritated by Darcy's rude jabs and her father's unwavering patience.

Archie was bent over the worktable as she approached. "Eustace tells me you're close to having the amplifier finished."

He glanced up from his worktable and wobbled as if she'd pushed him. "You've been misinformed. I still have minor adjustments to make and tests to run."

Fate bit her bottom lip–worried he'd tell her they were still months away from leaving for Oldwilde. "How much longer will it take then?"

"At least seven days, but possibly five."

"Oh... that's great!"

Archie returned to his work.

Disappointed there wasn't more to distract her from having to return to the galley where she'd have to suffer Darcy's company, Fate walked over to Brune's workstation. "What're you working on?"

"Farouk's cage."

Fate leaned in to watch Brune engraving tiny symbols onto the bars of an octagonal frame the size of a golf ball. "Where's the cage part of the cage?"

Brune paused, raising an eyebrow that mocked her. "This is the cage."

"You have seen how big Farouk's gotten, right? That thing is microscopic in comparison. He wouldn't fit in that even if he was the size of a finger monkey." She shuddered at the memory of his hulking head and slavering fangs. "I sure miss the little Farouk who mixed up his words."

"We all do." Brune straightened and removed the magnifying glasses she was wearing. She reached for a page of diagrams. "This is Archie's design. It's an expandable cage engraved with binding sigils. He designed it to be portable. All we have to do is throw it at Farouk and trigger the trap with an incantation."

"So you're saying this little cage will enlarge enough to fit over Bigfoot Farouk?"

"Yup."

"I like the sound of that. How soon before it's ready?" Fate glanced back at Eustace, where he was chatting quietly with Darcy. The nightmare was still fresh in her mind and the terror of losing him refused to go away. Insidious fear had infected her mind, filling her with a dreadful sense of urgency that time was running out for Eustace. There was no getting around it. As long as Farouk was out there, her nightmare could become a reality.

"I should have it finished by tomorrow," Brune said, pulling Fate from her unwelcome thoughts. "I still have hours of engraving before I'm done with all these sigils."

"Maybe we should put some protective wards in place between now and then. Finn wanted to do it, but apparently that involved a bunch of live chickens running around with their heads cut off."

"What?"

Fate waved her off. "Never mind."

Brune's stare became peevish. "Do you even know how to place protective wards?"

"Not exactly, but Archie does. His defensive wards are doing the job for the sanctuary." Fate turned to the scientist. "Right, Arch?"

"Defensive wards are not the same as the wards needed to repel a demon of Farouk's power," Archie replied. "I would have to research the subject."

"But you have binding sigils that work on him," Fate pressed. "How much of a stretch is it to come up with repelling wards?"

Archie blinked at her. "Binding sigils are universal."

Fate frowned. "How is it Finn could place his crushed chicken bone wards without doing this so-called research you're going on about?"

Brune smirked. "Do you know anything about druids?"

"Duh," Fate snapped. "I'm the one who made Finn a druid."

"Then you should know that druid's have an innate ability to tap into the root of all magic through the Dark Speech," Brune explained. "Combine that with the Elder race runes and you've got yourself the panacea of all wards, which is why he doesn't have to custom design them the way we have to."

"Super," Fate muttered.

Brune's hazel eyes narrowed on Fate. "What are you so nervous about?"

"Farouk, what else? The shelter may be keeping Kaliena and her minions out, but it doesn't work where he's concerned." Fate glanced over her shoulder. "He could be here right now, blending into the shadows, watching our every move. He could be planning to destroy your expandable cage!"

Archie and Brune exchanged a look.

Fate caught the concern in their eyes. "I'm not being paranoid! You know I'm right."

Brune set down the engraver. "No argument there. But if Farouk were here, he would've made his move by now. He wouldn't let me get a single sigil further."

"Maybe he wants to see you put in all those hours you were talking about, and then demolish it right before you finish it. He's cruel that way."

Something swiped near Fate's head. She ducked and drew her sword. Archie teetered backward as he tried to hold his scanner steady. Brune grabbed one of his arms and righted him.

Fate's heart pounded out of control. "What're you doing? Are you trying to tranq me?"

His neck squeaked as he shook his head. "Simply reading your stress levels." He glanced at the graph. "Your cortisol is spiking. The increased levels are suppressing cognitive function. Or it could be the emanations. I'll need a blood sample to determine–"

"I'm not crazy!" Fate yelled.

Brune took a step forward cautiously. "Prove it. Sheath your sword."

Fate hadn't realized she'd drawn her sword. She gripped the hilt, shifting her gaze back and forth between them. They looked like two dogcatchers circling a rabid dog with nets and tranquilizer guns.

"I can't be here!" And with that, Fate activated her teleporter.

24
BY THE KING'S COMMAND

FINN GRIPPED THE SPIKE on the dragon's back, fighting the g-forces as it swooped down into the valley. "Take it easy, Sithias, or you're going to toss us!"

"I'm trying my bessst, but the extra weight's throwing me off. I'm not exactly usssed to this dragon body, or carrying people on my back, let alone a tree troll!" Sithias's words were more of a deep snarl, but understandable.

"It's not a complaint," Finn yelled into the glacial wind whipping around them. "Just a warning."

"It's complaint!" Leif bellowed. "You best hope I die if I fall, because I kill you otherwise."

Sithias growled his displeasure.

Tove leaned against Finn's back and spoke near his ear, her skin brushing softly against his as she did so. "I know Beldereth is the northern most kingdom in Oldwilde, but it's early for snow. Isn't this the harvest time?"

Uncomfortable with the familiarity she had begun to use with him since his return, Finn straightened to put a few inches between them. "I'm not sure," he replied stiffly. "Time passes differently where Fate and I were. But if you say it's harvest time, the leaves should only be beginning to turn color."

She withdrew. "I suppose winter can sometimes come early."

"No, I don't think so." Finn pointed beyond the snow-covered valley. "Something's not right. The mountain range to the south is bare. There should be as much or more snow on the peaks as there is in the valley."

Sithias flew over the River Torle, which was flanked by high canyon walls. There was so much snow and ice Finn couldn't see the rushing water of the mighty river. From what he remembered, the River Torle never iced over. His muscles bunched with tension as they rounded the winding rock walls, which opened into what should be the crystal blue lake of the Windmere Loch. Instead it was a frozen, hollowed-out lakebed.

They rose higher as the castle and its township came into view near the end of the great basin. A thick, unnatural mist clung to the majestic castle, covering most of the structure and its protective walls in a gray gloom, save for the highest towers.

Dread settled in the pit of Finn's stomach. He'd been looking forward to reuniting with his good friend and mentor, King Rudwor. Now he was unsure of what he would find within the walls of Beldereth.

Finn called out to Sithias. "Head for the tallest tower. There's a courtyard behind it big enough for you to land in."

Sithias flapped his leather wings harder to gain height, a move that rocked his passengers precariously from their perches. Leif let out another string of threats.

Gray mist swirled beneath them as the white stone of the huge tower came into clear view. Sudden movement along the balcony caught Finn's attention. He raised his hand when he saw the warriors lining up along the railing. He waved, then gulped when he saw bows drawn and aimed straight at them.

"Sithias, climb higher!" he yelled.

But his warning was too late and the sky filled with a barrage of arrows. One of them hit the mark and Sithias lurched to one side, plummeting with a pained growl. Finn clawed at the air, trying to grab hold of Sithias in the hopes he regained flight. There was nothing to hold onto. He was falling through a sea of mist.

Something caught his ankle and he banged into Tove and Leif. Grysla wrapped her huge arms around them, protecting them with her body. They hit the ground, a jarring blow that Grysla absorbed for all. Sheets of snow billowed around them.

Finn groaned as he reoriented himself. "Thank you, my friend," he signed to Grysla. The tree troll gave him a grave nod as they stood, each of them unharmed. Concerned for Sithias, Finn searched the surrounding drifts, but a white dragon didn't exactly stand out in so much snow.

Tove jumped from the boulder she stood on, quickly scaling the rocky terrain before stopping to crouch. As soon as she waved him over, Finn knew she'd found Sithias. He rushed over, growing more and more tense with each step.

There was no dragon. Sithias had shifted into human form, though one with wings, which were splayed wide and broken. He stared blankly at the gray sky with the shaft of an arrow rising from his chest. His blood-soaked shirt was wet through and through in bright red contrast to their frosted surroundings.

Scared they'd lost him, Finn dropped down next to him. "Sithias, can you hear me?" When there was no answer or movement, Finn passed his hands over Sithias's face while snapping his fingers.

"Of course I can hear you. And I'm not blind either." Sithias's mouth pulled back in pain. "On the other hand, I can't move. Not even to shiver."

Finn gulped with relief. "Are you saying you're paralyzed and have no feeling in your body?"

"No, I'm absolutely f-freezing, but any movement is excruciating. In case you haven't n-noticed, I've been shot and am laying in a sssnowy wasteland."

At a loss for how he would provide vital shelter for Sithias, Finn glanced around. He needed to get Sithias warm and start tending to his wound. "We'll figure something out." He looked at Tove and Lief, as if they would know.

Leif shrugged. "What? I know nothing. You said we'd be welcome."

Tove didn't add to that, but Finn could see she didn't disagree.

The ground shook as Grysla made the descent over to them in one massive step. She gently slid her enormous hand underneath Sithias and scooped him off the ground. Despite the smooth movement, Sithias yowled and promptly fainted. "Do you know of a safe place?" the tree troll asked.

Finn shook his head. "The castle's the only–"

"By the king's command, you are under arrest!" a woman's voice shouted.

Several dozen Beldereth knights emerged from the mist, surrounding them with drawn swords and fiery arrows aimed at Grysla. Finn held his hands up. "Hold on, we're friends. Don't you recognize me? I was the king's First Knight. Tell him I'm–"

Before he could finish, Grysla bellowed, a baleful sound filled with fear. Cradling Sithias with one hand, she swiped her arm at the warriors threatening her with fire. Those still standing let their arrows fly, riddling Grysla with flames that lit and spread over her like oiled kindling. The tree troll roared, smashing through the line of knights, thrashing at her blazing limbs.

Leif drew his crossbow, shooting the nearest knight in the neck before the others besieged him. He drew his sword, fending them off with barbaric swings that would only spare him a few more minutes of life. Tove's eyes went black as night as she drew her sword, cutting in between the knights in a blur of swift movements that had them swinging at air.

Unwilling to fight the knights he'd once sworn loyalty to, Finn did the only thing he could. He invoked Air. The sound of his voice rumbled through the canyon as the rune power poured from his mouth in red-gold sparks. The wind answered his call with a shriek rushing in from the North. A hurricane of blustering snow crashed into them, scattering Leif, Tove and the knights through the air like dry leaves, pelting against Grysla–who turned her back against the stream to protect Sithias–dowsing the blanket of flames racing over the tree troll's legs.

Bracing himself against the violent tempest, Finn thanked the elements before commanding them to leave. The winds abruptly dissipated to a gentle breeze. Snowflakes swirled around the castle like a snow globe. Finn marched over to the knights as they dug themselves out of the drifts. "Which one of you is Meara?" he called out.

At first there was no answer, then a knight stepped forward. She removed her helmet, releasing a cascade of blonde hair. "Finn? Is it really you?"

"Aye, it is, and I can vouch for my friends here."

Another knight stepped in next to Meara, shoving the visor of her helmet up. Finn didn't recognize her, but knew by the fine lines around her eyes that she was an older officer. If Fate were there, she'd probably know the woman since she'd trained as a Beldereth warrior for months. "We do not suffer giants on Beldereth soil." The officer's severe gaze moved to Tove and Leif. "Nor barbarians who attack the royal guard."

"They're with me, and one of my friends took an arrow." Finn looked at Meara. "You remember Sithias, don't you? He's been shot and needs medical attention *now*."

Grysla leaned down and held Sithias out for them to see.

Meara gasped when she saw the arrow in his chest and signaled to several other knights. "Take him to our healers," she ordered.

The knights moved cautiously toward Grysla, who bent to hold Sithias within their reach. They retrieved him none too gently. Sithias yelped in pain as they carried him away and disappeared into the gray mist.

Finn breathed a sigh of relief. "Much appreciated. Now, can we talk about allowing the rest of my friends inside?"

The officer moved in between him and Meara. "Where's the dragon?"

Finn stiffened. He couldn't tell them Sithias was the dragon. During their first stay in Beldereth, no one had known Sithias was actually a snake using a mermaid's glamour to change shape. And with all this hostile behavior, he didn't trust them to welcome Sithias if they learned he was anything other than human. "It dropped us and flew off," he finally replied.

"Was that another one of your so-called friends?" the officer asked. Her fierce tone led Finn to believe she wasn't a fan of dragons either.

"No, it was under my control. That is, until we fell under attack."

The officer studied him with a cold look. "Will it be back?"

"No, I can promise you won't see it again."

She stared at him, and then snapped the visor of her helmet shut.

"I'll take you to see the king, but only if the giant and your barbarian friends give us their weapons and agree to surrender."

"I keep weapons!" Leif shouted, his face turning red with rage.

Finn clenched his fists. "You'll lay them down and be quiet about it."

Leif's red face purpled with defiance, and just when he looked ready to argue, Tove drove her elbow into his gut. Grabbing his stomach, he buckled over as she flung her bow and arrow onto the snow. Then she proceeded to relieve Leif of his crossbow, sword and the dagger in his boot, as well as the hunting knife in his belt, piling them all at her feet.

Finn waved his arm. "As you can see, we're happy to cooperate." He frowned at Leif. "Most of us anyways."

The officer ordered her knights to surround their new prisoners. "Follow me," she told Finn. After they made the hike to high ground and passed through the gates, the knights herded Grysla, Tove and Leif across the courtyard toward the dungeons while Finn headed in the opposite direction toward the great hall. As he passed through the long corridors, the tension and fear he'd sensed from everyone–all the way from the servants to the guards–was evident within the walls of the castle. He didn't know the reason, but something had gone terribly wrong during his absence.

Two guards pushed through the tall, heavy doors of the great hall. "Wait here with the prisoner," the officer told her knights.

"Prisoner?" Finn called after the officer as she removed her helmet and slipped past the screens blocking his view of the hall.

Rudwor's thick Scottish brogue boomed, echoing off the high arches of the ceiling. "You've what? Do you know who that is? Leave and let him pass!"

The officer's hurried footsteps announced her return. She didn't look at Finn, but merely told her guards to step outside the door with her.

Finn chuckled as he eased up to the screen and peered around the edge, his gaze resting on the dais, where Rudwor sat at the dinner table with his niece, Valesca.

"Laddie, get yourself in here!" Rudwor stood, his burly arms held wide and deep belly laugh filling the vast room. He clapped as Finn crossed the vast stone floor. "You always did know how to make an entrance. It's been a long time since I've seen my guards worked into such a froth!"

He rounded the table and met Finn with a bear hug that squeezed the air from his lungs. Gripping Finn by the shoulders, he held him out at arm's length. "Let's have a look at you." Rudwor's light brown eyes twinkled with mirth. "Ah, there's the lady slayer I remember." He made a show of glancing around. "Speaking of which, where's that fiery lass of yours?"

"Long story," Finn sighed.

"I see we have much to discuss." Rudwor gestured for him to sit down. "Come, have a seat and fill your belly while you're at it. You remember my niece."

"Aye. How are you, Valesca?" Finn tipped his head at the fine-boned young girl, whose mind was every bit as fragile as her delicate form.

She raised rounded eyes the color of muddy pools and looked at him, though she didn't meet his gaze. Instead, she stared at the top of his head. "He's shiny, uncle. I haven't seen anyone with that much light before. Is he an angel?"

Rudwor smiled at her indulgently. "Aye, love, he's one of the good ones."

The king's servants–all pretty young women, of whom he was notorious for surrounding himself with–moved in to help serve Finn, but Rudwor dismissed them with a wave of his hand and an order to take Valesca with them. Then he piled a turkey leg, some boiled turnip and bread onto a platter and shoved it in front of Finn. "Feast, young sapling. And then you can tell me what's brought you here and explain the reason for the questionable company you've been keeping."

Finn's throat went dry. He hadn't expected Rudwor to get down to business in such short order. He reached for the pitcher, poured himself a cup of ale and downed the malted draft in a few big gulps. "Before I get into why I came, I first want you to know the tree troll, the girl and her brother are trusted friends."

Rudwor's expression hardened. "I'll have to differ with you on that one, laddie. Giants are not to be trusted. Those unholy behemoths have been the bane of my existence for too long now."

Finn raised his hands to show he wasn't arguing. "I know the Mount Helgunth rock giants have been Beldereth's enemies for centuries, but why tar all giants with the same brush? Grysla has shown me nothing but kindness. In fact, she's the one who shared the Elder race runes with–"

Rudwor banged his meaty fists on the table, rattling dishes and spilling goblets. "Giants are the reason your plate is filled with such meager fare. Last spring the rock giants dammed the River Torle, drying up the loch and tributaries my farmlands rely upon. Our crops suffered the worst drought in recorded history, and what little harvest we managed to eke from the dry earth was all but destroyed by an early winter brought down upon us by the frost giants of the North."

He took a breath to calm himself. "Stores were already low after the Three Year Winter that snake of a sorcerer, Gorm, brought down on

Beldereth. To be thrown back into the ice this soon has destroyed the spirit of the people, especially amongst the troops. I've lost a legion since this all began. Everything outside these walls belongs to the giants now. Most of the troops I sent never returned, and those soldiers who did haven't been the same."

Finn sat back in his chair. "I'm sorry. Had I known what was happening, I never would've brought Grysla and her family here."

Rudwor dragged his fists from the table and gripped the arms of his chair. "Your timing couldn't be worse, and I'll not be able to bend the law, no matter how much you vouch for them."

Finn leaned forward. "Maybe I didn't speak strongly enough. This is my *family* we're talking about. Grysla and Tove are every bit as important to me as you are."

Rudwor drew air between his teeth and shook his head. "Sorry, lad. My hands are tied."

"That's it? Are you saying you're going to hold them prisoner indefinitely?"

"No, nothing of the sort." Rudwor's eyes filled with regret. "I'm saying they'll have to be executed."

25
STALEMATE

FATE REMATERIALIZED IN FRONT of the troll vault Finn had used to enter Oldwilde. When she saw where she was, the tears flooded in. She hadn't known where she would go when she tripped her teleporter, but it appeared her heart had chosen. Not that she was surprised. After all, her deepest wish was to flee her troubles and be with Finn.

She dried her tears with the back of her glove and glanced at the kind face of the tree troll carved over the dark mouth of the entrance. The temptation to run after Finn was overwhelming. With Brune as her proxy, the Keep no longer had a stranglehold on her. She was free to leave. All she had to do was step inside and activate the portal. Which could prove challenging. It's not like she knew the meaning of the Elder race runes, nor was she versed in troll speak the way Finn was. Still, she wasn't averse to trying.

Her stomach clenched with guilt as she stepped into the shadows of the vault. What kind of coward was she if she left Eustace and the others to face Farouk and Kaliena's army without her? She took another step, telling herself all she wanted to do was have a look at the last place Finn had been. All she needed was a moment alone to think. To calm down, and this was the perfect place to do that.

Fate felt her way through the dark tunnel's curved walls. The tunnel seemed to go on forever before she realized it moved in a spiraling pattern. At last she approached the end, which glowed with a soft flickering light.

The sound of steps made her stop. Someone was approach-ing the entrance of the tunnel from deep inside the vault. Could it be Finn? Had he decided to return? Her pulse raced as she watched a shadow slide over the earthen floor. She started forward, when a large form filled the opening.

It wasn't Finn. The blinking lights and sharp angles of the silhouette told her it was one of Kaliena's retrofitted killing drones. How stupid of her to think that Kaliena wouldn't know when one of the portals had been used. Of course there was a drone lying in wait for when one of them returned like the idiot she was.

Adrenaline flooded Fate's bloodstream. She had to deactivate the drone before it saw her and reported her presence to Kaliena.

Fear triggered the indwelling power stored within her core. In one move she harnessed its full might by using her hands to direct the energy. The power obeyed, hurling outward in an invisible stream of energy that slammed the drone into the wall with such force it burst into shrapnel.

Fate raced to the end of the tunnel and peered around the corner to make sure there weren't any other drones inside the large cavern. After determining all was clear, she breathed easier and walked all the way inside, her attention drawn to the high ceilings gleaming with Elder race runes.

Her gaze dropped to the domed mound and its spiraled path. Would walking the path to the top center activate the portal and transport her to Oldwilde? The urge to do so became stronger than ever and she set a foot on the path.

All at once, the hair on the back of Fate's neck stood on end. She dove to one side as electrical fire surged through the space she'd been standing in. The blast hit the mound in a burst of earth and rock, decimating the bottom bands of the runneled path.

Fate screamed with rage. The portal was destroyed!

She turned around to unleash her fury on the desecrator, but stopped when Jessie marched into the cavern.

Jessie aimed her weaponized arm at Fate. Her modulated voice boomed within the cavern and echoed off the walls. "Surrender or die."

Fate considered tripping her teleporter to avoid another battle with her best friend, but the power building beneath her ribcage emboldened her. Maybe there was still something left of Jessie underneath all those layers of mechanized metal. It couldn't hurt to try and reach her before the imminent arrival of the reinforcements Jessie had no doubt already sent for.

Fate strode toward Jessie. "That old line again? If you still want to be a writer, you're going to have to change up the dialogue. Do we need to get out our trusty old Thesaurus?"

Jessie held still, staring back through the machined armor she was encased in. Fate focused on her friend's one exposed eye, searching for any sign of emotion.

There was none. The mechanics on Jessie's arm clicked as the gun slipped back inside the arm bracer and steel daggers slid from the hard surface of her gloves.

"Okay... so witty banter isn't your thing anymore." Fate backed up. "I can see you're into the whole Wolverine slash and kill approach."

Jessie charged, her daggered fists slicing vertical lines in the air before leaping at Fate with a wild rake of her claws. Fate drew her sword and parried. Sparks flew from the collision of blades. Jessie brought her other arm round in an uppercut swing that would've dug deep into Fate's solar plexus had she not possessed the speed to escape the killing blow.

A surprising thrill rushed through Fate at her lightning quick reactions to Jessie's swift attacks. Her experience of time seemed to have shifted to the point where Jessie's actions now looked like someone trying to run underwater. Whereas, Fate was in her element, fully conscious of the subtle currents swirling within the folds of space and able to ride them to her advantage.

Fate deflected a series of deadly strikes with such ease, she yawned. Since she had no intention of hurting Jessie in any way, she realized this could go on indefinitely. In one great leap, Fate flew over Jessie's head and landed on the wall, where she grabbed hold of a knotted whorl in the wood to maintain her vantage point.

She glanced down at Jessie. "Do you realize this time last year we were working on our Nightingale armor for Comicon? That whole time we were hot-gluing molded pieces of plastic onto our bodies–suffering serious burns for our art–we were daydreaming about having the kind of power and skills we're using in this latest scuffle."

Jessie bent her knees, like a cat ready to pounce at a bird trapped in an open cage. But then she blinked, and not the kind of blink it takes to moisten one's eyeball. This was the blink of someone snapping out of a trance.

Hope swelled in Fate's chest. "We've really come a long way, Jessie. Look at us. We're the kickass girls we always wanted to be. We're both super strong and fast. We can fight like nobody's business. And best of all, we look pretty darned cool doing it."

Jessie squinted at Fate, her one eye blinking over and over.

Fate sprang from the wall and landed in front of Jessie. "How smooth was that? There was a time–not too long ago–when I would've twisted my ankle making that jump *and* I'd be whining about the pain like a toddler."

Jessie's eye filled with questions as her gaze traveled over Fate's face.

"Think of all the fun we could have together again," Fate continued. "I'm talking movie marathons and blanket forts complete with a fully stocked popcorn bar. Heck, I'll even throw in some Karaoke because I know you love it... being that you're the only one of us who can sing."

Jessie tilted her head and continued to stare at Fate.

"Jessie?" Fate leaned forward, excited, but ready to dodge a sudden swipe. "Do you remember when we swore to be best friends forever?"

Jessie's arms dropped to her side as the daggers receded into her suit.

Fate sighed with relief. "You do remember. I knew you'd–"

Crimson flames struck Fate, throwing her across the cavern. She crashed against the wall and dropped to the ground. Pain throbbed through her body as she struggled to catch her breath. Dazed, she crawled onto all fours and lifted her head.

Wodrid stepped in beside Jessie, a fireball hovering over his open palm. Energy radiated around the outer edges of his robe, a full display of the magic he possessed. Though something was different about him this time. He wasn't leaning on his silver staff to compensate for the false leg he wore. From what she could see, the leg she'd severed from his body had grown back. She had no idea the elixir could perform such a miracle!

"Wodrid, nice to see you back on your feet."

Wodrid's smile was venomous. "I'd say the same about you, but I'd be lying."

"Huh, you've always been so good at it. What's stopping you now?" Fate gripped the wall and stood.

Wodrid's expression hardened. "How is it you're getting back up from that hit you just took? It should've killed you." He wagged a finger at her. "Looks to me like someone found a cheat."

Fate ground her teeth together. Best to let him wonder and worry about how extensive her new powers were.

Wodrid heaved a sigh of frustration when she remained silent. "And here I thought I could saunter in, kill you and rip the Rod of Aeternitis from your neck."

Fate shrugged. "Sorry to foil your diabolical plans, but I don't have the Rod anymore."

Wodrid's pale complexion turned chalkier. "What?"

"Yeah, I gave it to Finn, and since he's now in Oldwilde, you and your handsy girlfriend are basically hooped."

Wodrid's face flushed with rage, all the way to the tips of his elven ears. Fate smiled as she watched him connect the dots. "That's right. He was the one who used the portal. Which by the way, was destroyed by my friend, Jessie, here."

Wodrid's glare flicked from Fate to Jessie. When his gaze returned to Fate, she crossed her arms with a satisfied smile. "I suppose that leaves us at a stalemate."

The red jewel on the end of Wodrid's silver staff flared bright and hot. He shook his head. "The game's not over yet." He aimed the tip of his staff at her and fired.

Fate spun out of the way. Heat filled the cavern as she dodged the advancing wall of flames. She twisted round to look at Jessie. Her friend stood stiff, as if stricken by a computer glitch that rendered her unresponsive to the battle waging in front of her.

Wodrid marched forward, conjuring a constant stream of fire. The searing blaze rose on all sides, cornering Fate against the back of the vault. Smoke stung her eyes. The air burned her lungs, tasting of ash as she pressed her spine to the wall and searched for an opening. But there was none. The inferno stretched the length of the vault and rose to the scorched ceiling. Hissing flames curled down at her like thousands of giant fingers. Her only escape was to use her teleporter.

Or she could go straight through.

She still didn't know the extent of her powers and wasn't sure she was strong enough to take Wodrid down. Or smart enough. The ancient sorcerer had a million tricks up his sleeve, but a demonstration of her powers might make him think twice before taking her on again.

Fate stared at the raging fire. "This is going to hurt."

Tensing every muscle, she called on her invisible strength and bolted into the flames. They burned, instantly charring her skin where the armor didn't protect. Fire surged over her neck and face searing deep, melting skin down to raw muscle. Incredible pain shuddered through her, tearing an inhuman sounding scream from her throat.

Fate pushed through the barrier and stood in front of Wodrid, whose shock had momentarily paralyzed him. The pain stopped, leaving within its terrible wake a tightening in her ruined face and neck. The sensation grew stronger and stronger, joined by a cooling shiver as the damaged cells of her skin fully regenerated.

Before Wodrid recovered his faculties, she snatched the staff from his hands and bent the silver rod until it snapped in half. She flung the pieces at his feet.

A visible jolt ran through him, as if he'd been rudely awoken. His furious gaze dropped to the broken staff. Roaring with rage, he called one of the pieces to his hand and in the same instance speared Fate's solar plexus with the jagged end.

Pain exploded through her core and she gasped for air. She looked down and didn't move. Blood poured from the wound. The heat of it spread over her skin as it spilled and pooled inside her armor.

Wodrid leaned within inches of her face. "Die already." Pure hatred dripped from his voice.

His words sparked terror in her. Was she dying? Had he destroyed the corset? Was this its one weakness? She coughed and her mouth flooded with the taste of iron. Raising a hand, she touched her tongue and drew bloody fingers away from her mouth. At the same time, the pain throbbing through the length of her torso came to an abrupt end and she felt the same tightening as she had on her face.

Raising her head, she glared at Wodrid, while pulling the staff from her body. The tugging sensation of the silver rod was nauseating as rapidly repairing tissue and muscles clenched to close the wound. Ignoring the urge to vomit, she yanked the rod all the way out of her abdomen.

Wodrid staggered toward the tunnel. "How?" Open fear shone in his eyes. "What did you do?"

Without a word, Fate marched toward him. Wodrid darted into the tunnel just as she'd hoped. She was done with him for now. Waiting a minute to ensure he was gone, she turned to Jessie. "Whoa, can you believe what just happened? It's still early and I've got a whole lot more to learn about this upgrade, but I'm thinking there's a pretty strong chance I can't be killed!"

Jessie remained motionless, though her gaze was fixed on Fate.

Fate took a few more steps in her direction but held her distance. Jessie may not have joined Wodrid in the fight, but that didn't mean she should let her guard down. "I don't want to fight you, Jessie. I'll let you leave and go back to Kaliena if that's what you want."

Jessie didn't move.

"Or... you can come back with me. Would you like that?" Fate chewed on her bottom lip as Jessie stared back.

The seconds ticked by.

At last, she answered in that emotionless, modulated tone of voice Fate had come to hate. "Yes, I will go with you."

26
ALL YOU HAVE TO DO IS DIE

FINN WOKE WITH A pounding headache and the rancid taste of ale on his breath. Rising with a groan, he glanced around to see where he was. From what he could tell, he'd either passed out on a daybed in Rudwor's bedchamber, or someone had put him there. The events of the previous night were muddy at best. The most he could remember was a constant stream of clanking his mug against Rudwor's and a whole lot of singing off-key.

Hoisting his legs over the edge, he planted his feet on the cold stone floor, shuddering as he stood. The room wobbled around him. He staggered for the table, gripping hold of it to stay upright. Nausea roiled in his stomach. Hanging his head, he swallowed the bile burning at the back of his throat, fighting the urge to vomit.

He lifted his head after a few minutes. Where was Rudwor? Still holding onto the table, he turned to the king's massive four-poster bed. His friend was sprawled in the middle of the mattress and he wasn't sleeping alone. It was hard to tell just how many women were lying beneath the puffy quilts, but from the heads barely poking above the covers, Finn counted at least three sharing Rudwor's bed. Possibly five if he counted the uneven lumps near the edges.

Finn shook his head with a rueful smile. Same old Rudwor.

Or maybe not.

Less cheery details of the evening came back to him. The king had not budged on his judgement to execute Grysla, Tove and Leif. In fact, the subject had become forbidden at one point. Finn's desperate attempts at softening him up with drinks hadn't worked.

Finn hobbled across the room. He pulled on his boots and jacket and headed for the door. This wasn't over. There was no way he'd allow harm to come to his friends, even if that meant incurring Rudwor's wrath.

A chill smacked him in the face when he left the warm room and stepped out into the hall. The frigid air sweeping through the castle was a stinging reminder of the brutal winter the giants had brought down over Beldereth. He fully understood why Rudwor had deemed all giants to be his enemy.

If only he could get his friend to see that Grysla was different.

Another bout of nausea stopped Finn in his tracks. He grabbed the wall for support. There'd be no coming up with any bright ideas while he was dealing with a hangover. The most he could hope to accomplish at the moment was to check on Sithias.

He moved on, taking it slow through the hallways, passing servants bundled in winter furs. These were not the healthy, rosy-cheeked people he remembered. Their faces were wan and colorless. And their eyes held the hollow look of poverty.

It had been easier to pass off Rudwor's complaints the night before. After all, the stout, burly man had the constitution of a grizzly bear and didn't seem reduced by the hardships he'd described. Finn should've known better though. Rudwor had not only survived the Bane of Duenthorn and its savage yearlong winters, the man had actually thrived.

But now it was plain to see the king's people were suffering famine and tremendous hardship.

Finn turned the corner and headed toward the stillroom, where he knew the healers kept their store of herbs and prepared their medicines. When he reached the door, two female guards crossed their spears to bar his way.

"I'm here to check on my friend Sithias. He's under the king's care," Finn explained.

Both guards stared past him, even when one of them spoke. "We have orders to keep the prisoner under heavy guard."

"Prisoner? Sithias isn't under arrest. The king knows him. Sithias is a guest here, same as me, and he should be treated as such."

"You'll have to take it up with the officer in charge."

"And where might I find–"

"You can direct any protests to me."

Finn turned around to see the same officer who'd taken his friends to the dungeons. She was a tall woman with a stern face. Her height matched his own and even though she'd shed her armor, she was armed and gripping the hilt of her sword.

"I'm here to see Sithias, but I've been told he's under arrest. I'd appreciate knowing why, because I don't think you realize he's been welcomed by the king as a guest."

The woman's steel gray eyes narrowed as she perused him. "That was before our healers discovered your deceptive friend is actually a snake masquerading as a human."

Finn swallowed. Sithias must have lost control of the glamour's magic at some point. "He's harmless. You can take my word on that."

The officer gestured to his guards. "Arrest him."

The dull throb in Finn's temples escalated into a jagged pounding. He staggered backward until he hit the wall. "Wait! Does the king know about any of this?"

The guards rushed in, wrenching his arms behind his back as the cold metal of iron shackles clamped down on his wrists. Panic thrummed along Finn's nerve endings as the horrors of his imprisonment in Asgar's dungeons slammed to the forefront of his mind. Adrenaline flooded his veins. He would not suffer that same humiliation and torture ever again.

Finn broke the chains, dodging the reach of the guards. "Stay back," he warned them. "I don't want to fight you, but I will. I won't go back to the dungeons."

The officer gripped her sword, her eyes darting at his broken chains with veiled fear. "If you mean that, stand down. You'll make things worse for yourself by resisting the royal guard."

The bile in Finn's queasy stomach churned. Blood rushed to his head, thudding so loud it was all he could hear. Fear raced through him, clouding all reasonable thought. "I won't be locked up! If you come near me, I can't be held responsible for what I'll–"

A thick, meaty arm snaked around his neck, squeezing off the air, lifting Finn off his feet. "Settle down, laddie," he heard Rudwor say.

Thrashing his legs, Finn clawed and pounded at Rudwor's forearm. But the huge man held tight until dark spots swam across his vision and all went black.

Finn opened his eyes to a blur of light and shadows. It felt like his bed rocked as if he was on a ship caught in a storm. Nausea gripped hold. Pouring with sweat, he gagged before lurching to one side of the bed to retch. When he was done, he flung himself back onto the pillow, only to hear the sounds of someone else heaving.

He turned in the direction of the noise. Sithias was sitting up in the bed next to him, gagging into his hand. "Are you sick too?" Finn muttered.

Sithias gulped and shook his head. "I have a weak stomach around the vomiting of others."

Finn heaved a tired sigh. "You're on the mend otherwise?"

Sithias touched his chest. "It hurts when I breathe too deeply, but yesss,

I'm on the road to recovery. It's just a good thing dragon's have dense bones or I wouldn't be sitting here talking to you."

Finn lifted his head to confirm they were alone in the stillroom. "Where are the guards?"

"Outside the door."

"And the healers?"

"Sent away after Rudwor dumped you on the bed."

"He left?"

Sithias nodded.

"Then we need to leave before he returns." Finn threw the blankets back, ready to leap from the bed when he saw his ankle was shackled to the wrought iron bedpost. "Bollocks! I suppose I'll have to break this one too."

"I wouldn't, sir. Rudwor left a warning."

"And what was that?" Finn seethed.

"He told me to tell you that you'd best stay put or your friends in the dungeon would find a swift death."

Finn bit down on the explosion of rage in his chest. How had everything turned upside down so quickly? If there was one person he'd been certain he could count on, it was Rudwor. "He told me they're slated for execution, and now most likely you too," Finn growled under his breath. "I have to get us all out of here."

Sithias's chin quivered. "Me? Why me?"

Finn frowned. "They found out you're not human."

"How can that be? I've been wearing the glamour this whole time." Sithias worriedly pulled on the tip of his goatee. "Although... come to think of it, I was rather delirious with pain when they extracted the arrow and I might have slipped into a hissing fit. That would explain why the healers were screaming and backing away. Hmm, and here I thought it was an impressive show of empathy on their part, but looking back now, it could very well be I momentarily reverted to my natural state."

Finn stared at him incredulously. "You didn't know you were under arrest?"

Sithias's amber eyes rounded with fright. "I had no idea. I assumed the guards were there to... protect me." He drew the quilt up under his chin. "Oh dear, whatever will we do?"

Finn's fury turned swiftly to a desire to summon the elements and rain holy hell down upon the kingdom. When he envisioned the destruction he was capable of causing, his anger fizzled into frustration. How could he add to the hardships the kingdom had already endured? Not to mention, a heinous act such as that would permanently seal himself as an enemy of Beldereth, and at a time he desperately needed Rudwor's assistance. Retaliation was not an option he could exercise. The situation required diplomatic finesse, not brute force.

"If only we could get Rudwor and Grysla in the same room," Sithias mused. "Then he'd see her for the gentle giant she is... a creature who only wants peace."

Finn sat straight in the bed. "Aye, that's it!"

Sithias raised his eyebrows in confusion. "And... what would that be exactly?"

"We're going to negotiate an end to this war with the giants."

"Uh... we? As in you and I?" Sithias sank deeper beneath the quilt. "But how?"

"Don't fret, Sithias," Finn assured him, "yours is the easy part. All you have to do is die."

27
A PLAN TO FIX EVERYTHING

"HELP HIM!" FINN HOLLERED. He rattled his chains and hurled the pewter water pitcher at the door. "He's dying!"

The officer and guards burst through the door, swords drawn as they assessed the situation. When they saw Finn still chained to the bed with Sithias convulsing in the other bed, they sheathed their swords. The officer eyed Sithias with suspicion then gestured to one of her guards. "Send for the healers."

Sithias arched his back, contorting in one last overly dramatic death throe before he fell still and rigid as bedrock. That last move was a bit much for Finn, but when did Sithias ever temper his performances? Though he had to admit, the gray pallor spreading over his friend's face and the blue tinge surfacing around his eyes and mouth were convincing indeed. If he didn't know Sithias was using the glamour to mimic death, he'd be horribly alarmed.

"He's dead! My friend's dead!" Finn yelled, staring at the officer with all the outrage he felt at being made a prisoner. "This is your fault! If you hadn't sent the healers away, they would've been here to save him. This is a terrible injustice. I demand to speak to the king!"

The commanding officer seemed at a loss for words.

The healers rushed into the stillroom, circling around Sithias's bed as they bent over him. After checking his pulse, they backed away with grim expressions. One of them shook his head at the officer. "The patient is gone."

Finn jerked his leg. The chains banged against the bedpost, clanging loudly through the silence. Everyone jumped. He pointed at the officer, who backed away in reaction to the black glower in his eyes. "This is on you. I hold you personally responsible."

Rudwor stormed into the room. "Back off, lad. She's just a soldier following orders. If there's anyone to heap this unfounded anger of yours onto, it's me."

Finn scowled at the king, finding it easy to continue his tirade. He didn't have to fake how deeply hurt he was by the huge chasm of distrust Rudwor had carved between them. "What do you expect? You refuse to believe my friends are to be trusted. Hell, you might as well tell me I'm every bit as untrustworthy!" Finn jerked on the chain. "Oh wait, that's exactly what you've done."

Rudwor dismissed the officer and ordered the healers to remove Sithias's body. He watched them leave, then sat down in the chair next to Finn's bed. The folds around his eyes sagged in sad lines as he sighed with exhaustion he'd been hiding until that moment. "I want to let you loose, son, but first you need to tell me what's got you so worked up. I haven't seen you such a broodin' nightmare since we first met. At least then you were under the control of that Mugloth character, but I thought that was behind you."

Finn slumped onto the bed and stared at the ceiling. "It's simple. I don't take to being locked up."

"No, there's more to it than that."

Finn closed his eyes against the flash of the foul floor of the cell he'd been chained up in. Every scummy stone was burned in his brain. The aches of the sores made by the irons echoed in his bones. "Some time after you and I said our farewells, I was taken as a prisoner of Asgar." He glared straight ahead, seeing only those prison walls. "I don't know how long I was in the dungeon, but it was long enough that I thought I'd die before the day of execution. They left me in shackles to rot with a stopper in my mouth to keep me from calling on the elements. I didn't receive so much as a drop of water."

Rudwor's eyes filled with outrage. "What kind of king allows such cruelty, even to prisoners?"

"One who blamed me for his mother's death." Finn shrugged. "He wasn't wrong. She's dead because of me, but he didn't know what an evil snake she truly was."

Rudwor stroked his beard. "I'll unlock you, so long as you promise to behave from here on out."

Finn smiled grimly. "Aye, you have my word I'll do my best to…behave."

Rudwor withdrew a key from his breast pocket and leaned toward the shackle around Finn's ankle. He stopped with the key poised near the lock. "I'm sorry about Sithias, and I know you're upset about losing him… "

Finn held up a hand in surrender. "I know your healers did everything they could. I don't blame anyone. Not even the officer I took my anger out on."

Rudwor freed him from his chains.

"But if you care how I feel at all, you'll consider saving my other friends," Finn pressed.

"That's impossible, lad. I have a kingdom of people to answer to.

Suffering out this brutal weather, scant food supplies and too much loss of life has hardened their hearts. They need something to channel their rage into, and this giant you delivered is exactly what they've been waiting for."

Finn rubbed his ankle to chase away the lingering bite of the shackle. "Did you know Grysla is the last of her kind?" He didn't wait for an answer. "That girl in the dungeon with her is her daughter. Grysla raised her. This was the child of the humans who killed Grysla's entire family. Yet this tree troll found it in her heart to forgive by showing that little human nothing but love and kindness. Tell me, is that like the giants you're at war with?"

Rudwor ran his thick hands over the tops of his legs with a pained grimace. "What would you have me do, lad? If I free the giant, the people will revolt." He shook his head. "Beldereth won't survive the dissention that will cause. Not with half my troops out there hunting giants and the other half busy defending the walls against their attacks.

Finn pulled his boots on and stood. "If I told you I could negotiate with the giants to bring about an end to this war, would you at least announce a stay of execution?"

Rudwor frowned with confusion. "Negotiate? With *giants*? Are you daft?"

"I've never been clearer," Finn assured him. "I know troll speak and I'm marked with the Elder race runes. The giants will take notice of that."

Rudwor rose to his full height and loomed over Finn. "And promptly squash you beneath their ruddy flippers like the vermin they think we humans are."

Finn shook his head. "I know it's hard to see, but this could be an age old misunderstanding between you and them."

Rudwor's face flamed crimson. "This is no misunder-standing! This is an extinction of our kind. They want us wiped from this place."

"Give me the chance to talk to them. What have you got to lose?"

Rudwor slapped his meaty hands on Finn's shoulders, rocking him off balance. "You, laddie, I could lose you! That's a gamble I won't make."

"I'm not giving you a choice here. I plan to do this whether you agree or not."

Rudwor stared back. "Aye, I know. You've got that thrawn look in your eyes."

"Then it's settled. All I need from you is that stay of execution."

"It won't be an easy decree to pass," Rudwor grumbled.

"But you'll do it."

Rudwor nodded. "Aye, I'll get 'er done. But you best deliver and be quick about it."

Finn was quiet as he gauged Rudwor's overall demeanor. "I have just one more favor to ask."

"Boy, you're killing me!" Rudwor smoothed his hand over the top of his bald head with a look of defeat. "I'm not going to like this one, am I?"

"No, I'm pretty sure you're going to hate it."

Finn stood on the veranda outside the great hall, staring into the raging blizzard. He leaned into the glacial wind, trying to make out the sharp ridges of Mount Helgunth in the distance, but snow flurries made it impossible to see the imposing mountain. The frigid air was enough to cut a person in half, but the cold was the least of Finn's problems. His main concern was to make peace with the giants and end this war so Rudwor's army would be free to help him gain other alliances. Without Beldereth's mighty strength on side, there's no way the other kingdoms would join the army he was building.

Of course, he hadn't even told Rudwor about the impending doom Kaliena's army was about to unleash upon Oldwilde, but that subject would have to wait until after he'd solved the king's most pressing problem.

Finn gripped the balustrade, frustrated by the continual rise of roadblocks since his arrival in Oldwilde. He'd been naïve to think everything would fall into place with little to no trouble.

His thoughts turned to Fate. He could only hope she wasn't being plagued with any more complications than what he'd left her with. Which was more than enough as it was. It killed him not to be there fighting by her side. And now she was depending on him to have the alliances in place before Archie punched a hole through the universe to bring their war with Kaliena to Oldwilde.

A voice, nearly drowned by the howling wind jarred him from his thoughts. Finn turned to see the lead officer waving him inside through the cracked door. He walked inside, pushing against the tall doors to shut out the blustering gale forcing its way in. A cloud of snow swirled around him, scattering over the marble floor as he strode to the middle of the hall, where a dozen guards surrounded Grysla.

The tree troll had to stoop even within the high vaulted ceiling of the great hall. Her head hung low as she dragged the thick, heavy chains attached to the irons binding her wrists to her ankles. The tree troll's eyes lit to a bright green when she saw him.

Finn stopped in front of the officer. "I was promised a meeting alone with the prisoner."

The officer gave him a disapproving frown as she gestured for her guards to leave. "We'll be outside the door. You have ten minutes."

Finn trailed after them, waiting for the door to close before turning to Grysla. Racked with guilt at seeing her shackled, he shook his head. "I'm so sorry you've been treated this way. I had no idea what we were walking into when we came here."

Grysla's craggy face softened into a smile as she signed the words for forgiveness.

"How are Tove and Leif?"

The tree troll's smile turned apologetic, while the branches of her fingers curled into claws.

Finn swallowed. "Pretty angry, huh?"

Grysla nodded.

Finn sighed. "I don't blame them one bit. But I have a plan to fix everything." With that, he launched into what he'd learned from Rudwor of Beldereth's war with the rock giants and the frost giants. "There's only one solution to this," he continued. "You and I need to go to Mount Helgunth and negotiate a truce. Mostly you, as far as the negotiating is concerned, but I'll be there with you. To represent the humans."

Grysla held up her shackles and glanced over her shoulders at the door with the guards on the other side.

"I know, it's not looking like a possibility at the moment, but it will be as soon as Sithias gets here with the key." Finn paced the floor. "He was supposed to be here already," he grumbled.

The words were no sooner out of his mouth, when a white mouse with brown wings whipped past his head and landed on one of the gnarled branches protruding from Grysla's head. "Sssorry I'm late," the mouse squeaked, his tiny chest heaving while gripping a large iron key. "You have no idea what I went through to get this extremely heavy chunk of metal!"

Sithias let the key drop as he bent over to catch his breath. Finn caught the key before it hit the floor and went to work unlocking Grysla's irons. Sithias straightened, arching his back as he rubbed a sore spot. "Did you know the jailer carries the keys with him? I had to follow him around while he jangled them at the prisoners, taunting them with the keys to their freedom."

Grysla nodded grimly.

"Awful fellow, that one," Sithias continued. "He doesn't seem to do much of anything else but make a nuisance of himself. It wasn't until that sluggard had to use his hands for other activities–of which I wish I could forget–that I was able to steal the key. Fortunately, I knew to take the largest one."

"Brilliant, Sithias," Finn said as he unlocked the last iron.

Grysla slipped the shackles off and set the chains down on the floor quietly.

"Ready for the next step?" Finn asked Sithias.

Sithias launched into the air, flapping his little wings furiously. "Not in the least. I hope you're fully aware of the sacrifice I'm about to make. I ask that you *pleassse* make haste with your negotiation. Otherwise, I'll be driven mad by the incessant jangling echoing off the walls of the dungeon, and once that happens, I cannot be held responsible for what I may do."

With that said and accepted by Finn, Sithias elongated to an enormous height, his limbs thickening and distorting as his soft fur gave way to bark and his head sprouted a crown of branches. He teetered off balance for a moment before adjusting to the added weight of his massive form.

Grysla stared wide-eyed at Sithias as Finn stepped back to compare the two tree trolls. The only difference between them was the color of their eyes. Sithias's eyes never changed. They were always the same telltale color of amber, but Finn was certain no one else would notice that small detail. "All right then, let's move. We don't have much time before the guards return. Grysla, you step outside while I lock Sithias in the chains."

The tree troll did her best to tip toe across the floor, but Finn felt the vibration beneath his feet and hoped it wasn't strong enough to reach the guards. Gesturing for Grysla to hurry, he snapped the shackles onto Sithias's ankles and then his wrists. Grysla squeezed through the tall double doors out onto the veranda, and just as she drew the last leg outside, the guards stormed through the door on the opposite side of the great hall.

Snow gusted in through the open door as the tree troll stood and hid on the other side of the wall. Finn shoved the key into Sithias's enormous palm and stepped back.

"What's going on in here? Why are the doors open?" the officer demanded to know.

Finn shrugged. "The doors burst open from the wind. I guess I didn't shut them tight enough."

The officer eyed him suspiciously, marched over to the doors, squinted into the snow whipping into her, but stepped no further than the threshold. Two guards rushed over to help her close both of the heavy, wooden doors.

She ordered her soldiers to escort the giant back to the dungeon. Sithias let out a gruff whimper as he turned and tripped over his chains. Stumbling to regain his balance, the room shook as his crown of branches hooked into the chandelier, ripping the fixture from the ceiling. The massive metal ring hit the marble floor with a jarring clang, scattering broken candles everywhere.

"Sorry," Sithias muttered, his voice deep and rumbling the same as Grysla's, if and when she chose to speak.

"Get it out of here and back to the dungeon before it destroys anything else!" the officer yelled. She stopped in front of Finn. "I don't know what you're up to, but be warned, I'll be watching you." She turned abruptly and left Finn standing in the middle of the mess Sithias had made.

Finn made sure she was gone before heading back to his room in case the officer carried through on her threat. Once he was inside his suite, he locked the door, gathered his provisions, slipped out onto the balcony and whistled a message into the air only Grysla would recognize.

Within a few minutes, her massive hand rose above the railing and Finn stepped onto her palm. The tree troll set him on her shoulder and turned in the direction of Mount Helgunth, where they would soon face Beldereth's oldest and most loathed enemy.

28
TROJAN HORSE

"HERE WE ARE." FATE stopped in front of the locked hatch of the shelter. Jessie hadn't spoken a word since they'd left the tree troll's vault. "I'll just pop inside, explain that you're out here, and somehow convince them to let you come in."

Jessie's wide hazel eye shifted from the hatch and back to Fate.

"Okay then," Fate said when Jessie remained silent. "Be right back."

The moment Fate teleported into the shelter, Gerdie squealed with delight and skipped over to her with the doggit hopping beside her. "You're back! Where did you go?"

Eustace rounded the corner, relief flooding his face. Archie and Brune turned away from the workstation, both staring intently with an air of tension. Darcy didn't appear, which meant one of two things. She was either still holed up in bed, or didn't care that Fate had freaked out earlier and left.

"Are you feeling better?" Eustace scrutinized her with what seemed like more than his usual fatherly concern.

"I am, and I have news. Some good, some bad." She muttered the last part.

Brune edged forward, her hand resting on the hilt of her laser gun. Archie followed timidly behind her.

"I went down to the surface, back to the tree troll vault," Fate began.

Concerned faces stared back.

"You went to the surface?" Brune yelled. "Why the hell would you do that? Especially since Kaliena would've known the portal had been activated recently. Did she have drones stationed there? Because that's what I'd do."

Fate pressed her lips together to keep from yelling back. She was determined to remain calm, especially since they were all looking at her like she'd completely lost her head. "As a matter of fact, yes, there was a drone there. Which I destroyed, on the spot."

Brune's eyes narrowed on her, but Fate continued before she could say another word. "I was about to leave when Jessie showed up. There was a bit of a fight between us... and the portal was destroyed." She mumbled the last bit of information so quickly no one noticed. "But then Wodrid came, and I'm proud to say, I kicked his smug, elven ass. He ran out of there like a crybaby. And the good news is, Jessie didn't help him fight me. I got through to her. She's on our side now."

The concern on everyone's face turned to horror. Brune was the first to break the momentary silence. "Do you have any idea how insane all this sounds?" He gaze shifted to Archie. "You need to test her. She's succumbed to the emanations."

Archie blinked, making the white beams of light radiating from his eyes go off and on in rapid succession as he inched forward nervously.

Fate held out her hand to stop him. "I'm not crazy, and I can prove it. Take a look at who's waiting on the other side of the hatch."

Archie tottered back to his workstation, swiped the instruments on his control board and brought up an image of Jessie.

"You brought the enemy to our doorstep?" Brune shouted.

"She's not the enemy anymore. Jessie wants to be with us now." Fate moved toward Archie. "You can remove all of Kaliena's gadgets, right? You can free Jessie from her control, I know you can."

Archie's neck squeaked as he tilted his head in consideration of the question. "I cannot answer that without knowing how extensive the cybernetic invasion is. I do know that Kaliena's controlling influence is continual, which means there's likely a permanent disruption to the brain's neural networks." He pressed a finger to his chin. "Though Kaliena's source of power is through her use of multidimensional magic. Therefore, I may be able to break the connection with a series of counter spells in conjunction with a thorough systemic flushing and brainwave repatterning."

Fate nodded like she thoroughly understood what he meant. "See, Brune? We can get Jessie back. Think of all the intel we'll be able to gather from her once Archie's got her all cleaned up and back to normal."

She could see the wheels turning in Brune's head. "Maybe," Brune admitted reluctantly, "but it's incredibly risky. What if Archie can't do it? We might as well open the doors and let Kaliena walk inside because she's going to know all our business the moment Jessie steps inside here."

"Besides our exact location–which she already knows and is Kaliena-proof, thanks to Archie–what else is there to discover?" Fate asked.

"The portal amplifier, for one," Brune was quick to say.

Fate glanced down at her feet. "Oh yeah, about that. Um... the portal we were going to amplify was kind of... destroyed."

Archie, Brune and Eustace gaped at her in disbelief.

"That was the bad part of the news." Fate squirmed beneath their stares.

"But there are other portals into Oldwilde. I can name one off the top of my head. It went to the island of Innith Tine. We can use that one, right?"

Archie's many hands were already flying over the control panel. "Unfortunately, that vault is deep below the subsurface and entirely inaccessible."

"Can't we use the teleporters?" Fate asked.

Brune planted her fists on her hips. "How do you expect us to visualize where we're teleporting when we've never been down there?"

"We've been to the core. How much different can it be?"

"The tracks the vaults move along within the lower levels are fully encased in iron walls fortified with energy disruptors and binding sigils to keep all multidimensional magic from activating," Archie explained. "Meaning, the portals lie dormant until they return to the surface."

"Oh." Panic streaked along the ends of Fate's nerves. How could she have been so rash? Maybe she really was a victim of the emanations.

Archie returned to his control panel, his fingers blurring in a flurry of activity as one holographic image after the other flashed in and out of view. He finally stopped on a mosque made of shifting white sand. He pointed excitedly at the mosque. "This one may work, though it doesn't open into Oldwilde."

Fate and the others crowded around the image. "No, it has to be Oldwilde, Archie." Her voice rose to a fearful pitch. "That's where Finn is."

Eustace placed his hand on her shoulder. "Give Archie a chance to speak, Doodles."

Archie pointed at the image. "This portal opens into Shalamoraize, a continent situated on the southern most tip of Oldwilde. The two land masses are connected by a small peninsula."

"We can work with that." Fate sighed.

"I will have to complete the amplifier sooner than anticipated," Archie continued. "The vault is due to slide beneath the surface of the Keep in two days time."

"But you'll be able to work on Jessie too," Fate pressed.

Archie shook his head. The metallic creak of his neck grated on her and she bit her lip to keep from yelling at him to oil the thing. "I do not have time for both."

"Good," Brune interjected, "because when it comes right down to it, I'm not comfortable with letting a Trojan horse inside our last refuge."

"Since when do we give up on our own?" Fate asked.

"Since Kaliena can see through Jessie's eyes and give her the order to take us all out."

Fate glared at Brune. "If it ever came down to that, I can handle Jessie."

Brune stepped within inches of Fate's face. "Oh really? You're saying if you had to choose between us and Jessie, you'd actually be able to kill her?"

Fate swallowed down the instant ache that formed in her throat. "I will do whatever is necessary to protect every single person in this room. Even you and Darcy, my two least favorite people in the universe."

"Ouch, you hurt my feelings." Brune rolled her eyes. "Please, do you really think I care what you think of me?" Her eyes narrowed into a glower. "Jessie stays outside."

Fate looked at Eustace. "Dad, this is Jessie we're talking about. We can't give up on her."

Her father's tired expression grew sad. "I'm sorry, but I agree with Brune. Given what I've seen Jessie do since she's been changed, it's too much of a risk."

Shaking with anger, Fate turned her back to Eustace and Brune. "Archie, I'm taking Jessie to the infirmary. Make sure you've transmitted the counter spells and whatever instructions your robo-medics need to flush her system and repattern her brain. I want everything ready by the time we get there."

Before anyone could say a word, she teleported out of the shelter and rematerialized next to Jessie outside the hatch. "Come on, Jessie, follow me."

Jessie fell in step with Fate's rapid jog down the long corridor. Her heart raced at the thought of restoring her friend to her former self. This had to work. Her heart couldn't take the disappointment of having to accept she'd lost Jessie forever.

Fate pushed through the double doors of the infirmary. The medic robots were waiting with an array of equipment gathered around an operating table. "The patient will lie down," one of them instructed.

Jessie eyed the complex apparatus warily.

"This is all going to help you be free of Kaliena's control," Fate explained. "That's what you want, right? To be free. To be your own person again."

Jessie didn't move, only her eye as it settled on Fate. She nodded and lay down on the table. Fate drew in a nervous breath as the medics went to work, plugging tubes into the exoskeleton of Jessie's armor. The sparkling, golden liquid inside the bags dripped down the tubing like melted honey.

One of the medics handed Fate a ledger with several spells listed out in chronological order, along with a silver cylinder the length of a cigar. Fate held it up. "What's this?"

"The wand," one of the medics replied.

"Really? I didn't know we used those around here. How does it work?"

"The wand is calibrated to emit elemental, color and sound frequencies to match the invocations of the spells," the medic explained very matter-of-factly.

"Oh. Well that doesn't sound very magical." Fate stared at the wand with disappointment.

"Magic is a science."

"I think I liked it better when magic was a mystery. And sparkly." She stepped closer to the table. "So should I start saying the spells and waving this unexciting wand now?"

The medics moved around to the top of the table and began plugging cords into Jessie's helmet. Once they were finished, one of them nodded at Fate. "The purifying solution appears to be clearing the multidimensional magic contaminating the subject's system. We will now attempt to repattern the brainwaves to a neutral state." The medic turned the dials on the machine, which made a whirring sound. The medics stepped away from the table at the same time. "You may commence with the spells."

Fate smiled down at Jessie, where she stared straight at the ceiling, completely devoid of emotion. "Okay, Jess, we'll have you back to your old self in no time."

She took a step back, aimed the wand at Jessie and began reading the spell aloud. *"Gold for Power, Silver for Will, and Bronze for Energy."* As she spoke each color, a range of tinkling sounds like that of metal wind chimes echoed through the room as rays of gold, silver and bronze streamed from the end of the wand and settled in shimmering layers of dust over Jessie's body.

"Ooh, there's some sparkles for you." Fate paused to see if there was any reaction, but Jessie continued to stare at the ceiling.

"No worries. We've got two more spells to go." Fate pointed the wand at Jessie again and read the spell. "*Fire wards the nerves–*"

Flames surged from the wand and blasted over Jessie.

"Whoa!" As soon as Fate broke away from speaking the spell, the fire dissipated. She frowned at the medics "This thing's dangerous!"

"The fire is of an energetic state only," the medic replied. "It is unwise to speak any other words once the spell is initiated. Please continue."

Fate cleared her throat and aimed the wand. "*Water wards the blood.*" Soft mist sprinkled down on Jessie. Feeling better about the spell, Fate continued. "*Air wards the breath.*" A gentle breeze rushed from the wand. "*Earth wards the bones.*" A puff of silt drifted out over Jessie, clinging to her armor as if magnetized.

Fate moved close and leaned over her. "Jessie? Are you there?"

Jessie's gaze moved to Fate and she gave the slightest nod. At least that's what Fate took the tiny movement as.

Encouraged, Fate took a few steps back again. "Last one." She couldn't stop smiling as she took aim with the wand and invoked the next spell. *"I call upon the highest powers far and near to banish what is not welcome in thee–"*

A tangled, violet stream of particles burst from the wand, encompassing Jessie in a cocoon of chaotic light, while a bright, burning sigil formed above her head.

"*By this light and sigil, I command what has caused harm in thee to leave.*"

Jessie convulsed as the light snarled around her.

Fate looked at the medic. "Is that supposed to be happening?"

The medics checked the instruments Jessie was plugged into. "The possessing energetic signature is resisting the command. The subject is experiencing rapid physical decline."

Fate marched forward, holding the wand like a sword. "Get out of her!" she screamed. "Leave Jessie alone!"

Jessie's back arched in a tortured spasm as the twisting light crackled around her.

"Is she in pain?" Fate asked the medics.

"Affirmative. The subject's pain receptors are elevated."

"How do we stop it?"

"There is nothing to be done while the spell is active."

Fate gripped the wand. "But it won't kill her, right?"

"Unless the subject's own will power is strong enough to expel the energetic possessing signature, death is imminent."

Fate rushed to Jessie's side. "You can do this, Jessie. I know you can. Kaliena has no power over you. Come on, kick her out."

Jessie shuddered beneath the churning encasement of light.

Fate frowned at the medic. "Any improvement?"

"Negative. Vital organs are beginning to shut down."

Fate's heart thudded out of control. "I have to stop the spell. How do I do it?"

"Spell breaking instructions were not included."

Fate ran to the intercom. "Archie! I need to know how to break the last spell, and I need it *now*!" She kicked one of the beds, bashing it against the wall. Unable to watch Jessie as she thrashed on the table, Fate paced the length of the room.

"Message received," the medic informed her after a few eternally long minutes.

Fate skimmed the ledger as she hurried over to Jessie and pointed the wand. "*Break the powers and the spell which cast them. The spell is now reversed. It is done.*" It was so simple, she felt as though she should've known it.

The violet light dispersed in a flash of filmy mist. Jessie's body stilled and Fate hurried over to her. "Jess, can you hear me?"

Jessie didn't respond. She was either unconscious, or... Fate couldn't bring herself to think the worst. She turned to the medic. "Is she still alive?"

"Vitals are returning to normal."

"Oh, thank–"

A hand clamped around her throat, choking off her words. Jessie rose to a sitting position, her one eye trained on Fate, cold and empty. Fate grabbed Jessie's wrist to break free, but Jessie's grip tightened all the more. The metal edges of her glove sliced into Fate's neck.

"Did you really think you could take what is mine?" It was Kaliena speaking through the modulated voice box of Jessie's headgear. She stood, lifting Fate off her feet. "You tiny humans are incapable of recognizing true power. Your feeble fight for survival might be considered amusing had I not grown bored with your pitiful performance long ago."

Fate's lungs burned from lack of air as the weight of her failure caved in. Her friend was lost, which, god help her, left no reason to temper her strength.

In one swift move, Fate brought her feet up. Climbing the front of Jessie's armor, she pushed off with a violent kick, breaking free of the steely grip on her neck and somersaulted through the air before planting her boots on the floor a few yards away.

Her friend's body staggered backward from the sudden jolt as a thick, blue-green haze seeped from Jessie's armor. Six tentacles of mist split off from her sides as more haze concentrated around her head and congealed into Kaliena's face. Her expression wavered over Jessie's blank face, contorting into lines of fury. "Whatever enhancements you've gained will only delay the inevitable. You cannot win," Kaliena warned.

Squeezing her fists until her arms shook with fury, Fate considered punching through Jessie's armor and ripping it to shreds as a demonstration of her newly acquired power. But that would do nothing to rid Jessie of Kaliena's control. And it might even kill her. Fate refused to give up hope as long as Jessie remained Kaliena's prisoner.

Fate's only alternative now was to leave. With nothing to fight and no one else to hunt with the others safely locked within the shelter, Kaliena would be forced to call Jessie back. Grinding her teeth against the anger eating a hole in her stomach, Fate brought the shelter to mind and teleported there before she did something she'd regret for the rest of her life.

29
FOREVER THE GOOD FATHER

WAITING FOR ARCHIE TO complete the portal amplifier was pure torture. With each passing hour, the walls of the shelter closed in tighter around Fate. She paced the perimeter of the room like a caged tiger, wishing she could find the patience to continue helping Eustace research Shalamoraize, where the portal would be taking them. But she couldn't sit still any longer. She needed to move, take some sort of action that would propel things forward. If she thought it would help, she'd assist the scientist in his efforts. Unfortunately, she didn't have a head for gadgets the way Brune did.

"Wanna play hide and seek with me and the doggit?" Gerdie asked.

Her fine, elfin features lit with a hopeful smile and Fate didn't like letting her down. "I can't right now. I have other stuff I have to do. Really important stuff."

Gerdie's smile vanished. "It doesn't look like it."

"Well, I'm thinking... about all the important stuff I have to do."

Gerdie's shoulders slumped with disappointment. "Guess I'll have to call B–"

"Hey, Gerdie, I've got something much more fun to do." Eustace strode forward with a chocolate frosted cake, lit with candles. "How does a birthday party sound?"

A brick of ice formed in Fate's stomach as a chilling sense of déjà vu flooded in. She'd seen this before. This very scene came straight from the nightmare she'd had the day before.

"Dad, what's this?" She rushed to his side. "Is that for Gerdie?" *Please say it's for Gerdie.*

Eustace gave Gerdie a wink when the little girl puffed with excitement. "Not this one, but we can certainly celebrate Gerdie's birthday next." His gaze moved to Fate. "This one's for you, Doodles. As you've reminded me–more than a few times– you're technically eighteen after being trapped inside the *Book of Fables* for half a year. From what I've been able to calculate, there are still a few more months to go before it's October 31st back home, but I think it's high time we celebrated this important milestone."

A high-pitched buzz filled Fate's head as he spoke the same words from her nightmare. The candles on the cake blazed as bright as flares, hurting her eyes. She shook her head. Was she asleep? Was this another dream?

Wake up!

"I think a dose of chocolate is exactly what you need to take the edge off," Eustace continued. "I had no idea chocolate cake would prove to be such a challenge for the food replicator." He chuckled. "It only took ten attempts to get it right."

Panic fired through Fate's nervous system. *No, this isn't happening!*

Lines of confusion crinkled around Eustace's eyes. "Hey, are you feeling all right?"

Fate's mouth was bone dry. "I'm just not very hungry at the moment," she croaked.

He set the cake down and felt her forehead. "You're ice cold."

"It'll pass. I'm fine."

Eustace frowned with concern. "No you're not." Pulling her gently by the elbow, he guided her to sit down.

Gerdie hovered near the cake. "Can I blow out the candles?"

"Yes, go ahead." *Something different from the nightmare.* A spark of hope.

Gerdie squeezed her eyes shut, her mouth moving silently as she made a wish. Taking a big breath, she blew out all the candles.

"Run and get some plates, Gerdie," Eustace told her.

"Be right back!" Gerdie skipped off toward the galley.

Eustace sat down next to Fate and reached in his pocket. "Well, if chocolate's not going to fix this, then maybe this will. Close your eyes."

Tears burned behind her shut lids as she held out her hand. *It's not a miniature of my cat, Oz. It's not a miniature of my cat, Oz.*

Eustace set something cold and metallic in the palm of her hand. "Okay, have a look."

Fate's heart thudded with terror as she opened her eyes to the miniature clockwork cat curled in her hand. Just like in the nightmare, it rose to a sitting position, peering at her with glinting emerald eyes. Its soft meow rang shrill in her ears and its purring sent icy shivers racing along her arm.

She wanted to throw the thing on the floor and smash it to bits beneath her boot, if only to break the pattern of the nightmare. But how could she? Eustace would never understand.

Eustace leaned forward with a smile. "I tried to get Archie to add orange striped fur to make it look more like Oz, but he said it would get caught in the cogs and wheels."

Fate tore her gaze from the clockwork cat to look at Eustace. His face swam behind a storm of tears. Wiping her eyes roughly, she tried to smile. "I love it. Thanks, Dad."

Relief smoothed her father's furrowed brow. "Oh, I'm glad to hear it. For a minute there, I thought I'd made matters worse." He patted her knee. "I know how much you're hurting with not being able to help Jessie. And you miss Finn... "

Fate sniffed. "I do, but I'm glad you're here with me. I don't know what I'd do without you."

Eustace brought her into a warm bear hug. "The feeling's mutual, Doodles."

Fate sank against his shoulder, for the briefest moment feeling as though this was the safest place in the world. But fear loomed large, banishing all sense of well being.

Gerdie raced across the room with plates and a cake knife.

Eustace let Fate go. "Slow down, Gerdie. Hasn't anyone ever told you not to run with sharp objects?"

Fate smiled sadly. *Forever the good father.*

Gerdie skidded to a halt. "Nope. Can I cut the cake?"

Eustace held out his hand. "How about we cut it together?"

Gerdie handed him the knife. Holding the handle, Eustace positioned her in front of the cake, allowing her to put her little hand over his while he sliced the cake into generous portions. "So Gerdie, what did you wish for?"

Gerdie twisted around to look at him. "I thought we weren't supposed to tell."

"Only when it's your birthday cake. Did you make a nice wish for Fate?"

Gerdie stepped aside with a guilty smile. "No, I didn't."

Eustace handed her a plate. "That's all right. What was your wish?"

Gerdie stuck her finger in the frosting and licked it off. "I wished for Boo to come to the birthday party."

Fate lost all equilibrium. The walls swayed and the floor dipped as her heart plummeted into the cold pit of her stomach. She reached for her sword, squeezing the hilt until the room steadied. Glancing everywhere, she searched the shadowy corners for the burning eyes. Slowly, she stood and drew her sword.

"Who's Boo?" Eustace asked.

"My new friend."

"Is that so?"

"I think he's a Bandersnatch."

"Oh really." Eustace held out a slice to Fate. He set the plate down when he saw she was ready for a fight. "Fate, I know you're not yourself right now, but... "

Fate turned in circles. "Dad, I'm fine."

"No you're not. Sithias told me about the Amazonian girdle you're wearing and how it's affecting you."

Fate stopped and looked at him. "He what? Sithias had no right to tell you that! Ooh, when I get my hands on that rat, I'm going to–"

"He did the right thing. He wanted me to continue his research and find a way to remove the girdle without harming you."

"You have no idea what you're talking about. I'm fighting a war out there. This power is what's kept me alive so far."

"It's also what's driving you to do things you wouldn't normally do."

The scrape of claws against metal had her turning toward the hatch. She gulped down her raging terror and spoke quietly. "Dad, not now. I think Farouk's here."

Eustace blanched. "Where?"

Fate poured sheer will and determination into every muscle and turned in a slow circle. She would prevent the worst from happening. "I don't see him ye–"

Bolts of silvery fire lanced the air as Farouk's claws emerged from a shadowy shape sifting through the wall. Two eyes gleamed from within the moving darkness before his form fully materialized into the hulking, feral creature she'd come to fear.

The air wavered around him, blurring her vision as his evil emanations rolled toward her in waves. Nausea and weakness set in. Her arms shook from the heaviness of her sword, loosening her grip.

Farouk crept forward, his snout curling back in a snarling grin. Black smoke leached past his fangs as he leveled his malignant gaze on Fate. "*Here we are again, ready to repeat the same tragic scene. I know what you're thinking. Is it another nightmare, or is it happening for real this time?*"

"It doesn't matter!" Fate yelled. "I won't let you hurt him this time!"

Farouk's voice scraped the inside of her skull as his large head swung toward Eustace. "*Oh, but I will do so much more than hurt him.*" His barbed tail whipped threateningly behind him.

Fate charged at the demon, but as soon as he cast his ruinous gaze back on her, her energy withered and her knees crashed into the floor. Her sword clanged loudly next to her.

Brune rushed in, firing her laser gun.

Gerdie screamed when Brune shot what she thought was her friend.

Tears streamed down her face as she called out Boo's name. Eustace ran over to pull her away from the horrific scene.

The slicing ray of Brune's gun barely singed Farouk's hide before he dematerialized and vanished from the spot. Remembering how Brune had been slain in the nightmare, Fate grabbed her sword and drove her blade upright behind Brune with all her strength. Farouk appeared there in the same instance.

Her blade found its mark beneath his ribs. A sinister shriek filled the room. With his attention on his wound, Fate's strength returned. Encouraged by yet another change to the nightmare, she jumped to her feet and shoved the sword all the way to the hilt.

Growling ferociously with black smoke flooding from his gaping maw, Farouk turned his burning gaze fully on her. She couldn't think, nor could she move. A spike of pain hit the top of her head as the stench of sulphur permeated her every pore. Her stomach roiled with nausea, draining her further. She watched helplessly as he drew his arm back, claws ready to shred her throat.

Something struck Farouk and he lurched backward, releasing Fate from his deadly thrall. Hitting the floor, he wrestled against a pronged wire stuck in his neck. Blue bolts of electricity pulsated over his coarse fur. Archie struggled to hold the gun and keep the trigger pulled, but Farouk's weight and flailing wrenched on the cable between them.

Knowing the spindly scientist would lose the battle; Fate rushed to his side, grabbed the taser gun and held the trigger firm. She had to keep the electricity going. It was the only thing keeping Farouk from dematerializing. "Brune, take your shot!" she yelled.

Brune aimed her laser gun at his chest, this time scorching a line in Farouk's fur before holding it steady to sear an ever-expanding hole quickly becoming lethal.

Farouk's howl reverberated off the walls, chilling Fate to the marrow. But for the first time since dealing with the devious demon, she swelled with confidence. She could finally cross this one off her long list of enemies.

Farouk stopped struggling and fell still, but Fate kept the electricity going while Brune continued firing. The stink of burnt fur and charcoaled meat drifted off his carcass. When at last the red-hot glow in his eyes dimmed to black, Fate took her finger off the trigger. "I think it's safe to say we can stop beating this dead horse."

"We can't trust anything when it comes to Farouk," Brune argued.

Fate waved a hand in front of her face. "Please stop frying him, the smell could gag a maggot."

Brune's hand shook as she holstered her laser gun. Fate noticed a trace of sadness in her tired expression.

"You're not actually upset about this, are you?" Fate asked.

Brune frowned at the demon. "He was my only friend for most of my life. I'd hoped to get him back into his cage before it came down to this."

Gerdie raced across the room and kicked Brune in the shin. "You killed Boo! I hate you!"

Brune opened her mouth to speak, but instead, shook her head and walked in the direction of the barracks. There was a drag in her step Fate had never seen before.

Eustace trailed in behind Gerdie and kneeled next to her. "Don't blame Brune. She did what was necessary to protect us."

Gerdie stomped her little foot. "Boo was a friend. He wouldn't have hurt anybody."

"Didn't you see how he attacked me?" Fate asked.

Gerdie's bottom lip trembled. "All I saw was you swinging your sword at Boo."

"I suppose you could see it that way. But Boo–I mean Farouk–was threatening to kill Eustace."

Gerdie looked at Eustace, who was obviously stunned by this new piece of information.

"I couldn't let that happen," Fate continued. "You wouldn't want to see anything bad happen to Eustace, would you Gerdie?"

Gerdie sidled in closer to Eustace and took his hand. "No, I don't want Eustace to be hurt." Her voice had grown small and worried.

Eustace cleared his throat. "Fate, is that why you've been so on edge lately?"

She nodded. "I'm certain Farouk caused that nightmare I had earlier. He planted absolute terror in me so I'd seem crazy to the rest of you, and he somehow orchestrated the same events of the nightmare all over again. Dad, I thought for sure I was going to lose you–" She choked on the painful lump in her throat.

Eustace stood and held out both arms. "Doodles, you know I'll always be h–" The air punched from his lungs as a look of pained surprise froze on her father's face. "Oh dear," he gasped.

Fate stopped breathing. Time stopped as she watched Eustace lift off his feet and float in the air. She didn't know what she was seeing, until the moment Farouk rose from the floor, his barbed tail impaled into her father's spine. In one swift move the demon jerked his tail free and vanished, leaving Eustace to drop lifeless to the floor.

30
DESECRATION

GRYSLA SCALED THE SHEER, rocky terrain of Mount Helgunth with relative ease. Finn felt a bit sheepish that the tree troll was doing all the work. His only concern at the moment was to not fall off her shoulder, which gave him plenty of time to turn his mind to Fate.

My bonnie bride.

Finn spoke the words out loud. He smiled, despite the glacial winds battering them from all sides, as if to thwart their progress. But he hardly noticed the bitter cold. The remembrance of his recent union with Fate consumed his thoughts.

He closed his eyes, conjuring that moment in the garden when he'd laid her down, his imagination so rich, he felt the warmth of her breath fanning his skin, the heat of her lips on his mouth. Her face flashed bright in his mind, both devilish and angelic as she gazed back, her wild curls spilling over the green moss like flames. A hot, sweet ache burned at his core.

A thunderous clap resounded through the mountainous terrain, jolting Finn from his daydream.

"What's wrong?" he asked when Grysla stumbled.

The rumbling avalanche of rocks crashing toward them answered his question.

Grysla did her best to fend the boulders off, the force of which threw Finn off her shoulder. She fought to keep them both from being buried, but the barrage of rocks barreled at them too hard and fast.

Calling upon the Elder race runes, Finn invoked Earth, as did Grysla. The ancestral power of the giants of old exploded inside his chest. The heat rushed up his throat. Red-gold micro-sparks poured from his mouth and flew on the wind.

Finn and Grysla's voices boomed and echoed against the mountainside, a deep, unified sound that drowned out the roaring winds and crashing rock, and spoke to the ground beneath them. The earth quaked in answer as massive slabs of granite broke through the earth's crust in front of them, forming a protective wall.

The avalanche slammed into the barrier with ear-splitting cracks and force. Could the wall even hold the sheer volume and weight? Rocks spilled over the tops of the granite slabs, raining boulders down upon them. Grysla bent over Finn, taking the full brunt of the rocky onslaught.

At last, the deafening sound of the avalanche faded, leaving only the shriek of the snowstorm, but this time Finn felt the bitter cold carried within them. He tensed against a convulsion of shivers. Either he'd lost his preternatural resilience to extreme weather the Elder race runes endowed him with, or the temperature had suddenly dropped dramatically. He hoped it was the latter.

Grysla straightened, her large craggy head turning from side to side. Many of the branches growing from her crown hung in shredded pieces. Worse yet, a rapid spread of hoarfrost crystallized over her tough wooden hide. When she spoke, Finn barely heard her usually resonant, gruff voice. "This is the work of frost giants. You must–" Her stiff movements halted and she stood as still as stone.

Frozen.

Shaking uncontrollably now, Finn spoke the Elder race rune for Air. The rune's power roared from deep inside. A hurricane of wind answered his call, sweeping around him and Grysla, forming a wall of churning air. As he stood within the calm eye of the storm, Finn recognized the blizzard for what it truly was. The North winds carried malevolent spirits upon their violent currents. The snow flurries congealed into distorted, snarling faces, their teeth gnashing, claws raking against his air-bound shield. He could only surmise the frost giants had combined black magic with their rune powers, something Grysla would never do.

While his air shield had effectively cut the arctic wind-chill, the temperature remained at subzero levels. With his teeth chattering and a slur in his speech, Finn called upon Fire, the one element Grysla feared and refused to use with any greater force than to light a small campfire. The power ignited in his chest in an explosion of welcome heat and spread throughout his limbs. Fiery embers surged from his mouth as he commanded the element to fill the frigid air container.

Currents of warmth flooded in around them, melting the coat of frost covering Grysla. The tree troll broke free of her rigid stance and smiled down at him gratefully.

He gave her a relieved smile. "Welcome back, my friend."

She nodded, though her gentle expression turned grave when she noticed the evil spirits present within the raging storm.

"Aye, I was every bit as surprised to see black magic being used with the rune powers. I suppose that means any attempt at negotiations will be useless."

Grysla kneeled and placed a hand on the ground. Her fingers grew longer and dug deep beneath the snow into the soil. Tilting her head to one side, she stared off in the distance. Moments later, she withdrew her hand and stood. "The rock giants are clean. There is no darkness here in this mountain, only a desire for peace. The evil lives in the North winds."

Finn frowned in confusion. "If the rock giants are peaceful, they have a nasty way of showing it. That land slide didn't happen on its own."

"They feel threatened by our presence."

"We haven't done anything to them. Though I'm mighty tempted to go on the offensive at this point."

Grysla snapped off the broken branches of her crown. "We cannot attack. We must demonstrate our peaceful mission through submission."

"I was afraid you were going to say that."

Grysla gestured the sign of running water. "Be like water. Flow where the land takes you."

"I take it that means we keep climbing."

The tree troll nodded and offered her shoulder.

"Thanks, but I'll reach the peak on my own two feet. I wouldn't want the rock giants mistaking me for a lazy or superior-minded human who uses giants for his own selfish needs."

Grysla agreed, gesturing for him to walk in front of her. Finn held the elements of Air and Fire in place as they made their ascent. The storm hammered at them with a growing ferocity. Baleful shrieks issued from the swarming spirits as they worked to hinder all visibility. Luckily, his air shield held, though not without effort. When Grysla realized he was tiring, she too called on Air and layered her own barrier of wind around them, allowing him to drop his. Renewed strength pumped through his fatigued limbs as he focused only on keeping them warm.

At last they came to a level area just below the peak of Mount Helgunth. Through the monstrous faces thrashing in the snowstorm, Finn made out the towering craggy tips of what appeared to be a castle carved from the rock. Dark holes blurred in and out of focus, presumably windows set within recessed terraces.

Grysla pointed off to one side of the megalithic structure. "Enter there."

"Without knocking?" he asked.

"They are expecting us."

Finn didn't move. "When did you get to be on speaking terms

with them?"

Grysla shook her head. "No words. Only feelings."

"Yours, or theirs?"

Grysla shrugged.

Finn sighed and walked in the direction she wanted him to go. As they drew closer, the furious tempest waned and with it the sinister faces in the lashing snow vanished, as well as their howling shrieks of anger. Grysla released the element of Air with a word of gratitude for the protection they had enjoyed. As the air shield receded, the storm calmed to mild gusts. The snow flurries thinned, drawing back the veil of blindness they'd been forced to navigate through.

Finn thanked Fire for warming them and released the element. The air that rushed in was icy, but not the deadly arctic gale they'd managed to escape.

Grysla stepped toward the entrance and signaled Finn to follow. He glanced around, searching for any sign of the rock giants. There were none. What he did see, were the Elder race runes carved into almost every surface in sight, many of which he did not recognize. He decided the unfamiliar runes were most likely wards against the frost giants' North winds. A further mystery, since Finn had assumed the rock giants and the frost giants were allied in their war against Beldereth.

As soon as Finn and Grysla passed through the threshold of the massive opening, the sound of rock cracking against rock echoed behind them. They turned in alarm as the surrounding terrain shifted and moved. Enormous chunks of rock broke away from the castle walls, while what seemed were huge piles of boulders rose from the ground to form huge figures of stone now towering over them.

Finn was in awe at the sight of them. These were not giants. These were titans. Even the shortest of them made Grysla appear small. Composed entirely of irregular pieces of stone and covered in carvings of the Elder race runes, the rock giants loomed over them with hard, glowering faces.

Finn edged closer to Grysla. "What do we do now?"

Grysla made the sign for silence as she arched her back to stare back at the giants. Adrenaline streaked along Finn's spine. The tree troll was frightened, something he'd never seen before, unless it involved fire. But then again, Grysla was entirely unfamiliar with being the smallest in a crowd. He did his best to not think about how easily they could be crushed into the ground.

Grysla scribed a series of runes in the air, a message of peaceful intentions with a humble request to be granted the opportunity to explain why they had so boldly trespassed onto their mountain.

The rock giants continued to stare down at them. The seconds ticked by without response, a torturous wait that built to an unbearable air of tension. Then one of the rock giants made a long, drawn out sound, musical in nature, though low and gravelly. The other giants joined in, each answering in the same way but in varying octaves.

Their combined voices reverberated through the ground, a sensation Finn felt in the soles of his feet and up the length of his legs and spine. When the vibration hit his brain, sparks filled his vision, along with a kaleidoscope of images, which formed words in his mind.

You may speak with our queen. Upon passing the test.

The giants brought their sonorous hums to an end and gestured for Finn and Grysla to enter their domain. Darkness swallowed them as they walked deep inside with the echoes of rumbling footsteps bringing up the rear.

Unable to see anything, Finn squinted into the black while wondering what sort of test they would be facing. He didn't have to wait long for his answer. Rays of light sifted in to reveal a cavernous space so vast it seemed to stretch on forever. Grysla was no longer beside him. He turned in circles, searching for her, but she was nowhere in sight.

There was only one rock giant remaining. The others had vanished along with Grysla. Before Finn could sign the question of where his friend was, the giant hummed, sending a message through the earth to let him know the tree troll was being tested and that he would be next.

While this did nothing to ease his concerns, Finn settled down at least enough to take a breath and look around. Several miles across from where he stood, a waterfall cascaded its frothy waters into a lake, which narrowed into a river. Off in the distance, an ethereal golden light poured from the center of the cavern, shimmering sparks over the blue water. The source wasn't sunlight, but it was every bit as bright and powerful. Gigantic bridges, crude in design, crossed the lake, while massive staircases spiraled upward to parts unknown. Most everything else in the cavern appeared to be natural formations, that of stalactites dripping from above, some of which formed majestic stalagmite pillars connecting the cave floor with the arched ceiling. It was plain to see the giants respected what nature had already put in place by how very little they had changed the cavern's landscape.

The giant interrupted Finn's observations to inform him it was time for the test and directed him along a wide path. The path turned in a downward spiral, a familiar pattern commonly used by all species of giants. They revered the spiral as sacred because it appears everywhere in nature, from shells of the tiniest sea creatures, up to the biggest hurricanes and even further out to the spinning of galaxies.

The smell of wet rock grew stronger as they continued down the path, a trek seemingly without end. After what felt like an hour of walking, the path leveled out and opened into a sweeping cavern. A still pool filled the whole of the cathedral-like space. Rising from the center of the water was a colossal, crystalline tower, its brilliant light casting golden hues over the rough walls and surrounding stalagmite pillars. The sight took Finn's breath away with its sheer beauty.

He looked up at his escort. "What is this place?"

The rock giant hummed a cryptic answer, a sound, which quaked throughout the cavern, rippling the water. *This is your test.*

Finn was at a loss. "What am I supposed to do?"

The rock giant receded toward the path they had come. When Finn tried to follow, he was directed to stay where he was. He wondered how Grysla had fared with the test. Had she passed? He could only hope as much. It wouldn't do if they'd come all this way just to fail in their mission. It was paramount he pass this mysterious test. But he needed to know more about this place and there was only one way to do that. Bending, he placed his hand on the cold rock and pushed his senses into the earth.

His connection to the Earthmind was instantaneous, a familiar link which pulled his awareness deep underground, where all was peaceful. The sheer enormity of the mountain's earth energy overtook him, dwarfing all human concerns as he drifted toward the heart of that greater existence he had once been a part of.

Finn's awareness expanded, flowing beyond the base of the mountain, joining with the heartbeat of the land, extending all the way to the steady thrum of the ocean. The immense sentient power of the mountain reined him in, drawing his questing spirit back, directing him to its vast network of crystal caves, all of which converged at the base of the crystal tower he'd seen at the center of the still pool.

Musical notes rang from the massive store of crystals, singing stories of dead giants whose bones of rock had transformed into these crystalline records buried deep beneath the mountain. Riding the harmonic currents, Finn reached the core of the tower, where suddenly, harsh chords rang out of tune. He wanted to escape the discordant sounds, but he held his awareness there while searching for the cause.

Then he saw it. The massive crystals were pocked with great, jagged gouges. Invasive tunnels ran throughout the mountain. Made by trespassers, there to steal what was sacred to the rock giants, and in doing so, had damaged the very spine of the mountain. Part of the mantle had collapsed at the base. Any further desecration to their burial grounds would bring the whole of the mountain down.

Finn broke his connection to the mountain and stood with a lingering sense of sorrow. The giant emerged from the darkness and Finn signed what he'd learned.

The rock giant gave him a solemn nod and beckoned Finn away from the pool while humming a resonant invitation to meet with the queen. As he followed his escort back up the spiraling path, Finn's thoughts raced. Was this Beldereth's doing? He'd seen statues carved from this very same crystal at the castle. There was no mistaking its color, a golden citrine shot through with veins of carnelian red. Rudwor had called it Gofannon's meldachite, a highly prized crystal used to fortify the metals in weapons and armor. The king prided himself on how his army's swords were unbreakable, and their armor impenetrable.

Anger burned in Finn's chest. How could Rudwor sanction the mining of a burial ground for his kingdom's gain? Yet, his friend had seemed genuinely mystified by the long-standing feud between Beldereth and the rock giants. More than likely the mining had been going on long before Rudwor ever became king.

Finn increased his pace to keep up with the giant's long strides when it suddenly occurred to him Beldereth probably wasn't doing the mining. The dwarves of the Brynmoor Highlands were well known for their mines. They were also the best metal workers in the region. If memory served right, they supplied Beldereth's armory. Not that the rock giants would care if the kingdom wasn't directly involved in the desecration of their burial grounds. Whosoever held possession of the crystal would be considered an enemy.

Finn's spirits grew heavy. How was he supposed to negotiate a truce if Beldereth appeared every bit as guilty as those greedy dwarves? Defeat put a drag in his footsteps and he fell behind. He hadn't expected yet another layer of complications. This was only the first leg of his mission. How many more problems would he encounter?

For the first time since leaving Fate, he found it hard to see his way back to her.

31
THE ROCK QUEEN

FINN WAS SO DEEP in thought during the lengthy trek back up the spiraling path, time passed faster than before. He glanced around in surprise at the thundering sound of the waterfall in the main cavern. His escort beckoned him across a bridge toward a cavern gleaming with warm light. They passed through the enormous threshold and came to a long set of stairs snaking around a high tower.

His guide traversed the stairs one step at a time. In contrast, Finn had to hoist himself up each step and jog the length to the next one. He stopped after a time to estimate how many more he had to traverse. There were at least ten more tiers of stairs to the top. Clenching his jaw, he pushed on, wishing he still possessed the power to fly.

When at last he reached the top, his escort and several other rock giants stood waiting patiently outside a towering stone henge, its center filled with blinding golden light. Grysla was there too. She smiled and signed her joy at seeing he was safe.

Happy to see his friend, Finn stepped in beside her. "I take it you passed the test too."

The tree troll nodded.

"Do you know what's next? I thought we'd be meeting the–"

Grysla shushed him and made the sign for a crown, indicating the queen was inside the circle.

Pressing his lips tight, he bowed his head slightly to show respect.

The rock giant standing next to Grysla stooped to look at them and hummed instructions to enter the ring of standing stones. Finn squinted against the brilliant light radiating from the center of the henge as he strode forward with Grysla at his side. The deeper they moved into the light the more blinding it became, making his eyes water. They continued on in spite of their inability to see, when suddenly they stepped, as if through a door, into a softly gleaming space.

Sitting on a massive stone throne–plain in design and covered in a mossy cushion–was a giant unlike any of the previous rock giants. This one was the color of sun-kissed clay. The rounded, feminine curves were smooth and polished like glazed pottery. Finn wondered if the rock giant queen might have been the inspiration behind the Neolithic mother deities he'd seen in history books. Though she was not faceless like those ancient statues. Wise, slanted eyes stared from beneath a broad forehead. The nose was wide, anchored by a full mouth curved in a gentle smile.

Finn found himself smiling back as he gazed at the queen.

She tilted her head and her eyes, composed of glinting onyx, focused on him. For the beat of one second, he thought she would hum a message the way the other rock giants had. Instead, her large belly lit with the same golden light he'd seen from the bottom of the tower. The internal glow revealed the striations of warmly colored feldspar crystal with every conceivable Elder race rune embedded within. The light pulsed down her generously rounded legs, the ends covered in mounds of rough crystal, which had grown and spread over the whole of the tower's stone platform. The queen was encrusted to the base of her throne, not mobile like her kingdom of rock giants, but Finn suspected her connection to the mountain was all encompassing.

His suspicions were confirmed the instant the light traveled across the crystalline slate to where he and Grysla stood. Vibrations drummed through the soles of his feet and shot to the top of his brain with a fleeting high-pitched ring.

The queen's sonorous voice filled Finn's head with the universal language of giants as she continued to fix her gaze on him. "*You are unlike the humans we call enemies. The Elder race runes have blessed you with our speech and voice.*"

Finn nodded and started to speak, but the queen continued.

"*Had you failed the test, you would be dead.*" Her face remained smooth and peaceful, an incongruous sight to her frightening words.

Finn swallowed. He'd been so focused in his overall mission it never occurred to him his very life had been hanging in the balance.

The queen's gaze shifted to Grysla. "*You risked much by gifting the runes to a human. We could have you put to death for such an act.*"

Grysla hung her head.

"*You are forgiven. This human has shown to be worthy of the gift. You may now speak of the reason for your trespass.*"

Finn breathed easier as Grysla indicated with a quick gesture that she would be the one to explain their mission. The tree troll did this with mostly sign language and minimal speech, her arms swaying gracefully like branches in the wind as she communicated Finn's desire to negotiate peace between the rock giants and the king of Beldereth.

The queen listened with the same unsettling, placid expression.

When Grysla was done, the giant remained quiet for an uncomfortable amount of time. Her answer finally sliced through the tension and was not what Finn had hoped to hear. "*As long as these thieves steal from the bones of our ancestors, war will continue.*"

Finn took a step forward, much to the obvious distress displayed in the darkening color of Grysla's eyes. "I say this with the deepest respect, but your actions have caused much suffering in Beldereth. Innocent families are close to starving."

"*Humans are the reason we had to leave our wide open ranges and recede into the confines of this mountain. Humans are why our numbers have dwindled. Humans have no respect for the earth and her bounties. It is clear they will never appreciate the gifts they receive until they lose them.*" The anger in the queen's words was not reflected in her gentle visage, something that troubled Finn. She was impossible to read, whereas he had to guard his thoughts against the telepathic connection she'd bound them within.

"I understand why you feel the need to teach them a lesson, but to what end?" Finn argued. "All you've done is breed contempt in their hearts. They think your kind are bent on wiping them from the face of the planet. There are no lessons to be learned here. Only more hatred and fighting."

The queen sat as still as the stone she was made of. When she didn't reply, he continued. "The king of Beldereth is willing to speak with you about a truce. Will you agree to meeting with him?"

"*Not when his people continue to invade our sacred tombs and the very life source of our mountain.*"

"Beldereth is not the one drilling holes in your mountain," Finn pressed. "You can look to the Brynmoor dwarves for that."

"*The Beldereth soldiers dress in armor made with the bones of giants who once ruled this land with benevolence toward humans.*"

This was the stalemate Finn had feared. His hands curled into fists as he fought to contain his frustration. "This is true, but I can honestly say I don't think they know the actual source of the crystals used to make their weapons and their armor invincible. They call the crystal Gofannon's meldachite, after the dwarf who discovered its metal strengthening properties. Once again, the dwarves are the ones you should be at war with. Not Beldereth."

"*We waged war on the dwarves long ago, centuries longer than our fight with Beldereth,*" she replied. "*But they are like the vermin you humans detest. Dwarves know how to chew through rock with ease and burrow deep, where we cannot go.*"

Finn glanced at Grysla, hoping she might have something helpful to add.

The tree troll lifted her arms and shrugged. He sighed. "I didn't know. I can't say as I blame you for wanting to halt the demand for more crystal."

"*The dwarves will not stop until they have destroyed this mountain and what little is left of us. Even if the demand ended, there is no end to their greed.*"

Finn looked at the queen in defeat. "I don't know what else to say... " He trailed off, wondering how he and Grysla would exit themselves without incident.

"*You may leave unharmed,*" the queen said in answer to his question.

Finn bit down on his disappointment as he moved to leave. He'd failed. All was lost without Rudwor to help him build the alliances they needed to defeat Kaliena's army. His thoughts raced haphazardly as he grasped for something. Anything to keep from walking away empty handed.

Grysla was already leaving. Finn moved to join her when the inkling of a solution broke through the jumble in his mind. He stopped and faced the queen again. It was a long shot, but any idea–regardless of how crazy–was better than giving up. "What would you say to joining forces with Beldereth against the dwarves to stop the mining?"

The queen leaned forward in her throne, the only indication of a reaction beyond her unperturbed expression. Finn's heart pounded out the seconds as she stared back. Then she tilted back into her usual repose and he worried she'd decided against his offer.

"*Tell your king,*" she said at last, before pausing for yet another excruciatingly eternal second, "*we are agreeable.*"

Finn relaxed somewhat. "I'm mighty pleased to hear it, though the king will need a show of good faith before he'll agree. I think the best place to start is to have the frost giants end this super storm."

"*That, we cannot do.*"

All the air went out of Finn's lungs. "What? Why?"

"*This land belongs to the frost giants now. Desperation drove us to do something we once swore would never happen. We handed our territory over in exchange for cursing Beldereth with an endless winter and building a wall of ice around Brynmoor Highlands, though this has not kept the dwarves sealed inside their under-ground cities. They have found ways to continue raiding our burial grounds.*"

Anger boiled beneath Finn's skin as he narrowed his eyes on the queen. "Are you aware of the evil presence in the North winds?"

"*We are.*"

"Yet, you allow this darkness to spread across the land? This goes against everything the Elder race runes stand for. You need to banish them back to the North!"

Grysla gestured for him to tread carefully.

"*We honor our agreements,*" the queen replied.

"Even when it poisons everything around you?"

"*We did not know the frost giant king walks the black path until after the pact. It cannot be undone.*"

"I can undo it." The words were out before Finn even gave himself a chance to think about how such a feat would be accomplished.

The queen's expression remained undisturbed, though her dark, gem stone eyes widened ever so slightly. "*I cannot hear you on this matter, though you are free to do what you wish.*"

Finn accepted this roundabout permission she'd given him by bowing his head. "Aye, I understand."

A slab of crystal, as tall as Finn, broke away from the surface near the base of the queen's throne. It was filled from top to bottom with runes. "*Deliver this treaty to your king. I will know he has accepted the agreement when he places his heart hand on the crystal.*"

Grysla stepped over to the slab and picked it up.

Finn clenched his teeth and nodded. While this wasn't exactly what he needed to bring about an immediate truce between the rock giants and Beldereth, the treaty was at least a step in the right direction. He gestured a respectful farewell to the queen and turned on his heel to leave.

But he wouldn't be going back to Beldereth yet. The treaty would not be enough to convince Rudwor to lay down arms. He would first need to show evidence of the rock giants' intentions for peace. So instead, he would be heading North, where he would have to face the evil king of the frost giants.

32
What It Means to Fight a God

FATE STARED, UNCOMPREHENDING, INTO Eustace's eyes. They were the color of slate–flecked with warm olive and gold tones–forever wise, caring and always inquisitive. For as long as she could remember, whenever she'd looked into them, the world became a safe place.

But not now.

He couldn't see her.

She crawled across the floor for his fallen glasses. The hard-ness of the floor bit into her knees as she moved back beside him and placed them on his nose, gently hooking them behind his ears. Then she stroked a messy tumble of silvery bangs off his forehead, careful to brush each strand neatly into place. She straightened his tie and smoothed down the front of his sweater vest.

Sitting back to look at him, she hugged her legs to her chest, avoiding the red pool soaking into the back of his tan blazer. She was numb all over, and she clung to that numbness with all her spirit to keep from accepting what she refused to believe.

Eustace was fine, merely stunned. He'd stir any minute now, turn his head and tell her not to worry. He was her tall pillar of strength. That's who he was.

A torrent of childhood memories crashed in: *Riding on his shoulders and feeling like a giant. The same nightly bedtime stories until they could both recite her books word for word. His fumbling fingers and the clumsy braids she wore until she grew old enough to do her own hair. The sparkly polish he used to let her paint on his nails. The goodbye nose kisses they gave each other everytime he delivered her safely into the hands of her teachers.*

Eustace's face swam behind a rise of tears. She squeezed her eyes shut to hold them back. "This isn't real," she whispered. This was another nightmare, one of those terrifying dreams she couldn't wake from. She needed to concentrate, find a way out.

She swallowed down the sick feeling spreading through her stomach. "Wake up," she choked. Her voice sounded muffled and distant behind the blood pounding in her ears.

A far-off voice said something and Fate looked up to find others close by. Gerdie was sobbing into her hands. Brune stood over her sister with hands resting on her little shoulders, a dismal stare in her eyes. Archie blinked dolefully as he teetered in place. Darcy inched forward, her face furrowed with concern.

"Did you hear what I said?" Darcy asked. "You're not asleep."

Fate focused on Darcy's oily, unkempt hair and laughed–a high-pitched hysterical sound that jangled her nerves. "Now I know this is a nightmare if you're in the dream." She forced her deadened legs to move and rose from the floor. She staggered and her stomach tightened into sick knots.

Darcy didn't take the usual offense. The concern in her stormy blue eyes only deepened. "I know what you're feeling. I know how much it hurts, Fate. I'm here if you need to–"

"What are you talking about?" Fate screamed, more against the thing clawing at her insides than at Darcy. She couldn't let it out. It would kill her. "Eustace is fine! He'll get up, you'll see!"

Darcy shook her head. "No he won't. You have to accept it. *He's gone.*"

Those words were the sharp claws Fate had been hiding from. Her heart hammered like it would break her ribcage. Blood throbbed inside her skull. Her head was ready to explode. Grabbing at her pounding temples, she glared at Brune. "Tell her to stop talking like that!"

Brune's expression softened and her eyes watered. "I wish I could... but, I can't."

Agony tore into Fate, shredding her heart into raw strips, a tearing pain unlike anything she'd ever experienced.

It was too much. Too big. Too strong. It was killing her.

"*NOOOO!*" An unnatural, thunderous shriek rang through the chamber, wild and guttural such as Fate had thought herself incapable of making. The others edged away from her with fear on their faces.

A mass of fury churned in Fate's belly, scorching her insides. She glanced down at her waist. The corset glowed crimson beneath her shirt. Lifting the bottom of her top, she touched her abdomen, where the corset's intricate design blazed through the skin in interlocking shapes of serpents and birds of prey. Intense heat coursed along her veins, spidering over her chest, racing like wildfire up her neck and into her face.

The fire in her blood raged to her brain, blinding her with visions of the old god, Ares. Eyes of radiant light blazed from within a gleaming helmet of gold as the god of war looked down on a battlefield. The cries of both the fallen and victorious carried above the deafening clash of swords and shields.

They fought in a swamp of blood like worms at the Olympian's feet. Fate felt the god's insatiable appetite for war and slaughter as if it was her own.

In that moment, she surrendered to the thunderous power, utterly and completely. A thirst for destruction and violence washed over all personal cares and concerns. A hunger for battle thrummed through her bloodstream, dissolving all fear, dread and hesitation. Savage hatred flooded over the unbearable pain of loss and sorrow, filling her limbs with unbridled strength, elevating her senses beyond all human limitations. Through the eyes of Ares, she saw everything for what it truly was. Expendable. Trivial. Inconsequential.

Nothing else mattered but the glorious strife created by war.

Fate summoned the very atoms around her, an instinctive command, to coalesce and form into the invincible armor of Ares. As she waited the few seconds it took for the golden armor to mold around her like a malleable second skin, she pushed her heightened awareness outward, searching for the red-eyed demon–its kind an age-old nemesis of the gods.

Barriers flew in place the instant she probed the Keep's depths for the fell creature, like false shadows thrown to avert her gaze. The elusive beast was far craftier than she expected.

Rage blazed in her belly as she breathed in the lingering stench of its presence. If she couldn't unleash her might on the demon until it chose to reveal itself again, she would have to find something else worthy of her attention.

She scanned the Keep surface.

There.

A fleet of ships filled with vile things whose life force bore the signature of unnatural means–the product of witchcraft and the alchemy of men. Lowly beings led by a queen who thinks she deserves godhood.

She and her spawn would do.

Seeing through the layers of iron walls, Fate turned and strode in the direction of the fleet.

"Fate, stop! You can't just leave him here!"

Fate ignored the insignificant human and continued on, her attention on rearranging the atoms in the wall so she could move through them.

"Wait, maybe you can save Eustace with the elixir!" another human shouted. This voice was more forceful, filled with experienced authority.

Anguish ripped through the ferocity churning in Fate's core. The disruption was fleeting, but enough to hold her there with a modicum of curiosity. She turned to look at the human who'd spoken–a female, strong of jaw with sharp, cunning eyes. A soldier. "Tell me of this elixir,"

Fate demanded.

The soldier stepped around a weakling child, pushing it toward another female who also happened to be there. "Kaliena has huge stores of the elixir of life," the soldier explained. "She's been harvesting hundreds of thousands of dead soldiers from derelict ships and using the elixir to build an army."

A blue-skinned being with many arms flashed in Fate's mind. *Kaliena.* She welcomed the rush of exquisite hatred the momentary image incited. The desire for utter destruction pumped in her veins. She would decimate Kaliena's abhorrent, undead army and destroy every drop of this elixir she was abusing.

For a split second, Fate considered striking down the humans in the room, but her desire for a real battle had her racing through the walls. Upon phasing through the outer wall of the sanctuary, she leaped into the Keep's expanse and rose to where one of the gargantuan rings spun in rotation. The forcefield protecting the atmosphere was visibly weak, the air thin, though not a problem for Fate.

Down below, legions of ships littered the sky in numbers too great to count. Fate's pulse raced, her heart pounding like a war drum. The urge to rain holy hell upon them coursed throughout her being, but she held her position. While she relished the battle ahead, she wanted even more to win. To do that she needed to pull this spreading weed from the roots, which meant first destroying Kaliena's supply of elixir.

Closing her eyes, Fate cast a wide net with her senses, probing the Keep's surface and its depths for large stores of the life-giving elixir. A bright, blue-green light filled her vision the instant her awareness skimmed over it. The basin of a coliseum, a hundred times bigger than the one in ancient Rome, had been dug out and filled with the luminescent, aquamarine waters of the elixir. The cool scent of rain carried on the negative ions lifted off the surface of the immense well. She welcomed the purifying air in her lungs and on her skin.

When Fate opened her eyes, she was standing on the edge of the great pool. She bent to scoop the sparkling liquid. Taking a sip, she swallowed the sweet elixir, feeling her cells enlivened throughout her entire body. She stood and flicked the water off her hand. It seemed a shame to destroy such a precious resource. Not that she would ever need the elixir with her regenerative powers. All the same, this was the weapon of a formidable enemy. The elixir must be destroyed.

Drawing her sword, she willed the fire of disease and death to come forth. The blade ignited with black flames. She stepped to the very edge and dipped the sword's point into the water, watching as the dark fire spread across the surface of the clear, shining blue water like an oil slick.

Something hard and sharp rammed into Fate, dumping her headlong into the infected pool. The weight of her armor dragged her to the bottom. Darkness swarmed in around her, pressing against her power with a force of its own. She was trapped within the gloom of death and the paralyzing fear that came with it.

Fate shoved off the floor of the pool, expecting to launch skyward and explode through the surface, but her superhuman strength was eroding at a rapid speed. If she didn't escape, she would die like any mortal.

With her lungs screaming for air, she turned from side to side in a frenzy, searching for a way out. Deep within the murk, she saw lingering glints of aquamarine light spidering out, like veins of gold. She pushed toward the light, her efforts slowed by the press of water, the weight of her armor and sapped limbs.

She reached one of the thin ribbons of light, clawing at the elixir in such a panic she flooded its purity with darkness. Precious air escaped from her mouth as she cried out in anger and pushed toward the next thread of light. She slowed when she got there, but she was unable to hold her breath any longer. The bubbles pushed the elixir away from her lips, above her head.

Knowing she would draw breath at any second and flood her lungs with the diseased water, she cupped the life-giving light in her palms, guiding it to her mouth. Slowly, carefully. In one painful gasp, she sucked the liquid into her mouth, not sure if it was life or death she'd swallowed.

Vitality surged through her veins, restoring her strength. Fate pushed off the bottom, tore through the gloom and burst free. Dripping with fetid, black ooze, she hovered above the pool, looking down on the last glinting specks of elixir with a sting of regret that confused her. Something deep inside wept for its loss.

She shook it off. There were more pressing matters to attend to than some nameless sorrow. Her attacker could still be nearby.

She no sooner had the thought when a dark blur came out of nowhere and slammed into her. Fate hit the tier lowest to the pool, her back cracking on stone. Ignoring the biting pain, she twisted to the right, avoiding the iron fist that came hammering down. She swung her leg around, driving the heel of her boot hard enough to send her attacker flying back.

Fate stood, her gaze locked on her opponent, who'd crashed into the top tiers of the coliseum, crushing stone to rubble on impact. She detected the presence of a human encased within the steel armor, enhanced with ensorcelled machinery. She sensed a warrior spirit akin to her own, but the human's mind was trapped within a sleeping spell to allow an outside controlling force to take over. The blue-green halo the suit emitted could only be Kaliena's energy signature.

The warrior rose and hung suspended in the air, arms raised as the suit's mechanisms shifted, becoming a new shape. Light burst from the ends. Rays of energy drilled across the space between them.

The hot slice of one of the beams pierced Fate's armor, slicing into her arm. Angered by the burning pain, Fate evaded the onslaught by rocketing straight up. She held at the apex for a heartbeat, then dove toward the warrior, gauntlets curled into fists.

Fate smashed the warrior into the ground with such force the stone pulverized into a cloud of dust. And she didn't stop there. She punched the warrior's head deep into the rock again and again, until the warrior fell lifeless and the energetic halo surrounding the suit died out.

Satisfied the warrior no longer posed a threat, Fate lifted off and summoned her sword from the bottom of the pool. Its blade stabbed through the black murk and rose to her hand, clean and shimmering. Climbing higher, she scanned the expanse for Kaliena's army.

The fleet of ships blotted out the horizon.

Gripping her sword, she raced toward Kaliena's armada, landing on one of the airships floating on the outer edge of the fleet. Lighting her sword with the fire of destruction, she slashed the balloon beneath her feet, vaulting to the next ship as the first exploded into a ball of flames and plummeted to the surface. She did this over and over, delighting in the ruination of each vessel. Upon slicing her way through more than a dozen ships, Fate hovered above the debris, listening to the dying howls and shrieks of the undead trapped inside the burning wreckage.

But this gratifying moment of distraction cost her.

Ensorcelled fire smashed into her backside with such force she catapulted across the expanse. Gasping for air as she tumbled head over heel, Fate slammed into the side of a tower, crashing to its base before she could right herself.

The fall hurt, but not enough to keep her from rising to her feet within seconds, shooting skyward in search of her attacker. Off in the distance a massive ship, bigger than any of the others, barreled forward. It was flanked on either side by enough ships to fill hundreds of miles. Sheathing her sword, Fate plunged straight at them, her gaze fixed on the lead ship's bow.

Kaliena's form came into view as she drew near. She could tell a sorcerer stood next to her by the crimson flames blazing from the tall staff he held and knew he was the one who'd blasted her out of the sky.

Fate slowed; ready to show them what it means to fight a god. The indwelling power housed within her solar plexus insisted on being used in full force. Balling her hands at her sides, she directed the building power into her fists and punched the energy outward. The air visibly buckled and wavered, rippling across the expanse, building in strength as it advanced.

The lead ship bucked, like a colossal wave had crashed over its hull, throwing its occupants off their feet. They slid across the deck, smacking hard against the sides. Using this small opening, Fate swooped in and landed on the bow, sword ready to take heads, but Kaliena's soldiers swarmed the deck from below, blocking her target.

Several of them fell victim to the blinding sweep of her fiery blade before even realizing she was there. Though this did not keep them down. They rose as if knocked back by a strong wind.

Kaliena and the sorcerer moved aside, allowing hundreds more to close in around Fate. She couldn't tell what they were behind their spiked armor, but the stench of their necrotic flesh was unmistakable. Unlike the warrior she'd fought, these *things* lacked substance. Reaching into the well of infinite knowledge she possessed, she focused in on the black mist curling through the cracks of their armor. These were wraiths–hostile spirits, which animated whatever corpse was inside the armor.

Necromancy was at work here, a purposeful alternative to the elixir–a wise contingency that made these particular soldiers impossible to kill. But the pent-up energy, coupled with the nameless anguish she'd buried, surged through Fate's limbs and would not be denied. Her hunger for battle was insatiable.

The circle of wraith soldiers tightened, every blade aimed to spear her from all angles.

Fate imagined a twin to the sword she held. Feeling the girth of the hilt form in her left hand, she tested the weight and balance of both swords together. They felt right.

Twisting to deflect a strike from the wraith closest to her, a thrill streaked through her when everything moving around her slowed. She suddenly existed on another plane, one that allowed her to watch the reduced movements of her opponents while she moved in between the spaces, faster than they could possibly comprehend.

She brought her swords down on them in sweeping arcs, her blades slicing through heavy armor like flimsy tinfoil, slashing through desiccated ribs as easily as shredding paper. Each wraith fell, dark smoke billowing from gaping holes –only to be sucked back inside to reanimate the corpse and make it rise again.

This was of no concern. Fate dashed between them, more of a ghost than the wraiths themselves, cutting them down at the knees, shearing off their rotting arms, immobilizing more and more of them as she pushed into the fray.

After awhile she grew bored with simply slowing them down and began severing heads, a solution that forced the wraiths to abandon the corpses they inhabited. She was ready to focus on Kaliena and her sorcerer.

Fate finished the slaughter within minutes of her decision to bring this part of the battle to an end. She rose above the deck, now piled high with squirming, dismembered body parts and fixed her gaze on Kaliena, who stood ready to fight with scimitars gripped in each of her six hands. The sorcerer next to her raised his staff, its scarlet flame growing bright as he prepared to fire on Fate.

Kaliena gestured for him to stand aside. She moved forward, a gait so smooth and light, her feet barely touched the floor, a fearlessness conveyed by the relentless pace in her step. Kaliena's expression remained as indecipherable as a statue carved from pale blue marble. Only her dark eyes darted, as if they alone were made of flesh.

The power inside Fate swelled, pumping a new surge of bloodlust through her veins, but this was different. Her whole body vibrated with a knowing. She could kill with a mere thought.

Fate resisted. Where was the satisfaction in that? She lived for the challenge of the fight and the satisfaction of seeing her opponent cut down. But an even stronger power refused to be dismissed. She could feel it reaching out with long, invisible fingers, which wrapped around Kaliena's neck.

Dropping one of her scimitars, Kaliena grabbed her throat, her eyes wide with shock. The sorcerer rushed to her side. When he couldn't help release her from the stranglehold, he aimed his staff at Fate and hurled a ball of fire.

Fate raised her hand to deflect the crimson flames, when a deafening boom reverberated throughout the expanse. A shock wave crashed into her, catapulting her backward, the impact vibrating bone-deep. She spun out of control, hurtling toward the outer rings. A net of electricity hissed and crackled between the colossal rings, scorching the air with the smell of ozone.

Beyond the rings, the vast sea of glinting stars stretched into blurred lines, caused by a vortex opening amidst them, spinning like a whirlpool, enlarging with each rotation. Fate watched in horror as its violet light spilled across the heavens, filling her line of sight. It was only when the stars vanished and all that was left was this churning, gaping maw of light did she fully realize what she was seeing.

A portal had opened, and the Keep was about to be swallowed whole.

33
DEATH IS A BRUTAL THING

FINN LEANED INTO THE blistering, glacial winds, unable to see more than a few feet ahead in the blinding snow. Thankfully, he knew how to fend off the deathly chill he'd suffered on Mount Helgunth. He called upon Fire to warm his core and supply his limbs with the life-giving heat he needed to keep moving.

The further he pushed into the North, the more grateful he was he'd convinced Grysla to travel back to the outlying region of Beldereth and hide until he returned to deliver the treaty to Rudwor. The tree troll's fear of using Fire would have been his friend's undoing. The closer to the frost giants' kingdom, the more concentrated the malevolent spirits in the winds became, dropping the temperatures to ungodly levels. The gruesome faces within the snowstorm formed startling flashes. A tactic designed to keep him from remaining focused on holding the Fire element steady within his mind.

He could only hope he reached the kingdom soon. He'd traveled a full day already over challenging terrain, and was exhausted. If he rested, he'd very likely fall asleep and lose his defenses altogether. In less extreme situations, he would've put wards down to shield him while he recharged, but that was impossible in these winds. The fine bone powder used in the wards would be blown away before it even touched the ground.

Finn pushed on, each step more laborious than the last on the uphill climb. As he crested the top of the rocky incline, the vicious spirits lashed at him with even greater force. They pressed in from all sides with a frenzied shrieking. He shuddered as they clawed through his shield of heat and he feared this might be the end of him.

Stumbling forward, Finn came to an abrupt halt, squinting through the snowstorm. Unless his eyes deceived him, a gargantuan castle lay in the valley below. The sharp points of countless towers pierced a heavy layer of gray clouds. A massive bridge connected the surrounding terrain to the castle entrance, its arches stretching into pillars cemented to the ice floor by frozen waterfalls that had once flowed freely between the columns.

Digging for the last of his strength, Finn half ran and half staggered toward the bridge, leaving the snowstorm and its nasty spirits further and further behind with each step. The air grew calm and devoid of snowfall. The temperature became tolerable again–downright balmy compared to what he'd escaped.

When Finn reached the bridge, he slowed to check for guards, scrutinizing two gigantic sentries flanking the entrance to ensure they were statues and not frost giants ready to spring to life. As far as he could tell, there was no sign of the giants themselves. Probably because there was no need for guards to be stationed outside. Who would be mental enough to journey into the freezing North to confront frost giants on their own turf?

"That would be you, boyo," Finn muttered through frozen lips.

Finding his legs again, he jogged along the bridge toward the entrance, his boots slipping over the ice as he progressed. The castle appeared to be made of stone like any other, though it was a solid white, covered in a translucent coat of sparkling frost, its terraces and windows dripping with icicles. There was a magical beauty in the iced structure that only winter could bestow.

He passed through the massive archway into a darkened hall and crept along until he reached a great hall the size of ten football fields. Rows of squared columns spanned the length, each engraved with Elder race runes, as well as Nordic runes. The ceiling curved incredibly high overhead, transparent as ice, with an ethereal light shining through. Snowflakes fluttered lazily from the frozen canopy, but disappeared halfway down their long spiraling descent, saving the stone floor from being covered in thick drifts of snow.

Growing more and more nervous by the absence of frost giants, Finn stayed within the darkness just outside the archway and reached out with his senses before going any further. The force of his own probing bounced back, setting him on edge. If he didn't know better, something, or someone was blocking him. He considered retreating, but the thought of leaving without accomplishing what he'd set out to do held him in place.

Finn walked into the hall, regardless of the alarms going off in his head. He hadn't taken more than a few steps, when the whole room burst to life with the movement of frost giants stepping out from behind the pillars.

Unlike the rock giants, these were more human looking, but only because they were not made of ice like Finn had expected them to be. The similarities to humans stopped at their colorless skin. Yellowed incisors curled over their top lips like the tusks of a boar. Braided snow-white beards encrusted with frost hung long over the bronze breastplates of their armor. Horned helmets curved over their foreheads, keeping their cold, pale blue eyes in shadow. They weren't anywhere near as large as rock giants, though twice the size of Grysla and fully capable of crushing him all the same.

A sharp, cutting voice echoed throughout the hall, speaking in the ancient language of the Elder race. "Announce yourself, trespasser."

Finn glanced from one grim face to the other to see who had spoken. A movement from the far end of the hall answered his question. He hadn't noticed the massive throne situated beneath the row of peaked windows along the far wall. A frost giant seated himself, commanding Finn to come forward with a curt gesture.

Finn cautiously strode the length of the hall, unnerved by the frost king's appearance. His armor was coated in ice, as was his face, which was black and half rotted as if from frostbite. Jagged shards of ice grew from his shoulders and crowned helmet. He was stiff, unable to move easily, like the ice slicked over him was more of a prison than a formation natural to his kind. But it was the king's eyes Finn found the most disturbing. They were blood red and rimmed in darkness, open windows of the evil harbored within the giant.

By all accounts, the king appeared to be possessed by a malevolent influence. It would explain why he didn't look like the other frost giants. None of the others were confined by an overgrowth of ice. Nor were their eyes clouded by wickedness.

"I am an emissary for the King of Beldereth and am here on a mission of peace," Finn declared in the Elder race language.

The frost king's expression remained stern and uncom-promising. "Beldereth is part of the North now and of no other significance to me."

"You've brought an endless winter to the kingdom. It's killing the people who live there," Finn pressed. "The North has no right to invade a kingdom that depends upon the natural course of seasons to survive."

"The North moves where I will it. Who are you to tell me of my right?"

Finn ignored the question. "I know about your alliance with the rock giants. They are willing to make peace with Beldereth, but before my king will sign the treaty, winter must first come to an end."

The frost king leaned forward with some effort. The ice coating his armor crackled, even as his face remained frozen in a forbidding scowl. "How is it a human speaks the language of giants?"

His red eyes narrowed on Finn, sparking bright with a sinister light. Pushing off the arms of his immense throne, the king rose with even greater difficulty, his iced armor cracking as chips of broken ice showered over the floor. "Take him to the tower."

The nearest frost giant bent and swiped Finn off the floor, his massive fingers tight around his torso as he strode out of the hall. They passed through several dim corridors before the giant ascended a flight of spiraling stairs. Finn strained futilely against the giant's grip. His first instinct was to call upon Fire to burn his captor's hand, but a show of hostility this early on would kill any hope for peace.

The giant pushed open a set of large double doors and tossed Finn inside. He managed to land on his feet and caught a look of terror in the giant's eyes as he retreated and pulled the doors shut. Finn made a quick sweep of the room for whatever scared the giant, but saw nothing inside the chamber to cause such fear.

A fireplace with an ornate, towering mantel blazed with welcome warmth. Iron discs filled with many burning candles hung from long chains. They were positioned much lower to the floor than they should be for the comparative height of the ceiling and would hit any of these giants in the knees, so the makeshift candelabras were obviously hung for someone his size. In fact, the whole chamber appeared to be furnished for a human.

A wooden slab crudely carved with simple designs served as a desk. The rough surface was filled with bottles of crushed, dried herbs and what appeared to be different sorts of colored tinctures. Some held preserved specimens, such as snakes, frogs and bats. Wisps of steam emanated from a large black pot set beside an open book.

He glanced at the pages of the book, a chill passing through him when he recognized the sketch of upside down druidic symbols arranged in a summoning circle with a skinned cat at the center. Someone here was practicing black magic. Most likely whatever evil was in league with the frost king.

"I see you know how to read magic," a woman's voice spoke from behind him.

Finn reached for his flute as he twisted around to face her.

He caught the gleam of her bone-pale skin before she emerged fully from the shadows. She wore a cloak of raven feathers draped loosely around her bare shoulders. A black leather choker adorned with a large ruby clamped snugly around the thin stem of her neck. The polished skull of a wildcat crowned her long ebony hair, its fangs resting on her smooth brow. Her features were sharp and her dark, slanted eyes piercing and somehow familiar.

She eyed the flute in Finn's hand, her ruby pendant glowing as red sparks crackled from her fingertips. "With a weapon like that, I suppose I should have known there was more to you than a mere bloodthirsty soldier." Her gaze rose to the runes inked on his temple. "You've learned to blend the Elder race runes with the druidic oghams. Impressive."

Finn tightened his grip around the flute. "What do you want?"

"What do I want? Hmm." She strolled to the fireplace and stared into the flames. "Justice. That would satisfy me greatly."

Finn frowned as the red sparks from her fingertips ignited into a ball of fire. She turned to face him, her hands cupped around the wild blaze, the weapon of choice for practitioners of sorcery. And why was he getting the feeling this was personal?

"You recognize sorcery," she said, as if in answer to his thoughts. "You've fought other sorcerers."

It wasn't a question, but more of a statement of fact. Finn didn't answer either way.

She strode toward him, stopping in the middle of the huge room. "You took the hand of a sorcerer just before your king drove a dagger between his eyes."

Finn's heart jolted. Adrenaline pumped through his system. How did she know about his battle with the sorcerer, Gorm? He would've noticed the sorceress if she'd been there. And she didn't strike him as the type to stand on the sidelines.

Her face twisted with fury as she hurtled the ball of fire at Finn. "That was my brother!" she screamed.

Finn dove to one side. Scalding heat raked past him. Transforming his flute into a wind sword, he deflected the next fiery blow with its blade.

"He was my twin!" She stretched her arms wide, drawing the shadows of the room together into a cloud of darkness that swarmed behind her. "I felt the cut of your blade when you sliced off his hand. The pain was as much mine as it was his."

Finn stood motionless, determined to take her hand too, if it came down to that.

The dark mass sleeved itself over her entire body, distorting her features and form into something hulking and misshapen. Her voice rumbled into a guttural roar. "Do you know what it's like to feel death come over someone you're inextricably linked to? Death is a brutal thing. It's cold and dark and filled with nothing but fear. Gorm was always so strong, but in those last seconds he was terrified and tried to leech my power so he could live."

She pointed at Finn. "You and your wretched king did that!" Shadowy tentacles lashed at him, striking Finn's hand. Its frigid touch burned on contact, blackening his skin with frostbite.

Twisting away, he brought his wind sword down, slashing through the shadows, cutting them from the root. But it was a useless effort as more tentacles snaked in, replacing those that fell away in dusty particles.

Retracting the wind blade on his flute, Finn blew a series of piercing notes to summon the winds. The sorceress closed in, the shadow around her swelling high over his head, curling downward. Just when it seemed he'd be swallowed in its dark tide, the glass panes shattered in a spray of glinting shards. Finn covered his face, backing away as a fierce gale crashed into the chamber. Pressing against the wall, he commanded the winds to take the sorceress and her monstrous entity. The preternatural volume of his voice shook the room, loosening slabs from the ceiling, which crashed to the stone floor in rubble.

The sorceress screamed as the winds tore at the shadow beast. Her face froze in an expression of terror as she struggled to hold onto it, but the wind ripped it from her body, along with her cloak of raven feathers. She turned to Finn, her long ebony hair whipping violently around her pale face. The fear vanished, replaced by a look of pure malice. Her dark eyes filled with blood. Crimson tears streaked her cheeks as she chanted words he couldn't hear over the crashing winds.

He knew she was conjuring something terrible. Finn roared another command. The storm responded instantly, snatching her off her feet. She tumbled over the currents, pitching end over end like a rag doll. Finn directed the winds by punching the air. The sorceress slammed into the far wall in a spray of blood.

When he released the winds, the sudden silence jarred him. But the ghastly sight of the sorceress shook him far more. He hadn't meant to lose control and embed her within the wall of stone. The look of shock fixed on her half buried face unleashed the gruesome memory of the war goddess he'd killed in the same way. He could still see the enraged scream on the giant deity's burnt, petrified face.

He'd sworn he would never use the elements for that kind of violence ever again. Yet here he was, falling back into the darkness that had driven him to kill in such a horrific manner.

The doors to the chamber yanked open, banging with a loud echo against the sidewalls. A horde of frost giants thundered inside, all stopping to gape at what Finn had done to the sorceress. Gripping his flute, he prepared for battle as they closed in around him.

34
DESERT OF THE LIVING SANDS

FATE GASPED FOR AIR and choked on a mouthful of sand. Coughing on the grit, she pushed off the ground with sore, weak arms and sat in a kneeling position. She touched her throbbing head, wondering how she'd ended up face down eating dirt. She squinted against the sun glaring off white sand, her eyes dry and grainy with each blink.

Where was she?

Dunes stretched out in every direction as far as the eye could see. She rose shakily, teetering off balance, dizzy from the sensation of the desert moving around her. Planting her feet firmly in place with knees bent, she glanced around, only to wobble again as waves rippled through the sands and crashed against the small rock island she stood upon. Were her eyes deceiving her? Or was the ground actually moving like the waters of an ocean?

Fate rubbed her eyes, hoping to change what she was seeing. It didn't help. The sands undulated and rolled, rising and falling in giant swells. Her heart thudded as a dreadful realization set in. She would never be able to traverse this strange desert without being buried alive under a wave of sand. She was stranded on this rock.

Bewildered and feeling sick to her stomach, she sat back down, her mind grasping for logical answers. Was this a dream? The sweltering heat of the sun bearing down on her told her otherwise. How in the world had she gotten there?

Fate ran her fingers over her wet forehead and looked at her palm. Her breath caught in her throat when she noticed a glowing round symbol spinning within moving interlocking rings beneath the surface of her skin. She blinked at it, unable to comprehend how it had got there.

On her left wrist was a braided handmade bracelet of silk and plaid wool with two silver charms. She liked the look and feel of it. Had someone made it for her? Possibly one of her fans from the book signing?

Feeling runnels of sweat trickling down her back, she undid the top two brass buttons of a double-breasted military jacket she didn't recognize. The color was a robin's egg blue and fit like it was tailored for her. Spots of blood stained one sleeve. Her chest tightened. Whose blood was this? The horrible, queasy feeling that arose was too much to deal with in amongst all the confusion, so she returned her attention to the uniform she was wearing.

At her waist was a sort of utility belt with gadgets she'd never seen before. Attached to the belt was an empty gun holster and steel scabbard with ornate markings. She was also wearing snug leather breeches stuffed into tall combat boots, both of which were dark and soaking up the heat.

Nothing could explain how she'd come to be dressed as she was, and lost in a totally unbelievable place. The last thing she remembered was being at the Seattle Public Library signing books. She'd been dressed in a skirt and blouse then, not this mysterious uniform. She also remembered an uncomfortable scuffle between some of her fans and she'd decided to leave. Her last memory was of telling Eustace she would sneak out and take the bus over to Jessie's house.

Disbelief muddled the ability to think straight as she stared at the impossible ocean of shifting sands. Increasing anxiety fired along her nerve endings, making her sweat all the more. All she wanted was the safety of home and her father's stabilizing presence.

What was she going to do?

The answer didn't come. She was too paralyzed with fear to do anything but hug her knees to quell the uncontrollable quaking from within.

The rock beneath her bucked violently, the impact so powerful she was thrown into the air. She hit the edge, her hands flailing for anything to hold onto before she fell into the heaving sands. Grabbing hold of a craggy outcropping, she hoisted herself back onto the rock. She was no sooner up, when another jolt sent her flying like a pancake being flipped over a frying pan.

Fate landed on her back. Pain streaked along her spine as she turned onto her front and seized hold of a rounded indentation. The rock lifted and rolled. She slid, scrambling against gravity and the doom of the pitching sands ready to consume her. Her arm hooked into a hollow groove. Sharp edges dug into her armpit, but she held tight in spite of the pain as the rock continued to roll.

A sonorous growl rumbled through the rock and Fate suddenly knew true terror. A seemingly endless stream of scales and horns knifed along the surface of the sand. She screamed until her throat and lungs burned. The monster's unearthly roar pierced the air with a hair-raising shriek as it snaked skyward. Its massive head pitched downward, its fleshy maw of slime and fangs stretched wide, plummeting toward her.

Fate flattened herself to the rock, when a blinding flash appeared out of nowhere. The monster's gaping mouth lurched to one side with an angry screech. A robed figure had latched onto its head by driving a spear deep between its dusty scales. At first she thought she'd imagined it, because of the way the rider ghosted in and out of view. But someone was there. She could tell by the way the snakelike monster whipped its head back and forth, and the long spear glinting at the back of its mouth as her rescuer held firm, pushing it deeper.

The violent thrashing seemed to last forever, until the rider produced a sword out of thin air and stabbed the thing in a smooth spot on the top of its head. The monster dropped like a sack of wet laundry next to Fate. A strangled gurgle rushed past its slack jaw, blowing the rank air of its last breath over her.

Her hammering heartbeat calmed from what felt like a heart attack, even as she breathed in the horrid stench. Gratitude didn't come anywhere close to her feelings toward this robed stranger for saving her life. Words could not express the tremendous relief and hopefulness flooding her system.

But her elation was short lived. The stranger leaped from the dead monster onto a boat suspended in the air, leaving the creature to sink beneath the heaving sands.

Fate waited for the boat to descend toward her, until she realized she was about to be left behind. She jumped to her feet, her knees trembling with renewed fear as she waved her arms and yelled. "Please! Don't leave me here!"

The stranger bent over the edge, paused for a minute and then stepped away. The boat lifted and turned.

"Take me with you!" she cried. "Please, I beg you, don't leave me here to die!"

The boat drifted directly over her.

"Yes, thank you." Her voice had diminished to a shaky whisper.

A rope thwacked the top of her head. She tied it around her chest, praying her knotting skills were enough to hold until she was hauled safely aboard. As she rose into the air, Fate noticed the rock she'd been stranded on was not a rock at all. She'd been hanging on for dear life to the enormous skull of some long dead predator. Just one of its petrified fangs was larger than the monster that had tried to make a meal of her.

When she reached the boat, the stranger lifted her over the edge and set her down on the deck. Fate let out a sigh of relief as she wriggled out of the rope, letting it slide down her body to her feet. She mustered as much of a smile as she could under the circumstances. "Thank you so much. I don't know what I would've done if you hadn't come along."

Her rescuer was obviously a man, tall with broad shoulders. Eyes as blue as the sky with a starburst of white at the center watched her from behind layers of ivory cloth concealing his head and face. She blinked, trying to regain focus, but couldn't because of the way the outer edges of his robe shimmered in and out of view.

"Well, I guess it's no mystery what would've happened," she said when he didn't reply. "I would've been worm food. Right? I mean, that was a sand worm you just killed. I've seen them before. In movies, but never that up close and personal. Unless it's in 3D, which is the way I prefer any such life-threatening encounters."

She was babbling, and his silence only made it worse. Taking a breath to continue, she thought better of it and pressed her lips together to stop her out of control chattering.

He finally deigned to speak. "We call them, Sulayfirs. It means desert dragon in your language." He took care over each word to make them recognizable to her, but the effort did nothing to hide his thick Arabic-sounding accent.

"Sulayfir," Fate repeated, though she couldn't mimic the same inflections of speech.

His eyes crinkled with a fleeting smile before turning serious. "What are you doing in Dunebala without proper transportation?"

"Dunebala?"

"The desert of the Living Sands."

She dropped her gaze to the wooden deck. "I - I'm lost, and I don't know how I got here."

He eyed her suspiciously. "No one simply appears in Dunebala."

She gulped, wishing she hadn't blurted out her own ignorance of the situation. The last thing she should be doing was casting an air of mystery to a stranger who was already distrustful of her presence.

He gave her a dismissive wave before she could think of how to backtrack. "It matters not. Your future is all that's important now."

"Exactly," Fate agreed. "A wise man once said something along the line of, the past is gone, the future hasn't happened yet, but the present is a gift. Get it? A gift is a present you give someone, but the present also means right now."

"Ah, that is profound. I am certain this wise man would find our customs to be in alignment."

"How so?"

"Saving your life today was a gift I gave to you–"

"Mhmm, of which I'm extremely grateful. Believe you me."

"And now that gift must be repaid."

Fear trickled down her spine. "Come again?"

He kneeled, and before she knew what was happening, he'd clamped a heavy brass ring around her ankle. She jumped back, hopping on one leg in an attempt to remove it. When she failed to do so, she stomped her foot down and frowned at him. "What is this? What did you just do?"

"You now owe your entire life to me, your savior, through a life of servitude."

"Excuse me? You do know this is the twenty-first century, right? People don't own other people anymore. That hasn't happened since... like the 1800's."

He raised a dark brow as if to infer she was wrong, but rather than argue, he strode to the helm and took the wheel. He turned the boat, which responded with a surge in speed as it glided swiftly above the rolling dunes. The sudden movement rocked Fate off balance and had her grabbing the windward side of the boat for support.

Nausea stirred in the pit of her stomach, partly from seasickness–in this case airsickness–but mostly from the frightening and baffling course of events taking place around her. How was any of this possible? Why was this happening? Was any of this real, or had she completely lost her mind?

The latter seemed most likely. She'd probably gone insane after too many years of living in the fantasy worlds she'd been dreaming up since childhood. In all likelihood, she wasn't even a published writer. What authors have fans that show up dressed like characters from their books and then get so carried away with their roles they end up fighting in a tangle of limbs on the floor? Only her crazy imagination could cook up such a far-fetched scenario.

But this situation was a whole other level of imagination. Everything appeared so real. The smooth wood beneath her hands was solid. The sun beating down on her was hotter than any summer sunshine she'd ever had the displeasure of experiencing. And most certainly, the desert dragon's fangs had appeared hyper-real and perfectly capable of ripping her to shreds.

The boat dipped, making her stomach lurch. Fate covered her mouth, swallowing down the rising bile, which only served to intensify her motion sickness. Rushing to the edge in an unstoppable bout of nausea, she hung her head over the railing and vomited over the side of the hull.

She stayed there, waiting for the queasiness to subside. The desert surged below her, revealing wreckages of other flying boats and even what looked like city structures when the waves sank low. But then the waves would swell and bury the ruins under tons of sand again.

"Stand away from the edge." The stranger's tone was forceful and commanding.

Fate ignored him, stubbornly staying where she was. She might not be able to control what was happening, but she could at least disobey the orders of a man who thought he now owned her.

A black shape erupted from the sandy waves. A beak of razored teeth snapped the air within inches of her nose. Fate jerked her head up, stumbling backward into the middle of the deck as a frustrated howl sounded from below.

"As I said, stand away from the edge."

She glared at him. "You might've told me why, rather than sounding like you're power-tripping. I'm a human being, not a dog, and I don't take well to being ordered around."

He was quiet a moment, but his voice was no less commanding when he did speak. "You'll follow orders if you wish to survive the remainder of the trip."

"Or what, you'll drag me by the hair like the caveman you're being?"

"No, but if you do not listen to me, the desert will take you."

Fate set her fists on her hips. "Oh! So, you're threatening to throw me overboard if I get out of line."

His expression was hidden, but his grip tightened on the wheel. "If that is what you wish to think."

Shaking with a mixture of anger and fright, Fate turned her back to him so he wouldn't see the hot tears rising in her eyes. She stood still, her watery gaze fixed on the bow, refusing to focus on the pure helplessness of her situation because if she let her mind go there, she would turn into a useless, quivering blob. This was her reality at the moment–psychotic break or not–and she needed to accept it and deal with it.

The boat tacked to the right and she grabbed hold of the mast to keep from tipping over. How the heck was the boat flying? Sails in the shapes of fans extended horizontally from each side of the hull. Other than the shivering, mist-covered sails, nothing else indicated the boat's form of flight. Was it magic? She resisted the urge to satisfy her curiosity by asking questions. He wasn't her tour guide. He was her captor.

She slid to the floor and sat with her back to the pole. Her gaze settled on the brass anklet. Drawing her foot toward her, she tugged at the ring, making it jingle with beads filling the inside. There was no give to the decorated metal and pulling it hurt her ankle. She turned the ring, searching for a break and hinge, but it was solid. Sliding the ring to her calf, she pulled her boot and sock off and tried shoving the anklet down over her bare foot. The diameter was too small. How in the world had he gotten the anklet over her foot, let alone her boot?

"You cannot remove the soul ring," he said from behind her. "You would need my blessing for that to happen."

Fate bit down on her anger as she pulled her sock and boot back on. "Do I need your blessing to get a drink of water?"

"You are free to move about as you please."

"Free!" Fate laughed harshly as she stood. "That's funny. *Not.*" She glanced around. "Where's this water I'm *free* to drink?"

He pointed at a row of glazed clay jugs. "There, next to that crate of food. You may eat if you are hungry."

"Really? I'm allowed sustenance?" Fate grumbled as she wobbled over to the crate. She really needed to get her sea legs back. Dropping down next to the crate, she grabbed a jug and uncorked it. As she gulped down a mouthful of water, she considered dumping its contents in an act of rebellion, but hesitated. "How long are you planning on keeping me out here?" Dying of thirst wasn't something she wanted to experience.

"Only the Moulghazal knows." His eyes reached skyward as if in search of something.

Fate shook her head. "Whatever *that* is."

"The Moulghazal is a rare and sacred sky whale. My people are in great need of her presence."

Fate busied herself with replacing the cork in the jug so he wouldn't see she was intrigued. She huffed and rolled her eyes. "A sky whale? You really expect me to believe there's a big blubbery whale floating around out there." She leaned forward, hoping to hear details.

He continued to gaze at the clear blue sky. "When Moulghazal migrates south every spring, she creates the ranemist my kingdom relies on to stay above the clouds. For some reason, Moulghazal did not arrive this year, so the replenishment did not happen and now the city is sinking."

Fate stared at him round-eyed. If it weren't for the fact she was riding in a flying boat, she would've dismissed his outrageous story. "Is ranemist what makes this boat fly?"

His gaze dropped to her and he nodded. "If I do not find her soon, I will be forced to turn back before my supply is depleted."

"What will happen to your city if you don't find her?"

Pain showed in his eyes. "The hungry desert will swallow my kingdom as it has so many others."

Fate remembered the ruins she'd glimpsed within the shifting sands and gulped. "Do you think something bad happened to Moulghazel?"

His gaze hardened and he looked straight ahead. "I cannot entertain such poisonous thoughts, and I would thank you to silence your curses."

"That wasn't a curse."

"No? I expected *you* would understand the power of the spoken word."

Fate frowned in confusion. "I have no idea what you're talking about."

His stern expression turned to one of disbelief. "You lie. Your maraja is god-touched, and I can plainly see you are endowed with the power of the Word."

"My what is what?"

"I see the powers all around you." He waved a hand to illustrate something surrounding her.

Fate stood and braced her legs against any sudden tilting. "If I'm so powerful, how come you had to save me from being eaten?" She held her arms out to show she was harmless. "And for that great privilege, I've become your prisoner. Honestly, I'm beginning to think the desert dragon might've been the better way to go. At least then it would've been over quick."

His eyes fixed on her waist with contempt and she glanced down for a second to see what he was looking at, but there was nothing out of the ordinary. His gaze moved to the phantasms he believed he was seeing around her and his shoulders stiffened. "Clearly, I made a grave mistake. I should have let you die, but that's easily remedied."

The steel in his words sliced the air between them and Fate backed away as he stepped around the wheel with his saber drawn.

35
SMOKELESS FLAME OF THE HINN

FATE DUCKED, ESCAPING THE bite of his blade, and grabbed one of the water jugs. She brought it up in time to shield the next blow. The clay jug exploded in her hands. Water splashed over her face and soaked into the front of her jacket. She staggered backward, instinctively reaching for a sword, instead feeling the emptiness of the silver scabbard at her side.

But she could use that.

Ripping the scabbard from the utility belt at her waist, Fate blocked the strike as his sword came down. The shrill clash of metal pierced her ears, heightening the flow of adrenaline pumping through her system. He countered with a diagonal strike, the point of his blade slicing one of the brass buttons from her jacket before she parried and kept the momentum of the killing blow from ripping her chest open.

His robes billowed around him, hiding his moves behind veils of fleeting invisibility, but not before she caught the look in his eyes. The shock she saw there emboldened her. Rather than withdrawing, she held the scabbard by both ends and pushed ahead, deflecting each strike with greater force.

Something had awakened inside. A fire she hadn't thought possible. Yet the stirring felt somehow familiar. She whipped the scabbard around in a full arc, meeting his blade with such force the impact struck the hilt from his grasp. Taken off guard, he paused for a split second, an opening she used to drive the point of the scabbard into his solar plexus. He flew back, slamming against the mast with a gasping groan.

Stopping to take a breath, Fate rested the scabbard on her shoulder like a baseball player. "Guess you weren't expecting *that* from your helpless prisoner." To be honest, she hadn't expected it either. To say she was blown away by her surprising new abilities would be an understatement. But she wasn't about to let him in on that little secret. Best to act like her unnatural strength and sword fighting skills were entirely normal. "Now that we've established the pecking order around here, I order you to remove this shackle. And pronto." She tapped the brass ring around her ankle with the scabbard.

Coughing, he rose to his feet with both hands pressed against his abdomen. The covering around his head and face had fallen down around his shoulders. His black hair hung long and straight, tumbling over a simple cotton overcoat to the middle of his back.

Fate's mouth fell open. He was young, probably the same age she was. The gleam of his sun-kissed skin reminded her of creamy caramel sauce. His features were flawless, as if carved from marble and smoothed to perfection. His strong, defined jaw was clean-shaven and only served to display the generous curves of his mouth to distraction. Despite the furious angle of his dark brows, his azure eyes blazed with a magnetism she'd been more resistant to when his face had been covered.

A plume of heat flushed her face. She looked away and cleared her throat. "And no funny business," she warned, doing her best to sound tough.

He didn't move to undo the anklet.

Fate frowned at him as he removed the wrappings he'd used to conceal his face and threw them on the deck. He pulled the hood of his shimmering robe up over his head and tugged it down over his forehead, shading his eyes from the sun. "It is not our custom to revoke a life debt."

"You were about to revoke it by killing me!" she yelled.

Lifting his chin, he stared down the straight line of his nose at her. "Because you were lying about who you are."

"Really? Is this how you treat everyone who isn't an open book the instant they meet you?"

He crossed his arms and remained silent.

"A person has a right to privacy," she pressed.

"Not on my ship. Trust is paramount to survival in this desert. Without it, death is sure to–"

The boat heaved upward with the screech of rending wood, knocking them both off their feet. Fate hit the floor next to him, sliding the length of the deck toward the stern. Sand rained down over them, followed by an enormous shadow spreading over the tilting boat.

Smashing against the sidewall, Fate grabbed the railing, lifting herself enough to peer over the edge. Her pulse stuttered. Blotting out the sun with its massive wingspan was a leathery creature shaped like a colossal stingray. Its ribcage glowed with scarlet streaks that webbed across its membranous wings, the lava-like color coalescing in its gullet as it thrust skyward and lashed its barbed tail against the shifting sands with a resounding boom. Red lightning crackled across the dunes, spreading outward in concentric ripples.

Her captor thrust a coil of rope in her hands. "Tie yourself to the boat!" When Fate continued to stare at the creature, he pulled her by the shoulder, forcing her to look at him. "Now, before the wind comes!"

With hands shaking, Fate tied the rope around her waist and then to the railing. She was pulling on the last knot when the wind slammed into them, capsizing the boat. Sheets of sand and searing heat raked over her as she dangled in the turbulence, battered in all directions like a ball of yarn being clawed by a cat. Biting down on the pain of heat and sand blasting her exposed skin, Fate squeezed her eyes shut against the blinding dust storm and used the sleeve of her jacket to cover her mouth to keep from suffocating.

The violent gust passed as suddenly as it came. Fate glanced at the bottom of the boat from where she swung. Vaporous mist poured from a jagged hole in one side, but the damage didn't appear to be keeping the boat from rolling upright and pulling her along with it. She banged against the other side of the hull, reaching for the railing to get a better handhold when her captor bent over the edge and grabbed her by the forearm, helping her the rest of the way.

"Thanks for saving me. Again," she muttered, knowing the gesture no doubt doubled her prison sentence.

His face was grim and covered in a layer of grit and dust, his long hair white and stiff. She glanced down at the thick, chalky film clinging to her clothes and touched her hair. It felt as tangled as a tumbleweed, and probably looked like one too.

"I did not do it out of kindness," he grumbled. "The hull sustained extensive damage and I will to need your help to sail to the nearest refuge."

Fate bunched her fists at her sides. "I take it back then. I'm not thankful."

Ignoring her, he lifted a hatch in the floor, closing it before disappearing below deck. Uncomfortable with being left out in the open, Fate turned in circles, searching for signs of the monstrous creature that had tipped the boat over. The tension in her muscles eased when she confirmed it was gone. Given that it hadn't stayed to finish them off, she could only assume the boat had merely been in its way when it erupted from the sand. She drew in a deep breath to steady her nerves, unsure if she could handle any more encounters with Dunebala's wildlife.

The sound of the hatch banged open, making her jump. She turned, frowning as he pushed a leather bag onto the deck. It looked heavy and clanged with metal contents when he slid it to one side. A rolled parchment and compass followed before he climbed all the way out and let the hatch drop with another loud thud that rattled her frayed nerves. He sat down next to the wheel and unrolled the parchment, which turned out to be a map. Fate stepped closer to have a look as he lined the compass up with the map's cardinal directions.

It was a map of Dunebala with only a few islands, each of which were tiny specks on the paper in comparison to the vast expanse of the desert. Peripheral borders indicated neighboring territories, but there was no way of knowing how close they were to any of them. "I suppose we'll be heading to the nearest bordering country now."

"You really have no idea where you are, do you?" He pointed at the center of Dunebala. "We are here, in the deepest part of the desert." He traced a finger in a straight line to one of the specks. "This is where we need to go. That is *if* we have enough ranemist to make it there."

He stood and moved to the wheel, referencing the binnacle and its navigational instrumentation. Turning the wheel, he swung the boat in a new direction. "Come here."

It wasn't a request.

Fate joined him at the wheel.

"Put your hands on each of these pegs," he instructed.

She squeezed in front of him, placing her hands where he told her. He held his position behind her, his arms flanking the outside of her arms and chest grazing her back. His voice grew softer as he spoke next to her ear. "Hold the wheel steady. You must not let it waver, but you must also watch the compass at the same time. Keep the bow in line with the needle, which must stay on this number."

Fate glanced at the compass, which had markings that looked nothing like any numbers she was accustomed to. She mem-orized it as an upside down 'v'.

A strong breeze buffeted them from the left and the wheel turned of its own accord, moving them a few points off the mark. She pushed the wheel back until the needle lined up with the inverted 'v'.

"Good, you know to readjust with the slightest wind." He walked over to the leather bag and tied a rope around his waist before lifting it over his back. "I will do my best to patch the tank and make any other necessary repairs."

Fate stared at him in alarm. "Wait. You're not going overboard, are you?"

"I cannot access the damage from the inside. It must be done from outside the hull."

"Where you'll be asking for one of those things to take a bite out of you."

"We cannot run out of ranemist." His jaw tightened. "If that happens, it will not matter whether either of us is inside or outside the boat." Slinging the heavy tool bag over his back, he swung his leg over the railing and dropped over the side.

They sailed for three days before the sharp peaks of the rock island sanctuary knifed over the horizon. The days had been long, filled with unbearable heat and constant tension. They'd slept in shifts, and only for an hour at any given time. The slow pace they'd been forced to keep due to the low supply of ranemist had made them easy prey for every nightmarish creature the desert had to offer.

Fate had become the official helmsman, manning the wheel while Azrael fended off the growing number of attacks with his spear and saber. His name had been the only information he'd been willing to offer since their fight, and only because she'd threatened to start calling him Elmo. Not that she'd been inclined to strike up conversations with the man who'd previously tried to kill her over what he said was a lie, when in fact her supposed lie was a major lapse in memory on her part.

The long stretches of silence had been torture. She des-perately wanted to know what had caused her to be trapped in this living hell, and how she'd come to possess this incredible strength and mind-boggling ability to fight. As much as she missed being at home with her father and cat, she was at the same time excited by her newly discovered powers. Though of late, a growing fire in her belly was turning her thoughts to an unfamiliar bloodlust that frightened her.

But maybe this strong desire for action and killing monsters was a result of standing still at the wheel for hour upon endless hour, watching a tiny needle to keep the ship on course while more and more beasts circled.

The boat lurched to one side. Yanking on the wheel, she turned the bow back in the direction of the rock island. Azrael raced to the edge, his spear raised over a spiked fin rising above the starboard side. He stabbed the behemoth, only to be thrown backward as it rammed the ship with an angry roar. He hit the deck, losing his saber in the fall.

The saber skidded across the wooden planks and banged into Fate's boot. In a moment of weakness, she grabbed the weapon and abandoned her post. Running across the deck, she leaped onto the railing just as the beast's head came into view. She thrust the blade into its black bulging eye, then sliced the hinge of its yawning jaw before jumping back on deck. Neither blow was lethal, but she'd targeted what she hoped were sensitive areas.

Sure enough, the creature thrashed and sank beneath the sands.

She turned, flashing Azrael a triumphant smile. He stood behind the wheel, his dark brows furrowed in an angry scowl. "What?" she scoffed. "I thought you could use a break. I know I needed one. Staring at that compass needle for days on end was making me crazy. It was time to change things up."

"It was not your decision to make."

Fate wiped the ichor dripping off the curved blade with a rag. "Who made you boss?"

He squeezed the pegs of the wheel and stared straight ahead. "This is my ship. I dictate the rules."

She strode over and handed him the sword, hilt first. "I suppose you have a point." Shading her eyes, she squinted at the rock island. They were getting closer. In less than an hour they would finally step onto terra firma. "For now," she added.

They sailed the remainder of the way without another word, the silence broken only by the thud of grasping tentacles or the scrape of claws against the hull. Fate had learned not to be too alarmed by the sounds. It was only when the ship was being rocked, or pulled down, that there was something to worry about.

When they reached the island, Azrael steered the boat between several towering pillars of smooth, black rocks. They were twisted and spindly up close, as if centuries of wind and sand had found holes in solid rock and had worn away at them, leaving these skeletons, which would one day disintegrate into sand. Azrael hadn't exaggerated when he'd said the desert was hungry.

"Take the wheel while I tie us off," he called out.

She did as he instructed, holding the direction as he leaped to the bow and hung from the very tip with rope in hand. He lassoed a metal post at the tip of an outcropping and pulled the boat alongside a wide terrace that was obviously manmade.

"Others have been here before?" Fate asked.

"My people have been using these islands for thousands of years as way stations for travelers in need. There will be food, water and barrels of ranemist down below." He jumped onto the shelf and Fate followed him down a sheer staircase carved straight from the rock.

Azrael stopped near the bottom of the stairs suddenly and reached for his saber. "Do you smell that?"

The air was arid and relatively devoid of smell, but when Fate took a sniff, she wrinkled her nose. "Is that sulphur?"

Azrael descended the last few steps. "We call it the smokeless flame of the Hinn."

Fate fell in behind him, her stomach clenching with dread. She didn't know where or when, but she'd encountered the sulphurous stench before and she couldn't shake the feeling something terrible and sad had happened as a result of its presence.

Azrael moved slowly down the dark narrow corridor leading off the stairwell, his saber poised for whatever this Hinn was. Staying behind him, Fate edged forward. The smell grew noisome, stinging her eyes, coating her throat with a sickening taste. Her skin prickled in a rash of chills and her head spun dizzily.

They rounded the corner into a cavern dimly lit by a flickering lantern. A hazy mist hung thick in the air. Debris littered the floor. Tables and chairs were tipped as if thrown by a strong wind. Shattered boxes lay open with spoiled food. Shallow pools of water held the shards of countless clay water jugs.

Azrael gripped Fate's wrist, pulling her along as he backed up within the mouth of the entrance. "We must leave," he whispered.

The fear in his voice raised the hair on her arms, and she was about to ask what was wrong, when a movement drew her gaze to the darkest corner of the cavern. A pair of eyes stared back, flaring like molten lava from within a heavy cloak of writhing shadows.

Fate's mouth went dry as her heart pounded terror throughout her veins. A sharp ache drilled the inside of her skull. Nausea gripped hold. Grabbing her abdomen, she struggled to breathe, but her surroundings tipped sideways, until she realized she was falling. Hot pain raked across one side of her face.

Azrael kneeled over her. His face was blurred, his mouth moving. He was saying something she couldn't hear. She blinked, trying to bring him into focus, when a chilling voice invaded her mind, obliterating all else.

"*Hello, Fate. Did you really think forgetting what you lost would erase me as well?*"

Wave after wave of buried sorrow crashed in on Fate. A sob from the deepest part of her being tore through her chest, scorching her lungs with its ferocity, ripping her throat to ribbons. The cry became endless; a banshee's wail that dragged her down into the bottomless depths of an ocean of darkness.

36
THE KEY MASTER

INEXPLICABLE GRIEF CRUSHED FINN and he fell to his knees, sinking into the deep snow as he clutched at the agony ripping a hole in his chest, his brow breaking into a sweat despite the glacial temperatures. Pulling the hood of his fur coat off his head, he breathed deeply of the frosty air and stared into space.

It was Fate. She was back in Oldwilde, and in trouble.

Surprisingly, his first instinct was to shield himself from the intense sorrow with the Sovereign Symbols the monks of Almsdeep had taught him to use to prevent being an emotional sponge to whatever Fate was feeling. His extraordinary link with her had been that strong from the beginning, and had always wreaked havoc with his own wellbeing. But he'd purposely let his defenses drop upon his return to Oldwilde. It was the only way for him to know when she arrived.

He was all at once relieved she'd made it through the portal, but also tormented. What had gone so terribly wrong to drop her into such unbearable despair?

Finn no sooner asked the question when the heartrending onslaught ended as abruptly as it had begun. As if Fate ceased to be.

Alarmed, he rammed his fist into the snow, pushing his senses into the earth, radiating his reach beyond the northern reaches of Beldereth in search of her spirit's radiant red-gold flame. When he didn't find her in any nearby lands, he probed further into the southern regions, skimming over dense forests, sparkling lakes and sprawling valleys until he reached the ocean.

He'd been wrong. She was nowhere to be found in Oldwilde.

Forcing down his growing panic, he expanded his search beyond a cluster of islands off the shores of Asgar and crossed the ocean to a place of hostile deserts. He swept along the endless dunes, his senses stretching outward, hoping to detect the tiniest spark of her presence.

Without warning, he hit a barrier not unlike the fiery divide, though this one was not formed by its own sentience. This was an ocean of seething wild magic that pushed back with meteoric force. The impact shot through his brain like a bullet tearing through his skull.

Finn jerked his hand from the snow, severing the con-nection, violently and swiftly. Drained and dizzy, he drew a shallow breath, his body shaking with frustration as his worst fears rushed to the forefront. Had something gone wrong with the portal? Had Fate survived the passage only to die upon her arrival?

"No!" he growled. "She's alive!"

Unwilling to accept any reality other than her ultimate survival, Finn stood and pushed through the snowdrifts, his sights set on the ravine below. It was the last stretch before he reached the outskirts of Beldereth and Grysla with the rock queen's treaty. The king would have nothing to argue against, especially since the frost giants had agreed to end the kingdom's everlasting winter. They'd been surprisingly grateful to Finn for killing the sorceress who'd spelled their king with her own personal vendetta.

Finn hastened his descent, leaping from one mound to the next, his feet barely touching the ice crusts as he picked up speed. Upon passing through the ravine, his view opened onto the valley with its winding path of what used to be the River Torle. Further still was the empty lake basin of Windmere Loch with Beldereth situated at the very end of the lakebed.

The dark swollen clouds that had hung heavy over the kingdom for so very long were now shredding into ragged strips. Sunshine streamed through their thinning veils, warming the air. Finn continued his downward climb as the snow grew wet and slushy. He would've been happy for having completed his mission, but he was too anxious about Fate to enjoy this major feat of peace between giants and men. His only thoughts were returning to Beldereth, freeing his friends from prison, then setting out to find Fate amidst those godforsaken deserts.

The ground shook beneath his feet, stopping him in his tracks. Another familiar thud told him Grysla was drawing near. The tree troll's crown of gnarled branches crested over the next hill within several more quaking steps. Finn raced down the slope to greet her.

"Good to see you, my friend." He smiled wearily.

Concern filled Grysla's smoky green eyes. "You are troubled."

"It's Fate. Something awful has happened to her." Finn swallowed down the ache rising in his throat. "I can't feel her anymore. I'm mad with worry."

"You will be leaving soon."

"Aye."

Grysla tucked the rock queen's crystal tablet under her arm and nodded solemnly. There was nothing else to say. She'd always understood his bond with Fate and had even been the one to encourage him to leave Tove, in spite of knowing her daughter was deeply in love with him.

They continued the remainder of the trek to Beldereth in silence and at a swift pace. When they arrived several hours later, the sun was setting, casting hues of dusty rose and pale violet over the fluffy cloud tufts. Shadows from the castle towers crawled over the length of the cobbled road, now bare of snow. Melting icicles as long as a man hung from the turrets, glistening like smooth crystals in the last of the light, the water dripping onto the stones below with the patter of soft rain.

A horn blew from the parapet as Finn and Grysla approached. The drawbridge lowered down over the empty moat, still white with remaining snow. Guards poured over the bridge, their spears pointed at the tree troll.

Finn stormed over to the closest guard. "Stand down! We carry a peace treaty from the rock giants. Winter is gone because of–"

The butt of a spear driving into Finn's gut knocked the air out of him. "Take them to the dungeon!" the guard ordered.

Finn bit down on the urge to argue and fight back, allowing them to push him roughly inside the castle walls. He hadn't come this far to ruin his chances for peace by fighting them. Grysla hugged the stone tablet close to her burled chest and hung her head low as they corralled her into the confining halls, propelling her forward with the tips of their spears.

Fury boiled in Finn's chest at the injustice his friend was being forced to endure. Why couldn't they see this gentle giant for what she was? "There's no need to use force!" he shouted. "Where's Rudwor? I demand to speak to him!"

The guard behind him jabbed Finn hard in the back. "Shut your mouth!" she commanded. "You have no rights here. Not when you were allowed to leave by the king's good grace and then bring another vile giant back with you." Malice dripped from her voice.

Finn shook from the effort of containing his building rage. Obviously there was no reasoning with the guards. He would have to bite his tongue, and his anger, until they granted him an appointment with the king.

The walls closed in around them, suffocating the light as they descended into the bowels of the castle. The harsh jangle of keys and clang of chains echoed against the grimy stonework as they forced Grysla to lay the crystal tablet down before proceeding to shackle the tree troll to the wall.

When they clamped the manacles around Finn's wrists and ankles he broke into a cold sweat, shutting his eyes against the horrors of his incarceration in Asgar. But he couldn't escape them. His head filled with the miserable screams of fellow inmates. The phantom pain of being gagged with his mouth wrapped around a wooden knob ached anew in his jaw. Memories of gnawing hunger and thirst returned to haunt him, while the shame of living in his own filth sickened him to the point of nausea.

Unable to handle the thought of being locked up again, Finn lost all control and went wild–kicking, flailing and straining against his restraints. The guards descended upon him with the ends of their spears, beating him from all sides.

Grysla's enraged roar filled the space as she thrashed against the irons holding her to the wall, but even her great strength was not enough to break them. Like every weapon in Beldereth, the shackles and chains were forged with Gofannon's meldachite.

Before Finn could recover his wits, he was chucked into the cell with Grysla so hard he skidded across the floor and banged into her feet. The guards filed out, locking the enormous rusted gates behind them.

Groaning, Finn rolled onto this back, only to see Grysla leaning over him. She shook her head.

"I know. I shouldn't have lost my cool like that," he muttered as he sat up and wiped the blood from his mouth.

Tove spoke from the next cell. "What are you doing in here with us?" The green irises of her eyes smoldered to darker hues within an angry frown. "You should be out there convincing the king to let us go."

Leif bellowed from one of the cells further down the row. "What I say? I was once troll hunter. I know what is to hate giants. We are left to rot down here!"

The chains and shackles holding Sithias clattered to the floor as he transformed from being a tree troll into his natural state. He slithered between the greasy bars of Tove's cell and entered Finn's, his large feathery wings unfurling as he coiled and swayed in place. "I did my bessst to reassure them your plan was sound, sir." He dipped his head closer to Finn. "This isss part of the plan, right?"

"Did that look planned?" Finn grumbled.

Sithias kept his expression blank and blinked innocently.

"Well, at least we have you," Finn admitted with a sigh. "Do your shrinky thing and fly out of here, would you? Find Rudwor and tell him we've delivered the rock queen's treaty. And be sure to mention that the frost giants ended winter due to our efforts."

"Gladly." Sithias cocked his head at a rattling sound coming from the outer corridor. "Ah, hear that?"

"Aye, the guards are returning." Finn lowered his voice. "Best make yourself scarce before they come inside."

"No, that annoying sound isn't the guards. It's that hideous jailer, and he's come for the hundredth time to taunt us by jangling the keys to our freedom under our noses." Sithias slipped through the bars and slithered over to the gate. He winked at Finn with a wide grin. "I'll be but a minute."

The gates cracked open, followed by a long bony arm shaking a huge ring of various sized keys. A wheezy chortle ensued as a tall, spindly man with thin, oily hair, a bulbous nose and dark, beady eyes stepped inside. "Did ye miss me?" he goaded.

Without stopping the incessant clang of his keys, he wiped his runny nose on his soiled shirt and shuffled toward his caged prisoners, while failing to see Sithias waiting off to one side. "Look what I've got. Do ye want yer keys?" He laughed again. "What would ye give to have 'em? Yer food? If ye go without for the next week, I'll consider letting ye have 'em."

Sithias weaved silently in behind him, his wings spreading so wide it looked as if they belonged to the jailer. A hiss near his ear made the man's eyes grow round. He turned around and yelped when he saw the giant snake.

Whipping his wings in one powerful thrust, Sithias lifted off, lashing his tail around the man's ankle at the same time. The jailor cried out for help, his limbs flailing as Sithias hauled him to the top of the high ceiling and shook his body by the one leg. The keys in the man's hand clanked loudly.

"How do you like the sssound of that?" Sithias flapped his wings furiously. "It's not nearly as nice when you're not the one in control of making that racket, is it?"

"Guards! Help!" the jailor shouted.

Sithias whapped him against the wall. The iron ring and its contents clattered on the stone and echoed sharply throughout the dungeon, but the jailor held onto his precious keys all the same.

"Drop the keys, and I'll let you go," Sithias offered.

The jailor writhed. "I be the only key master here!"

"We'll sssee about that." Sithias dropped the man from the ceiling, then swooped to catch him by the leg just as his head grazed the floor. The jailor howled, rubbing his sore crown as Sithias heaved him back to the ceiling.

"Next time, I might not catch you," Sithias threatened.

The jailor's face purpled with blood, his veins standing out on his forehead as he pressed his lips into a thin line of indignation. Sithias loosened his grip, letting him slide.

"Aye, have it yer way!" the jailor shrieked.

The keys hit the stone floor with a pleasant jangle.

Sithias descended, letting go of the jailor six feet above the ground to ensure he landed in a pile of tangled limbs. He then slithered over to the keys, his form shifting into the jailor's twin as he did so. Sithias retrieved the keys and turned to the jailor who rose to his feet with a pained grimace.

He yelped in shock. "What witchery is this?"

Sithias shook the keys under the jailor's protuberant nose. "Bessst not to question such things."

The man shrank from his doppelganger, his bony shoulders shaking in fear.

"Follow me," Sithias ordered the jailor. He winked at the others as he strolled over to the cell he'd been caged within. "Which key opens this one?"

The jailor pointed a trembling finger at one of the keys. Sithias unlocked the cell. "Get in."

The man's small, rat-like eyes rounded and he made mewling noises as he scuffled into the cell. Sithias banged the door shut behind him, locked it and jangled the keys. "Now then. What would you give to have these keys?" Sithias jeered.

Finn huffed impatiently. "Enough, Sithias. You're in danger of becoming this creep. It's time to get us out."

Sithias's smug smile vanished. "Oh, dear. I throw myself into my roles a little too much at times. I apologize. It's the cursse of all great actors." He held the ring of keys up. "I can free you now that I'm the key masssster." A taunting smile crept back onto his face as his gaze returned to the jailor.

A tear ran down the jailor's cheek.

"No, don't bother," Finn told him. "We'd be forced to fight the guards once we made it to the top and that would only worsen matters. We need to do this right. Go find Rudwor."

Sithias shrugged. "As you wish." He headed for the gates and slipped through the opening.

Finn settled into the damp, musty hay piled in the corner of his cell and rolled a tattered blanket into a pillow. Tucking the smelly roll behind his head, he heaved a weary sigh, hoping to catch a bit of sleep before Sithias returned with Rudwor. Though resting might prove difficult with the jailor's sniveling and snorting a few doors down.

"How can you sleep right now?" Tove asked from the other side of the bars. She strode to the adjoining corner where Finn was resting.

"It's called exhaustion," he muttered.

"I don't care." Tove's stare was furious. "You didn't warn us about what we'd be walking into when we agreed to help."

"How was I supposed to know Beldereth was warring with giants?" Finn argued. "I was across the universe at the time."

"With Fate," Tove swore under her breath.

So that was it. Guilt knifed into Finn. It was bad enough he'd roped his friends into this miserable predicament, but knowing Tove was still hurting over his decision to leave her for Fate made the guilt a hundred times worse. She didn't deserve the heartache he'd caused her.

He rolled onto his side and looked into her darkened eyes, searching for the emerald spark that should be there. "I'm sorry I hurt you, Tove. I'd give anything to take back the pain I caused you."

She glanced down, hiding the telltale colors of her eyes behind the dark fringe of her lashes. When she finally lifted her gaze, her irises had lightened to a dusty sage and the angry lines furrowing her brow had smoothed. "I wish you could too," she whispered.

Finn started to reach out for her hand, but thought better of it. A show of affection, regardless of how friendly on his part, would likely be taken as an opening to pick up with each other again.

Tove was never one to hide her feelings for him, and had demonstrated them with fierce passion. The remembrance of how she would slip into his bed and the inviting press of her body rushed in unbidden. Heat flushed through his core with the memory of her glossy dark hair splashed over his bed of furs. Resisting the fiery green light in her eyes as she looked up at him had been torturous. Under any other circumstances, he would've given in if his heart hadn't pulled on the reins for reasons he hadn't been aware of at the time. Perhaps, in another life he could've been happy with Tove. But even these fondest of memories could not compare with what he shared with Fate, and the ache for his brown-eyed beauty grew all the more acute.

Attempting to plump his makeshift pillow, Finn faced the opposite direction and stared at the wall, his heart reaching out to Fate as he did so. She was nowhere to be found. He pressed a fist over the fear gnawing a hole in his chest. Why couldn't he feel her anymore? The need to rush out and find her fired painful streams of adrenaline through his weary limbs. But the burst of frenzied energy was short lived. Fatigue claimed him, and he could no longer fight the heaviness of his lids as he quickly succumbed to sleep.

37
THE UNEARTHLY MIRROR

FATE OPENED HER EYES to the glittering brilliance of stars filling the night sky. Momentarily disoriented, her first thought was that she'd never seen the stars so clearly before. She was used to the light pollution of the city and had therefore never paid much attention to the sky, except when she'd been in the country visiting her grandmother. But even then, the starlight had not compared to this breathtaking display. What a shame it was that all this beauty hovered above her every night and went unappreciated.

"You're finally awake." Azrael's voice slammed her back to earth, along with the harsh reality of her circumstances. He was no doubt ready to take his turn sleeping.

"Did I oversleep?" she croaked. Her mouth was dry as paper. He leaned into the golden light of the lantern and held out a tin canteen. Sitting up to take it, she gulped back every drop.

"That was not sleep," he replied. "You have been un-conscious the entire day. There was no waking you."

"Sorry. I suppose I needed more sleep than the usual hour you've been giving me." She glanced around, realizing they were anchored to the rock island they'd been struggling to reach for the last three days. "Looks like we made it just fine. Why are you getting so upset about me catching a few extra z's?"

"Because everything is not fine. The stores of food, water and ranemist have been destroyed." He stared at her with a confused frown. "Do you not remember arriving here earlier today?"

"Should I?"

"Yes, you were well aware of being here and quite alert, that is, until we encountered the Hinn."

Fate's stomach tightened. "The Hinn?"

"A foul demon made of fire and smoke. They were said to be extinct long ago. Had I not seen the devil dog with my own eyes, I would not have believed one to be alive today and here in Shalamoraize."

His description conjured two glowing red eyes that burned from the darkness. A chill raced along her spine and she shivered. What was happening?

By all accounts, she should remember encountering something that frightening. How could she be missing even more blocks of time?

Azrael's blue eyes glinted in the light as his expression hardened. "This is all because of you."

Fate gulped. "I don't know what you mean." Yet she knew he spoke the truth. Too much was hidden from her awareness for her to feel comfortable about any of this.

"The Hinn came for you."

The air squeezed from Fate's lungs as she glanced over her shoulder. "Is it here now?"

"I have tethered the ship on the very edge of the way station, though we will need to be on guard for attacks coming from the sands. As for the Hinn, we are as safe as we can be here on the boat. Fortunately, I have a mother who never believed the demons of old were truly gone. She taught me in the art of wards and banishment spells."

Pulling a blanket tightly around her arms, Fate drew in a shaky breath. "Where do you think it is?" she half whispered.

"I suspect down in the grotto where I left it. I conjured a barrier at the entrance, though I do not know how long it will hold."

Fate glanced down at the blanket, worrying her hands until each corner was twisted into taut points. "I guess I should be thanking you for not leaving me down there with it." She looked him straight in the eyes. "Thank you."

"No need." He shifted with apparent discomfort. "I believe I have misjudged you."

This surprised her. "How so?"

He dropped his gaze, but before he did, she caught a look of shame. "I took the opportunity to divine your true nature while you were sleeping."

Fate stared at him in horror. "Exactly how did you go about doing that?"

Azrael reached for an ornate wooden box inlaid with white abalone, which sat atop a pile of leather bound books she hadn't noticed until that moment. Lifting the lid, he retrieved an object small enough to hold hidden in the palm of this hand. He positioned the round piece between two fingers for her to see. Encrusted within the beautifully intricate bronze metalwork were eight teardrop diamonds, each surrounded by smaller diamonds, which caught the light in dazzling flashes. Within the center of the design was a black gleaming surface.

"This is the Unearthly Mirror of the Talfaelah. A gift from my mother," he explained. "It is an object of tremendous rarity and was made for many purposes, such as seeing into the soul of others when the mirror is placed over the heart."

"What did you see?" She desperately wanted to know, but hated having to ask someone else–especially him–to fill in the missing pieces for her.

Azrael returned the mirror to the box and closed the lid. "I saw many troubling things, but not the one I most expected to see."

"Which was?"

"That of a deceiver, such as what I thought you were when we first met."

She rolled her eyes at the heavens with an exasperated sigh. "Sorry to disappoint."

"No, it is I who must apologize... for how I have treated you."

"I wasn't apologizing. You tried to kill me."

"Reprehensible behavior on my part."

"I might be persuaded to let it go, so long as you tell me everything you found out about me. I can't stand being in the dark any longer. I need to know how I got here and why I keep losing time." She sat straight, her heart thudding nervously.

He crossed his legs and rested his elbows on his knees. "Let me begin by saying I have never seen this much disparity in any one person's miraja. You appear to be from many different places all at once. It appears your soul has fractured into pieces to allow those parts of you to be in those places. This would explain why you cannot remember what came before you arrived in Dunebala. The parts of you that left have taken those memories with them."

"What places are these?"

"I cannot say with certainty. One of them is far from here–an ancient source of powerful magic that is part of the stars. Another is here, but not of this world because it resides behind the fiery divide."

Fate's throat constricted. None of this was helping. She was growing more lost by the minute. "Did you see anything else? Like maybe something better than me breaking into a bunch of pieces?"

He dropped his gaze and fell silent.

"Oh, don't tell me it gets worse."

Leaning forward, he looked at her, his expression earnest. "Your powers are not your own. They are borrowed."

This angered her. Her powers, while shocking, were the only good part of this whole miserable situation. Knowing she could defend herself in this deadly world was the only thing making her feel relatively safe. "I don't care what you say," she argued. "They're mine to use as I please now."

"Do you not care to know what the source of your power is?"

"Not if it means giving them up."

"You misunderstand. No one can take them from you."

Fate relaxed somewhat. "Good to know. Please continue."

"The power of an ancient god is wrapped around your waist. Have you not noticed?"

She laughed uncontrollably. There was a hysterical pitch to it, but she didn't care. She was enjoying the outlet. "Do you know how ridiculous that sounds?"

He waved his hand impatiently. "You won't laugh once you have taken a look."

His serious tone dampened her laughter. "Fine," she muttered, and ducked her head beneath the blanket to unbutton her jacket. The pungent smell of her unwashed body after sweating in the sun for three days wafted into her nose and she had to hold her breath. Tugging on her undershirt, she lifted it to expose her skin and gasped. Intricate patterns of light laced across her abdomen from deep within, shimmering beneath muscle and skin. If she didn't know better, she would almost say it looked like she was wearing a glowing corset.

It also explained the fiery sensations of bloodlust that had been churning at her core.

Fate pushed her head from beneath the blanket, her mouth hanging open as she puzzled over yet another mystery. "You're right, there's something–" She stopped and frowned at Azrael. "Did you have a look while I was asleep?"

He held his hands up with a wild shake of his head. "No. There was no need. I can plainly see it in your miraja."

"Even now?"

"Yes."

She squinted at him suspiciously, but decided there were more important matters to focus on than his possible impropriety. "Any chance that x-ray vision of yours can tell me what this is and how it got there?"

"My sight only shows me what you are. Not what came before." He gestured at the pile of books sitting next to him. "I have been searching the ancient texts of my people, but none have revealed answers."

"Hand me one of those. I happen to be a writer and well versed in doing research."

Azrael looked ready to protest, but refrained and did as she asked. Fate set the heavy book on the floor in front of her. The edges of the weathered, brown leather cover were bejeweled with rubies inlaid into the same elaborate metalwork she'd seen on the mirror. "I'm all for sparkles, but you people really take your jewels to a whole new level."

"They are not used for adornment," he replied with an edge of irritation. "Gemstones hold magical properties."

"Doesn't make them any less pretty though." Fate opened the book to pages filled with hand-written text she didn't recognize. "I can't read this."

"I was going to say that, but you seemed determined to... help."

"So much for that." She slammed the book shut with a frustrated huff. "Well, at least I know more than I did before."

"I have not told you everything."

"There's more? Wow. I would've thought missing soul parts and lighting up like a glowworm was plenty enough."

Azrael stroked his chin as his expression turned pensive. "Tell me about your ancestral line, and as far back as is recorded."

Thrown off guard by the question, Fate had to think about it for a second or two. "Uh... I don't know much about my mother's side, other than they came from a long line of librarians who eventually became bookstore owners. Our surname on my dad's side is Welsh. *Floyd.* Yes, it's as boring as it sounds, and it means gray." She watched Azrael for any indication of the enlightenment he sought, but all he did was frown.

"This is all you know of your ancestry?" By all appearances, he seemed appalled. "I can trace my line back by thousands of years."

Fate returned his frown. "Good for you, but that's not how we roll where I come from." He looked about to speak, but she interrupted him. "That's a weird question. Why are you asking in the first place?"

"Because only a descendent of a god–regardless of how diluted with human blood she may be–can survive being god-touched, as you are."

"Whoa. Are you saying what I think you're saying? That one of my ancestors was a god?"

Azrael nodded solemnly. "If you did not have a god in your lineage, you could never be the vessel for the power that now dwells within you. It would have destroyed you on contact."

"Oh." Speechless and baffled, Fate stared past him into the darkness, her mind racing in a hundred different directions at once. Had her grandmother ever mentioned anything unusual about their family history? Or did this god originate on her father's Gaelic side of the family? And how had she recently become 'god-touched'? Was this the reason her soul had shattered into pieces, taking her precious memories with them? These were by far the most nagging questions.

It was all too much to take in, and way too overwhelming. As anxious as she was to learn the details of her lineage, what really mattered at the moment was finding a way to restore her lost memories. That's where she would find answers to her most urgent questions. "How do I get my soul parts back?" she asked at last.

Regret shadowed Azrael's face. "This is not something I can help with. My mother is the only person I know who has performed soul retrievals successfully."

"Will you take me to her?"

"I would, but without ranemist, we are marooned here." He ran his hand through his dark curls. "Not that we will last much longer without food and water. Though thirst and starvation will be the least of our problems if the Hinn breaks free of my wards."

"What about the Moulghazal? Is there a way to call it to us?"

Azrael lifted his troubled gaze, studying her in that quiet, serious way of his. "The Moulghazal's migratory path has remained unchanged for hundreds of years. She never deviates from it."

"I know you don't want any cursey, negative talk when it comes to the Moulghazal, but is it possible something happened that might've thrown her off course? Where I come from, whales sometimes beach themselves and no one really knows why. I know there's no beaches in the sky, but is it possible she may have grounded herself?"

He didn't look happy about her line of reasoning, but at least seemed more open to listening. "If any of this were true, it would explain the Moulghazal's delay. But it matters not. The Moulghazal is a mountain that should not be moved by the whims of anyone such as you."

Fate was at a loss once again. "Am I hearing things? What could I possibly do to make a floating whale do anything it didn't want to do? Especially on a whim. I generally save those for chocolate and popcorn binges, and the occasional risky lipstick color."

Azrael's brooding stare darkened all the more. "Stop this pretence. I know you possess the power of the Word."

Fate threw up her arms. "You said that before and I didn't know what you meant then either, so for Pete's sake, just explain what the power of the Word is. If any of it sounds familiar, I'll be sure to tell you."

Azrael nodded in spite of the suspicious look he continued to give her. "The ancient texts of our people say that in the beginning was the Word, and the Word was with God, and the Word was God."

"Oh hey!" Fate blurted. "One of my people's books says that too!"

"Yes, because it is truth. In the beginning, there was nothing. Only the

Word was in existence before all this was created. In the earliest of times, the different beings of the world knew how to use the power imbued in words to manifest whatever they needed out of nothing. But as time passed, a greedy few began to horde the power of the Word, until at last, the knowledge was lost to the masses. To this day, most live in ignorance of how words are the tools used to add dimension and substance to this world and thus craft our reality."

Fate tapped her chin as she listened intently. "Are you saying the power of the Word is magic we could all be using to have whatever we want, whenever we want?"

"When used correctly, yes."

"Well that proves it. I don't have this power. If I did, I wouldn't be stuck on this boat. I've been dying to go home from the moment I landed in this monster-ridden dust bowl."

He shook his head. "I have seen drawings of the old ones with the power of the Word–a radiant gold light emanating from the crown of the head."

"Like those pictures of saints I've seen in church windows?"

"I know nothing of this. Only that you have the same light as the old masters."

Fate felt around her crown in the hopes of feeling this mysterious light. Her head felt the same. She dropped her hand with a sigh. "A lot of good it's doing me." Azrael grew quiet and stared off into space. "Nothing to say?" she asked.

His expression was thoughtful as he turned his head toward her. "The power of the Word must be harnessed by a calm, decisive mind. You, on the other hand, use the power to weaken yourself with confusion and fear." He gave her a revolted frown. "I will never understand how a simple-minded girl came to be endowed with the original creative forces."

"That's insulting! Didn't your mother ever teach you that if you don't have anything nice to say, don't say anything at all?"

He held up a hand. "I did not say it to insult you. I simply speak the truth."

Fate crossed her arms and scowled. "I think you're confusing simple-minded with disoriented. If I had all my soul parts, I'd have a better handle on all this because I'd remember how I got here. And did it ever occur to you that I might just be a master at using the power of the Word like your old ones?"

A look of apprehension replaced Azrael's judgmental expression.

"Yeah, you might just want to be more sensitive to my feelings.

Otherwise I might... " she scrambled for the right word, "smite you... once I figure out how to 'harness' the Word." She punctuated her tirade by clawing air quotes in the air.

"Forgive me. I may have spoken too soon."

"Darn right, you did. Now here's how it's going to go down. You're going to teach me everything you know about the power of the Word and how to use it. Then, after we've run a few tests, I'll use the Word to get us out of this dry, dirty desert, and far away from that nasty Hinn."

Azrael's blue eyes rounded with surprise.

Fate stood, letting the blanket fall at her feet as she stood over him. "Allow me to introduce myself–since you've never even bothered to ask my name. I am Fate, and I'll be the one deciding what happens from here on out."

38
TRANSIENT TRUTHS

THE SUN WAS AT its highest peak when Finn and Rudwor reached the oracle high in the mountain of Alderath. The four-hour hike had been arduous, and showed in the king's labored breathing and sweaty red face. Finn, on the other hand had barely noticed the steep climb. His impatience to reach the Well of Eyes had pushed him forward with an overabundance of strength and speed, hindered only by Rudwor's need to stop frequently to catch his breath.

"Laddie," Rudwor said through gulps of air, "I swear you'll be the death of me. If not from this climb, then from the next heroic scheme you happen to dream up." He bent, resting his meaty hands on his knees.

"Did you forget the oracle was your idea?" Finn reminded him. He left his friend to rest while he surveyed the rundown temple. Many of the columns were cracked, some broken, having fallen to rubble. The elevation was high enough that there was still snow, though melting slowly with the warming temperatures. "Did something happen here? Has the temple always been in ruins?"

Rudwor stood straight with a grimace as he rubbed his back. "I ordered the priests away from here when I first learned of the scryer's treachery. By the time one of them finally convinced me to let them return, winter had struck and there was no going back to tend to the place." He moved forward stiffly as he took in the disarray. "Hmm, I didn't expect a few years of neglect would do this though. Maybe an avalanche hit the temple. Something like that would account for this kind of damage."

Finn rushed toward the entrance, anxious as to whether the destruction extended to what was inside.

"What's your hurry, boyo?" Rudwor called after him.

Finn didn't bother to answer as he picked through the rubble. The king knew what his hurry was. His heart thudded with a growing dread as he approached a circular pool filled with dark water. When he reached the tiled edge, he kneeled, dipping his fingers in. An oily sludge clung to his skin when he withdrew them from the frigid water and wiped the muck off.

Rudwor's heavy footsteps echoed throughout the dim chamber before he stopped next to Finn. He squinted at the pool's glossy black surface. "I can't see the beast. The water's usually clear as day."

Finn's energy flagged along with his hopes. "It must be dead." He clenched his teeth against the panic burning in his chest. During the climb he'd been certain he'd find out what had happened to Fate and where he could find her. He stood and kicked a broken pillar into the water, disturbing the still surface with concentric waves that rippled beneath the sludge.

Rudwor rested his hand on Finn's shoulders and squeezed. "Sorry, lad. Though I can't say the same for that treacherous beast, and I'm not surprised it's dead after the priests left. I never wanted it to live after how it betrayed my brother. Our family suffered greatly from its vendetta."

Finn jerked his shoulder free of Rudwor's grip, his fists clenched as he paced back and forth. "Why'd you bring me here if you knew this is what we might find?" he growled. "Fate needs me! I should be out there looking for her. Not wasting time climbing mountains for you again."

Rudwor's round face darkened with a warning stare. "Hold on there. I never asked you to go to Mount Helgunth. You went of your own accord."

"Because you were holding my friends in prison!" Finn shouted. "I couldn't just let you execute them. And out of respect for our friendship, I went about it as peaceably as possible."

Shame flickered in Rudwor's eyes, but only for a second. "I'm not proud of that, but a king's decisions extend beyond personal matters. I thought you understood that."

Finn's rage burned hotter than ever. "I've done nothing but jump through hoops for you since I got here, and now after all I've done to bring peace to your kingdom and end winter, I come to find I'm no further along than I was before."

Anger deepened the exertion lingering on Rudwor's red face. "I made you First Knight, Finn. You may have left Beldereth for reasons best for everyone concerned, but your allegiance to this kingdom came with your return. What you did was your duty, and nothing less."

Finn stopped pacing and glared at Rudwor. "I didn't come here to pick up where I left off. I came to tell you war is coming and that you need to prepare."

Rudwor's eyes widened and then he shook his head. "Why would you wait all this time to tell me something like that? You've gone mad, laddie. I don't know what happened while you were away, but we need to get you to the Springs of Almsdeep. The monks helped you before and they can help again."

Finn moved in front of Rudwor, his whole body shaking with fury. "I don't need the monks. What I need is for you to be my friend–not the king–and listen to me."

Rudwor puffed up his barrel chest and began to speak, but Finn cut him off with a low growling sound. "To answer your question, I waited because I needed to help *all* my friends, and that included you. Beldereth was under siege and in no position to fight another war unless I helped."

"And I'm grateful you did, so much so, I've pardoned your friends," Rudwor reminded him.

Finn brought his face within inches of Rudwor's face. "A pardon that still has them under heavy guard."

"To keep them safe from giant haters."

"Maybe so," Finn conceded, "but they're prisoners all the same."

"All in good time, lad. We'll deal with that when we return. My main concern at the moment is what put this idea of impending doom in your noggin."

Finn sucked the cold air between his teeth to control his building impatience. "I've been to a place you can't possibly comprehend or begin to believe, so I won't go into the details of it. But what you do need to believe is that I witnessed the building of an army bigger than you or any of your ancestors have ever faced before." He let that sink in as he watched Rudwor's stunned reaction. "And if that's not bad enough, this army is made up of the most unthinkable, monstrous, hard-to-kill creatures I've ever seen."

Stepping back to give him some breathing room, Finn watched a mixture of fear and confusion play over Rudwor's face before a look of disbelief settled on his broad features. Finn threw up his arms. "You don't believe me."

"How can I? I would've received word from my allies of an army such as what you've described if any of this were true."

"You haven't heard because they only just landed a few days ago," Finn argued. "Word will come, but by the time you hear about it, it'll be too late to stop them. We need to prepare now. You have to gather your allies and take the war to this army before it comes to you."

Rudwor let out a heavy sigh as he gave Finn a pitiable stare. "Lad, let me take you to Almsdeep where you can–"

The sound of water slapping the pool's edge stopped him and they both turned toward the noise. Horns pierced the oily black surface, followed by an enormous, horse-shaped head covered in iridescent scales that were peeling away, exposing sickly gray skin. Overwhelming sympathy for the once magnificent sea creature washed away Finn's anger.

He moved to the water's edge as the scryer glided closer. The creature's eyes were as large and gentle as any horse, but fogged by a milky coating that obscured the blue of its irises. It stopped within a few yards of him, its half blind gaze lifting to meet his. The scryer's voice sifted into his mind, soft and gentle. "*You have come with a question of the heart.*"

Finn nodded, despite his concern for the creature's well being and a desire to right the injustice it had suffered. He remembered the story of how it had been stolen from the sea by one of Rudwor's ancestors, to be held captive in this well for centuries and used as the royal scryer.

The creature bobbed lightly as it tilted its head. *"Have no concern for me. My time is near its end. Ask, and you shall be the one who receives my last gift."*

Finn swallowed hard as he reached for the handfasting bracelet he'd made. "What happened to Fate, and how do I find her?"

The scryer's gaze dropped to the dark surface of the water. After what seemed an eternity of waiting, the creature whispered its visions into Finn's mind. "*The one you love no longer exists. She is reborn as an old god in the desert of living sand. Though you are unmade by this and your connection forever severed, your paths are destined to cross. But be warned, young druid, you will meet your death if you try to find her there. Your search begins with finding the fallen star and the blight it carried to this world. The desert of illusions is where you must go. Do not believe everything you see there, lest you lose your way. Keep the shape shifter close, for when the whole of the world is at war and all seems lost, the power of the Word will be the only salvation.*"

Finn stared speechless at the creature, his heart pounding as he fought the fear the scryer's message had ignited and the cryptic words that echoed in his mind.

No longer exists, unmade, forever severed, your death, blight.

With so much of the message wrapped in mystery, he wanted desperately to deny the whole thing as a false prophecy. Yet he sensed the truth in every word, and that's what scared him most. He wanted to ask more questions, but the scryer closed its clouded eyes and sank below the murk before he had the chance.

The scuff of Rudwor's footsteps startled Finn from the paralysis he'd been thrown into. "Don't let the scryer's doom and gloom message discourage you, lad," he told him. "Remember the silver lining at the end. The scryer rarely ends its prophesies on an up note, so I'm hopeful."

Finn turned away from the pool. "You heard that too?"

"Aye, I suppose it wanted me to know of the coming war." He gestured for Finn to leave with him. "Tell me everything you know about this fallen star and the blight that came with it."

Finn's legs felt heavy as he followed Rudwor out of the temple. "It's not really a star," he explained. "It's a gigantic structure as big as the moon, built by an ancient race of beings who have pale blue skin and six arms. It's called the Keep because the entire thing is filled with powerful objects of magic."

"Sounds outlandish," Rudwor said as they began the descent down the long, winding steps carved into the mountain's rocky incline.

Finn shrugged. "No more outlandish than the gruesome faeries and mermaids I've encountered here."

"When you put it that way," Rudwor huffed, his face already flushed from the first trek of their hike. "And what of this blight?"

"That would be the massive army I told you about. A sorceress named Kaliena found a way to make an elixir that brings the dead to life. She made vats of the stuff and used it to reanimate legions of dead soldiers, though none of them were human. I don't know what they were when they were alive, except to say they may as well have been demons come straight from hell. And they were hard to kill."

Rudwor stopped, this time out of shock, rather than to catch his breath. "Sounds like we'll need all of Oldwilde to fight these things."

"Aye, I'm afraid so," Finn confirmed.

Rudwor rubbed the sweat from his brow and continued the descent. "The treaty with the rock giants was timely, lad. Do you think Grysla and her band will be willing to help me form an alliance with the giants after all they've suffered at my hands?"

"I have no doubt they will. They know about the impending danger. It's why they came with me."

"Good... good," Rudwor murmured. "While I'm handling the negotiations with the giants, I'll have my army march for Asgar. Beldereth had been allies with them for centuries."

Finn's gut clenched into a tight ball as soon as Rudwor mentioned Asgar. He'd never blamed King Tynan for throwing him into the dungeon for killing his evil mother, but he riled against the thought of ever returning there. "You'll want to have Queen Kaura send word to her people on the Eldunough Islands," Finn said, moving his focus elsewhere. "Their fleets are large and formidable."

Rudwor nodded. "Aye, good thinking."

"You may even want to see if King Tynan would be willing to approach the Serpens."

Rudwor stopped again, so abruptly, Finn ran into him. "That abominable race with dragon blood?"

"Aye, the very same."

Rudwor stomped down the steps. "No, no, no. There's a reason nobody crosses the River Torle into Mount Fargrum. The Serpens are hostile and cold-blooded reptiles. And after what you told me about Moria's lifelong grudge and the world of hurt that snake brought down on the kingdom, I could never ally with the likes of them."

"Believe me, I know what they are, but maybe hostile and cold-blooded is exactly what we need to defeat the undefeatable."

Rudwor grew quiet, except for grunts of physical effort as he navigated the steep decline. They were nearing the bottom, where the royal guard awaited them, before the conversation picked up again.

"How are you doing with the scryer's vision of your bonnie lass?" the king asked.

"Not well," Finn ground out between clenched teeth.

"I suppose not." Rudwor nodded to the royal guard when he reached the last step. They waited for Finn and the king to pass by before filing in behind them.

Finn continued on in silence, too tormented to share his bleak thoughts aloud. The scryer had said Fate no longer existed, that she was reborn as an old god. This had to be the work of Hippolyta's magical girdle. Which meant Eustace had failed to find a way to remove it safely before its powers consumed her. He shook his head, wishing his bride wasn't so incredibly headstrong and stubborn.

Yet, those very same qualities might just be what will save her in the end. He could only hope so.

His one solace was in knowing they were destined to meet again. The scryer had spoken truthfully about their severed connection. Regardless of how many times he reached out with his awareness, she was hidden from him. Though he refused to believe this spiritual divide would last forever. They had overcome so much already. He simply could not allow himself to accept that they would not find a way back to each other.

He was part of her, and she part of him.

Finn's heart pounded out his deepest fears as the most troubling part of the scryer's message pricked his mind like a poisonous needle. *You are unmade by this and your connection forever severed.*

Was this the beginning of the end for him? He'd been born from Fate's imagination, her love and overpowering desire to meet him in the flesh.

He wasn't made of the same stuff she was. What happens if she's been taken over by something so powerful, she no longer remembers him... no longer loves him? Would he be unmade? Would he begin to fade into the nothingness he came from?

The terrifying thought sapped his strength with a sudden vengeance. Grabbing at the ache in his chest, he stopped and hung his head.

The royal guards tramped past him. He lifted his gaze, seeing that Rudwor was walking ahead, not having noticed Finn had slowed down.

Rudwor glanced over his shoulder. When he saw how far behind Finn was, he waved him forward. "Catch up, lad!" he bellowed. "We've got much to do!"

Finn forced his crippling fear down into the shadows and quickened his pace, weaving through the soldiers before falling in stride with Rudwor.

Rudwor slapped him on the back, a blow that was meant to be comforting, but threw Finn off balance with the force of it. "Don't let the scryer's message get you down in the dumps. Prophecies are transient truths. Some parts are unchangeable, because they've already happened, but the parts that haven't happened yet are merely strong probabilities. You have the power to shift them towards the outcome you desire."

"I like the sound of that," Finn said, his spirits lifting somewhat.

"You'll be fine, laddie," Rudwor assured him. "Besides me, you're the strongest man I know." He smiled mischievously as he glanced at the female warriors marching alongside them. "But that's only amongst men. I'm not sure I can say the same if I include women."

Finn smiled, thinking of Fate. "Aye, I know what you mean."

They passed through the castle gates into the courtyard. "Assemble my officers and bring our guests to the great hall," Rudwor ordered.

The royal guards dispersed to different parts of the castle as Finn and Rudwor headed to the great hall. They no sooner pushed through the massive doors before several officers joined them around a long table, though no one sat. A few minutes later, several royal guards escorted Sithias, Grysla, Tove and Leif into the hall.

The tree troll had to stoop to pass through the entrance and then gingerly found a place to stand straight where she wouldn't hook the chandeliers with her crown of branches. Sithias, having assumed the human form everyone there was accustomed to, scurried over to stand by Finn. Tove eyed Finn from across the room, but moved to stand next to Grysla, with Leif shadowing her like the protective big brother he was.

"I've called you all here to announce our findings on Mount Alderath,"

Rudwor said, his voice booming throughout the large hall.

Finn only half listened to the king's descriptions of the coming war and the alliances Beldereth would form. His mind was circling around how he might change the course of the scryer's predictions.

"Sssir, are you all right?" Sithias whispered, his amber eyes wide with concern. "You're troubled. Is it about Fate? Has something happened to her?"

"It's bad," Finn said under his breath. "The power of the girdle has taken over. She's not herself anymore. It's why I haven't been able to feel her presence."

Sithias drew in a sharp breath. "Oh dear, I was afraid of that. Did the scryer give you any indication of being able to save her?"

You are unmade by this and your connection forever severed.

Finn shoved the haunting words aside with a shake of his head. "I have to believe there is." He gave Sithias a quick sidelong glance. "The scryer mentioned you."

Sithias's hand flew to his chest with a look of surprise. "Me? Whatever did it say?"

"To keep the shape shifter close, and that when the war was at its worst, the power of the Word will be the only salvation."

Sithias frowned with confusion. "I can still shape shift because I have the mermaid's glamour, but I lost the Words of Making when we left Oldwilde and went to the Keep."

"Then why would it have said that?"

"Could it be referring to my writerly talents? I *am* a powerful storyteller."

Finn screwed up his face. "I suppose maybe."

Sithias stood a little taller and smiled. "I never looked at my writing that way, but yes, I have the power of the Word. I move people deeply with my stories." His gaze turned dreamy. "Is it possible I'm destined to save the world with the might of my pen?"

Finn had his doubts, but he wasn't about to dampen Sithias's heroic vision in case he was wrong.

"Grysla." Rudwor's commanding tone brought Finn's attention back to the assembly as the king continued to address the tree troll. "We owe you a great debt for delivering the rock queen's peace treaty to Beldereth. Your goodwill and capacity for forgiveness is immense after enduring the chains we imposed upon you. Your actions speak highly of your character, and I welcome you and your family to our kingdom as trusted friends and allies."

The tree troll tipped her heavy head toward the king and smiled. Tove and Leif watched Rudwor with guarded expressions, but remained silent.

Rudwor bowed back. "And now I must ask even more of you, Grysla. Would you be my emissary to all giant kind to help form the alliance all of Oldwilde needs to fight and win the coming war?"

Grysla clasped her huge hands together and gave him a solemn nod.

Relief showed on Rudwor's face. "Very good. We will discuss the details over the next few days." He turned to his officers. "Return to your troops. Prepare for the march south to Asgar. We leave in a fortnight."

The great hall cleared, leaving Rudwor alone with Finn and his friends. The king pulled a seat at the table and sat down. He looked tired as he directed his weary gaze at Finn. "I suppose you'll be leaving us soon."

"Tonight," Finn replied.

Sithias gasped with surprise. "Can't we have a last meal together?"

Rudwor slapped the table, his energy suddenly back. "Aye, we must have a celebratory feast! We have much to toast to."

"No," Finn said. "I can't risk the hangover I know you'll do your best to make sure I get from a night of toasting every wee thing you can think of."

"I wouldn't do that," Rudwor protested.

"Remember the first night I got here?"

Rudwor waved him off. "Ack, I was too mullered to remember that night."

"My point exactly."

Rudwor rose from his seat. "This is it then?"

"Aye, I need to go. There'll be no rest for me until I find Fate."

Rudwor pushed the chair aside and strode over to Finn with his arms held wide. Pulling him into a bear hug, he squeezed until the air rushed from Finn's lungs. The king let go and held Finn by the shoulders at arms length, his light brown eyes shining with love. "Find her, young sapling, and then you'll find the peace you deserve."

"Thank you. I'll be seeing you soon." The words came in a choke from his tight throat. Finn hated leaving his friends this way, but delaying the urgent tugging of his heart for even one night would be too painful.

"Damned right you will." Rudwor moved on to Sithias with his hand outstretched. "I'm trusting you to take care of him." He shook his hand so vigorously, Sithias wobbled off balance. "He's as much a son to me as if I fathered him myself."

The moment Rudwor let go of his hand, Sithias rubbed his shoulder with a pained smile. "You can count on me, your highnesss."

Rudwor walked over to Grysla, Tove and Leif. "We won't be letting Finn's leaving stop us from that celebratory feast, will we?"

"No need for arm to be twisted," Leif was quick to reply.

"Ah, a man after my own heart." Rudwor gestured for him to follow him out. "In fact, why wait for supper? Let's begin the toasting in my chambers."

Without so much as a parting glance, Leif followed the king out of the great hall.

Finn and Sithias rounded the top of the table to join Grysla and Tove. Bending low, the tree troll gave Finn a concerned smile. "Stay safe, Shining One," she said, avoiding troll speak so Sithias could understand.

"You as well," Finn told her.

"Sorry," Sithias interjected, "I don't mean to interrupt the goodbyes, but what is all this about the Shining One?"

Finn shrugged. "It's the name the animals in the Twisted Bone Forest gave me when I was lost in the snow before Grysla found me. I guess to them my spirit was much brighter and larger than other humans." Though he was certain some tarnishing had taken place after Mugloth's influence.

"It still is."

Finn glanced at Tove, surprised by how readily she'd picked up on his thoughts.

Sithias cleared his throat. "Uh, I think I'll go to your room and pack your things." Grysla followed behind as Sithias hurried to the door, her footsteps vibrating though the stone floor.

Tove stepped in, unsure at first, but then she rushed to hold Finn. "You'll find her, I know you will," she whispered in his ear.

Wrapping his arms around her waist, he closed his eyes. "I'm not sure, Tove. I've always had an inner compass when it comes to Fate, but it's gone. I don't know how to navigate anymore, and I'm afraid it's going to be the end of me."

Tove pulled back to look into his eyes, her expression both fierce and loving. "Fate does not define you. Only you have the power to do that."

He shook his head. "It's not that simple. Something's happening to me. I can feel it, like a loose thread got caught on a thorn, and every step I take away from that thorn means more unraveling."

The brightness in her irises shifted to a darker shade of green. "Don't talk like that. You're strong and more powerful than you know. Always remember that."

He nodded, but it was an empty gesture and he could tell she knew it too.

"Let me go with you," she offered.

Finn was more tempted to accept her offer more than he cared to admit.

Tove had saved his life once before, and she was ready to do whatever it took to do that again. He wanted that kind of support more than anything, but ultimately, her presence would only confuse matters. "No, I have to do this on my own. And you're needed here."

He could see she was ready to argue. Instead, she cupped his face in her hands and kissed him. Fire coursed through his body as his lips parted in response, their tongues meeting, silky and wet and soft.

Finn broke away, his breath coming in heavy waves as he held her by each shoulder to break contact with her warm, pulsing body. A move that was more difficult than it should have been. But she was entrancing. Her olive-toned skin gleamed and her irises glowed bright green as dark ribbons of hair fell over one eye. If his heart weren't bound to another, he would succumb to her wild beauty with everything he had. "Tove, I can't do this with you." His eyes misted over. "Fate and I... were wed before I left."

The light in her eyes extinguished and she stiffened beneath his grip.

"I'm sorry, Tove, I should've told you when I first came back."

Finn expected a justifiable storm of anger from her, but Tove edged backward, her eyes dead as she turned and sprinted for the door, leaving him standing in the vast emptiness of the room alone and sadder than anything he'd ever known.

39
ASHES OF DESTRUCTION

WARM, SULTRY AIR BUFFETED beneath Sithias's membranous wings, tickling along the edges as he glided over the lush jungles of the islands below. He'd always loved flying, but he had to admit he enjoyed it even more in dragon form. His massive leathery wings, though not as pretty as the soft, tawny feathers given to him by Elsina when he was a hatchling, were more powerful by far.

Not that he would ever admit any of this to Finn. Sithias wasn't about to become the default beast of burden simply because carrying someone was basically effortless. Unless it happened to be a tree troll. Grysla was heavy. Thankfully, Finn was his only passenger.

And a rather sullen one at that. Finn had been in a mood ever since his goodbye to Tove–his eyes dark and shadowed. A low, involuntary growl rattled along the length of Sithias's throat. That seductive sylph had set her sights on Finn from the moment they'd first arrived in the Twisted Bone Forest, doing her best to turn his head.

Finn was so utterly in love with Fate and consumed with missing her he hadn't noticed the girl's attempts to draw him in. But with each obstacle and delay they'd encountered, Sithias could see that Finn's heartache was wearing on him. No red-blooded male could be blamed for wanting to take comfort in what was being so readily offered, especially from a girl with such otherworldly beauty as Tove.

Had Finn taken comfort? Sithias growled again. He didn't want to think of what that would do to Fate.

"What's with the growling?" Finn asked.

"Oh, merely a bit of indigestion," Sithias replied, trying to keep the deep snarl out of his voice. An impossibility coming from a dragon.

"Then I'm glad I'm not in your mouth like I was the first time you turned into a dragon and pretended to eat me," Finn grumbled. "The smell was foul enough when your stomach was settled."

"You weren't exactly a tasty morsssel yourself, being that you were in dire need of a bath after being held in that filthy dungeon."

"Don't remind me."

"Sorry, sssir. I know it's a sore subject."

Finn grew quiet again and Sithias worried his friend's spirits would continue to spiral. The scryer's warning to avoid searching for Fate and wait until their paths crossed wasn't helping either. Who wouldn't feel powerless to create immediate change with a directive like that? But something had to be done to shake Finn out of his misery.

A sudden, stabbing blow to the ribs sent Sithias twisting through the air. His frightened scream came to his ears as a deafening roar. Claws tore through his tough hide of scales, the pain burning deep into the muscles of his left hindquarter as enormous shapes blocked the reeling blur of jungle and sky. He was falling, unable to right himself with more attacks coming from all sides.

Finn grunted with the effort of hanging onto his spiked back. Sithias flapped furiously to level out, only to have Finn plucked from his perch and carried away in the talons of a giant hawk. He no sooner spied one of his attackers, when a terrible, high-pitched scree cut through the silence, followed by the hot slice of claws down the ridges of his back.

Dizzy with pain, Sithias arched his spine, his wings collapsing at his sides as the air blasted past and the ground rushed up to meet him.

The slow drip, drip of water woke Sithias. Opening his eyes to the enclosure of a rusted, iron cage, he blinked and shook his head to make sure he wasn't dreaming.

No. He was indeed inside a cage and back in his natural state. Coiling his tubular body and folding his wings as tight as possible, he rose as far as the cage would allow, hissing from the knifing pain of the bloody gashes he'd received in the attack. He peered through the small openings of the cage to see where he was.

Light sifted in through a broken ceiling of hewn stone. Rotting beams stretched overhead, each breaking the sunlight, casting long shadows over a dirt floor dotted with patches of moss and tall grass. Decaying statues of winged warriors stood as pillars, their arms held above their heads to hold the ceiling. Heavy chains dripping with condensation hung across the other side of the once opulent chamber. A depression in the earth held a shallow pool of rainwater, its surface rippling from countless water drops falling from the chains.

A moan close by had Sithias peeking through the other side of his cage.

It was Finn, waking up inside another cage. The moaning stopped and Sithias wondered if he'd passed out again.

Nothing of the kind.

The cage shook, lurching in place as a furious, inhuman snarl came from Finn and echoed throughout the cavern. Afraid he might injure himself, Sithias called out to him.

The rattling ceased. "Sithias?" Finn's voice was hoarse, weak sounding. "I thought those hawks killed you."

"Fortunately for me, a dragon's hide is thick. Those awful raptorsss would have easily made mincemeat of me if I'd been in any other form."

Panic laced Finn's tone. "Shrink yourself and find out why we were attacked."

"Because dragons are the sworn enemy of my kind," a male voice said from somewhere within the cavern.

Finn banged against the confines of his cage. "Show yourself!"

Sithias pressed his face close to the holes, searching for the owner of the disembodied voice. Tall, slender forms came slowly into view along the edges of the walls. A string of soldiers comprised of both men and women closed in around them, swords drawn as they advanced. Each of them were fair skinned with flaxen hair framing fine, youthful features and wide eyes as gray as rain clouds. Their grace and beauty lent an alluring quality to their form, with faces that were hard to look away from. The only other person Sithias knew who had this same beguiling presence was Princess Kaura of the Eldunough Islands, who was now queen of Asgar. Could it be, this was where they were?

"Please kind sir, Princess Kaura sent us with a message," Sithias said, gambling on his assumptions.

One of the soldiers stepped closer to Sithias's cage. Unlike the others, he wore a modest silver crown adorned with a single sapphire. "Kaura is my sister, and she would never send word by way of a dragon."

"But as you can see, I'm not a dragon. Nor do I ever have to be again." Sithias struggled to smile. "I have many personas I can be. Do you like stories? I'm quite happy to perform one of my plays. Actually, I'm famous for them where I come fr–"

"You are Serpen kind," the prince interrupted, "and obviously a trickster of the highest order." There was no malice in the young man's tone, nor any indication of hatred on his serene expression, yet his attitude remained resolute.

"I assure you, I'm no trickster. My power to change shape really isn't impressive at all. I use a sssea nymph's glamour to do it," he winced at the hiss he'd let slip, but continued his jabbering all the same. "And apparently, these kind of glamours are a shell a dozen beneath the ocean. I'm sure I could scrounge one up for anyone who's interested."

The prince held out the pearl and coral necklace. "You mean this one?"

Sithias gasped. "Oh my."

"He's harmless," Finn interjected. "Sithias and I are trusted friends of your sister, and I can prove it."

The prince strode toward Finn's cage. "How so?"

"Queen Kaura dispatched a messenger hawk to you this last summer, asking you to send soldiers to help free a prisoner her husband, King Tynan, was planning to execute. She asked for discretion in the matter, but your soldiers were too late to save the prisoner."

The prince stared at Finn. "How do you know this?"

"Because I was the prisoner scheduled for execution." Anger laced Finn's words. "If Sithias hadn't come along, pretending to be Tynan's mother in dragon form, I wouldn't be here to tell the story."

"Open the cage," the prince ordered.

A soldier unlocked the door and Finn started to step out.

"Stay," the prince told him as he studied Finn's face. He stared for a moment then stepped back. "Close it."

"No, wait!" Finn shouted.

The soldier slammed the door with a reverberating ring of metal, but before he could anchor the lock, Finn kicked it, throwing the soldier back. Swords bristled toward the cage as Finn burst from the cage.

Sithias went rigid with fear when he saw the black look in Finn's eyes. His friend looked ready to make permanent enemies of this kingdom of mighty warriors, which would most definitely hinder Rudwor's plans for an alliance. "Finn, think about what you're about to do!" he called out.

"They want to lock me up like a bloody animal!" Finn growled. "I won't suffer being anyone's prisoner again. Not ever!"

Finn moved in a sudden blur, closing the space between him and the nearest soldier. Kicking him to the ground, he pounded his fist into the man's face with unbridled rage. Sithias cringed as blood splattered beneath each terrible blow.

A female soldier rushed in from behind, striking Finn on the back of his skull with the hilt of her sword. Finn buckled forward, then turned in a heartbeat. His returning blow sent her flying to the far wall. Her body crumpled to the ground.

Finn spun toward the next soldier, plowing both fists into the man's chest, sending him hurling through the air, slamming him into several soldiers charging forward. They hit the ground in a tangled pile.

Two soldiers rushed Finn from behind, grabbing him by both arms, allowing that split second the prince needed to position the deadly point of his sword on the soft cleft of Finn's throat. Finn instantly strained against them, but stopped all struggling when the prince pushed the sharp, glinting tip into his vulnerable flesh. A thin line of blood trickled down over Finn's heaving chest.

"Do you wish to die here and now?" the prince asked.

The defiance flushing Finn's face vanished, replaced by something akin to grief. At that moment Sithias knew his friend's mind had turned to Fate and the grievous thought of leaving her when she needed him most. The poor boy would do anything for her, even if it meant incarceration.

The prince held a cold gaze on Finn as he spoke to his soldiers. "Put him back in the cage."

Finn's face twisted with fear, but he held still, his breathing increasing to a rapid, shaky pant as the soldiers pulled on his arms. Sithias looked away, unable to watch his surrender any longer, but screams of pain had him pressing his face back to peer through the grate–fully expecting to see that Finn was resisting again. But nothing of the kind was happening. In fact, Sithias had no words for what he witnessed next.

Finn's entire body seemed lit from inside. Radiant sparks of golden light spread over his body as a flameless fire burned his skin down to glistening red muscle. Pain etched his face, his mouth open in a silent scream as muscle gave way to bone. The fire flashed bright, racing along the skeletal structure in a blink, disintegrating all bone into sparkling gold dust. A network of veins and nerves connected to vital organs, eyes and brain floated in place of all previous substance for all but a second, before the delicate pathways burst into spiraling sands of gold.

Throughout this, the soldiers holding onto Finn's arms shrieked, their hands and forearms consumed by the fire in the same way. Though more slowly, so that by the time Finn was gone, they had lost only those body parts. They staggered backward; their gray eyes round with utter shock as they stared at the cauterized stumps of their arms.

Stunned silence filled the cavern for what seemed an eternity. Bewildered and lost, Sithias stared at the glinting gold dust curling in the air like fireflies on a hot summer night. Was this the unraveling Finn had been so shaken by whenever he'd used the teleportation device? Tears welled in Sithias's eyes and he squeezed them shut, unable to look upon the last remnants of his dear friend.

The prince's voice spoke within inches of his cage, making Sithias nearly jump out of his scales. "What wicked sorcery is this?"

Sithias opened his eyes to see the prince staring at him from the other side of the grate. "Finn's n-not a sorcerer. He's... a Druid," he stammered.

"I've never seen a Druid with that kind of speed and strength."

"He is... *was* marked with the Elder race runes." Sithias sniffed and hung his head.

The prince turned to the last standing soldier. "Fetch the healers, and find O'Deldar."

The female soldier seemed not to hear him. She stood with eyes fixed on the cloud of swirling sparks, her sword hanging loosely in her hand with the tip dragging on the ground.

"Go!" the prince commanded, jolting her from the frozen stare with his harsh tone. He watched her sprint across the chamber as he stroked the smooth skin of his chin, deep in thought.

"O'Deldar is here?" Sithias asked.

The prince whirled to look at him. "You know O'Deldar?"

"I was part of O'Deldar's plan to defeat Moria," Sithias explained. "Though Finn was the one who... set her on fire. Not that he was proud of it." He muttered the last part.

The prince pointed at the sparks. "*He* was the Unholy Piper?"

Sithias nodded sadly. "That's what he was trying to tell you."

The prince looked truly intrigued. "My sister was miserable over his demise, having known the truth behind Moria's deceptions upon the kingdom. She would be greatly comforted to know he survived after all."

Sithias heaved a sigh, his eyes watering as he rested his head on his coiled body. The prince grew quiet, most likely realizing the irony of his words and kneeled next to one of the unconscious soldiers.

The soldier sent to find O'Deldar returned with a host of robed figures, all of whom spread out to attend to the injured soldiers. Some had woken, and those who could walk, were assisted by the healers and taken from the chamber. The others were carried away.

Just as the last soldier was being removed, another robed figure, much smaller in stature than the rest, entered and strode over to the prince. They spoke in hushed tones before the conversation ended abruptly. The robed figure stormed across the chamber and stopped in front of Sithias's cage, staring at him from within the shadows of his hooded robe.

"Sithias?"

Sithias lifted his head when he recognized the man's voice. "O'Deldar?"

The old Druid pulled his hood back and smiled, his dark eyes crinkling. His brown skin stood out in sharp contrast to the fair-skinned race he lived amongst, though his salt-and-pepper beard did much to soften his raw-boned features. O'Deldar was not a tall man, especially in comparison to the prince and his soldiers, but he emanated an air of majesty even the prince could not match.

"Release him at once," O'Deldar ordered.

The female soldier who'd retrieved the priest jumped to attention and unlocked the cage. Sithias slithered from the cramped enclosure, stretching and flapping his wings. Several feathers fluttered to the ground. He would no doubt lose many more before the day was out. His grief over losing Finn was already unbearable.

O'Deldar shot the prince an angry look. "Return his glamour."

The prince stepped forward, holding the glamour out at arm's length. Sithias weaved his head through the loop of the necklace and transformed into the tall, skinny young man he'd presented himself as when he'd met O'Deldar. He hoped the white hair and bone-pale skin would be more acceptable to the prince and his people. Though he decided to keep his wings, minus the toga, harp and golden circlet of leaves of the playwright and actor, settling instead for a plain tunic. Not that he would be in the mood to perform anytime soon, regardless of how much he may have taken Asgar by storm with his rocketing stardom.

"Leave this to me," O'Deldar said with undeniable authority.

The prince's gaze flicked from the priest to Sithias and back again, but in the end departed without a word.

O'Deldar waited for the chamber to clear before his attention moved to the sparks whirling near Finn's cage. Sithias followed him over to them, his heart beating hard with a desperate hope, hindered only by the dread that hope would be smashed once and for all. "Is there any chance you can bring Finn back?" he asked.

The old priest narrowed his eyes on the glinting specks of light. Reaching out, he touched one of the embers. The tip of his finger singed on contact. Sucking in a sharp breath, he snatched his hand back and looked at Sithias with a sobering frown. "I wish I could, but these are the ashes of destruction. I regret to say, there is no life left here."

40
RAIN

HARNESSING THE POWER OF the Word proved much trickier than Fate had expected. She slumped against the railing of the boat, holding her nose as she stared at her last disastrous attempt. Azrael stood opposite her on the other side of the deck, the lower half of his face veiled to obstruct the nauseating stench of rotting fish wafting around them.

She'd been trying to summon the Moulghazal by reciting a chant Azrael had provided in his native tongue. The words had been difficult to pronounce, and she'd made a mess of them. But when clear blue skies had misted over with swirling gray clouds, Azrael was certain the Moulghazal had arrived.

He couldn't have been more wrong. The precious ranemist they needed to fuel the ship was not what poured down over them. The heavens opened like a giant trap door, dumping countless dead fish onto the deck of the boat. If anything, Fate had successfully summoned the contents of the Moulghazal's stomach, rather than the creature itself.

They'd both ducked for cover, waiting for what seemed an hour for the revolting slap of slimy carcasses piling onto the deck to cease. By the time it was finally over, the smell was more than Fate could take and she'd retched over the side of the boat.

"Well, I think it's safe to say this one makes the accidental sandstorm and the water turned to seaweed soup look like a stroll in the park," she said at last.

Azrael stared back with a blank look. "Regardless, I feel we're getting closer to calling the Moulghazal."

"That's what you said the last two times." Fate clamped her hand over her mouth, forcing down another bout of nausea. "Except this one stinks in every sense of the word."

He bent, grabbing for some of the fish pressing against his legs and hiked them over the side. After doing this for a few minutes he stopped to look at her. "The fish will not move themselves. Get to work."

"Ew, it's bad enough I'm up to my hips in them, but you're crazy if you think I'm touching these slimy things with my bare hands!"

"Do you really expect I can clear the deck all by my–"

The ship lurched upward, throwing Fate off balance. She belly-flopped onto the fish, her face and hands slipping over rancid scales, fins and fogged, bulging eyes as she struggled to stand. Another blow sent her rolling to the other side as the ship tipped on its side, burying her beneath the fish. Overwhelmed by disgust, she held still as they slid past her body and over the edge. When the weight of them lifted, she burst through the surface gasping for clean air. But the ship continued to tip and gravity took over.

Fate dropped into a freefall, her arms flailing for something to grab hold of. A hair-raising roar from below made her look down and she screamed when she saw the terrible maw stretching wide to catch her.

Azrael grabbed her by the forearm, his grip painful as she slammed against the hull of the boat. He pulled her back into the boat and she clung to him in a moment of weakness. Instead of pushing her away, he held her close within the cradle of the boat's sidewalls.

The ship righted itself with a sudden jolt, knocking them from each other's arms. They hit the deck and it was all Fate could do to rise to a sitting position. Azrael was on his feet in an instant, rushing to look over the edge. The tension in his shoulders visibly relaxed as he turned and leaned against the railing. "The dharakir is gone. There was enough of a meal from the fish to satisfy it."

Fate gave him a weary thumb's up. "Yay." She glanced around at the small number of fish left scattered in random corners of the deck. "I suppose that's one way of cleaning up that stinky mess."

Azrael busied himself with flinging the few remaining fish over the edge. "Except you touched them with more than just your bare hands." The veils he'd had wrapped around his nose and mouth had fallen away, allowing her to catch the hint of a smile on his face.

She was reminded of the feel of his arms around her.

"Yes, well there's that." She looked away, hiding the smile that came in response. Blowing out the last of her stress in one long exhale, she stood, holding her arms out to examine the muck she'd been smeared with and wrinkled her nose. "But we're still left with the stink. How're we going to get rid of it? It's not like we can use what's left of the drinking water to clean ourselves off."

Azrael rubbed his hands together. "The deck needs to be swabbed as well. The smell will only get worse as the sun bakes the fish oil and blood into the wood."

"We have a bucket of seaweed soup you could use," Fate offered. "Which of course will only add to the fishy smell."

"I fear you are going to have to do your best to conjure water with the Word." He sounded every bit as uncertain as she felt.

"Ooh, such risky business."

"Rain would be best. We can catch the water in the empty barrels and clean the deck with much less effort."

Fate shrugged. "Sure, and we can strip and shower off while we're at it, too."

His blue eyes blazed with interest as his gaze trailed down the length of her body. Feeling a little like she was being undressed with his eyes, she blushed and fidgeted with her hair. When she felt the grime in the curl she twined around her finger, the heat in her face intensified. She must look a fright, and realized she was imagining things. After all, the majority of Azrael's actions and attitude toward her had been aggressive and angry.

He suddenly looked uncomfortable. "I will look to my books to find the chant for summoning a rainstorm."

"That's all fine, I have nothing against your chants, but we're three for three when it comes to absolute debacles. I'm beginning to think me trying to speak your language is what made them all go kerflooey. Don't you think it's probably best I stick with speaking English? But only if you can translate for me."

Azrael frowned as he thought about her idea. "It seems sacrilege... but I am forced to agree you may be right. You have truly slaughtered my language." He moved to the big wooden box holding his sacred texts.

Fate took that as a yes and paced the length of the deck while he rifled through the pages of one of his books. After a few minutes, he set the book down, raced across the deck and dug inside one of the supply boxes. When he found what he was looking for, he returned with a bowl and a burlap sack that looked like it might contain flour or something along that line.

Azrael sat back down in front of the book and gestured for her to sit opposite him. Placing the bowl in front of her, he set the burlap sack next to it.

"Are we going to bake a cake first? I prefer chocolate, just so you know." She chuckled, but sobered when he tightened his lips as though he would yell if he didn't do so.

"These rituals are not to be taken lightly. Each word is sacred and to be revered. If this is not how you spoke them before, then this is why the last three chants failed."

"All right already," she muttered, "I'll be more reverent."

Opening the bag, he reached in and drew out a handful of pink rock salt. "You will place as much salt as you can hold in one hand and pour it into the bowl with each sentence. Do you understand?"

"Yes." She squelched the urge to roll her eyes.

"Repeat the chants after me." He gave her one last warning glance. "Word for word."

She nodded amiably, in spite of wanting to slap him for his patronizing tone. "Mhmm, got it."

Satisfied, he bent his head over the yellowed pages and recited the first sentence.

"*Born of earth and sea, I offer this salt to the skies and call the rain.*"

Fate scooped the rock salt as she repeated the line, letting the pink crystals fall through her fingers into the bowl.

"*With this salt, I take control of air, earth, water and fire.*"

As Fate spoke the words and poured more salt, she sensed a change in the air.

"*Let this salt pour with rain from far and near to cover all.*"

The air grew heavy with moisture as she recited the last line. Gray swollen clouds accumulated out of nowhere upon saying the last word. Juicy raindrops smacked the deck, dotting the wood with dark splatters. Fate held her face to the sky and stuck her tongue out to taste the rain. She let the sweet water trickle down her throat and looked at Azrael. "We did it!"

He stared back in awe.

"Stop looking so surprised," she scolded playfully.

Azrael flashed a smile that rendered her breathless. His teeth were bright pearls against his mocha-colored skin, his eyes shining like the bluest ocean. Raindrops dripped from the ends of his long ebony hair, the water wetting his face until his mahogany skin glistened. She'd never denied his good looks, but the display of joy in his face made him all the more devastatingly gorgeous.

He jumped to his feet, and shocked her by extending a hand to help her up. Hesitantly, she took his hand and rose, unable to tear her gaze from the entrancing curve of his mouth.

"I am not surprised," he told her. "This is respect for what you have done." His voice deepened with emotion.

Her heart skipped a beat, flushing a wave of heat over her neck that pooled in her cheeks until they burned. "I'm just doing what anyone in my position would do." She cringed inwardly at her breathy words.

Azrael's gaze roved over her face. The intensity of his grin faded into a warm, inviting smile. Fate held her breath as he leaned in. Her heart hammered. Was he about to kiss her? But then he took a step backward and she fell forward into the empty space he left between them.

That's when she realized she'd been the one leaning in.

She turned her head, hiding a pained expression. Her face was so hot the rain should be steaming on her skin. "Uh… so how long will the rain last?" she asked, scrambling to regain her dignity by saying something to fill the sudden awkwardness.

Azrael walked to the stern of the ship and returned with two mops, one of which he gave her. "I do not know. For now, let us use this abundance of water to clean the deck."

Avoiding eye contact, Fate grabbed the mop and went to work swabbing the wooden planks. She pushed the mop around like a crazy person, grateful for an activity to pour her mortification and frustrations into. What had she been thinking by allowing herself to feel anything but contempt for a man who'd imprisoned her, tried to kill her and then treated her like an idiot?

She was suffering from Stockholm syndrome. That was it.

Perfectly acceptable, given the conditions. It wasn't her fault he wasn't a repulsive troll. She did what any girl would do in the presence of such a handsome face. But not anymore. She was done being sucked in by his spellbinding blue eyes and hot chocolate skin.

A hand on her shoulder startled her, making her whirl around with the pole of the mop held like a sword, ready to fight. Azrael lifted an arm to block her blow. Glaring at him from behind the dripping curtain of her long hair, Fate relaxed her grip on the mop. The mild look of alarm on his face vanished as he too took a more relaxed stance. "I was calling out to you, but you did not hear me. I had no idea you enjoyed mopping to such a degree."

Fate started to disagree, but decided to let him think what he wanted. "What is it?"

He gestured with a sweeping arm toward the deck and a line of water barrels. "The deck is clean, thanks to your efforts mostly. The barrels are full with fresh water and sealed." He walked over to a tub, which she hadn't noticed he'd brought up from the below. It too was full of water. Some bottles with oils, the color of olive, amber and violet, and stuffed with flowers and fruits, had been set beside the tub.

"Your bath awaits." He said this with a slight bow of his head. "You will find clean clothes in the box there. They are my sister's, and should fit you."

Fate dropped the mop and walked over to the tub, her hands already unbuttoning her soiled jacket. She slipped it off, shedding the undershirt, down to her tank top. Kneeling next the oils, she uncorked the amber colored bottle with the moss and citrus rinds, and breathed in the honeyed, woodsy scent. A happy sigh escaped past her lips as she poured a teaspoon of the oil into the water.

Hooking her fingers in the waistband of her trousers, she tugged hard at them as the drenched fabric stuck to her skin. The momentary struggle, brought her back to the moment, and she was shocked by her lack of modesty. She glanced over her shoulder, prepared to demand privacy, but Azrael had already retreated below deck.

Fate shed the remainder of her clothes, leaving them in a messy pile on the floor. She stepped into the tub–welcoming the cool temperature of the water against the balmy, evening heat of the desert–and sank into pure fragrance and silk with a soft moan of delight.

The rain pattered down lightly over her as she dipped below the surface and submerged herself in tranquil silence. If she could hold her breath, she'd stay right there forever. Or at least until her skin wrinkled into a prune.

She rose slowly and ran her fingers through her hair, now slick with perfumed oil. Tipping her head back, she stared up at the raindrops showering down in glittering streams from a vast blanket of night. She let out another happy sigh and decided she would soak until she was permanently scented with the aroma of amber oil.

"Are you dressed?" Azrael called out from below deck.

"Foiled," Fate muttered. Leaning over the edge of the tub, she opened the box and drew out a blanket. Glancing from side to side, she wrapped it around her chest, grabbed the clothes and dashed for the supply area sheltered by a canvas tarp.

"Give me a minute!" she cried out, while drying off. Fumbling with the clothing he'd supplied, she drove her legs into a pair of thin, lightweight leather breeches before sliding her arms through the holes of a sleeveless hooded vest. They fit well, even the boots. The last article of clothing was a cloak, made of an otherworldly gossamer material. It was the same material Azrael used to make himself invisible whenever he was fully veiled by the cloak. She passed her hand beneath the translucent cloth, watching how the delicate weave reflected her surroundings.

Smiling, she whipped the cloak over her shoulders and clasped it at her neck. Feeling human once again after a much-needed bath, and even a little regal in her new clothes, she strode over to the hatch and peered down at Azrael. He must've bathed as well, because he was looking every bit as freshly washed as she felt.

"You will spend the night down here," he offered. "Until the rain ceases."

Fate stared at him in surprise. She'd been made to sleep on deck with only a few scratchy blankets as her mattress. In fact, she hadn't even stepped below deck. "Sure, why not?" She did her best to sound nonchalant, in spite of a growing curiosity.

She climbed down the ladder, gasping at the luxurious trappings of his sleeping quarters. The walls were draped with jewel-toned silks, the floor covered in Persian rugs and silken cushions. Four inviting mattresses curtained off with sheer netting flanked each side. Hanging from the draped ceiling, were many brass lanterns, each cut with elaborate patterns to diffuse the light and cast interesting shadows over the cabin's decadent contents.

There was a door, slightly ajar, on the other side of the ladder. Behind it, she saw a second bathtub surrounded by water barrels. Now she understood why Azrael had always appeared bathed, while she, on the other hand, had soured into a sweaty mess beneath the sun.

"Huh, look who's been living in style while I've been roughing it upstairs," she stated, her tone flat with annoyance.

Without bothering to look sheepish–as she would've preferred–Azrael sat down on a cushion and held up a platter of dates, cheese and olives. "Will you join me for food?"

Why was he being so nice all of a sudden? Was it fear of her power, or was it finally kindness? Her stomach growled, and she decided those sort of questions could wait. "I've never been one to say no to food."

He stopped her before she could take another step. "Leave your boots there. I have left slippers for you."

Fate removed the boots and slid her feet into the satin slippers. *Nice.* She plopped down onto one of the cushions.

"It is a meager offering, of which we will need to make last until our circumstances improve."

Fate nibbled on a date, savoring its sweetness. "I'm not a big eater. Unless we're talking chocolate yumminess. Or popcorn. Then all bets are off. Just stand back and don't get in my way."

"I know nothing of these kinds of food."

"Then you are missing out, my friend. There's nothing better." She popped an olive in her mouth, rather enjoying the salty contrast to the sweet date. "But this isn't bad either." She reached for the cheese, which melted on her tongue, delighting her taste buds with a pleasing blend of sour and bitter. "Mmm, not bad at all."

"Allow me." Azrael took the knife, cut a strip of date, and then halved an olive. Taking both pieces, he wrapped them in a thin slice of cheese and handed it to Fate.

"Oh, I see where you're going with this." She grinned and took a bite. The delectable fusion of salt, sweet, sour and bitter exploded in her mouth. Closing her eyes as she chewed, Fate moaned. "Heaven. Pure heaven."

When she looked at him, the same devastating smile lit his face. Her throat closed and she coughed on the food as it stuck halfway down. After that, she grew shy without knowing why exactly and her appetite shrank beneath all her nervous energy. They ate in relative silence, until Azrael had eaten enough as well.

"We should rest for the night." Azrael stood with the platter in hand and returned the leftover food to the storage bins. "When morning comes, we will call Moulghazel. This time in English."

Fate nodded. "Where should I sleep?" She blushed, nervous about his intentions.

"Take one of those."

Relief flooded through her as Azrael gestured to the right side of the room. He moved to the nearest lantern and extinguished the light. Fate kicked off her slippers, then removed her cloak before lying down on the mattress. Covering herself with the cloak, she curled onto her side, watching the room dim as each lantern's light was doused.

She lifted her head. "Would you mind leaving one light on?"

Azrael left the last lantern burning and strode to the opposite wall. Fate blinked sleepily as he shed his cloak, his slippers and then his shirt. Her eyes widened at the sight of the tattoos covering his bare, chiseled back–circles within circles woven together to encompass intricate mandalas composed of geometric designs, broken only by softer lines of lotus leaves with all-seeing eyes at their centers.

He turned and sat on the bed. His lean, muscled chest and arms were solidly inked with a continuation of the beautiful patterns on his back. Her gaze traveled over his torso, slowly, raptly, then stopped at his eyes. He was staring straight back.

Fate's face burned hot as she clenched her eyes shut. When she opened them again, Azrael was lying down on his back with his arms resting behind his head, his gaze fixed on the ceiling. She started to breathe again.

Huffing with a strange, edgy impatience that began surging through her limbs, she flung herself onto her other side, at the same time, trying desperately to put the image of his muscular chest out of her mind.

After an hour of tossing and turning, she chanced another glance in

Azrael's direction. He hadn't moved from his reclining position, and from what she could tell in the weak light, he was still awake too.

"Do you know any good bedtime stories?" she asked.

Azrael rolled onto his side and rested his head on his hand. "I learned many epic tales sitting at my mother's heels."

"Me too. It was kind of a thing with my father and I. He read stories to me every night." She laughed slightly. "Even when I got too old for it." Fate's eyes watered with an overwhelming case of homesickness she'd been denying, but could no longer hold back. "It always helped me get to sleep."

"Then I will tell you a story. Though it is one that will take more than this night to complete."

"I always did love a good series." Hugging her pillow, she settled on her side to face him.

"I must warn you, this story will stir dreams, and not all of them peaceful."

Craving a distraction from her sudden-onset-heartache, Fate blinked the tears from her eyes. "I'm a seasoned story hound. I can handle it."

"Very well. Then close your eyes and I will take you back to a time when gods chose to be born into mortality in order to makes sons who would be endowed with the strength to fight the demon plague."

Her eyes popped open. "Demons like the Hinn?"

"Yes, like the Hinn, as well as many other kinds of demons. One such son of the gods was Prince Kelael. He was chosen by the wise old wizard, Dagon, at the age of seventeen for his superior strength, and given great weapons of magic to destroy the demons."

The tented room seemed to darken and Fate thought she caught a glimpse of two red eyes glowing from within the thickest shadows. She clamped her eyes shut and sank into the soft, rhythmic cadence of Azrael's voice.

"*In another kingdom, the sad, fatherless King Elzanar wished for a child. He was staring into the flames of a fire beneath the stars when he made this plea. The gods took pity and granted his request by gifting him with an infant born of fire in that moment. The king snatched her from the flames and named her Sarayna. She was everything the king had imagined, and even more. She grew to be a young woman of unsurpassed beauty, whose spirit shone brighter than any jewel. When she came of age, the king challenged that whomever could lift and wield the great scimitar of the gods, would be granted Sarayna's hand in marriage.*"

A curious longing came over Fate. Holding the pillow tight, she stroked the silk and wool bracelet of unknown origins on her wrist. The differing textures against her fingers were calming and comforting. Her lids grew heavy as she drifted near sleep.

"*Hearing of this, the old sage took Kelael to see the scimitar. Overcome by a desire to brandish the divine weapon, Kelael lifted the mighty sword with ease and skill. King Elzanar was pleased and in turn arranged a festive wedding between Princess Sarayna and Prince Kelael.*"

A flurry of colorful images played across the field of Fate's mind–twirling skirts, satin ribbons and flowers. As she sank deeper into the waking dream, fleeting impressions of pretty maidens and handsome young men with intertwined ribbons dancing around a thin fir tree stripped of its lower branches flashed in her mind's eye like freeze-frame photos.

Smiling drowsily, she welcomed the visions, wondering which one was Sarayna, and which was Kelael. As she focused on the dancers, one came forward. Breathless and excited by the dance, he smiled at her through a tangle of bronzed-gold hair, his eyes as lustrous and green as rain-washed leaves. He was stunning, and everything she'd ever dreamed of.

Fate's heart climbed into her throat as she reached out to keep him there, but as with all dreams born of deep slumber, they were uncontrollable and impossible to hold.

41
FREEDOM

A CONSTANT THUDDING OVERHEAD woke Fate from a dreamless sleep. Groggy and rubbing her eyes, she rose to see Azrael climbing the ladder. After opening the hatch, he was instantly pelted with a mass of dark, wriggling things spilling over his head and shoulders.

Curious, Fate inched forward, her skin crawling with apprehension as she stared at the squirming floor. It took several seconds before her mind registered what she was looking at.

Worms. Thousands of them!

Screaming, she bolted to the far end of the room with her back pressed to the wall.

Slamming the hatch shut, Azrael jumped off the ladder, the muscles in his arms and back bunched with tension as he scanned the room for threats. When he didn't see one, his shoulders relaxed and he gave her a baffled look. "What is this screaming about?"

Clamping her hand over mouth, she pointed at the bottom of the ladder.

He looked at the worms and then at her. "The earthworms?"

Fate worried her hands together and nodded.

"They are harmless."

She finally found her voice again but it came out as more of a croak. "Th-there's so many of them."

He waved his hand at the floor. "This is nothing. There are far more on deck. It would appear we have more cleaning to do." He listened to the thumping of worms hitting the deck. "As soon as the deluge has ceased."

Fate convulsed with revulsion. "I'm not going up there! I won't touch a single one of those slithering mucilaginous tubes of hideous goo!"

Azrael blinked in confusion. "Why are you so afraid of them?"

Unwilling to relive one of the most horrific experiences of her life, Fate stared at him with indignation. "The real question is, what are they doing here? Is this a common event in the desert? Do you normally have worm storms here?"

Azrael thought for a second. "Not in my lifetime. If I were to guess, I would say this came from you."

"Oh no you don't. You're not blaming this on me."

"They came on the heels of the rain. A rain which was summoned and is not natural to Dunebala, except every thousand years." Azrael studied her with a pensive expression as he stroked his smooth chin. "What does the rain mean to you?"

"Nothing."

He shook his head. "Whether we realize it or not, all things, be it food, people, places or weather, affect us in ways that are either pleasant or uncomfortable. So I ask you, how does rain make you feel?"

"Well, it's kind of mixed. Rainy days, which are fairly common where I come from, were a great excuse to stay inside and write, or draw, or spend the day baking brownies with my friend, Jessie. And sometimes my dad would make popcorn in four different flavors for us if he wasn't working, and we'd have a day-long movie marathon." She smiled wistfully as the ache for home returned. "I loved those rainy days."

Azrael's blue eyes softened. "Was there anything you didn't like about the rain?"

"Being out in it, duh. I don't like getting wet. I mean, who does?"

"I welcomed the rain last night. It was a rarity I will not soon forget."

"I suppose I can see your point, given where you live," Fate agreed. "But when the rain shows up more than the sunshine does, it can get old. Plus, I really hate how the worms come out after the rain." She rubbed the rash of goose bumps breaking out over her arms. "It made walking to school feel like I was navigating a minefield. I never knew when I was going to step on one and get its squishy innards on my shoes."

"There, that is why the worms came after the rain." He tapped his temple with the hint of a smile. "Your buried fear weaved itself into the chant."

"Hmm, I guess that makes sense."

"This is why you must treat the power of the Word with utmost respect. Careful consideration of what you choose to use them for means the difference between harmony and utter disaster."

She nodded. "Yeah, I got the message. Four times. But I'm still not going near those gore noodles."

"Very well." He sighed and turned to scooping the worms into a shallow pan.

Unable to watch, Fate stared at the drapes covering the ceiling, distracting herself with the beautiful paisley patterns and rich colors. The thud of falling worms stopped as abruptly as it began, and Azrael climbed up to lift the hatch. Fate shuddered upon hearing the wet plopping of more worms spilling through the hole. After several minutes of scraping this additional batch into a pan, he carried the load of worms up the ladder and closed the hatch behind him.

The tension in her shoulders eased somewhat, but she was unable to relax fully. Now that she knew she truly possessed this precarious power of the Word, she was even more unsettled than before. How had she come to have such a power? She should remember if something that remarkable had happened to her. Yet, she could think of nothing. Everything between leaving the book signing at the Seattle Public Library and her mysterious arrival in Dunebala was a big fat blank.

She ruminated on this for nearly an hour before the hatch door opened and Azrael called down. "Fate, climb on deck. You must see this." There was an excitement in his voice she'd never heard before.

She inched toward the ladder. "Is it safe? Are they all gone?"

"Yes, yes, the worms are gone. Please, come up!"

Fate climbed the ladder, hesitantly poking her head above deck as she scanned for signs of wriggling escapees. Surmising the coast was clear, she stepped on deck and joined Azrael near the bow of the ship. "What's up?"

He touched the small of her back, gently guiding her to look in the direction he was pointing. "See those clouds in the distance?"

Fate squinted into the early morning light. A stretch of swirling, misty clouds grazed the horizon. There was an orange glow at the center, which she assumed was the sunrise reflecting burnished rays off the rise and fall of the swelling dunes. "Is that what's left of the rainstorm? Wait, don't tell me it's coming back. Do I need to do another chant?"

"No, do you not see it?" Azrael's blue eyes blazed with anticipation.

Fate focused on the clouds, noticing they seemed to be much closer, as if blown by high winds at a tremendous speed, yet nothing stirred the sands below. "Not really, except that maybe they're moving unnaturally fast."

"That is the Moulghazal." He laughed, a pleasurable sound that tingled along her spine. "She answered your call. You did it."

Fate stared into his eyes, caught in the dazzling brilliance of his smile. When he saw she was speechless, he wrapped his arms around her, pulling her close as his mouth brushed the shell of her ear. "Thank you, Fate. You have not only saved us from certain death, but you have saved my people as well." The heat of his whisper against her skin made her go weak in the knees.

He let go, and she had to grab the railing to keep from tipping over. "We must leave now to catch the wake. Take the helm while I untie us and release the sails."

She nodded and stiffly took her station, grateful for the wheel to hold onto to keep her upright. With her heart pounding, she watched Azrael rush to the ropes and push them off from the rocks. When they were well away, he released the struts. The sails unfolded, spreading out to either side as the last stores of ranemist shimmered over the stiff canvas.

Azrael slid in behind her and took the wheel. "We will steer the ship together. Let us hope the shadow we cast over the sands goes unnoticed."

The warmth of his chest radiated against her back as his arms brushed her skin. Her head swam, and she had to concentrate to keep from leaning into him.

As the ship moved at a dangerously crippled height across the undulating sands, Fate finally made out a solid shape amidst the rolling clouds of mist. Her curiosity peaked; she rose on tiptoe, watching as the mist curled away in places, offering glimpses of the behemoth swimming within the thick churn.

A haunting, sonorous call echoed out over the desert as the sky whale crossed the sun, casting an enormous shadow that darkened the entire deck as they moved directly beneath. Fate tilted her head back, her jaw dropping as the glowing belly of the colossal creature passed over them. An internal fire lit the whale's underside entirely. Steam rolled off the heated, leathery skin and billowed up and around its massive outspread fins.

The air grew humid as tendrils of mist trailed down over them, leaving beads of dew over every surface. Heat pressed in, saturating the air with a heavy wetness until Fate's clothes clung to her skin. The salty scent of brine carried on the eddying mist reminded her of vacations near tropic shores with her dad and Jessie. Did the whale's migratory pattern include a dunk in the ocean?

She released the wheel when the ship rose suddenly and swiftly. "What's happening?"

"Moulghazel's ranemist is soaking into the sails and lifting us out of harm's way," Azrael explained. "We can now ride in Moulghazel's wake all the way home."

Her stomach tightened. "Home?"

"Yes, the city of Biraktar. It means jewel of the skies." His tone turned wistful as he described a place high above the menacing desert, filled with golden towers and glittering glass domes of azure, tangerine and violet. It sounded truly beautiful, and his love for his home was evident in the far off look in his eyes.

But what would become of her after they arrived? Would his mother actually help her retrieve her lost soul parts? Or would she be relegated to the slaves' quarters? She was, after all, still his prisoner as long as the soul ring bound her to him. Why had she let herself be blinded by his irresistible good looks? Obviously, the silly crush that had followed was a momentary weakness, considering how badly he'd treated her in the beginning.

Her insides seized with distrust as he continued on about his city. She had to figure out a way to free herself before they arrived in Biraktar. But how? Azrael had said she needed his blessing to unlock the soul ring. Well, there was no time like the present to press the issue. He was in a grateful mood, and she wasn't sure how long that would last.

"Uh, your city sounds amazing," she interrupted. "I can't wait to get there to see it for myself." Looking pleased, Azrael started to pick up where he left off, but she cut in before he could say another word. "How long before we arrive in Biraktar?"

"Normally it would take a fortnight or more." Smiling, he shook his head in amazement. "With Mouldghazal's speed, we should arrive by tomorrow."

"That soon, huh?" She frowned.

"What is it?"

Fate pushed past the barricade of one of his arms to put some much needed space between them. When she was well away, she turned and pointed at her ankle. "I think it's time you removed this thing." She wasn't asking. This was an order.

Azrael's gaze dropped to the soul ring resting over her boot. All joy vanished from his face as he looked at her. "I cannot."

"Cannot, or will not?"

He hesitated before answering, allowing just enough time for Fate's anger to come to a full boil. "Both."

"Both?" she yelled. "You said all I needed was your blessing to unlock the soul ring. I've earned that in spades. You said it yourself. I saved you and your people by summoning Moulghazel. If anything, this thing belongs on your ankle!"

He surprised her by nodding. "I agree." He reached into a silk pouch hanging from this belt, pulled out another soul ring and held it out to her.

"How many of those do you have?"

"Take it," he pressed.

Fate frowned at it. "And do what? Stack it on top of the other one?"

"No. Place it on me."

"What? Why?"

"I owe you a life of servitude for the greatest of all gifts you have blessed me and my people with."

Fate backed away as he stepped forward. "No, no, no. Take mine off, and we'll call it even-steven."

Azrael held still to keep her from withdrawing, his thumb smoothing over the patterns etched in the brass ring as he did so. "This is the only way, Fate."

Fear and anger twisted together in her gut. "None of this makes sense," she seethed. "What kind of life is it for either of us to be indebted to each other this way? Keep your freedom. All I ask is that you give me mine."

His blue eyes filled with regret. "You are too valuable to release."

"What... this is all about *money*?" She choked on the words before her voice pitched to an infuriated scream.

"Never," he was quick to say. "You are a priceless treasure, of which my people will benefit from for years to come."

Fate's breath came in short, ragged bursts as her future, according to Azrael, unfolded in front of her. Every part of her, body and soul, railed against the shackles she envisioned. "Do you actually think you can control me while holding me against my will?"

"You will have the adoration of all my people and your every need will be met. You will be treated like a queen."

"I don't care if you promise me Willie Wonka's chocolate factory. A gilded cage is still a cage. I'm not a thing to be owned. I'm a human being who values freedom above all else. Without it, I'm a slave."

Undaunted by her protests, Azrael held out the ring. "Take this soul ring and place it on me. A life for a life. We will be equals. This is the best I can offer."

Fate grabbed the ring from his hand. Shaking with rage, and bent on showing him how it felt to be shackled, she rammed it against his shin. Surprisingly, the metal softened for the briefest second and the ring melded around the ankle of his boot. She let go in shock, staggering backward from a pinching in her solar plexus, as if an invisible thread was tugging her insides.

"What was that?" She glanced down, smoothing her hand over her diaphragm, expecting to see and feel something that would cause the pulling sensation. There was nothing.

Relief smoothed the tension in Azrael's face. "That pulling sensation is the etheric cord connecting us. We are bound together as long as we wear the soul rings."

"Great, frenemies," Fate grumbled.

"I do not know this word."

"Friendly enemies."

He took a step closer. "We can be more than that."

She gave him a sidelong look. "I prefer frenemies, thank you very much. I'm in no mood to be besties."

Azrael appeared further confused, but ignored her last comment by saying something she never could have predicted in a million years. "Then return with me to Biraktar as my willing bride."

42
RESURRECTION

SITHIAS CAREFULLY BRUSHED THE last of Finn's ashes into his suede cap. Several remaining embers circled over the fine particles he'd been unable to scoop from the cracks in the earth. Tears swam before his eyes as the soft glow of the sparks flickered above the ground. He still couldn't believe what had happened to Finn.

The finality of it was too painful to accept.

O'Deldar placed a hand gently on his shoulder. "Come away, Sithias. Finn is no more. There is nothing else to be done."

None of this was comforting. Sithias sobbed into his hand as he clutched the ashes in his other hand. "How did thisss happen?"

The old Druid kneeled next to him. "You know as well as I that Finn was brought into being with the Orb of Aeternitis without the benefit of the Rod's balancing force. Unfortunately, he was living on borrowed time. It was only ever a matter of time before the creative energies turned destructive."

Sithias sat straight. "But he was wearing the Rod." Wiping his eyes dry, he set the hat of ashes down and began searching the ground with a frenzy.

"Are you certain, Sithias?" O'Deldar asked.

"Yesss!" Sithias replied, his tone impatient as he ran his hands over the ground.

"If this is true, the Rod should have been a stabilizing force for the Orb's creation."

"That's what Fate thought too. It's the very reason she gave Finn the Rod." Sithias's fingers rolled over the tiny bar of smooth cold metal. The chain was gone, having disintegrated along with Finn. "Found it!" Pinching it between his finger and thumb, he held it up for O'Deldar to see.

The Druid's dark eyes widened. "This is truly puzzling." His gaze shifted from the Rod to the few embers hovering over the hat full of ashes. "What happened that prompted Fate to give him the Rod? Her reasons must have been quite compelling. The spell that forced her to gain the Rod at any cost would've left residual effects upon her, rendering her unnaturally possessive of the Rod."

"Oh, you don't know the half of it," Sithias replied. "But out of concern for Finn, she was more than willing to give him the Rod."

Sithias drew a deep breath, and in one long sentence explained as much as he could about the Keep and how Archie had embedded a teleportation device connected to Finn's brain. He gasped for air to finish. "Finn was deeply unsettled by the dematerialization process of teleportation. He described it as a terrifying unraveling in which he felt he was losing pieces of himself each time. He had the device removed for fear he'd be dismantled completely by it."

"Ah, I see. This was the catalyst." O'Deldar stood, quiet in thought as he paced in circles. At last he stopped and looked at Sithias. "Was there anything else that may have contributed?"

"Well, there are a few that stand out, I think." Sithias sucked in more air, quickly summarizing for the Druid how Finn had been imprisoned in Asgar. A traumatic experience that had driven him mad when he was locked up in Beldereth, and then caged by the Eldunough prince.

Sithias shook his head sadly. "But I think what really broke him was when his connection with Fate severed abruptly. He was distraught with thinking she was surely dead."

O'Deldar pulled at the end of his wiry beard. "I believe it is this that ignited the destructive forces. Fate is his source of creation. The Orb drew upon her desire and imagination to mold him into flesh and spirit. Without her to anchor the magic in this world, Finn had nothing to hold him here."

Sithias rose slowly. "Are you saying Fate isn't alive?"

"How could she be? If anyone would know, it's Finn, and you said he was certain she died."

"B-but the prophecies... " Sithias's chin trembled. Was his sweet miss truly gone as well?

"What prophecies?" O'Deldar asked.

Sithias gulped back the tears. "The scryer in the Well of Eyes on Mount Alderath told Finn that Fate is alive, but not the same as she was. He was to go to the desert of illusions, which is where we were headed before we were attacked. So you see? She's likely *not* dead."

"Prophecies are tricky things. They are more often riddles we put our own meanings to." The Druid's expression softened. "But yes, it's possible Fate lives."

Sniffing, Sithias nodded.

"You said prophecies. That was only one."

"Yes, there was another." Feeling more hopeful, Sithias described the time he and Finn met Aradif. "You might call him a genie, one of the nicer ones," he explained.

The old priest's face darkened with a disapproving frown. "I've never known any of the Djinn to be nice."

"Oh. Well, he fed us. That's nice, isn't it?" Sithias squirmed under O'Deldar's stare. "You're so right. Aradif tortured me with a camel, and he made Finn think Mugloth was back. It was terrible. But afterwards, when we were dining in his tent, he told Finn that his oracle saw him fighting Kaliena in the Marajaran Desert. Which is the desert of illusions, by the way."

Remaining quiet, O'Deldar stared at the two sparks circling the ashes. Something about the dwindling number of embers clawed at Sithias with an urgency he didn't understand.

"Aradif's prophecy wasn't a riddle," Sithias pressed. "He spoke with absolute confidence. He said he would meet Finn in the desert again and watch him fight Kaliena to the death. Oh dear, I forgot about that part."

"Who is Kaliena?"

Sighing, Sithias picked up Finn's ashes and cradled them in his arm. "What does it matter anymore? With Finn gone, we've already lost the war."

The two embers chased the ashes, coming close to his face. O'Deldar caught Sithias by the wrist before he could bat them away. "Hold still." The Druid took the hat full of ashes from Sithias and moved a few feet away.

The embers followed.

O'Deldar set the hat back on the ground. "We must work quickly."

"To do what?"

"Save Finn." O'Deldar yanked hard on a chain around his neck, breaking the clasp as he did so. He let the crystal hanging on it fall next to the hat. "I should have seen it earlier. These last specks of light are Finn's life force. Not the dying sparks of a ruinous fire."

Standing like someone ready to catch a ball, Sithias trembled with hope. "What do I do?"

"We must gather the four elements together. Bring me some water from the pool."

Sithias lurched toward the shallow pool before realizing he had nothing to hold the water in. Scrambling back and forth in a panic, he finally spotted a rusted cup. Upon scooping up the water, he raced over to O'Deldar, his movements so jostled he nearly lost all the contents. He set the cup down. "Is this enough?"

"Yes, yes," O'Deldar replied.

Sithias was alarmed to see O'Deldar had emptied the ashes back onto the ground within a circle he'd carved into the soft earth. Then he placed the cup of water on one side of the ashes, directly opposite the crystal.

An ember blinked out, leaving one waning speck of light left.

"Oh no!" Sithias gasped.

"I see it." O'Deldar's voice sounded tight, betraying the same fear pounding in Sithias's chest. The Druid looked up at him. "I need something representing air."

"Tell me. I'll get it!"

"One of your feathers will do."

As if on cue, a large contour feather dropped and fluttered next to O'Deldar. Sithias shrugged. "You can thank my anxiety for that."

The priest positioned the feather within the circle. Holding his palm upright, he muttered a word Sithias didn't catch, summoning a flame he placed opposite the feather.

Sithias held his breath, praying the last ember held long enough for O'Deldar to complete whatever it was he was doing.

The Druid placed the Rod in the middle of the ashes and shifted his gaze to Sithias. "Is it possible you have something of Fate's?"

Sithias patted his body down. "I have nothing!"

"Has she ever given you anything? It doesn't matter what it is, as long as it came from her."

"Oh! The glamour." Sithias shuddered at the memory of Fate ripping the heart from the sea nymph who'd nearly killed him in her attempt to protect her treasures.

"Let me have it."

"Gladly, if it will help Finn." Sithias removed the pearl and coral necklace, returning to snake form the moment he handed it over.

O'Deldar set the glamour onto the ashes, allowing it to encircle the Rod. He was silent a moment. Too long for Sithias's liking, but he held his tongue and waited all the same.

At last, the Druid spoke:

"*Spirit of Aether, come forth. Bind now with Fire's light, Water's blood, Earth's bone and Air's flight. Shining One, return to your vessel of clay. Unite with Sol in perfection of body and mind, and transmute into soul. Join the sea, the mountains and skies for more than this day. Hear the deepest call of your heart, lest death hold this desire apart. Answer me, and make it be.*"

Coiled tight and holding still, Sithias stared at the weak, flickering light of the ember. His hopes sank as each second ticked by and nothing changed. Was he watching the last of Finn's life force sputtering out of existence? "Oh dear, it doesn't seem to be work–"

O'Deldar shushed him and leaned forward, his dark eyes fixed on a glittering haze gathering slowly around the ember. A tendril of haze slithered downward, touching the Rod, melting the tiny gold bar on contact. An impossible amount of liquid gold spilled over the ashes, covering the pile entirely. Swirling inward, the molten gold flowed and undulated upward, steadily taking on a distinctly male, human form.

Awestruck, Sithias gasped as the basic form sharpened into detail. Sculpted hair fell around familiar facial features, while the texture and shape of clothing formed over the rapidly developing body. Within seconds, the golden shine faded, giving way to the color of skin, hair and garments.

Finn stood before them, staring blankly into space as if caught in a daydream.

O'Deldar rose and circled him before stopping to face him. "Finn, wake up."

Finn blinked, his smooth features furrowing into a look of disbelief when he saw who was speaking. "O'Deldar?" He smiled. "You're alive! I can't tell you how good it is to see you."

"I feel the same seeing you." O'Deldar smiled warmly.

Finn glanced at Sithias with a look of relief before his gaze locked on the iron cage. He turned his back to it. "Thank you for talking the prince into letting me go."

A frown of concern replaced O'Deldar's smile. "You don't remember what happened?"

Finn laughed half-heartedly. "Aye, I remember perfectly. They were about to lock me up for good, and I was fighting against it. Not with any real courage, mind you. I haven't been able to–"

O'Deldar placed a hand on Finn's arm to stop him. "There's something you must know, and I need you to remain calm about what I'm about to say."

Finn stiffened visibly. "What is it?"

"You... " At a loss for words, the old priest sighed heavily. "You ceased to exist."

Finn stared past him, his green eyes filling with utter fear and confusion. "I-I don't understand," he stammered.

"It would seem the creative force that brought you into being, disintegrated."

Finn's chest heaved like he couldn't get enough air. "Are you saying I disintegrated into nothing?"

O'Deldar nodded solemnly.

Finn hung his head and a horrible silence descended, broken only by the hollow sound of dripping water. Hurting for his friend, Sithias slithered a little closer. "But you're back, sssir. And I for one am grateful beyond measure. As I know Fate will be."

"Fate?" Finn lifted his head, his face contorted with agony. "According to the scryer, she's not who she used to be. She doesn't know I exist. She's *forgotten* me. I'm back to being a figment of her imagination. Given she even remembers writing about me all those years."

"You don't know that for sure," Sithias reasoned.

"I do, because I can feel it right here." Finn punched his gut.

O'Deldar gestured for Sithias to ease off. "Finn, you must remain calm. Strong, raging emotions are what triggered your uncreation."

Finn's jaw flexed with tension, his fists clenched as he glared at O'Deldar with eyes fast growing dark. "What does it matter? There's nothing to hold me here if I've lost Fate."

"I know the depth of your feelings, and I understand the connection you had with her, but you cannot allow anyone else to determine your very reason for living," O'Deldar insisted. "You must build your life around a greater purpose."

Sithias nodded emphatically. "He's right, sir. I hate to say it, but there's more at stake here than what's happening with you and Fate. Remember what Aradif's oracle foretold about you defeating Kaliena. All of Oldwilde is on the brink of destruction and you may be the only one to stop it."

Finn turned on his heel, his back bunched with fury as he paced the length of the chamber like a feral dog on a leash. O'Deldar looked at Sithias with a concerned questioning gaze. "I think it's time you filled me in on who this Kaliena is."

Sithias sagged with exhaustion, but dug into his reserves once again to explain the details of Kaliena's rise to power and the legions of horrifyingly unearthly soldiers she'd raised from the dead.

"Do you know when they are due to arrive?" O'Deldar asked.

"If Fate is here, that means Kaliena's army is here," Finn replied, his voice a deep growl. "The plan was to bring the entire structure of the Keep through the portal."

"I see." The lines around O'Deldar's eyes tightened. "Why would Kaliena advance her legions all the way from Shalamoraize to Oldwilde? Is it rich fertile lands she wants?"

"Not likely," Finn replied dryly. "She's driven by the power the Rod will afford her once she combines it with the Orb. That's the main reason I agreed to take it with me. To keep it as far from Kaliena as possible until we could build reinforcements here."

O'Deldar swayed off balance as if struck by a blow. "She has the Orb?"

"Aye, and she's after the Rod with a vengeance." Finn felt for the chain at his neck, pulling his shirt away from his chest when he didn't feel it there. "Where is it?" He looked at O'Deldar in alarm. "I was wearing the Rod."

Visibly shaken, the old Druid sat down on the ground next to where he'd resurrected Finn. He slouched forward, leaning his elbows on his knees as he stared at the thin dusting of gold left on the earthen floor. "I used the Rod to recreate you," he said at last, his face drawn and aged all of a sudden.

Finn crouched next to him. "Are you saying the Rod is part of me now?"

"Yes, only the Rod could bind with the creative energies of the Orb left in the last traces of your essence. The fact it was made of gold made the transmutational process of fusing with the four elements all the easier," O'Deldar explained.

Finn still seemed uncertain. "Will this keep me... whole... for good?"

The priest lifted his gaze from the floor. "It's possible, but I cannot be completely certain of that. Which is why you must guard your emotional state with greater vigilance than you've ever known."

Sithias couldn't stand seeing Finn's dejection. "Are there any positives to this?"

O'Deldar regarded Finn carefully. "I suppose you would now have the power to unlock the full might of the Orb, but only if you are the one in possession of the Orb." The Druid's expression grew even more troubled. "I don't think I need to tell you that this Kaliena must never capture you."

The green of Finn's irises darkened. "Aye, if that happens, we're all lost."

43
WELCOME TO BIRAKTAR

FATE LEFT AZRAEL'S SHOCKING proposal hanging unanswered between them the entire day. Not because she was considering saying yes, but because she feared how he'd react to a resounding no. As far as she could see, silence was her safest option for the moment.

Azrael on the other hand didn't seem at all bothered by her failure to give a prompt answer. Like most males in the middle of a romantic pursuit, he probably assumed she was playing hard to get. But how thick was he?

For starters, they were both far too young to be entertaining the idea of marriage. Even if age wasn't an issue, how could he think she'd agree? Super powers or not, she didn't belong in this terrifyingly vicious world and she'd said so time and again. Did he truly not understand how miserable and homesick she was?

And it didn't help that riding in Moulghazel's wake meant listening to the creature's eerie, melodic moan. There was beauty in the whale song, but it was mournful sounding as well, and only heightened her longing to be home, safe and happy with her father.

"Fate, come look!" he called from the helm. He turned to look at her, ensnaring her within that hypnotic smile of his again. She kept her pace to a begrudging trudge to ensure he wouldn't detect the affect his smile had on her.

"What?" She tried to keep the tone of her voice flat and uninterested, despite his contagious excitement.

He pointed into the swirling mists lighting the night sky and parting away from the bow of the ship. "Do you see it?"

"All I see is clouds."

He moved in behind her, his hands a warm caress on her shoulders as he directed her gaze into the middle of the churn. "There."

A small whale tail broke through the mist before swiftly diving out of sight. "Is that a baby whale?"

"Moulghazel birthed a calf. This is why she was delayed." Azrael returned to the wheel with a look of pure joy lighting his sky blue eyes. "We are doubly blessed, and all because of you."

"I had nothing to do with making a baby whale, so I wouldn't go that far."

"We will never truly know," he agreed. "Regardless, there will be much to celebrate upon our return." He fixed his elated gaze on Fate. "This heralds good fortune for our wedding."

"I haven't said yes."

"You will."

"You don't know that for sure."

Azrael didn't argue any further, but his air of confidence remained annoyingly unshaken. He glanced at the black, starry sky and tied off the wheel to keep the ship on course for Biraktar. "It is late. Come below, we will eat and turn in for the night."

Fate followed him down the ladder. When she reached the last few rungs, Azrael took her by the waist and placed her gently on the floor. Blushing beneath the intensity of his gaze, she brushed past him and took a seat on the cushions. When he joined her a few minutes later, it was with two platters overflowing with generous portions of sweetmeats, herbed flatbreads, cheese and dried fruit coated in crystallized honey.

He set the platters down between them. "We will be arriving in Biraktar by mid-morning, so there is no longer any need to ration our stores." He poured a dark amber liquid into a bronze goblet and handed it to her.

The sweet, tang of mulled citrus and berries warmed Fate's throat without a strong alcohol taste, much like the few sips of wine her father had allowed her to have on special occasions, only this was tastier. They ate the banquet of simple, yet delicious food in relative silence. Unwilling to encourage his notions of impending marriage, she refrained from commenting on just how much she enjoyed the exotic spices baked into the breads and meats. When she was finished, she rose and announced she was ready for bed.

Nodding, Azrael cleared the platters, doused the lights and moved to his side of the room to retire for the night. They were both settled into their respective beds, when his voice penetrated the darkness. "Do you wish me to continue the story of Kalael and Sarayna?"

"Yes please." The lids of her eyes–made heavy by wine and a full stomach–closed the moment she settled into the softness of her bed. Azrael's low, melodic voice proved to be an even stronger tonic as he picked up his story from the night before.

"*Kalael and Sarayna's marriage was a happy one for many years, but it was a love destined for tragedy. The demon plague was spreading and Kalael, who should have been fighting them back with the mighty weapons of magic the wizard Dagon had given him, was too taken by his wife's beauty and kind nature to set foot on the war path. As darkness soaked the lands, Sarayna's shining spirit drew the attention of the demon king, Dregkaan. Born of fire himself, he saw past her mortal cloak to the indwelling flames of the divine power that had created her, and knew this was a life force he could feast upon for an eternity.*

"Dregkaan sent his demons to attack the borders of Kalael's kingdom to lure him from the castle. With Kalael gone, the demon king slipped with ease past the guards posted outside Sarayna's bedchamber. But what Dregkaan did not know was that Sarayna had been blessed with a protective glamour, for when the demon laid eyes on her, he was lost in the sight of her angelic visage. He could not tear his gaze from the way her dark lashes feathered against satin skin, and the luscious blanket of ebony locks spilling over her pillow. In that moment his hunger for her became more than mere greed. She touched his heart and he felt what no demon ever should. He felt love.

"Did this inspire him to take pity and leave her there? Nothing of the sort. Dregkaan lifted the sleeping Sarayna into his arms and he carried her down into the underworld of his infernal kingdom to make her his queen. When Kalael returned the next day and found his beloved wife had been taken, his tortured cry was heard throughout the land as he swore vengeance upon the demon king."

Wanting to know what happened next, Fate struggled to stay awake, but she slipped between waking and dreaming. Terrifying visions of a horned king with no face except eyes of fire amidst blackened bone and hellfire burning behind a charred ribcage of burning organs warped her dreams into a nightmare. She became Sarayna, feeling an awful heat emanating from the demon's core as the rough bones of his arms scraped against the bare skin of her limbs. Stifling a scream, she twisted in his grasp and gasped at the sight of a severe castle surrounded by razor-sharp rocks and an ever-present gloom. If she didn't escape then and there, this was to be her home.

Fate jolted upright, her spine rigid. She gasped in panic.

"I warned you this story would stir dreams," Azrael said from within the darkness.

She put a hand over her pounding heart. "Yeah, but you never said anything about nightmares that feel as real as being awake."

The dark room filled with the sounds of Azrael moving around. The light of a lantern chased away the fearsome shadows and he returned to his bed. "I should have left the light on for you." His smile had her heartbeat racing once again, but for very different reasons.

She returned his smile, then quickly turned to face the wall in a rush to stamp down her confusing emotions. Why was she slipping back under his spell? Like Sarayna, she was being carried off to a foreign place to be made her captor's wife. She should be looking for any opportunity to escape, not flirting and blushing everytime he flashed his entrancing smile.

Fate yawned, despite the animosity coursing through her. This shouldn't be happening. She'd always been immune to the so-called charms of the boys she'd gone to school with. None of them had ever managed to turn her head. Her disappointment in every boy she'd ever met was the very reason she'd invented Finn McKeen. It didn't matter that he was imaginary and existed only on paper. He was the only one who'd ever made her blood rush.

If only Finn was as real as this utterly unbelievable situation she'd found herself in.

Hugging a pillow tight to her chest, she willed him to the forefront of her mind, sighing with relief as his familiar form crystallized within her imagination. Finn strode eagerly toward her, tall, lean and muscular. She relaxed into his strong embrace, lifting her face to his like someone soaking in the sun. Her skin tingled beneath the brush of his mouth over her eyelids as he left a trail of kisses along her cheekbone, jaw and neck.

A tousle of bronzed gold hair slipped over his forehead as he pulled away to stare into her eyes. His expression of love broke her heart. She lost herself within the color of his eyes, greener and more lustrous than any leaf in nature. This was her perfect dream boy–blindingly handsome, mesmerizing and passionate.

Unable to hold back any longer, Finn kissed her, deeply, gently. Her own hunger unlocked, Fate pressed against him, kissing back hard and fast to answer the building need inside her. They tumbled together with limbs entwined, swept away by the tide of a wild, unrelenting ocean of love–

"Fate, wake up."

Breathing hard, she opened her eyes to see Azrael bent over her. "What?" she gasped.

"By the sounds you were making, you seemed to be having another nightmare."

Her face burned hot. "Oh, thanks," she muttered wryly. She pulled her cloak over her head. "Sorry I woke you."

"You did not. I have been up for hours and was about to wake you. We have arrived in Biraktar."

Rubbing the sleep from her eyes, Fate sat up fast. "How did that happen? I only just got back to sleep."

"No, you slept all through the night. Join me on deck." He turned and climbed the ladder.

Still shaken from being yanked from her blissful dream, Fate grabbed at the ache in her chest. The dream had been more real than any she'd ever had. The ghost of Finn's touch lingered on her skin. If she closed her eyes, she could still feel the heat of his bites and kisses on her neck.

She shook her head, admonishing herself for wishing for the impossible. She'd slept in her clothes again, so there was nothing to delay her from facing the inevitable. Slipping her feet into her boots, she clamped her cloak around her shoulders and took a deep breath. "Deal with the here and now," she muttered as she climbed the ladder.

When she stuck her head through the hatch, she stopped on the top rung to gaze at the brilliance beyond the parked boat. Towers built of gold in the shapes of rope twists with fluted caps stretched high into the sky. Sunlight glittered over jewel-toned glass domes, spraying a prism of colors–plum, ruby, fuchsia, emerald and cobalt–over every surface, while saturating the surrounding clouds of ranemist with pastel hues of the rich shades of the city. Cotton candy tufts of mist swirled around the topmost peaks of each tower, diffusing the sun's light into a shimmering haze, disrupted only by flocks of white birds.

Fate stepped on deck with her mouth hanging open. A patchwork of gold encrusted the cobblestone streets. The play of light and color shifted over the shining architecture like a kaleidoscope, and she quickly realized the floating city was turning slowly.

Azrael sidled up next to her. "Welcome to Biraktar."

"This is so much more than you described." Her voice was a breathless whisper.

He looked pleased by her astonishment. "Biraktar's beauty is beyond words." He threw a rope ladder over the side. "Come, I want you to meet my family."

Fate's wonder and excitement vanished with the reminder of why she was there. Reluctantly, she climbed down after him. The robed guards armed with scimitars who met them, were tall, muscled men with beards and fierce brown eyes.

They kneeled before Azrael. "Welcome back, your highness," said the man at the front of the line. He raised his gaze with a deep look of respect at the sound of whale songs resonating through the air. "And we are grateful to you for Moulghazel's return."

Azrael nodded solemnly, before striding past them.

Fate looked at Azrael. "You're a king?"

He laughed. "Not even close. I am the youngest of nine sons and far from ever being the crown prince."

"But you're a prince."

He shrugged. "Yes, for what it is worth."

Stunned by this new discovery, Fate glanced back at the ship. There was nothing majestic about his modest boat, especially after the damage it had incurred. The hull was riven with countless claw marks and one side had been patched with an oiled tarp and a few spare boards. It was a miracle they'd actually stayed airborne.

"If you're a prince, why would you risk your life like that? Don't you have people who'll do that for you?" she asked.

"Of course. Many of our best captains and warriors have been searching for Moulghazel, and many did not survive. But who am I to say that my life is more valuable than theirs? It was my honor and duty to do what my father asked of his people."

Doubly surprised by what she was learning, Fate stared at Azrael. "Wow, I can't believe your dad asked you to join the search."

Azrael stopped walking and turned to her. "He did not. I chose to go. Why does this surprise you?"

"Well, maybe because you didn't strike me as the altruistic type when we first met."

His gaze grew intense. "There is much you do not know about me." Releasing her from the uncomfortable stare, he continued on, leading her deeper into the inner city.

The streets grew thick with people dancing with colorful ribbons and ringing bells. Earthy scents of incense drifted from side altars as they sang and laughed. Fate couldn't help smiling at all the happy faces they passed by.

"Is it like this all the time around here?" she asked.

"No, this has been an unhappy place for a very long time. They rejoice for Moulghazel's return, because it means our city will escape the hungry desert for a good number of years." The gratitude Azrael had displayed the night before returned to his eyes, and he took her hand. "Come, there will be plenty of time to celebrate later. My family must meet you."

They wove through the crowds, jostled along the way by carefree dancers, kissing couples and children running with toy carvings of whales held high as they imagined them swimming through the air. All the while, Moulghazel's melodic throaty song reverberated throughout the very foundation of the city.

It wasn't long before they reached a palace of unmatched beauty at the very center of the city. Unlike the other buildings of gold, this was a luminescent white, covered entirely of abalone tiles set in elaborate patterns with pearls lining the entrances, windows and archways. Fate slowed to take it all in.

The palace guards bowed their heads as Azrael led her inside and down a series of peaked hallways bedecked with scalloped arches, hand carved trim and flourished pillars. Every inch of these surfaces was inlaid with intricate, polished gemstone tile designs of lapis, jade, citrine, opal and tourmaline, to name just a few. Painted indentations glittered with diamond powder. Elaborate, tiled geometric patterns covered the floors with the same richness of Persian carpets, except this was pigmented stone, worn smooth and satiny by centuries of foot traffic.

Azrael stopped in front of a pair of double doors framed within an ivory, scalloped arch. Fate reached out to trail her fingers over the solid pattern of interconnected starbursts hammered into the door's gold surface. "These are my family's private living quarters," he informed her before pushing one of the doors open.

She stopped him. "Wait. Is there anything I need to know before we go in? Am I supposed to bow, or curtsy or something?"

"No, not in here," he assured her. "We are very informal in our home. The only formalities you need be concerned with are when seen in public with the king and crown prince."

"Okay... "

They entered into what appeared to be a common room, subdued by pastel colors of blues, sage, rose and buttery yellows. Plush pillows and cashmere throws made up a large, horseshoe shaped seating area. Thick carpets invited bare feet. Luscious green palms along the far walls curved high overhead, their leaves fluttering in the soft breeze of an open veranda. A long table of dark mahogany surrounded by a few dozen heavy-set chairs flanked one side of the room. On the other side, hallways led off to parts unknown.

A group of five women, of various generations, from Fate's age to forty, gathered on one end of the seating area. They spoke softly while sewing beads to bolts of silk cloth. Four men in their early thirties lounged with hands resting on the tubes of standing brass pipes sitting close by. They all turned to see who entered, and then left what they were doing to gather around Azrael.

One of the men spoke in Azrael's native tongue, saying something Fate didn't understand. He slapped him on the back with a smile to match Azrael's, though his eyes were brown. He sneered at the other three men while delivering a message that made them roll their eyes.

Azrael laughed with a shake of his head before rattling off something she could only guess at. By the other's response, he was giving them a hard time, but in good humor, which they received warmly.

The women asked several questions of Azrael with a mixture of excitement and then concern over his travel-worn clothes, before they sent the youngest of them to either fetch something, or possibly deliver a message.

When they finally noticed Fate standing off to one side by herself, Azrael waved her over. "This is Fate," he announced in English. "She is new to Biraktar and not familiar with our language, so please make her feel welcome by speaking in her tongue when in her presence."

Fate stepped in beside Azrael and waved. "Hello."

The one with Azrael's smile looked her over with an appreciative eye. "She's a beauty, brother. Where did you find her?"

Azrael smiled proudly. "I saved her from a Sulayfir."

One of the others threw Azrael an exaggerated look of surprise. "*You* fought a Sulayfir?"

Azrael pushed him with the playful roughness of brothers. "It was not my first, and you know it."

The brother laughed as he regained his footing. "Ah, you have brought home a grateful slave girl who happens to be... *most* beautiful." His gaze dropped to the soul ring around her boot. "How convenient."

Fate tensed.

Azrael's jovial demeanor turned serious within an instant. "You are mistaken, brother. I am as indebted to Fate, as she is to me. Indeed, we are all indebted to her. It is because of her that Moulghazel has returned."

The laughter died in their eyes and each brother's dark gaze narrowed on Fate.

"What nonsense is this?" the first brother asked as he grabbed the bottom of Azrael's cloak to look at his ankle. He staggered backward, as if he'd seen something repulsive. "You allowed a common foreigner to bind you over what you have every right to claim as your own doing?" Rage rolled off him in waves.

He turned to the third brother who'd been more of an observer up to that point. "Go find father and the others. We must deal with this before word passes beyond these walls."

The brother left at the same moment a woman entered. Dressed in turquoise and coral silks, she had the same vivid blue eyes as Azrael. The sparkling gold charms trimming the neckline and shoulders of her dress rang softly with an uplifting jingle. At first glance, she appeared as youthful as Azrael, but her age and maturity became evident as she moved closer.

"Welcome home, my son," she greeted Azrael, without needing to be told to speak in English. She hugged him, but her gaze rested on Fate with the hint of a smile playing on her lips. "Come with me, we will take refreshments in my chamber."

The outraged brother blocked her way. "No, we have summoned father."

She stared back serenely, her smile unfolding like a summer flower. "You know your father is not one to be summoned." Gesturing for Azrael and Fate to follow, she stepped around his brother. "You know where to find us, once the king decides to speak with Azrael."

Leaving the other women to stare after them with open mouths, Fate hurried past the upset brothers into one of the doors leading off the common room. Azrael's mother's gait remained unhurried as they passed many doors before turning into a winding stairwell. The climb seemed long, but there were windows along the way, allowing first a view of a courtyard garden and then rooftops.

They entered a round chamber lined with walls of bookcases. At the center of the room were several tables buried beneath stacks of books, parchment, quills, ink and amber bottles of plant-infused oils. Bundles of cut herbs and flowers hung from the ceiling to dry, scenting the room with an earthy, floral aroma. Shelves built into the far wall displayed numerous wooden bowls, glass jars and clay pots filled with a wide variety of crystals, feathers, shells and gemstones.

Azrael's mother led them to a balcony set with a small table and three chairs, as though she'd fully expected the guest count. "Have a seat. I made tea."

Fate stepped out onto the balcony, immediately awed by the vista. The city stretched out below them, sparkling in the sun like a cluster of jewels mounted within the finest, wrought gold. Thick clouds of ranemist encircled the metropolis, curling over the outer edges in spiraling eddies. Beyond the thickening mist, the shifting sands of Dunebala spread to the distant horizon. After seeing the splendor of Biraktar from this new, breathtaking vantage point, she easily understood Azrael's love for this place.

The sounds of dishes being set down pulled Fate's attention from her momentary sense of wonder, and she sat down. His mother took the seat opposite her, pouring tea into glazed clay cups.

Fate took a sip of the rich brew steeped in citrus and spice. "Thank you, your highness. It's very tasty."

"I am only one of many wives. You may call me Mahelia."

Fate smiled nervously. "Azrael has spoken of you often. He's been telling me your fairy tale of Kalael and Sarayna."

Mahelia raised a brow at her son with a playful smile. "Has he now?"

Azrael shifted his gaze to the floor. "Do not start, mother."

"Azrael loved that story when he was a little boy. He made me tell it over and over without ever tiring of it. I had other tales to share, but this was the one he always wanted to hear."

"Hmm, didn't you say you learned *many* epic tales sitting at the heels of your mother?" Fate teased.

Azrael looked at the ceiling. "Yes, yes, I may have stretched the truth a little."

Mahelia patted his arm. "It is my favorite as well." Her smile faded somewhat. "Unfortunately, it is not a fairy tale."

"Are you saying those things really happened?" Fate asked.

"Mother… " Azrael's tone held a warning.

Mahelia looked at her son. "She must know this, just as you must learn to accept that all I have taught you has been to prepare you for what lies ahead."

Azrael's jaw clenched.

Mahelia's gaze moved to Fate with a sudden fierceness that burned away her gentle demeanor. "You know deep inside of what I speak."

Fate gripped her cup so hard the tea sloshed over the edge. She set it down with a terrible sense of relief at being able to admit her fears. "Something bad is coming, isn't there?"

Mahelia reached across the table, took Fate's hand and nodded. "Yes. It has already broken you into pieces, but it is not done. It wants more."

Fate's breath stalled in her chest. "What is it? What's after me?"

Mahelia's gaze turned sorrowful. "The deepest of all darkness."

44
BENEATH THE SURFACE

"CAN YOU HELP MAKE her whole again?" Azrael asked his mother. His uncertainty worried Fate, especially after he'd assured her his mother could retrieve her soul parts. Would she always be missing these huge chunks of memory? The thought terrified her.

Mahelia studied Fate with the same scrutinizing gaze Azrael had demonstrated when he was seeing lights and other mysterious phantasms around Fate no one else could see. "I will do my best, but we must perform the ceremony now. Your father is biding his time, but he will expect to see her at the dinner table." She rose and strode to one of the tables covered with books and a stack of candles.

Azrael and Fate trailed after her, watching her clear the long table and spread a silken cloth over the surface. She instructed Fate to lie down on the tabletop. Fate did as she was told, but not without a rattling of nerves. This was all happening so fast. She'd barely stepped foot in Biraktar and she was already in the middle of some sort of controversy, at least as far as Azrael's brothers were concerned.

Yet, she felt safe with Azrael, despite her reluctance to trust him completely. And Mahelia seemed genuinely compassionate and caring. Something about the woman made it easy to surrender her apprehensions. Besides, what other options did she have?

Zip, zero, nada.

Mahelia placed crystals at the center of Fate's collarbone and several more along her torso, before placing the remaining crystals around her body in a full circle.

"Should I be feeling anything?" Fate asked.

"Such as?" Mahelia replied.

"Uh... I'm not sure. Like maybe some weird tingles or heat from all these crystals."

Mahelia laughed softly. "Not likely. The circle of crystals work as anchors to hold what's left of your soul here, while these ones transmit signals of your soul signature out into the ether."

"Hmm, that sounds more technical than I would've expected."

"There is a certain science to this work, though there are always surprises along the way." Mahelia leaned over her and put her finger to her mouth. "I will need you to close your eyes now and become quiet within yourself."

Fate glanced at Azrael, who nodded encouragingly. Taking a deep breath, she squeezed her eyes shut and tried her best to relax.

The silken rustling and tinkling of the charms sewn to Mahelia's dress were calming sounds that mingled nicely with the smell of burning sage, lavender and cedar. A soft, melodic chanting whispered around her, unraveling the tense knots in Fate's back, loosening her stiff limbs. Tranquility flooded through her, rising to her busy mind. A drowsy, heavy feeling pulled her to the edge of sleep as Mahelia's dulcet tones threaded through the air.

Fate floated within serene nothingness for a time before light pierced the black. The light grew larger, until at last she could see the gleaming pages of an open book. But this was no ordinary book. It was enormous and loomed over her.

The yellowed pages were spotted with age and penned in old-world calligraphy. She read the first line: *In the morning of the world when the very air swelled with magic, an enchanted island floated against the currents of the ocean.*

Curiosity welled up within, even as an undeniable sense of familiarity rose to the forefront. She'd read those words before. But where?

Suddenly, the inked words lifted off the ancient pages and a flurry of letters swirled around her like thousands of tiny butterflies before combining together into a scene bursting into a symphony of sights, scents and sounds. The story had come to life, and she was part of it!

Her pulse raced as the fable of *The Lonely Sorceress* played out before her. At last, the rich reality came to a heartbreaking end, and the story's fantastical creatures and captivating scenery shattered into a storm of letters, which returned to the book's pages.

In that same moment, she knew she was imprisoned within the book's world. Someone touched her arm, asking if she was all right. When Fate turned to see who'd spoken, everything she thought was impossible dissolved when she saw her dream boy standing over her.

Finn McKeen, real and in the flesh.

Her shattered heart began to piece back together as everything she'd experienced inside the *Book of Fables* surged back in poignant detail. As painful as it was to relive her travels through the cursed book's eight fables, a strength she hadn't known was missing, returned. Restored memories of her friendship with Sithias and Gerdie filled her with even greater fortitude.

Her spirits soared when her connection with Finn emerged into reality. Though this did nothing to protect her from living through losing him all over again. At least she knew he wasn't a mere ghost of her imagination. Finn was as alive as she was, and she'd known the feel of his arms around her, the touch of his lips on hers.

Determination coursed through her veins. She would find her way back to him. But how?

The moment she asked the question, the image of a structure unlike anything she'd ever seen before materialized around her. Ancient buildings stretched out for miles, all resting on the flat plains of enormous, turning gears. Colossal rings encompassed the massive complex system of moving parts, each sweeping in circular rotations, crackling against a surrounding force field. Beyond the protective sphere, lay a sea of glittering stars.

Memories of the Keep flooded back, along with her initiation as Keep Guardian. Faces flashed in rapid succession: Eustace, Jessie, Gerdie, Darcy, Mason, Lincoln. And Steve, who'd turned out to be the deceptive sorcerer, Wodrid. Chills raced over her skin from visions of Kaliena's awakening and the sorrow of losing Lincoln and then Jessie to Kaliena's control.

But there'd been one bright moment in it all. She'd reunited with Finn.

Fate braced herself as more memories returned–the battles against one horrendous army of undead creatures after the other, and with no end in sight. The futility of it all is what had compelled her to use the power and strength of Hippolyta's magical girdle for herself. But then the shame of her hasty actions returned in the face of Finn's unhappiness at what she'd done.

And he'd been right. The power she'd borrowed may have equalized her against Kaliena's relentless attacks, but there had been a price to pay for what she'd gained. Possessing the power of a god had become her Achilles heel the moment she'd unlocked Farouk's cage and freed a nightmare held at bay for thousands of years.

Darkness swarmed in around her, and from within the churning shadows emerged Farouk's red burning gaze glinting from behind thick tendrils of smoke sifting between razored fangs. Sulphurous heat waves rippled off him, tainting the air with a sickening stench of rot and death–emanations filled with hate and malice that weakened her life force.

The mere sight and smell of the demon paralyzed her with terror. Yet an even greater fear lurked beneath that terror. Something far worse than her own death, and it was something she could not look at. Her heart hammered so hard inside her ribcage she thought she would die.

A woman's soothing voice penetrated the emptiness. "Fate, follow the sound of my voice."

Fate turned in circles, unable to locate the source of the voice within the pitch black.

"There is no need to stay here," the woman assured her. "Come away with me."

A hand took hold of Fate's, gently pulling her through the darkness.

"Open your eyes. *Now.*"

Fate found herself staring at the bundles of flowers and herbs hanging overhead. Azrael leaned in to block her view, his blue eyes filled with concern. Mahelia removed the crystals she'd set on and around her body.

Azrael helped Fate sit up and wrapped a soft, cashmere shawl around her trembling shoulders. "How do you feel?" he asked.

"A little like I've been squeezed through a tube of toothpaste and flushed down the drain."

He gave her a quizzical look. "You may have lost your way in there, but I see you managed to retain your confounding form of speech."

"And you wish I hadn't?"

"Maybe a little." He smiled warmly.

Mahelia placed the bowl of crystals on the end of the table and set her hand on Azrael's shoulders. "It is time to clean the desert from your skin and dress for dinner, my son. I will help Fate do the same."

Azrael hesitated, glancing first at Fate and then at his mother. "There is much to discuss, considering where she came from and all that was awakened there."

"You saw all that?" Fate blurted out, before remembering he had the ability to *see* what most couldn't. Her face warmed with knowing he'd also seen her relationship with Finn. "Is everyone in Biraktar able to see my private business the way you two are?"

"No, only those of us with *jann* blood are attuned to unseen forces," Mahelia assured her.

"Who are the *jann*?" Fate asked.

"We are part of the Djinn. Those born of a universe invisible to humans."

Goose bumps shivered over Fate's arms. "You're not human?"

"I am part human," Mahelia replied. "My son has even less *jann* blood than I."

"Oh." Fate looked at him, trying to see what part wasn't human.

"I am mostly human," Azrael offered hastily.

Unsure of what to do with this disquieting information, Fate nodded.

"Sure, okay."

Azrael's discomfort grew. Clearing his throat, he spoke to Mahelia. "The prophecy is coming true. We must discuss this."

Mahelia gave him a warning glance, which made Fate all the more nervous. "What prophecy?"

"The mother of the great goddess, Kali, has awakened. We have felt her unquenchable thirst for power radiating across the great ocean of stars ever since," Mahelia replied.

"Kaliena," Fate whispered under her breath.

"Yes, the very same," Mahelia confirmed. "And now she is in the Marajaran Desert with her abominable army."

Fate swallowed down the fear rising in her chest. "She escaped the Keep? How is that possible?"

"The same way you arrived here. Through a giant tear in the universe, which allowed the ancient Obiectus to pass through to this world." Fate was surprised to hear Mahelia refer to the Keep as the Golandon builders used to. Her knowledge of Kaliena's origins was authentic. And unless Fate was mistaken, Mahelia's expression held a disturbing hint of judgment and blame.

But Fate was too distracted to dwell on what Mahelia was thinking. Her head was swimming with a confusion of questions. How had she ended up in Dunebala if the Keep was in the Marajaran Desert? What had happened to her father and Finn, and all the others? Had she done something to cause this terrible occurrence? She rubbed her throbbing temples. "If I came here with the Keep, how come I'm not on it right now?" She looked at Mahelia through a swell of tears. "Everyone I love was in the Keep! Oh no," she moaned. "I have no idea if they're alive or dead. Why can't I remember what happened?"

Mahelia pulled Fate's hands down between them. "The part of yourself that holds this memory was too far away for me to retrieve."

"But I have to know what happened to them. I have to!"

Mahelia studied Fate, as if measuring her strength.

"What?" Fate pressed.

Mahelia's eyes softened with heartfelt sympathy. "The only reason a soul part drifts that far away, is to protect you from a memory too painful to live with."

Despair welled in Fate's chest, squeezing off the air in her throat. "Are you saying they're all... *gone?*" She choked out the last word.

"I cannot know this. I can only see what is part of your miraja."

Fate found her voice and it came as a shout. "But you said you knew

Kaliena and her army are here. There has to be more you can see!"

Mahelia shook her head. "I witnessed only what you saw when your lost soul parts returned. The rest of my knowledge concerning Kaliena and her army came from my *jann* relations."

Tightening the shawl around her shoulders, Fate stared at the floor, locked between needing to know if her father, Finn and the others were still alive, yet terrified to take action in case her worst fears were confirmed.

Azrael's voice grew low and tense when he spoke. "Have you spoken of this to father?" he asked his mother.

"Not yet. Moulghazel's return was my first concern. Thanks to Fate, our kingdom is blessed with the renewal of our most precious resource, and we will now be able to face the impending war with the full might of our military fleets."

The volume in his voice rose. "War?"

Fate raised her gaze to watch them.

Mahelia's grave expression was sobering. "A war unlike any this world has ever seen."

"What do you mean?" he asked, though it was obvious by his closed fists he didn't want to hear the answer.

"Age-old enemies will be forced to form unlikely alliances in order to defeat Kaliena's legions. Our world's survival is dependent on a unification of the whole. Any break in the chain will be the end of all we hold dear."

Clenching his jaw, Azrael stared out the window as he absorbed the terrible news.

Mahelia's sobering demeanor lifted, and she playfully turned her son toward the door. "There will be plenty of time to dwell on this tomorrow. Refresh yourself for dinner and tonight we will celebrate the blessings at hand."

Nodding, Azrael left willingly this time. Mahelia gestured for Fate to join her. "Kindly follow and I will take you to my private chamber to wash and dress."

Fate slipped off the table with a weary sigh and followed her down the spiraling stairs. They passed several servants, whom Mahelia stopped and spoke softly to in her native language. By the time they reached the ornate doors of her bedchamber and pushed through them, the room was filled with female servants laying out a selection of beautiful dresses on the bed and throwing fragrant petals into a small pool set in the private courtyard outside the room.

Too drained and tired to speak, Fate walked into the courtyard, her gaze fixed on the pool. "Take your time," Mahelia said as she closed the doors behind her.

Fate stripped off her dusty desert garb. All that was left was the mysterious braided bracelet she'd been wearing. She ran her fingers over the wool and silk strands, her pulse racing as she recognized the tartan pattern from Finn's First Knight uniform and the silk ribbon keepsake he'd given her.

Finn had made the bracelet for her! But when?

Frustrated by the remaining holes in her memory, she slipped the bracelet off. Setting it carefully on the pool's edge, she stepped into the lukewarm pool. Aromatic oils slicked the surface of the water with rainbows of color. She sank into the soothing bath, inhaling the sultry scents of jasmine, gardenia and honeysuckle. Her muscles responded immediately, unknotting little by little. Dunking her head beneath the water, she indulged in the feathery tickle of her long hair sliding against her shoulders and welcomed the silence wrapping around her.

Yet her mind was anything but quiet, refusing to allow her this one brief respite from a constant stream of inner turmoil. Somehow, luxuriating in a bath without knowing if her loved ones were alive and safe only served to fill her with unbearable guilt. For all she knew everything that had gone wrong was due to one of her many rash decisions. She'd certainly abused her powers before and made mistakes that had caused untold grief, starting with using the Words of Making thoughtlessly, which had resulted in Finn's internment inside the giant oak.

She broke the water's surface, her chest heaving with quiet sobs. Why hadn't she learned her lesson yet? What was it going to take for her to finally accept that grasping for powers beyond her capability to control always compounded the trouble she was trying so desperately to escape? She gulped down the sharp, painful lump in her throat as the answer slapped her in the face.

The worst has already happened. You just can't remember.

That's when she knew she had to leave Biraktar and find the Keep. Even if it meant sailing straight into Kaliena's clutches.

Fate splashed her face with water, washing the tears and then straightened her shoulders. "Get a grip," she muttered gruffly. Water slicked off her oiled skin as she stood and reached for one of the large cotton cloths sitting next to the pool. Wrapping the towel around her, she put her bracelet back on and returned to the bedchamber.

Offered a choice of dresses, Fate simply pointed at the nearest one, a deep scarlet with gold embroidery. The servant girls took her towel, gasping at the magical girdle emanating light beneath her skin.

Mahelia shushed them, and they worked quickly to dress Fate. First helping her to slip into the fitted top and long skirt before wrapping the sari around her waist with the longest end draped elegantly over her shoulder. They sat her down and brushed her hair, fussing over details Fate had no interest in. When they were finished, her hair was braided down one side and the weight of a beaded headdress rested on her forehead.

One of the servants tried to remove the bracelet Finn had made her. Fate jerked her hand away. "I want to keep it on."

The servant looked at Mahelia, who gestured for the servant to leave Fate alone. Thanking them, she sent the girls on their way. "You look beautiful," Mahelia said.

"Thank you." Fate didn't bother to look in the standing mirror.

Mahelia watched her. "You are upset."

"Just a little." Fate allowed her tone to drip with sarcasm.

"What bothers you the most?"

"Hmm, I'd say it's a toss up between finding out I'm responsible for waking up Kaliena and unlocking the cage of a monstrous demon, both of whom have caused cataclysmic catastrophes in my life and the lives of everyone I've ever known and loved. And the worst part is, they're only just getting started and about to spread even more misery over the entire world."

Mahelia tilted her head, surprising Fate with a smile. "There is another way to tell this story."

"Oh for sure," Fate agreed. "I pretty much skated over all the gory details, but I can get into them if you'd like."

"I meant a better way to look at this."

"There isn't one."

Mahelia leaned in toward her. "Ah, but there is. You are forgetting that if you had the power to set all these horrible things in motion, then you also have the power to put an end to them."

Fate frowned. "With what?"

"You have the power of the Word."

Fate laughed harshly. "You mean the Words of Making?"

"You call it by another name, but it is the same power nonetheless."

Fate stared at the brilliant plum and orange hues of the setting sun outside the window. Temptation seeped in as she thought about the Words of Making and what that meant. The power was hers to use again now that she'd returned to their place of origin, and the desire to write a whole new story that ended happily rushed into her heart. Did she dare use the Words of

Making for a quick fix that could remove all the problems she faced?

Fate shook her head. "No. I already burned my hand on that stove, and more than once. I can't go making the same mistakes again."

"Maybe so, but you succeeded in summoning Moulghazel with the Word."

"After first getting dumped on with a boat load of stinky fish and icky worms!" Fate shuddered at the memory.

"The power of the Word can be mastered. I will teach you," Mahelia pressed.

"No, you don't understand. I can't be trusted with that kind of power. It *always* backfires." Remembering what she'd done to Finn, Fate curled her fingers into a fist.

The gentle plains of Mahelia's face darkened into a fierce scowl with such speed it was startling. "You are a mere child who knows nothing."

Shadows swept into the room, bringing a chill as Fate shrank from Mahelia's malicious gaze. Whatever part of her that wasn't human had suddenly emerged.

Mahelia stood over Fate, a foreboding figure comprised of shadow and light. "You may be able to fight Kaliena with the power you stole from a god." She jabbed the air with a spectral finger that pointed at Fate. "But you cannot fight the Hinn. It has set its sights on you. This is a curse like no other. Have you ever seen a cat play with a mouse? The Hinn is the same. Its patience is limitless, and it will torture you in ways you could never imagine. By the end, you will beg for death."

Fate shivered. "That darkness you mentioned. It's not Kaliena, it's the Hinn, isn't it?"

Mahelia's blue eyes glittered sharply like stars against the blackest sky. "Yes, the Hinn comes for you now. I feel its presence closing in."

"Why me?"

"For all that you are, or for nothing at all. Knowing the mind of a Hinn is to ask for madness."

"How do I stop it? There has to be a way."

The menacing shadows dissolved–and with it, Mahelia's dark shroud –allowing the waning light of the setting sun to return, bringing welcome heat and color to the room again. The serene woman Fate had first met stood before her once more. "There are ways."

Fate waited for her to elaborate on them, but Mahelia remained silent. Fate's stomach twisted into a cold knot when she realized she'd stepped into a bargaining situation. "Oh, I get it, you want something from me in return for your help."

Mahelia sat down next to Fate. "There must always be fair exchange."

"That's what you're calling this?" The heat of anger flushed Fate's face. "And here I thought bringing your precious Moulghazel back to Biraktar was more than enough to win your gratitude."

"That would be true under any other circumstance. But these are dangerous times, which as you know, call for extreme measures."

Fate huffed with exasperation. "What do you want from me?"

Mahelia stood and walked over to a table holding a display of jewelry. Retrieving a white satin box, she handed it to Fate. The lid was ornately beaded with pearls and silver sequins. Fate opened it to reveal a gold necklace with a pendant in the shape of an open flower, or possibly a sunburst. Within the center was a winged serpent made of sapphires. Her fondness for Sithias gave her an instant appreciation for the design, not that she wanted to wear the overly fancy piece of jewelry.

"This is your protection against the Hinn," Mahelia told her. "The sapphires represent the sacred constellation that is the great serpent in the sky we call, Aradif, our Guiding Star. He only appears to those deserving of his help."

"A choosy constellation is supposed to protect me?"

"You misunderstand. The serpent is a symbol of both creation and destruction. Wearing this calls forth the protection of Aradif, while also strengthening your creative and destructive powers, depending on how you choose to use them."

Fate picked up the pendant, turning it to catch the light in the gemstones. "Will this keep me from getting weak and disoriented around the demon?"

Mahelia nodded. "Yes, this is what you need to stabilize your powers when in the presence of the Hinn."

"Sounds good to me." Fate moved to clasp the necklace around her neck, but Mahelia stopped her.

"Not yet."

"Oh right. We haven't finalized your shady deal yet."

Mahelia returned the necklace to its box. "Tonight, you will attend dinner with the king and the other wives, as well as his sons. The king will first display his dislike of you as a common foreigner, as well as scold Azrael for his decision to be soul bonded to you. After he has declared his disapproval to the family, he will then announce there to be no other solution but for you and Azrael to be wed during the four day celebration for Moulghazel's return."

"Whoa, hold on there. I can't marry Azrael. You both saw I'm in love with Finn. Nothing will ever change that." A thrill ran through her knowing Finn was in the flesh and out there, wherever the Keep was. If she weren't being hunted by Farouk and in dire need of Mahelia's protective necklace, she'd leave in a heartbeat to search for him. Though she suspected she wouldn't make it very far. A nagging sense of danger told her she'd only glimpsed a tiny portion of Mahelia's power.

Mahelia's expression remained unperturbed. "Most marriages are arranged for reasons beyond that of the couple involved, and are rarely based on love. But I see the way Azrael looks at you. He will grow to love you."

Fate was flabbergasted. "But I'll *never* love him. My heart belongs to Finn." She clasped her hand around her wrist, holding onto his bracelet for strength.

"Do we really ever let go of our first loves? Most would say no."

Fate opened her mouth to argue, but Mahelia's grim look of warning decided her silence. "Enough. You will be gracious and agreeable at dinner. And you will be my son's bride tomorrow, with the same grace you display tonight. Only then will you wear the necklace that will prevent you from becoming prey to the predator. Thereafter, you will swear to protect this kingdom with the power of the Word, but *only* under my direction. Do you understand?"

A chill snaked up Fate's spine as she nodded reluctantly.

"Good, let us begin then." Gesturing for Fate to follow, Mahelia strolled across the room. She stopped to hold the door open for Fate with a warm smile.

Fate sped past, her gaze averted. She couldn't look at Mahelia anymore. Not after seeing the heartlessness lurking beneath that thin veneer of feigned kindness.

45
DEATH CAMP

THE GIANT HAWK BEARING Finn on its back, swept over the desert, its shadow skimming over white dunes. Hot winds raked Finn's skin as he shifted in the saddle and bent to one side to call out to Sithias. "How are you doing down there?"

There was no immediate answer. Nervous about his friend's welfare, Finn asked again, this time shouting.

"How do you think I'm doing?" Sithias replied at last, his voice an anxious squeak. "I'm being hauled around within the deadly talons of a bird of prey who would no sooner have me for dinner than look at me!"

Finn didn't blame him for being upset, given the circumstances. O'Deldar had decided it best they leave without delay, and had secretly arranged for one of their military hawks to transport them to the Marajaran Desert. The soldiers had instructed Finn on the fundamentals of riding a hawk, which had gone smoothly enough. But when it had come time for the winged snake to land in the saddle behind Finn, the hawk had gone into attack mode. The only reason his traumatized friend had survived was because he'd managed to fly out of reach to avoid the tethered hawk's snapping beak.

After several hours of the soldiers working to familiarize the hawk with Sithias, the raptor still would not allow him on its back. It took even longer before they finally figured out the bird would only consent to carrying him in its enormous claws. Sithias immediately announced he would fly there himself. Of course, they all knew that would never work. He couldn't match the speed of the hawk, nor would he survive the heat over that much desert country.

Needless to say, Sithias begrudgingly agreed, but that didn't stop either of them from being terribly ill at ease with the arrangement. Time was of the essence, and they were out of options since Sithias couldn't shapeshift after O'Deldar used his glamour in Finn's ressurection spell.

"We should be there anytime now!" Finn yelled into the wind.

"That's what you said four hours ago!" Sithias whined.

Well, that was certainly true enough. Finn scanned the horizon, expecting the same empty expanse when suddenly the top edges of the Keep's massive rings rose into view. They were still miles from the Keep, but it looked gigantic cradled in the dunes, even from afar. He'd only ever viewed the Keep's surface from the sanctuary's lofty position within the nexus of the rings, which had been like viewing a large, sprawling city from an airplane. But seeing the entire structure from the outside, and the sheer immensity of it, was mind-boggling.

Grabbing the reins, he adjusted the hawk's course to the left when he saw the fleet of airships hovering in and around the rings, and spoke the command for climbing higher. The hawk responded with a sudden downward thrust of its gigantic wings, causing Sithias to shriek with fright as they rose higher and higher into the sky.

"What's happening?" Sithias yelled.

Finn didn't answer. His attention was riveted on the Keep. He leaned forward in the saddle as the hawk closed the distance within seconds of his first sighting. Blinding flashes of sunlight reflected off the shiny surface of the rings. Steering the hawk to avoid the glare, Finn squeezed the reins, his concern for Fate and everyone else increasing to a rapid hammering in his chest.

The rings were half buried within a crater that stretched for miles. A clear indication the structure had come through the portal with enough force to drive the main girth of the gargantuan rings deep into the earth. By some miracle of lingering magic mixed with science, the massive round construct of the Keep remained hovering within the center of the partially buried rings, its gears still rotating the ancient vaults across its complex surface.

"Is that the Keep I'm seeing?" Sithias called out. "I knew it was big, but this is humongousss!"

"Aye." More nervous than ever, Finn directed the hawk even higher and retrieved a spyglass from one of the saddlebags. Quickly focusing the lens, he brought the outer periphery of the rings into sharp view, where unrecognizable debris lay in strewn clusters. Thousands of structures set within orderly patterns surrounded the scattered detritus of the site, all of which were crawling with movement. Kaliena's army had taken over the Keep's perimeter.

Finn swiped the reins, turning the hawk away from the Keep. Only when they were a safe distance away, did he guide the hawk to finally descend and land.

Finn slid out of the saddle and onto the sand. The hawk turned its head, fixing its sharp yellow gaze on him. He stroked the bird's neck. "Thank you for seeing us safely here."

Sithias said something but his voice was too muffled to understand. Finn bent to look under the hawk. Poor Sithias was pressed into the sand, held down beneath the hawk's heavy talons. Finn pulled hard on the reins until the giant raptor stepped off the snake. "What did you say?" he asked.

"I said, speak for yourssself!" Sithias hissed. Pointing a furious glare at the hawk, he shook out his crumpled wings, losing several feathers in the process. "It's a wonder I wasn't crushed to death or suffocated just now!"

"Are you all right?" Finn asked out of courtesy, even though his friend was clearly in one piece.

"I think so. Physically, that is," Sithias grouched. "I can't say the same for my emotional state. I'm certain I'll be plagued by nightmares of my recent trauma for the ressst of my life."

Allowing Sithias to go on about the ordeal at his leisure, Finn unpacked their supplies. Once he finished, he removed the harness from the hawk's head. The second he released the leather straps, the bird of prey lifted off. Finn turned his head away from the flurry of sand kicked up by its enormous wings. The hawk disappeared swiftly out of sight.

"Did you catch sight of Kaliena's ground troops?" Finn asked.

"No I did not. I was far too busy fearing for my life while in the clutches of that monstrous beast."

"They're camped out all around the Keep. The place is mobbed with soldiers, which I fear will make finding a way into the sanctuary next to impossible."

Sithias's amber eyes went round with terror. "Are you saying we flew out here for nothing?" He slithered toward the direction the hawk had flown. "Why would you let the hawk go if we can't get into the sanctuary? Call it back, call it back!"

"The hawk's halfway to Eldunough by now."

Sithias slumped his head. "Then we're doomed to die a horrible death." He lifted his head. "Unless we can summon Aradif. He is, after all, expecting you."

"Any ideas how we'd go about doing that?"

Sithias blinked at him wordlessly.

"Exactly," Finn affirmed. "Besides, I didn't get the impression Aradif was the type to answer a summons. Given how things played out before, he probably already knows we're here. And my guess is he's waiting for destiny to take its course before he steps in. *If* he steps in, since he never promised to help. He was simply sharing his premonition."

"Destiny is highly overrated. Some helpful intervention is what we need," Sithias grumbled.

"Agreed, but until then, we're going to have to fend for ourselves." Finn strapped on the pack O'Deldar had supplied him with and drank a swig of water. Offering the canteen to Sithias, he stared back at the Keep. From where they'd landed, only the top of the rings were visible above the horizon.

Sithias handed him the canteen and he tucked it in the pack. "What's your plan, now that we're stranded?"

"We walk back to the Keep."

Two more feathers fell from Sithias's wings. "Straight into Kaliena's death camp?"

"We're not just going to walk in and hand ourselves over. That would be mental of us."

"Thank goodness! For a moment there, I thought you'd lossst your head."

Finn stared back with annoyance. "I'm quite aware of what's at risk here, Sithias. If we were unfortunate enough to get caught, it wouldn't take long for Kaliena to figure out the Rod is part of me." He shook his head. "I don't even want to think about that."

"The whole world would come to an end! That's what would happen," Sithias finished for him.

"Aye, I was hoping to avoid heaping on anymore pressure, so thanks for voicing my fears out loud." Finn sighed.

"Sorry, sir," Sithias mumbled. "What is your very carefully thought out plan then?"

"I figure by the time we reach the outskirts of the Keep it'll be after dark, which will give us the cover we need to scout out the situation. I'll check out things on the ground while you fly into the rings to see what condition the sanctuary is in."

Sithias listened intently, before straightening his spine. "Wait, back up. You want me to fly over Kaliena's army in the dark?"

"Would you prefer to do it in broad daylight?"

"Well, when you put it that it way…"

Finn nodded tiredly. "Let's be off then," he said as he took the first step of their journey.

True to his prediction, they arrived near the outer edges of the site a few hours after sunset. They knew they were close when the ridges of the dunes ahead began to glow with the firelight of countless campfires.

Finn slowed down, creeping on his belly to the nearest rise. Sithias slithered next to him, his large wings folded tight to his back. He hissed at the sight of the thick ring of countless fires mixed with strobes of light shining off the hulls of thousands of airships hovering overhead.

"This is bad. Very, very bad," Sithias whispered. "You never mentioned all those ships."

"Aye, sorry about that."

"Do you actually expect me to fly past that fleet without being seen?"

"Flying is the only way to reach the sanctuary, given the entrance is up there and not buried." Finn punched the sand. "It's a shame we don't have those visibility disruptors anymore."

"I still have mine. I kept it hooked on my glamour, and then tucked it in the band of my hat when I gave the glamour to O'Deldar to use in the spell to bring you back." Sithias tapped his suede hunter's cap with his tail. "What happened to yours?"

"I carried mine in the pocket of my army pants. It must've been destroyed when I…deconstructed." He couldn't say the word without wincing. "Only the original contents, like my flute, remained in the pockets when I was remade."

"How terribly unfortunate."

"I'll make do. At least you have yours."

Sithias glanced at the war camp and heaved a sigh. "No, you'll need the visibility disruptor more than I will if you're down there."

"Are you sure?" Finn asked, surprised by Sithias's un-expected display of courage.

"It's easy to forget I was Elsina's spy before I became the acclaimed storyteller I am now. But I was known amongst the soldier hawks for being rather stealthy."

"I'm sure you were." Finn repressed a chuckle, thinking there couldn't have been much need for espionage on the sorceress's peaceful island. In fact, the only time Sithias had done any real spying was when he and Fate had first arrived in the *Book of Fables,* and even then he'd defected to leave the boredom and join them in their "adventure", as he had called it.

Sithias plucked the visibility disruptor from the band of his hat and gave it to Finn.

Finn hooked the device onto his belt with a grateful smile. "You may have just saved the world with this heroic sacrifice."

Sithias stared at the visibility disruptor longingly. "We can only hope," he squeaked.

"Don't fret, boyo. You can do this."

The snake bobbed his head and gulped loudly.

"All right then, I'm going in," Finn said, fearing Sithias would lose his nerve altogether if they didn't take immediate action. "Let's plan to meet back here just before dawn. Agreed?"

"I'll be here." Sithias stared back with a look of dread. "Unlesss... I'm dead."

"You'll survive." Giving him a wink, Finn activated the visibility disruptor. Sithias blurred in and out of vision for a split second, an indicator the device was working to make him invisible.

Sithias unfurled his wings and lifted off into the night sky.

Without wasting another second, Finn descended into the crater, his boots sliding over the loose sand, hastening his approach to the hollowed out bottom. The descent was long, his speed increasing to the point of losing his footing. He tumbled the rest of the way, hitting a solid structure protruding from the ground along the outer edge of the crater.

Catching his breath, he stood, checking to see if he'd been heard. Thankfully, he'd landed unnoticed, so he turned his attention to the obstruction that had halted his fall. A pillared archway, broken on its edges, leaned sideways, as if a giant had cracked it off a building and thrown it. More fragmented pieces of once ancient edifices were strewn throughout the crater, each embedded in the ground like the one beside him.

Finn's stomach sank. These were shattered remnants of vaults from the Keep–hundreds of them dislodged and demolished on impact.

His gaze rose to the massive rings arching into the darkness. The Keep floated hundreds of yards above the ground, indescribable in its enormity–a colossal ball of magically infused metal that had somehow remained functional, despite the loss of so many treasured relics of powerful magic. He could only hope those lost objects of power had been buried irretrievably in the desert sands. He hated to think how they could be used to add to Kaliena's military might.

Finn crept further into the encampment, where huge scraps of torn metal had been pieced together into sharp-angled shelters. There were countless rows of them, all ordered in repeating lines. Soldiers milled in and out of the shelters, congregating near the light of the campfires. He couldn't see them in any great detail from where he stood. They were growling black outlines against the flames, their monstrous shapes distorted by horns, spikes and twitching tails, making it obvious they weren't human.

A foul stench of rotting meat hung in the air. There was no escaping it, and he could only guess that most of the soldiers had probably only been reanimated to the point of functionality. Leaving tissue and organs partially necrotic.

Finn moved deeper into the center, but stopped at a massive barrier. It was a long wall that curved out of sight to either side, built to the height of a hundred-story building. Disturbing shrieks and snarls came from the other side.

He followed the line of the wall to a gate made of open metal slats. His gut clenched tight. The lights of the airships illuminated an area the size of ten football fields, sectioned off into sturdy structures caging nightmarish creatures. He didn't have names for most of them, only that they were massive and the most vicious looking things he'd ever seen.

Some he might call dragons, except these were not the majestic winged beasts of flighty imagination. These were malformed leviathans–all fangs, spikes and claws. Others were titanic ground beasts with crushing hooves and horns as sharp as spears. Those were the largest of them, while others of smaller stature paced their pens. Most resembled wildcats and wolves, but in shape and movement only, because they had scales and leathery skin. Manes of quills grew from the huge heads of the serpentine felines, while long thorns bristled from the spines of the reptilian canines.

The running stomp of footsteps had Finn turning and pressing his back to the gate. Several soldiers tramped straight toward him. One of the soldiers strained to hold onto the leash of a gruesome creature with a head made of tentacles. Scrabbling on all fours, its tuberous belly snaked over the ground, claws gouging clumps of hard sand in its fervor to move faster than the soldier would allow. The thing stopped within a few feet of Finn, its hideous head raised and tentacles stretching toward him. It knew he was there.

Tensing every muscle, Finn held his breath.

The soldiers loomed over him, giants in their own right, with hoofed feet and decaying skin as black as charcoal. Thick necks of corded muscle held large heads with curling horns. Smoke drifted off their shoulders as they leaned in toward where their bloodhound had sniffed him out. How could the thing smell him over the rotting stench of the soldiers? But then again, maybe it wasn't his smell it was sensing.

The soldier holding the leash spoke to the others, his voice a guttural growl, his speech entirely alien to Finn. The others replied with short, gruff sounds.

Finn reached for his flute.

A gurgling clicking came from the bloodhound as its whole body stiffened, its tentacles quivering and glowing a deep crimson. The soldiers crowded in close to Finn and he flattened himself to the gate. But they knew the bloodhound was sensing something they couldn't. One of the soldiers swiped his claws through the air, grazing Finn on the chest, ripping his shirt.

Finn blew the notes into his flute, transforming it into his wind sword. Taking a wild swing, he sliced the soldier's arm off. It fell to the ground with a thud. The other soldiers stared at the appendage as the soldier snarled and lunged toward Finn. Leaping high, he grabbed hold of the gate, watching all of them claw blindly at the empty space he'd vacated.

But then the bloodhound rose on its hindquarters, clicking and pointing its shivering tentacles at Finn. The soldiers clamored onto the gate, climbing after him with more speed than was comfortable. Finn scaled the gate to the very top, then jumped onto the top of the nearest pen.

The massive beast inside bellowed, ramming its horns into the ceiling of its cage, throwing him off balance. He landed on his belly. The beast bucked into the ceiling again, the full force of the blow hitting Finn like a punch to the gut. Gasping for air, he jumped to his feet and leaped to the next cage, just as the soldiers landed behind him. They gave chase without the aid of their bloodhound. Not that they needed the creature anymore. Every cage Finn landed on disturbed the monsters inside enough to let them know where he was.

He needed to get out of there, and fast.

The deep pitch of horns being blown echoed throughout the encampment–a signal alerting the legions of intruders. More horns sounded from all directions, spreading the alarm, a unified tumult joined by the roar of entire armies on the move.

Taking a long run at the wall, Finn leaped, catching the top of the wall with one hand. Swinging his leg up over the edge, he dropped to the other side, landing on the sloping roof of one the ramshackle shelters. He slid the length of the roof, scratched by jagged edges of metal before reaching the bottom and falling. But it wasn't ground he hit. He slammed into a wall of armor, knocking to one side a soldier rushing out of the enclosure.

Finn's weight hadn't been enough to floor the goliath. Growling low, the brute glanced from side to side, searching for what had crashed into him. Scrambling to his feet, Finn gripped his wind sword, keeping one eye on the alerted soldier and the other on a way past the thick churn of soldiers flooding into the open.

Haloed blue-green light seeped from between the cracks of the soldier's helmet and armor as he drew his sword and stepped toward Finn. Swinging the long blade, he came within inches of Finn's neck. Ducking backward, Finn edged along the wall, hoping to convince the soldier his invisible attacker was gone. But while the rest of the army rushed off in all directions, this one soldier remained.

The soldier advanced slowly, cornering Finn between the barricade and the shelter built against the massive wall. He could either slip into the soldiers' quarters, where his movements would likely be every bit as confined, or fight his way past the giant. Yet something told him his wind sword might not be an effective weapon. He was close enough to see through the slats of the helmet to a skull engulfed in ensorcelled blue flames. The soldier was nothing more than a skeleton, brought to life by Kaliena's elixir. Even if Finn managed to slice through the armor, there wouldn't be any vital organs to stab.

Finn spoke the Elder race rune for Earth, commanding the element to rise beneath him. The ground answered with a quake, followed by a surge of sand so forceful Finn and the soldier shot high into the air. The sand collapsed beneath them just as suddenly. The soldier dropped on the other side of the wall into an open muddy pit of reptilian creatures that tore into him on impact.

Finn flailed, hoping to avoid the same bloody end by willing himself to land on one of the covered pens. Much to his surprise, he swept off to one side, crashing on top of the nearest cage. A shriek thundered from the beast he'd disturbed as he rose shakily to his feet. He stood there, bewildered and wondering if he'd imagined redirecting his fall to such a dramatic degree. He shook his head, knowing without a doubt he should've fallen straight down the same way the soldier had.

Was it possible he had the power to fly again now that he was back in Oldwilde, where magic existed in abundance?

Remembering the freedom he'd experienced when he'd possessed the ability to fly, he jumped as high as he could and continued to lift higher. He hovered in place, still trying to wrap his mind around the miracle. How long had he been able to do this? From the moment he'd stepped off the troll mound in the Twisted Bone Forest? Or had the power returned gradually?

"You idiot," he laughed. He hadn't even bothered to test it out. He'd simply accepted the loss of his power to fly after he'd crossed the fiery divide and had assumed it was gone forever.

Grinning, Finn stared down at the mobs of soldiers rushing around, tearing everything apart to find the intruder. He rose higher, spotting hundreds of tentacled bloodhounds snaking in amongst the throng. At least he was too far up for those creepy things to sense his presence.

But the thought died there. Each and every one of the bloodhounds rose on their haunches, their shivering tentacles glowing bright red and pointing skyward. A terrible chorus of clicking sounds rose in volume, dampening all other noises until all went quiet and every undead abomination stopped and turned their attention to the center, where Finn hung suspended in the air.

46
A DISCOVERY OF POWERS

FINN LAUNCHED STRAIGHT INTO the sky, narrowly escaping the sudden onslaught of fireballs, laser fire and flaming arrows, all of which collided in an explosion of fireworks within the space he'd vacated only seconds before. He climbed higher until he reached the topmost arch of one of the rings. Glancing over his shoulder, he dodged to one side to avoid the fireballs shooting from the airships. Fire crackled against the bottom side of the ring.

He descended slowly, landing topside. The ring's girth was at least a football field wide, providing more than enough shelter from the barrage from below. Not that they could see what they were firing at. At least he didn't think they could. But when he thought back to how close he'd come to being blown out of the air, maybe he was wrong about that.

"Best to find the sanctuary," he muttered, since there was nothing to keep the airships from rising above the rings.

Using his spyglass, he followed the line of the other five rings, searching for the nexus point, where the entrance to the sanctuary was positioned. As he moved the spyglass along the curving lengths, he pushed down the nagging worry that access to the sanctuary might be buried under tons of sand. Things were complicated enough without having to deal with that particular problem.

He stopped the spyglass on a dark hole where all the rings overlapped. Adjusting the lens, he brought the shredded opening into focus. Bloody hell! The hatch had been blown open and Kaliena's airship was stationed directly outside the hole.

She must have broken through the defensive wards Archie had used to seal the opening from invasion. And now she was waiting like a cat, ready to pounce when the mouse poked its head through the hole.

Shoving the spyglass into his pocket, Finn lifted off. He flew until he reached the next ring. Staying hidden behind the outer edge, he reached the middle of the ring and landed. He crept forward to peek inside.

Fireballs exploded against the inner wall of the ring a few feet from where he stood. Diving out of the way, he pressed the front of his body flat against the horizontal plane of the ring, his breath coming hard and fast.

They could see him. Had his visibility disruptor stopped working? He flipped the switch on the device to test it. His surroundings blurred in and out of focus, indicating it was working.

They obviously had some other way of detecting his presence.

Finn stood. He had no other choice but to make a dive for the opening and hope he was fast enough to do it without getting killed.

A terrible thought stopped him in his tracks. What about Sithias? He'd been so busy dodging bullets, he'd forgotten about his friend and the danger he'd sent him into. Finn quickly chased the fear spreading like frost through his gut. He had to believe Sithias would never be that brave. He would've seen the death trap outside the sanctuary for what it was and would've turned tail instantly. Sithias was no doubt waiting for him where they'd left their supplies. Once he got inside, he'd fine a way to get Sithias to safety.

Finn bent his legs like a runner waiting for the blast of the gun to start the race. Staring at the finish line, he dove straight for the opening of the sanctuary. With every muscle in his body held taut, he sped through the air faster than he'd ever flown before.

A red-hot beam sliced into his arm as countless lasers crossed his path, throwing him off his trajectory. Fireballs sizzled near his head, burning his skin with sprays of sparks. Keeping his sights on the sanctuary's opening, he corrected his course and picked up speed.

He was almost there when Kaliena's ship moved to block his way. The bronze wolf masthead of her ship loomed in front of him. Finn's blood ran cold as both Kaliena and Wodrid moved to the front of the bow to face him. Her stare was cold, impassive, like she didn't really see him. Just that he was a pest that needed to be removed. The red jewel of Wodrid's staff flared with magic as he conjured a fireball in his hand. A vicious smile formed on his pale face, letting Finn know things were far more personal between them.

Something sharp and powerful slammed into Finn, throwing him into a tumbling, wild free-fall. Disoriented, he fought to right himself, but only in time to see Jessie hurtling toward him. Metal fists punched his chest, knocking the air from his lungs. Pain drilled into his ribcage as he spiraled downward.

Pulling every muscle tight, he leveled out, his hand digging for his flute. Jessie charged again as Finn blew the notes to activate his wind sword. But she latched upon him in seconds, constricting his arms to his sides, her body armor biting into him as she pulled him toward Kaliena's ship.

Finn struggled to break free, but she was locked onto him like a vice. The strength of her cybernetic suit was astounding. Plus, she had every available weapon built into the suit to kill him with if she wanted to. So why hadn't she? It didn't make sense.

Kaliena must want him taken captive, not dead.

Adrenaline fired through his veins as O'Deldar's warning rang in his head, "*You now have the power to unlock the full might of the Orb... Kaliena must never capture you.*"

But how could Kaliena have known that Fate had given him the Rod? Terror iced through him. Could Kaliena sense the Rod was part of him?

Finn strained to loosen Jessie's hold. She didn't budge an inch. He looked into her wide hazel eye, the only part of her humanity left exposed by the exoskeleton encasing her. She stared past him, her vacant gaze fixed on the ship.

A projectile blurred behind her, crashing into her back with enough force to jar her grip, giving Finn the opening he needed to bust free. He shot across space, closing the gap between him and the sanctuary within seconds. Without looking back, he careened through the jagged entrance, skidding across the floor until he smashed into the large meeting table in the center.

Panting hard, he straightened, turning to see Brune standing near the edge of the hole, her back to him, both fists resting on her hips. Finn joined her in time to watch Jessie ripping herself free from the harpoon Brune had launched at her.

Brune waved her palm over the panel, triggering a force field filled with glimmering symbols. A timely shield, which deflected the swift barrage of fireballs from Kaliena's ship. She gave Finn a worn smile. "Welcome back."

"Isss it over? Did he make it?" Sithias hissed from the back of the dark room.

Brune tilted her head back in exasperation. "Yes, you can look now."

Sithias slithered out of the shadows with a grin so wide it showed his fangs. "Sir, you made it. I was so terribly afraid they had you."

"I could say the same for you," Finn said. "How did you get past Kaliena's ship without being seen?"

"Oh my, it was touch and go there. I'd managed to sneak past all the other airships, but when I was just about to enter the sanctuary, her behemoth of a ship materialized out of nowhere. They shot at me! Can you believe it?"

"Aye, I can actually."

Sithias's wings quivered, shedding a handful of small feathers that floated up around them like snowflakes.

"Did Brune save you too?" Finn asked.

"No such luck! Brune didn't know I was out there."

"How did you make it then?" Finn's curiosity was burning now.

"Well, there I was, my life flashing before my eyes–oh and what an exciting, wonderful adventure much of it was. A bit of a snore before you and Fate came along, but–"

"Come to the point, would you."

"Right, well there I was, under fire from every direction, and me without a clue as to how to survive the next second. All I could think of was how much I missed my shape shifting powers, because then I could become a tiny fly that Kaliena and her henchmen couldn't see anymore. And you know what happened then?"

"You changed into a fly."

Sithias's excitement deflated. "Oh. How did you guess?"

"Because I can fly again. I'm not sure when it happened, but our powers must've been restored some time after we returned to Oldwilde."

Sithias chuckled lightly. "How silly are we for not checking? There were so many times we could've used those powers! That awful hawk comes to mind for one."

Finn joined in the laughter. "I know. We really–"

"Glad you're both back and all," Brune interrupted, "but we should get back to the barracks. I don't like leaving Gerdie alone for too long."

"Isn't Eustace with her?" Finn asked. "Or Fate?" He knew not to expect she'd be there after what the scryer had told him, but he could hope.

Sithias lost his smile and Brune's expression turned more wearisome, kick starting Finn's heart into a chaotic beat. "What?"

Brune sighed. "Eustace is dead."

Shock rocked Finn to his foundation. "How?"

"Farouk killed him. In front of Fate." Brune's gaze fell to the floor, but not before Finn caught what looked like guilt in her eyes. She probably blamed herself for seeking out the key that unlocked his cage, even though it had been Fate who'd turned the key and released that nightmare.

Finn pushed against the sorrow aching in his chest. She must be utterly devastated. He needed to be with her. To hold and comfort her. "Where is she?" he asked at last.

Brune shook her head. "We don't know. After Eustace died, she changed into... something else."

Finn knew she was referring to Hippolyta's magical girdle, and he dreaded Brune's next words.

"The power Fate stole consumed her completely," Brune went on. "I can't know for sure, but it seemed like she disappeared, because what stood in her place wasn't her anymore. She acted like she didn't know us, or even that Eustace had just died. And her powers amped up all of a sudden. Mind-blowing powers, like growing full body armor out of nothing. When she left here, she walked straight through these walls like they were air. We haven't seen her since."

Finn's head swam with disbelief and an urgent need to find Fate, but the scryer had been very specific: *Be warned, young druid, you will meet your death if you try to find her. Your search begins with finding the fallen star and the blight it carried to this world.* He hung his head and sighed.

Sithias weaved in next to him. "Come, sir, let's go to the shelter, where you can sit down with Brune and Archie to discuss the next course of action."

Finn trailed after Brune and Sithias, down the long winding corridors, past the residence quarters. From what he could see thus far, there hadn't been any obvious damage to the interior rooms when the Keep had crashed to Earth. "I would've expected to find everything a wreck in here after seeing how deep the rings have driven into the ground."

"The builders designed all living quarters to oscillate with the movement of the rings and gravity generators," Brune replied without slowing her pace. "We didn't feel so much as a bump when we landed."

"What a relief!" Sithias exclaimed. "I couldn't bring myself to think of what damage the library might have sustained."

"It's fine," Brune said.

They passed by the large glass doors of the garden, a painful reminder of the blissful time Finn had shared with Fate. Picking up the pace, he strode by the doors, his gaze on the floor as doubt knifed into his heart. Were those few hours all they would ever have together? It certainly seemed as though the forces of the universe were bent on setting every possible obstacle in their way.

Regardless of circumstances, he couldn't ignore that neither of them was stable. He was at risk of literally disintegrating at any given moment. And according to Brune, Fate was something else. He'd witness a small fraction of the power Brune said had consumed her, and it hadn't been pretty. What if the girl he'd fallen in love with truly didn't exist anymore?

Was it over for them?

He was so deep in thought he didn't realize they'd stopped in front of the hatch to the shelter. Brune passed her guardian seal over the panel. The grinding sound of iron sliding open echoed throughout the corridor as they passed through the entrance.

"Why don't you move back into the residential quarters?" Finn asked. "I only ask since Archie's wards are working to keep Kaliena out."

"I don't know. I suppose we've all grown accustomed to close living quarters. Or maybe it just feels safer to stay together." Brune stepped inside.

Gerdie was in the common room playing hopscotch with the doggit. She stopped to stare at Sithias, her brown eyes growing round with a mixture of wonder and fear, before running to Brune. Wrapping her arms around her big sister's leg, she pointed at Sithias. "That's a snake!"

Sithias drooped. "I sssee her memory hasn't improved."

Brune shook her head. "If anything, it's getting worse."

"What a shame." Sithias tsk, tsked.

Brune kneeled down to Gerdie's level. "Did you finish your dinner?"

"Most of it." Gerdie didn't take her eyes off Sithias. "I like its wings. Can I pet them?"

Sithias looked horrified. "First off, I'm not an it, nor am I available for pettting!"

Gerdie's chin quivered. "It's a mean snake!"

Brune shot Sithias a warning glance.

"No, no, I'm quite nice," Sithias recanted.

"I don't believe you." Gerdie pressed her lips together, her eyes brimming with tears.

"Maybe I should go to the library, where I can research remembering spells," Sithias offered.

Brune stood and nodded grimly. "That would be best. If you don't know quite where to begin, I'm sure Darcy can point you in the right direction. She's in the library so much now, we hardly ever see her."

Sithias blinked sadly. "I take it she's still miserable over losing Mason."

"That's not something you ever get over," Finn muttered.

"None of us are handling our recent losses all that well." Brune shrugged. "Except maybe Archie. He's too much of a machine to be affected by emotion."

Given the tremendous turmoil Finn was in, he almost envied Archie's ability to avoid the plague of human despair.

"You know where to find me," Sithias muttered to Finn as he slithered off in a hurry.

Finn nodded, but his attention was on Archie. The scientist hadn't glanced from his worktable. His six hands moved in a flurry of activity, a few typing over his keyboard, while the rest flipped rapidly through a series of holographic images, leaving one hand to scratch at his chin pensively.

Brune took Gerdie's hand. "Time for bed."

"But I'm not tired!" Gerdie protested.

"Your crankiness says otherwise," Brune disagreed as she tugged her resistant little sister toward the sleeping quarters.

The doggit's ears swiveled in Gerdie's direction before it hopped after her.

Finn walked over to Archie. "What are you working on?"

The bright beam of Archie's glowing eyes shifted to Finn. His many arms continued without interruption. "I am manually operating the maintenance drones to repair the surface gears and damaged vaults."

"The Keep surface must be in ruins. I saw the wreckage of vaults on the ground."

Archie returned his gaze to his work. "Yes, there was nothing to protect the vaults on the surface once the last ring stopped generating the force field."

"Aye, it's a shame so many magical objects are lost in the sand. That is, unless Kaliena's soldiers have already dug them out."

"I have reason to believe they have not. My sensors detect they are buried deep."

"Did your sensors pick up on what happened to Fate?"

"Before or after I activated the portal?"

"After?"

"I do not know. I have no further recordings of her after we passed through the portal."

"But you have recordings of Fate before then?"

"I do."

"Let me see them!"

While continuing his other work, Archie used one hand to trigger a holographic screen, which he pulled aside and positioned in front of Finn. An image of an enormous coliseum came into view. Glowing from its center was a vast shimmering blue lake, which Finn recognized instantly as the elixir.

Nothing happened for several seconds, but then near the water's edge, a golden glow appeared, taking on a human shape, and in full shining armor. Finn blinked in disbelief when he saw that it was Fate. Her skin gleamed with an inner light. Her eyes shone so bright, they were nearly white as she gazed out over the lake.

"When was this?" Finn demanded to know.

"After Eustace ceased to be alive," Archie replied matter-of-factly.

Finn's mouth went dry as he watched Fate materialize a sword out of thin air and light its blade with black flames. Her face was hard as stone as she dipped the blade into the water and watched its dark fire cover the surface until the life-giving light of the elixir died and the liquid rotted into black sludge.

Jessie rocketed across the landscape so fast she was a blur before ramming Fate into the mire. Hovering over the infected water, Jessie's head moved from side to side, watching to see if Fate surfaced. But she didn't.

Finn leaned forward, his heart thudding with fear as each minute ticked by. Had she drowned? He jolted backward when Fate shot out of the water. Huge wings of light lifted her high above the lake. Jessie pounded her with lasers, which cut into Fate's armor. Yet Fate withstood the assault.

With one mighty sweep of her light wings, she plunged through space, hitting Jessie so hard she flew across the coliseum, crashing into the upper tier. Fate swooped down like a terrible bird of prey, driving her gauntleted fist into Jessie's head, pummeling her down into the rubble until the lights on her exoskeleton blinked out.

Finn gulped back the bile rising in his throat. Fate would never hurt Jessie that way. *Seeing* what Fate had become was so much worse than hearing Brune's description of her terrifying transformation. Apparently, today was a discovery of powers on all fronts, though Fate's were an unwelcome sight. He wanted to look away, turn it off, but he needed to see this through to the end.

Fate sped across the Keep's expanse, destroying airships with shocking ease as she made her way to Kaliena's massive flagship. The deck filled with frightening, wraithlike soldiers as Fate approached. She landed in the middle of them, hewing limbs and heads, mowing them down like they were bugs she delighted in squashing. When the last of them dropped, Wodrid conjured his infamous fireballs, but Kaliena waved him aside, each of her six hands gripping a scimitar as she strode forward to fight Fate.

Folding her light wings until they vanished, Fate stood still. Kaliena closed in, then stopped. Dropping one of her scimitars, she grabbed her throat, struggling to breathe. Fate was strangling her without so much as touching her! Wodrid rushed in, launching his fireballs at Fate, which she swatted away like pesky flies.

Finn magnified the scene, zeroing in on Fate's face. Her cold, impassive expression chilled him to the bone as he searched for the tiniest sign of the girl he loved. But he never found it, because a sudden flash washed her features into nothing but static.

He lurched at the image. "What just happened?"

"The portal activated," Archie explained, "disrupting all sensors."

"So that's it? You don't know what happened to her after that?"

Archie turned his gleaming gaze to Finn. "I have two theories."

"Which are?"

"Fate was either thrown into the desert far from the point of impact, or she was caught within the portal vortex and destroyed."

The last of Archie's words hit Finn like a knife in the heart. "No, she's alive. The scryer said she was reborn as an old god and that our paths are destined to cross again."

Archie blinked. "Highly doubtful. After running simulations on numerous prophecies, I have come to the conclusion they are mere probabilities with a fifty percent chance of actually taking place."

Finn backed away from Archie as the scientist continued with a litany of other calculations. He didn't want to listen to his grim percentages. He needed to believe in what the scryer had said. That he would see Fate, because it was meant to be.

But try as he might, doubt loomed large and he couldn't shake the mountain of fear that caved in on him.

47
WEDDING DAY

THE FOURTH DAY OF celebrations for Moulghazel's return echoed off the streets as Fate stood on the balcony of her tower room, staring at the horizon with a terrible ache in her heart. She'd suffered through three days of preliminary wedding ceremonies–forced to endure blessings for the happy couple by a host of priests, attend feasts with a wedding party that merely tolerated her presence because it was the king's command, as well as mingle and dance with countless relatives who did little to hide their disapproval of the unusual union.

Fate had worn a plastic smile throughout each tortuous day's events. Her face actually hurt from the effort. She'd wanted to run so many different times, to give her guards the slip when she'd been escorted through the streets of Biraktar and hide amongst the crowds until she found the dock, where they kept the boats. But she was never alone. Servants filled her bedchamber and guards stood outside her door. Not to mention, Mahelia was always there, even when it appeared as though she wasn't. Whenever Fate made so much as a move in the wrong direction, the woman appeared from around a corner or emerged from some shadowy corner as a reminder she was being watched closely.

But now the dreaded day of the wedding ceremony had arrived, and the gravity of what she'd agreed to hit home. The servants had spent half the day preparing her for her gown, starting with the mandatory removal of Finn's bracelet. It broke her heart to do it, but Fate had tucked it into a small bag holding the clothes she'd been wearing when she'd first woken in Dunebala. All she could do was pray no one disturbed the last of her meager belongings.

Upon a bath of the servants scrubbing her with rough sea sponges, all the while taking curious peeks at the magical girdle illuminating her waist, they'd slathered her down with aromatic oils that made her gleam like a polished pearl. Once they'd finished priming her skin, she was told to lie down on a table, covered only in the silken undergarments they'd provided, at which point the wives of the king and Azrael's brothers painted her hands, feet and limbs with henna paste. She'd then had to wait hours for the intricate tattoos to dry, lest she smear them and bring bad luck upon the marriage before it had even begun.

After the wives had deemed her ready, the servants returned to clothe her in a dress she would've considered absolutely beautiful, had circumstances been different. The long, off-the-shoulder sleeves and bodice was embroidered with lace of silver thread easily rivaling that of the richest Venetian lace, and continued over the top of the skirt before flaring to the floor in lavish layers of shimmering gold silk. But as it was, Fate hated the sight of the dress.

Finally, another few hours were spent taming her wild curls into a loose, silky cascade of ringlets falling over her back and bare shoulders. The last touches came with khol around her eyes, a feathering of rouge on her pale cheeks and a lustrous dab of red on her lips. Gold earrings dangled to the base of her neck, and an elaborate gold ornament draped over her forehead, were the final pieces of adornment before the servants guided her to the standing mirror.

Fate barely recognized herself as she stared at her reflection. She looked every bit the exotic, beautiful princess they'd designed her to be. But this was someone else. She wasn't that girl. Every cell in her body rebelled against the mold they'd poured her into.

That's when the hard, cold reality hit her.

She was to be married to Azrael in less than an hour, and forced to swear her allegiance to the kingdom. The very thought filled her with panic, so much so, her skin felt like it was burning from the inside out. This wasn't a situation where she could get away with making hollow promises. The soul ring sitting on her ankle was proof of that, and she'd allowed herself to forget it. Both the wedding and the pledge would be binding oaths she'd never escape.

She'd been fooling herself into thinking she could outsmart Mahelia by agreeing with this, all so she could get the necklace to shield her from Farouk's power to weaken her. For the first time since she'd made the deal, Fate knew she was in way over her head.

Her only option was escape. Even if it meant certain death. She couldn't live a single day in an unwanted marriage and under the thumb of a tyrannical, supernatural mother-in-law.

Gripping the balustrade, Fate glanced from side to side. No exits. The only way out of this tower was down–a long, long way down. If only she could fly the way she used to when she'd been trapped in the *Book of Fables*. Her problem would be solved.

But if she had the Words of Making, what was stopping her from creating the ability to fly again? Better yet, she could write herself back inside the Keep sanctuary! Finn would be there. And Eustace. Sithias and Gerdie too. Her excitement grew. She was even anxious to see Brune and Darcy.

Fate marched back inside her bedchamber. "I need a pen and paper," she told one of the servants.

The girl frowned, tilting her head to one side. None of the servants understood English.

"Never mind, I'll find it myself," Fate grumbled. She surveyed the room. There was no desk or bookshelves. No paper of any kind that could be used. Not to mention anything to write with. But she wasn't daunted. She'd been in similar situations during her time in the *Book of Fables*. She'd simply have to get creative with whatever was around.

Her gaze landed on the vanity table and the sharpened coal stick the servants had used around her eyes. She rushed to the table, grabbed the stick and a linen cloth from the servants' basket. Sitting on the stool, she scribbled out the words: *I am now inside the sanctuary of the Keep.*

She shouted them aloud, her heart racing and breath coming fast as she waited for her surroundings to shift and morph into that of the sanctuary.

Nothing.

Staring at the words scrawled on the cloth, she yelled them out again.

Still nothing, except that the servants were edging away from her, whispering to each other with confused expressions.

Fate's eyes brimmed with tears as she scratched out a different set of words. "*I now have the power to fly!*" she screamed. She pushed off the stool, knocking it over in her hurry to jump, fully expecting to lift off. Instead, she landed hard on one foot, twisting her ankle before falling to the floor in a pile of lace and chiffon.

Mahelia appeared, clapping her hands to gain the attention of the servants before ordering them out. The room cleared in an instant. "What are you doing?" Her voice cut through the silence like a knife.

Fate sobbed freely. Black tears of coal hit the skirt of her dress.

Mahelia dropped a towel on Fate's lap. "Control yourself. The ceremony is about to begin, and you look a mess."

Fate's head spun with crushing disappointment and bewilderment. The Words of Making should've worked. "I don't care. I can't go through with this."

"You *will* do this," Mahelia insisted.

"Or what? You'll kill me?"

Mahelia didn't answer, but the longer she stayed silent, the more nervous Fate became. "Stand up," she said at last.

Fate rose shakily to her feet. Mahelia righted the stool and guided Fate to sit down. Taking a cloth, she began dabbing away the smeared eye makeup.

"You said I have the power of the Word." Fate sniffed, swallowing down her dismay. "But I don't, so there's no need to keep me here anymore. I'm useless to you."

"Look up," Mahelia directed. Her voice was calm as she drew the lines back in around Fate's eyes. She stood back to view her work. "You said it yourself. You have never been able to control your power over the Word."

"I could at least do basic things like shift from one place to another. Or fly." Fate muttered the last part.

"The power of the Word works best when you are truly connected to the object of your desire and the outcome you are trying to achieve. A part of you, deep down inside, did not want what you think you most desire."

Fate scowled at her. "Have no doubt. I really, really wanted this."

Mahelia took a cloth, dunked it in the water pitcher and wiped at the black tearstains on Fate's skirt. They came out easily enough, much to Fate's chagrin.

"Maybe you did," Mahelia conceded. "I suppose then, it is time I told you that the soul ring binds you against doing anything that would cause grief to Azrael or anyone he loves."

Fate stood and backed away. "So that's it! The soul ring's to blame!"

Mahelia retrieved the lace pallu from the bed and draped it over Fate's shoulder with a pleased smiled. "It is good you are learning your place."

Fate went rigid, her whole body shaking with fury as she glared at Mahelia.

"Come, it is time for the ceremony." Mahelia beckoned her with a sweep of her arm. "The kingdom awaits Prince Azrael's new bride."

"No."

Mahelia's smile didn't fade, but the warmth in her blue eyes turned icy. "You will do as I say."

"Or what?"

"You do not want to find out." She wagged her finger at Fate. "Not ever."

Fear coiled taut in the pit of Fate's stomach. She didn't want to test Mahelia's warning, not with the soul ring chaining the full might of her powers. Sure, she could attempt a fight, knowing she could at least access the superhuman strength and speed Hippolyta's magical girdle granted her. But how effective would that be against Mahelia?

Swallowing down the acid burning the back of her throat, she followed

Mahelia out through the door. A troop of guards waited outside in the hallway. Falling into place on either side, the guards marched them down the stairs to ground level. Fate moved with Mahelia's entourage as if in a nightmarish dream, her feet heavy like she was slogging through mud.

Sorrow dug in deeper with each step. What did this mean for her and Finn? If they ever found each other again, would he forgive her for being manipulated into marrying someone else? She hated to think how devastated he would be.

Shame replaced bitter sadness. Maybe it was best if she never saw him again. Her heart shattered in a million pieces to even consider such a thing, but it would kill her to see the look on Finn's face if he were to find out about this marriage.

They stopped outside a huge set of arched doors, carved in the shape of a gilded winged snake centered within a cobalt sea of silver stars. Fate thought of Sithias and how impressed he would be by this grand temple raised in the honor of a celestial god that looked like him.

"Wait here," Mahelia told Fate, who continued to stare at the effigy reminding her of her dear friend. Mahelia moved in front of Fate, blocking her view to grab her attention. "Look at me."

Fate dragged her dulled gaze to Mahelia.

"Stand straight, hold your head up. You are about to be presented to the entire nobility."

Fate raised her chin. Not in obedience but defiance. "Are you afraid I'll embarrass you?"

Mahelia dismissed the guards. As soon as they rounded the corner, she narrowed her gaze on Fate, her dark brows creasing ominously. Shadowy tendrils crept around the edges of her body, sucking the light from the tangerine dress she wore, turning the silk to a muddy brown. She grabbed Fate's wrist, her grasp burning like ice. Chills seeped deep into the bone. Fate pulled away, but Mahelia's hold only tightened as she leaned within inches of Fate's face. "I can torture you in countless ways no one else would ever detect. I can cause pain that feels like a spike running through you, but leaves only the scar of a needle point."

She let go just as suddenly, and the pain ceased. Fate pulled the sleeve back, expecting to see frostbitten skin, but there wasn't a mark. Trembling, Fate gave her a silent nod.

The shadows receded and the cheery color of Mahelia's dress returned. Her face smoothed into a pleasant smile. "I will see you inside." She turned and slipped through a side door.

Taking in a shaky breath to calm her frayed nerves, Fate squared her shoulders and clenched her fists, deciding in that moment she would never allow that horrible woman to touch her again.

The side door opened and the crown prince walked toward her with two guards. He was dressed in a brocade tunic of royal blue and gold. His gaze ran over her, slowly and with open appreciation for what he was seeing. "You may not be a princess, but you certainly look like one."

Fate gave him a polite nod to hide her distaste for this whole charade.

Smiling gallantly, he held out his elbow. "I have the honor of giving you away."

Fate stiffened with untold grief. Eustace was the only one who should have that honor. Anguish twisted inside her chest, tightening until she couldn't breath.

"Are you feeling unwell?" the prince asked.

Gulping for air, Fate pushed the sorrow away, allowing absolute numbness to take its place. Feeling nothing was preferable, especially in this awful place. Pulling her mouth into a cold smile, she looked at him. "I'm fine."

The prince gestured to the guards to open the huge doors to the temple. They swung wide, revealing an enormous cathedral filled with royalty, all dressed fancifully in a rainbow of festive colors. An overabundance of flowery garlands dripped from the highest arches. Lined all the way down the ornate, gold-leafed walls, stood large urns with fragrant bouquets exploding with color. The opulence of it all was overwhelming.

Those in attendance stood to watch as the prince escorted Fate down the aisle. Whispers and gasps of surprise could be heard from every direction, but she fixed her gaze on the saffron-colored robe of the bearded priest who stood at the very end reciting something.

When they reached the end of the aisle, the crown prince backed away. Several young children carrying a long garland of flowers skipped in behind Fate, their eyes lit with excitement as they spun to face the entrance. The congregation turned as well, a ripple of movement among hundreds in attendance that signaled something important.

Azrael strode down the aisle, a handsome sight clothed in silvery white. His tailored, knee-length overcoat was made from the finest silk brocade, fashioned to fit his broad shoulders and narrow waist to perfection. His long hair fell down his back, smooth and glossy as raven's wings. Something about the way he carried himself was different. He moved with a boldness she hadn't noticed before, eyeing her with an intensity that quickened her pulse.

When he stepped beside her, a palpable heat radiated from him, one that enfolded her and made her knees wobble. He swallowed thickly as his gaze roved over her face, hair and shoulders. Passion blazed in his blue eyes like never before. Her breath caught in her throat as her heart skipped a beat.

The priest gestured to the children, who responded by placing the flower garland in a circle around Fate and Azrael. They ran off to one side, stifling their giggles. The priest reached out and took the end of Fate's pallu and did the same with Azrael's stole, which he then tied together in a knot.

Fate's chest tightened. She'd allowed herself to be swept away by Azrael's open affection for her and had let Finn fall from her thoughts. It may have only been for the span of a single heartbeat, but it was enough to make her ill with guilt and sorrow. Finn was the only one she wanted to be tied to. Certainly not this former enemy, regardless of the fact that he seemed in love and only too willing to marry her.

The priest reached for a silver pitcher filled with ranemist and poured the liquid haze into a small, copper bowl. He spoke what must have been a prayer, given his hushed, reverent tones. When he was finished, he set the bowl down between them.

"Do as I do," Azrael whispered, his mouth curving into a gentle smile. He circled the bowl of ranemist, gesturing for Fate to do the same. They made four full rounds before stopping to take their original positions to either side of the bowl.

Mahelia stepped forward and gave them each a tiny satin pouch. Azrael's eyes shone with joy as he took it from his mother. She smiled at them both with what looked like equal amounts of love, but Fate knew it was a lie and the charade nauseated her.

Azrael untied his pouch and indicated for Fate to open hers as well. Taking her other hand, he poured a handful of glittering jewels onto her open palm. "This symbolizes all that I am handing over to you–my wealth, my royal station, my protection and my love." His lips curled into a loving smile.

A confusion of feelings flooded in, compounding her guilt. His declaration and vulnerability rocked her off guard. How was any of this fair to Azrael? His parents had forced a marriage upon their own son, who had decided to pin his heart on a girl in love with someone else.

Azrael's smile faltered as he held out his hand and waited for Fate to follow suit. Gulping down her remorse, she poured the jewels into his palm. He released a tense breath. "Please, tell us what you are handing me," he encouraged.

Fate's mind froze. She couldn't match his pledge, nor would she lie.

If nothing else, he deserved her honesty. But what was she willing to give him beyond what she wanted to save for Finn, and Finn alone?

Blinking the tears burning behind her eyes, she searched for her voice and finally spoke. "This symbolizes all that I am handing over to you." She paused to clear her tight throat. "I hand you my respect, my friendship, and... " She trailed off, unwilling to promise her body, or her love.

But she sensed everyone expected her to offer more than what she'd already stated. This offering needed to be of equal value to what Azrael had vowed. Otherwise, she risked shaming him in front of the entire nobility. She bit her bottom lip, knowing her next words would bind her to him every bit as much as the soul ring had. Mahelia had already told her she would be expected to swear her allegiance to the king and defer her use of the power of the Word over to Mahelia's control. Handing them to Azrael was a far better gamble. She took a deep breath and declared the last of her pledge, "My allegiance and my power of the Word."

A flurry of confusion rose from the audience.

"Did I say something wrong?" Fate whispered.

"No," Azrael whispered, his jaw clenched. "Though, this is not the place, or time, to declare a power no one here has seen since the time of the old masters."

He looked at the priest, who was staring at Fate with equal measures of awe and bewilderment. Speaking in his native tongue, Azrael said something that had the priest raising his arms to hush the attendees. Once the cathedral grew quiet, the priest nodded to Azrael.

Azrael's posture relaxed as he kneeled and poured the gemstones into the bowl of ranemist. His expression softened as he raised his gaze to Fate. "All that is yours is mine." He gestured for her to do the same.

Fate kneeled and let the gemstones fall from her hand into the bowl. "All that is yours is mine," she repeated. Her voice came out faint and spiritless.

She caught the pained flinch at the edge of Azrael's eyes as he rose and extended his hand to help her up. She felt a pang at having hurt him with her lackluster attitude, but he knew she was being forced into an arrangement she didn't want. How could he expect anything else?

The priest stepped forward and proclaimed them married. Smiling, Azrael squeezed Fate's hand, raising their arms high for everyone to see. She forced a smile as everyone jumped up, clapping and singing. A troop of drummers burst through the entrance, adding to the celebratory noise, dancing with their drums as they filled the aisles, unifying everyone's clapping in a thunderous, festive beat.

Taking Fate by the hand, Azrael led her down through the dancing guests, who shouted out congratulatory messages as they passed by. Fate glanced around in surprise. Her ill-timed declaration had either been accepted or forgotten. But then she caught Mahelia's pointed stare from the top of the aisle. She was obviously furious with Fate's unexpected vows.

This time it was Fate's turn to smile with satisfaction, and it put a spring in her step.

The next few hours flew by in a blur of dancing with all of Azrael's brothers, cousins, uncles, and finally the king. Dinner was eaten at one long table, while watching dazzling performances by troops of aerial dancers overhead. Mahelia sat with the other wives several seats down from the king and his sons, making it easy for Fate to avoid her gaze.

Upon finishing the meal, the wedding cake was wheeled in by a handful of servants, a grand presentation which received much praise from the guests, and deservedly so. It was a large sculpted masterpiece of Moulghazel flying in a cloud of whipped cream. The sky whale was iced in a soft powder blue color, elaborately trimmed with white chocolate dots, florets and scallops.

"Are we expected to feed each other messy bites of cake?" Fate asked, cringing inwardly at the tradition she was accustomed to.

Azrael tried to control his expression, but he was obviously appalled. "Why would we do that?"

Too ill at ease to explain, Fate shrugged. "Just wondering."

The servants sliced into the cake and served pieces, of which Fate and Azrael received first. She took a nibble of the dense, moist cake. It was banana. Not bad, but she would've preferred chocolate.

Azrael set his cake down and leaned in toward her. "I have a gift for you." He signaled a servant forward. Fate recognized the white satin box immediately, but the necklace he lifted from the box was not the protective talisman Mahelia had shown her. It was made of gold and similar in design, with one exception. The sapphires didn't form a winged snake. Diamonds in the shape of concentric circles were inlaid at the center.

Mahelia had switched them out.

"This necklace has been passed down through my mother's line," Azrael said as he clasped the fine chain around her neck. "It has protective powers, and now it is yours." His fingers lingered on her skin for just a moment before he sat back to admire the jewels on his new bride.

Fate glanced down at the necklace to hide her anger. She'd done everything Mahelia had told her to do, only to have the woman renege on their agreement. She knew why, but if Mahelia was going to blame anyone for her plans going awry, she should hold herself responsible. It's not like she clarified whom Fate was to swear her allegiance and power of the Word to.

The guests sitting nearby complimented Azrael on his gift. Fate lifted her gaze. "Thank you, it's lovely." She glanced down the table at Mahelia, whose smile became superior the moment they locked eyes. Fury burned at the back of Fate's throat.

The war was on.

Angling herself behind others to block Mahelia from view, Fate looked at Azrael. "I'm afraid I don't have anything for you." She tilted her head, feigning playful contrition.

The intensity she'd seen in his eyes earlier returned. "You are my gift." He took her hand in his, pulling her toward him for a kiss.

Fate's first instinct was to resist, but she needed Azrael's support if she was going to gain any leverage over Mahelia. Closing her eyes, she thought of Finn, imagining the touch of his soft, warm lips. Buried longing rose to the surface, fueling her response with an eagerness that left her breathless.

A thunderous boom reverberated outside. The entire hall quaked, jarring Fate from her momentary escape. Plates rattled, glassware tipped, spilling blood red wine over table linens. Panicked guests shrieked, running for the doors. Another booming quake shook beneath them, knocking many people off their feet.

Azrael stood and tugged Fate in next to him. "What's happening?" she asked.

Guards rushed in, weaving through the frightened crowd to reach the king and the royal family. "I do not know." He took Fate by the hand and pulled her into join the circle. All she could do was stand by cluelessly, as the guards reported to the king and his sons. She didn't need to speak the language to know they were in danger.

The king listened solemnly, his dark eyes glowering with rage. All the wives watched, their faces stretched with fear. All except Mahelia. Fate suspected there wasn't much that scared that woman. At last, the king spoke, his tone commanding as he issued orders. The guards dispersed, leaving a dozen soldiers to escort the royal family out of the hall.

As Azrael fell in behind them with Fate in tow, she tugged on his arm. "Are you going to tell me what's going on?"

"We will be taking cover underground."

She was about to ask from what, but her question was answered as they hurried outside and ducked between buildings. The sky was filled with Kaliena's ships.

48
PAPYRI GRAECAE MAGICAE

LOOKING AT THE NUMBERS, it doesn't appear Kaliena has moved her troops out yet," Finn surmised as he set his elbows on the table and rested his chin on his hand. His vision blurred as he stared at the holographic image of the massive gathering of Kaliena's forces in and around the Keep. Stress and too little sleep were taking its toll. He needed to end this meeting soon so he could rest awhile. "That means there's still time for Rudwor to arrive with his allies. At least then, we have a chance of containing the fight here in the desert, where there'll be less damage to innocent bystanders."

"You're wrong on all fronts," Brune said. "Kaliena's been moving her fleet out in every direction, as well as ground troops since the day we crashed here."

Finn shook his head. "Well, the numbers she sent couldn't have been all that large. Not with what's still here. There's got to be hundreds of thousands of soldiers on the ground, and that's not counting how many troops the airships are holding."

"One million, seven hundred and thirty nine thousand to be exact," Archie said without looking up from his complex workstation.

"And don't forget about that pen of caged war beasts down there," Brune reminded him.

"Aye, I saw them. Up closer than I would've preferred. Where did they come from anyway?"

"Kaliena sent her soldiers through the portals of three hundred and eighty one vaults to capture the creatures," Archie informed him.

Brune pushed away from the table. "Yeah, everytime I hear that, I know this is a war we can't win."

Finn frowned at her. "Nice attitude."

Brune threw up her arms. "How many soldiers would you say are coming to our rescue?"

"I don't know exactly, but if I had to guess... it should be around two or three hundred thousand." Finn averted his gaze to hide his lack of confidence.

Brune laughed, a sharp sound full of bitterness. "That's a pretty disparaging guess, considering you might be off by a hundred thousand." She paced the length of the room, her shoulders shaking with silent laughter, before she stopped to look at him. "Okay, let's say it's three hundred thousand on our side, we're still massively outnumbered, and that's by soldiers capable of capturing monsters of myth and legend like they were rounding up cattle."

"I know it looks dismal, but we can't be giving up this early on," Finn pressed. "Not when brave men and women are on their way to fight a war we talked them into."

"I get it," Brune conceded. "You didn't know what they'd be facing. But we've been here for weeks, watching Kaliena's army dig its home base into the sand, training the beasts and building war machines beyond even Archie's knowledge."

"I continue to run analysis on the information I receive," Archie was quick to say. "Not all my maintenance drones return from their outings, which keeps my data incomplete."

Brune gripped the hilt of her laser gun as she stared into space. "We've watched recordings of them testing some of those weapons on their own troops. I'm talking canons with explosive fire that strips flesh from bone, wind blasters that cut giants in half, and camouflage generators that can make an entire army invisible to us."

"I suspect sorcery is behind most of the designs," Archie added. "Though alchemical formulas would be necessary for many of the others."

Finn did his best to remain calm in the face of this troubling information. "I thought that's what Kaliena needed you for, Archie. How is she pulling all this off, if that's the case?"

"Kaliena is well versed in the use of multidimensional magic, while Wodrid is a sorcerer of great knowledge," Archie replied. "As for the alchemy, it's highly probable Kaliena accessed library archives I had previously programmed into the system to create the elixir."

"I still don't buy it," Brune interjected, her voice hitting a more stressful pitch. "I think Kaliena's been using the Orb to augment her efforts. How else can you explain the titans? Even Archie can't figure out what powers them."

"Titans?" Finn asked. "I think I would've remembered seeing titans while I was down there."

"That's because they haven't been unwrapped yet." Brune gestured to Archie. "Show him." The scientist's fingers flew over his control panel. "Did you notice all those makeshift shelters while you were down there?" she asked Finn.

Finn nodded. "Aye, army barracks, I assume."

"Those aren't barracks, they're hangars for the titans. Six in total. The only reason we know about them is because of the intel the maintenance drones brought back, which Archie pieced together."

Six 3D images of mechanical giants rotated in front of them. They were each different in design and roughly put together, obviously comprised of salvaged parts from Keep wreckage and made operative by means that mystified even Archie. Brune was most likely right about Kaliena's use of the Orb. "How big are they?" Finn asked.

"Let's just say they could use the rings around the Keep as hoola hoops," Brune quipped.

Finn whistled under his breath. "That's big."

Brune rounded the end of the table, looking at him through the transparent images of the titans. "I know I don't have to ask if you remember Jessie's cybernetic suit and how it's been fitted with weapons..."

"Actually, we just bumped into each other an hour ago. So no, I don't need a reminder."

"Well, these things are outfitted the same way, but with added goodies," Brune said.

Archie tottered over to the table and began educating Finn on each titan's specialized weaponry. Finn listened at first, but couldn't keep his mind on the details. Not when his thoughts were consumed by how he'd doomed the armies he'd recruited. They would need something of incredible power to shift the balance back to their side.

"Fate. We need Fate," he whispered.

Archie cocked his head to one side and stared at him. "Did you have a question?"

"Uh, no." Finn arched his back and stretched. "In fact, I think I need a break."

Brune nodded. "We can pick this up later."

"I'll just see what Sithias is up to before I turn in." Finn strode out into the hall, grateful for a quiet moment to gather his thoughts. Not that it helped much. His mind remained a jumbled mess of questions. Why was Brune being so defeatist? On the surface he could see why she'd fallen into despair.

Yet Brune, of all people, should've considered Fate a major solution to what they were up against.

He still couldn't get the image of Fate's effortless attack on Kaliena's ships out of his mind. And he was still incredulous over her ability to strangle

Kaliena with a mere thought. If Archie hadn't activated the portal at that exact moment in time, Fate would've killed Kaliena.

He wondered what the repercussions of Kaliena's death might've been. Would her army have disintegrated without her as the controlling force behind their might? Possibly Wodrid would want to continue in her place. Though if there were one thing Finn was certain of, having Kaliena out of the way would've given them a far greater advantage over what they currently faced.

Finn entered the library and found Sithias sitting at one of the large tables, hunched over several stacks of paper. He was human again, a long, lanky man in his late thirties, and dressed in what Sithias considered librarian attire, with round glasses perched on his pointed nose and argyle sweater vest over a starched shirt and bow tie. He peered over his spectacles as Finn approached. "I can see by the miserable look on your face that Brune and Archie gave you the full brunt of all the bad news they've been gathering."

"Aye, the situation's dismal at best." Finn sat down across from him. "From what I can tell, Fate's the only one who has the power to turn the tide in our favor."

"That's exactly what I thought after I watched the recording," Sithias agreed, his white eyebrows arching above his wire-framed glasses like furry caterpillars. "I said the very same thing, but Brune wouldn't consider it. She said Fate was every bit as dangerous and unpredictable as Kaliena." He clucked his tongue.

Darcy walked over with an armful of books and set them on the table. "I say dangerous and unpredictable is exactly what we need right now." She glanced at Finn with a dull, almost bored expression as she sat down. "Welcome back, such as it is."

"Thanks." He tried for a smile, but it fell flat.

Sithias huffed. "Our small band is divided it would seem. Even Archie backed Brune up with a tedious list of calculations predicting Fate's propensity toward rash and destructive behavior that would be to our ultimate undoing."

Finn chuckled in spite of the ever-present tension. "Well, neither of them is wrong there. We both know she's been rash and destructive more than once."

Sithias let out a little laugh. "Oh yesss, but her intentions have always been in the right place."

"Aye, that's my lassie. She's a real ball of fire."

"And it'sss why we love her." Sithias's smile faded and he sighed.

"Unfortunately, Brune and Archie's reservations may be more valid than we would like to admit."

"What? How can you say that?"

"Remember how I handed over all my research to Eustace on finding a way to remove Hippolyta's girdle from Fate safely?"

"Aye, and I agreed it was a wise move."

"More than you know. I've been going over Eustace's notes, and it appears he looked into areas I never would've considered." Sithias shuffled through the stack of pages before stopping on one. "Apparently, there's been an ongoing war between gods and demons since the dawn of time, and demons have spent much of that time devising ways to disarm the gods of their weapons of power. One such demon was Dantalion, the Great Duke of Hell, who commanded legions of demons in the war against the gods. He was known for being a man of a thousand faces, be they men or women."

"Okay, he was a shape shifter. But what does any of that have to do with removing the girdle?" Finn asked.

"As we know, Hippolyta's girdle was designed to meld with the wearer to ensure the power could *not* be stolen. There's only one way that girdle is coming off."

"If the wearer dies. Is that why Hercules killed Hippolyta?"

"Yes, but his reason for doing so was far more interesting than the event itself. He did this because he received news of Dantalion's Key and the demon's plan to unlock Hippolyta's girdle, imprison her in Hell to torture her for knowledge of the gods, and then rise to rule as Hippolyta by wearing her face *and* the girdle."

"Are you saying Dantalion's Key will unlock the girdle without killing Fate?"

"It would seem so."

This was the best news Finn had heard in a long time, and with it came a plan of action. He would get that key, find Fate, have her use her powers to bring this war to an abrupt end, and then free her of the girdle's all-consuming influence. "Is the key here in the Keep, in one of the vaults?" he asked, growing excited. "I'll get it. Just point me in the right–"

"Dantalion's Key isn't anywhere in the Keep," Darcy cut in.

"Are you sure?"

The sympathy in her eyes said it all. "Eustace had me doing the research on Dantalion's Key to find its location. It's definitely not here. But if you're ever wanting to know anything about demons and where they live, I'm your girl."

Sithias slid a piece of paper in front of Finn, his finger tapping on an underlined sentence written in all caps. "Darcy narrowed the location down to one likely place."

Finn leaned forward to have a look. "Hadean's Kingdom?"

"Just one of the many kingdoms in a godforsaken realm called Hell," Darcy confirmed.

Finn sat back and folded his arms. "Are you really going to sit there and tell me Hell is an actual place?"

Sithias stared back with frustration. "Where do you think Farouk came from?"

"I don't know... I suppose I never gave it much thought."

"Even if we could get our hands on the key, it wouldn't matter. Eustace discovered something far more troubling."

The hope that had begun to spark in Finn's heart extinguished. "Tell me everything."

Sithias gave Finn a look of concern. "You look terrible, sir. Maybe this can wait until you're more resssted."

Finn crumpled Eustace's note in his fist, squeezing the paper into a tight ball. "How can I sleep knowing there's more?"

Sithias pulled at his bow tie with a loud gulp. "All right then. Eustace's research led him to the discovery that humans are entirely incapable of wielding the immense power of a god's weapon or garment. Unless... that human is the descendant of a god. In essence, the power surging through Hippolyta's girdle should've killed Fate on contact. Except it didn't."

Finn's grip on the wad of paper loosened and dropped on the table. "How is that possible?"

"That's what Eustace wondered, a question that led him down a rabbit hole of even more startling discoveries." Sithias rummaged through the notes, casting large stacks aside before resting on a leather-bound diary. "Here it is. This was written by a great, great, great, great, great–" He sucked in air. "Great, great aunt on Fate's mother's side, who was a Keep Guardian, and took over the job of recording the family tree, which went all the way back to the time of Alexander the Great."

Finn frowned. "Were there really *that* many greats?"

"I may have lost count, but you get the picture," Sithias muttered as he opened the diary to a page marked by a frayed satin ribbon. His eyes darted over the words. When he found what he was looking for, he raised his gaze with an anxious expression. "Are you ready to have your blood curdled?"

Filled with apprehension, Finn looked from Sithias to Darcy. She looked every bit as grim as he felt, though doom and gloom was her usual state, so maybe that meant nothing. "Drop the melodrama, Sithias. Just read what it says."

"Very well." Shrugging with a shake of his head, Sithias began reading the passage:

"*I have tracked the family bloodline to the exhaustion of every available written text, both inside and outside the Keep, each of which lead relentlessly to the most ancient of Greek myths. I still find the end results of my research to be entirely unfathomable. Yet there is no escaping the fact that Ananke seeded this family. Do not assume this is an ancestor named after the primordial deity known as the first goddess, mate to Chronos, both of whom were born from the void we know as the Chaos Region. Ananke controls Fate, the force of circumstance over–*"

"Hold on," Finn interrupted. "She doesn't mean *our* Fate does she? That would be impossible... "

"Fate is capitalized in the entry, but I think in this case the author isn't referencing a person. Although the context changes later and that's where–"

"Don't say anymore. Keep reading."

"*In the beginning, Ananke was incorporeal, an omnipotent entity whose amorphous form coiled around the universe to create distant worlds of earth, sea and sky, as well as to control the celestial rotation of the heavens, which she used to rule over the lives of lesser gods and humans alike. After eons of existence in this form, Ananke wished to leave a part of herself in the world of mortals, and did this by individuating a small part of her immense form into one chosen human embryo.*

And so, Ananke was born into this selected bloodline, of which she had specific plans. Her mortal life was lived as any ordinary woman, who played as a child, fell in love, gave birth to many children, and grew old and died. While this life was unremarkable, in and of itself, the act of this one incarnation is what steered the course of her descendants toward the inevitability of becoming guardians of the Keep."

"Wait, none of this makes sense." Finn folded his arms. "Why would some omnipotent god want to live as a mortal and then orchestrate a family business she's had nothing to do with since that one life? I think we're wasting our time here."

Sithias looked less convinced. "Remember, Ananke has been controlling destinies since the beginning of time, so why is it such a stretch to think she hasn't been working behind the scenes all along?"

Finn laughed cynically. "How do we even know this mythological goddess is even around anymore, let alone controlling our fates? I truly believe we have a choice in the matter. We're not puppets that can be made to dance just because something outside of us wants it."

"I'm not saying I believe we're being toyed with, but... " Sithias busied himself with picking invisible lint from his sweater vest to avoid Finn's defiant stare.

"But what?" Finn pressed.

"This last passage is more than a little disturbing in its accuracy."

Everything in Finn resisted what Sithias was pushing him to look at. "Read," he finally said through clenched teeth.

Sithias glanced at him with hesitation, then quickly dropped his gaze to the page. "*I had thought my search was over after tracking our lineage to these primeval roots, however unbelievable they may be. But as fate would have it, I discovered one last piece of information that will be of great importance to those who come after me. I found a disturbing prophecy written on the Papyri Graecae Magicae, which was once archived in the Library of Alexandria before it came to be stored within the Keep.*

"The translation reads: The mother of all gods, Ananke, has grown weary of watching from afar the mortals whose lives are lived in uninspired mediocrity, with very few heroes to mark the passage of time. With this tremendous disappointment weighing upon her, Ananke vowed to demonstrate what true greatness is by seeding a bloodline that would inevitably distill the ultimate culmination of heroic qualities in one being, all of which would be brought about by a series of pressurized, preordained circumstances.

"This descendant, of undetermined time of birth, can be recognized by a history of extraordinary happenstance, both fortuitous and unfortunate. Character traits, which are truly bold, courageous and protective, will be misconstrued as rash, fearful and thoughtless. An inborn hunger for strength, power and mastery will be frowned upon by those who cannot know the driving force of Ananke's plan, the impetus behind every action taken to achieve higher levels of excellence. Only when it is too late, will they see this to have been the necessary preparation for becoming a vessel strong and worthy enough to hold Ananke. If any doubt remains, let it be known this vessel will be given the name of Ananke's daughters. Some called them the Moirai, others named them the Fates."

Sithias looked up from the diary, his amber eyes filled with dread as truth rang in Finn's ear until his mind numbed with white noise.

49
THE SLAUGHTER

FATE PACED THE FLOOR, furious that Azrael had shoved her into a small room with the other women while the men strategized with the generals. Kaliena was her enemy too. She'd tried to tell him she could help with vital information, but Azrael closed the door without saying a word.

Energy crackled at her core, hot and pressurized, needing to be released through action. Fate pulled at the neckline of her dress, wanting to rip the restrictive garment off and find some clothing more suitable for the fight to come. Turning on her heel, she stopped to avoid bumping into Mahelia.

"Be still," Mahelia hissed under her breath. "You are upsetting the others."

"Oh, I'm sorry," Fate seethed, her voice piercing the silence. "I wouldn't want to upset them with my anger at being relegated to a roomful of useless women."

"Azrael knows what you are. He will come for you when it is time."

"Why not now? Unlike the rest of you, I happen to know who's behind the attack and what we're up against. Those misogynists should be listening to what I have to say."

"The war room is not a woman's place in our culture."

"Then it's a stupid culture."

Mahelia's blue eyes narrowed. "We women have more power than you know, and without being forceful."

Fate snorted. "You're one to talk. You've done nothing but force me into a corner." She leaned in close to Mahelia's face, emboldened by the power collecting beneath her ribs. "I won't be caged. Not by anyone."

"You have proven that well enough." Mahelia's lips lengthened into a bitter smile. "I am rarely outsmarted, but I must admit, you surprised me with how you managed to slip from my direct control."

Fate matched the bitterness in her smile.

"Measure your confidence," Mahelia warned. "Azrael is my son. He has always followed my guidance. You may be his wife, but he will never listen to you over me."

Fate stared back. "We'll see about that."

The door opened and Azrael strode over to them. "Father has ordered the entire fleet on the offensive. My ship is ready for us."

Fate nodded. "Let's go."

Azrael's eyes shone with admiration. "I knew you would want to fight." He turned and led the way out.

When Fate saw that Mahelia fell in step with them, she stopped in her tracks. "Your mother's not coming with us, is she?"

Azrael tugged on her arm to keep them moving. "Of course she is."

Fate dug her heels in. "Why?"

"We will need all the help we can get, and my mother's unique gifts will give us a tremendous advantage."

Mahelia angled in behind him, smiling coldly at Fate.

"Fine, lead the way," Fate conceded.

Azrael fell into a hasty jog, which Fate found difficult to keep pace with. The soles of her satin shoes were slippery upon the smooth marble floors. Stopping, she kicked off the shoes and ran to catch up to them in bare feet. "I hope you've got a change of clothes waiting for me on the ship. I'd hate to see this beautiful lace torn to shreds."

"Everything we need is being supplied as we speak." Azrael pushed a heavy, unadorned door open, which led onto a narrow lane used for refuse. They ran down the length of the alleyway, staying within the shadows to keep from being seen by the airships hovering above.

Just as they turned the corner into another back alley, a deafening crack resounded from above. Dust and rubble crashed in front of them, which Azrael dodged, while pushing Fate and his mother back. A series of explosions boomed from all directions, shaking the ground beneath them as they picked their way past the debris. Fate stepped on a jagged piece of glass and covered her mouth to squelch the urge to scream in pain.

Azrael swept her off the ground and kept running with her in his arms. While it was a gallant move, she felt uncomfortable on several levels. She disliked the involuntary thrill it gave her to be so close to him because it brought a weight of guilt on her as her thoughts turned to Finn. But mostly, she didn't like being made to feel helpless, because she wasn't.

"You can put me down now."

He didn't slow down. "Your foot is bleeding."

"I'm fine." She wriggled to get free, until he was forced to set her down.

He frowned with concern. "You are being stubborn."

"Didn't I tell you? Stubborn is my middle name." Testing her weight on the foot, she winced as pain shot up the arch into her shin. "See? I can walk."

Azrael stared doubtfully at the blood pooling around her foot.

"Let her walk if that is what she wishes," Mahelia said as she hurried down the alleyway.

Fate moved forward, skipping with her good foot to avoid putting weight on the injury for more than a few seconds. But then with each step, the pain lessoned and she was soon running ahead of Mahelia, leaving Azrael to catch up in surprise. "How is this possible?" he asked.

"I heal fast," was all she could say, hiding her own delight at this latest discovery of her mysterious powers.

They arrived at the loading dock, which was under heavy fire and being defended by a circle of Biraktar ships. The defensive line was holding with a steady stream of cannon fire. They knew to cripple the larger ships and their ability to hold altitude by targeting the rotating fans beneath the hulls, and aim for the balloons of dirigibles, many of which were in flames and sinking out of sight.

Fate recognized Azrael's ship and ran straight for it. Hiking her skirt up, she scaled the rope ladder and jumped on deck. She headed straight for the hatch and climbed into the cabin below. Her desert clothes, armor and weapons were laid out on one of the beds. Anxious to shed her gown, she stripped down to the scant, silken undergarments the servants had clothed her in. She let out a relieved sigh, grateful that she needn't worry about an unwelcome wedding night and being seen in them.

Azrael landed below deck with a jarring thud. Fate whirled around, hugging her arms over her half naked body. His blue eyes widened as his gaze ran the length of her body. Heat scorched her face as she grabbed her cloak to cover herself.

Clearing his throat, he looked down at the floor then strode to the bed, where his desert armor was arranged neatly. "I... I came down to do the same."

Fate nodded. Slinging the cloak over her shoulders, she turned her back to him, managing to put enough clothes on to cover what she wasn't comfortable exposing. As she strapped on the scabbard and slid her sword in the sheath, she felt more like herself again. As gorgeous as the wedding dress was, it had been something she didn't belong in. She was much more at ease in warrior gear.

Now all she needed was Finn's bracelet to feel complete. The bag she'd stuffed it into sat next to the bed. Sweeping it off the floor, she dug inside, feeling around for the silk and wool braid. Nothing. She flipped the bag inside out and shook it. The bracelet was gone, and her heart broke, knowing the servants had removed it.

Taking a breath to calm herself, Fate turned around just as Azrael slid a light cotton tunic over his muscled torso. She looked away, but not before he caught her staring.

A nearby explosion reverberated through the hull. The shockwave pitched the ship violently. Both of them charged up the ladder. Azrael raced to untie them from the dock as Fate ran to the helm and grabbed the wheel.

Mahelia held onto the railing of the sidewalls as the boat lurched into space. "I see you've become accustomed to working together," she observed.

Neither of them answered. Azrael focused on unfurling the sails, and Fate had nothing to say to the woman. At least nothing she wanted to say in front of Azrael.

"I'll be changing below deck if you need me," Mahelia said to Azrael.

Giving her a distracted nod, he joined Fate at the helm. "There." He pointed at a gap between enemy ships. "I will work on catching clean air to increase our speed."

Fate turned the wheel, jolting the boat into action and rocking Mahelia off balance, nearly causing her to fall. The woman shot her a dark glance, which Fate returned with a smirk.

Azrael pulled at the ropes, straining to keep the sails taut. The ship streaked through the air, slipping past the enemy line in a shot, launching past clouds of smoke, out into the clear blue. He rushed back over to Fate. "Circle around, we'll come at them from behind."

"With what?" she asked. They weren't exactly packing cannons like the Biraktar military ships. And from what she could see, the enemy fleet outnumbered them by a hundred to one, and had already devastated the city. Most of the glass towers and domes were shattered. Smoke filled the air from massive fires coming from the city center. The jewel of the skies was in ruins.

"With the power of the Word." Azrael slid in behind her, gripping the pegs of the wheel.

Fate looked over her shoulder at him. "That's wildly risky, don't you think? This is no time for experiments that could backfire very horribly. Do I really need to remind you of the boatload of fish and worms? I didn't think I'd ever get that smell off my skin."

Azrael's dark brows knitted into an incredulous frown. "You can end this with a few well chosen words, here and *now.* Think of the lives that will be saved."

Fate ducked under his arm to escape the close quarters he'd enclosed her within. "Thanks for heaping on the pressure. What if this ends up killing everyone in your city?"

"Biraktar is now your city as well."

Fate backed away. "No, I can't risk the lives of an entire city. If anything went sideways I couldn't live with knowing it was my fault."

"Can you live without trying?" Mahelia asked from behind Fate. She was dressed in desert garb and completely unarmed. Though Fate suspected she didn't need weapons to be lethal.

The ship shook with a thunderous boom off the port side. They passed through a blast of fire and billowing smoke as Azrael veered the ship in the opposite direction. Fate and Mahelia both lost their footing and slammed into the sidewall as the ship tacked into the wind and climbed at a rapid, steep grade.

"We are under attack!" Azrael shouted.

Fate gripped the railing and pulled herself up. Five small vessels shaped like sharks barreled toward them. They were fast and closing the gap.

Mahelia ran to the stern, her arms outstretched. Wind whipped her cloak and long hair violently skyward, building to such a degree that Fate was forced to move to the bow of the ship, where Azrael gripped the wheel. The edges of Mahelia's form blurred, expanding beyond her body, becoming as dark and immense as thunderheads. Fiery embers spewed from her arms and swirled into the blackness devouring the clear sky.

The oncoming ships flipped and spiraled out of control the second they entered the churning black cloud. The darkness spread in waves with sparking embers coating their hulls, scorching them down to charred, steel frames, burning through the sails, disintegrating everything into ash faster than flash paper as they fell from the sky like crisp leaves.

After the last ship fell, the turbulent, smoky darkness of Mahelia's unearthly shape fused into human form. She turned and strode across the deck toward Fate. "I have done my part. What will you do to help?"

Fate swallowed. She'd known Mahelia was formidable, but this was terrifying. She gripped the hilt of her sword. Heat flared and spread through her solar plexus, filling her with the need to do battle. "Get me on any one of those ships and I'll fight. I have no problem with that."

Mahelia stared back. "Why fight one by one when you can defeat them all with the Word?"

Fate glanced at Azrael, hoping he might realize the risk. He'd taken them high above the sky battle and his tension had eased somewhat, though his gaze remained ever vigilant, watching for more sneak attacks. "I'll try if that's what you really want."

"It is," he replied. "I believe you can do this without incident, but only with mother's guidance."

Fate sighed with frustration. Would he always side with Mahelia?

Mahelia reached into her satchel and drew out a pointed silver rod, a roll of thin gold sheets and a wooden board the size of a greeting card, with a coating of wax on one side. She placed the items in Fate's hands.

"What am I supposed to do with these?" Fate asked.

"You scribe the Word with them."

"Uh, you'll have to help me out here. I'm not exactly familiar with this outmoded form of communication."

Mahelia uncoiled a sheet of the malleable gold metal. "Place this on the waxed side of the tablet and press the point of the stylus into the gold to scribe with."

Fate wrinkled her face at the archaic tools. "I'm guessing you missed the memo, but pen and paper are one of the marvelous inventions of modern times. How about I use these museum pieces to conjure a few nifty notepads and pens? I promise, your mind will be blown."

Mahelia's expression remained firmly disagreeable. "No, you will use these. Each sheet was originally lead and has been alchemized into gold. They are strong conductors of energy and will transmit your words with greater accuracy and force."

"Oh, well when you put it that way." Fate rolled her eyes. "I suppose you're going to dictate what you want me to write. Emphasis on *dictate*." She muttered the last part through clenched teeth.

Mahelia's gaze flicked to Azrael, before resting on Fate. "I think we would all agree it is best, given your past failures."

The remark was intended to hurt, and hurt it did as Fate's thoughts returned, as they so often did, to the grievous mistake she'd made that had resulted in Finn's imprisonment inside the oak.

Azrael cranked on the wheel, jolting the ship in a downward swoop to escape the fire of an advancing ship, toppling Fate to the floor, a fall that had her writing tools scattering across the deck. "Do whatever it is you have planned!" he shouted at Mahelia.

The ship righted and Fate scrabbled across the floor, grabbing the stylus and gold sheets, but she didn't see where the tablet had landed.

"Here," Mahelia said from behind.

Fate stood and took the tablet she extended. Patting the gold sheet over the waxed side of the tablet, she held the stylus poised. "Go ahead."

The boat swerved, but this time Fate gripped the railing, waiting for the velocity of the sharp turn to end. She considered loosening her grip on the tablet and letting it fly from her hand, but most likely Mahelia had an extra supply in her satchel.

"Write the words exactly as I say them," Mahelia instructed.

The ship shuddered in the same instance of a jolting blast and loud rending of wood, the impact so great, Fate and Mahelia were thrown several feet across the deck.

"We are hit!" Azrael strained to turn the wheel against the air currents pushing them downward. Ranemist billowed over the port side of the boat.

Sliding on her back, Fate skidded to a stop as she squeezed the writing tools to her chest. Without waiting for Mahelia's unwelcome guidance, she scribbled a short sentence and yelled it out. "*The hull of the ship is whole and undamaged!*"

The ship responded to Azrael's attempts to level out and all visible signs of ranemist leakage ceased. She jumped to her feet and rushed to stand beside Azrael, but the look on his face chilled her. He was staring straight ahead, his jaw slack with horror as he pointed.

The ranemist surrounding the burning city was filling with sprays of bright red. At first Fate didn't know what she was looking at, but then she saw the tethers coming from the largest enemy ship and the harpoons digging into Moulghazel's back as the whale rose into view. The cacophony of war muffled the whale's sonorous cries of pain, but there was no ignoring the sorrowful sound underneath all the noise once Fate knew what was happening.

"We have to free her!" She began pressing out a line in the gold, but Mahelia grabbed her wrist to stop her.

"It is too late for Moulghazel," Mahelia said. "We must protect the calf.

Fate's vision watered with frustration. "No, I can save Moulghazel."

Mahelia pointed in another direction. "See those ships? They are after the calf. We cannot allow them to kill it." She looked at Fate, her face as hard and cold as stone. "Scribe these words. *Now.*"

Fate couldn't find a reason to argue and merely nodded with the stylus ready.

"*Spirits of the desert, take all but one of these ships into your black grip. Crush the bones of my enemy into dust. Feed them to your ravenous dwellers. Make them suffer my wrath until they beg for death, but let that not be the end. Condemn their souls to eternal punishment for the sin of murdering our people and our sacred Moulghazel.*"

Chills crept along Fate's spine as she wrote Mahelia's vengeful words. She looked up from the tablet. "Heavy on the overkill, don't you think? Can't we just say something like, 'All enemy ships are falling into the desert and becoming lunch for the sand monsters?'"

The iciness in Mahelia's blue eyes remained as she watched the slaughter. "It is my city that is dying, so I must be the one to choose the words. You can never know the grief Azrael and I feel at this moment."

"I'm no stranger to grief," Fate stated flatly. She glanced at Azrael. His hardened gaze softened somewhat but she could see he agreed with Mahelia. "Very well," she agreed, despite the sick knot forming in the pit of her stomach. Taking a breath, she spoke Mahelia's vengeful words aloud.

Nothing Fate had experienced to this point had prepared her for what happened next. The desert rushed into the sky all at once. Walls of churning, grinding sand slammed into the enemy ships. Hideous shapes formed within the sand, sifting in and out of view, behemoths that snaked with gaping maws, which latched onto the airships and shook them in their mouths back and forth. Other leviathans of indefinable shape hammered ships into the desert floor with fists as gargantuan as mountains.

Fine dust filled the air, stifling Fate's breathing, leaving the taste of iron on her tongue. Covering her mouth with her scarf, she fumbled in her pocket for her protective goggles, unable to tear her gaze from the sight of Moulghazel falling with the ships she'd been harpooned by and the awful trail of blood-filled ranemist that streamed behind her.

The storm of sand spirits calmed all at once, and every bit as swiftly as it had begun. A haze of dust remained, though not thick enough to obscure what was left behind. Biraktar's military fleet peppered the sky, some burning and slowly sinking as they lost precious ranemist.

A lone enemy ship streaked past them, rocking their ship in the air currents it stirred, a harsh breeze that flapped their sails with a loud snap.

Fate pointed at the ship. "Hey, they're getting away!"

Mahelia joined them at the helm. "Let them."

Confused, Fate read back over the words Mahelia had dictated. "Wait, you wanted all but one ship to go down." How had she let that slip by while she'd been writing? "Why?"

Mahelia didn't bother to answer and looked at Azrael. "You know what to do. Ensure you give them enough lead."

Azrael nodded and cranked on the wheel, turning his boat in the direction of the fleeing ship. "Not to worry," he said. "They will not know we are following."

"You plan on following them?" Fate glanced back at the scattered military ships, most of which were in need of dire repair. "But not alone, right?"

"Only us," Azrael replied. "We cannot risk taking what is left of our fleet into another battle without first knowing what we face. For now, the people of Biraktar need military aid and our sister cities must be alerted."

"I can already tell you what we're facing," Fate pressed. "Those ships that attacked Biraktar are a tiny drop in the bucket of what makes up Kaliena's forces."

Mahelia wiped the dust from her face while giving Fate the saccharin smile she hated so much. "I must see this for myself before I let the king know where and when to send our fleets."

"Are you insane? We can't sit around waiting for reinforcements to come. We're going to need them as soon as we get there." Fate shook her head, knowing it was useless to argue with the woman. Instead, she reminded herself she was returning to the Keep, where she knew Eustace would be, and possibly even Finn and Sithias. Yet, as much as she desperately wanted to see each of them, an unnamable fear of what awaited her at the Keep clawed at her insides and cried out for her to stay away.

50
STAY WHOLE

FINN WOKE WITH A start, his heart racing and sweat pouring off him. Despite the comfort of his old bed in the residential quarters, his dreams had been tortured by visions of Fate possessed by Ananke. A ruthless being of absolute power that cared nothing for the innocent lives lost in the war she waged against her enemies.

Closing his eyes, he fell back against the pillow, attempting to calm his nerves with deep breathing, but all he could see was Fate with eyes of shining white, wings of blinding light and her gleaming blood-splattered armor.

"Screw it," Finn grumbled as he whipped the covers back and rolled his legs over the edge of the bed. Despite the need to catch up on some much-needed sleep, his mind wouldn't allow him to rest after what Sithias had discovered about Fate. In fact, there would be no quality shut-eye until they had figured out a way to prevent the prophesy from becoming a reality.

Grabbing his clothes, he dressed and headed back to the library. He was halfway there when a deafening clang pealed through the hall, shaking the walls and floor. Finn broke into a run straight for the shelter, but was thrown against the wall as another massive quake shuddered through the entire structure of the ring. Rising from the floor, he raced toward the open hatch, which was spiraling shut.

"Hold on!" he yelled.

Brune waited long enough for him to jump through, then sealed it shut. Sithias and Darcy both looked out of breath as they unloaded stacks of books and papers onto the table in the galley. Gerdie followed Brune back over to Archie's workstation with the doggit hopping close behind.

Another ear-splitting crash shrieked around them. The floor jerked out from under their feet, slamming occupants and furniture to one side of the room. Finn grabbed hold of Gerdie's arm, pulling her close to save her from being crushed by a heavy bench.

The quaking stopped and Finn set Gerdie down next to him. Brune rushed to her little sister. "Are you all right?" she asked.

Gerdie nodded, her brown eyes round with shock.

"I take it Kaliena's patience has run out. But do we know the specifics of what's happening out there?" Finn asked.

A cabinet in the corner tipped over and Archie rose stiffly from out behind it. "She released one of the titans." He wobbled creakily into the middle of the room to pick through the scattered debris of what used to be his workstation. "The titan was cutting through the ring between the sanctuary and residence quarters before I lost visual. I estimate we have twenty-one minutes until the main halls are fully invaded. And ninety-three minutes before they penetrate the hatch and terminate us upon entry."

Brune hunted through a jumble of weapons and armor, and began suiting up. "It doesn't make any sense. Kaliena's left us alone this whole time, and we've done nothing to make her think we're a threat. Why would she bother with us now?"

Finn looked at Sithias, who knew exactly what was on his mind, because he shook his head no. "She wants me."

Both Archie and Brune stopped what they were doing to stare at Finn. "Of course," Brune said at last. "You have the Rod. I should've remembered that."

"I do and I don't," Finn replied hesitantly. "I had an incident while I was on the Eldunough Islands, where I sort of... disintegrated into dust, and O'Deldar used the Rod of Aeternitis to put me back together. Except that the Rod became part of me, so it's now me Kaliena needs to unlock the Orb."

Archie tilted his head, studying Finn pensively. "Ah, I understand now. The Rod's energies combined with the elemental powers of the Elder race runes are telegraphing emanations easily sensed by Kaliena. You are like a beacon of light she cannot resist."

Brune stormed across the room. "You came here without telling us this? We've been sitting ducks the whole time you've been here. You've killed us all." She kept her voice low for Gerdie's sake, but she might as well have yelled it out, for the palpable fury behind her accusation.

"If I had known how much the crash had disabled your defenses, I never would've come," Finn admitted. "But I can turn this around. Open the hatch and I'll surrender myself."

Sithias pushed a messy pile of books off his lap and stood, stepping over countless pages covering the floor. "No, sir, you mustn't. O'Deldar told you all would be lost if Kaliena captured you. She would have ultimate power over everything."

"I've been thinking on that, and I don't agree with what O'Deldar said. Kaliena can't make me unlock the Orb. I'll die before I ever agree to do such a thing."

Brune laughed bitterly. "You're as dumb as you are hand-some, which is too bad for Fate." She looked him over with a shake of her head. "Kaliena will find a million different ways to make you do what she wants. By the time she's done with you, you'll be begging to do her bidding."

"You're not getting it," Finn pressed. "I'm not doing this in the hopes I'll win out on a battle of wills with Kaliena." He swallowed down the panic that was already rising. "I seem to have developed an allergy to being locked up ever since my time in the dungeons of Asgar. I will literally unravel the moment she puts me in shackles, and whatever is left of the Rod will disintegrate with me."

He strode over to the hatch, shoved the galley table out of the way and glanced at Brune. "Open it. We're losing precious time."

Sithias ran across the room, stubbing his toes on equipment in the process. "Sir, please don't do this. There has to be another way!"

"You know there isn't." Finn leaned in and whispered. "The rest is up to you, concerning Fate. After what we read in her ancestor's prophecy, we both know she's on her way here to defeat Kaliena. But I need to know you're going to find Dantalion's Key to free her from being fully possessed by Ananke. You'll be cutting it close, because you'll first need to allow her to put an end to this war."

Sithias bobbed his head up and down. "I will, but what about you? There has to–"

"Don't fret over me." Finn swallowed back the hard lump in his throat. "I... I can't be the reason we lose this war. Remember Aradif's words. He said I would fight Kaliena to the death. Well, now we know this is how I do it."

Sithias's amber eyes brimmed with tears. "No, I can't believe–"

"Sithias, work with me here." Finn patted him on the shoulder. "There's more I need you to do. For now, you must leave here and get word to Rudwor and O'Deldar to turn back. I don't care how you do it, just do it fast."

Sithias sniffed. "Are you sure?"

"We both know Kaliena's army will massacre them. Fate's the only one who can overpower them." Finn gestured to Brune to open the hatch.

Sithias's Adam's apple bobbed up and down in a big gulp as he turned to Brune. "I'll return as soon as possible to help in whatever way I can."

"We'll hold the fort until then," she said with a nod.

"And I'll keep researching for the exact location of Dantalion's Key while you're away," Darcy assured Sithias. "I've become something of an expert on demons lately."

Sithias sighed. "Thank you."

Brune swiped her hand across the panel. Her gaze flicked sadly from Sithias to Finn. "Best of luck to you both."

As the iris slid open, the growling sounds of Kaliena's troops could be heard from the breeched residential quarters. In the blink of an eye, Sithias shrank into a fly and zipped past Finn as he stepped hesitantly through the opening and waited for the hatch to close behind him.

The thundering of heavy footsteps grew louder as Finn strode toward the clamor with his hands held in surrender. Jessie was the first to round the corner, with Wodrid falling in step behind her. She raised her arm and her body armor slotted an automatic weapon over her gloved hand, its laser beam shining a red dot on Finn's chest.

"I'm not here to fight," Finn announced. "Take me to Kaliena and leave the others. They're of no threat to you."

Wodrid sauntered forward, the icy blue of his eyes raking over Finn with each step. "It's not for you to decide who lives." His cold gaze moved to the hatch. "And since you seem to think otherwise, it's best we kill them while you watch. You need to learn your place, once and for all."

Finn grabbed the sorcerer's arm, jerking him within inches of his face. "Go ahead, but you'll be doing it over my dead body. And we both know Kaliena would be more than a wee bit displeased with losing the one chance she has of unlocking the full power of the Orb."

He let go of Wodrid, who turned a seething gaze toward Jessie and the armored monsters standing behind her. "Take him."

Soldiers with serpentine features swarmed around him. Reptilian hands gripped Finn by each arm. Their talons dug into his flesh as they slapped a manacle around his neck and shackled his wrists. Finn stiffened immediately, adrenaline firing through his veins as his panic heightened. It took every ounce of self-control to stay halfway calm and keep at bay that awful sense of the very fiber of his being disintegrating. He wanted to save that moment for Kaliena to witness, if only to see the look of sheer fury in her eyes before he was gone.

Pulling on the long chains, Wodrid's henchmen jerked Finn down the corridor, leading him to where the walls had been torn asunder. Across an enormous divide was the other half of the ring, with several stories of floors exposed, framed by mangled iron and run through with a tangle of ripped cable. Electric-blue light sparked brightly against the darkness of night. When they reached the jagged edge, a small airship rose into view and a plank was thrown across from its deck to where they stood.

As Finn stepped onto the plank, he caught sight of the titan–the one that had sawed through the ring–and he stopped to stare. Its size was incredible. The iron giant's waist hit the topmost curve of the tallest part of the ring and its head was lost in the black sky.

Snarling behind him, a soldier shoved Finn so hard he lost his footing and skidded over the rough surface of the deck. The ship lifted off and headed for Kaliena's flagship with its miraculously repaired alabaster buildings rising from its middle, an architectural marvel that gleamed in the moonlight like a palace in the sky. The windows of the towers reflected the small ship's searchlight in bright flashes as it maneuvered over the broad deck and descended. Guards rolled a ramp into place for them to disembark.

"Take him to Kaliena," Wodrid ordered the soldiers as he strode down the ramp, his scarlet cloak sweeping behind him like blood poured into ink.

Finn noted every detail as they pushed through the main entrance, making a mental map to be used as a speedy exit if the right circumstances presented themselves. Not that he was counting on escaping, but hope sparked eternal and there was no dampening an inner cry for freedom.

They pushed through a set of ornately carved ivory doors, turned left, and then right before entering a large chamber lit with warm light and rich furnishings. Kaliena sat on a gilded throne in an ebony gown girdled with a silver armor breastplate. When she saw Wodrid leading the way with Finn in chains, she rose from her seat and stepped off the dais, her six arms bent outward like a black widow spider.

Advancing across the room, she set her dark, predatory gaze on Finn and circled around him. Her every move was laced with deadly power as tendrils of aquamarine energy trailed in her wake. She stopped in front of him, and Finn felt her awareness probing his mind–invasive and painful as a steel rod to the brain. Sweat beaded over his brow and top lip as he fought to build a wall of resistance. She passed several hands between them in a snakelike pattern to draw his gaze into hers. But he knew he'd be trapped in those glimmering black eyes, so he focused on the skin at the base of her throat, so choked with the elixir's life force energy it was a blue, pearlescent gleam.

She finally gave up and withdrew, a sudden extraction every bit as painful as the initial invasion. "How did you do it?" she asked.

Finn drew a shaky breath upon release. "Do what?" His voice was little more than a whisper.

"You know what I ask."

He did, though he wasn't about to make this easy for her, nor was he anxious to bring his inevitable demise to a swift conclusion.

"The Rod of Aeternitis," Kaliena said when he didn't answer. "How has it become part of you?"

Finn remained defiantly silent.

Wodrid charged forward, the red jewel of his staff flaming. "Answer her!" When Finn didn't respond, he launched a jet stream of fire.

Kaliena spun around, her arms lashing out to shield Finn from the blast. "Leave!" Her voice filled the room and quaked through the floor.

Wodrid glared at her, his mouth opening and closing, though voiceless before he whirled and stormed out the door.

Kaliena turned back to Finn. Her tone was a malevolent hiss when she spoke. "You may think you hold the key, but you are wrong." She reached behind her neck and unclasped the chain holding the Orb of Aeternitis. Her lips formed sinister words as she swung the gold pendant from its chain in wide, rhythmic circles. "The Orb is what made you."

Fear iced over Finn's skin. She knew everything about him, despite his efforts to guard his deepest secret.

Kaliena continued swinging the Orb in ever expanding circles. "The Orb can also take you apart and remake the Rod."

Finn started to speak but a sudden wrenching in his solar plexus, like an iron fist pulling cruelly at his insides, squeezed off his words. The pendant glowed and sparked with jagged points of light, piercing his eyes like fine splinters of glass. He tried backing away, but the guards yanked on his chains and held firm.

Kaliena watched with a detachment that was more chilling than if she displayed enjoyment from what she was doing to him. "This is a fight you cannot win."

Gasping for air, he doubled over. The weight of his body gave way to insubstantial nothingness. Death fired through his veins as every molecule began to unravel. Searing white-hot pain burned along the threads of his nervous system. He raised an arm, staring in horror at the radiant sparks flaring from his fingertips as skin and bone disintegrated and spiraled through the air like fireflies, drawn inexorably toward the Orb.

He squeezed his eyes shut against the sight. This wasn't how it was supposed to happen. He'd been willing to sacrifice himself, but only in the knowledge his actions would deprive Kaliena of her ultimate goal. Instead, he'd handed himself over like a pig to slaughter and given her exactly what she wanted.

He railed against the injustice of it all, unable to accept the reality of what he'd done. The fight may be lost, but he wouldn't just give in. He inwardly recited the mantra the monks of Almsdeep had instilled in him. *Stay*

Whole. Stay Whole. Stay Whole.

He checked his hand. His fingertips were reforming. The destructive force halted in its vicious spread. He shouted the mantra aloud, over and over again, until he began feeling the weight of his body return.

Kaliena's dark eyes widened in surprise, and she lost the rhythmic swing of the Orb for all but a heartbeat–just enough time for Finn to invoke Air. The rune power burst from his mouth in a stream of fiery red-gold sparks, his voice thundering over the dunes like a roar of giants.

The winds answered his command with a distant howl. Within the time it took Kaliena to look in the direction of the terrible sound, the room's wall was torn away. Thrashing air rushed in, slamming the whole of the ship against one of the colossal rings, toppling the high towers. Glass shattered, spraying cutting shards as the lower structures crumpled inward. Finn's guards went flying, dragging him with them as they clung stubbornly to his chains. Kaliena hurled past them, nearly falling overboard before catching hold of the edge.

Squinting against the pelting sand, Finn dug into his pocket for his flute and blew the notes to make it into his wind sword. He cut his chains and launched skyward, tossed on the violent currents of the storm he'd summoned. Putting his back to the wind, he climbed higher, watching the hurricane pummel the fleet of ships. The lighter vessels spun and careened into the larger ships, which tipped sideways. Finn could barely hear, over the shrieking tempest, the cries of falling soldiers, but he watched with satisfaction as they hit the ground far below.

Returning his attention to Kaliena's flagship, he flew high overhead and stopped to hover over the damaged vessel. It was crammed against the inside curve of one of the enormous rings. The stationary position had allowed its captain to right the ship. Wodrid and Jessie stood next to Kaliena. Soldiers rushed back and forth around them, hauling debris to the sides to chuck overboard.

Adrenaline pulsed through Finn's veins. For the first time since Kaliena's rise to power, he actually felt like he could win this fight. Maybe even end it. Her fleet was crippled and her defenses were down.

Finn called upon Earth. Rune power burst inside his chest, hissing past his lips in a surge of heat and fiery sparks. He watched as the sand dunes heaved into a thrashing cloud of dust and climbed high over the ships, a mountainous tidal wave that crashed over them. Half the fleet went down in one fell swoop, burying the ships beneath tons of sand.

Unable to see through the sandstorm, Finn descended. He wanted to watch Kaliena's ship go down with his own eyes. But when the dust cleared enough for him to see clearly, he stopped and hovered, his every muscle tense and rigid. Kaliena was staring up at him. She waved her arms, and before he knew what was happening, a gigantic metal hand swiped through the churning sand and closed in around him.

He'd forgotten about the titan.

Finn shot through a narrow opening between its fingers, barely escaping the deadly crush sure to follow. The titan's other hand lashed out, grasping at air as he dodged its clutch. Straining to climb as high and fast as he could, Finn broke above the storm, where the air was relatively calm. But he didn't stop there. He continued to climb, until he felt safe enough to stop and check below.

The sandstorm swirled around the titan's shoulders, its arms outstretched toward him, before dropping its grasping hands and turning its gaze to the rising dunes. Another wave of sand was building and rolling toward Kaliena's ship, destroying another section of her fleet as it pressed forward. The titan stepped into the tidal wave, blocking the sands from hitting her ship, effectively dispersing the force and impact of the wave barreling toward the remaining ships in the area.

Finn's hopes for an abrupt end to the battle sank with the sand sliding down around the titan's legs. And with his dwindling spirits went the energy behind his elemental summons. The dunes settled, along with the howling storm. He thanked Air and Earth for answering his call all the same.

The dust thinned and the air slowly cleared, allowing a better view of the destruction he'd wreaked. More than half of the ground encampment was buried under earth. Splintered pieces of ships scattered the surface. Wanting to remain out of the titan's reach, Finn held his distance, though he was more encouraged than he'd expected to be, by the results of his elemental summons.

Stirring the desert's wrath several more times could very well finish this. It wasn't like the titan could protect all the remaining ships at the same time.

But then the sands began to swell, as if mountains were forming from underneath. Finn watched in confusion. Were the elements rallying to his call with his renewed hope? Yet something told him this was not the case, and his suspicions were confirmed as five more titans pushed through the sand and rose to stand guard over the tattered remnants of Kaliena's army.

51
MARRIED?

FINN FOUGHT THE WEIGHT of defeat bearing down upon him. One titan had turned the tides against them, but six titans made Kaliena undefeatable, regardless of having lost two-thirds of her army in the storm he'd summoned.

Fate was still the only one who could turn this around. And it needed to be now, before the remains of Kaliena's troops recovered from the storm. The scryer had warned him against seeking her out–that it would be the death of him if he tried–but he was tired of heeding the warnings of prophecies. He had to believe his destiny was his own and not predetermined by another's vision.

Dawn was only a few hours away and the desert was at its coolest as Finn hung suspended in the air. He was almost chilly, though that would soon end as soon as the sun rose. The dark skies were already lightening to a dim gray along the eastern horizon. He needed to clear the area before he lost the cover of darkness. But which way should he go? If Fate was heading toward the Keep to face Kaliena, it made sense to wait there for her. Though that would be suicide. He was already pushing it by staying this long.

It was decided. He would go to her. That was if he could first reconnect with her. His heart ached remembering the anguish she was in when he had first sensed her return to Oldwilde. Knowing that Eustace's death had been the source of her untold grief, as well as her frightening transformation, didn't lessen his fear for her. Sharing her sorrow had been agony, but the sudden, inexplicable severing of the extraordinary link between them had been unbearable because he'd had to face the very real possibility that she might have died.

He'd been afraid to attempt connecting with her ever since, lest his greatest fear be confirmed. Believing she was still alive and that they would meet again is what had made it easier to move through each day. It was why he'd clung to the scryer's prophecy for as long as he had. At least then there was still hope.

But he could put this off no further.

Finn sped away from the growing light, putting the Keep behind him by a few hundred miles. He descended, landing in the soft dunes, where he kneeled and pressed his hand on the cool sand. He drove his senses into the earth, allowing his awareness to radiate outward in all directions while questing for her spirit's fiery signature. Confining his search to Shalamoraize, he skimmed over the white rolling dunes, which seemed to stretch forever.

He pushed further and further out, until all at once, he crashed into the same barrier of thrashing wild magic he'd come up against the last time he'd tried to reconnect with her. But this time he could see it for what it was, a protective wall holding back the release of countless sand monsters that swam the desert sands like sea creatures in a vast ocean.

This had to be the divide Fate was trapped behind. It was the only answer he would accept. Nor did he entertain the notion she hadn't survived the deadly desert behind the barrier.

Finn waited, and time passed. The sun climbed into the sky, scorching his back as he pressed his palm deeper into the rapidly warming sand. Doubts wormed their way in, but he held to the passage Sithias had read to him. If Ananke was the driving force behind Fate's every action, then the Keep was where she would demonstrate her ultimate culmination of heroic qualities in one being. Which meant she would be doing everything in her power to get there.

Without warning, the link to Fate raced up his arm, hitting his chest in an explosion of cinnamon-scented wildfire and cool splashes of brisk, autumn air. Her essence blazed through his veins straight to his heart, soaking into his tortured soul like a much-needed balm. The force of her presence took his breath away, at the same time, filling him with immeasurable relief.

She was alive!

More than that, he sensed her longing and deep love for him every bit as strongly as his own for her. She was with him again. Maybe not yet in body, but she was with him in mind and spirit. Tears of gratitude filled Finn's eyes as he launched into the sky and catapulted toward her.

"I'm coming, love. We'll be together soon."

His heart hammered out a chaotic beat when he saw a schooner-sized ship in the distance. Mist billowed in and around the white sails extended to each side of the hull. The vessel was unlike any of the airships in Kaliena's fleet. Wary yet hopeful, he slowed down, wondering if Fate was aboard the ship.

Climbing higher, he moved directly above it, but was still unable to see the occupants. He descended until he saw a young man steering the helm. A dark-haired woman stood at the bow. Finn scanned the deck for Fate.

She wasn't there.

His certainty fogged with disappointment. He'd been so sure she was near. He would have to push on. Maybe there were more ships headed in the same direction. Surely Fate would be on one of them. Sighing heavily, Finn began to lift away, but a movement near the stern stopped him. Someone was emerging from below deck.

The moment the sun caught the red highlights of the auburn-haired girl who stepped into view, he knew it was Fate. Dressed ruggedly in desert garb, she was even more beautiful than if she'd been wearing the most elaborate gown. She lifted her face to the sky, her gaze hard as she stared into space. There was something different about her. Her skin still gleamed from the dormant power within, but she'd lost the luster of innocence, replaced now by a restlessness that smoldered beneath her carefully composed expression. He opened to her, immediately hit by the force of restrained fury.

Although she radiated absolute rage, Finn was at least grateful to see she wasn't the frightening, otherworldly being he'd seen in the recording Archie had played for him. By all appearances, she was back to her normal. Endearingly human, flawed and so very irresistible.

Finn dropped swiftly from where he'd been hovering high above them and landed on deck. His breath stalled in his lungs, his muscles tight with desire as he stood before Fate. Her brown eyes widened and her lips parted in a shock-still moment that grabbed hold of his heart.

Expecting her to run into his arms, he waited. She didn't move. Instead, she glanced over her shoulder at the woman storming across the deck toward them. The guy at the helm tied off the wheel and drew his saber as he fell in step beside the woman. The two were related. Finn could tell by the same dark coloring of their hair and skin, and their striking blue eyes.

"Who are you?" The woman's voice was deadly quiet, but tinged with menace. A malevolent energy poured off of her.

Finn slipped his hand in his pocket, reaching for his flute in case he needed his wind sword. "Fate knows me," he answered.

The guy stepped in next to Fate. Too close, as if he had a right to her personal space. "Is this true?" His English was forced, not his first language.

Fate's surprised expression closed as she tore her gaze from Finn. "Azrael, this is Finn."

Azrael's head jerked in Finn's direction–startled–like he'd heard a gunshot. His blue eyes raked over him from head to foot. Stepping in front of Fate to put himself in the middle, he lifted his chin, leveling a commanding stare on Finn. "What are you doing here?"

Finn leaned sideways, trying to see Fate. Why was she hiding behind this guy? "Fate," he said, speaking directly to her. "I've come to get you, love. We need to go."

She kept her gaze on the floor and didn't answer.

"Fate? Talk to me." Finn started to step around Azrael, but was promptly shoved back.

"She will not be going anywhere with you. Leave now, before I am forced to make you go." Azrael reached around to hold Fate behind him, a possessive gesture that ripped at Finn's heart.

Mine, she's mine, Finn thought as the blood pounded in his skull. Yet he was bombarded by doubt. If Fate was truly his why was she allowing Azrael to come between them? "What's going on, Fate?" he yelled. "Who is this guy?"

The question hung in the air for what felt like an eternity, and with each second that passed, Finn grew fearful of the answer.

"I am her husband," Azrael stated.

His words hit Finn in the gut like a hard sucker punch. The air went out of his lungs as an invisible fist gripped his throat. His head fogged with disbelief, his mind racing to disprove what he'd just heard.

Fate edged out from behind Azrael. A shadow of sorrow crossed her face when their eyes met. "I'm sorry, Finn, I... I didn't have any other choice."

"No choice?" He choked on the words. "What about us?" He dropped his gaze to her wrists, hoping to find the bracelet he'd made her. She wasn't wearing it. "We pledged ourselves to each–"

"Don't." Fate's voice was tight and sharp and filled with warning. Misery dulled her eyes. "Please go."

Incredulous, Finn stared back, searching for an inkling of reservation in her gaze. But she was resolute. He'd seen that look enough times to know her mind was made up. Yet he was plagued by a million questions. How had she come to be with this stranger, let alone *married*? Other than being obviously ashamed of her situation, what reason did she have to stonewall him? Was she being forced? Everything in him said yes. So if this was the case, what insidious hold did these people have over her?

Protective rage swelled in Finn's chest. Squaring his shoulders, he folded his arms and planted his feet wide. "I'm not going anywhere, lass." As much as it pained him to be near Fate when another man had claimed her, he wouldn't desert her.

Azrael's hand tightened around the hilt of his sword, the azure of his eyes glinting with growing fury. "You will do as Fate says."

"I'm no more happy to stay than you are to have me here, but something not unlike the end of the world is fast approaching," Finn explained. "Brutal forces are brewing a few hundred miles from here to the southeast. Massed battalions of monstrous soldiers, beasts and iron giants are advancing over the desert, and they'll be destroying everything in their path. Unless we can work together and bust it up, big style."

The woman shot him a feral look and moved in to stand next to Fate like some sort of guard dog. "We are well aware of the enemy you speak of. They left our city in ruins."

"Then you know what must be done." Finn waited to see if these two strangers knew the full extent of Fate's powers.

"We do," the woman replied.

"Do you really?" Finn challenged. "Because I've seen first hand what we're up against, and I don't think you have a clue what it is."

"I have come to realize this war will not be won with a battle between armies," she said. "True power will be the only end to this war."

"Aye, but where do we come by this power?" he asked, playing dumb.

Unnatural shadows moved over the woman's face, and Finn could've sworn for the briefest second that dark tendrils flared along the edge of her body. "This is not for you to know. Now go. Leave us."

"No," Finn refused. "The only way I'll leave is if Fate can give me reason enough to go."

He looked at her and swallowed, his breathing shallow as he waited for her to speak.

Fate's hardened gaze smoothed as she put her hand on Azrael's chest, an act of tenderness that tormented Finn. "Let me talk to him," she requested. "Alone. It's the only way we'll be able to get him to leave."

Azrael gazed straight back, his expression a sudden, open display of his affection for Fate. It was all Finn could do to keep from punching the lovesick look off his face. "Please do so quickly," Azrael told her.

Nodding, Fate gestured for Finn to follow her below deck. He landed next to her within the dimly lit space and only glanced at the lavish drapes, lanterns and plush rugs. His gut twisted as his gaze landed on the curtained off beds lining the walls with their silken pillows and sheets.

Unable to contain his emotions a moment longer, he grabbed hold of her arms. "Fate, I'm going starkers. What the bleeding hell is going on here? You married that brooding dobber? And who's that thrawn woman? There's something off–"

Fate jolted against him, quieting him with the press of her lips against his, a starving demand that sent electric shivers racing over his skin. A soft strangled cry rose in her throat when he pulled her close, his own hunger a ravenous match to hers as their tongues met in an achingly sweet caress. A hot pulsing sensation thrummed between them, partly passion, partly something else, something larger than either of them could ever express. Their once-lost connection fused in that moment, and Finn sank into the knowing that Fate was his, and he was hers.

Peaceful warmth unfurled in his chest as he took her face in his hands and kissed her cheek gently. Leaning into the hollow of her neck, he breathed in the perfume of her skin and hair. "I've been tortured with missing you."

"Me too," she whispered breathlessly. "I've been miserable."

He pulled away, but only enough to see her face. She seemed afraid to look at him and wouldn't meet his gaze straight on. He nudged her by the chin. "Look at me." She did so, but the guilt welling in her eyes tore at him. "Don't be hard on yourself. I know you had your reasons. Just tell me how this happened."

Fate stared at the floor as she hastily recounted the fright of waking up in the deadly desert of Dunebala and how Azrael had saved her life. While Finn was grateful to him for rescuing Fate from certain death, he grew even more hostile toward the guy when Fate told him about the soul ring he'd clamped onto her ankle. Yet she excused this as his custom.

Despite his growing resentment, Finn chose to listen without interruption as she described her encounter with Farouk and how Azrael had saved her a second time by throwing wards that kept her from falling within the demon's clutches.

Finn couldn't hold his words any longer. "I don't care what you say about him, no amount of heroics will ever absolve Azrael for enslaving you. Calling it a soul ring doesn't make it something else. It's still a shackle and he's–"

"I wouldn't be here if it wasn't for Azrael." Fate glanced down at her hands, worrying her fingers together. There was something she was hiding. "I don't hate him. He's been fair with me."

Jealousy burned a hole in Finn's gut. How deep did her feelings run for this guy? "He had designs on you, Fate. The bastard doesn't deserve your forgiveness. Especially since he ignored the fact that you belong to someone else." He paused, waiting for her to say something. "You did tell him about me, right?"

Fate lifted her eyes and they were filled with tears. "I didn't have any memory of you when I first met him."

Finn fell speechless as she went on to explain that every recollection of their time together in the *Book of Fables* had been lost to her, even her discovery of the Keep and her struggles before their ultimate reunion. Worse yet, she hadn't said a word about losing Eustace. But then he remembered the overpowering grief he'd felt from her, the wretched sorrow that had brought him to his knees on Mount Helgunth. It had happened just before the painful severing of their connection.

"Have you gotten all your memories back?" he asked.

"No, there's still a big chunk missing."

Namely Eustace's death. Finn's heart ached knowing her devastation. Brune had said she'd changed, completely transformed into something else immediately after Farouk had murdered Eustace in front her. It's no wonder she'd lost herself.

And that was the opening Ananke needed to emerge. Brune had thought it was Hippolyta's magical girdle that had taken over, but he was certain its job had been to make Fate the proper vessel for containing Ananke's godforce. Yet, at this moment, Fate wasn't the fearsome being he'd seen in the recording. If anything, she was more like she'd been when they'd first met–unsure of herself and still testing her courage.

Indeed, she was relatively calm and at peace, despite the troublesome circumstances she was currently entangled in. Telling her about Eustace would only shatter her into countless tiny pieces and Ananke would surely surface. If the memory was lost to Fate, it was because she wasn't emotionally ready to deal with the reality of losing her father. It was best if the memory came back when she was stronger, and he could guarantee he'd be with her when it did return. Things were far too precarious at the moment to do anything to the contrary.

"How were you able to get your memories back? Do they trickle in bit by bit?" he asked.

"No, I had help." Fate stared at the ceiling and frowned. "Azrael's mother, Mahelia. She knows magic, and she helped me recover most of what I'd lost."

"The woman is Azrael's mother? She looks too young. I could tell they're related but I thought she might've been his sister."

"That's probably because she's not entirely human."

Finn nodded. "I could tell something was off about her. What is she then?"

"She said she has *jann* blood. She's one of the Djinn–a genie–but not the wish-granting kind, unfortunately."

"She's one of the *jann*?"

Fate looked surprised. "You know who they are?"

"I met one of them when Sithias and I entered the Mirajaran Desert. His name was Aradif and he–"

"Aradif? Are you sure of the name?"

"Aye, we were his guests for dinner. That's to say after he put us through a grueling test that just about killed us, but that's another story."

Fate stared off, lost in thought. "Mahelia spoke reverently of Aradif. She said Aradif is a sacred constellation in the shape of a great winged serpent in the sky. She called it their Guiding Star. The Aradif you met couldn't be what she was talking about, right?"

"I can't be certain, though he was mighty powerful. The illusions he created for our tests were gobsmackingly real."

Fate shrugged. "I guess it doesn't really matter if he was or wasn't."

"Well, you seem to think otherwise. Let's say he's one and the same, how would that change things?"

"I'm not exactly sure yet. I just know it'd be nice to have an edge over Mahelia."

"She's dangerous, isn't she?"

"More than you know. She's powerful. Scary powerful. I watched her generate a flameless storm that burned through ships like they were made of magician's paper." Fate sighed wearily. "At first she seemed harmless, all there to help with her zen smiles and medicinal teas. But I found out just how cold and ruthless she actually is after she was working her mojo on me and found out I wasn't simply a useless peasant her son had recklessly bonded himself to. She zeroed right in on my history with the Words of Making, which I had no clue about until my memories returned. And now Mahelia's appointed herself the dictator over my 'power of the Word', as she likes to call it."

"You don't have to do what *she* wants. The power is yours."

Shame splashed across her face. "You of all people know how I badly used the Words of Making. I can never trust myself with them again.

"If you think Mahelia can be trusted over you, then you've definitely been brainwashed."

"Mahelia is horrible but as much as I hate to admit it, we both want to see Kaliena go down, and she understands how to use the Words of Making to make that happen. And just so you know, I tried using the Words of Making to escape, but it didn't work. Apparently, the soul ring binds me to Azrael. I can't do anything that would go against his wishes."

Finn bit down on his building fury and ground his teeth together.

"They've enslaved you, Fate, and you're acting like the prisoner they've made you into."

"I'm not disagreeing, but if you're going to blame anyone, it should be Mahelia. She reinforced my fears and used them against me, especially when it came to Farouk. She said he would never stop hunting me. We both know she wasn't exaggerating." She paused, waiting to see if he would argue the point, but he'd seen the nightmare that was Farouk and remained silent. "Mahelia promised to give me a necklace that would protect me against him, and that's the only reason I went along with her shady plans."

"What necklace?"

"A flashy necklace I would *never* choose to wear, with Aradif's protective talisman on it. But then when I pledged my allegiance and my power of the Word over to Azrael, she was furious, because she'd told me to swear those two things to the kingdom so she could be the one to control my powers. As my punishment for pledging them to Azrael as part of my vows, she didn't give me the protective necklace she'd promised me."

Finn's chest tightened. "What else did you pledge to Azrael?"

Fate reached for his hand and rubbed her thumb over his fingers. "Only my respect and my friendship. You're the only one I've pledged my love and body to."

His muscles went limp with relief. "Does that mean you haven't–"

Fate pressed her finger to his lips to stop him from saying the words. "I may be married to him, but not like that."

"Does he know that's how it is?"

"I haven't exactly had the chance to spell it out to him yet. The city was attacked right after the wedding, and we've been stuck on this boat with mommy dearest ever since."

"Too bad the attack hadn't come before the ceremony, but I suppose I can thank Mahelia for putting a damper on things."

Fate frowned. "Do you really think I would've gone ahead with the honeymoon if Kaliena's ships hadn't shown up?"

"No," Finn replied tightly.

"You do!"

He brushed aside a long wavy curl dangling in her eyes and caressed the flush of color on her cheek. "Sorry, I know in my heart you wouldn't have. It just drives me mad having you in this insufferable circumstance, especially after seeing how he looks at you."

"He doesn't love me."

"Beg to differ with you, love. He's smitten, and I can't say as I blame the lad. He's fallen under the same spell I'm under, you saucy minx."

A smile tugged at the corners of her lips as she gave him a sidelong glance. "You make me sound like a witch or something."

"Or something." Finn swallowed, his thoughts turning to Ananke's blood pumping through Fate's veins. She was clearly oblivious of the true nature of her ancient roots. He wondered how to broach the subject, or if this was even the time to tell her what he'd learned.

Instinct told him to wait. Her ignorance of what had happened to Eustace must be what was protecting her against Ananke taking over again. He could see now that her memory loss was a blessing in disguise. For all he knew, Ananke's full emergence might have destroyed Fate in the process.

Now that he understood what Fate had been through, he'd been a fool to think letting Ananke out to finish this war would end with Fate safely returning to normal. Thankfully, there was no longer any need for that. The Words of Making could be used to everyone's advantage. But that meant leaving her with Mahelia, unless he could figure out a way to free her from Azrael's hold.

"Enough about me," Fate said. "Tell me what happened after the Keep came here. How is my dad? And the others? Where's Sithias?"

"Everyone is as fine as they can be, what with Kaliena's army camped outside their doorstep." Finn couldn't hold her gaze as he lied about Eustace and the recent invasion of Kaliena's troops, made possible when the titan cut through the ring. Nor did he want to tell her about the dismantling he'd suffered during his imprisonment on the Eldunough Islands. Best to stick to less volatile matters. "Do you have any memory of us... together in the garden?"

"Do you mean the picnic Sithias and Gerdie crashed?"

Finn's heart sank as the memory of what they'd shared pulsed through his veins. "What about the bracelet I gave you? Do you remember why I made it for you?"

Fate's complexion blanched. "I had it, but Mahelia's servants... I think they might've thrown it out." She bit her bottom lip nervously.

"Oh, well don't bother yourself about it." He hated seeing her upset.

"Tell me why you made it."

"You could say it was my way of tying the knot. A handfasting of sorts."

All the air went out of Fate and her eyes welled with tears. "Oh no, I took it off. I let them make me take it off. I knew if I did I might lose it, and I was right. It's not in my bag."

Finn pulled her into his arms. "It doesn't make a lick of difference.

Not to me. As far as I'm concerned, you're my bride. Not his. Not ever."

Tears slipped down her cheeks and she nodded–desperately, frantically.

He squeezed her tight, kissing the top of her head as she relaxed in his arms. They held each other in silence, soaking up one little ounce of joy until peace flowed between them.

"Hate to say it, but we're running out of time," Finn whispered at long last. "Mahelia and Azrael won't tolerate my presence much longer."

Fate looked up at him, her eyes clouding with the unspoken question hanging between them. What happens next? As much as he wished otherwise, Finn knew the answer. "You're going to have to stay here for now. From what you've said, the soul ring won't allow you to leave with me. Unless Azrael is fine with that, and we both know he's not."

She nodded solemnly, but betrayed her distress in the way she clutched at his shirt. "What about you? Where will you go?"

"I need to correct a mistake. I sent Sithias to stop Rudwor and his allies from coming here after I saw what we were up against. I'm not entirely sure that was the best decision anymore. I think we could use all the friends and help we can get. Do you think you could use the Words of Making to send me to him?"

Fate dug into the satchel at her waist and pulled out a strange looking board with wax on it. "Sounds fairly harmless. I suppose I can manage that at least."

"Then it's decided. I'll meet up with Sithias and bring back all the reinforcements we worked so hard to gather."

"I always knew Rudwor would be on board, given how he feels about you."

"You'd be surprised how difficult that actually proved to be." Finn sighed wearily. "As it turns out, that particular obstacle proved beneficial, because in the end, we were able to convince the rock giants to join as well. We've also allied with Kaura's people of the Eldunough Islands. As for Asgar, Rudwor was confident he could convince Tynan to sail their combined legions to Shalamoraize. And with Asgar allied to Beldereth, it's possible Tynan could get the Serpens to join the fight as well."

Fate's eyes rounded. "The Serpens? Do you mean Moria's dragon race?"

"The very same."

"But they're vicious and vengeful people."

"Which is exactly what we need to defeat Kaliena."

Concern darkened Fate's expression as she stared past him. "Mahelia mentioned a *jann* prophecy about Kaliena. She said age-old enemies would be forced to form unlikely alliances in order to defeat Kaliena's legions, and the world's survival was dependent on unification of the whole. Any break in the chain would be the end of everything." Her gaze returned to Finn. "You have to make sure the allies get here. Winning this war can't fall on my shoulders alone. I'll crack under the pressure."

"You're a lot stronger than you know. And you're not alone in this. Have you forgotten that Sithias also has the power to use the Words of Making? Though he's been known to be awfully miserly with it. He learned too well from your mistakes."

Fate's worried expression smoothed into a wistful smile. "That's exactly why I gave him the power. I knew he'd use it wisely." She frowned. "Wait, does that mean I can fly again?" she asked, looking like she was about to slap her forehead for being an idiot.

"Aye, and don't go feeling foolish about not clueing in. Sithias and I only realized the restoration of our powers yesterday, and we've been back for weeks."

She was still puzzling over it. "But I tried to fly with the Words of Making and couldn't."

"Most likely because you were trying to escape and the soul ring blocked your power," he reminded her. "But promise me, if things go seriously awry, you'll use whatever power you can access." She nodded as he pulled her into his arms. "I'll come back for you, love, so promise me you'll stay alive at whatever cost."

"I promise," she whispered breathlessly.

He ran his hand over the curve of her waist and gently tangled his hand into the tumble of curls resting against her back. He kissed her long and slow. The heat coming off her took hold of him and his body tightened instinctively.

An infinity later, Finn drew back. The effort was excruciating.

"Send me off now, love, or I swear I'll never leave," he said, his breath ragged.

Fate reached for the tablet reluctantly. He knew the pain of parting was beyond her as she pressed the stylus into the wax, her hand shaking with each word that would take him from her.

Finn didn't register through his dizzying haze of desire what was said when she spoke the Words of Making aloud. Within seconds, she and the cabin with its silken drapes and cushions melted away into formless gray hues before swiftly rearranging into bright, hard shapes that darted around him in a blur of movement.

Harsh, crashing, booming sounds shattered the silence. Shock paralyzed him as he tried to grasp what was happening and where he'd been sent. And then the realization hit him. The war had begun, and he'd landed right in the middle of it.

52
BIRD'S EYE VIEW

THE AIR SEEMED TO leave the cabin the second Finn was gone, sucked away by his sudden absence. Fate's breath deserted her, leaving her lungs aching. She pressed a hand to her chest, trying to push away the hollow feeling. He'd promised to come back for her, but she didn't trust the unpredictable conditions that could break his vow at any given moment.

She walked stiffly to the ladder and hung her head with one foot on the rung, her body unwilling to climb above deck, where Mahelia and Azrael waited. She hadn't realized just how thin her courage had been all along. Not until Finn had dropped out of the sky. Seeing his face and the green of his eyes, lit bright with his excitement to see her, had filled her with indescribable joy and more strength than she'd known in a long time.

"Fate?"

Raising her head, she found Azrael standing at the top of the ladder, his brow furrowed with controlled anger. "I have granted you plenty of time to convince him to leave. I will not wait any longer."

She willed herself to breathe and climbed the ladder. Azrael kneeled to better see into the shadowy cabin after she reached the top. "Where is he?"

"Gone. I sent him away with my Words of Making when he refused to go."

Azrael stood, the tightness in his expression relaxing. "Where did you send him?"

"What does it matter as long as he's off your ship?"

Mahelia closed in beside him. "It matters if he remains nearby."

Fate clenched her fists, digging her nails into her palms. "He's fighting the same war we're fighting, so it's possible you might lay eyes on him again." She huffed in frustration. "If you must know, he's gone to gather reinforcements."

"Biraktar and our sister fleets will be more than enough to keep Kaliena's army distracted while I formulate the words that will destroy the abomination," Mahelia replied, her tone tempered by carefully composed patience in the presence of her son.

"We'll be there in a few hours," Fate said. "I don't see how your fleets can beat us there. And how would they even know where to go? It's not like we called it in. No offense, but you're all living in the dark ages here."

"While we were waiting for you to finish with him, mother communicated to my father all he needs to know to send the fleet here." Azrael strode to the helm and untied the wheel.

"And how was that accomplished?" Fate grumbled. "A quick trip on her broom?"

Azrael gave her a quizzical look and shook his head. "You never cease to confuse me with your confounding form of speech."

"I used the winds to carry my message–a simple thing when you know where to direct them," Mahelia explained.

Fate looked at Azrael. "You couldn't have used that when we were running low on ranemist and dangling over Dunebala like lunch for the monsters?"

"I am not blessed with the same powers my mother is."

Fate bit down on another snide remark directed at Mahelia. She couldn't risk alienating Azrael. He was upset by Finn's appearance and she could sense him distancing himself already. Best to nip that in the bud before his feelings bloomed into full-blown detachment.

She joined him at the helm, brushing her shoulder against his. "I'm sorry our wedding day was hit with disaster. It was a beautiful ceremony and something I'll never forget."

Azrael kept his head straight but his gaze flicked downward as she spoke. "I'm grateful to you for saving my life and for all the help you've given me to regain my memories. I'll never forget the kindness you've shown me."

He didn't reply, but his tense posture relaxed slightly.

"I meant what I said in the ceremony," she continued, "that you will always have my respect and friendship."

"Clearly not your love, however." He maintained a hard stare straight ahead. "You saved that for *him*."

Fate started to speak, but Mahelia interrupted. "Come with me, Fate. You and I must prepare for what is to come."

Stubbornness straightened Fate's spine as she put a hand on his arm. "My husband and I need a little more time to sort things out. Right, Azrael?"

The muscles in his jaw flexed. "Go with her, Fate. We are at war, and that is my only concern."

Letting her hand drop from his arm, Fate followed Mahelia below deck. Everything in her resisted being alone with the woman, but she didn't have much choice if she wanted to learn how to master the Words of Making. Though once she had, there would be no more doing Mahelia's bidding.

Mahelia laid out the tablets and began placing the thin sheets of gold on each one. Fate sat down on the cushions. "I wasn't aware we were about to write a book."

"We must allow for every contingency."

"Wouldn't it be better to write something based on what's happening in the moment?"

Mahelia sat opposite her. "You are such a child in regards to magic and how it works to mold the world into what it is. Most importantly, what we want it to be." She laughed bitterly, a soft laugh but sharp around the edges. "This power you've stumbled upon is wasted on you. Oh what I would do with it, were it mine."

"Actually, the thought makes me shudder." Fate frowned at the woman. "And since we're speaking honestly here, I won't be writing and speaking anything aloud that I don't fully agree with. So don't go getting any bright ideas about tipping the scales in your favor. We work together to stop Kaliena and that's it."

Mahelia's lips pinched tight as her brow arched with fury. "Do not think you can undermine me? You may have pledged your power of the Word to Azrael, but he is my son, and has always deferred to my wisdom. You cannot sway him otherwise, especially after seeing you with the man you truly love. Azrael is slow to open his heart but when it shuts, the door locks forever."

"I wouldn't be alive if it wasn't for Azrael. So trust me when I say I have no desire to hurt him. And I certainly don't enjoy seeing him upset by Finn's unexpected appearance."

"The only reason Azrael didn't take his head is because he cares what that would do to you."

Fate gulped. "I appreciate that."

Satisfaction settled over Mahelia's expression. "Let us begin. We have much to do."

The time passed quickly enough, with Mahelia meticulously composing every form of attack possible. But Fate was horrified by the descriptions and worried they were too extreme. Mahelia's imagination surpassed her own when it came to devising ways of destroying Kaliena and her army. On the other hand, Fate was relieved to have the tablets prepared and ready to be spoken aloud.

"Wouldn't it be better to just read one of these aloud right now, versus showing up and giving them the chance to blast us out of the sky?" Fate asked.

Mahelia stuffed the last tablet in her satchel and stood. "I want to see the destruction with my own eyes."

"Well, there's that," Fate agreed.

"And we must account for any unexpected variables, which could possibly turn the Word against us."

"Uh huh, so my first suggestion for writing something based on what's happening in the here and now wasn't as crazy as you previously made it out to be," Fate said as they both headed for the ladder.

Mahelia set her foot on the ladder. "There must always be room for flexibility, but we flirt with defeat by being unprepared when under attack."

"You have a point," Fate muttered as she followed her up the ladder.

When Fate poked her head above deck, she stopped to look around in surprise. The skies were filled with hundreds of ranemist-powered ships, some flying the golden banners of Biraktar, and others with flags of crimson, purple or green. She climbed all the way up, unable to take her eyes off the impressive show of force. The ships extended to either side, and behind them, as far as the eye could see. "Whoa, they got here fast."

"All military ships are built for speed," Azrael replied.

Fate strode across the deck to stand beside him at the helm. "We must be getting closer to the Keep by now."

Azrael pointed. "We are still several leagues away, but it is well within view."

Fate looked out over the bow, letting her jaw drop as she stared at the massive rings filling the length of the horizon. The round iron structure of the Keep, hovering within the center of the rings, actually appeared small from this distance. Which was unbelievable, because she knew how immense the Keep surface was.

She grabbed the spyglass and brought the Keep into focus. "It looks like there's towers all around the rings. How would they've gotten there?"

"I suspect those are the iron giants Finn spoke of," Azrael offered.

"Iron giants?" Fate's nerves pulled tight. "Are you sure? Because I count six."

"We will know better when we are closer." Despite this, Azrael slowed the ship, allowing the fleets to barrel past them like they were standing still.

"Why are we slowing down? I thought we were trying to get closer for a better look."

"This vessel is not built for battle. We will let the military ships take the lead and move in under their protection," he explained.

"Oh. I suppose that's prudent," she muttered, but was hardly content with his cautious stance. The sleeping power dwelling beneath her ribcage had awoken, pumping fiery bloodlust into her veins. She sprinted to the bow, enviously watching the armada racing by them, blackening the dunes below with an enormous sprawling shadow.

Azrael increased speed once they were safely positioned within the middle of the fleet. Fate gripped the hilt of her sword and leaned into the hot wind. There were so many ships ahead of them it was impossible to see anything beyond the spindrifts rolling off the ranemist in their wake. She glanced back at Azrael. "Can we climb any higher than this? A bird's eye view would be better than sitting blindly in the middle of all these ships."

Mahelia nodded in agreement. "An improved vantage point would be preferable."

"Take the helm," Azrael instructed Fate. He glanced at Mahelia. "I will man the sails while you call winds strong enough for us to scud upward currents."

Mahelia raised her arms. The winds answered in a sudden burst, hitting the vessel with shocking force. The wheel wobbled in Fate's hands as she tightened her grip on the pegs and strained to keep the ship on course as the bow pitched upward. The initial climb was swift and precarious as she navigated between the masts of the bigger ships.

"Level out," Azrael shouted once they'd cleared the fleet.

He tied off the sails and returned to the helm to take over. Fate gladly relinquished the wheel and raced to the bow. Countless airships moved below them in a steady stream. The front line was fast approaching the periphery of the Keep. Kaliena's ships advanced with guns blazing. Fiery cannonballs blasted across the closing gap between the two armies. Deadly red laser beams streaked from smaller fighter ships darting past the heavier airships.

The Biraktar ships answered with heavy fire. Blazing flames and thick spouts of black smoke filled the front line of defense as the rear part of the fleet split off, spreading wide in each direction to encircle the Keep. Explosions boomed across the desert expanse like war drums that reverberated in Fate's chest, calling her to battle with each thunderous crack. Her breathing quickened, her pulse pounding adrenaline into her limbs until she could no longer stand still. She leaped onto the very tip of the bow, leaning forward and ready to launch into the air with her sword leading the way.

"Fate, get down from there!" Azrael called out. "You will fall to your death!"

Fate glanced back and threw him a grin. "Didn't you know? I can fly."

Azrael deserted his post and rushed over, his eyes wide with panic. "What could make you think such nonsense? Please, get down!"

Mahelia strode forward slowly, her eyes narrowed on Fate. "She is capable of far more than you know, my son. The power of an ancient war god runs through her veins and calls her to the fight." She stopped behind Azrael. "You must use the soul ring to keep her safe."

Azrael nodded solemnly. "Fate, I forbid you to leave this boat. I command you to stay with me."

Fate returned her gaze to the battle in the distance. She refused to be held prisoner any longer. But when she moved to jump, the sensation of something strong and forceful coiled around her waist and ribs, holding her fast. The more she fought against it, the more it squeezed her ribcage, constricting her ability to breathe.

Furious, she whirled around to face him. "You can't do this to me," she rasped.

Azrael held a hand out, his eyes wide and imploring. "Stop fighting me and come down from there."

Shaking with rage, she closed her eyes, willing the power building inside to break the chains of the soul ring, but force behind Azrael's will only grew stronger. Dizzy from lack of oxygen, she swayed. Azrael caught hold of her wrist and yanked her off the ledge, catching her in his arms before she dropped to the floor.

She opened her eyes as he swept her feet out from under her and carried her from the edge. He set her down on the bottom step of the helm's platform. Gently, he brushed her unruly curls back from her face, his brow furrowed with concern. "You stubborn, stubborn girl. Do you have any idea what you were about to do?"

Sweet air filled her lungs as she yielded to the warmth in his eyes. For as angry as she was with him, she knew he was only thinking of her safety. Mahelia was the one to direct her fury toward. She had manipulated Azrael into all of this. Well, two could play that game.

Caught in the moment, Fate pulled Azrael into a kiss. His first response was to freeze, but all that he'd been holding back erupted at once, and he kissed her back with more passion than she ever expected. She recoiled, horrified by her impulsive actions and what she'd dared to ignite between them. He stared back searchingly, his breath shallow and shaking.

"Sorry, I'm feeling a little queasy," she lied. His jaw clenched as he nodded and extended his hand to help her up. She stood and rubbed her stomach. "I'll be fine. We should really be focusing on what's going on down there."

"Yes, we should," Mahelia said, her gaze pointed as she glanced back at them from where she stood on the starboard side of the ship. She turned back toward the battle below. "The titans are on the move."

Fate and Azrael rushed to lean over the edge. All six titans were wading through Biraktar's fleet, snatching ships from the sky, smashing them together as though they were flimsy toys. Any fire they took did little damage, certainly not enough to bring them down.

Azrael gripped the railing, his knuckles showing white through his dark skin. "It is time for the Word."

"Agreed." Fate held out her hand, expecting Mahelia to pull out the tablets they'd prepared.

Mahelia would not be rushed. "We must wait until we have located Kaliena's ship."

"Are you nuts? We can't stand by while Biraktar's entire fleet is systematically destroyed," Fate argued.

Mahelia didn't move. "If we use the Word too soon, Kaliena may find a way of undermining us before we ensure her destruction."

Azrael closed the gap between him and his mother, his tone low and furious as he reverted to his native language. Fate didn't understand what was said, but he was obviously commanding Mahelia to save what was left of the fleet.

"Our intervention is unnecessary," Mahelia replied calmly. "Look, our remaining ships are retreating as I knew they would."

Azrael looked over the edge, as did Fate. Sure enough, the ships were scattering in all directions. There was no order to their movements, only swift retreat. With the view cleared of Biraktar's legion, Fate noticed another battle taking place on the ground.

The clash of swords, hammers, axes and shields resounded in the air, a noise that had always been there beneath the blasts of cannons coming from the fleets. They were too high to see which battalions were fighting Kaliena's ground troops, until Fate noticed a horde of giants made solely of rock advancing toward one of the iron titans. She stared, stupefied, for the briefest second. Those were the rock giants Finn had mentioned.

"Hand me the spyglass, Azrael," she said under her breath.

He gave it to her, and with shaking hands she focused the lense, stopping when she spotted Beldereth's army of female warriors. Rudwor and his allies were down there. But how could they have arrived within a few short hours?

There could be only one answer. Sithias had used the Words of Making to get them there. Fate's heart hammered with dread. Had she dropped Finn directly into the middle of battle without warning? She tried doing the mental math to figure out if he would've had time to meet with Sithias and Rudwor from the moment she'd sent him away, but fear clouded her thinking.

Fate tried to remain calm, but she couldn't keep her fists from shaking at her sides when she turned to Azrael. "You have to let me go. Those are my friends down there on the ground. They need my help."

Mahelia edged into her line of sight with a self-satisfied smile, pointing her finger at Fate. "There. This is what I have been waiting for, an emotional investment too painful to ignore. We can now use the power of the Word, and the results will be swift and exact."

Fate frowned at her. "That's the real reason you were waiting? What about all those ships you allowed to be destroyed? We could've saved them!" She turned to Azrael. "That's it! Your mother's certifiable and I'm done playing her game. Please, let me go down there to help my friends."

Azrael stared straight back at Fate with what could only be regret. "Do what you must."

"Thank you," Fate cut in anxiously.

"I was speaking to mother. You will stay and follow her direction to the letter." Whatever pull Fate had gained with Azrael had vanished, along with any warmth he'd shown her, leaving only icy calm in its place. And with that, he turned his back to Fate and returned to the helm.

53
ON THE SAME SIDE

FINN CROUCHED LOW, HIS stance defensive as he activated his wind sword. The surge of bodies locked in battle disoriented him all the more. Arrows hissed overhead, a steady hum over the clash of metal on metal. Grunts, roars and growls rose from ally and enemy alike. There was blood everywhere, a lake beneath them, turned to red grit in the white sands. The impending war had been a faraway thing, but now it was here and happening all too swiftly.

Eldunough hawk riders wheeled overhead, shooting flaming arrows into the thick of Kaliena's ground troops. The blue capes of Beldereth's female warriors weaved in swift blurs between the long red shields of the Asgar knights pressing forward. They worked in unison, the men blocking the brutal onslaught of Kaliena's inhuman soldiers as the women hit their marks with a steady stream of arrows. But these were creatures born at the very heart of multidimensional magic, and even though the stench of death still clung to them, the elixir of life used to reanimate them made them extremely hard to kill. Regardless of how skilled the knights of Eldunough, Beldereth and Asgar were in battle.

A beastly soldier with the head of a lion and stag's horns protruding from its bristled mane stormed through the melee, swiping knights aside as though they were made of straw. Finn dodged the deadly lash of its bloodied claws. Swinging around in a wide arc, he sliced its hand clean off with his blade of wind. The beast howled, its muzzle wrinkling into a vicious snarl, searching for the culprit before fixing its gleaming yellow eyes on Finn.

Unwilling to wait for its next move, Finn leaped, sweeping the point of his wind sword down between its twisted horns. The skull parted like a cantaloupe, soft and swift, before the blade struck the hard, iron breastplate of its armor. The beast toppled backward, crushing enemy soldiers beneath its massive weight.

Alert and fueled by adrenaline, Finn rushed into battle, cleaving necrotic arms, heads and legs from torsos. Blood sprayed the air around him in a fine mist, the awful tang of iron slipping past his lips with each inhale. Wiping his eyes, he spit blood from his mouth and pushed on, killing the abominations with barely a second's notice of what he sliced his blade through.

A familiar bellow rose above the clamor, a sound Finn knew well. Rudwor was somewhere deep in the middle of the fray. Not surprising. Rudwor always relished a good fight. Finn moved in the direction of his friend's roars, cutting through the crush in a frenzy of sword work, hacking thoughtlessly like a man cutting a path through the densest jungle.

He found Rudwor extracting the red blade of his sword from the gut of a lizard-faced soldier, while at the same time, spiking his halberd into the soldier's skull–an effective kill. His friend's face was red-raw, his eyes shining with the same savage fire pumping through Finn's veins. Rudwor was a big man, but seemed larger than life as he mowed through the enemy line.

Finn worked his way over to him. When they locked eyes, Rudwor grinned wide. "Laddie! What took you so long?" He drove his sword into a fanged creature of decayed, patchy fur and kicked it in the chest to pull his blade free. "I was beginning to think you might've left me to clean up this mess on my own."

"I thought about it." Finn smiled through a grimace as he sliced off the head of a soldier with the skin of a charred corpse. "But I knew you couldn't make it without me."

"Oh, those are big words, boyo. You'd better back them up by making sure I come out of this with not so much as a wee knick off my baby smooth skin."

"I'd thought I did that when I sent word to have you turn back, but I can see Sithias failed to convince you."

"Why would I want to miss all this?" Rudwor drove his halberd into the forehead of the next enemy in line.

Finn chuckled, but the laugh was knocked out of him when a winged, green-skinned soldier with wooly gray hair swooped from the sky and rammed the blunt end of his spear into his chest. The impact sent him tumbling backward into the horde, clearing a path to each side, which the soldier thundered down, his muscular arms flexing as he twirled his spear around to aim the point at Finn.

Pain fired through Finn's ribcage as he gulped air into his tortured lungs. The soldier loomed large over him, his oversized spear ready to spike him clean through. But the soldier suddenly arched and he went stiff, his milky blue eyes staring straight ahead in shock. Blood splattered Finn's face before he noticed the source–a steel arrowhead sticking from the soldier's spurting neck. He just stood there, arms raised over Finn for a prolonged second and then collapsed.

Finn rolled to one side to avoid being flattened beneath the behemoth, then turned to see Tove holding her crossbow aimed where the soldier had stood. She sprinted over to Finn, extended a hand and pulled him to his feet in one quick move. They smiled, but there was no time for words as the battle closed in around them. Putting their backs to each other, they fought the endless crush of enemy soldiers.

Grysla barreled toward them using her tremendous size to smash enemy soldiers beneath her feet. Leif used the path she cleared to take down the rest with his crossbow. His aim was every bit as true as his sister's, but nowhere near as fast on the draw.

A battalion of soldiers dressed in black armor stormed in. Finn didn't recognize the serpentine ironwork of their breastplates, and by the look of their helmets, made in the shape of dragonheads, they could only be Kaliena's troops. He careened toward them, his wind blade arching to cross swords with the first soldier in line.

Tove rushed in, knocking Finn back, the force of which matched his own supernatural strength. "They're our allies!" She yelled to be heard above the tumult, but even as she explained her gaze flicked to them with distrust.

"Those are the Serpens?"

She nodded as the legion of black knights thundered by, smashing into the enemy line, hacking viciously, moving as one like a massive steamroller flattening everything in its path. A roar so deep and loud, it vibrated in Finn's bones, drew his gaze to the skies. An enormous dragon sailed overhead with a spiked head twisting from side to side, its yellow eyes scanning the ground. It plunged into the throng. A hideous howl rose above the clamorous horde as the dragon's leathery wings twitched violently. Then it launched skyward, carrying the mangled remains of one of the monstrous ground beasts Finn had seen in the cages. The dragon ripped the creature in half, dropping the shredded pieces onto the battlefield before soaring upward, hunting for its next victim.

For once it seemed as though they might have a chance to win the war.

"I never thought I'd be grateful to come face to face with the Serpens and one of their dragons," Finn shouted to Tove as he glanced around warily, but the enemy was being forced back by the Serpen army. He took a breath, happy for the temporary reprieve from fighting. "They're like a machine."

Tove's stance remained coiled and ready. "They scare me."

"Aye, I can see why," Finn agreed. "Let's hope our alliance with them holds after the war is over."

"I wouldn't count on it," Tove warned.

The ground quaked, catapulting Finn back into fight mode as he searched for the threat. A dozen rock giants stampeded by, trampling enemy troops into the blood-soaked dunes as they headed toward the Keep. Enemy ships fired on the giants, but their explosions glanced off their granite heads harmlessly. The rock giants pushed forward, swiping the flying vessels aside, intent on more important targets.

The titans.

They were on the move and taking out an armada of ships Finn didn't recognize. He could only guess they belonged to Azrael's people. In a moment of panic, he searched the skies for the ship Fate was on. But it was impossible to discern one vessel from the next from his place on the ground. His first instinct was to fly straight into the battle raging above them, but logic kicked in. Azrael and Mahelia had plans to use Fate's power with the Words of Making. They wouldn't risk being in the thick of it all. Yet none of this was comforting. He hated leaving her alone with those two. Someone else should be there to back her up.

"Where's Sithias?" Finn asked Tove.

"I haven't seen him since he shrank into a bug."

"That figures," Finn grumbled. "Maybe Rudwor knows where he went off to."

He turned in a circle, looking for Rudwor's shiny bald head. A buzzing zipped past one ear and Finn brushed it away dismissively. He could hear Rudwor's bellow a fair distance away, but he couldn't see the giant of a man amongst the thrash of spears, swords and shields.

The buzzing returned, this time near his other ear. "Did I hear my name?" a tiny voice asked.

Finn turned to see who spoke and was greeted with a white dragonfly the size of a hummingbird, hovering in front of him, staring back with amber bug eyes. "Sithias! I'm surprised to see you."

"Where would I go?"

"I would think as far from here as you could get."

Sithias zigged to one side, his little head shaking back and forth. "That would be rather cowardly of me when everyone else has volunteered to be here."

"You aren't exactly known for your bravery."

"I'll have you know, I'm risking my life every bit as much as the rest of you. I was nearly sucked into the nostril of a hideous beast!"

Finn looked over his shoulder to ensure the Serpens were still keeping the enemy line at bay. "I'm sure it's been dodgy for you too, but I've got a job for you if you're willing."

"A special mission?"

"Aye, and it involves Fate."

Sithias's wings jerked excitedly. "You found her? How is she?"

"She's well, but not exactly herself. She doesn't have any memory of what happened to Eustace."

"You didn't tell her?"

"No, not after what Archie showed me in the recordings. Eustace's death is what triggered Ananke's emergence, and we have to avoid that at all costs. Fate's not ready to hear it. We'll lose her forever if the time's not right."

Sithias cocked his little insect head to one side. "But I thought we decided Fate's incredibly scary power is the only thing that can stop Kaliena."

"We don't need that anymore. Fate has the Words of making, and she's prepared to use them."

"Oh, and that's because we both know how well *that's* worked in the past."

"And that's exactly why I need you to go and be her guide. She's in a rather sticky... predicament, and I don't trust the people she's with."

Tove grabbed Finn's arm. "Get ready to fight. The Serpens can't hold the line. It's breaking."

Finn's hand tensed around his wind sword as he nodded. "There's no time to explain, Sithias. Just find her. The entire direction of the war lies in her hands, and she's going to need a friend to help her make the most important decision of her life."

Sithias worried his delicate insect arms together. "Oh dear, what makes you think I'm the one for the job? Wouldn't it be better if you went?"

"I want nothing more, but my presence would only complicate things for her." Finn bit down on his frustration. "Now go. And Sithias, keep yourself a secret. Fate's the only one that can know you're there."

"Where is she?"

"Above us. On a small ship. It's not militarized, so look for a lone ship that's holding back from the fight."

"I'll find her, sir." Sithias zipped away before Finn could say another word.

A terrible crash resounded above the din. Finn jerked in the direction of the sound. Five rock giants had brought a titan to all fours and they were bludgeoning it with clubs that looked as though they'd been hewn from the side of a mountain.

A pack of barbarians broke past the Serpen line. Their heads resembled goats, if goats had fangs. Rotting flesh hung from their skulls and skeletal torsos. Many of them bristled with arrows wedged between their fossilized ribs, but this didn't slow them down. They stood six feet taller than the Serpens, and they were fast and brutal as they slashed through the black knights like cleaving blades of grass. The shriek that came from them pierced the air, sending shivers down Finn's spine.

Regardless, he charged toward them, slicing off the curved tip of the first goat's saber. Screeching with fury, the goat barbarian raised its blade, bringing it down crudely like an axe. Finn dodged and swung upward, cutting a line up the middle of its chest, splaying it open. The barbarian fell to its knees and Finn severed its head.

Tove darted in between the goats with her sword drawn, having traded in her bow and arrows, since they'd proven ineffective with this brood. While they used brute force, she used speed, chopping arms first, then springing to the shoulders, taking her victim down with a twist of her knees before driving the point of her blade down the middle of the skull. It worked, and she slew two in the time it took for Finn to glance her way.

The air went out of Finn's lungs from a blow behind. He hit the ground, rolling onto his back as he struggled to breathe. A knight bearing the Asgar shield stood over him and brought his sword down. Finn lurched to one side. "We're on the same side!" he yelled.

The knight pulled his helmet off, throwing it to the ground. Tynan glared down at him, his dark brows pinched with rage, his pale skin running with sweat and black curls sticking to his forehead. "You! You're the Unholy Piper," he seethed. "You were supposed to have died in the teeth of my treacherous mother!"

Finn was speechless. Not once had he considered what it would mean to face Tynan, the king of Asgar, who'd thrown him in a dungeon to be tortured by thirst, starvation and the degradation of living in his own filth. All while a death sentence hung over his head. If Sithias hadn't pretended to be Tynan's mother, he would've been executed.

"Didn't Rudwor explain my role behind the alliance?" Finn's voice broke and wavered. Seeing Tynan like this brought back in full force all the horrors of his time in prison. He shook from a sickening mixture of loathing and remembered powerlessness, a paralyzing quandary that pinned him to the spot.

"Rudwor said nothing of your involvement!" Tynan's nose flared, his mouth twisting in a fit of fury. "I *cannot* fight by your side!" He swung at Finn. The point of his blade sliced Finn's cheekbone, and would've cut deeper had it not been for the beast that gored Tynan with its long tusks and flung him to one side with a violent jerk of its head.

The scaled, horse-shaped creature trampled over Finn. Stunned with pain, he ricocheted off the beast's enormous hooves, each rock-hard blow worse than the last. His bones ached to the marrow, its rough scales tearing the skin on his arms and face as he fought to escape each crushing step. He caught flashes of Tove and Leif firing arrows into the monster. Grysla charged the beast, ramming into its hindquarters to force it off of Finn, but the move only served to rock the creature. Its hooves stomped on his back, smashing him into the ground. Ribs cracked as he cried out in agony. Blood filled his mouth, coating his tongue with a coppery tang.

Blinking through swollen lids and blood dripping in his eyes, Finn started to rise. Through the red blur, he saw Jessie land nearby, her weaponized arms raised, blasting red lasers into Leif, then Tove. Grysla was next. He cried out to them, powerless to help them as Jessie marched toward him. Finn scrabbled sluggishly to one side, trying to get out from under the beast, but it stomped wildly, caging him within the confines of its thrashing legs. Jessie shot it in the chest. The beast reared. A hoof the size of a boulder descended on Finn's head, and a bone-cracking sound filled his skull, silencing the war into a sudden void.

54
THE WEIGHT OF THE WORLD

FATE WATCHED KALIENA'S FLAGSHIP sail into view directly beneath them as Azrael steered his ship into position. She used the spyglass, focusing in on the bow of the deck, where Kaliena and Wodrid stood, safely removed from the carnage taking place on the ground.

The titans had cleared the sky of Biraktar's armada. What remained of the fleet had retreated, and there wasn't a single ship in sight. The smoke from the wreckage of ships left drifting aimlessly had thinned, allowing her to see hundreds of Eldunough hawk riders soaring over the ground troops, shooting flaming arrows into the thickest clots of the enemy horde. A black dragon, she assumed belonged to the Serpens, wreaked sheer destruction on Kaliena's army. If the winged leviathan wasn't sweeping down over them with great rivers of fire, it was tearing gigantic, monstrous beasts into bloody ribbons of meat.

Two titans had been taken down, toppled by the much smaller rock giants, and beaten into shrapnel. This might have been encouraging, since the rock giants outnumbered the titans, but the other four titans had grouped together, their backs to each other like one colossal pillar, and no amount of force could knock them over. Fate cringed as the rock giants rammed against their legs, only to be pulverized beneath the titans' gargantuan iron boots.

Unable to watch any longer, she turned to Mahelia. "Our allies are literally being crushed down there. We have to do some-thing, and quick. Which one of the tablets should I read?"

Mahelia raised a brow with a curious expression. "Which one speaks to you the most?"

Fate glanced down at the row of tablets arranged neatly near her feet. Her heart thumped with panic and uncertainty. They'd written seven distinct scenarios describing Kaliena's destruction. As far as she was concerned, any one of them would do the job, and she had no preference of one over the other, especially since they now knew exactly where Kaliena was and what she was doing. There was literally nothing that could possibly interfere with what they'd written on the tablets. "I don't have a favorite. Can I just close my eyes and point?"

"I told you before, you must be emotionally invested for the power of the Word to be truly exact in its effect."

"I am!" Fate snapped. "Isn't it enough that Kaliena took my best friend from me and turned us into mortal enemies? Don't worry, I have *plenty* of reason to hate Kaliena!" Her desire to leap from the ship and face Kaliena burned in her center, molten and mercurial.

"Hatred is a volatile thing. Results can be unpredictable if you are unpracticed in controlling your rage. True power comes from one unwavering emotion, and that is love."

Fate stared back in disbelief. "There's no way I can feel even an inkling of love for Kaliena. Not a single drop."

"This is not about how you feel toward Kaliena. This is about what you want for yourself, your friends and the world at large. Do you wish for peace? Do want to know that everyone you love is safe from harm?"

"Of course. That's all I've ever wanted." While this was the truth, it wasn't enough to calm the bloodlust forcing Fate's hand to the hilt of her sword. She wanted to fight. She *needed* to fight.

"Then this is what you must focus on," Mahelia pressed. "Think about the world you want to create. Feel the love and peace of that vision in your heart. Only then can you read from one of these tablets and know that the words written there will overpower Kaliena's all consuming vision for destruction."

Fate laughed harshly. "What a hypocrite you are! You had me speak the words to not only destroy the ships that attacked Biraktar and killed Moulghazel, but you also condemned their souls to everlasting hell. Talk about vengeful! And yet here you are, telling me to do the exact opposite, when all I want right now is to take my sword and cut Kaliena's throat with it." The power collecting behind her ribs scorched her insides at the thought and it was all she could do to stand still a single minute longer.

Mahelia's expression remained unperturbed. "Can you honestly say you did not want to see the enemy punished after what they did to Moulghazel, the most loving and gentle of creatures?"

Fate couldn't argue. The sky whale's slaughter would haunt her memories forever.

"There is a time and place for vengeance," Mahelia continued. "But as long as you fear for this friend who is under Kaliena's control, the energy behind the words you speak– regardless of what they say–will be less focused and open to distortion, than when your very heart has been ripped from your chest by something so agonizing all you are left with is hatred. Only then can you funnel vengeance to your liking."

As much as Fate hated to admit it, she was beginning to understand what Mahelia was saying. She sat cross-legged in front of the tablets and skimmed over what she'd been instructed to write. There were tablets that summoned fire in three very different but terrifying forms, and two more that called upon the winds to deliver horrors from hidden dimensions. Another tablet cast a pestilence upon the enemy so gruesome it made Fate want to hurl just to speak it. And the last dismantled the fiery shield that kept the desert monsters of Dunebala contained and commanded them to invade the pristine sands of the Mirajaran Desert. Each frightened her equally, any of which could go horribly wrong and at the very least result in unknowable, lingering consequences.

"Choose," Mahelia said. "You know deep inside which one is right."

"*Please,*" Fate hissed under her breath, "leave me alone to think."

Mahelia did as she asked and joined Azrael at the helm, where they turned their backs to her and spoke in hushed tones.

Fate stared at the tablets, her mind freezing into a block of ice. This was a decision too huge for one person to make. The indwelling power building at her core surged, calling her to rise and surrender to the siren of war. Brute force she understood. All it required was the march of one foot in front of the other, the slice of her sword and the will to conquer. Fighting with words designed to change the course of destiny itself was too complex. So much could go wrong, and she didn't want to be held responsible.

Her temples throbbed and a buzzing filled her head. Fate closed her eyes and clapped her hands over her ears. The buzzing muffled and she realized the noise wasn't in her head. She opened her eyes to an oversized dragonfly hovering in front of her.

"Hello, misss! I'm so happy to see you!"

"Sithias?"

"At your service. Finn tells me you could use some help."

She sighed, feeling the tightness in her shoulders relaxing in the presence of her dear friend. "You have no idea how much. You talked to Finn? How bad is it down there?"

"I did, and the battle... it's worse than anything you can imagine. You, I mean we, need to do something quickly. But I've been told to keep my presence here a secret."

Fate checked on Mahelia. She was still deep in conversation with Azrael. "You've got that right." She raveled her long hair into a loose knot, sweeping it to one side before lifting the hood of her cloak. "Hide in here." She tapped her shoulder. When he landed, his vibrating wings tickled her neck and she giggled. "Stop that!"

Mahelia and Azrael turned to look at her.

"Just testing out my voice," she told them with a dismissive wave of her hand. "Don't worry, I'll let you know when I'm ready to do this." She waited for them to return to their conversation before whispering to Sithias. "Lose the tickly wings, please."

"A mouse it is." Sithias transformed into a white mouse with wings. He sat down and leaned forward with his whiskery muzzle resting on his tiny pink hands as he studied the tablets. "This looks interesting. What have we here?"

"These are Mahelia's alchemized gold tablets. They amplify the Words of Making."

"As if the Words of Making need amplifying." Sithias tsk, tsked with a shake of his head. He was quiet while he read each one. "Oh my, I must say this is much darker and bolder than your usual machinations."

"You think I wrote these?"

"It's your handwriting."

"Wow, thanks for assuming I'm capable of thinking like Hitler. This came from Mahelia's diabolical mind."

Sithias pointed at Mahelia. "I take it you mean her. Who's that with her?"

Fate gulped. "Azrael, my husband." She mumbled the last part.

"Your husband?" he squeaked loudly.

"Shh! Keep it down."

"Oh, it's all too clear now. I can see why Finn decided to stay out of thisss messy debacle."

"Did he seem... angry?"

Sithias tapped his chin. "Hmm, he didn't mention your recent marital status, but I didn't notice any undue rage. He was however deeply concerned with your present situation and the company you're in. Which I can see is every bit as complicated as he alluded to. How did this come to be?"

"It's a long story." She let out a heavy sigh. "Longer than we have time for."

"You're right. We must deal with Kaliena first. But after that, I want to hear every sordid detail."

"Over a meal made entirely of chocolaty goodness."

"Oh, of course. A story like this deserves to be accompanied by the most delicious of comfort foods known to mankind."

Fate couldn't help smiling. "I'm so glad you're here, Sithias." Her gaze returned to the tablets and her smile faded. "These are the worst possible scenarios ever."

"I'm so relieved to hear that, misss. I'm traumatized just reading these descriptions. I can't begin to imagine the countless ways in which any one of these could go wrong."

"It does feel like we'd be trading in one nightmare for a worse one."

"Indeed."

"Can you think of a better way to stop Kaliena?" Fate asked. "Something that doesn't involve the possible annihilation of every living thing within a thousand square miles?"

Sithias grew quiet. "I have a confession to make," he said after a few minutes. "I blame myself as much as you do for Finn's imprisonment within the oak. I was there when you dreamed up the idea of summoning the Green Man to rid the grove of the dark faery. I helped you with the wording, yet you've always blamed yourself, solely and completely, for how badly it all went afterward. It's the very reason I've remained ever cautious in my use of the Words of Making you so generously endowed me with."

"Don't be so hard on yourself, Sithias. How could you have predicted what would happen?"

Sithias tilted his head to look at her, his nose twitching as he did so. "I could ask you the same question."

She didn't know what to say to that. Nothing would ever erase her guilt. Not after living with it for so long. "It doesn't matter, Sithias," she said at last.

"It does to me, and that's why I want you to let *me* say the Words of Making that will turn the tide in this war. That way if everything turns upside down, you won't have to hold yourself responsible. Let it be my turn to carry the weight of the world."

"No, I couldn't do that to you."

Sithias held up his little paws with pink fingers spread. "Think about it, that's all I ask. In the meantime, let's put our heads together and think of what those Words of Making will be. Do you happen to have anymore of those alchemized gold tablets?"

Fate smiled slyly. "As a matter of fact I do. I pocketed one of the sheets when Mahelia wasn't looking." Positioning herself to keep Mahelia and Azrael from seeing her movements, she slipped her hand into her satchel and pulled out an extra tablet and the rolled gold sheet. She smoothed the sheet over the wax side of the tablet. "Now for the hard part. Any ideas?"

Sithias stroked his whiskers, twisting them into points as he concentrated.

After a few seconds he stopped fiddling with his whiskers and dropped his arms. "I have nothing."

"I know, right?" Fate huffed. "It's too much. This is a job for a council of wise men and women. Not two bumblers like us."

"Fate, it is time to speak the Words." Mahelia stood directly behind Fate, making her jump with an uncomfortable spike of adrenaline.

Fate slid her stolen items under the tablet closest to her knee and looked over her shoulder at Mahelia. "Jeez, let a person know when you're coming up from behind. You startled me. Make some noise. Clear you throat or something."

Mahelia's stare grew suspicious. "What are you doing? We have been listening to you mumble to yourself."

Sithias edged behind Fate's neck to stay hidden, tickling her with his hands and feet. Struggling to keep a straight face, she squirmed. "If you must know, I've been doing my affirmations. You know, telling myself I can do this. That I'm brave enough and strong enough." Fate resisted the urge to roll her eyes at her lame explanation.

Mahelia didn't bother to respond and returned to the matter at hand. "Have you chosen one of the tablets?"

"I prefer the elementals over the others, so I've managed to narrow it down to two."

"Show me."

Fate scanned the row of tablets hastily, reaching for the one hiding her tablet and another describing fire. "It's a tough decision. Do I call the dark winds to unleash the parasitic wraiths from the Ashroth dimension, or summon the elemental dragon, Volcanis, to spew the black fire that'll turn everyone into molten lava?"

"*Choose.*" Mahelia's tone was sharp and angry. She was done with niceties for Azrael's sake.

Fate stood with both tablets in hand and held Mahelia's cold gaze. "Give me five more minutes to think. I promise I'll have my choice down to one and I'll read the Words then."

Pressing her lips into a tight line, Mahelia walked over to Azrael.

Fate turned her back to them. "You heard the witch, Sithias," she whispered. "This is it. We have to come up with something *now*."

Sithias skittered back onto her shoulder. "I've put my mind to it, and I think I have it."

Holding onto the blank tablet, Fate stuffed the other two into her satchel and drew out the stylus. "Go ahead, give it to me."

"Don't you want to discuss it first?"

"There's no time. Whatever it is will be better than Mahelia's apocalyptic solutions."

Sithias hesitated at first, but then he whispered each word into her ear with great care. As Fate pressed the message into the gold sheet, she wondered why she hadn't thought of the solution he offered on her own. But she'd been so bent on destroying Kaliena she couldn't see any other way out. She finished writing the last word and smiled. "You're a genius, Sithias. This is it. This will work."

"Oh my!" But he didn't seem to be convinced and worried his paws together. "I hope so. I really, really hope so."

She glanced back at Mahelia, who was watching her intently. Feeling more trapped than ever, Fate leaned against the side rail and hung her head. Should she risk reading the tablet in Mahelia's presence? Her stomach tightened into a ball of fear. No, as soon as Mahelia realized she wasn't reading from one of the tablets she'd dictated, she would do everything in her power to stop Fate.

"Sithias, you need to get me out of here. *Now.*"

"Can't you fly? Any powers you gave yourself with the Words of Making should've returned by now."

"I know, Finn told me, but I'm bound to Azrael. I haven't been able to fly away, because he wants me with him."

"How awful!"

Fate turned slightly, peeking past the hood of her cloak. Both Mahelia and Azrael were walking toward her. "We're out of time, Sithias. Change into something that can carry me out of here. Do it now!"

Sithias jumped from her shoulder, his furry little body enlarging fluidly, first into snake form before expanding to greater and greater proportions. His feathered wings solidified into pale leathery wings. Spikes sprouted from his scaled back. He arched upward before wheeling back around, a majestic white dragon that swooped down and clutched Fate within its talons.

The tight grip around her ribs squeezed the air from her lungs in a sudden burst as she rose high above the ship. Azrael shouted, charging across the deck with his saber drawn, ready to fight the dragon that had stolen his bride. Mahelia stood very still, her robe and dark hair blowing in the wind stirred by the dragon's wings.

For the first time since Fate's destiny had become entangled with Azrael's, she felt free. But this was a fleeting moment of joy, because her gaze drifted to Kaliena's flagship as Sithias circled in a steady, downward spiral.

The massive deck came into view. Kaliena and Wodrid strode from the bow of the ship to where Jessie had landed with a limp body she dumped onto the floor. Fear stopped Fate's heart. It was Finn who lay bloodied, beaten and still at Jessie's feet.

55
Wisdom in Action

PANIC POUNDED IN FATE'S blood, igniting the patiently waiting power brewing in her core. It uncoiled, swift as a striking cobra, pushing her to force Sithias to loosen his grip. He angled his horned head to look down at her. "What are you doing?"

"They have Finn! Let go and drop me down there!" Fate wrestled to free herself. She couldn't tell how badly Finn was wounded from where they were, or if he was even alive, but she had to know, and now.

Sithias ignored her demand. "Thisss is very bad, indeed."

Fate frowned as she struggled to pry his clawed toes back. "Obviously! So get me onto that ship!"

"You don't understand, misss. The Rod is part of Finn. The only way for Kaliena to get it from him is to rip the scattered particles of the Rod from every molecule of Finn's body and reassemble them."

Fate's heart dropped to her stomach. She shook her head, trying to understand how such a thing could've happened. But this wasn't the time for explanations.

Sithias dove straight down. "I'll land with you and do my best to look vicious and scary."

"No, the Words of Making are the only thing that will save Finn now. I'll read them!"

"Are you sure, misss? I can set down somewhere safe and read them myself. After all, this was my brainchild and I'd prefer to save you from taking responsibility for any harmful oversights I may have missed."

Fate reached into her satchel for the tablet. "I trust your brainchild, Sithias. I should've read these words the second I wrote them down."

Sithias gulped loudly. "Very well, go ahead, mi–"

He lurched suddenly and violently, his words cut off by a pained growl. Sithias plummeted, and before Fate could tell what was happening, she was freefalling. The air rushed past, whipping the tablet from her grasp. She tried to catch it, but it fell out of reach. Sithias tumbled beside her, red ribbons of blood spilling from a harpoon embedded deep within his ribcage. She followed the line of the chain to Azrael's ship.

Sithias came to the end of the chain and he swung back and forth, tipping the ship with the heavy weight of his dragon form. Seeing her friend dangling helplessly from Azrael's ship filled Fate with rage. The warring energy generated by the magical girdle, combined with the fury she'd been holding back, built to unbearable levels. Nothing in the world was going to stop her from surrendering to its urgent call any longer. Not while so many lives hung in the balance.

Spreading her arms and legs to keep from spinning out of control, Fate summoned all her willpower to fly. She tightened her muscles, lifted her chin in defiance of gravity and shot upward. Testing her speed, before fixing her eyes on Sithias, she reached him and hovered close to his face. "Sithias!" she cried out.

He opened his eyes, barely able to lift his head. "I'm all right, misss. Go to Finn. He needs you more than I do."

She moved directly under the ship to stay hidden from Azrael's view. "I can't leave you here like this."

"Not to worry. I plan to shrink into something too small to be harpooned. I just need a minute to rest."

Fate looked at the harpoon sticking from Sithias's split hide and the torn meat of muscle stretching away from the thick iron spear. Too much blood pooled around the wound, dripping in rivers over his white scales. Tears rushed to her eyes. "I can't."

"You mussst," Sithias insisted. "Now go, before it's too late for Finn."

Leaving Sithias was the hardest thing Fate had ever done. She hurtled through the air faster than she'd ever flown before. Speed. Action. Combat. These, she could do without thinking. She clung to those base directives and pushed all other thoughts from her mind.

Fate landed on the deck of Kaliena's ship directly behind Wodrid. The sorcerer jerked around to look at her. Fate charged before he could conjure a fireball. He blocked her sword with his staff, but his strength was no match for hers. She struck his staff down between them, his arms shaking from the effort before twisting her blade with a flick of her wrist, a movement that jarred his grip loose. The staff flew across space, clattering on the floor several yards away.

The look of astonishment in his ice blue eyes was surpassed only by the shock of Fate's blade ripping through his chest. She yanked her sword from his body, leaving him to fall slowly to his knees, where he sank to the floor like a tired old man lying down to take a much-needed nap.

Kaliena shrieked. Not with grief, or even rage, but with fear. The whites of her eyes showed absolute terror when she saw what Fate had done. Her scream shifted, becoming a panicked command, which propelled Jessie into action. Her friend shot across the gap between them, body-slamming Fate with the hard, sharp edges of her armor. Racked by bruising pain throughout her chest and hips, Fate wrestled to push Jessie off as they rolled over each other. But there was no breaking free. Jessie seized her, crushing her arms and legs within the powerful clamp of her cybernetic suit.

Survival burned at the forefront of Fate's brain. Something primal, yet intelligent beyond all comprehension took over. The atoms in the air coalesced around her, forming a malleable shield of armor around her body. Golden. Invincible.

Her awareness expanded to encompass everything all at once. Suddenly, Fate could see more than what was in front of her, as if she were standing outside herself, yet very much present within her physical body. She gripped Jessie's arms–sensing the daggers unsheathing from the shifting mechanisms of her armor–and blocked the blades before they could slip beneath her helmet and snick her arteries.

In the same instance, she saw Kaliena standing over Finn's unconscious body, swinging the Orb, chanting spellrich words designed to tear him apart. The otherworldly sorceress was closer than ever to combining the Orb with the Rod. If Fate didn't do something to stop her within the next few seconds, she would not only lose Finn forever, but the world–the entire universe –would become Kaliena's to ruin.

The indwelling power surged, vibrating throughout Fate's entire body, pressing to be fully unleashed. The energy fired through her nervous system, blazed up her spine and exploded at her brainstem. Images of Ares in all his radiance blotted her vision, filling her with a ravenous hunger for battle and bloodshed. The sensation was both thrilling and frightening. All it would take was a second's surrender and the power would take over. Consume her. And that's what scared her the most.

As much as she wanted to accept the full power, Fate resisted. She couldn't risk losing all control. This warring force, no matter how staggering, was indiscriminate. It didn't care who died and who lived. There was no way for her to know if she could deliberately protect Finn, or keep from killing Jessie. Both would become casualties of war, either by her blade or another's.

But she couldn't be in two places at once, despite her astonishing ability to simultaneously view more than was humanly possible. A sick realization welled inside the pit of her stomach. She'd lost the Words of Making when she'd dropped the tablet with the words Sithias had dictated. Now Jessie was her only obstacle to stopping Kaliena. Jessie's directive to kill Fate made her relentless. Fate could use her full power to kill her best friend, but she wouldn't be able to live with herself. Not even to save Finn.

Jessie pinned Fate on her back using her knees. Fate's newly grown armor was the only thing keeping the spikes in Jessie's armor from stabbing into her shoulders. Jessie's steel fist collided with Fate's jaw, throwing her head back, dislodging her helmet. Another blow to the face cracked down. Fate's cheekbone crunched beneath Jessie's glove. The next punch met with her nose and mouth. Burning, agonizing pain flared across her face. Blood gushed down her throat, coating the back of her tongue with a coppery bite.

Fate twisted away from the next punch. Jessie's fist smacked the floor next to her ear. Calling upon all her strength, Fate pushed with both arms and threw Jessie off. Her friend landed on her back, but rebounded in a blur of movement and flattened Fate before she could rise. There was no stopping her.

Fate blocked another hit with her forearm. As they strained against each other, she searched for an inkling of humanity in Jessie's eye, the one last part of her friend that wasn't covered in metal. Her gaze moved to the Dragon Eye, the conduit in which Kaliena had used to infect and control Jessie with the machinery that had stolen her humanity. Fate reached up and tore it from Jessie's face in a moment of pure rancor.

Jessie let go, screaming in agony with hands covering her face. The ear-piercing pitch of her modulated cries tortured Fate as her friend collapsed onto the floor in a sparking heap of convulsions. Fate rose to her feet, wanting to help in some way, but knew she couldn't. Whatever blend of magic and science was needed to heal Jessie was beyond her. The only one she could help now was Finn.

When she turned toward Kaliena and Finn, her feet turned leaden as horror twisted in her gut. The Orb swung with such velocity all that was visible was a ring of brilliant light over Finn. His skin was lit from beneath with the same golden light crackling from the Orb. Blinding sparks pierced through, scorching him from inside. His mouth stretched back in a silent scream of agony as skin sizzled down to muscle and then bone. The destructive light blazed along his bones and organs, disintegrating all that was left of him in one last fiery flash, leaving behind only whorls and eddies of sparkling gold dust drifting in the air.

Fate staggered in place, her mind whirling with disbelief. She couldn't be too late. Not when it had only been a matter of mere seconds. She refused to believe the awful truth staring her in the face.

No, no, no. This can't be happening!

With fury boiling beneath her skin, Fate lunged forward, driving her sword into Kaliena's back. The blue-skinned sorceress arched in a spasm of pain, her six arms outstretched, writhing like a spider pinned to a wall with a needle. Fate pushed her forward, driving the blade all the way through until she saw the sharp tip appear on the other side. The Orb fell from Kaliena's grasp, its light extinguished the moment it hit the floor.

Fate yanked the sword from Kaliena's body. The sorceress swayed and then collapsed. Fate dropped her bloody sword and turned to where the last sparks of Finn swirled over a pile of ash. Trembling uncontrollably, she reached for the Orb and stared at it. How could such a small thing grant the ultimate power of creation and destruction? She squeezed the tiny piece of round metal until her arm shook.

The Orb was at the root of all her troubles. Yet without it, Finn never would've been made flesh and bone. He would've remained a fuzzy figment of her imagination. Her gaze returned to the glowing embers of Finn's dwindling life force. Several blinked out of existence and she knew that whatever was left of him would be lost and irretrievable if she didn't use the Orb to recreate him. But how? She wasn't a sorceress, and she certainly didn't know any spells.

But she had the Words of Making.

Fate's pulse pounded urgently as she reached in her satchel. It was empty. There was nothing to write with. She raised her fists in frustration, a scream building in her chest. And then she saw the blood on her hands. Kaliena's blood. She crawled over to where the sorceress lay bleeding out on the deck and dipped her finger in the rich red pool she supplied.

Fate didn't have to think about what she finger-painted onto the wooden planks. Her heart knew the words. When she was finished, she dangled the Orb by its chain, swung it over the crimson words and spoke, *"I summon the creative power of the Orb of Aeternitis to make Finn whole, alive and well, here and now."*

The Orb glowed with a soft luminescence. Not the sharp jagged light that had destroyed Finn. As the Orb spun in circles, the glow left tracers of golden light in the air like a sparkler and slowly descended to the floor, splashing over the deck, pooling in a glimmering haze that drifted toward the ashes. The twinkling haze thickened into liquid gold, which flowed and undulated upward, steadily taking on a distinctly male, human form. Loose wisps of hair formed over the smooth head, falling around facial features swiftly sharpening into familiar detail. The shape of clothing formed over the rapidly developing body. Within seconds, the golden hue faded, giving way to the vibrant color and texture of skin, hair and garments.

Finn opened his eyes like someone waking in the morning, relaxed and sleepy. Whatever grievous injuries he'd suffered in battle were gone. He was clean of blood and bruises. Fate's heart broke with gratitude when he looked at her and smiled. She flushed with renewed passion. It was as if she was seeing him for the first time again, and she savored every detail of his face. The sweet curve of his lips, the squared line of his jaw, the robust color of his skin and his eyes... like liquid pools of green. Not just any green, but every hue of the earth's most lush forests.

His peaceful expression held for only those few seconds of reverie, quickly replaced by a frown of concern. "Fate, what's happened to you?" He rushed over to her, cupping her chin in his hand as he ran a thumb over her split lip. "Who did this to you?"

She touched her nose, wincing at how tender it was and what a terrible sight she must look. "Jessie gave me a beating. But don't worry, I'll heal in no time at all."

Finn looked her over, his frown deepening as he studied her gleaming armor. "Aye, I suppose you will." His gaze flicked to Kaliena and then to Jessie. "You did this?"

Fate nodded sheepishly as she slipped the Orb's chain over her head.

"Is Jessie... ?"

"I couldn't bring myself to check."

Finn walked over to Jessie and kneeled next to her. She'd gone still, but thin bolts of electricity crackled over her body armor. He gently opened her eye and leaned in. "She's alive."

Fate let out a shuddering sigh of relief.

Finn stood. "I don't suppose we'll know what sort of condition she's in until she wakes. If she wakes. Maybe Archie can help."

"You're right. We need to get her to Archie. Will you take her? There's one last thing I have to do."

Finn stared back warily. "And what would that be?"

"I need to end this war."

"With the Words of Making."

"Don't look at me like that. I can do this. In fact if you must know, Sithias is the one who came up with the words, and it's the perfect solution. Sublime, actually." She sighed wearily. "I hate to admit it, but I never could've come up with it myself. So there's no need to worry about how this will roll out."

Finn's expression softened. "I'm sorry, love. I can see I've made you doubt yourself. I had no right to–"

"No, that's all on me. I haven't used enough caution in the past, and you paid for my mistakes. I won't do that–"

The ship pitched and tilted sideways, knocking them both off their feet, throwing them into a high-speed slide across the deck. The tallest structures of the elaborate city built onto the flagship broke away with a deafening crack. Glass windows shattered as walls caved under the pressure. An avalanche of debris rolled toward them. Fate launched skyward, fully expecting Finn to follow. Instead, he caught Jessie by the arm as she slid past him, but he was unable to hold onto her and she tumbled toward the edge. Finn pushed off the steep incline of the deck obviously expecting to take flight. Instead, he plummeted down.

Fate plunged straight for him and grabbed hold of his flailing arms. She held firm, while searching for Jessie, but she'd either fallen off the ship or was buried beneath the detritus. Tears burned her eyes but she fought them back, refusing to believe the worst. She had to trust that Jessie's body armor would protect her. Once she had Finn to safety, she'd look for Jessie.

"Fate, watch out!" Finn shouted.

She barely dodged the swipe of a titan and flew out of reach. Three titans were on the march, smashing enemy ground troops, as well as their own, into the desert sands. The titan that had attacked tilted its head back to watch her. Kaliena stood in its outstretched palm, her many arms pulsating with renewed energy, which ran in blue-green rivulets over the titans hand. She was alive and still very much in control.

Fate tensed. "I guess it was asking to much to think I killed her."

"She must've had enough elixir with her to heal." Finn groaned. "I wish I could help, love, but I seem to have come back useless. Set me down so you can deal with her, once and for all."

"You're not useless. Don't ever say that again," Fate argued.

"I can't fly." Finn raised a sleeve to examine his arm. "The Elder race runes are gone from my skin. I've been remade as I was when Brune first conjured me. I'm completely ordinary in strength and speed."

Fate spotted Azrael's ship, where it hovered high above them and sped towards it. She set Finn on the deck and landed next to him. Azrael rushed over, his expression relieved but clouded with confusion as he took in her golden armor. "You are safe. I harpooned the dragon that took you, but when I hauled the beast aboard you were gone." He breathed a shaky sigh as he reached for her gauntleted hand.

Fate put her hands behind her back and glanced around for Sithias. Her gaze landed on a large smear of blood. "What did you do to the dragon?" she asked hesitantly.

Azrael shook his head and frowned. "It was strange. I turned my back for all but a second's breath. When I looked again, the dragon was gone. Yet the harpoon was left behind."

"That was no ordinary dragon," Mahelia said as she climbed up from the lower deck and joined them. She gave Finn a cursory look then fixed her gaze on Fate. "You used the power of the Word to conjure something that would help you escape, didn't you?"

"Actually, that was my good friend, Sithias."

Finn took a step toward Mahelia. "You don't have to defend yourself to these people, Fate."

Mahelia didn't budge, but merely shoved one of her dreaded tablets at Fate. "Read and end this war before it ends the world as we know it."

Fate folded her arms. "No, I'm not reading any of your doomsday fixes."

Mahelia handed the tablet to Azrael. "Order her to read. She cannot disobey you."

Azrael took the tablet and stared at it. "Fate, I order you to read from the tablet."

Fate's arm reached for the tablet of its own volition, a small action that sapped her resolve. "Please don't do this, Azrael."

Finn pushed Azrael back forcefully. "Grow a spine, boyo, and stand up to your mother. You know this is wrong!"

Azrael cracked his fist in Finn's face. Finn staggered back and then lunged. They fell to the floor, wrestling and punching each other, but Azrael was holding back, at least for the moment, and he had strength Finn could no longer match.

Fate grabbed hold of Azrael by the collar and tossed him aside. They both looked at her, Finn with a cut above his eye and Azrael with a bleeding lip. "We don't have time for this. People are dying down there!"

She turned to Mahelia. "I'm ready to use the Words of Making. If you really want to help, you'll give me a clean sheet to write with."

Mahelia stood stubbornly in place.

Azrael rose from the floor and straightened his clothes. "Do it, mother."

Mahelia's cold gaze moved from Fate to her son, before pained disappointment broke her hardened expression. Reluctantly, she reached into her satchel and drew out a fresh tablet, a rolled gold sheet and stylus. "I wash my hands of you." She was speaking to Fate as she thrust the items in her hand, but Fate sensed the message was meant more for Azrael.

Fate stepped aside as she spread the sheet over the wax.

"Do you need any help, love?" Finn asked as he stood and rubbed his red knuckles.

She gave him a smile. "I've got this." The words had been burned in her brain since she'd written them the first time. Now that she was writing them again, it was without doubt or fear. These words were right. She only wished Sithias was there to witness his wisdom in action. Her stomach tightened with not knowing if he'd recovered from his wound or had crawled off somewhere to die. There was so much to worry about. She felt spread thin. There simply wasn't enough of her to go around.

But she could at least honor Sithias by speaking his Words of Making to bring much-needed peace to the world. Fate walked to the starboard side and leaned over the railing. They were too far up to see anything of real detail, but the cacophony of war rose from the battlefield–raging hatred, cries of despair and dying screams.

Fate looked at the tablet and spoke. Not loudly, because there was no need. The power was in each carefully chosen word. "*I return all sentient beings not of Earth to their place of origin, never to return to this world or any other, forevermore.*"

Breathing deeply to calm the building suspense, she bent over the edge to have a look. The first thing she saw were the four titans, which immediately threw her into a fit of doubt. But her discomfort was short-lived. They weren't moving. The eerie aquamarine gleam of Kaliena's power no longer fueled the light in their eyes. The titans were hollow, dark towers of iron that would no doubt weather the storm of the elements for thousands of years, but would one day crumble to dust.

Kaliena's fleet of ships listed in the air, now unmanned and slowly sinking to the ground. The abrupt silence from below had Finn, Azrael and Mahelia rushing over to join her.

Finn whistled softly. "You did it." His eyes twinkled with joy as he turned to her. He moved in to hug her, but her armor was a deterrent and he stroked the side of her face with the back of his hand instead. "Thank you."

She smiled. "It wasn't me. Sithias is the one to thank... wherever he is." She blinked back the sting of tears.

Finn's smile dimmed. "I'm sure he's fine, love." His voice cracked, betraying his own fears.

Fate steeled herself to keep from unleashing her anger on Azrael. He was only trying to defend her from a dragon he'd thought was going to kill her.

He gazed back in horror. "How was I to know that beast was your friend?"

"Please just take us down so we can search for our friends." Fate sighed.

Azrael's remorse was obvious as he walked over to the helm in silence. Mahelia gripped the railing until her skin stretched tight over the bones of her knuckles as she watched her son. When she glanced back at Fate, her blue eyes were hard chips of ice. "You dishonor your husband by flaunting your lover in front of him this way."

Fate stepped up to her. "I'm done with you, Mahelia. And everything you forced me into."

Mahelia glared back, her shoulders and arms shaking with rage. Shadows curled off her body, tendrils of pure malice that stretched toward Fate. "You are bound to Azrael and his family... to me," she hissed.

Finn pulled on Fate's arm. "Leave it alone for now," he warned.

Fate gave him a sidelong glance. "This is something I need to do."

Finn let go and backed away as she returned her gaze to Mahelia, but the air wavered around Mahelia, suddenly blurring Fate's vision. She rubbed her eyes as the shadows thickened and wreathed around Mahelia's body. "Only death will break your oath and bond." Her voice grew low and guttural, becoming a deep growl. "You will never be free of me as long as you live."

"Step back, Fate." Finn reached into his pocket for his flute and blew the notes to transform it into his wind sword, but nothing happened. He examined the flute, turning it over and over. "*Bollocks!*" he swore under his breath. "The Elder race runes are gone from that too."

Azrael deserted his post at the helm and ran over. "Mother, please. Let her–"

Mahelia lashed out with an arm made of absolute darkness and struck Azrael down. He dropped like he'd been shot in the heart and didn't move. Without so much as a care, she turned back to Fate.

Flames flickered from her body, blackening her skin, burning away her long dark hair. Nausea gripped hold of Fate as Mahelia's bones cracked and bulged. Her features twisted and elongated beneath her charred skin as it peeled away from bristled fur, matted with blood and ichor. The sickening stench of brimstone tainted the air, choking Fate, stealing her breath and strength. She'd seen this before. When Farouk had posed as Mason.

Fate's mind swam. How long had he been pretending to be Mahelia? Had she been in the demon's presence from the beginning?

Finn ran over to Azrael, grabbed the hilt of his saber and charged at Farouk. The demon flung the ghastly remains of his disguise aside and swung his large wolf's head in Finn's direction. He ripped the saber from Finn's grip with a barely visible lash of his tail and lunged at Finn, his fangs bared as he bit down.

Summoning what little strength was left, Fate flew at Farouk and bashed into him from behind, forcing him off Finn. The demon skidded across the deck. Letting go, she rolled to one side, sluggish and slow. She rose and staggered, barely able to stand under the weight of her heavy armor.

Farouk recovered in a blink. His lightning-quick movements were beyond her ability to register and he was on her within seconds, squeezing her neck with claws digging into her skin. His eyes flared an angry red as his muzzle stretched back in a feral growl. Black smoke drifted between fangs dripping with thick slaver.

In that moment Fate's armor dissolved away, a visible sign that all her defenses had deserted her and she was going to die.

Farouk's voice invaded her thoughts. He chuckled, a grating sound that scraped her brain and pierced her ears. "*This is not the day you meet your death. You and I have only begun to play.*" He hooked a talon under the chain holding the Orb, tugged it from her neck and vanished within dark folds of fetid smoke.

56
AN ORGANIZED LIE

FINN GRIMACED AGAINST THE burning pain in his neck where Farouk had bit him. The medic bots in the Keep had cauterized the wound and patched him up, but apparently the healing would take longer than usual due to the venom in the demon's bite. He could handle that much. After all, it was a small price to pay compared to all the soldiers who'd lost their lives in the war.

What bothered him most was losing the elemental powers of supernatural strength and speed the Elder race runes had granted him. They had become part of him, like breathing, and he felt lost without them.

Rudwor stepped into the ripped opening of the sanctuary, where Finn waited for Fate to return with another load of injured soldiers on Azrael's ship. Finn had been with Fate when they'd finally found Jessie beneath a mountain of rubble. After they'd delivered her and dozens of other wounded to the infirmary, Fate had asked him to stay with Jessie while the medics cleansed her friend's system of Kaliena's magic. Finn would've preferred to stay on the ground where he could be of more help, but Fate was torturing herself for not getting to Jessie sooner, and being the only one who knew how to fly the ship meant she couldn't do it herself.

She needn't have worried though. After a series of spells, the cybernetic suit Jessie was encased in unlocked and she was extracted safely. She would likely sleep for days, so there was no reason to sit by her bedside any longer. Especially since Azrael was in the bed opposite her.

Azrael had been unconscious since Farouk's attack. Something was wrong with his heart. Finn felt badly for him. No one should have to witness what Azrael had seen–the horrifying destruction of his mother and not knowing exactly when she'd been taken from him and replaced by a vicious conniving demon. Yet Finn hated being anywhere near Azrael. He'd chained Fate to him against her will and it baffled Finn to no end to see her fretting over the guy.

Just how deeply did her feelings run for Azrael? Did she love him?

The king slung his burly arm around Finn's shoulders and squeezed. Finn winced as the bandage tugged on his wound. "I must say this is a wondrous yet baffling construction. I can't begin to imagine what that round ball of metal and mystery is." He waved his other arm at the Keep, with all its moving parts and elaborate vaults, floating at the center of the colossal rings.

He let go of Finn and faced the sanctuary with his hands on his hips. "This room alone is mystifying enough with all these priceless treasures lying about on the shelves like everyday dishes in a cupboard. But I've explored the endless halls behind those doors there, and am stupefied by the grand scale of it all. Every room is filled with oddities galore. Have you seen the machines that make food out of thin air?" He didn't wait for Finn to answer. "And the bedchambers are fit for a hundred kings! If I weren't expected back in Beldereth, I'd stay here to live out the rest of my life in luxury. Though I don't know that I'd ever grow used to the mechanical people–all those extra arms, blinking lights and no personality. They're unsettling, but efficient. I'll give them that! Better than my grumbling servants back home."

Rudwor shook his head in disbelief. "What I can't get over are the healers and how they use those peculiar whigmaleeries to close a gaping wound without thread and grow new skin over what should surely leave a scar. I'm gobsmacked!"

"Aye, robots are new to this world, and the Keep takes some getting used to for sure," Finn agreed.

Rudwor turned his attention to the ground. "Has there been any sign of our friends on the last few deliveries?"

"Still waiting." Each load that didn't include Sithias, Grysla, Tove and her brother, Leif, chipped away at what little hope he had left.

Rudwor let out an impatient huff. "The waiting is always the hardest. They've run out of room in the infirmary and have started putting the wounded in the sparring arena." He rubbed his shiny bald head worriedly. "I checked for familiar faces but have only seen a handful so far."

"Was Tynan amongst them?" Finn would prefer to be asking out of concern, but it was mostly out of dread. The man had tried to kill him on the battlefield.

"No, I fear the king of Asgar may not have survived."

"That's sorry news. I'd hoped to hear otherwise." Finn bit down on the lie, but he didn't wish to blemish Rudwor's good memory of Tynan. "We were fighting side by side when one of Kaliena's creatures stampeded us. He was gored and I was trampled. I thought maybe he might've survived as I did."

"I didn't know!" Relief shone in Rudwor's eyes. "Sounds as though some angels were watching over you, laddie. I wish I could say the same for Tynan."

Finn nodded grimly. He would've died had it not been for Fate using the Orb to recreate him. Something he should be grateful for, if not for the fact that Farouk had shown up to claim it. The disastrous ramifications of that unforeseen development only added to his exhaustion. Thankfully, Farouk had been unaware the Rod was part of him. He didn't want to think what the demon would've done to him had he known.

"Ah, here comes the ship. Let's hope our friends are on it this time," Rudwor said.

Finn gripped the edge of the wall and stretched to catch the rope being tossed to him by one of Rudwor's soldiers. He tied it off as Fate lined the boat up to the platform. Her cuts and bruises had healed, but she looked tired–sad to be more specific–and she didn't move from the helm as the wounded were carried off. He knew why. She was ready to head back down because she still hadn't found Sithias.

Finn started across the ramp when Tove limped toward him. He reached out to help her across. The dull, broken look in her eyes confirmed what he hadn't wanted to know. His dear friend Grysla had fallen in battle. "Your brother too?" His voice cracked with emotion, but he was careful to remain outwardly calm for Tove.

Tove stared past him and nodded.

There was nothing he could say that would be of any comfort to her. He took her in his arms and wept for the kind, gentle tree troll that had taken him in as family. And he wept for Tove's loss. Her entire family was gone, taken from her all at once, because he'd asked them to join the fight. He remembered Tove's arguments against it, but Grysla had been all too willing to help and he'd taken advantage of her generous spirit. Tove pushed him away, her stare empty as she turned and followed the other wounded.

Rudwor set a hand on Finn's shoulder to stop him from going after her. "Leave her be, lad. She can't give you what you want right now."

"I don't want anything from her. I only want to help her through this. She shouldn't be alone."

"But she is alone, and there's nothing you can do to make her feel any better about that." Rudwor's gaze moved to Fate. "Now there's a lass who'll have your help."

Finn tensed as he looked at Fate. Her shock over Farouk's deception had catapulted her into a frenzy of activity, as if she could somehow escape what had happened by throwing herself into saving as many people as she could. But each time she returned without Sithias, the more drawn and sad she looked. She needed to rest, but he feared there would be no peace for her for quite some time. Once she entered the sanctuary walls expecting to see Eustace, the awful truth would come out.

Rudwor studied Finn. "Something's eating you, boyo. What is it? Did you two lovebirds have a spat? My advice is to agree with everything she says, even if you don't. Trust me, it's always easier that way."

Finn slumped against the wall. "If only it were that simple."

"Dealing with women is a complicated affair."

"This isn't just complicated, it's convoluted. For starters, she's married to the guy who owns that ship. The worst of it is, her father was murdered in front of her and she has no memory of it, but she's about to find out I didn't tell her the truth when she last asked about him."

Rudwor blew air between his teeth with a shake of his head. "Why didn't you tell her?"

"Because I fear her reaction will allow an ancient goddess to fully possess her again, and this time she'll be lost to us forever."

The king stared back in surprise. "There's an answer I didn't see coming."

"Like I said, the whole thing's convoluted."

"Not so much," Rudwor disagreed.

"Are you serious?"

"Deadly serious. Deal with the most pressing issue first. Don't let her find out about her father."

"And how do I do that?"

"Make excuses. Tell her he had to go somewhere else."

"Fate will never believe that. Eustace isn't from here. He doesn't know anyone outside the Keep."

"Then tell her he went back to where he came from."

Finn pushed away from the wall and paced. "I hate to say it, but that could work. I'll need you're help on this though. And now."

"Of course. What do you want me to do?"

"Tell Brune what we talked about and have her get everyone else on board with the same story. I'll bring Fate along shortly."

"Aye, consider it done."

Finn waited for Rudwor to leave, then crossed the plank and jumped on deck as the last of the wounded was carried off. Fate was winding the rope and preparing to make another run to the ground when he strode up behind her. "I think it's time you took a break, love."

She turned with a start. "Oh." Her voice was a weary whisper when she realized it was him. She cast her gaze downward. "I can't stop yet. There's still more wounded down there. We can't just leave them."

"The worst of them have been brought up already. I think the rest can wait a few hours while you rest a bit."

Fate's mouth slanted in a sad line. "You don't know that. Someone could be close to dying out there. A few hours could kill him."

"You mean Sithias."

Tears brimmed in her eyes. "He's down there somewhere. Don't ask me to give up on him."

Finn brushed his hands down the sides of her arms. "I'm not. I only want you to take a moment. When was the last time you ate?"

She shrugged. "I'm not hungry."

"Please, Fate. Come inside, have a bite to eat and then we'll both go back down."

"But you're supposed to be with Jessie." Her eyes widened with fright. "Is that why you wanted me to come in? Is Jessie–"

"She's fine and sleeping peacefully."

Fate let out a shuddering sigh.

"You can see for yourself after you've eaten." Finn took her hand and pulled her along. She didn't resist, but the fear in her eyes didn't ease. He led her down the long halls to Brune and the others. As they passed the towering, double doors of the library, Fate slowed down. Her chin trembled and Finn knew she was thinking of how much Sithias loved the library. He tugged her gently and they continued on in silence until they reached the shelter.

The hatch was standing open. Rudwor was talking in hushed tones to Brune and Darcy in the galley while Gerdie skipped in circles with the doggit in the common room. She noticed them enter before the others did and ran over with a big smile.

"Fate, you're back!" Gerdie exclaimed. "Finn said you learned how to fly a boat that floats on air. How does it do that?"

Fate bent level with Gerdie, her smile thin as she did so. "It's fueled by something called ranemist."

"Ooh, can I see the boat and the ranemist?"

"I have to use it to help the injured soldiers, but after I'm done, I'll take you out for a ride." Fate straightened and glanced around distractedly.

Gerdie jumped in place and clapped with the doggit doing the same.

"Where's Eustace?" Fate asked.

Gerdie stopped jumping. "You don't know?"

"Know what?"

Gerdie's expression saddened as she reached into her dress pocket. "Here, you're gonna want this back." She placed a miniature clockwork cat in

Fate's hand. It raised twinkling emerald eyes to look at her and meowed.

"This isn't mine," Fate said.

"Yes it is, silly," Gerdie pressed. "Eustace gave it to you for your birthday. You named it Poz, short for pocket Oz, after your cat from home. You forgot to take him with you when you left, but I've been keepin' him company for you."

Every muscle in Finn's body tensed. Out of all the times Gerdie's memory has failed her, why couldn't it have been now?

Brune hurried over. "Gerdie, go sit down for dinner."

"Aw! I don't feel hungry right now," Gerdie grumbled. But she obeyed and moved slowly to the table, dragging her feet loudly over the floor.

Finn held his breath as Fate's strained expression turned to anger and confusion. "Where's my father?" She wasn't asking. She was demanding.

Rudwor and Darcy's conversation ended abruptly and the room grew uncomfortably quiet. Finn started to speak but Brune took over, and for once, he was grateful. "Eustace isn't here, he had to leave and go–"

"Sorry, am I late for dinner?"

Everyone turned toward the familiar voice to see Eustace standing just within the hatch. "Dad!" Fate ran across the room. Eustace folded his arms around her, squeezed and kissed the top of her head. "Hey, Doodles. I missed you."

Finn watched the unexpected reunion in utter confusion, his heart pounding with fear. Brune and the others looked every bit as terrified. They were all thinking the same thing. With Sithias missing, Farouk was the only other one capable of assuming Eustace's form.

"How'd Eustace come back?" Gerdie asked. "I thought he was–"

Brune shushed her and whisked her off to the barracks. The rest of them watched, frozen in fear as Eustace held Fate in a long hug. Then he looked at Finn and winked.

Sithias.

Finn started breathing again. He didn't know whether to be relieved Sithias was alive and well, or outraged at their friend for letting them worry for so long. After a few seconds consideration, Finn decided he could choke him to death. First for the awful scare he'd given them and then for making a decision like this on his own. If Fate discovered the truth of his deception, she'd be doubly devastated. Sithias's acting would have to remain impeccable, and Finn wasn't sure he had that much confidence in him.

Fate released her father and turned around, beaming with relief. She was finally beginning to relax and Finn was grateful to see it. "What's for dinner?"

she asked. "I'm suddenly starving to death."

"It's pizza night," Gerdie complained as she walked back in with Brune.

"*Gourmet* pizza night," Darcy corrected her. "I came up with a new killer combo. Roasted zucchini, bell peppers, red onion and chipotle chicken sprinkled over a spicy cranberry sauce base, topped with goat cheese."

"Yuck." Gerdie pouted. "I don't know why we can't just have cheddar cheese like before."

"Because we need our veggies too." Darcy sat down next to her.

"It doesn't matter. They're not even real vegetables," Gerdie argued. "The food simulator only makes them look and taste like them. And they taste bad."

"She isn't wrong, Darcy." Brune sat down on the other side of Gerdie. "The nutritional value is all the same, whether it tastes like vegetables or cheddar cheese."

Darcy bit into a slice of pizza, smiling as she chewed. "But this tastes so much better."

Rudwor claimed the seat next to Darcy, giving her the rakish grin usually reserved for the bevy of pretty girls he was accustomed to having around him. He took a bite and swallowed. "Creativity in the kitchen, now there's a lass after my own heart."

Darcy looked straight ahead and frowned.

Finn slipped in next to Fate, where she sat by her father on the bench. She reached for a slice of pizza. "Wait, where's Archie? I know he doesn't need to eat, but I just realized he's not here."

"He disappeared the same time Kaliena's army vanished," Brune said.

Fate set her slice on the plate. "Oh... " Her shoulders slumped. "That's my bad. I didn't even think about Archie when I read the Words of Making to send all sentient beings not of Earth back to where they came from, never to return."

Brune looked surprised. "So that's how you did it." She nodded with a thoughtful smile. "Smart."

"It wasn't me," Fate was quick to say. "Sithias is the one who came up with the solution. It was brilliant really, because it allowed the Keep to stay with all the bots and magical machinery we've come to rely on. I just wish I'd had the same courage and wisdom to add something to make Farouk disappear too." Her expression hardened into a quizzical frown. "I still don't understand why he didn't. Shouldn't he have gone back to whatever hell dimension he came from?"

"Farouk is a Persian Shedreakai demon," Brune reminded her. "His kind were homegrown here on Earth by ancient sorcerers."

"Figures there'd be some loophole where Farouk's concerned." Fate stared at her food. "Either way, I wish Sithias was here to see how well he did with getting rid of Kaliena and her troops."

'Eustace' patted her back. "Don't lose heart. Sithias is stronger than you think."

Fate's expression filled with hope. "You really think so?"

"Sithias is an adventurer at heart. How else do you think he can write such impressive plays and perform them like no one I've ever seen."

Fate stared back, puzzled. "You like his plays and his performances that much?"

Finn held his breath, seeing that her question had flustered Sithias.

'Eustace' cleared his throat. "Uh... well, I've always been grateful for Sithias and how he broke the monotony of our research in the library by reciting excerpts from his plays."

Fate laughed quietly. "Yup, that sounds like Sithias. He'll ham it up for any willing audience." She looked down at her plate and bit into her pizza, not noticing how appalled Sithias was by her remark. "Mmm, this is yummy, Darcy."

"Thanks." Darcy gave her a nervous smile as her gaze moved between Sithias and Finn.

Fate finished her slice and stood. "I think I'll go to my old room and lie down for an hour before I head back out." She glanced at Finn.

"Go ahead, I'll look in on you when I'm done eating."

She nodded wearily and left.

"It's time for you to go to bed too," Brune told Gerdie.

"I'm not tired," Gerdie argued, but Brune picked her up and carried her off to the barracks.

Finn glared at Sithias while he waited for both Fate and Gerdie to be well out of earshot. "What do you think you're doing pretending to be Eustace? Do you have any idea what you're playing at? If Fate figures out you're not Eustace, she'll be–"

"She won't find out." Sithias frowned seriously. "I know what's at stake. We have to keep her from being upset with the truth so that Ananke can't take full possession of her."

Finn huffed with frustration. "We had a better plan, Sithias. We were going to tell Fate that Archie had found a way to send Eustace back to his world where he'd be safer. What you're doing is beyond risky. Fate knows her father too well. At some point you're going to slip worse than you just did and she's going to realize it's you. Once that happens there'll be no keeping the truth from her."

"Not to mention how royally pissed off she's going to be at the rest of us for what she'll see as an organized lie," Darcy added. "I was there when Fate lost herself to that uber powerful, stone-cold deity after Eustace died. I don't have words for how scary that was. Thank god she wasn't interested in any of us at the time. But when I think how bad it's going to be when she's furious with us... " She trailed off with a haunted look in her eyes.

Brune rounded the corner. "We're going to need a contingency plan for when that happens."

Sithias stamped his foot, which didn't suit Eustace's dignified appearance at all. "There's no need for all this concern, or a contingency plan! I'm a professional thespian. I know how to stay in character. Fate will *never* know from me, unless one of *you* let it slip."

Finn shook his head at Sithias. "That may be well and good, but Fate's beside herself with worry over you, Sithias. Everytime she goes down to the ground and doesn't find you, the worse she feels. She needs to know you're alive too."

Sithias stared at the floor. "Oh, dear."

Rudwor filled his plate with more pizza. "There's only one thing to be done now that we're in the thick of this. Sithias needs to make an appearance and do double duty by being himself and Eustace for as long as necessary." He stuffed an entire slice into his mouth and chewed.

"Do you think you can you do that?" Finn asked Sithias.

He stared back with wide eyes. "*Yesss*, I'll do anything to keep my miss from suffering."

Finn jabbed a finger at him. "You just hissed. Eustace doesn't hiss!"

"You're making me nervous! But I promise, I can do thisss." He gasped and covered his mouth. "Oops!"

Finn clenched his fists in an effort to keep from shouting. "You've got the looks down, all the way to the color of Eustace's eyes, but I'm warning you, Sithias, this will have to be the most stellar performance of your life. Our lives depend on it."

Sithias bobbed his head up and down urgently; making Eustace's neatly combed bangs tumble down over his glasses.

Rudwor leaned back from his empty plate and rubbed his belly. "I have every confidence in Sithias."

Sithias brushed the hair from his eyes. "Thank you," he muttered.

"But he won't be able to pull off this deception indefinitely," Rudwor continued, causing Sithias to sag. "Is there a plan to declaw Fate before it's too late?"

"Aye, there is." Finn relaxed somewhat as he put his mind to solving their dilemma. "We need to find Dantalion's key to safely unlock Hyppolota's magical girdle. The power Fate gains from it has made her strong enough to be the vessel for the ancient goddess, Ananke. As long as Fate remains calm before we can remove the girdle, Ananke won't have the opening she needs to fully emerge." He held a hand up against the questioning looks. "It's a long story, which I'll leave to Sithias to tell."

"Did you forget the key is in the Hell dimension and warded against every possible means of capture?" Darcy asked. "I still haven't found a way in."

Finn set his hands on the table and stood. "Please keep looking."

"This is all news to me," Brune said. "Why wasn't I told?"

"You've been so busy with Gerdie and all the repairs around here since Farouk's attack," Darcy told her.

Brune frowned. "Regardless, I want to be fully informed. I'm still Keep Guardian. Not to mention every single one of you is overlooking the obvious."

"What's that?" Finn asked.

"The Words of Making." Brune made a face and shook her head like they were morons. "There's no need to go hunting down some elusive key when Fate has the power to remove the girdle herself."

"Believe me, I've considered that." Finn looked at Sithias, whose sudden discomfort became apparent by the way he averted his gaze. "As you know, the Words of Making work on intention. Fate doesn't know it yet, but she'd be going up against the will of Ananke, and frankly I don't want to see how badly that could go. To be honest, even if Fate wasn't the one who used the Words of Making to remove the girdle, I'd be hard pressed to trust there would be no serious consequences. From everything we know, not even the gods fought against Ananke because she controlled their fates and everyone else down the line."

Brune looked up and sighed. "And here I thought the dust was settling now that Kaliena's out of the way."

"Sithias and Darcy can fill you in on all of Eustace's research," Finn told her. "I think it's best I check on Fate."

"Aye," Rudwor chimed in, "it's going to be up to you to keep the lass distracted and as content as possible." He directed a flirtatious grin at Darcy. "I can give you some pointers on pleasing the lasses if you need it." Darcy's repulsed expression did nothing to wipe the confident smile from his face.

Finn strode for the door. "Thanks for the offer, but I'm good."

Sithias rushed after him, leaving Darcy to fill Brune in on Fate's bloodline and the impending doom of Ananke's emergence. "Sir, I want to apologize for taking matters into my own hands. I should've found a way to speak with you about it first."

"It is what it is, Sithias." Finn could barely hold his gaze. Talking to Sithias in Eustace's form was disconcerting, to say the least. "I know you had everyone's welfare in mind. And most of all, I'm glad to know you're all right. Fate wasn't the only one who was worried about losing you."

Sithias managed a sheepish smile. "Thank you, sir."

Finn winked. "Drop the sir. Eustace would never use that term with me."

Sithias straightened his posture, fully embodying Eustace's quiet dignity. "I will." His voice deepened with conviction. "Don't worry about me. Now go. I'm relying on you to take care of my daughter."

Finn stared back in surprise. If he didn't know better, he would've been truly convinced he was talking to Eustace. "Aye," he replied, playing along with a new sense of confidence. "Fate's well being is all I want and I can promise I'll do whatever it takes to see her safe and happy."

57
INTO THE MIDNIGHT SKY

FATE STEPPED FROM THE shower, wrapped herself in a towel and loosely braided her wet hair to one side. The act of rinsing the blood of her enemies and desert grime off her skin had done her more good than she could've expected. She felt cleansed of the hatred and fear that had been pumping through her system like poison. Even the fire of Hippolyta's girdle had dimmed and was only a soft glimmer beneath her skin. Despite this and a list of other troubling factors still present in her life, putting an end to the war had lifted a weight she hadn't realized was crushing her little by little.

She felt liberated, as if she'd been granted a fresh start. A strong sense of well-being had replaced the constant, nameless fear she'd been haunted by for far too long. Her relief was indescribable. Eustace was alive and well. Finn had survived the war. Jessie was in recovery. While nothing had changed for Gerdie and her failing memory, she seemed happy to have her big sister, Brune, taking care of her. Even Darcy appeared to be more at peace and settling into a life she'd been resisting from the very start.

All of Fate's other worries had been a senseless waste of energy, which was why she'd allowed herself to stop worrying over Sithias. Something in her father's voice, when he'd assured her Sithias was stronger than she knew, had filled her with certainty. Sithias was fine, and for whatever reason, he'd been detained and would return as soon as he could.

She dropped the towel and let the grandmotherly-faced chamber bot she'd grown familiar with help her into a simple white nightgown. Fate climbed onto the large floating bed and sank against the stack of freshly plumped pillows. She nestled in and took the steaming cup of hot chocolate being offered. From the first frothy sip, welcome warmth spread through her chest and she closed her eyes, savoring the rich dark flavor.

Months of exhaustion flooded in, washing away whatever strength she'd been hanging onto. There would be no leaving this bed until she'd slept–the sleep of the dead, no doubt. She blinked drowsily as her thoughts drifted haphazardly, touching on her most recent experiences, still raw and unprocessed.

Mahelia's face swam behind her closed lids. Visions of her kind smile distorted into darkness, twisting into the gruesome eruption of Farouk from beneath her skin. Fate's eyes flew open, her breathing coming hard and fast as she caught her cup from spilling her now-tepid chocolate onto the sheets. She set the cup on the nightstand and pulled the covers to her chin, shivering as Farouk's words echoed in her mind. "*You and I have only begun to play.*"

The weight that had lifted from her shoulders bore down once again. There was no telling how long Farouk had been toying with her while wearing Mahelia's face. It chilled her to think he could hide behind the face of anyone she knew, especially someone she loved. And there was nothing she could do to prevent that from happening. Darcy had certainly been fooled when Farouk had cloaked himself in Mason's skin. Azrael had been equally clueless. He hadn't once suspected that Farouk had replaced his mother.

She still felt for Darcy and her loss, and she couldn't begin to imagination how devastated Azrael must've been to discover his mother was gone. Fate wondered if he would awaken and if his heart would ever heal fully from Farouk's attack and insidious deception.

She blamed herself for not knowing, for not being able to fight Farouk. She had the incredible power of a war god, yet Farouk had rendered her powerless each time he'd chosen to reveal himself to her. And she would remain vulnerable as long as she was wearing the girdle. She had to figure out a way to remove the thing. It's not like she needed the power it gave her anymore. Kaliena was no longer a threat.

Plus, she had the Words of Making, which she would need to use very soon. As far she could see, that was the only way to get the Orb back from Farouk. It wouldn't be long before he discovered the Rod was part of Finn and use it to destroy him the way Kaliena had done.

Her temples throbbed as her mind scrambled to discern what those words should be. Nothing sensible came to her. Exhaustion jumbled her thoughts. There was so much to think about, and the urgency of it all pressed in from every side. She started to rise from bed but her body protested with limbs too heavy to lift. Fatigue won out.

"A few hours of sleep," she muttered. "That's all I need and I'll be good as new."

Her lids hadn't closed for more than a split second before there was a light rap at the door. The chamber bot trundled to the door. Finn leaned in through the doorway. "Need some company?"

She smiled through sleepy lids. "Yes please." Her heart beat faster just watching him stride toward her. The warm light of the lanterns caught the gold of his hair falling loosely over his brow as he kicked off his shoes and situated himself on top of the covers next to her. Her breath locked in her throat at his beauty. In the low light, his eyes were the color of soft green moss resting in the deepening shadows of trees.

Finn leaned close, his gaze sweeping over her face as he brushed her hair back from her forehead. The touch of his fingers sent tingles of pure pleasure rippling over her skin. Desire roused her weary body, and suddenly the energy that had abandoned her, returned in full force, banishing all her aches and pains.

He bent and kissed her, his lips soft as satin, urgent yet yielding. Fate's head spun in a delicious spiral of hunger and heat. She pressed her hand to his chest, feeling the rapid beat of his heart behind a solid wall of muscle and kissed his neck. The scent of sandalwood soap clung to his skin beneath the taste of salt. She dug her fingers into his back and arched against him. Her need for his skin against hers burned away every troublesome thought.

"Make love to me," she whispered against the smooth shell of his ear, while unbuttoning his shirt.

Finn's breath came in unsteady bursts as he pushed her nightgown off her shoulder, kissing all the way up to her neck before recapturing her mouth with his. The air hummed between them with magic, hot and thick, as he slipped beneath the covers with her, hastily with clothes still on. Fate surrendered herself to his exploring hands. She pressed against his arousal, feeling the connectivity they shared–*had always shared*–like never before.

Scorching hot pain circled her ankle and the connection snapped.

Fate tore herself away from Finn and scrambled to the other side of the bed, clutching her ankle in both hands. An angry raw burn marred her skin, a wound caused by the soul ring.

Finn frowned at her scalded skin, his chest heaving from a mixture of passion, confusion and anger. "Seriously? The soul ring's keeping you from being with me even though Azrael's out cold and may never wake?"

Fate bit her bottom lip. "I don't get it. That's never happened before."

"Obviously it's because you wanted to give yourself to me. It's not like we've had the chance to be together like that until now." The muscles in his jaw flexed as he shook his head. "What happens if Azrael dies? Will that free you from this god-awful shackle?"

She stared back in horror. "You're not actually thinking of killing him, are you?"

"Of course not." He let out a heavy sigh. "His prognosis isn't good though. It's possible his heart could give out, and if that happens, I'd like to know if you'll be free of him."

"I think so." She glanced down at the burn. "Look, the skin's already turning pink. It's healing almost as fast as it happened. Maybe we could pick up where we left off and–"

"No, I won't have you in pain while we're... " Finn climbed out from under the sheets and glared at the wall.

Fate reached for his hand. "Don't go. I don't want to be alone with my thoughts right now. I can't get everything that's happened, or will happen, out of my head."

His tortured gaze softened. "You're killing me, lass. Do you have any idea how agonizing it is for me not to be able to show you how I feel?"

"I do, actually." Her body literally ached for his touch. She tugged on his hand. "Please stay."

"God help me, I can never say no to you." He resumed his place on top of the covers and gestured for her to tuck in beneath his arm.

Fate rested her head against his chest. "This isn't so bad, is it?" she murmured. Relaxing within the safe cocoon of his arms and listening to the steady beat of his heart worked like a tranquilizer and she grew instantly sleepy.

Finn set his chin on the top of her head. "Not too terrible at all."

Fate smiled drowsily. "It's working."

"What is?"

"My mind is blank for the first time in ages." She yawned and wriggled to get even closer to him. "I can't remember the last time I wasn't kept awake by a million horrible things to think about."

He stroked her arm. "We have tomorrow to face what's ahead. For now, close your eyes, my sweet lass, and dream of sunshine over fields of flowers. Or whatever suits your fancy. Just know I'll be by your side for as long as there's life in me."

The comforting cadence of Finn's voice lulled Fate deeper into sleep, until she was wrapped in a velvet darkness strewn with glittering stars. A fire-tassled comet streaked over a calm sea sparkling with the mirrored light of the sky. On the shore, a dark horse with a single horn cantered near the water's edge, kicking a spray of crystal dust and sea foam behind its strangely cloven hooves.

Misty vapors streamed from its flowing mane as the black unicorn slowed and stamped to a stop in front of her. His eyes glistened milky white, a disturbing untamed stare, which moved to meet hers. Stretching his neck with nostrils flared, he sniffed the air between them, tossing his head as he edged nervously toward her.

Equally nervous, Fate held her hand out until the creature allowed her to touch the spiral of his horn. His feral gaze calmed as he lowered himself in a silent invitation to ride. The skin at the back of Fate's neck prickled and she hesitated. The unicorn was both beautiful and terrifying in its darkness and deformities.

Blackhearted. That's what he was.

Yet the air around him thrummed with a raw, dangerous magic she couldn't refuse because of the irresistible promise of freedom and power held within it.

She no sooner mounted his back and wound her fingers in the thick rope of his ebony mane before he lurched into a gallop. They raced along the length of the beach, an endless spur of glinting black sand that curved into the midnight sky, and Fate lifted her face to the stars, breathing in the crisp, cool air as she left all the fear and chaos of her life far behind.

READ THE FIRST CHAPTER OF

Book 4 of Her Dark Destiny

FATE'S FURY

T. RAE MITCHELL

I
BENEATH THE SKIN

Fate bounded out the door of her personal suite, thrilled and excited. Finally, some good news. Jessie was awake and talking! Her relief was overwhelming after being forced to accept the loss of her childhood friend to Kaliena's control. Even though the cybernetic suit had been removed safely, the wait for Jessie to wake had been excruciating. The possibility that she could be a mindless, empty shell when she woke had been a constant concern.

But if Jessie was asking for her, that could only mean her friend had recovered fully intact. Fate chewed on her bottom lip, wondering if Jessie remembered the brutal fights they'd had.

Their last fight had been especially vicious. Fate still winced with the memory of Jessie's sharp metal fists smashing the bones in her face. The blow would've killed Fate, or disfigured her for life, had it not been for the regenerative powers Hippolyta's magical girdle granted her. Not that Fate would ever hold any of that against Jessie. Her friend hadn't known what she was doing.

Fate rounded a corner, accidentally bumping into a man who was a solid wall of sinewed muscle. "Watch it," the Serpen knight growled, before shoving her so hard she hit the wall.

Weeks of suppressed rage blazed in Fate's core, a volcanic heat that overrode all sense of reasoning. Twisting around in a flash, she used the wall to propel herself into the air feet first, her boots aimed at his head. She grinned when her heels struck his jaw and knocked the sneer off his jiggling lips. The blow flattened him before her feet hit the ground. Stunned and lying on his back, he stared at the ceiling.

Fate planted her foot over his neck and leaned forward. His forehead beaded with sweat as his dark eyes found hers. She applied more pressure when she caught the same scarlet glint in his eyes she'd seen in Moria, their Serpen Dragon Empress, whose thirst for vengeance had ruined the kingdom of Asgar.

"Watch your manners," Fate told the man. "Remember, you're a guest here. If you can't behave, I'll throw you to the desert."

The red-faced soldier fumed, his mouth tightly closed as he nodded.

Fate ground her heel into his Adam's apple, making him struggle for air before finally lifting her foot. The other Serpen knights quickly cleared a path for her as she resumed her speedy pace down the hall. The crowds thickened at the lower end of the Keep's residential suites, and Fate was forced to dart and weave her way through the populace once again.

Three weeks had passed since the Great Desert War–as many were now referring to it–and she still felt invaded by the thousands of people milling within the walls of the ancient structure. This latest run-in with the Serpen soldier served to magnify the intrusion. But these were the surviving remnants of allied forces. Despite the large numbers, they really only occupied a small percentage of the Keep's available residential suites. If only she'd been able to convince Brune to open a different section, instead of putting them where she and her friends had been living.

Housing them wasn't the most pressing issue though. As each day passed, their unexpected guests were beginning to act as if they owned the place. Such as taking over the sparring arena, which Fate was accustomed to having all to herself. They were also taking liberties by trespassing beyond closed off sections within the colossal rings.

Even more alarming, was the trespass into the vaults on the Keep surface. Fortunately, they couldn't enter most of them. To do that, they needed the Keep Guardian seal, which only she was equipped with, as well as Brune and Jessie after she'd made them her proxies. Any vaults they could walk into were safe from thieves since the treasures inside were either locked or hidden by a riddle to solve. But Brune had found entrances damaged from failed attempts to force their way in.

While the situation troubled Fate, Brune had become absolutely livid. If Fate hadn't signed full guardianship over to Brune, she would be the one feeling the relentless, painful call to protect the Keep at any cost. All the more reason to cut Brune plenty of slack for being extra cranky lately.

At least they had the support of Rudwor and his knights of Beldereth. Fate was grateful for Rudwor's decision to stay longer than planned, assigning his knights as peacekeepers to prevent things from escalating whenever fights broke out. So far the Eldunough soldiers, who were recovering from injuries and the riders who'd been grounded after losing their hawks, appeared to be civilized and respectful. Though they'd remained neutral as to whose side they leaned toward.

The Serpens were causing most of the trouble, bulldozing their way through the halls, cutting in on food lines and hoarding weapons they found in the armories. She wasn't surprised though. When she'd faced their dragon empress in the *Book of Fables*, she'd seen first hand what a warring race they were. But their rude behavior seemed to be contagious, because the Asgar army was growing hostile as well. Having taken the heaviest hit in numbers of soldiers, morale was lowest amongst them. King Tynan's death had only served to leave them directionless and rebellious.

Fate ducked into the infirmary, her step quickening as she moved past bed after bed of critically injured soldiers. When she reached the private rooms at the very back, she slipped through the door and closed it behind her.

Jessie was sitting up in bed talking to Eustace. Her long dark hair hung in smooth waves over her shoulders. She was smiling and animated–a human being again. No longer the killer automaton Kaliena had turned her into.

"I hear someone was asking for me," Fate interrupted.

They both turned to look at her. Jessie's smile widened, crinkling her warm hazel eyes into gleeful crescents. Giddy with excitement, she waved Fate over. "That would be me! How's it going?"

Seeing Jessie's beautiful face was a welcome sight after being hidden behind ensorcelled machinery for so long. Fate ran over to her, arms held wide as she dove in for a hug. "How am I? How are you?" She squeezed Jessie hard, afraid to let go.

Jessie tapped her back lightly. "Finding it hard to breath," she gasped.

Fate let go."Oh sorry!"

Jessie rubbed her arms. "Whoa, who turned you into Captain Marvel?"

Fate glanced at her father and sighed. "How much time do you have?"

"Loads. Apparently, I'm being held for further tests," Jessie informed her.

"Lucky you." Fate sat on the end of the bed and crossed her legs.

Eustace patted Jessie's hand and stood. "I'll leave you two to catch up."

Fate chuckled. "What? You don't want to hear this all over again?"

"Not so much." Eustace reached around to rub the small of his back with a pained grimace. "Especially since I have a pile of research waiting for me in the library."

"What sort of research?" Fate wasn't aware of any urgent need for cracking the books open. Was he making unnecessary work for himself? She hoped this wasn't the case, because she really didn't like how tired he looked lately.

Eustace seemed caught off guard by her question. He grew stiff and nervous all of a sudden, which made her tense. "Oh, I uh... I've been helping Brune find remembering spells for Gerdie."

Fate frowned. Why would he be nervous about that? Something was off.

What was he hiding? Her stomach tightened into a knot of suspicion. She narrowed her eyes on him, watching as he squirmed under her scrutinizing gaze.

Was she looking at her father, whom she loved with all her heart? Or was she looking at Farouk? The demon could be lurking behind any face. After all, Farouk had fooled Azrael by hiding behind his mother's face. And Darcy had never suspected she was sleeping with the demon when he'd pretended to be Mason.

If there was one cringy picture she didn't want in her head, it was that one.

She shook it off, telling herself to stop being paranoid about everyone around her. She'd even begun to worry if Finn was Finn. Every now and then, she sensed the same sort of secretiveness from him as well. This constant underlying fear was wreaking havoc with her sanity.

Jessie waved her hand in front of Fate's eyes. "Hey, where'd you go?"

Fate blinked. "Oh, I was thinking about something I need to do." She glanced at Eustace, who was about to make his escape. "You should have Sithias help with the research."

Eustace froze in the doorway without turning around.

"He's practically been living in the library since he got back," Fate continued. "Come to think of it, I haven't seen him in the last few days. I really need to find out what's up with him. It's weird for him to be so antisocial."

"Will do," Eustace replied, offering a limp smile as he glanced back at them.

"Is it me, or does your dad seem a little on edge?" Jessie asked, after he left.

Fate stared at the empty doorway. "He's definitely not himself." She didn't voice all of her thoughts. "I think something's bothering him."

"You going to talk to him about it?"

Fate nodded. "Yup."

"Good, but first things first. I want to know how you powered up." Jessie plumped up her pillows before settling back into them.

"Well, it's probably easier to just show you." Fate lifted her shirt enough for Jessie to see Hippolyta's magical girdle lighting her waistline from within.

Jessie's eyes rounded as she leaned forward to study the girdle's interlocking design. "What exactly am I looking at? Is that a pattern of snakes and eagles?"

"It's a magic corset."

"But it's under your skin!"

"Yeah, it melded into me only a few hours after I put it on."

"Does it come off?"

Fate shook her head, clamping down on a growing desire to remove the girdle. Ironically, the very thing that had given her the superhuman powers she'd wanted so badly had also become her Achilles' heel. How could she have known that whenever Farouk chose to fully reveal himself that her godlike powers would be weakened by his presence?

Jessie's green eyes grew wide. "Whoa, that's some serious business. Are you okay with having it be a permanent fixture, just stuck there under your skin like that?"

Fate let her shirt drop back in place. "I pretty much have to be."

"Do you have other powers besides super strength?"

"I guess you could say I'm invulnerable."

"As in nothing can kill you? Like, if your head gets cut off you'll grow a new one?"

Fate chuckled. "Either that, or I'll be a talking head rolling around on the floor."

"I got one! Maybe your veins will shoot out your neck like long spider legs and creep over the floor feeling around for your body." Jessie laughed at Fate's horrified expression.

"Gross, I'm not The Thing!" Fate shrugged. "I don't know what I am exactly. I'm basically the same, except for this fiery burn in my belly whenever I get angry. It kind of makes me want to go postal on people."

"You always did have a bit of a short fuse."

"Believe me, this is more than a hot temper. I get Hulk angry. It's because the girdle was made by Ares."

"The god of war?"

"Uh huh."

Jessie leaned back against her pillows again, watching Fate with a quizzical frown. "What is it with you and gods of war? Didn't you say that Miranda chick was a goddess of war?

"Who?"

"You know, the one who gave you all those kickass wind and lightning powers."

"*Murauda.*" Fate smiled wryly. "And yes, I seem to have a type when it comes to ancient deities."

"Huh, I wonder why that is?"

Fate hesitated, unsure if she should share what Azrael had told her when they'd been in the Dunebala Desert.

"You know, don't you?" Jessie pressed.

"It's going to sound crazy," Fate warned.

Jessie laughed. "Shooting through a secret portal into a gargantuan storehouse of magical objects and being made a power-hungry sorceress's cyborg bitch sounds like an everyday thing to you? Nothing will ever sound crazy to me anymore."

Fate laughed too, but curiosity cut her laughter short. "Do you remember everything that happened while Kaliena was controlling you?"

The twinkle in Jessie's eyes vanished and she glanced down at her hands.

"Sorry, Jess, if it's too fresh to talk about, I can wait until you're ready."

When Jessie looked up, her eyes were glassy with tears. "Yeah, it's too soon. I'd much rather hear about your stuff."

Fate waved her hand to show it was no big deal. "Right, back to me and why I'm a war god magnet. Are you ready for this?"

Jessie nodded, looking all of a sudden like the little girl Fate had first met in kindergarten. Her heart ached for what her friend must have endured under Kaliena's iron grip.

"From everything I've gathered, humans are too weak to contain the massive energy housed in an instrument of a god, such as this lovely magical girdle, which according to the history books, Ares made as a special gift for his daughter, Hippolyta. The only way for any human to survive wearing, or wielding such an object, is to be a descendant of a god."

Confusion played across Jessie's face. "Are you saying you're a descendant of Ares?"

"I don't know, maybe. There's no way to know for sure."

Jessie stared at her like Fate had suddenly sprouted an extra nose. "That's *huge*! How did you find out?"

Fate pointed at Azrael, who was lying in the bed next to Jessie's. "Him. He told me."

Jessie's mouth fell open as she glanced over at Azrael. "You know him? I've been doing nothing but staring at him since I woke up." She fanned her face. "I cannot get over that long black hair, mocha skin and gorgeous face. He's totally hot! So tell me, who is he?"

"That's Azrael, and... we're married." Fate muttered the last part under her breath.

Jessie laughed cynically. "You wish! Wait a minute. What about Finn? Does he know you've been crushing on this guy enough to wish you're *married* to him?"

Fate stared back. "It's no joke. And yes, Finn knows all about it."

Jessie shook her head in disbelief. Then her gaze settled on the back of

Fate's hand, taking in the henna tattoo that was only now beginning to fade. She glanced over at the tattoos on Azrael's neck, exotic markings, which were similar in design to Fate's. "Whoa, what the heck happened while I was away?"

"A lot. Too much, now that I'm looking back on it all," Fate admitted.

"Start from the beginning." Jessie reached for a cup of water and took a sip, her eyes wide with anticipation of what Fate would say next.

"When the portal opened to send the Keep into this world, it didn't land in Oldwilde as planned. Instead, it crashed in the Mirajaran Desert on the continent of Shalamoraize. Picture it like shooting for the British Isles and hitting the Middle East."

Jessie nodded–a hint that she remembered and had been fully aware of the situation. Fate pretended not to notice and continued. "I somehow got thrown even further away and ended up in Dunebala, the Desert of the Living Sands."

"Oh wow, what was that like?"

"Don't even get me started on that awful place. It's enough to say, Dunebala was a miserable, blistering hot, dustbowl full of sand monsters that wanted to eat me. And that's where I met Azrael. Super romantic, let me tell you."

Jessie made a face. "Ew yeah, I suppose you were both sweaty and covered in sand."

"Oh, I was a stinky mess for sure. But Azrael... he was fresh as line-dried laundry, because *he* was taking baths everyday." Fate held up her hand when Jessie started to ask why. "We didn't exactly get along when we first met. I actually kind of hated him in the beginning. Mostly because he enslaved me for having saved my life, but also because he tried to kill me for not being honest, when in actuality, I'd lost my memory. The last thing I remembered, before making my big face plant in Dunebala, was the book signing at the library, so you can imagine how freaked out I was."

"Totally!" Jessie folded her arms and frowned at Azrael with disappointment. "So he's an angel-faced jerk."

"He was at first." Fate glanced at him, her heart softening as she watched the steady rise and fall of his chest. "He wasn't so bad once I got to know him."

Jessie pointed at Fate and gasped. "You like him! Are you in love with him?"

"No!" Fate knew the denial had come way too fast and loud. "I don't *love* him. But I do care about him."

Jessie took another sip of water. "Tell me everything."

There was no getting out of it now. Jessie was like a dog with a bone when there were secrets to share. Fate shifted uncomfortably as she recounted how Azrael had saved her from becoming a desert monster's snack, which resulted in the soul ring around her ankle.

Jessie leaned forward. "Let me see it."

Fate lifted her leg to show the thick brass ring around the ankle of her boot.

"Wow, another magical thingy you can't take off." Jessie shook her head, and then looked at Azrael. "I suppose it could be worse though."

"How do you figure?"

"He could've been an old toothless dude with long dirty fingernails."

"Ew!" Fate screwed up her face.

Jessie fell back into her pillows, laughing.

"It's not funny, Jess. This is serious. As long as I'm wearing the soul ring, Finn and I can't be truly together."

Jessie's playful grin turned to curiosity. "Well how come? Especially when there's no way to know if Azrael will ever wake up?"

"Finn and I can't be *all-the-way* together." Fate's face warmed with embarrassment. "The soul ring burns my skin every time we get any closer than a hug and a kiss, if you know what I mean."

Jessie's mouth fell open. "Are you saying you were actually ready to get horizontal with each other?"

"I've been ready for a long time now." Fate wondered whether to tell Jessie what Finn had told her. That they'd made love before he left for Oldwilde to organize the army that fought Kaliena's undead legions. Of all the memories she'd lost and still eluded her, this one pained her the most. She decided to hold onto this one personal secret and continued on with what she felt most comfortable telling her friend. "I don't remember any of it, but Finn made a pair of hand fasting bracelets for each of us and we declared ourselves married."

"What? No way!" Jessie squealed. "Are you wearing it? Let me see!"

"I don't have mine anymore. It was taken from me when I married Azrael."

Jessie clapped her hand over her mouth. Her eyes were round as marbles when she finally lowered her hand. "Do you realize you're married to two guys? Fate Floyd, that makes *you* a bigamist."

Fire exploded in Fate's belly, burning hot with rage. She closed her eyes and clenched her fists. "Don't say that! It's hard enough for me to wrap my head around being married at all. Let alone to two different guys."

"Sorry," Jessie muttered.

Fate sucked in enough air to cool the anger boiling beneath her skin. "It wouldn't be so bad if I could actually remember Finn giving me the bracelet and the promises we made to each other. You know what's weird? I loved that bracelet, even though I didn't have a single memory of Finn. Yet I knew it had been made with love, because I could *feel* it."

Jessie shifted nervously. After an awkward stretch of silence, she asked, "How'd you lose your memory?"

"Azrael's mother told me I have a memory too painful to live with, which made my soul shatter into lost pieces." When Jessie looked confused, Fate waved it off. "Her words, not mine. Anyway, she said the most damaged part of my soul drifted too far away for her to retrieve. She said it's a form of self-protection, and whatever that traumatic event was must've happened just before the Keep went through the portal."

"Sounds complicated. But at least you got most of your memories back, right?"

"Most of them, I guess." Fate stared into space. "As for what caused the amnesia, I'll probably never know what that was."

"It sounds like Azrael and his mother were a huge help getting you back on track." Jessie glanced over at him again. "Is that when you started to like him?"

Fate resisted the urge to look at Azrael. Seeing him in such a vulnerable state made her sad and stirred feelings she wasn't fully prepared to deal with. Mostly because of how unfair it was to Finn to be indulging in emotions that caused her to feel confused and divided. "Let's just say I eventually grew to respect Azrael after I learned more about him. But I never *ever* fell in love with him." Her chest tightened. "Finn's the only one I love."

"That's good to hear."

Startled by Finn's voice, Fate turned to see him leaning within the doorway sporting a teasing smile; his muscled arms crossed and tousled waves of bronzed-gold hair falling over his emerald green eyes in the most irresistible way.

Heat flooded up Fate's neck, warming her face. "You're not supposed to sneak up on two girls talking. This is sacred space and there's no boys allowed," she admonished him.

Finn nudged his chin at Azrael as he strode all the way into the room. "What about him? He's a boy."

Fate frowned, despite the smile tugging at the corners of her mouth. "Unconscious boys don't count."

Finn leaned down and kissed the side of Fate's neck. The warm touch of his lips shot delicious tingles down her spine. He stood to face Jessie with his hand lingering on Fate's shoulder. "Hey, Jessie. It's good to see you're back. Fate's been miserable without you."

Jessie wriggled with delight. "I can see why. Nobody else can get brownies out of the food simulator like I can."

Fate nodded. "You know me too well."

Jessie winked. "Always have. Always will."

Fate continued nodding, but what she really wanted to say was that nobody knew her at all. Not Finn. Not Eustace. Not Sithias. And not even Jessie. She was changed. Changed by the power embedded beneath her skin. More so, she was being changed by something else, something nameless that was buried deep down inside. Something she very much wanted to stay buried. But it was rising, pushing to the surface little by little, and that terrified her.

This concludes the
first chapter preview of

Fate's Fury

Acknowledgements

So much goes into writing a book, and while it's just me adventuring with my characters in solitude every day, it's the support of others that ultimately helps me reach the finish line.

First and foremost, I must thank my good friend and editor, Nora Mader. She went above and beyond on this one, polishing 175,000 words into a smooth, clean read. Thank you, Nora!

Thank you to my husband, Tony, and my son, Tyler, for your undying patience and support during the many trying times throughout my writing process. I could never reach that glorious last line without your encouragement. And as my first round readers, thank you for your honesty to help make my stories the best they can be.

Most of all, thanks to all of my Fate fans. You are the reason I continue writing, and though I've kept you waiting for each new installment, your staying power is what keeps me from giving up whenever the writing gets tough. Thank you from the bottom of my heart for cheering me on by wanting more books from me!

Bestselling author T. Rae Mitchell is an incurable fantasy junkie who spent much of her youth dreaming up worlds and bringing characters to life. While most kids outgrow such things, T. Rae didn't and sometimes took playing make-believe a bit far. Like the time a wizard hid a bottle of dragon beans in the back yard and left her son convinced he could grow his own dragons. Needless to say, the beans failed to produce and disappointments were had. That's when T. Rae decided to funnel her crazy imagination into writing young and new adult fantasy.

Sign-up for T. Rae Mitchell's
Exclusive VIP List
for upcoming notifications:
www.traemitchell.com/sign-up

You can also find T. Rae Mitchell on...

Instagram: www.instagram.com/t.raemitchell

Facebook: www.facebook.com/mitchelltrae

Bookbub: www.bookbub.com/authors/t-rae-mitchell

Goodreads: www.goodreads.com/author/show/6926344.T_Rae_Mitchell

Twitter: www.twitter.com/TRaeMitchell

Pinterest: www.pinterest.com/TRaeMitchell

www.ingramcontent.com/pod-product-compliance
Lightning Source LLC
Chambersburg PA
CBHW010446310726
48979CB00018B/2830/J